Communes Brit

A History of
Communal Living
in Britain
1939 - 2000

Chris Coates

*History is wildly contingent and unpredictable. Many
alternate paths leave from the current moment, as they
have from every previous moment too. Bitter struggles,
military accidents, secret conspiracies, and the best-laid
open plans, not to mention the vagaries of weather,
nature, disease, and human culture have all pushed
and pulled to bring us to this moment.*
Chris Carlson, *Nowtopia*, 2008

*A dream you dream alone is just a dream
A dream you dream together is reality*
Yoko Ono and John Lennon

Diggers & Dreamers Publications

Diggers & Dreamers Publications
2012

D&D Publications
BCM Edge, London
WC1N 3XX

www.diggersanddreamers.org.uk

ISBN
978-0-9514945-9-2

Distribution
Edge of Time Ltd
BCM Edge, London
WC1N 3XX
www.edgeoftime.co.uk

Design and Layout
Jonathan How
www.coherentvisions.com

Contents

Preface

All of us who enjoyed *Utopia Britannica* – Chris Coates's earlier volume on communitarian history – will have eagerly awaited this follow-up. In some ways this must have been an even tougher challenge. Records are often scanty and only someone as personally familiar with this rich current of communal living could have succeeded in tracking down the many colourful experiments. The result is a remarkable account of an alternative approach to modern life, starting at the time of the Second World War and coming right up-to-date. Along the way we meet pacifists and true believers, urban squatters and long-term groups in country houses, artists and therapists, diggers and dreamers – all bucking convention in their own ways. A comprehensive directory at the back of the book with 1110 entries catalogues communal groups of all shapes and sizes from Atlantis to the Zanzibarians. This fascinating book will undoubtedly find its way onto the bookshelves of communal homes. Let us hope, too, that it will be read more widely, as telling evidence that there are, indeed, different and fulfilling ways to organise society.

Dennis Hardy,
Emeritus Professor of Urban Planning
Adelaide, Australia
Author: *Utopian England* and *Arcadia for All*

Introduction

... despite all the failed communes and the failing ones, despite the problems and the disappointments, communality is still a beautiful idea and often a beautiful reality, and it's infinitely worth doing. There ought to be a law in favour of it.

Clem Gorman, *People Together,* **1975**

The history of communal living has existed in the margins and footnotes of other stories down the centuries. Communes Britannica is an attempt to bring that history out from the sidelines and, if not put it centre stage then at least, bring it into the footlights and shine a light on it. The second half of the 20th century saw a blossoming of communes, not just in the cliché of the 1960's and 70's so-called hippie communes, but from the late 1930's onwards there is a continuous communal thread that can be traced from the wartime pacifist communities through the classic back-to-the-land big house communes to the low-impact and cohousing communities at the turn of the new millennium.

When talking to people about communal living the question of defining what is or isn't a 'commune' comes up very quickly. In some ways I have chosen to try and sidestep this debate – my personal thoughts are that this is a somewhat academic exercise. There seems to me to be a matrix of communal set-ups which in its centre has groups that clearly fit into everyone's idea of what a commune is. And then there are all kinds of variations – as the edges get greyer – which make one ask exactly how communal they really are. That is why the subtitle of this book is 'A history of communal living' and not 'of communes'. It is also my take on the history and there are clearly other tales and narratives that others would tell. I have tried to take a broad look at the period telling the story of the 'communes movement' in so far as it existed at any one time. I have used individual communities as illustrations of different aspects of communal living rather than give detailed histories of every group I came across – the story of each and every community could be a book in itself!

Writing and researching communal living has been a voyage into something of an archival desert – there is no single starting point for anyone wanting to research the counter-culture ... radical politics ... the alternative society ... the underground – call it what you will – of the late 20th century. The groups themselves are often unaware of their own forebears or even recent history. Few have gone to any lengths to preserve or catalogue their past – only Findhorn who have placed their records in the Scottish National Library have gone any way to making their heritage available to future researchers or would-be-communards. I have spent time tracking down collections of magazines and newspapers from the period (about the only publicly accessible complete set of Peace News magazine is in the Library of the Religious Society of Friends on the Euston Road in London). Other records exist in odd corners of other collections dotted around the country – or in the back drawers of filing cabinets in communal offices ... or in cardboard boxes in former members' attics. At one point in my research I was sent a 'commune in a box', the whole paper life and death history of a London-based communal group from 1960. Everything: legal documents, correspondence, even the notes from the communal noticeboard. The person who sent it to me was a former member who had kept everything for 40 years 'in case their experience might be of use to others.' It came to me completely by chance. There is a crying need for some university to start a specialist archive before even more is lost.

It is an odd experience writing about your friends and your own life as history. It all seems so very recent, yet so far away at the same time – if that doesn't sound too strange. I hope I haven't placed too much emphasis on the things that I was personally involved in – or on the other hand played them down and not given them the dues they deserve out of some sort of false modesty. It has been a privilege to meet people from all walks of communal life, past and present, who have freely given me their time, their memories, their thoughts and particularly their communal family photos. Those who have dug out old boxes of memories – some of which they found difficult to recall. Without their generosity and trust the book would not be half of what it is.

The 'commune in a box'

News of Peace

In the years before and during the war, there has been a strong movement to found communities in Britain, arising largely out of the peculiar circumstances of the British pacifist movement at the beginning of the war. The communities which arose during this period were numerous, running to several hundreds. Some lasted only a few months – others are still alive and thriving after seven or eight years.

George Woodcock, *The Basis of Communal Living*

In April 1937 a communities conference was held in Bath, convened under the banner of the Community Service Committee. It brought together a wide cross section of people involved in community experiments from across the country. The list of speakers included: Nellie Shaw from the Whiteway Colony in Gloucestershire who had recently published *A Colony in the Cotswolds*, her early history of the Tolstoyan Colony; Alfred Higgins from the Brotherhood Church who had travelled down from Stapleton in Yorkshire to tell those attending of their attempts to live a Christian anarchist life based on the Sermon on the Mount; Brinsley Nixon, a founder member of Hugh's Settlement, who told of how they had set up an experimental community for the development of rural settlements in England and overseas on 120 acres at Quarley in Hampshire; John Middleton Murry who spoke of his Adelphi Centre in Essex as a 'training centre for Socialists'; and Ernest Bairstow, of the British Llano Circle, who wanted to form a federation of communal settlements based on the communities that now existed. The Bruderhof were represented by Emmy Arnold who described progress at the newly formed Bruderhof community at Ashton Keynes in Wiltshire. Other speakers broadened the definition of 'community' from land-based communal experiments to include various community building ventures. Bert Over described his Community Fruit Service at Bleadon in Somerset – a co-operative venture run without the use of money; the Order of Woodcraft Chivalry gave details of Grith Pioneer camps for the unemployed; and the Brotherhood Trust Extension Society told of their plan to acquire land and tools for co-operative communities and to assist in the transfer of surpluses between communities. The conference had brought together, perhaps for the first time, people involved in community experiments from all over the country.

Following the Bath event, the Community Service Committee was formalised as a clearing organisation, operated from 'Chancton', Dartnell Park, West Byfleet in Surrey, with no funds and 'no organisation'. The conference also seems to have set off a flurry of community building activity. At Kingsley Hall in Bow a series of meetings were arranged to discuss such things as "The Spiritual Basis of Community" and "The Structure of Existing Communities such as the Bruderhof and the Kibbutzim". At one gathering, held on 5th March 1938, George Kenworthy outlined a scheme for an experiment on 2,000 acres to be planned and laid out scientifically with a modern dairy farm, industrial sections, a distribution centre, a marketing depot and 'non standard housing'. The spring of 1938 saw the launch of a quarterly journal called *The Plough* by the Bruderhof carrying news of community activity from around the country. In October a series of community study group meetings were being held at the Dick Sheppard Peace Centre in Bayswater and a follow-up to the Bath conference was being organised for December at Kingsley Hall. An advert in *Peace News* on 29th October announced 'This year's community gathering at Kingsley Hall will be a council of action, rather than a conference.' The Saturday was to be taken up with a 'survey and review of directions in which community has developed in the last year', followed by a 'real hammering out of group plans' on the Sunday. The advert ended with a rallying call: 'It is felt the time for action may well be short, that the need is urgent and the way is open.' The papers from the two conferences were published under the title of *Community In Britain*. Whilst many of the conference papers were optimistic in the face of society's problems, there were also papers that acknowledged the real difficulties faced by those trying to form communities.

To leave your present way of living and adopt one essentially different is not easy; there is great risk in it. For a community may well fail, and then where will you be. Again this is not the point; you will be somewhere and that is all that matters; what is more you will be the richer, whatever you have given up, for an invaluable experience ... Community to those who have had time living separately, looks very convenient; if you are out of work the community will provide for you; if you are fed up with your job, the community will keep you while you look for another or take a well earned rest; if you want to get away from an uncongenial home life, community offers the opportunity; if you are tired of living alone in lodgings, community will give you companionship and regular meals (and perhaps) someone to look after your clothes and make your bed. All these things are true, a community will do all this for you ... the only valid reason for joining a community is the desire not to receive but to give. What you are prepared to give up is important not what you are prepared to accept. [1]   **R Howard**

In 1939 the British Llano Circle, a group of 'Voluntary Socialists' inspired by the Llano del Rio Co-operative Colony in California, started to produce *Community Life*, a journal with details of small communal experiments like the Elmsett Community, at Nova Scotia Farm, near Ipswich; Tythrop House Agricultural Establishment formed by Jewish Refugees at Kingsey in Buckinghamshire; and the Southend Community in Essex. Much of the talk in the pages of all these publications was about the impending war that most of the contributors could foresee and what contribution communities might make to the cause of peace. With the invasion of Poland by Nazi Germany in September 1939 the situation for communities changed: many focussed on providing space for conscientious objectors (COs). Local peace groups in many parts of the country set up land schemes for those given exemption to work on the land by the military service tribunals. For some groups the outbreak of war was catastrophic. The Jewish Christian Community in an old country house at Kenninghall, south of Norwich, was broken up when most members were sent to the internment camp on the Isle of Man and the Bruderhof communities in the Cotswolds would eventually be forced to close because of increasing anti-German feelings.

The surge in numbers, mainly of men, looking for places to work on the land gave a boost to community building activity. During April 1940 a series of meetings was held between the Bruderhof and the North-East Regional Committee of the Fellowship for Reconciliation to discuss how best to organise and encourage land-based communities. Members of the Fellowship had already set up a number of land-based schemes across the country at Ropley,

Hindhead, Alton, Lewes, Glastonbury, Ipswich and Shrewsbury. By November 1940 *Peace News* was carrying a regular Community Notes column with news from groups around the country as well as small ads of places needing people and people looking for places in communities. During March, April and May 1941 *Peace News* printed a two-page Community Supplement with one page devoted to theoretical writings on community and the other on news from communities. Adverts appeared from groups such as The Transpennine Christian Group who hoped to set up on a 70-acre farm just south of Wakefield; the Cheadle Hulme Community Fellowship, a group of three families and a woman teacher who had given up their individual homes and rented a large house just south of Manchester, and the Myddle Park Land Settlement in Shropshire where local Peace Pledge Union members were clearing 35 acres of rough land and erecting huts to take COs. Some were well organised groups that had established themselves on small-holdings or joined together with sympathetic farmers. From looking at other adverts it is not clear whether they are actual communities or the plans and dreams of enthusiastic individuals. There were organisations such as the Bureau of Cosmotherapy at Leatherhead in Surrey who wanted to set up an experimental small-holding along the lines of the 'most recent findings of nutritional science' or the Jiffy Club Cult in Derby who were promoting 'the only genuine mutualist co-operative scheme in existence'.

Pacifists on the Land

The situation for pacifists during the early part of the summer of 1939 was complicated. War hadn't yet broken out, but conscription for military training was already being introduced. The Ministry of Labour and National Service had made tentative proposals that a corps of conscientious objectors should be organised to be employed on essential services. None of the organised pacifist groups responded to this idea as they had no wish to co-operate with the Government to facilitate the working of conscription to which they were on principle opposed. Labour members of the coalition government wanted to

avoid the situation in the First World War where conscientious objectors had been imprisoned and persecuted. George Lansbury MP arranged for a deputation from the Council of Christian Pacifist Groups to meet Ernest Brown, the then Minister of Labour and National Service, on a number of occasions to explore how the new National Training Act would affect COs. It was put forward that it might be possible for an independently run scheme to be set up for COs to carry out some form of community service. Land or ambulance work was suggested. As the Quakers had already refounded the Friends Ambulance Unit, the Methodist Peace Fellowship took up the idea of establishing pacifist land units.

At the same time as these discussions were taking place the Forestry Commission in Bristol made an appeal to the Ministry of Labour and National Service for extra forestry workers and were told of the possibility of employing conscientious objectors. The Commission's plan was to bring in skilled foresters from Newfoundland and once that was done they were prepared to look at employing COs on forestry schemes around the country. After further talks on the nature of the work to be carried out, the Methodist Peace Fellowship agreed to organise a group of workers. The first unit was offered work in the Hemsted Forest in Kent, but no accommodation could be found for the workers. Such housing in local villages that might have provided lodgings was filled with war-time evacuees. Almost in despair a large-scale map of the Forest was scanned for anything suitable. In the very middle of the forest the map showed what looked like a dwelling-house, and on inquiry it was found that the house had not been occupied for several months, and was said to be haunted. The Methodist Peace Fellowship rented this "haunted" house for £12 a year. Four men were ready to go at once to set up the first pacifist forestry unit.

At first an ad-hoc committee was formed to co-ordinate the units. Meetings were held and attended by the Baptist Pacifist Fellowship, the Congregational Peace Crusade, the Presbyterian Pacifist Group and the Anglican Pacifist Fellowship. Out of these meetings the Christian Pacifist Forestry and Land Units (CPFLU) was formed. A 'headquarters' office was organised at Room 16, Kingsway Hall. From four men in a solitary derelict house in the middle of Hemsted Forest the organisation would grow in leaps and bounds. Within two years there would be fifty units with six hundred members at work on the land, and eventually the membership would number 1,392. Throughout 1940 inquiries for more workers came from regional officers of the Forestry Commission in Sussex, Hampshire and the Forest of Dean. These were matched to an increasing number of applications from COs. Difficulties with finding accommodation for the units were overcome with ingenuity. Men were housed in a variety of tents, caravans and railway coaches. In some parts of the country Youth Hostels were used. In one place, a unit was housed in the village schoolroom. Later, a variety of more permanent accommodation was found on farms and the Forestry Commission provided huts in more remote locations. Soon the numbers of COs applying for places in the units outstripped the work available and when the Forestry Commission started to stand down men during the summer season other work had to be found. Some men, using their newly acquired knowledge of the countryside, found jobs for themselves on farms with sympathetic owners. Others moved on to the many land-based communities being set up by peace groups and individuals around the country. The CPFLU started to find other work for units through the County War Agricultural Executive Committees (WAEC). A unit would be employed by a Committee, or 'loaned' by the Committee to a private farmer. The work usually consisted of ditching, drainage or clearing rough land. In 1941 the situation was radically changed when the Government bluntly told farmers that 'labour mattered more than prejudice'. From then on one County WAEC after another got in touch with the CPFLU, requesting workers. The units were winning a good reputation and it soon became possible to place in land service as many Christian COs as were available.

Much of this land work was heavy and demanded greater skill and strength than many of the COs straight from the office or university had. Training programs were started to help counter this and two training farms were set up by people involved with the Peace Pledge Union at Holton Hall in Lincolnshire and at

Goose Green Farm in Somerset. By the middle of 1942 CPFLU membership had risen to nearly 800 and the work of the units was expanded into other fields: on the south coast a unit repaired sea defences; one unit was set up in an epileptic colony; in London a Kingsway Unit was formed operating out of the Kingsway Hall headquarters which carried out civil defence and welfare work. The units varied considerably in size and set-up. Some were clearly short-lived workcamps that lasted the duration of a piece of work. Others were semi-permanent communities from which the unit would go out to work in the local area. It was in these more stable set-ups that a sense of community grew.

C.P.F.L.U. was not only influenced by this community movement but was itself an important part of it. Every Unit was in some sense a community, an experiment in living together and sharing a common life. The Units of course could not be ideal communities inasmuch as they usually consisted of men only, and of men all engaged in the same kind of work. But for those who shared in them they were adventures in the working out of a new social order. The expectation was high that the war would end in far-reaching changes in society. There was, for some at least, an almost apocalyptic sense that capitalism was doomed and that a new age would emerge from the throes of world conflict. For nearly all, the Unit was the expression of desire for a simpler way of life consistent with the principles of the New Testament.

L Maclachlan, CPFLU

A series of regional gatherings for unit members were held during 1942. These gave members from around the country a chance to meet each other and discuss wider issues of Christian experience and witness of the Church. Reports of these regional conferences were presented to the Central Organising Committee and there was an almost unanimous agreement that the movement should continue after the war to help in post-war social reconstruction in harmony with Christian principles and to help members to obtain or retain employment. Another suggestion made was that a weekly quiet time should be observed by all the units across the country during which their thoughts could be directed towards community life. There was a suggestion that a Units Magazine

CPFLU Unit sites – Top to Bottom
Harvington, Worcestershire;
Norton Grounds Farm, Mickleton, Gloucestershire;
Forestry Hut, Strathyre; Brinsbury Manor, Sussex

should be published, but paper control made the issuing of new periodicals almost impossible in war-time. However some of the units issued their own newsletters. These took the form of duplicated sheets appearing at somewhat irregular intervals and circulating in the larger units or in groups of units, often spreading out to a wider circle of readers in the homes of members, and among their friends, all over the country.

The members in one unit submitted a proposal to the Secretary 'That a Fellowship of Christian Pacifists be formed who have all possessions in common (while they continue living in their own homes and working at their own occupations), thus recapturing the economic as well as the spiritual fellowship of the early Christian Church.' They went on to say, 'Many of us have found in Units a spirit of brotherhood which we shall be loath to lose when the war is over. A small group of members in a certain Unit is already operating the following scheme; which though from its personal nature it could not be adopted by the Units Movement as a whole, yet could start as groups within the various Units. A growing cell working on these lines would in time have a profound influence on the social and economic conditions about which we are so concerned, and would present to the world a Christian community which would answer the question 'Why are professing Christians so little different from other people?'

They outlined their proposal in a seven point plan:
(1) Each member would receive sufficient for his immediate needs. Any surplus to go to a common pool.
(2) Each member should follow his own vocation, and should do the best in his power irrespective of payment.
(3) The economy of the fellowship would prevent members being faced with either of the two economic extremes which can endanger spiritual life-becoming too rich or too poor.
(4) In this fellowship the importance of the principles, relationships, and implications of Christian family life must be stressed.
(5) Members would be drawn from all denominations.
(6) In this fellowship would grow men and women who would influence the wider community wherever they lived and worked.
(7) We need not wait until after the war to make this conception a reality. We can start now.[2]

No community was formed as a direct result of the work of the CPFLU. Whether COs who had worked in the units had been inspired to go and join any of the other communities around at the time is also not known. Membership of the units peaked in January 1945 and fell away very quickly as the war ended with all units effectively ending work by the end of 1947.

The Committee pays tribute to the men of our Units who have faithfully worked and witnessed during the years that are past. They have endured hardship in work which has been strange and difficult; sometimes they have faced hostility from their neighbours, been misunderstood or ostracised. Yet consistently men have shown a spirit of quiet endurance and cheerful courage and sought by acts of true neighbourliness to prove the sincerity of their Christian convictions ... We go forward in the spirit and strength of comradeship to take our experience of life and work in community as a contribution to the post-war world.

CPFLU AGM minutes, April 1944

War and Socks

At the Tolstoyan Christian Anarchist Brotherhood Church colony at Stapleton near Pontefract the outbreak of war brought renewed conflict with the authorities. Whilst there were no men of military age at the colony in 1939, the two families there refused to be registered or have anything to do with ration cards.

The local man who brought the forms was very concerned about our welfare, but we reminded him that during the Israelites' 40 years in the Wilderness, manna had been provided by God. Of course there was some hardship – there was hardship for everyone. We had some reserves and we were able to get some butter etc occasionally. And we did not deal in the black market. Tea was fairly easy, and we stopped using sugar in tea, a practice we have kept up ever since. We ate peanut butter ad lib – quite useful and nutritious – but I never want to see another jar of it. **A G Higgins**

The knitting business, that was one of the mainstays of the community, also ran into trouble with wartime bureaucracy as all knitted goods and wool were subject to rationing. Lacking the necessary ration coupons the colony acted as a sort of go-between – using customers' coupons to buy wool from a supplier in Manchester which they then knitted up into socks and other woollen garments. This practice came to the notice of the Board of Trade who informed the colony that under the Defence Regulations all unregistered manufacturers of rationed goods, however small, had to make returns, something the Brotherhood point blank refused to do. Writing to the Board on 6th November 1942 to explain their position they said, 'We are a Christian organisation, which preaches and practices Christian methods in business and social life. We have no part or lot in the state, which substitutes thieving and murder for Christian methods, and consequently have never sought sanction from the state ...'

Following further demands for them to comply with the regulations Alfred Higgins replied:
It does not seem to have occurred to you yet that all actions should have a moral basis. It is because of a lack of any moral basis in the Board of Trade and the Government (which is alleged to look after the interests of the British people) that our people are plunged into an orgy of murder and rapine which you are pleased to mis-call 'a war for freedom' ... You tell me ... that I am committing an apparent breach of the Defence Regulations for which heavy penalties may be imposed. Your so-called Defence Regulations are designed to cover a multitude of sins. These regulations have no moral backing, they are based on a denial of the Ten Commandments, and you cannot expect any honest man to bow down before them.
Reply to Board, 3rd February 1943

And after the Board wrote again with the same old 'blah blah' Higgins wrote back:
Your letters to me are abominably rude – the incivilities of civil servants in making threats of punishment is characteristic of the Fifth Form Bully. I am always ready and willing to discuss things on Christian grounds, but I am not your slave.
Reply to Board, 8th April 1943

Following a further series of letters repeating the previous threats and delivering an ultimatum, which the Brotherhood either ignored or burned, nothing more was heard. The colony switched to asking customers to use their coupons to purchase wool themselves that would then be made up into garments in the colony's knitting shed.

The full story of the early days at Stapleton is told in *The History of the Brotherhood Church*, A G Higgins, Brotherhood Church 1982. See: www.thebrotherhoodchurch.org

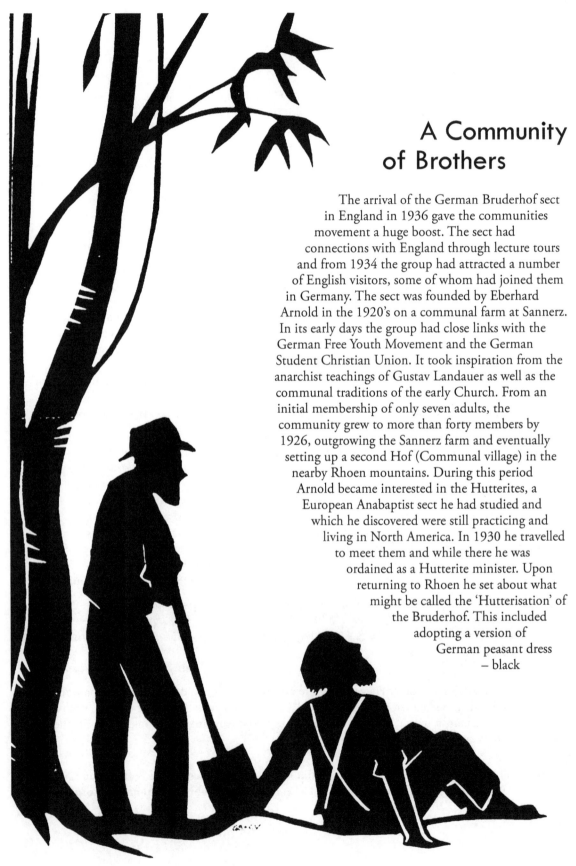

A Community of Brothers

The arrival of the German Bruderhof sect in England in 1936 gave the communities movement a huge boost. The sect had connections with England through lecture tours and from 1934 the group had attracted a number of English visitors, some of whom had joined them in Germany. The sect was founded by Eberhard Arnold in the 1920's on a communal farm at Sannerz. In its early days the group had close links with the German Free Youth Movement and the German Student Christian Union. It took inspiration from the anarchist teachings of Gustav Landauer as well as the communal traditions of the early Church. From an initial membership of only seven adults, the community grew to more than forty members by 1926, outgrowing the Sannerz farm and eventually setting up a second Hof (Communal village) in the nearby Rhoen mountains. During this period Arnold became interested in the Hutterites, a European Anabaptist sect he had studied and which he discovered were still practicing and living in North America. In 1930 he travelled to meet them and while there he was ordained as a Hutterite minister. Upon returning to Rhoen he set about what might be called the 'Hutterisation' of the Bruderhof. This included adopting a version of German peasant dress – black dungarees and blue shirts for men and long skirts and a spotted head-scarf, for women. When Hitler came to power in 1933 the themselves in conflict with the new National Socialist regime. B(pacifism and their Christian beliefs made them targets for the N community moved some of its members, mainly draft-age young Liechtenstein creating the Alm Bruderhof. It was during this per Eberhard Arnold died and for the following few years a sort of cc family leadership of the group was undertaken by Arnold's widov the face of increased persecution they looked for somewhere safe an initial step, the brotherhood leased the Ashton Fields Farm, at Keynes in Wiltshire and in 1936 purchased the entire estate, gradu increasing it to 500 acres. In the relative safety of England the comn flourished and, following further Nazi persecution, eventually moved members to the Wiltshire farm. The somewhat strange pacifist refugees initially welcomed: an article in the *Wilts & Glos Standard* in May 1937 compared them to Huguenot refugees, said they were fleeing persecution 1 'taking a stand against pagan blasphemy' and said that they were "not to be confused with the many modern colonies started on the wrong basis". Free from the threat of persecution, and for the first time farming on reasonably productive land, the Bruderhof were able to start a thriving community, although they would still rely on outside financial help for a long time. In less than two years they managed to establish a successful community on a scale unimaginable to most English pacifists at the time.

At the Cotswold Bruderhof there are 230 men, women and children of several nationalities,
Swiss, British and Dutch. As there are nearly ninety children, educational work is one of the ,
activities ... English, German and Swiss teachers, kindergarten teachers and nurses look after the
about fifteen people are engaged in this work. Apart from the housework, which includes cooking
baking, cleaning, sewing, etc., the members of the Bruderhof are engaged in the following branches
Firstly, farming and gardening. Nearly 200 acres are under pasture and there are also 100 acres of ara,
including ten acres of market garden. A tuberculin tested herd of Shorthorn dairy cattle is kept and part
milk is sold and some is consumed by the large household. Further livestock includes 120 Shropshire sheep,
horses, two working oxen and a pony. The community has a veterinary surgeon who looks after the cattle. /.
large poultry section of more than 1,000 birds is one of the most successful branches of the community's activitie.
In addition to this, thirty beehives are kept. The arable land produces the grain for the community's bread and
potatoes for the household, and also fodder for the cattle. Most important for the running of the household is the
market garden of ten acres which produces all the vegetables required. Some fruit trees have already been planted.
The entire farm and market garden are worked by modern scientific methods, although it is essential that the
natural conditions of rural life should not be destroyed. The other large branch of work is the publishing, printing
and bookbinding department ... **Community in Britain 1938**

In just two years, they had transformed the property into a model of progressive
agriculture. Two hundred people were living off what had been a family farm. Even
the neighbors, always wary of newcomers, admitted that the cash-strapped Germans
had done an amazing job ...
Homage to a Broken Man: The Life of J Heinrich Arnold

Bruderhof members were active in pacifist circles and lectured throughout Britain. In 1938 they held some fifty meetings in cities and towns around the country. At the end of 1938 a public company, the Friends of the Bruderhof Ltd, was established, in which supporters in Britain were able to buy shares and help the Bruderhof to invest in agriculture and buildings on the Ashton Farm and to purchase land for a new community. This was Oaksey Park, a 300-acre farm with a dairy herd of sixty cattle and buildings in good condition which enabled the immediate housing of some seventy people. The Oaksey community was close by and allowed the joint use of services such as the bakery and school. At this time it was felt necessary to give the movement an English name and The Society of Brothers was chosen.

The Cotswold community attracted many visitors with busloads of tourists arriving at weekends. Students and members of the Workers' Education Association, the Peace Pledge Union, the Fellowship of Reconciliation, socialists and communists, vegetarians and people from radical religious groups arrived in such numbers that the group was forced to set days aside for visitors and ask those intending to stay to inform them in advance. The community also took in twenty Jewish refugees from Austria, and thirty members of a Zionist youth group who came for a year of agricultural training before travelling on to Palestine to found a kibbutz. During the early days of the war the group maintained good relations with their neighbours. In October 1939 they were visited by a tribunal dealing with the status of enemy aliens which determined that as they were refugees from Nazi persecution all the members were eligible to remain where they were and carry on with their lives as before. The only constraint imposed upon them was that they should stay within the county borders. However, after the evacuation of the British Forces from Dunkirk in May 1940 and the fall of France, there was a deterioration in the situation for the Bruderhof in Britain. Relationships with local people had started to sour when the Oaksey Farm was being purchased. Some local landowners had objected to the sale of land to German nationals and had sent a petition to Parliament. One Oaksey village resident seems to have taken a particular dislike to the 'strangers in our midst' and appears to have been responsible for a letter-writing campaign in the local press, describing them as wearing grotesque costumes, attacking their pacifist beliefs and calling for their internment. The local MP weighed in to the debate and asked a question in Parliament. There were rumours that signals had been seen from the farm at night, and that they were some sort of German Fifth Column. A children's tree house was thought to be a lookout tower. Suspicion became near hysteria. One night drunken Home Guard soldiers arrived, searched the farm and ordered a fruit tree to put its hands up or be shot!

Attempts were made to counter the negative publicity: they addressed a meeting of the Cirencester Rotary Club and wrote to the local paper trying to explain their position on the war and offering help to local farmers. There were voices in defence of the Bruderhof, including the Home Secretary Sir Samuel Hoare and Lady Astor, saying that they were a peaceful anti-Nazi group that had found refuge in Britain. Things came to a head when the *Wilts & Glos Standard* printed calls for a boycott of the community's produce and further calls for German members to be interned – the editor then abruptly curtailed any further correspondence on the subject. In the end the Home Office decided that all foreign members would have to be detained in an internment camp and that travel was to be limited to a five mile zone around the farms. This news meant that the community would effectively be split and the sale of their goods made impossible. They decided that they had no choice but to emigrate. Two of the Brothers were sent to Canada and the United States to try and get permission to settle near one of the Hutterite colonies there. This attempt failed despite support from the Hutterites and Eleanor Roosevelt. An attempt was made to get the Shakers to allow them to take over the abandoned Shaker Village at New Lebanon. Over the next few months they looked into the possibility of finding refuge in Jamaica, New Zealand, Australia, and South Africa. When these efforts also failed, help finally came from the Mennonite Orie Miller, an old friend of the Bruderhof from Germany in the 20's. He had contact with the Paraguayan ambassador to the United States from the time the Mennonites emigrated to Paraguay in 1929. Through the ambassador, contact was made directly with the President of Paraguay, General Higinio Morínigo, who gave his permission for the Bruderhof to enter Paraguay under the same conditions that had applied to the Mennonite immigrants; in other words, they would be given the right to organise their settlements according to their principles, to speak their own language in their schools, and be exempt from military service. Preparations for the journey were begun. First the farms had to be sold. Oaksey was sold immediately, its inhabitants moving to the Ashton farms. A proposal was put forward by British pacifists to set up a company to buy the farms, it was planned that a hundred COs and their families would work them.

It is intended that it shall be a co-operative enterprise of
the Pacifist Community as a whole.
Advertisement in *Peace News*, November 29 1940

In the end, through help from the Home Office, the three farms at Ashton Keynes were sold to the London Police Court Mission, a charity which used them as an approved school. The Home Office also gave assistance in reserving berths on the Blue Star Line's transatlantic vessels, which carried meat and wheat from Argentina. Almost the entire community would make the treacherous journey across the Atlantic running the gauntlet of German U-Boats. Just a few members were left behind to wind up the community's affairs.

The story of the Bruderhof continues on page 51.

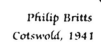

Philip Britts
Cotswold, 1941

Pacifist Islands

There were a number of accounts of living on pacifist farms published in the years after the war which give a flavour of life in various types of communal set-up. In *Island Farm*, published in 1946, Welsh naturalist Ronald Mathias Lockley tells the story of his co-farming experiment on the Pembrokeshire coast. Lockley, with his first wife Doris, had taken a 21-year lease on the island of Skokholm in 1926. Their plan was to be self-sufficient and make a living raising chinchilla rabbits. This idea had to be abandoned because they found the rabbits too difficult to handle. Lockley then began to study migratory birds and in 1933 established the first British bird observatory on the island. He described his research in several books which brought him to the notice of a wider circle of conservationists and naturalists, among them Peter Scott and Julian Huxley. At the outbreak of war the island was taken over by the military as it overlooked the approaches to Milford Haven and the Lockleys looked to return to farming on the mainland by taking a run-down farm at Dinas Cross to run as a co-operative farm. The farm had been advertised by the local War Agricultural Committee for some months with no takers and local farmers were sceptical of the venture. But Lockley gathered a small group of enthusiastic co-farmers who ended up taking on two farms.

Map of Island Farm – drawn by Phyllida Lumsden

We know for what purpose we are gathered together to-night. Ronald has explained it – to farm the two farms known as Island Farm and Inland Farm. Although we have all of us come here by different ways, the common bond of co-operation links us, joining us together as one great family determined to prove that the farm of the future is the co-operative farm, where each of us works for the common good, seeing our reward in the joy of united labour as much as in the good harvests which our team work will assure for us.

One of the members at the inaugural meeting of the co-farmers

Much of the book is taken up with details of farm work and the reclamation of the land and renovation of the buildings. The farms were set up as mixed farms with cattle, sheep, and some arable crops. The co-farmers were also keen to experiment with other more unusual crops. They started growing flax at the request of the WAEC and grew rye from seed sent by the Ryvita Company. They set up a hostel to accommodate single members, but also visitors and later gang labour from the Women's Land Army. The co-farmers were a moderate success in terms of farming, especially given the state of the farms when they started. The co-operative side of the venture proved harder as, after a while, some members wanted a more flexible, more individual, set-up. They argued that this was because 'the previous collective system did not give sufficient individual scope to each department, some of whom felt frustrated by other sections and who felt that they were supporting less enterprising sections of the community'. A proposal was put forward to constitute a new organisation – the Pioneers' Co-Farming Society. This would be an Industrial and Provident Society providing general services such as banking, marketing, buying and selling of agricultural goods and produce, hire of machinery and extra labour, and educational and social activities to individual farm groups. This would be extended to bring in local farmers who would be invited to form co-operative groups, affiliate to the central association and share its services. It was proposed to set up a number of separate groups: the Inland Farm group, the Island Farm group, a Market Garden Group, a Transport Group, and a Carpentry Group. Later a Wood-turners' Group and a Fishing-cum-Pleasure Boat Group were to be added. This grand scheme didn't materialise and in the later years of the war the farms were run on a more individual basis. The co-farmers were able to persuade some local farmers to set up a machinery pool to hire equipment from the local WAEC. This proved to be the beginning of the first machinery pool in Wales, an idea that caught on and within a year there were twenty such pools across Wales with 1,600 members – this was partly because the WAECs found it easier to deal with farmers collectively rather than individually.

The co-farmers harvesting flax

Looking back on the venture after the war Lockley said: 'Our experiment attracted many enquiries of which a great number were from members of the armed forces. What, they asked, could they do to get on the land with little or no capital and experience? Could we advise from the experience of our co-farming venture? The answers lie in the reading of this book. Our original collective farm – the 'Island Farmers' – was for its first year to act almost as a training school for the co-operators who were afterwards to launch out on their own, taking with them the experience and the sense of responsibility acquired with us. If the keen would-be farmer can do the same on the farm training centres which are now being set up by the Government, then there is a good chance for these beginners.'

After the war Ronald Lockley played a leading role in establishing the Pembrokeshire Coast National Park, and mapped out the long distance footpath around the Pembrokeshire coast. He emigrated to New Zealand in 1970 because he felt that successive British governments were not sufficiently aware of the threat to the landscape from industrial development.

Over on the other side of the country on Lodge Farm, at Thelnetham in Suffolk, John Middleton Murry, writer, literary critic, socialist, pacifist and at the time editor of *Peace News*, was busy trying to establish his own co-operative farm. In *Community Farm*, published in 1952, he chronicles the trials and tribulations of the early years on the farm. Murry had a previous history of community building. He and his first wife – the writer Katherine Mansfield – had spent part of the First World War living communally with D H Lawrence and his wife Frida in a cottage on the Cornish coast, where they discussed plans for a utopian community called Rananin.[4] Later, Katherine Mansfield died in somewhat mysterious circumstances at the Institute for the Harmonious Development of Man in France, a community run by the mystic G I Gurdjieff. In 1934 Murry had also set up a 'training centre for socialists' with Max Plowman, called the Adephi Centre, at Langham in Essex. Here they had planned to train "real socialists not socialist politicians. We believe that the essential element in the making of socialists is almost wholly neglected. This essential element is 'education into community.'" When war broke out, some of the conscientious objectors at the centre started a Farm Group in a nearby cottage and rented 70 acres of poor quality land.

His previous experiences in these ventures seem to have left Murry with a somewhat jaundiced view of communal living and the sort of people who are attracted to it. So much so that at the start of Community Farm he states that 'I have learned that 'community' is a dangerous word to use among young people of a certain type. Adolescent idealists, they might be called ... They are at odds with society, and 'community' appeals to them as an Elysium in which, without their having to do anything particular about it, the burdens of social existence will be lifted from them ... They appear to regard themselves as having a natural right to live at other people's expense, without troubling themselves about whether they are earning their keep.' This didn't stop him advocating community ventures as a way forward for pacifists at the start of the war. He was instrumental in the setting up of the Community Land Training Association. In a speech at its opening in 1941, entitled The Need for Community in our Time, he said 'At the cultural level community is based on a pooling of talents for the common weal. No doubt the process of over-coming deep-seated cultural egocentricity of an anarchical period will be slow and arduous ... I believe that community is the only antidote to totalitarianism.'

Following the sudden death of Max Plowman and the requisition of the Adephi Centre land by the military, Murry ploughed much of his capital into a final attempt to set up a co-operative farm – a project he claimed to have been thinking of for over twenty years. On 13 April 1942, he noted in his diary 'I have paid the deposit on the farm, which I am buying for £3,325. Buying it and capitalising it will take, quite literally, every penny I possess: so much at least and possibly more. But in my bones I feel it is a wise and good thing to do. It gives me a purpose in life, or rather commits me to the attempt, practically, to realise a scheme which I have long been convinced, theoretically, is the creative thing to do, today. My one regret is that I am 52, nearly 53, and a semi-invalid. I would give a great deal for a sound pair of legs.'

Murry gathered together a team on the farm made up of some members from the Langham Farm Group, pacifists who came from the training farm at Holton Beckering, plus a few local men to help out when extra labour was needed. He

*Community Farm
– illustrations by
Richard Murry*

also managed to transfer some of the animals and tools from the Adephi Centre. The team of co-operators were a mixed bag when it came to farming experience and skills, but they set about getting the 180 acres of Lodge Farm into working order. Many of the pages of *Community Farm* are concerned with the economics of small scale farming: what the price of beets are this year and what the Shorthorn Heifers and Red Poll calves are worth. Interspersed in this are chapters with titles like A Chapter of Cranks, and Artists and Usurers, which document the seemingly never-ending conflicts between members and between Murry and the other members. If we are to believe Murry, this conflict often led him to near despair 'By now 'community', as understood and practiced by most of the enthusiasts for it who had come my way, was almost as ugly a word to me as 'capital' was to them. It was a lofty excuse for evading personal responsibility. In this sense I was sick and tired of 'community'. Nevertheless, I was deeply attached to the idea.'

Richard Murry's illustrations in the book show an almost idyllic rural life going on amidst all this communal turmoil. It's hard to believe that things could have been as bad as Murry seems to make out, at least not all the time, although the recollections of the time on the farm by Murry's children are, in many ways, more cynical of the community members than Murry himself.[5] The farm continued as a community until 1947/8 when one of the few pacifists with any farming experience, Dugald Ferguson, took over as farm manager (he also took over the tenancy on Murry's death in 1957). Speaking in 2007 Ferguson said 'Murry was being criticised all the time, folks had these stupid notions you know. When folks were finding it hard on the farm they'd look round for a stick to beat him with. Ideas were like steam, they tended to rise and disperse. You never criticised other farmers in the same way. You might think the man you worked for was an old bugger but if you didn't like it, you went somewhere else. At Lodge Farm, if people didn't like a job they always had some principled objection to it. They'd never say I just hate doing it. When I came it was a life commitment I felt. I never seriously

thought about giving up and even when there was no community there after Murry's death and I took over the tenancy, I still felt I was building Lodge Farm up as a memorial to Murry.' **6**

The problems encountered on Lodge Farm were by no means unique. Cliff Holden who ran a pacifist community farm at Crossways, Cradley, near the Malvern Hills, funded by local Quaker John Jenkins, had a similar tale to tell. 'There were four of us and I gave the others ten shillings a week pocket money but nothing for myself. We lost money. Sending one boy to buy a cow he came back with a car and a radio. I threw them out and I worked the farm by myself for some months in order to make a profit to pay back John Jenkins.' **7**

Poet, playwright and pacifist Ronald Duncan kept a diary of his attempt to set up a co-operative farming community on a derelict farm near Welcombe in Devon. Extracts of the diary were published in *The New English Weekly* and later in its entirety as *Journal of a Husbandman*. Duncan's diary entries sketch out what would seem to be an all too familiar story. Things start off with a burst of ideological fervour: 'My intention is to found a community, an order based on agriculture. I know very little about farming, no more than the average person who has spent a good deal of time in the country but has not participated in its activities; in other words very little indeed ... By community I mean first a group of people co-operating instead of competing ... By 'based on agriculture' I mean that it should grow its own food, bake its own bread and weave its own clothes ... we are sick of ideas which never get anywhere but tepid flat pamphlets bulging with abstractions and suppositions ... Better to start here, where I am, than wait for a vague millennium.'

That is then followed by efforts to rally the members: 'I asked Leonard and John to come over to North Mill for dinner. This they did. And the whole night I spent going over what we were trying to do and seeing if I couldn't get their enthusiasm to persist into the day. It is too easy to make people interested in a project whilst discussing it over a good fire and good coffee. They see things done before they're thought of or begun. They agree it is a good thing to reclaim the farm and support ourselves entirely from it, and I said that if we could not do that, we ought to join the army ...' **12th March 1940**

The new community then has to cope with an influx of new people wanting to join: 'A Henry Stone has followed his first letter up by visiting us before I had

had time to answer. He is most enthusiastic for all our plans and intentions; in spite of the fact that I now describe the realities, difficulties and shortages of the place in the grimmest colour in order to discourage those who seek a retreat, a free ride. He saw that we live largely on rice and lentils. And told him that were he to stay for six months' novitiate he could expect no cash return and would receive only his bought rations and milk, butter, cheese, potatoes and a share in anything else the farm produced. The difficulty of his joining us is that he has a young wife and baby. I told him that although he may be prepared to live on short rations his wife may not be so willing in the long run ...'

25th September 1940

After 18 months things seems to be working out 'There are now ten of us; our average age is twenty-four; before the war we were all pen pushers, either paid or unpaid; none of us with any farming experience. Most have no money; a few enough to last a few months. The money is pooled, a steward is appointed to buy the provisions we cannot produce. For most days it is chicken rice for lunch which we buy at a penny a pound. But we have plenty of milk, eggs, bread and vegetables. The two babies thrive. It could be said that we are townees back on the land, not drawn to it out of sentiment or amusement, but by economic necessity. We are doing the right thing, for we have no other alternative; but we say we are reclaiming this land from choice, as a form of repentance and because it is a pleasure in itself.'

3rd January 1941

Then things start to take their toll; '... I went to Travel Bridge to see how Alfred was getting on. He was not. He was sitting in the hedge, drugged

with self-pity. I tried hard to encourage him, pointing out that it was now possible to see across the hedge and how useful the work was. But he complained that it was all drudgery and that it gave him no time to write. I restrained myself from asking him why he came here but I tried to point out that we had taken on the job of clearing a derelict farm and that our living depended on it. His reply was that poets and priests should be supported by the society in which they lived and could not be expected to dig with the others ...'

15th February 1941

After that people leave and things slide from there; 'Now that the Stones have gone, only John and I remain to do the work which was planned for half a dozen. Obviously we shall have to stop clearing land and concentrate on preventing what has already been reclaimed going back again. The general plan now is to concentrate on milk and to get those queer shaped fields back into three or five year leys. And to keep up fertility and balance the export of milk we are collecting swill from two camps and Bideford ... Perhaps this will work, keep the milk flowing and the rats out.'

10th September 1941

Towards the end the diary entries become more involved with the economics of small scale farming and reflective on the attempts at building community: 'As far as my own attempt to construct community goes, it was apparent that weeds, rats and wireworm were not our worst pests – the greatest waste, I say, came from our own lack of discipline. It is all very well discussing social orders in vague terms but the reality of them is in the precise practical arrangement of infinite details. Who milks the cow, who eats the cream, who puts the tools away and what can one do about it if he doesn't? The modern farmer merely sacks his paid labourer. In trying to create a small community, an order without a wage sheet, the solution of these practical matters of everydayness was the beginning and the end.'

8th January 1942

'For the last month I have been trying to get the farm in order so that I can run it entirely by myself. I cannot use all these tools nor tend to half of it. And so I have had an informal sale before which I collected the remnants of harness, tools, rabbit traps from hedges; and the Yeofords and other neighbours came down and many of my prized but surplus possessions went up the hill. My neighbours who for three years have not commented on my experiment in community farming have, now that I have abandoned it, expressed themselves plainly; as Yeoford said: 'Everybody makes mistakes. I once went in for keeping moor ponies.' '

5th October 1942

After the war Duncan worked as a writer and journalist. He helped Benjamin Britten finish the opera Peter Grimes, and wrote the libretto for The Rape of Lucretia. He was instrumental in setting up the English Stage Company at London's Royal Court Theatre in 1956 and he wrote the film script for the 1968 film *Girl on a Motorcycle* starring Marianne Faithfull.

Pacifist in the City

The pacifist land units had their urban counterparts in the Pacifist Service Units (PSU) – established from 1940 onwards as a somewhat loose confederation of organisations providing COs with socially useful work in major urban areas.

Initially all the Units were engaged in some form of emergency work arising from the Blitz. They offered rudimentary medical aid to people using the air raid shelters, and they helped in the clubs and play centres established by the local authorities for children in the shelters.

A Cohen, The Revolution in Post-War Family Casework

By 1942 there were nine full-time units in London with further units in Bristol, Cardiff, Liverpool, Manchester and Sheffield. The 'social work' was varied. 'Unit A' was working on various general duties at Guys Hospital, 'Unit B' in Brockley was doing community work on the Honor Oak Estate, in Hampstead, 'Unit L' was doing all the maintenance, secretarial and social work at Anna Freud's nursery. Other units developed play centres and youth clubs, whilst in Sheffield the unit offered themselves as guinea-pigs to the Sorby Research Institute for a medical investigation of scabies. Because of their beliefs the PSU workers brought a sense of moral purpose and a pacifist ethic to the work that they carried out. Some of the work of the units would go on to have lasting effects on social policy and practice after the war. The Liverpool Unit, 'Unit M', had started working with so-called 'problem families' from a base in a large empty Victorian house on Grove Street and developed a way of supporting them that would eventually come to be known as 'family casework'.

We used from the basement right to the very top attic. The dining room and kitchen were down in the basement. Upstairs we had an office and all the other rooms were where we had to be bunked out. I remember being on a bunk above Mike Lee. The top attic was used for discarded clothing to supply the needs of cases. It was very bare indeed. I mean to get a piece of knitted carpet to stand on when you get out of bed was marvellous! 3

Ken Richardson, Liverpool PSU member

None of the members of the unit had any background in social work, having come from jobs in the civil service, industry and commerce. The work was hard and often very challenging – they often worked with families that other social workers had given up on and faced hostility from other professionals, both for their pacifism and because they were seen as meddling amateurs. But gradually they were able to win over many through the success of their work. The Liverpool Unit carried on working after the war under the name the Family Service Unit. As well as the 14 semi-official PSU Units there were also more small informal service communities advertising for members in the pages of *Peace News*, such as the Ellerslie Community in South Wales and the West London Social Service Community, a small income pooling community who devoted any surplus money and energy 'to social and cultural service'.

As a result of the influence of PSU ideas on postwar social policy and social work practice, people who had previously been subject to a hostile social policy and an unsympathetic social work were brought into the mainstream of a kinder policy and a more informed practice. Undoubtedly there was a cost to the organisation; the utopian-idealist life-style became peripheral and then extinct.

A Cohen, The Revolution in Post-War Family Casework

Training Pacifists

The problem of conscientious objectors lacking relevant skills and experience for land work was identified very early on and a number of training farms were set up to help overcome this obstacle. Towards the end of 1939 the Pacifist Service Bureau had contact with two sympathetic Methodist Lincolnshire farmers, Bill and John Brocklesby, who offered to sublet one of their farms, the 200-acre Collow Abbey Farm, for the Lincolnshire Farm Training Scheme (LFTS). Two pacifists, Dick Cornwallis and Roy Broadbent who financed the project, and their families moved onto the farm, which had no electricity or mains water, and in April 1940 the first six trainees arrived. With John Brocklesby acting as their agricultural adviser, the scheme began. A total of 29 further trainees arrived during the year.

The basic training period was to be three months and in that time, depending on the seasons, they would have to learn to milk a cow by hand, feed chickens and pigs, harness and groom horses, to plough, harrow and drill and to drive both tractors (steel-wheeled Fordsons) and horses. Early rising, the noise and smell of farmyard animals and working right through the day at tedious, back aching jobs like singling sugar beet, were at first very difficult for the many physically unfit trainees.

John Makin, *Pacifist Farming Communities in Lincolnshire in World War Two*

Almost in parallel to this scheme, another pacifist training project was being formulated. At a conference looking at how to go about setting up and funding agricultural communities for COs, held at the Adelphi Centre in December 1940, the decision was taken to form a society. This society, called the Community Land Training Association (CLTA), was to buy and run a farm for training pacifists. An appeal for funds was made through the pages of *Peace News* and the Brocklesby brothers in Lincolnshire were asked to look for a suitable farm. They came up with the 310-acre Laurels Farm at Holton Beckering just a few miles from the Collow Abbey farm and by the spring of 1941 it had been bought for £8,500. The two farms would turn out to be the start of a cluster of pacifist farms in the area that would eventually grow to farm something like 1,000 acres in all. There were occasionally other places where COs could get training. In Somerset the group that had been set up to take over the Bruderhof farms eventually bought Goose Green Farm at Sutton Mallet and ran it for a few years as a training project with some sort of co-ordination with the CLTA. A report in *Peace News* in February 1941 stated that 'both the Goose Green and Lincolnshire Schemes are conceived as single enterprise in a chain of similar societies and training farms to be extended throughout the country'. But the Lincolnshire farms were the only ones that really took off, becoming something of a pacifist cause-célèbre, with annual reports on their progress being published in *Peace News* and various Community Service Committee publications, such as the *Community Broadsheets* published two or three times a year during the war. At the beginning of 1941 the LFTS purchased two further nearby farms at Bleasby Grange and Floral consisting of '286 overworked acres and two dilapidated houses'. By the end of the same year the CLTA had added to its acreage the neighbouring Holton Grange farm after 'a West of England farmer', Gerald Vaughan, had purchased it and let it to them rent-free for seven years. This doubled the number of trainees they could take. Trainees came from all walks of life. The register for Collow Abbey farm records clerks, engineers, teachers, students, printers, accountants, artists and journalists, as well as an ironmonger, a boiler house attendant, a typist, a decorator, a pilot, a bookbinder, a tailor, a shop assistant, a machinist and a grocer. Training could last anything up to a year and, as well as building up practical skills and physical stamina, there were farm talks and discussions on such topics as cropping plans. Trainees were divided up into farming groups and committees, each with responsibility for different areas of work on the farms. The hard work did not prevent the trainees from finding time for recreation. They attended pacifist meetings in Lincoln, had a 'first rate collection of gramophone records', played football with the locals and set up a branch of the county library at one of the farms. At first the new inhabitants of the farms were a cause for concern, both among the local villagers and the authorities. Not only were their appearances somewhat unusual for farm labourers; wearing cricket blazers, evening suits etc and with beards and uncut hair, but some of their activities raised a few eyebrows. Dick Cornwallis was an enthusiastic moth and butterfly collector and could be regularly found hunting butterflies with white nets during the day and out at night trying to catch moths by torchlight, leading to the suspicion that the 'conchies' were signalling to enemy aeroplanes. This led to a dawn raid by over a hundred soldiers on Collow Abbey Farm on the morning of 6th June 1940 and the whole group being arrested and taken to Louth police station in military trucks where they were questioned. The authorities eventually released them all after coming to the conclusion that they were harmless. Later relationships with the locals improved with the bookkeeper for the CLTA assisting local farmers and neighbours with official letters and documents. The groups also lent to, and borrowed machinery from, local farmers. As well as training 'official' Conscientious Objectors, the land-based communities acted as a network of safe-houses for those on the run from the authorities. A number of pacifist artists found their way to the Lincolnshire farms. George Todd and Peter Hancocks who had been together at Sheffield School of Art were later joined by the printmaker Joan Lock. In the Autumn – Winter 1942 issue of the *Community Broadsheet* it was reported by Victor Farley that the Community Farming Society '... supports over forty men, women and children living in two farmhouses and nine other houses and cottages in the district'. A year later the Society was looking at trying to form a nucleus of more permanent 'continuity men' who thought they might take up farming as a vocation and who could help with the training of others. In the same year the society purchased Holton Hall from the army as additional accommodation for single men. As the farms became more successful during this period the group moved from simply giving pocket money toward profit-sharing and talk turned to the long-term future of the scheme. In December 1944, at a two-day gathering held at Holton Beckering entitled the 'Aims and Purposes Conference', a series of idealistic proposals were hammered out and put to the directors of the Society. These included that all members should have 'maximum scope for self expression in the fulfilment of daily functions, having regard to his freedom of conscience...' and that they should recognise 'the evils inherent in a society based on interest-bearing money' and should aim to free themselves from this evil. Unfortunately the reality of the situation as the war drew to an end wasn't going to lend itself to some continuing pacifist farming utopia.

Throughout its time the CFS at Holton Beckering had lost money (loans were now being called in and gifts were no longer being made) and it would lose more as the economy switched to a peace-time footing and some of the protection afforded to wartime food production began to disappear. The last trainees began to return to their former jobs, if still available, or to continue their education. CFS could not last in its existing form. Consequently the Board of Directors of CFS agreed to break it up and rent land to people closely connected with the Scheme, so that one day they could buy the land and farm for themselves.

John Makin, *Pacifist Farming Communities in Lincolnshire in World War Two*

From Kindertransport to Kibbutzim

The evacuation of approximately 10,000 unaccompanied Jewish children from Germany, Austria, Czechoslovakia and Poland to Britain at the start of the war, known as the Kindertransport, was largely in response to 'Kristallnacht' on 9th November 1938 when Nazi mobs destroyed synagogues and smashed Jewish stores across Germany and Austria. The British Jewish Refugee Committee made an appeal to Parliament, and it was agreed to admit to England an unspecified number of children up to the age of 17. When the children arrived in England, they were disbursed throughout the country: some were taken in by foster families, some went to orphanages or group homes, while some worked on specially established farms.

Following the placing of an advert in the London Times, the use of Great Engeham Farm in Kent was given rent-free to the British Council of the Young Pioneer Movement for Palestine (Hachsharath Hanoar). It opened in June 1939 and housed 134 children and 30 chalutzim (pioneers training to go to join kibbutzim). It served primarily as a transit camp for up to 350 13 to 16-year-olds. After a few weeks at the camp the youngsters were moved to newly-formed Zionist agricultural training centres, or Hachsharot, set up in run-down stately homes and mansions around the country, where they took part in training and the relevant visas and entry papers for Palestine were arranged for them. In November 1939 Kent was designated off-limits to foreigners and the farm was forced to close. A group from Kent of around 65 children and 26 adults moved to Bydown House near Swimbridge in Devon.

Appeals went out in the local newspaper for items of clothing, books, pencils and magazines.
The vicar of Swimbridge, Revd H Rushbridger, made an appeal for items to be sent to
the vicarage or directly to Bydown. A piano was loaned for the musical activities.
The local Marks & Spencer store in Barnstaple donated essential items of clothing.

Helen Fry, Jews in North Devon during the Second World War

Around the house there were greenhouses, outhouses, a couple of cottages and a few acres of land that the refugees worked growing potatoes, cabbages and cereals. There was not really enough land for everyone to work and so some also worked at nearby farms and factories. In March 1940 an offshoot of the scheme was set up in a house in nearby Braunton which housed another 30 young men and ran through until December. In May 1940 Bydown was affected by the government's policy of interning 'enemy aliens'. All men and boys over the age of 16 were arrested one morning and transferred to the internment camp on the Isle of Man. The scheme finally closed in October 1941 when the lease on the property ran out.

Over in Northern Ireland there was another somewhat longer lasting refugee 'kibbutz'. In early 1939 members of Belfast's Jewish community took out a lease on a 70-acre farm at Ballyrolly outside Millisle on the Ards Peninsula, County Down. The setting up of a 'Refugee Settlement Farm' was agreed by the authorities on condition that once trained they would 'emigrate to Palestine or the dominions'. Funded by Jewish communities in Belfast, Dublin and Cork, the farm housed a community of some 200 Jewish refugees between

1939 and 1948. The refugees came from a number of places: some had previously been in a crowded hostel in North Belfast, 30 children came from the Kindertransport, a group of 35 Chalutzim, one or two families and some older refugees came after escaping from Europe.

The farm prospered. It had outstanding harvests of vegetables, potatoes, wheat, oats and barley. It kept beef and milk cattle, chickens and bees. Its population was swollen during the summer by children and students from Jewish communities in Dublin and elsewhere, keen to experience life on an Irish kibbutz. Local farmers were generous with advice and equipment.

Jane Leonard, Ulster Museum 2002

The farm had its own laundry, tool shop, shoemaker, carpenter, bricklayer, mason and plumber and was largely self-sufficient in food. It had its own synagogue and Jewish soldiers serving with American forces later in the war often joined the community for services. By getting the farm classed as a 'voluntary internment camp', the scheme avoided the problem of all adult men being sent to the Isle of Man when the Internment regulations came in. In February 1946 a group of about 60 Holocaust Survivors were the last group of refugees to come to the camp. They were flown from Prague to Belfast and brought to the farm for several months rehabilitation where they rested, regained weight and learnt English. The Refugee Settlement Farm at Millisle finally closed in 1948.

Other wartime refugee 'kibbutzim' certainly existed during the war. In Stalybridge in Lancashire there was a group known as Kibbutz Hakorim set up by the Socialist-Zionist youth movement Hashomer Hatzair. The group worked as miners in a local coal pit. In East Lothian 160 teenage Jewish refugees were taught forestry and farming skills at Whittingehame Farm School from 1939 - 41. A group calling themselves the 'Jewish Christian Community' were based at 'Zion' Archway House at Kenninghall near Norwich in 1939 where they worked six acres of land until they fell foul of the Internment regulations and were forced to disband.

*Millisle Chalutzim
Summer 1940*

The wear and tear of communal living

The anarchist writer George Woodcock catalogued a cross section of the wartime communities movement at the time. Freedom Press published his account in 1944 under the title *The Basis of Communal Living*. In the book Woodcock, himself a conscientious objector, protects the identity of the communities by referring to them anonymously only as community number 1,2,3 etc – a touch of paranoia brought on, presumably, by the fact that some communities may well have been harbouring COs still on the run from the authorities at the time. The picture that comes across from Woodcock's writing echoes the experiences of those in the CPFLU units, the training farms and other communities, of struggles with lack of skills and resources.

At Community 10 members were 'labouring gallantly under difficulties since only one of them had previous experience of farming'. While at Community 3 ploughing was being done '... with the aid of a pony and a very old horse which has to be rested at the end of every furrow'. Community 6 complained it was '... painfully short of implements and stock, and our immediate wants in the way of harness, wirenetting, pig troughs, beehives ... would fill a book', and funds were so short at Community 5 that they were no longer able to accept new members. Other groups were struggling with matching their principles to the reality of communal living, with one member of Community 13 stating that '... the anarchic principle is the only one consistent with freedom and individual integrity. But this does not presuppose absence of discipline, but rather a condition of 'unrepressed self-discipline ...' and yet others were trying to keep members: Community 9, which at one time had 20 members, was faced with dwindling numbers: 'Now there are plenty of jobs going at the minimum wage of £3 a week, and it requires a strong feeling of worthwhileness of a land settlement for a CO to put up with a very low subsistence and the nervous wear and tear of communal living.' Overall Woodcock paints a picture of a struggling, but thriving, communities movement during the war. This is born out by reports of communities in other places, most notably in the pages of *Peace News*, where some of the communities reported on appear to be more successful than some of those visited by Woodcock. One such group was Elmsett based at Nova Scotia Farm in Suffolk. Started in 1939 the group issued a statement of its founding ideology:

We realise that it is useless to try to redesign the superstructure of the old system while the foundations are at fault, and have decided that we must help to lay the foundations of a new order based on the principles of brotherhood and co-operation of all humankind. We therefore renounce the selfishness of the old order, and this can only be done by sharing our life together in a true community, working not for personal reward but for the benefit of the whole and holding all material goods in common.

Peace News, January 1939

Elmsett was an ambitious project, well organised and seemingly well resourced. As well as managing a mixed farm the group restored farm buildings and found time to organise a range of social activities. 'Imagine the dining room after the mid-day meal. Members of the community are reclining easily in chairs about the room, in various stages of repletion. The gramophone is playing Debussy's 'La Mer' as being the music most suited to sultry weather. This is the period of siesta before work for the afternoon recommences. Perhaps one of the girls is attending to some small item of sewing out of hours – perhaps not (this is not a hint)."

"The Community Day – Elmsett" in *Community in a Changing World*, 1942

Decisions were taken by consensus at community council meetings. There was an attempt to share unskilled work equally between men and women. They had plans to convert the farm away from livestock as they themselves moved to a vegetarian diet. The group operated an income pooling system, organised study groups, Peace Pledge Union meetings, and Sunday evening services and each week members sold copies of *Peace News* in Ipswich town centre.

Interviewed for the Channel 4 TV series *Far Out* in 1999, one of the members, Noel Hustler, remembered: 'Life at Elmsett was hard: We had very little money and tried to live off farming the small amount of land that we had. Most of us were urbanites and so found the early mornings, bitter weather in the winter, and punishing physical labour extremely arduous. But I loved it, I loved the arrangements and it was a new life. I had never met such a thing before.' Noel also recalled the personal relationships between members of the group. "It's obvious, I suppose, when you were remote from your family but living with twelve other people, three or four of whom are girls, that relationships would build up and, indeed, they did. Some of us had no inhibitions with regard to relationships. We were thoroughly fed up with the hypocrisy of social life as it went on in town and were glad to be free to be with whom we wished ... The fact that some people were sleeping together we accepted, be they a man and girl or two boys or whatever ... At the time the relationships that took place were so taboo that they just wouldn't have been accepted outside. What went on wasn't broadcast abroad, the village people never asked any questions ...'

Close by at the Frating Hall Farming Society near Colchester things weren't quite so successful as at Elmsett. In an article headed "Headaches, Heartaches, Highdays and Holidays" in the *Community Broadsheet* D Watson complained of the difficulties of living with others. Of trying '... to be tolerant in the face of persistent disruptive elements, to feel that through the insensitiveness and irresponsibility of some members, the whole edifice which has taken so much time, labour, and love to erect may any minute be pulled down; is a great strain ... As for the minor heartaches and irritations, they are daily occurrences. To discover the stoves have not been stoked nor the water pumped, or that somebody has 'swiped' the soap out of the bathroom after you have undressed, or worse still, the fishman doesn't turn up, to say nothing about having to hand pick chaff out of socks after threshing before they can be washed!' Although he does conclude with 'Only living and working and suffering together binds people's hearts to one another. As an advertisement for Practical Pacifism, this experiment in communal living, is the best thing I know.'

At the end of *The Basis of Communal Living* George Woodcock tried to draw some conclusions from his journey through the wartime communities movement. 'It seems evident that while many British communities have survived and even prospered, they have yet produced no effective challenge to existing society. Their success has been limited to the functional level, and they have most value as experiments in free and communal working relationships. In this restricted circle their achievements have real significance.'

A Community's Journey

In *Community Journey*, published in 1956, George Ineson tells the story of a group that would manage to continue beyond the end of the war. In the years before the war George had been training as an architect in London, moving in anarchist, socialist and pacifist circles. He joined the Peace Pledge Union and studied the life and works of Gandhi. With his friends and partner Connie he discussed various ideas for forming or joining a community. With other architecture students they planned a self-build community of timber-framed houses somewhere close to London where they could commute into the city to work. They planned to visit the Bruderhof in Wiltshire but never quite made it. At the outbreak of the war he found himself working for an architect in Cornwall where he had moved with Connie. They lived in a rented cottage in Newlyn where they seem to have become a centre for visitors of every radical persuasion. They joined a local group of the Peace Pledge Union and involved themselves in campaigning locally. George was called before the local tribunal and granted exemption from military service. He started working as a labourer on local farms. One evening he returned home to find the local police searching the cottage and questioning Connie about their political activities and enquiring if they knew another local pacifist who ran a small-holding a few miles away with the same bright blue coloured front door? The very next day they set out in search of the other blue door. On the gorse-covered hills known as Lady Downs, in a tiny four-roomed stone cottage, they met Gerald Vaughan and his three-year-old son Patrick. Gerald had led a 'strange and unconventional life' – he had been a sculptor in Dorset, an interest in D H Lawrence had led him to live in an empty cottage perched on a rocky crag above Zennor, he had travelled the roads of Ireland with a donkey and cart, spent a year living with the Bruderhof in Wiltshire and gave them most of the money he had inherited from his father (money his family had made from the tobacco trade). He had taken the small-holding on Lady Downs near Nancledra just before the outbreak of war. 'A friendship began which was to make possible our plans for starting a community ... His political beliefs were a cross between anarchism and socialism similar to our own, but against a very different and more intuitive background."

Gerald offered his small-holding as the starting point for a community. So in September 1940, along with a handful of other local pacifists, they began to work the 13 acres whilst still living in various surrounding villages.

We had no money to buy much in the way of implements and, as a result, we were learning the feel of the earth directly and intimately, scything the corn and binding by hand, planting and lifting the potatoes with the long-handled Cornish shovel. We had meetings now and again but no form of authority or discipline; we very soon met difficulties in personal relationships and discovered that we had no knowledge at all of how to deal with them. I remember deep and insoluble depressions coming over me at times ...

George Ineson

In 1941 the community bought another two small-holdings after Gerald inherited money when his brother was killed in the war. By this time the community had grown to twelve. The main income of the community was milk production from a few cows which they kept along with pigs, poultry and goats. They also grew vegetables for sale. They started income pooling and attempting to share all possessions, something that turned out to be easier to agree in principle than to carry out in practice whilst living in five separate houses. By the spring of 1942 the group realised that they faced enormous difficulties trying to make a living from such a small acreage of fairly poor quality soil. Added to which were the problems of trying to form a community whilst being geographically separated in different households. They decided that the only way forward was to try and find a larger farm where they could all live together. They handed in notice on their cottages and started to look for a suitable farm. This was to be financed by a generous loan offer from Gerald Vaughan who had decided that it was not possible to live in community without a shared religious faith and had bought himself a farm near St Just.

The group looked at a couple of farms in Cornwall, but found nothing suitable that was available to rent or buy. With the dates for the termination of their tenancies looming they wrote to a number of other communities asking for accommodation and hospitality while they continued to look for a suitable property. The appeal was answered by a small group living near Ross-on-Wye, but unfortunately there was not enough room for all the community members and they were temporarily dispersed. George and Connie Ineson and their young family moved to the community whilst other members found lodgings. Over the next year they continued their search, looking at over 50 farms from Cornwall up to North Wales without any success. On the point of giving up altogether, things were complicated further by the break-up of the little group they were staying with. Searching for other local accommodation they stumbled across another small group that had just set up, known as the Adams Cot Community, who invited the group to live with them. The three families at Adams Cot had been inspired by the Bruderhof and after George and Connie had been with the group less than a month one of the members returned from visiting the Bruderhof and declared that he was leaving to join the Brothers in Wiltshire; he had reached the conclusion that it was a "mistake and waste of energy" to try and start small communities with no experience. He also wanted to withdraw the money he had put into starting Adams Cot. At almost the same time a land agent rang and offered a farm belonging to an 'esoteric religious group' in the Forest of Dean, somewhat reluctantly George Ineson went to inspect the farm overlooking the River Severn.

I then discovered that the occupiers of the farm ... were, in fact, a community; moreover, it was a community that seemed to be working successfully, yet without the narrow intolerance so often associated with a successful community. I spent the afternoon talking to them and did very little inspecting – it hardly seemed necessary. I explained that I had no money, but that I had reason to believe that Gerald would buy the farm for us ... Anxiously I asked whether I could have the first option for a few days; the owner smiled in a friendly way and said there was no need for me to worry about that if God intended us to come the others would not buy.

George Ineson

The farm consisted of fifty-five acres, eighteen covered with beech and oak woodland. There were three houses set amongst the trees at one end, overlooking the River Severn. The farm been named Taena by the previous owners. Plans were made to move, with some of the members of Adams Cot choosing to join with them, whilst others went to join the Wheathill Bruderhof. Having at last found a suitable property and having just witnessed the break-up of two small groups the soon-to-be Taena Community spent 'endless discussions' thrashing out the common basis on which the community would-be founded.

They came up with seven points of agreement:
(1) That the community should accept as guests any who are interested, as probationers any who wish to try out our life, and as members any who reach with us a sense of unity and common agreement.
(2) That the settling of all matters should be by discussion and by waiting until a common mind is found.
(3) That the community should never regard itself as permanent except in spirit and should keep itself open to change of form, place and work.
(4) That the corporate activities essential to the life of the community should include a communal meal and meetings for discussion and study in addition to those for business matters; it is essential that meetings dealing with problems of the life itself be restricted to members.
(5) That as many outside contacts as possible should be built up.
(6) That it should be the aim of the community to build up a system of education for the children.
(7) That the giving and taking of criticism and advice in the right spirit is essential to the life and growth of the community.

Because society is disintegrating from within and man has lost himself in a maze of technical achievements, we are concerned to build up a new society on the basis of an active belief in the brotherhood of man.
We feel that, for us, this means trying to make brotherhood live in the flesh at this point of time and not pushing off our responsibilities on to others by merely talking about possible future states.
So we come together to clear the ground and dig the foundations.

George Ineson

The second half of Community Journey depicts the years of the Taena community from moving in (in the late summer of 1943) up until 1951, seen very much through George Ineson's eyes. It is part diary, part dream log, part spiritual adventure. It tells of the group's delving into various esoteric ideas: members studied the works of Carl Jung, Krishnamurti and Rudolph Steiner and tried meditation and Yoga. It tells of a "maelstrom of cross relationships", of jealousies and resentments that threatened to undermine the community. It tells of political disagreements and questioning of each other's levels of commitment to the group. It rather strangely (given the detail that Middleton-Murray, Ronald Duncan and Ronald Lockley go into) says little of day to day farming life. The little Ineson does say though paints a now familiar picture. 'The farm was a difficult one to work; the fields were mostly on a slope, we had a small T.T. dairy herd of about ten cows, and in addition to food for the cattle we grew about four acres of potatoes; for many years these were to be our only sources of income. It was sufficient, but only just so; we were under-capitalised and there was a constant struggle to make do with worn-out implements and machinery.'

The most intriguing and surprising story that unfolds is the journey that they take from an almost atheistic community to embracing Roman Catholicism – this takes place over a number of years of seeking for a spiritual core of community life. They start off with times for quiet individual meditation and move to common prayer and even building their own small chapel. They made links with a couple of monastic communities and exchanged ideas on communal living with the monks there. At the same time the community was still struggling financially. In May 1947 Ineson records in his diary 'The financial situation is still deteriorating – to make the situation more critical, one of the cows has just died suddenly from eating a poisonous plant. We can't see how it is possible to last much longer.' They discussed the possibility of setting up a 'much looser, co-operative village scheme' as a way forward. Faced with both financial and spiritual crises, the community were drawn to Prinknash Abbey, a Benedictine monastery on the edge of the Cotswolds between Gloucester and Stroud, where the abbot was interested in the idea of a lay community growing up alongside the monastic community. After much soul searching and property viewing the group was able to buy Whitley Court, a 135-acre dairy farm close to the Abbey, with financial help from another benefactor, Catherine Englehart. In May 1952 they moved from the Taena Farm to Whitley Court where they would go on to establish a thriving community based on close links with the Abbey.

Now that we had been given this radical, reconciling unity we were at last free to begin the work of construction – a work in which we are still engaged. To build up a community does not imply a master plan which is progressively applied to every detail; this is the way of the twentieth century architect and is as disastrous in the life of a community as it is in the art of building. It is the growing point that we have to find; as soon as the organism is alive our work consists in solving a multitude of small problems as they arise and we no longer have to worry about the design. The world to-day has lost its growing point and every craftsman considers himself to be the architect; as a result we are building a tower of Babel instead of a cathedral.

George Ineson

The group was visited by sociologists researching communes in the early 1970's who commented that the group's '... ideas, sufficient as they had been as a response to the world of the late 1930's, were no longer enough to support the sense of purpose and identity of their project. Emotional crises came to be experienced as more turbulent and challenging than they had been in the past...' [8] and that in response 'the commune set out to build a monastic type of contemplative institution for men, women and children. A written constitution was adopted; forms of membership were specified; officers were

appointed, and leaders were elected. Participation in ritual events, prayer and religious instruction became the new basis of solidarity.'

Taena/Whitley Court is pretty much the only community to survive from the wartime period through to the next flowering of communal living in the late 1960's and early 1970's.

After 21 years as a close group with all possessions owned communally we changed to our present decentralised setup which is more like a very small village. Interests and lifestyles vary from family to family.
Organised meetings consist of a weekly mass and a weekly meeting in one of the houses.
Originally left wing, pacifist, political basis, we travelled through Zen and Yoga to the Roman Catholic church but are now very mixed in outlook and belief. One of the houses runs monthly retreats with meditation, Hatha Yoga, T'ai Chi Chuan dance and craftwork. There are also Hatha Yoga and T'ai Chi Chuan classes held here for people in the neighbourhood. We live in six houses on a 135-acre dairy farm and two of the families live on organically grown garden produce. Visitors are welcome.

Taena entry in *Alternative Communities* directory 1978

TAENA ~ Whitley Court ~ Upton-St-Leonards ~ Gloucester ~

Pacifist Theatricals

... reviving old traditions and experimenting with new forms ... they have remained true to their aim of working in theatreless districts ... they run their organisation co-operatively for they are completely united in their respect for their work ...

Review of Compass Theatre, *The Times* 1950

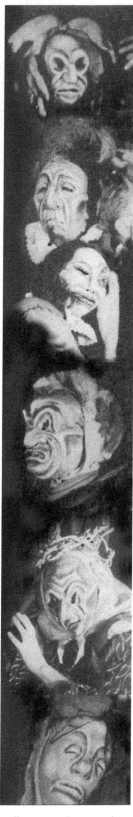

During the war years a number of small theatre companies formed to take theatre out around the country and deliver a decidedly political, and at times definitely pacifist, message. Two of these companies grew out of and had close links with pacifist land communities. The work that they pioneered was to be a precursor of much post-war community theatre and later 1960's and 70's fringe theatre.

The Adelphi Players were founded early in 1941 by R H Ward, a close friend of Max Ploughman, at the Adelphi 'socialist training' Centre set up by Ploughman and John Middleton Murry at Langham in Essex. They toured non-theatre venues performing a combination of 'neo-Elizabethan' play, 'intimate theatre' and self-penned plays.

The Compass Theatre company were formed in 1944 by John & Anne Crockett, two members of the Taena community at Warren Farm. As well as taking theatre to non-theatre venues, the company also developed a style that drew on dance, movement and the use of masks. They also did early theatre in education work in schools.

Both Companies were supported by CEMA, the Council for the Encouragement of Music and the Arts, a sort of civilian version of the Entertainments National Service Association (ENSA), which would turn into the Arts Council after the war. Both groups continued to perform into the 1950's when support for their work was withdrawn by the Arts Council

In their choice of repertory and their commitment to an egalitarian, community company existence, they pre-empted significant developments within oppositional, post-war theatre. Ultimately, in their breaking of new ground in terms of the venues and audiences they played to ... they helped to create the social and cultural conditions which facilitated the eventual growth of regional and community theatre after 1945.

Peter Billingham

For the full story of The Adephi Player and The Compass Theatre see:
***Theatres of Conscience 1939-53*, P Billingham**

At the pacifist farm at Holton-cum-Beckering in Lincolnshire The Holton Players grew out of evenings of music and play reading put on by the COs there. One of the founders was sculptor Roy Broadbent, father of the actor Jim Broadbent. After the war the Players continued in an old Nissen hut until it burnt down in 1960. In 1970 a chapel at Wickenby was purchased and converted into the Broadbent Theatre.

See: www.broadbent.org

Illustration from masks used by Compass Theatre

A Bomb to End All Bombs

I witnessed, only a few weeks ago, the total extinction of a city and of most of its inhabitants. The Japanese who once lived in the city were my enemies and I had good reason to wish them harm. My purpose in visiting them that sunny August morning was to kill; indeed, my whole business in life was to kill; and therefore I should have been satisfied at having killed so many in so short a space of time. When it came down to the point, however, not even the enormity of the spectacle, nor the certain knowledge that the war against Japan was over, was enough to obliterate the horror at so vast an extermination. **9**

Leonard Cheshire, letter to press, Armistice Day November 1945

Wing Commander Leonard Cheshire VC was the most decorated bomber pilot in the war. He was Commanding Officer of RAF 76 Squadron and succeeded Wing Commander Guy Gibson as commander of the legendary 617 'Dambusters' Squadron where he helped pioneer a new method of marking enemy targets for Bomber Command, flying in at a very low level underneath enemy radar to lay a trail of fire for other bombers flying at altitude to follow. 617 Squadron also pounded German defences with the Barnes Wallis' Grand Slam or Earthquake Bomb in the run up to D-day. By the end of the war he had completed 102 missions and was awarded the Victoria Cross for sustained courage and outstanding effort over an extended period, rather than a single act of valour. During the summer of 1945 the new Labour Prime Minister, Clement Attlee, sent word to Cheshire that he was to fly as a British observer on a secret American mission over Japan and was to leave immediately for the Mariana Islands to meet with the other observer, Professor William Penney, who had worked on the Manhattan project. On 9th August 1945, flying at 39,000 ft, the two men would see the complete destruction of Nagasaki, one of the largest sea ports in southern Japan. In one monstrous ten-millionth of a second as he witnessed the detonation of the Fat Man nuclear bomb over Nagasaki, Cheshire's mind revolted against everything that the nightmare mushroom cloud implied. The same blast that killed 80,000 Japanese curtailed all desire in him to kill again. There must, he thought, 'be better things to do with one's life. There must be some power higher in the universe than that of nuclear physics.' **10**

After the war Cheshire searched for that 'something better' to do. He considered studying geology. He suggested to some ex-RAF colleagues that they should form an experimental aviation company, claiming that 'Air travel removes national boundaries and nationalism, it links the common man of one nation with his counterpart in another and they find that they, as individuals, have no axe to grind.' He issued a challenge to ex-service personnel through the press. Why, he asked, should they not form colonies where they could live again the communal life they had known in the forces? They could each contribute a lump sum of cash as backing for the project, each working for it according to their own trade or profession, and each receive a weekly payment of £4. 'We will take over a disused aerodrome, or any other suitable estate, and move into it. Our first task will be to make ourselves self-supporting. For least of all do we want to live on charity in any shape or form. Whatever we lack in skill or resources we will make up for in hard work and unity.' The challenge was answered by some 200 enthusiastic men and women from all three Services. A number of meetings were held in a large forty-five-bedroomed house near

Market Harborough; and the first V.I.P. (Vade in Pacem) colony was started. A second colony was set up in a house on a 300-acre estate that Cheshire bought cheaply from his aunt called Le Court, near Liss in Hampshire.

A short piece in the winter 1947/48 edition of *The Community Broadsheet* described V.I.P as 'An international organisation nonpacifist but standing officially for establishment of world peace.' Its aim was the 're-establishment of comradeship of the fighting services in time of peace.' The writer goes on to describe the way the community was run.

Leonard Cheshire teaching croquet to 'patients' at Le Court

Members pool their capital and the income derived from following their trades. There are no individual rewards other than a small basic wage until all general necessities of the colony have been met. After that those giving most work and offering the greatest skill, benefit accordingly ... Families live in flats or cottages and home life is promoted although considerable communal activity is encouraged. School and nursery are provided for those wishing to use them. Kitchen and catering, shop and homework are run by women who spend the rest of their time in arts and crafts, kitchen garden, farm or office, as their tastes suggest.

The article ends with a description of future plans to absorb 'a large waiting list into new communities at home and overseas' and a statement that 'The association as such has no politics, provided the objectives of the association are respected and the welfare of other members regarded, the rights and freedom of the individual are fostered and upheld by all means.'

Leonard Cheshire set off in a private Mosquito plane to various parts of Western Europe to build interest in what he hoped would become a series of affiliated colonies. He suggested they might even found a colony in South America. He had visions of an international federation of colonies linked by radio, aviation and a universal fellowship of interests. He declared later that he had conceived the idea out of two convictions: 'one, that the only personal security left in a world of squabbling, class-conscious governments lay in friendship with the ordinary men and women who surrounded you; and, second, that the only physical security left in a world of rapidly swelling atomic arsenals lay in the dispersal of the world's peoples into small, self-supporting groups.'

The colonies were not a success. As well as recreating the 'service spirit', they also recreated a service-like administration, nasty little typed notices and a constant atmosphere of standing orders and rosters. The decline of the colonies was gradual and Cheshire put on a brave face declaring at one point 'We have faced bankruptcy twice. We have more than once reached the point where it seemed utterly futile to continue any further. We have made more mistakes in a year than I should have thought it possible to make in a lifetime. But now, at last, we are enjoying a temporary rest from misfortune and I am leaving soon for Canada to arrange our first V.I.P. colony overseas.' [11]

Cheshire had not given the real reason for his visit to Canada. Worn out by the war and the constant rush of the post-war years, he had been ordered to go overseas and relax. As he rested for six months in Canada the two colonies in Britain slowly slipped into serious financial debt. Finally word came and he returned to England to wind the colonies up and use what little remained of his personal wealth in order to pay off the thousands of pounds of debt. Interviewed afterwards whilst recovering from TB in 1956 Cheshire thought that the colonies had failed 'because there was no incentive for the individual to succeed spectacularly in his own trade, since all profits were pooled. The colonists were human. They did not mind contributing their share: but they did not wish to contribute one cent more than that share. If they earned more, they had to pool it: therefore, either they did not earn it or they resented bitterly paying it into the pockets of others. Conversely, there were those others who were not in the least averse to doing nothing and being supported by the rest.' [12]

Cheshire was in the middle of the painful process of packing up and preparing to sell the Le Court estate piece by piece to pay off the V.I.P creditors when he received a telephone call from a cottage hospital matron. The matron told him that an ex-airman and ex-member of the colony, Arthur Dykes, was dying of cancer, that his bed was needed and she was sure that "with his contacts in the RAF" he would be able to find an alternative place for him. This proved harder than Cheshire imagined and after weeks of trying he finally moved Arthur into the now deserted house at Le Court. Dykes was the first of a number of 'patients' who could find no place in the new embryonic National Health Service and who found their way to Le Court once the word went round. As the household grew, helpers came, some through local contacts and friends, others who had been associated with the original colony scheme and within a year numbers at the Cheshire home had reached thirty.

Because there were little or no resources at hand the regime at the Le Court was decidedly different to that at any traditional nursing home. 'Patients' had to help out in the struggling, pioneering venture and the effect on those who came was dramatic. '... many who arrived in a state of acute apathy, hardly caring where they were put or what they were given to eat, soon began to take on a new lease of life ... it is true to say that, despite all that was lacking in terms of organisation and material comforts, the household had a sense of purpose, a vitality, and generally speaking was a happy community.' In the summer of 1950 Cheshire realised that there was a continuing need for the services being offered at Le Court and that something needed to be done to bring the finances of the 'Home' under proper control. 'I took the only step that seemed open to me – a traditionally British one in the face of an impasse – and formed a committee, in the hope that it would gradually assume overall responsibility for running and maintaining the Home.' [13]

As the committee took over running of the Home, Cheshire was persuaded to take a job with Vickers-Armstrong, in order to 'get some rest'. He started working as Liaison Officer alongside Barnes Wallis on the experimental futuristic supersonic swing-wing Swallow and Goose aircraft project at Predannack Airfield in Cornwall. But despite having his own Spitfire to fly round the country and a cottage provided on the Lizard Peninsula he missed the personal contact of looking after others. When a young man wrote to him saying that he was an ex-frogman and an epileptic – and because of his physical disability he had been unable to get a job and been thrown out of his digs – Cheshire immediately wrote back inviting him to come and stay with him in his own cottage at Mullion. He then went on to talk to the base commander into handing over a derelict sergeant's mess on a monthly tenancy to turn into a 'Home'. The buildings were in a terrible state. In his spare time, with help from the ex-frogman, volunteers from the Vickers workforce and some Cornish locals, Cheshire knocked down partitions, laid bricks, painted walls and dug drains – and slowly the second Cheshire Home, named St Teresa's, took shape. This was soon to be joined by another home close by, called Holy Cross, as 'patients' rapidly filled the space at St Teresa's. All this activity was hardly the rest that he had been sent to Cornwall for and eventually the strenuous work ended in Cheshire being hospitalised and diagnosed with tuberculosis. He was sent to a sanatorium at Midhurst in Kent where he would spend two years recovering. Just before he was taken seriously ill, Cheshire was planning to go on a nationwide speaking tour to promote his ideas and his newfound Catholic faith. After tossing and turning for nine months in a hospital bed, he decided he wasn't about to let a little thing like hospitalisation stop him from getting his message out. With the aid of a tape recorder, some willing war veterans and two buses 'loaned' by another sanatorium patient (another ex-bomber pilot) the Cheshire message of 'Practical Christianity' was taken around the lanes of Cornwall and the streets of Soho.

The Cheshire Bus

Back at Le Court the committee of the newly formed Cheshire Foundation Homes for the Sick had managed to enlist the support of the Carnegie Trust and plans were made for an extensive refurbishment and rebuilding of the premises both at Le Court and at St Teresa's down in Cornwall. By this time the emphasis had shifted from admitting 'patients' with a wide variety of medical conditions to focusing on providing a supportive home for the younger physically disabled. By the end of 1954 four further homes had been established at Bromley, East Preston in Sussex, Ampthill Park in Bedfordshire and at Staunton Harold in Derbyshire. Cheshire Homes were seen as pioneering a new approach to disability and, looking back on those early days, in 1981, Cheshire reflected on the lessons he had learnt from those first 'patients'. They wanted, he said, 'not to be treated as if they were helpless and waiting to have everything done for them, but, on the contrary, longing to be up and doing it themselves, to the very best of their ability. They wanted to feel useful and needed, to find a purpose and a challenge to their lives, to have sufficient independence and opportunity to lead a life of their own choosing. Above all, I found they wanted to be givers to society, not just receivers.' **14**

Akhtar, M & Humphries, S *Far Out: The Dawning of the New Age in Britain* Sanom & Co 1999. ISBN: 1900178222

Armytage, W H G *Heavens Below* Routledge 1961. ISBN: 0415412900

Arnold, E C H *Stories of the Cotswold Bruderhof* Plough Publications 1984. ISBN: 0874864895

Billingham, P *Theatre of Conscience 1939-53* Routledge 2001. ISBN: 0415270286

Braddon, Russell *Cheshire V C: A Story of War and Peace* Companion Book Club 1956

Cheshire, L *The Hidden World* Fount Paperback 1981. ISBN: 0006264794

Cocksedge, Edmund *Vagabond for Peace* House of Freedom Christian Community Pubs 1991. ISBN: 0646064819

Cohen, A *The Revolution in Post-War Family Casework* Lancaster University 1998. ISBN: 1862200459

Community Service Committee *Community In Britain* Bruderhof Press 1938

Community Service Committee *Community In Britain* Lower Byfleet 1940/42

Duncan, Ronald *Journal of a Husbandman* Faber & Faber 1944

Fetherling, D *The Gentle Anarchist: A Life of George Woodcock* Univ of Washington Press 1998. ISBN: 0968716350

Fry, Helen *Jews in North Devon During the Second World War* Halsgrove 2005. ISBN: 1841144371

Goodall, F *A Question of Conscience* Sutton, Stroud 1997. ISBN: 0750907401

Hardy, Dennis *Utopian England Community Experiments 1900-45* Spon 2000. ISBN: 0419246703

Hayes, D *Challenge of Conscience: The Story of the Conscientious Objectors of 1939-49* Allen & Unwin 1949 ASIN: B002N9WCSO

Ineson, G *Community Journey* Catholic Book Club, London 1956

Lea, F A *Community in a Changing World* 1942

Lockley, R M *The Island Farmers* Witherby, London 1946

Maclachlan, L *CPFLU: A History of Christian Pacifist Forestry and Land Units* 1952

Makin, J *Pacifist Farming Communities in Lincolnshire in World War Two* East Midland Historian, 2004 University of Nottingham. ISSN 13501615

McKie, E *Venture in Faith: The Story of the Establishment of the Liverpool Family Service Unit* 1963

Middleton-Murry, John *Community Farm* Country Book Club, 1953

Moorehead, Caroline *Troublesome People: Enemies of War 1916-1986* Hamilton, 1987. ASIN: B001608J70

Oved, Yaacov *The Witness of the Brothers* Transaction Publications 1996. ISBN: 1560002034

Plowman, M & Plowman, D L S *Bridge into the Future: Letters of Max Plowman* A Dakers 1944

Rigby, Andrew *Pacifist Communities in Britain in the Second World War* Peace & Change Volume 5, Issue 2, Peace History Society and Peace and Justice Studies Association 1990

Thacker, J *Whiteway Colony: Social History of a Tolstoyan Community* Sutton Publishing 1997 ISBN: 0952176009

Wallis, J *Valiant For Peace: Fellowship of Reconciliation* 1991. ISBN: 0900368403

Wellock, Wilfred *Off the Beaten Track: Adventures in the Art of Living* 1961. ASIN: B0007JHK20

Woodcock, George *The Basis of Communal Living* Freedom Press 1944

Notes

1   Paper from Community Service Conference, printed in *Peace News* December 1938

2   Quoted in *CPFLU: A history of the Christian Pacifist Forestry and Land Units* L Maclachlan

3   Quoted in *The Revolution in Post-War Family Casework* A Cohen

4   See *Utopia Britannica* C Coates, 2000 page 157

5   Colin Middleton Murry, *One Hand Clapping: A Memoir of Childhood* Littlehampton Book Services, 1975

6   http://new.edp24.co.uk (18.11.07)

7   Private correspondence with the author

8   The Taena community is 'Fern Hill' in *Communes, Sociology and Society* Abrams & McCulloch, 1976

9   Quoted by Russell Braddon in *Cheshire VC: A Story of War & Peace*

10 ibid

11 ibid

12 Leonard Cheshire *The Hidden World* 1981

13 ibid

14 ibid

Post-war Communal Blues

... the house is the home, the whole home and nothing but the home; that it is right and proper that ...
cooking, eating, washing-up, laundering, study, social intercourse and recreation ...
should take place in the house and nowhere else.

Lawrence Woolf, summing up the 1944 'Dudley Report' [1]

Despite, or because of, the enforced communality of the war years, there appears to be a broad agreement amongst most commentators and historians that there was a reaction against all things communal in the years following the war. Whilst the popular nostalgic view often longs for a return to some great 'True-Brit' community spirit that got us through the war, the argument goes that at the time folks couldn't wait to get back to living their private lives in their private homes. Scratch the surface of this view, however, and the picture is somewhat more complex. Many of the wartime communal measures were viewed by some in a positive light. In a report in 1943, the Hygiene Committee of the Women's Group on Public Welfare on 'domestic standards and urban life' extolled the virtues of the communal catering measures set up; initially to serve those bombed out of their homes in London during the Blitz and later spread across the country as local-authority-run 'British Restaurants'. These had been initially opposed by the catering trade, but eventually numbered over 2,000 all over the country. These, along with workplace canteens, free school meals and food supplements for children, made a major contribution to the overall improvement in the general health of the population during the war. The Women's Group report had been prompted by calls from the National Federation of Women's Institutes, after protests from their members about the poor health of evacuees from the cities. Of the British Restaurants the report said that they had 'made a useful beginning, and it is to be hoped that commercial interests will not be allowed to bring about their abolition after the war'.

Part of the popularity of the British Restaurants was that they fell outside wartime rationing regulations; they also helped thousands of working women to feed their families. Once the war was over the emphasis changed somewhat and women were encouraged by male politicians to return to their domestic duties. In a debate on Domestic Supplies in the House of Commons, future Labour Prime Minister James Callaghan said 'The housewife feels – and I am inclined to agree with her – that the emphasis should be turned from the direction of public feeding back to private feeding.' In reply, Dr Edith Summerskill, Parliamentary Secretary to the Ministry of Food, said that she felt housewives would be dismayed if cafes or canteens were to close, leaving them to provide an extra meal at home.[1] Food rationing continued up until 1954, but the appetite of the authorities for providing communal meals had faded long before that and the British Restaurants were closed down.

The Dudley Committee, set up to devise minimum standards for post-war housing, also expressed support for providing a range of community and communal facilities. In its 1944 report it bemoaned the lack of 'club buildings, shops, schools and other amenities' in prewar housing developments and expressed support for the concept of 'neighbourhood centres' that might include such things as 'places of worship, the branch-library, a cinema, public house, branch administrative buildings, the necessary clinics, smaller club buildings, and a group of shops'.[2] At the 1946 Labour Party Conference voices were raised in support of post-war housing being provided with an even wider range of communal facilities. Describing housewives as becoming an 'oppressed proletariat' it was suggested that future housing should be provided with 'communal central kitchens with a hot meals delivery service, properly staffed nurseries and central play rooms, district heating centres and even communal sewing centres'.[3] This was echoed in the July 1946 report of the New Towns Committee which recommended that, in planning new towns, consideration should be given to providing groups of dwellings with their own restaurants and clubrooms.

Layout plan of Reilly Greens from The Reilly Plan 1945

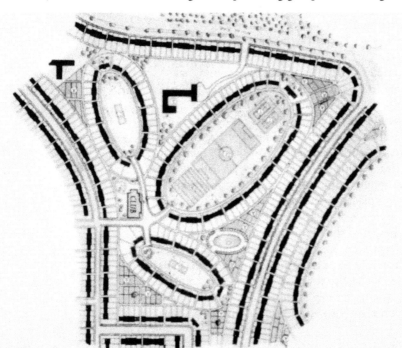

The most extensive communal proposals for post-war reconstruction were put forward by Sir Charles Reilly who had been Professor of Architecture at the University of Liverpool from 1904 until 1933. Reilly had designed a number of houses for Lord Leverhulme at Port Sunlight. Reilly's ideas for what became known as 'Reilly Greens' were developed during a period he spent working on post-war redevelopment of Birkenhead.

I suggested to the borough engineer that we should make a new layout plan together ... They were pleased with the idea and, chiefly wanting to get a semi-new planning principle adopted, that of houses [a] round greens... and the greens themselves arranged like the petals of a flower round a community building ...

Charles Reilly, *The Reilly Plan*

Reilly put forward a number of proposals; each using the same basic plan of grouping clusters of houses around a central green space with various communal facilities arranged in, on and around the green. These included: community centres, allotments, nursery facilities, communal kitchens and restaurants. In 1945 these ideas were expanded on with Laurence Wolfe and published in *The Reilly Plan*. The book went into great detail on some of the possible variations on communal life that might be lived in the new settlements.

Ordinarily the young couple do not take a whole house, but one of the kitchenless 'bridal suites' provided in the village green, and they either feed at the community centre or have their meals delivered in an insulated container. This means that both husband and wife can go to work or continue their studies ... just as if they were unmarried, until the sixth or seventh month of the first pregnancy, which may occur within about two years of the marriage.

The Reilly Plan

Reilly drew up a number of schemes for Birkenhead, including a plan for the Woodchurch Estate and large-scale plan for the redevelopment of large parts of the town, all based on the concept of the 'Greens'. But in the end none of the plans were adopted by the Conservative controlled council. It was left to others to champion the idea of communal housing estates. Reilly's plans were well received by some members of the architectural world. Clough Williams-Ellis writing in *The Adventure of Building* in 1946 saw the proposals as an extension of the way that services such as electricity, roads and streetlighting were already provided 'communally' and that Reilly's designs simply made it '... easy to extend this co-operation much further but in new and obviously sensible directions.' In December 1944 the Labour Party Conference passed a motion approving Reilly's 'ideas for community planning.' Reilly was a socialist and did work with other left-leaning clients such as the John Lewis Partnership. In 1945 he teamed up with the political economist Otto Neurath on a project to redevelop the Black Country town of Bilston. Neurath, an Austrian socialist Jew, had fled to England at the outbreak of war where he spent most of the war interned on the Isle of Man. He had served in the Bavarian revolutionary government in 1918-19, had been part of the 'Vienna Circle' during the 1920's and had a broad background in housing and planning issues. He had been secretary of the Austrian Association of Settlements and Allotment Gardens (Österreichischer Verband für Siedlungs und Kleingartenwesen or OVSK), a collection of self-help groups that set out to provide housing and garden plots to its members. He was also active in the Vienna Garden City movement. Through the 1930's Neurath had developed a pictorial graphic language which he called ISOTYPE to be used for presenting statistics and conceptual ideas to a wide non-academic audience. Working together, Neurath and Reilly became a very clear early example of what would later become known as community planning or community architecture.

Neurath's brief contribution to planning in Britain was to prioritise human happiness and to encourage planners to look at planning from the perspective of the people whose lives it affected.

Michelle Henning, *Imagining Post War Happiness*

The plan that Reilly drew up after the Austrian 'sociologist of happiness' had done his extensive consultations with the residents of Bilston was an adaptation of the ideas behind the Birkenhead schemes. The result was a combination of his original, organic 'flower petal' schemes outlined in The Reilly Plan and the hexagonal schemes of the Birkenhead plan. Each cluster of Greens was to have a clubhouse in the centre and it was proposed to incorporate a telephone system linking each house to the clubhouse to aid the establishment of a community network and so that meals could be ordered from the central kitchens. This feature was eventually dropped on technical and legal grounds. Once again the innovative proposals fell foul of post-war finances and politics and, although it was progressed much further than the Wirral scheme, in the end the Bilston plan was never built. A further private housing scheme based on the Greens

concept was drawn up by Reilly for workers at the Miles Aircraft Company factory on the Woodley airfield near Reading. This would also remain unbuilt.

It would fall to another West Midlands' town to realise a modified version of Reilly's vision. Dudley Town Corporation approached Reilly to prepare an outline scheme for the redevelopment of the 90-acre Old Park Farm along his 'village greens' lines to form part a plan for the town that would be enacted through special powers granted under the Dudley Corporation Bill of 1947 which enabled them to develop cultural

Proposed layout of Reilly Greens, Bilston

and communal amenities in the town. The scheme was carried out by a former student of Reilly's, Derek Bridgewater, and while more innovative features such as 'bridal suites' and telephone networks were absent from the plan, at least it made it off the drawing board and today forms a part of Dudley still known as 'The Greens'.

Nissen villas

Who cared if the huts were freezing cold, had condensation running down the inside of the roofs, were bare of any furniture, had no interior walls, no lighting and no running water and were made of wood, tin, or asbestos ... To the desperate families of the time it was somewhere to live!

David James – who grew up in Beech Barn Camp near Amersham

At the end of the war Britain faced a housing crisis: 110,000 houses had been destroyed by bombing, a further 850,000 had had to be evacuated because of structural damage, no new houses had been built for six years and building materials would continue to be rationed until 1951. On top of this, new households were forming at an almost unprecedented rate through a combination of the demobilisation of troops and the fact that during the war nearly a million marriages had taken place. Faced with a similar situation at the end of the First World War Harry Cowley in Brighton had started 'appropriating' houses for returning servicemen, a service he soon extended to civilians. He is remember for one incident when 'with a fake bomb in each hand he threatened to blow up an estate agent who tried to evict an elderly lady squatter.' **4** Harry and his self-styled 'Vigilante' colleagues, said to number 400 local war veterans, carried on their anarchist and anti-fascist activities throughout the 1930's. In May 1945, faced with the same chronic housing shortage, and the seemingly empty promises of 'decent homes for all', the Brighton Vigilantes (or 'the Secret Committee of Ex-Servicemen') once more started breaking into empty houses in Brighton and installing homeless families. By July, the activities of the Vigilantes had inspired others in seaside towns like Hastings and Southend to follow suit. Squats also started to spring up in major cities with groups in London, Liverpool and Birmingham.

This movement was the result of local initiatives rather than an organised extension of activity by the Brighton group. However, the press, by reporting each incident in some detail, helped to establish communication and from this a measure of organisation was fostered. By mid-July, leading members of the Brighton group – anarchists with experience of unemployment and anti-fascist struggles before the war – were travelling to other towns to address public meetings.

Andrew Friend, *The Post War Squatters*

Towards the end of 1945 and into the early months of 1946 the 'demob' of troops had begun to gather pace, adding to the housing crisis. Men were walking out of accommodation on military bases across the country to find themselves and their families literally 'on the street'. It is not clear from records quite when the first squat of military premises took place. But most sources agree that it was most likely to have been in Scunthorpe either in May or July of 1946 when a family moved into an unoccupied officers mess on an anti-aircraft camp just outside the town. Within days they were joined by other families who took over empty Nissen huts at the camp, 'booking in' by chalking their names on the Nissen hut doors. As the news spread other camps were occupied. Whether this was the first squatted camp or just one of many spontaneous squats is hard to tell – but the Scunthorpe squatters were interviewed by Movietone News and James Fielding, the 'chairman of the squatters committee', was filmed addressing the camera and giving a guided tour of the camp. 'My name is James Fielding. I'm a married man with four children and came to Scunthorpe on a job of work and spent many weeks of searching, which was fruitless, for accommodation ... I found that several of the huts had straw in them and that evidently sheep had wandered in, or had been put in by neighbouring farmers. I felt if it was right for animals to be put in, it was much more right that homeless human beings should have them ...'

Once the story had started to break in the press and on the radio those in dire need of housing started to follow the example of the 'Scunthorpe pioneers'.

... on the weekend of Saturday 10th August thirty families moved into army huts near Middlesbrough and were installed there before the local authority or anyone else knew what had happened. The invaders were not families of the workshy but those come to take jobs and were without accommodation. There had been no guard on the sites because it had not been thought necessary.

D Thomas, *Villains' Paradise*

At Seaham Harbour, on the same weekend, eight miners and their families were involved in an orderly take-over of a number of Royal Artillery huts; they elected a camp committee and started a rent pool to show that they were willing to pay for the accommodation. At the other end of the country at Harnham, near Salisbury, families occupied 32 empty army huts. On the following Monday one hundred squatters took over Vache Camp at Chalfont St Giles in Buckinghamshire, which had been earmarked for Polish soldiers and their families, and the White City Camp near Bristol was squatted by 50 families. Squatters had also occupied a disused miners' hostel near Doncaster, and another camp near Jarrow. As the week progressed squatters occupied sites near Newport, nine more around Bristol and condemned tenements in Edinburgh. Grimsby Council handed over the keys and turned on water and electricity to 22 RAF huts to house local families and there were reports of occupations in Warwickshire, Chesterfield, Durham, Ellistown in Leicestershire, Worthing, Coventry, Carlisle, Cowley, Chester, Barking, Eccles, Gloucester, Salisbury, Basingstoke and at a US Air Force camp in Watford.

A Northern Command spokesman reported that 'The army cannot prevent squatters from moving into disused military installations and it cannot turn them out'. The response of the various authorities was confused and very mixed. In Amersham the council issued a statement saying that it had requested that the Beech Barn camps be turned over to them for

Squatters in ex-army huts

housing and had received no reply from the War Office. While in Sheffield, the 'socialist' led council attempted to evict squatters from the Manor Lane gunsite camp, sending two lorries carrying demolition men accompanied by police, Aldermen, council officials and two double-decker buses to take the squatters to the local workhouse. They were forced to back down when the men working for the demolition contractor refused to knock down the huts with the squatters inside. In September, Aneurin Bevan, the Minister of Health, instructed local authorities to cut off gas and electricity supplies to property occupied by squatters. But by this time some councils were already directing homeless people to occupy empty huts and the squatters were organising communal cooking, nursery facilities and rotas to stoke the boilers left behind by the armed forces. On 10th October the House of Commons was informed that some 46,335 squatters were occupying 1,181 military camps across the country.

On 16th September 1946 Pathé News showed a film in news theatres across the country entitled Home Front Squatters of 'The Siege of London's Ivanhoe Hotel' in Bloomsbury. The film showed footage of police officers moving protesters along, members of the crowd throwing supplies up to people at upper floor windows and ended with a protester being led away by police. Squatting had come to the capital. The occupation of the hotel was part of a co-ordinated campaign supported by the Communist Party. It had started with 400 families moving in en-masse to Duchess of Bedford House – a seven-storey block of flats in Campden Hill. This was followed by occupations of premises in Upper Phillimore Gardens and Holland Park Road. Two days later 60 families had moved into Fountain Court in Pimlico, a small group had occupied a block of flats near Regent's Park called Abbey Lodge and the Ivanhoe Hotel 'siege' had begun. The government, spooked by the scale of the occupations, cancelled all police leave and issued instructions to the police to guard all empty buildings in the centre of London. Meetings of the newly elected Labour Cabinet were unsure how to proceed: they were worried that if they brought criminal prosecutions against squatters, juries might be unwilling to convict because of sympathy with the squatters' cause. Eventually they issued instructions for the squatters' leaders to be arrested and charged with conspiracy and incitement to trespass. In the afternoon following the arrests a demonstration of 12,000 people gathered in Leicester Square in support of the squatters. Soon after the arrests and with further threats of legal action the squatters agreed to move out.

Widespread support for the squatters came from trade unionists, who blacked work involving the wrecking of buildings as a deterrent to squatting in several northern towns, and had organised work parties to divert building materials to two squatted camps in North London and Yorkshire. Miners offered support by imposing an overtime ban when mine officials had tried to evict a family squatting in a colliery house. Public and press opinion had generally been in favour of the squatters whilst they had been taking over empty military camps, but after the mass London squats the government and the Tory press started a sustained publicity campaign against the squatters. In what amounted to a smear campaign the *Daily Mail* and the *Daily Express* gave front page coverage to unsubstantiated reports of people afraid to go out shopping for fear their houses would be squatted and of a rush to buy padlocks throughout suburbia. Aneurin Bevan made a statement suggesting that the camp squatters were somehow 'jumping their place in the housing queue' which was about as far from the truth as you could get as they were in fact moving into buildings which would mostly not otherwise have been used, and jumping out of the housing queue. The winter of 1946-1947 was particularly harsh and many of the squatters were driven out of their unheated Nissen huts and back into overcrowded accommodation. Despite the anti-squatter stance of the government, many local authorities supported the use of the camps as a temporary solution to their housing problem, although 'temporary' in some cases would last until the early 1960's. Councils carried out works to improve the facilities on the camps, connecting services, renovating the huts and in some cases erecting new wooden huts to provide extra accommodation.

Petersfield Rural District Council requisitioned the site in 1946, converting the army huts to make 146 units, capable of housing some 650 people and also providing a shop. They obtained some funds from Central Government to enable these conversions to take place, on the understanding that half the lettings would be made available to employees of the Engineers Supply Depot at Liphook. The site was renamed 'Superior Estate', but this seemed so pretentious that it was usually known locally as 'The Camp'. [5]

Pat Nightingale who lived at Superior Camp, Ludshott Common as a child

Whilst councils were getting their acts together, so were the squatters. Several camps around Sheffield had formed a 'Squatters Protection Society'. Representatives from camps in south-west Lancashire and Yorkshire had formed an area committee in Liverpool and were in discussion with others in London about forming a national federation. Around Reading, in Berkshire, there were ten squatted camps in all, and further camps just over the county borders in Hampshire and Oxfordshire. Fifty families occupying Nissen huts at an Anti-Aircraft Battery camp in Northumberland Road in Reading itself, sent a deputation to meet the Mayor of Reading at the beginning of September 1946. On the 8th September delegates from eight camps in the area, representing 250 families, met on the parade ground at Ranikhet Camp in Tilehurst to discuss forming a Berkshire Federation of Squatters. On Saturday 21st September they organised a demonstration in Reading, claiming that POWs were being looked-after better than former British servicemen.

In 1948 the government brought in the National Assistance Act which required local authorities to provide accommodation for the homeless. This did little to change the situation in the camps. In the Reading area the government allocation of new houses was 60 a year and there were some 720 applicants on the waiting list. While the mood of improvised holiday camp that had prevailed at many of the squats in the early days had gone and many of the huts were clearly in very poor condition, they would continue to provide homes to some for years to come.

... squatting worked. Time and again, councils were obliged to provide housing for those they saw as outsiders and queue jumpers, and to negotiate with them as the representatives of a legitimate interest in society. The squatters improvised and worked together in new ways, putting pressure on government and councils, so that housing remained high on the policy agenda for decades afterwards. Many of them had a lot of fun in difficult conditions along the way.

Paul Burnham, The Squatters of 1946

A Community in Paraguay

The Blue Star Line ships that started transporting the members of the
Bruderhof across the Atlantic to South America in late 1940 were all painted in
wartime camouflage. For four weeks at the height of the Battle of the Atlantic
the ships followed erratic courses, zigzagging to throw off the enemy U-boats.
While the crew practiced lifeboat drills and firing the ships' guns the
community of pacifist passengers whiled away the unaccustomed 'leisure' time
taking lessons in Spanish, playing chess and deck tennis and no doubt
wondering what the future held. The first group arrived at the Argentinean port
of Buenos Aires on 12th December 1940 and made their way up the Parana
River to the Paraguayan capital, Asuncion. They continued on to the
Mennonite colony at Fernheim in the Gran Chaco area who were to host them
while they searched for a suitable property. They would eventually settle on a
large estate 160 kilometres northeast of Asuncion, called Primavera, which they
purchased from a German settler.

*Estancia Primavera 'Spring Estate' consisted of a neglected cattle ranch surrounded by twenty thousand acres of
swampy grassland and virgin forest. Stands of sweet orange trees grew in the jungle, perhaps planted by Jesuit
missionaries long ago, but mostly the place was an untouched wilderness inhabited by howler monkeys, tapirs,
pumas, ostriches, parrots and boa constrictors. Now an entire village of Europeans with not much more than the
clothes on their backs had arrived to tame it into a liveable home.*

P Mommsen, Hommage to a Broken Man

By the summer of 1941 the whole community of 195 adults and 155 children
had made the perilous journey to the Primavera estate. The first to arrive had
lived in crude thatched lean-to buildings, constructed by Paraguayan workers,
each family being allocated a small roof space 'partitioned' off with hanging
screens. Using the considerable amount of tools, equipment and machinery
that they had managed to bring with them they set about establishing a new
community, Isla Margarita. They constructed a sawmill and started clearing
land for planting crops. Very soon it was realised that a second community
would be required and in 1942 Loma Jhoby (pronounced Lo-ma Ho-boo),
was set up about two miles away from Isla Margarita. As they became more
established they rented a house in Asuncion as an office to negotiate dealing
with the government and act as an agency for buying and selling goods to and
from local merchants. Later they opened a shop in the next-door house selling
decorative wooden products made at Primavera. In 1946 a third community
was set up on the estate called Ibate.

*The three Bruderhof communes at Primavera were established at a distance of two to three miles from one
another and although the production and service branches of all three were separate, all their economic activities
and income were managed jointly. Isla Margarita had its sawmill, wood workshops, a fruit juice factory, and
a bookbinding shop, while Loma Jhoby kept a beef herd and a slaughterhouse, and it was there that the central
hospital was later built. The third community, Ibate, had a bakery, shoemaker's shop, sewing workshop, dairy
herd, chickens, and the biggest central library in the Paraguayan settlement, which housed some 20,000 volumes,
mainly in German and English.*

Yaacov Oved, The Witness of the Brothers

The chief source of income for the communities was agriculture. They grew maize, wheat, sugarcane, manioc and rice. Initially the settlers used European farming techniques, but soon began to experiment with combining these with local methods, leading to increases both in productivity and crop yields. They cultivated market gardens for the supply of vegetables to the local population, and all around were tall citrus trees overloaded with fruit growing wild.

The Bruderhof would thrive in the post-war years in Paraguay. They set up schools and a hospital that would serve the surrounding area, with 10,000 patients on its books by 1954 and its doctors making long journeys on horseback to make 'house calls' to distant native huts. In 1945 they were paid a visit by the President of Paraguay, General Morinigo, who was suitably impressed by the settlers' economic achievements. They would survive the civil war that gripped the country in 1947. Numbers nearly doubled during this period; from a total of 350 in 1941 to 650 by 1951, largely through the birth of a new generation into the community. The Mennonite historian Joseph Winfield Fretz studied Primavera in 1950 and recorded that 'Eighteen different nationalities and ninety family names are found among the Hutterites in Primavera. About half of the members are English, a portion are German, and the rest are made up of a sprinkling of Swiss, Austrian, Dutch, Scandinavians, and others. Furthermore, the population is predominately made up of younger people; practically all married couples are under fifty years of age, most of them between the ages of twenty-five and forty. Children constitute a high portion of the total population and there are comparatively few old people. The diversity of backgrounds has provided new blood and invigorating spiritual and intellectual stimulation in the brotherhood.' **6**

Bruderhof in Paraguay in the 1950's: Top to Bottom
Watering wagon horses, Isla Margarita;
Unloading timber, Isla Margarita sawmill;
Brickworks, Isla Margarita;
Bruderrat – brothers' business meeting, Primavera

Though thriving as a community, in some ways none of their economic ventures were ever successful enough to provide them with a viable income to keep the communities going: they continued to rely on generous donations from sympathisers and the community sent regular begging letters asking for support – particularly for their hospital work.

We begged from business firms by correspondence (and for the commune's use we had specific expressions such as Sachwerbung for begging [for] things and Geldwerbung for begging [for] money etc.). We begged from benevolent associations and from the Hutterian communes in North America. We begged from old friends and made new friends in order to beg from them. We begged from old aunts and grandparents, and asked them to help the education of our children or with some relative's costly operation.

Roger Allain, The Community That Failed

The combination of the relatively enforced isolation, the struggle in primitive conditions and the sub-tropical conditions experienced by the group in Paraguay was in stark contrast to the pietist north European roots of the community. This contrast seems to have led to changes in emphasis in the Bruderhof communities during this period, leaning towards becoming more of a social movement than a specifically Church-based community. This led, in 1950, to a break with the Hutterites following an attempt to reconcile their differences. Summed up by Benjamin Zabloki in *The Joyful Community*: 'Neither side was willing to compromise. The Bruderhof felt that modernization was necessary to attract new members ... The Hutterians felt that the Bruderhof, in its over-concern with expansion, was losing touch with the essence of the Hutterian way of life.' After 20 years of unity and co-operation the links between the two sects were cut. This led to a period of liberalisation and expansion for the Bruderhof communities. Things overtly connected to the Hutterite link started to fade: Hutterite texts were dropped, beards were made optional and a younger 'clean-shaven' generation of male members started to appear. Women's dress code was relaxed 'slacks were no longer taboo, and were gladly adopted by the girls.' The 1950's saw a period of considerable expansion with new communities being set up: El Arado in Uruguay in 1951, Woodcrest in the USA in 1954 and Forest River in the USA in 1955. The formation of communities in the US also brought with it economic stability in the form of Community Playthings: a toy and play equipment making business that would become the economic mainstay of the communities for many years.

The years of the Bruderhof in South America came to a somewhat abrupt and startling end following a period of internal crisis that affected all the communities. The three communities in Paraguay were closed and the Primavera estate was sold to the Mennonites.

The Story of the Bruderhof is continued on page 70

Mutual households

During the War, huge amounts of land and property were requisitioned under the Emergency Powers (Defence) Act 1939 for a wide range of uses, including battle-training areas, airfields, mines, underground deep shelters, housing (of troops and civilians), railways, oil, fire services, factories, schools and hospitals. At the end of the war some property was returned to its original owner, a large proportion was transferred to other state functions such as the forestry commission or the new National Health Service, but for some no suitable use could be found. Many of the properties requisitioned were minor country houses and these were some of the hardest to find alternative uses for. By the early 1950's it was estimated that over 150 country houses had been demolished since the war. It is not clear how many of these were requisitioned properties or simply houses suffering from neglect. A small group of individuals concerned about this loss of architectural heritage got together to come up with a plan to find a viable use for empty country houses. Among the group were the poet John Betjeman, Sir Adrian Boult conductor of the BBC Symphony Orchestra, Lady Cynthia Colville and Sir John Ruggles-Brise. In 1955 they set up the Mutual Households Association with an office in Haymarket, London. In their first publicity leaflet entitled *An Experiment in Co-operation* they stated 'If you are amongst those who feel that the destruction of such houses, their surroundings and associations, is a permanent loss to the Country then you will welcome this leaflet. It describes an experiment in co-operation which is actively and successfully preserving and restoring these houses as residences and at the same time helping retired people on fixed incomes to meet increasingly difficult living conditions.' The idea was for groups of retired people to form a co-operative community within the country houses – each with their own private rooms (with private bathrooms for an extra charge), but sharing communal facilities in the rest of the house, very much like the pre-war co-operative housekeeping schemes. Each house was to have resident staff to do the cooking, cleaning, gardening, etc, and was to be run by a House Secretary who would be advised by an advisory committee of residents. The first Mutual Household was created at a house known as Danny at Hurstpierpoint in Sussex. This was followed by others at Gosfield Hall, near Halstead in Essex; Pythouse in Wiltshire; Otterden Place in Kent and Greathed Manor, near Lingfield in Surrey.

Cover of Mutual Household promotional booklet

AN EXPERIMENT IN *Co-operation*

GOSFIELD HALL *near Halstead, Essex. A house of various periods with many historical associations. The gatehouse shown here dates from 1545.* Drawn by J. E. R. Howard, a resident.

Unlike a hotel or institution a Mutual Household consists of a group of people of similar background who, while making their own home within the house, will also live together as a community. In addition to each resident's private apartment there are dining and drawing rooms, sitting rooms, libraries, etc. for their common use.

An Experiment in Co-operation

The Mutual Households Association was registered under the Industrial and Provident Societies Act as a non-profitmaking co-operative venture using rules formulated by the National Federation of Housing Societies. A set of internal rules 'for members residing in a Mutual Household' sent out by the association in 1960 covered such things as;

-   Use of the house car – charges are based upon costs and are charged on the mileage basis plus waiting time, irrespective of the number of passengers.
-   Additional heating – Mutual Households are adequately heated with central heating throughout and residents wishing for additional heating must make arrangements with the House Secretary, who will make an agreed charge.
-   Absences from the house – absences from the house entitle a resident to a refund of 30/- per week providing you have given seven days notice.
-   Gratuities to staff – are forbidden. In addition to leading to the dismissal and loss of valuable staff, gratuities are very unfair to other residents who may not be in a position to afford them.

The Mutual Households Association went on to 'save' a further five country houses across the south of England; Albury Park near Guildford, Aynhoe Park near Banbury, Great Maytham Hall near Cranbrook, Swallowfield Park near Reading and Flete House near Ermington in Devon. These properties were developed along similar lines to the original houses, providing a range of apartments and shared facilities, with the gardens of the houses open to the public. The combination of country house and co-operative retirement home

*Interior of
Mutual Household –
probably Gosfield Hall*

seems to have been remarkably successful with the organisation lasting for nearly 50 years. Along the way it changed its name to the Country Houses Association. Following a restructuring of the Association in 2004, all the properties were sold. The substantial sum of money raised by the sale of nine country houses was largely donated to the Country Houses Foundation, a charitable grant-giving foundation which was set up to carry on the work of preserving historic buildings.

To live in surroundings of such spacious comfort and elegance is quite beyond the means of all but a very small minority except through such a co-operative venture as Mutual Households

An Experiment in Co-operation

What did you do after the war, daddy?

Conscription for National Service continued right through until 1963. Conscientious objectors looking for alternative service could opt to take part in the Friends Ambulance Units Post War (PWS) and International Services (FAUIS). The PWS ran summer training camps for COs at Manor Farm in Birmingham and sent young men to do a variety of voluntary service, both in the UK and abroad. In 1948 radical proposals were brought forward to change the way the PWS worked and to carry out 'A New Experiment'. 'It is planned to establish first a permanent headquarters settlement in the country in England, where young Englishmen and young Germans (with other nationalities, possibly, later on if the initial work succeeds) can live together, work on neighbouring farms, and follow a broadly educational and social course in an international setting. The farm work is an attempt to meet some small part of the country's needs in agriculture.' [7]

In order to carry out this plan a more permanent base was set up in a large Victorian house called Dunannie next to the Bedales progressive school at Steep, in Hampshire. One of the 23 members who started off at the new 'Centre of Peace' was quoted in the local paper 'We are trying to do a kind of social first-aid, and we think that practical experience should be the basis of our religious and idealistic approach to the problems of internationalism. We want young people to learn, not just intellectually, what is involved in the building of world peace. We want to give to the potential young peace-builders an experience just as effective for their purposes as military training is for the fighting man.' [8] Young Germans came over and joined in with the activities which largely consisted of providing labour for local farms. Later other work was found: digging drains, doing house maintenance, helping out at the Bernhard Baron Quaker retirement homes and the Cheshire Home at Le Court. Summer training camps were set up at an old RAF camp at Havant. In April 1950 an International Weekend was attended by representatives from Africa, Ceylon, China and the USA. The gathering was opened by Gerald Gardiner from Springhead.

In 1951, faced with falling income, the decision was made to move to a larger farm at Melksham in Wiltshire in order to expand the in-house farming activities. For the next five years at Lavender Farm the PWS members carried out a range of farming and horticultural activities as well as repairing vehicles. There were plans for one final move before National Service ended. As the numbers joining the scheme started to dwindle, a house called Tunmers in Chalfont St Peter was used as headquarters. This was closer to London and the units' forestry activities in the South East. Activities at Melksham continued until the FAUIS was wound up in 1959.

The Unit was the making of me as an independent person. I came from a sheltered background and had never been away from home. In the unit I developed views of my own, and self reliance. I also learnt self-discipline and the fact that hard manual work never did anyone any harm! I learnt it was possible to put your ideals into action ...

David Hall, FAUS member 1949 - 51

The full story of the units is told in: *FAU The Third Generation*, R Bush

A common wealth

Another casualty of the post-war period was the small political party known as the Common Wealth Party. This had been founded in July 1942 out of an alliance made up of members of the 1941 Committee, a left-wing think tank set up by Edward Hulton, owner of the Picture Post, their 'star' writers J.B. Priestley and Tom Wintringham and the neo-Christian Forward March movement led by Liberal MP Richard Acland. The Common Wealth Party advocated three principles: Common Ownership, Vital Democracy and Morality in Politics. During the war years, the all-party coalition government with Conservative, Labour, and Liberal members had agreed that any by-election vacancies would be filled by the incumbent party unopposed. The intervention of the Common Wealth Party, standing candidates in Conservative seats with no other opposition, saw the election of left-wing Common Wealth candidates in a series of wartime by-elections in Eddisbury, Skipton and Chelmsford.

Common Wealth is the only revolutionary Party in Britain today. We should not be alarmed by this word. The achievement of Common Wealth's aims will require a social transformation which the historians would describe as a revolution.

K Heath, *Merseyside Common Wealth Newsletter* No1

The Party attracted many radicals to its cause: those who saw that from the ruins of war a new world might be created; and those who were critical of the lack of idealism and ambition shown by the Labour Party in the war time coalition. 'Common Wealth's appeal was overwhelmingly ethical, summoning up co-operative in place of economic man. The ethos of Common Wealth was conveyed, for example, in the slogan of Flight-Lieutenant Moeran, one of its candidates in 1943: 'Human Fellowship, not Inhuman Competition; Service to the Community, not Self Interest; the Claims of Life, not the Claims of Property'.' **9**

In the post-war 1945 General Election only one Common Wealth candidate was elected to the House of Commons. The failure to maintain its wartime momentum created a crisis and at the party's 1946 conference the party split, with two-thirds defecting to the Labour Party. During its short heyday the Common Wealth Party attracted a wide cross-section of left-leaning thinkers and supporters. One particular influence on the party came from the humanistic psychology movement. The psychologists Dr Don Bannister and Dr James Hemming were party members and through the work of another member, Norman Glaister, the party, in searching for a social organisation consistent with its principles, adopted an 'executive-sensory' model of organisation. This was derived from left/right brain theory, whereby an executive decision-making committee was shadowed by a 'Sensory Committee' whose role was to monitor and review decisions, carry out research and plan longer-term development. There were also those in the Party who were interested in communal living. Various articles appear in the party's paper, the *Common Wealth Review*, throughout the late 1940's and early 50's. There were stories about Kibbutzim in Israel, letters from the Bruderhof and in 1950 a Policy & Research Committee was set up to 'examine the possibilities and problems of community in modern times. The committee will be particularly interested in the experience of the numerous experimental communities which have tried to inject new life and a new way of living into the poisoned blood-stream of society.'

***Common Wealth Newsletter*, 1st November 1950**

An advert that appeared in the *Common Wealth Review* in September 1945 read:

COUNTRY HOME WITHIN 1 HOUR LONDON: Three families seek another to share expensive house (unfurnished), grounds, Montessori teacher etc. Some communal meals. Babies, young children; Cultural progressive outlook desirable. Some capital if possible. Please write fully BOX No 80.

Those who wrote in for more information received a duplicated sheet outlining plans for a co-operative community of like-minded families. 'We aim to live in real country, but near enough to 'belong' to a village. About an hour from a London terminus, preferably on the north or west side of town. The type of house we think will prove most suitable is a long, low Georgian one (enough ground floor living-rooms with garden access for children); ten acres upwards; about 20 bedrooms; orchard; company's water and electricity; several cottages; many bathrooms; and Aga or Esse cooker ...' [10]

The project was being put forward by a number of members of the Common Wealth Party who wanted to attempt 'new ways of living together'. The group included a book publisher, solicitor, election agent and a documentary film-maker and were seeking others to join them. The group had looked at nearly 30 houses before finding Barwythe Hall, a Queen Anne manor house near Studham in Bedfordshire, for sale for £11,750. After trying in vain to get a mortgage from several building societies the Dr Barnados Trust offered a seven-year mortgage guarantee which enabled the group to move in. Barwythe Hall, set in 22 acres of grounds, had 14 bedrooms, seven bathrooms and numerous reception rooms and outbuildings. The original three families: Edward & Nadine Moeran, Maxwell & Evelyn Martyn and Herman & Joy Scott sorted through the replies to their adverts looking for suitable recruits for their communal venture. They rejected a business man who had got his secretary to write, a man who approved of polygamy and a woman who wanted to bring her private maid. They eventually invited Fritz & Edith Eilers and their baby and Mrs Letia Lillico, a war widow along with her son and mother to join them. Each family was required to pay £7 a week to cover all running expenses including: mortgage, cost of cook and gardener and a fund for buying an extra cooker and washing machine. Each family furnished their own rooms and contributed items of furniture for the communal rooms. Apart from that the criteria for membership were somewhat vague. It was suggested that the qualities which the group were looking for were those who were 'progressive in outlook, congenial company' and had a 'sense of humour'. Writing in *Picture Post*, after a visit in 1946, journalist Hilde Marchant pointed out that whilst the criteria for joining were fairly lax the project appeared to have been thought about in depth for a long time. 'For many years these friends had theorised on the advantages of communal life for families like their own. Before the war they had studied experiments in communal settlements by pioneers with lofty principles. They had rejected them, for in most cases they had seemed to demand addiction to some cult or other – wholemeal bread, hand-woven quilts or contemplation – and the Moerans and Martyns regarded themselves as normal average citizens who wore sandals for comfort not for creed.' [11]

One of the families who had responded to the advert was that of Betty and Kenneth Allsop. Betty Allsop had got involved with the Commonwealth Party during the war whilst her husband was in hospital for two years recovering from having a leg amputated due to surgical TB. It was largely through her Common Wealth contacts that they became involved in the community project, although it would take a number of months before they felt able to join. The ups and downs of their time at the community are covered in *One and All: Two years in the Chilterns*, a slightly fictionalised version of their time there written by Kenneth (he changed some of the names and Barwythe to Berewordе) and published after his death. It was Betty who was initially the more enthusiastic of the pair about the advantages of joining the community, telling her husband 'You've no idea, darling, how stimulating it was to be able to talk to other women about things besides rations and clothes and cooking ... It's not so bad for you. You're out every day meeting new people and seeing new things. But since we left London I feel as if my brain has mummified.'

Once they had moved in though Ken warmed to communal life: 'Instead of going to bed early as we had intended we sat up until past one o'clock talking and drinking coffee that got progressively blacker and bitterer each time it was re-heated. I was prickly-eyed with weariness but I was enjoying it all too much to break away. It was exhilarating to be sitting around a spluttering wood fire in the warmth and security of a circle of new friends, while the rain shrrd against the panes and the wind made the trees groan.' The Allsops paint a picture of the pattern of daily life and the comings and goings at the community; of rotas for childcare and household chores shared amongst the women and working out at 'fewer hours than the average suburban household would require' and thus allowing every woman a 'full day free to go to town, as well as free time at the week-end'. The men were required to do eight hours a week helping in the garden, or with painting and odd DIY jobs. The community employed staff: two gardeners and later, to avoid arguments as to the best way 'to boil a cabbage, or bake a jam tart,' a cook who had previously worked in a communal kitchen during the war. They also catalogue the highs and lows of communal life. From conflict over pets: 'There were a few dogs and cats belonging to various people, but pet animals were not encouraged. There had been far too many quarrels and resentments in the past caused by messes within the house, for no pet-owner would believe it possible that his own animal was guilty, and, therefore, refused to accept responsibility for the clearing up', through to the difficulties of trying to work from home in a community: Kenneth found the pull of the community

Barwythe Hall Community –
photographs from an article by Hilde Marchant

sometimes hard to cope with and a distraction from his writing 'Always there were too many diversions, always there was an excellent reason for not shutting oneself away and working, and always if one did isolate oneself behind a locked door, there was the nagging guilty feeling that it was a desertion of one's community duties.'

There were also the potential pitfalls of relationships. Joy Scott, another resident reported; 'There was quite a bit of flirtation going on. Two couples swapped partners for a while. They tried to be discreet about it, but we all knew what was happening. Then when my baby was born, a very attractive midwife came to stay for a few days. All the men in the house were keen on her, and there were lots of secret meetings on the terrace. But attraction wasn't all one-way. The young good-looking village grocer was as welcomed by the wives as his deliveries to the concern of his wife and mother." [12] Visitors to the community were rather sceptical about its prospects: Hilde Marchant commenting that most members were from '... professional, middle-class backgrounds, and committed to socialism in a rather abstract way. They had a progressive, Reichian approach towards child-rearing but not much else in the way of a philosophy, and by modern standards it was a quaintly old-fashioned and illiberal community.' Another visitor, Betty Allsop's brother-in-law Nat Solomon, was even more harsh with his comments 'I thought it was phoney. I thought it pretentious and unreal and couldn't see it standing the test of time. To me, they were kidding themselves they'd discovered a new way of living. I was totally out of sympathy with it. At the time I was very left-wing anyway, but this seemed to me a way of opting out of society rather than trying to improve it.' [13]

The community lasted for two years before things came to a head, which would eventually lead to the group going their separate ways. Kenneth Allsop saw the end of the community largely as being to do with differences between individuals that were left unresolved. 'The reasons for the disintegration cannot be stated in complete detail. Certainly the money problem, which billowed into ever larger proportions ... was a powerful factor. But there were other fundamental causes which perhaps it would be simplest to label ideological. Probably sharpened by the financial worry, personal conflicts grew more pronounced. Most of the time they remained submerged beneath a makeshift day-to-day agreement to disagree, but now and then they exploded with a suddenness and force that revealed with discomforting clarity a bitterness that had not been apparent when we first moved in.' [14] Others such as Joy Scott saw the causes of the group's downfall somewhat differently 'The trouble was that the sort of people who lived at Barwythe – intellectuals or rather would-be intellectuals – didn't want to be bothered with all the drudgery that comes with a big house ... the place could get very dirty, with food all over the floor. I found that quite depressing. Most of the people were nice but by no means all of them. Some of the men were remote and treated the place like a hotel' [15]

The final decision on the group's future was taken after an epic meeting.

... Midnight came and went and discussion plodded on through the cigarette smoke, and when the momentum was slowing through exhaustion a vote was taken. By a majority of three it was decided that the community should be closed. The voting alignment was interesting, and, in a way, funny. Those who supported the proposal that the community should continue were the very people who all along had shown least enthusiasm for communal activity, who, in fact, had fairly well succeeded in transforming Bereworde from a community into a block of self-contained flats ...

Kenneth Allsop, One and All: Two years in the Chilterns

Anarchy and the Law

It is refreshing when courts are daily filled with people fighting each other over ownership of property, to read of a case in which people are standing up for the right of not owning it.

Freedom, December 1955

On 22nd November 1955 the case of "Wexham v Whiteway" was held before the Chief Registry Tribunal at the High Court in London. What was at stake was the existence of an anarchist form of land tenure that had lasted for over half a century, and with it the continuation of the Whiteway Colony, itself founded in 1898 by a group of Tolstoyan anarchists. When they took possession of the forty or so acres of Cotswold farmland, they needed to square the question of who should be the 'owner' of the property with their anarchist principles. This led the group, after the legal transaction was completed, to spike the deeds on a pitchfork smeared with paraffin and ceremoniously burn them. In the early years of the colony members were allocated plots by the community as a whole and when they left they were expected to remove their property (including any 'house' – most likely a shack, shed or railway carriage) and the plot would be allocated to a new colonist. The custom and practice that built up over the years was that money might change hands between the parting and the new member for the buildings on the plots, but not actually for the land itself, as that remained in communal ownership. This was confirmed at a meeting in 1925 when it was agreed that a meeting should always be held whenever land was being transferred 'to keep alive the bond of unity and common responsibilities, and principle of possession of land for use only.'

Mrs Wexham, who had lived at the colony for many years, claimed to know nothing of these 'normal' procedures and was attempting to register her bungalow and land at Whiteway with the land registry and so claim private ownership over the land. However paradoxical it seems for a group of anarchists to have to turn to the law to uphold their principles there was little else the group could do. Funds were raised and the case was contested.

Incredible though it might seem, the hearing proved that our ancestors had been using a form of ancient land tenure dating from 1200 AD. Further more, it proved that the Colonists as a whole were the licensees of their land, with their important monthly meeting held regularly from its very formation, the licensor.

Joy Thacker

While the judge found in favour of the anarchists they didn't follow his ruling to the letter – feeling sorry for the elderly Mrs Wexham the community waived the costs that the judge had awarded against her and paid their own costs in full. So anarchy ruled – with a little help from the law, and continues to do so to the present day, making Whiteway the longest surviving intentional community in the country.

I really felt that the old Whiteway was very much alive again. I think last night will remain one of the most unforgettable joys of my life to find the old Whiteway resurrected.

Gaspard 'Gassy' Marin

The full story of Whiteway is told in:
Whiteway Colony: The Social History of a Tolstoyan Community by Joy Thacker

Friends of the Future

In September 1948 in a session entitled 'Positive Plan of Action' at the second Common Wealth Party Sensory Summer School, held at the Forest School Camp site at Whitwell Hall in Reepham Norfolk, a proposal was put forward by Glynn Faithfull to set up a new group that would work alongside the Common Wealth Party. Faithfull hoped that this new group, to be called 'The Society of Friends of the Future', would recognise that: 'We are living in a world in which the waste of natural resources, physical and mental, already achieved or menaced by a third world war, seriously prejudices the life of future generations.' [16] and would act to 'save their fellow men as well as themselves from self-destruction, and form a society of people pledged to act on the positive criterion of their concern for the future.' Thirteen people signed up to be members of the new group and decided to wait until 100 members had been recruited before launching themselves into action. Over the next year the aims of the group were honed in a series of letters exchanged between key members. These were finally published in a leaflet in March 1949, in time for an inaugural meeting in the Alliance Hall, Westminster. The overriding aims were to be: 'a) To study the present dislocation of society and the means of remedying it.' and 'b) To act with a full sense of responsibility for the survival and further development of the human species.'

The Friends of the Future was the latest attempt to put into practice the Executive/Sensory ideas of group organisation developed by Norman Glaister from the ideas of Wilfred Trotter. Faithfull had met the older Glaister at the Order of Woodcraft Chivalry Camps at Sandy Balls in Hampshire where he had gone with his father, the progressive teacher and sexologist Theodore Faithfull, in the 1920's. Those involved in the Order were members of various overlapping networks exploring radical ideas around education, social organisation and psychology. Theodore Faithfull ran the co-educational Priory Gate School for 'difficult' or 'problem' children at Walsham Hall near Bury St Edmunds where he tried – through a combination psychoanalysis and recapitulation theory – to free the children from repression and allow them to grow naturally as individuals. The school ran as a branch of the Order of Woodcraft Chivalry stressing informality, open air teaching between May and September, outdoor activities, nudity and camping. One of the senior teachers, Dorothy Revel, wrote a book titled *Cheiron's Cave* published in 1928 as a blueprint for the 'school of the future'.

Such a school had to be a residential community in which full-time teachers work alongside practical craftsmen and children have the opportunity to choose to undertake paid craft work as well as their academic work. The school should include self-sufficient farms, forges, printing presses, and other artisan workshops as bases for craft work. Teachers and pupils should take on family roles in domestic, residential groups that may have either an intellectual or practical character according to the specialism and interests of the teacher ...

Dorothy Revel, *Cheiron's Cave*

Norman Glaister and Dorothy Revel were married in 1928, 'troth-plighting' themselves to each other at a Woodcraft moot at Sandy Balls in the New Forest and Glaister became psychiatric adviser to Priory Gate School. Glynn Faithfull became a gifted language student and during the war worked as an intelligence officer both in Italy and with Tito's partisans in Yugoslavia, where he fought alongside Alexander von Sacher-Masoch. As the British Army occupied Vienna, Faithfull called on the Sacher-Masoch family to tell them that their son was alive. It was there that he met and fell in love with Eva von Sacher-Masoch. Eva came back to England after the war and the couple were married in 1946. Later that year their daughter, Marian, was born. The new couple lived in Hampstead and Faithfull got work as a language lecturer and started to pick up his pre-war contacts. Joining Norman and Dorothy Glaister in their work establishing executive/sensory committees within the Common Wealth Party he became heavily involved in the Sensory Summer Schools held between 1947 and 1949. At the third summer school held at Abbey House, Glastonbury under the heading 'The Future of Humanity' it seems that ideas were put forward for something that would provide people with more 'continuous contact'; 'Perhaps a café. Something that would offer an opportunity for contact for more than two weeks a year.' Over the autumn of 1949 things would start to crystallise around the idea of some sort of 'School for Sensory Social Studies'. In October a party including Norman Glaister, Glynn Faithfull, Bonnie and Madge Russell and Chrystal Cates took the train to the north of Scotland to scout out a potential property at Findhorn on the Moray Firth. They rejected the location because it was 'too out-of-the-way', 'so far from London'. They continued to search nearer to London and in November a property was spotted at Ipsden in the Chilterns. Braziers, a Strawberry Hill Gothic mansion with castellated roof line and pointed gothic windows, was a Regency conversion of an earlier farmhouse and had been owned previously by the MP Valentine Fleming (Bond author Ian Fleming spent his early years here) who carried out extensive 'improvements to the building and grounds'. In 1911 it was sold to Sir Ernest Moon, counsel to the Speaker of the House of Commons whose widow was now selling it for £12,500. Glaister, who had some capital saved, had a survey and valuation carried out which mentioned roof leaks, possible dry rot and the poor quality of much of the decoration in the house and suggested a valuation of £8500 for the house, outbuildings and thirty acre estate. This was finally settled upon as the purchase price. Glaister wrote to Eva and Glynn Faithfull inviting them to join him 'I don't propose to plunge into it as an entirely private venture, but I do want to begin at once the search for people to share it, whether financially or in the matter of the work to be done at such a centre.' The purchase was completed in February 1950 and plans laid for what was to be called 'The School of Integrative Social Research'. Within weeks a Committee of Management and a Sensory Committee had been set up. The idea was to test whether by putting the Executive/Sensory theory into continuous practice a new synthesis of dual governance would lead to the creation of community cohesion and the formation of what Wilfred Trotter called the 'multi-mental organism'.

A brochure was written to promote the new 'school' explaining the ethos behind the project:

Braziers Park has been founded as a permanent college for those who wish to understand man's place and part in nature, to discuss with others the social and ethical aspects of his continuing development, and to co-operate in working out, wherever possible, the principles that may facilitate constructive action in the world today.

Original brochure for Braziers Park School of Integrative Research, 1950

It goes on to explain that the school would operate somewhat differently from other adult education establishments: 'In this adventure you are invited to participate. Anyone who visits Braziers Park, if only for a weekend, may expect both to learn and to teach something relevant to the betterment of social life. It is not possible to present a detailed picture of future activities, since these will be continually taking on new forms in response to new contacts ...'

Braziers Park

The house, especially at Christmas, was full to capacity (55) and with limited helpers and everything needing to run smoothly, much forward planning was necessary and early preparation of the festive fare. I felt honoured to be asked to help ... and there were carols and music and presents from the tree for all, and country dancing and party games, charades and plays, walks and plenty of good food and social fellowship and I was part of it and felt part of it too, for it was Christmas at Braziers and it was unique ...

Jean Westlake, 70 Years A-Growing

A fourth Sensory Summer School was held at Braziers in 1950 entitled 'Our Responsibility: The Development of Mankind as a Social Organism' and an official opening of the new school was held on November 11, 1950 attended by over 90 guests. Norman and Dorothy Glaister moved in along with Bonnie Russell, forming a small residential group. In the first few years as well as creative and artistic weekend courses in painting, modelling, music and writing, the events and courses focussed on the ideas that had led to the founding of Braziers 'philosophy, evolution, attitudes to religion etc'. They ran a combination of practical and artistic courses and more theoretical/intellectual offerings with titles such as 'The Art of Living' and 'Living with More Meaning'. They also organised children's summer camps and seasonal celebrations.

Braziers was also used for meetings and conferences by a whole range of groups active in the 1950's. War Resisters International met there, H.G.Wells' Progressive League held regular courses and there were weekend gatherings of MENSA members. The whole idea of the community and school was to attempt to put into practice the various ideas that the initial members had been exploring in the previous years in other forums.

Central to the running of Braziers was Glaister's executive/sensory concept. This was developed in a paper, originally written for but never published in the Lancet, entitled 'Implications of the Gregarious Habit in Man'. It was a shortened version of *Greater Things*, a book Glaister had written during the war. It was eventually printed "Stencil by stencil" in the Braziers' office and reprinted in booklet form for the community's 25th anniversary in 1975. At the back of the 1975 reprint there is a handy glossary explaining the various terms coined by Glaister:

Resistive – of the aspect of thought tending to preserve acquired
        characteristics
     – having a mind tending to put into operation, without further
        reconsideration, principles already accepted
Sensitive – of the aspect of thought tending to accept new stimuli
     – having a mind tending to assimilate new concepts before taking
        action
Sensory – of forms of social structure motivated by sensitive attitudes of
        mind
Executive– of forms of social structure motivated by resistive attitudes of mind

The sensory/executive concept was used both in the running of the community and in how courses and events were structured. In essence the sensory committee's role was to look into and explore new ideas and directions that the community might usefully follow and to keep the executive committee informed of the outcomes of these deliberations. It was the executive's role to run the organisation.

The early years were beset with difficulties: antagonism from the local village, some of whom believed they were 'either nudists or communists.'; problems in financing the project '... bills were far in arrears' and local tradesmen refused credit. At one point the group's lawyer advised them that they should close down. This led to what was referred to as 'The First Schism'. When Glaister asked others to share the financial burden there were some who were only prepared to contemplate this if the place became more of an arts centre and less a 'philosophical-sociological' centre, with Glaister and Bonnie Russell stepping down from their posts as Director of Studies and Warden. In the end the 'dissidents' resigned their membership and left. 'We were sorry to lose them ... The prospect was bleak, but we believed that we had something to give that people needed and that somehow we would succeed.' **17**

One venture to try and become more financially sustainable was the setting up of Braziers Farm. The idea was that this would be a separate Limited Liability Company that could sell its produce and that there would be a 'quid-pro-quo arrangement' between the farm and the school whereby the farm could call on labour from the school when needed and in exchange machinery would be

Braziers Park

available for the school to use and produce would be sold to them at below the market rate. Dorothy Glaister agreed to finance the farm by cashing some of her industrial shares and a farm worker was employed to manage the farm.

He had to be paid a farm worker's wage (albeit the minimum), which was about three times as much as the community honorarium. Twelve milk cows were bought and a tractor. Also the outhouses were altered and brought up to date. We had a milking parlour. Corn was sown in the fields to make straw and fodder for the cows, and the farm was set up.

Dorothy Glaister, *Braziers: A Personal Story* 1973

Part of Braziers aims were to get their ideas more widely known and over the years they have produced a considerable number of newsletters, booklets and research papers. In 1953, in *Braziers Park Social Research Papers and Bulletin* No 1, various observations were made on how groups worked and ways that had been tried to improve group dynamics. These included: working in pairs and reporting back to the group instead of depending on the lecturer to lead discussion; taking positive responses to ideas first to avoid negative responses having a disproportionately large effect on discussion; and the observation that 'the size and shape of the room affected discussions. People seemed to become inhibited in rooms felt to be too large or too small.'

In 1961 Norman Glaister died and the running of Braziers passed to Glynn Faithfull and Honor Fawsitt. Glynn Faithfull had separated from Eva von Sacher in the early 1950's and Eva and their daughter left and lived in nearby Reading. Marian spent her time split between Braziers and her mother's. Glynn spent many years working in Liverpool teaching Italian and commuting down to attend or run weekend courses. He took over running the Braziers Farm from Dorothy Glaister when it was struggling to

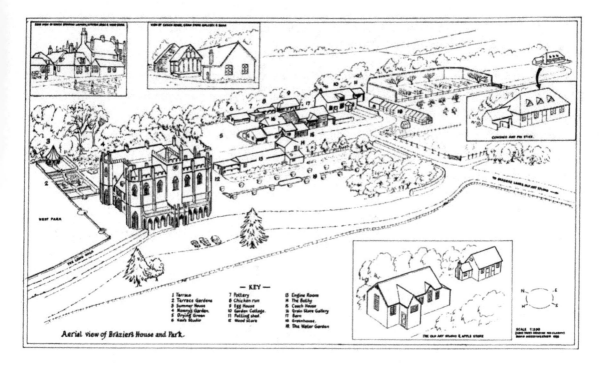

— KEY —

1 Terrace
2 Terrace Gardens
3 Summer House
4 Nanny's Garden
5 Drying Green
6 Ken's Studio
7 Pottery
8 Chicken run
9 Egg House
10 Garden Cottage
11 Potting shed
12 Wood store
13 Engine Room
14 The Bothy
15 Coach House
16 Grain Store Gallery
17 Barn
18 Greenhouse.
19. The Water Garden

Aerial view of Braziers House and Park

break even and the farm manager had left. In spring 1963 he married his
second wife Margaret and got a job at the Bedford College, in Regent's Park
which enabled them to move into Braziers on a permanent basis. During
the 1960's Braziers made links with the emerging counter-culture. They
were involved with the Communal Living Association who held at least one
gathering at Ipsden and they were closely involved with promoting the ideas
of the French Jesuit priest and philosopher Pierre Teilhard de Chardin.
There was also a direct link with the 'swinging sixties' through Glynn's
daughter, now known as Marianne and part of the Rolling Stones entourage
as Mick Jagger's partner and a budding singer in her own right. Glynn used
to tell of the day that Marianne brought Mick to Braziers to meet him. He
looked up from milking the cow and asked the young rock star 'and so what
do you do?' to which Jagger replied 'Oh, I'm in a band. It's just something
I'm doing in-between jobs.' Following the highly publicised Rolling Stones
drugs bust in 1967 Mick and Marianne hid out from the press at Braziers
on his release from Lewes prison.

Over the years considerable amounts of money have had to be spent by the
group on the upkeep of the rather amazing strawberry gothic building, one
of the few examples in the country. In 1951 the main building was given
historic listed building status Grade II and in 1985 it was re-graded as II
star. This added additional cost when it came to doing repairs and
renovations and in keeping up with new fire safety regulations. During the
70's the building was in such a poor state that there are records of at least
one member not wanting to live in the building because of its dilapidated
condition and of organisations refusing to hire Braziers because of the state
of the roof. On more than one occasion the burden of looking after a
historic building has led to discussion of selling up and moving to a more
suitable, presumably 'cheaper', property. Things were not really put into
good order until the 1990's when, after being reported to the authorities,

money was raised through an appeal and the sale of cottages on the estate and major alterations carried out.

Over the last ten years the expenditure on repairs and new work at Braziers has averaged some £60,000 a year, though this includes the exceptional case of the fire precautions. Even without this, the average is nearly £30,000 a year. As I am an engineer I have a feeling for machinery, buildings etc. To me, railway engines, motor cars, computers, buildings etc. have a personality: a life of their own. Braziers is a beautiful, gracious old building, a friendly building. But it had not been looked after in a friendly way since before the War. It had become run-down. Most people would say that there was no money, and this is true of course. But I would say that it is because the building had not been thought of as a member of the community. The community would not have treated its living members with the same disregard ...

Maurice Roth, *Research Communications* 19th October 1999

Braziers proved to be one of the few communities to survive from the post-war period through into the 1960's and 70's and while it appeared to some to be rather rarefied and intellectual in its approach, its aims and ideas still resonated. In an article in *Undercurrents* magazine in 1975 Bonnie Russell placed Braziers within the context of the newly emerging Communes Network, stating that a small group of people at Braziers had been working on a living experiment in which they themselves were the material. '... They endeavour as individuals to face and admit their own weaknesses as well as their own strengths ... conflict and stress are not shirked and when they arise, as they always do in any group or community, they are studied carefully and an endeavour made to turn them to positive use ... The aim is to achieve a better balance and understanding in our living together, to date results are encouraging.'

Along with the sensory/restive concept another idea that underpinned thinking at Braziers was Recapitulation theory. This was a 19th century psycho-sociological theory that was taken up by Freud and other psychoanalysts and applied to human development after birth.

'In the same way that the human embryo goes through all the stages of its evolution from amoeba to human being, so also the mind, before, but especially after birth, is continually developing and evolving from a lower stage to a higher, by means of experience'

Theodore Faithfull, *Psychological Foundations* 1933

Norman Glaister had been influenced by the ideas of the physicist Lancelot Law Whyte, author of *The Next Development in Man*, who he had met in 1946. Glaister came to his own conclusion that further stages of evolution were to be expected and part of the Braziers experiment was 'to pave the way for new developments in humanity's participation in the next stage.' Theodore Faithfull, Norman Glaister and Dorothy Revel had developed the ideas at the Priory School and through the Order of Woodcraft Chivalry, extending the idea into child development: encouraging children to enact the periods of human history in order that they themselves could develop fully as human beings. Recapitulation theory would appear at Braziers not only as an ideological basis but, in later years, echoes of it would appear on a number of occasions in practical form – for several years they ran an August Bank Holiday weekend "Festival of Evolution" course which involved a Timewalk around the estate followed by a day of evolutionary cuisine starting with a "Mesolithic breakfast" and progressing through the day to a "bronze age supper". Throughout the 1980's and 90's, the average age of Braziers members grew ever older and despite the help in running the school that they got from students who came to learn English, it was clear that they needed to attract a new, younger membership. In 1991 at an International Conference on Residential Adult Education, Glynn Faithfull suggested that residential colleges should be developed as training centres for senior leaders and counsellors, and that 'these colleges should provide courses in simpler living and redesigned patterns of human existence, which will consume less and pollute less ...' This idea chimed with those in the new Permaculture movement and moves were made to look into the establishment of a Permaculture training centre at Braziers. Glynn and Margaret Faithfull both died in 1998. Braziers has continued as a community, eventually attracting a new younger generation that have brought a new energy to the place, establishing innovative small festivals and new courses.

Let us hope that more of us in this world can come to see that living in community is not as difficult as we thought before; and that, given courage by this realisation, we can go forward to build a community which we need not be afraid of, which we can love because it and we will know what we are doing.

Glynn Faithfull, *Research Communications* No 9

The end of common wealth

In the post-war period the much reduced Common Wealth Party continued to be active in a number of domestic and international campaigns. In the Middle East, it worked for a two-state solution to the Israel/Palestine issue and at home it helped to form the Industrial Common Ownership Movement (ICOM). They also made common cause with other small parties campaigning for small parties to be allowed to make party political broadcasts. In 1956 with Plaid Cymru and the Scottish National Party they published *Our Three Nations* advocating the replacement of the United Kingdom by a 'cofraternity' of self-governing states. Some of its former members, including Acland and Priestley, helped in 1957 to form the Campaign for Nuclear Disarmament. Others were active in the early environmental movement, including the Ecology Party. The Common Wealth Party was finally wound up in 1993 shortly after its fiftieth anniversary.

A community in Shropshire

Now it is true that there should be a way of life to which man can give himself with wholehearted assent.
But the artificialities, the falsities of modern society make this impossible ...
the way out requires a radical break with what society depresses and violates the conscience.
But it requires more, it requires the building up of a new kind of society – a new kind of culture ...

Letter from Wheathill Bruderhof in *Commonwealth News* August 1950

When the Bruderhof left Wiltshire for Paraguay in the early years of the war three members, Stanley Fletcher and Charles and Hella Headland, had remained in England to complete the sale of the property at Ashton Keynes. With them were a few others who were considering joining the community. 'The last group left for South America and on that very day the first person with the serious intention of joining us arrived ... One after another, people came, including some we had never heard of before. We did not have permission to take them to Paraguay with us, so we knew we were running into a problem.' [18] Sale of the Wiltshire farm dragged on due to various negotiations over powers of attorney and other legal matters. Adding to this some of the sale documents were lost in an air raid that destroyed the solicitor's offices. By the summer they had been joined by ten pacifists and by Christmas 1941 a group of nineteen, including two families, had gathered together. This situation had been somewhat foreseen by those who had departed to Paraguay: just prior to leaving, Heini Arnold (who was Servant of the Word at the time) authorised those staying behind to become the nucleus of a new community because of the uncertainty as to the fate of those sailing for Paraguay. This new group wrote to the main Bruderhof group in Paraguay seeking guidance. While sitting in the empty community buildings waiting for both the completion of the sale and for a reply the group discussed starting a new community in England.

The buildings that once were occupied by the brothers and sisters were all around us, but they were in new hands, and many were not being used for the purposes for which they had been built. These buildings evoked fanciful plans of how it would be when we had our own place again ... We imagined the different work departments that would develop and the children's community that would arise, as more and more families came to us ... Above everything, the little group was held by a hope for the future. We left plans in preference to realism and set about finding somewhere to live, for we would soon have to leave our present abode.

Ten Years of Community Living

In January 1942 they set out in twos looking for suitable farms in the Midlands and Wales 'The return of such an expedition was eagerly awaited. As soon as the travellers were back, a full account had to be given of the places that had been seen that might be suitable – the buildings were described and accounts were given of the farming conditions.' [19] The story of the finding of Lower Bromdon Farm near Ludlow in Shropshire has the ring of communal myth making to it – one member, Charles Headland, told the driver of a car who had given him a lift that he was a pacifist, so shocked was the man on hearing this that he stopped and told Headland to get out and left him by the roadside. That night, looking for somewhere to stay, Headland came across a remote farm that turned out to be for sale. Lower Bromdon farm, set at nearly 1,000 feet high in the Clee Hills, consisted of 182 acres of mostly old pasture land suffering from neglect and officially classified as grade 'C' agricultural land.

Things moved fairly quickly and by March 1942 the group were able to move in. Like many of the other wartime pacifist communities they faced a struggle to get going due to starting with poor land, lack of farming skills and difficulties getting machinery due to wartime conditions. '… the exterior was depressing: a dilapidated farmhouse, ramshackle farm buildings, fields covered with weeds, mud everywhere and wretched buildings … but there was an atmosphere of faith and hope that was replete with an inner enthusiasm and joy …' [20] The twenty or so pioneers put up with spartan conditions and with a lack of furniture; sitting on boxes and single men sleeping on hay in the barns with overcoats as bedding. But they received a warm welcome from local farmers.

… our immediate neighbours were a great help in our first years. They gave us good advice and often came over to help. We reciprocated, not with skill, but with labour and an eagerness to learn. Our initial settling down would have been considerably more difficult but for the help of these friends and of the people with whom we did business in the neighbouring towns, and we sought continually to come into a close contact with them. Regularly neighbours came from the local villages to help in our farm, building and domestic work, especially at the time of the potato harvest. There were many occasions when the whole community gathered in the fields-haymaking, weeding the garden or lifting the potatoes. Such a time would often conclude with singing and a weary but cheerful gathering for a late supper outside the kitchen in the light of a hurricane lamp.

Ten Years of Community Living

They also received support from Paraguay where two members were sent from the community at Primavera to help the new group in England. By the end of the year the group, now numbering 33, was confident enough to give itself a name, The Wheathill Bruderhof, and to issue a report entitled 'The Founding of the Wheathill Bruderhof' setting out their aims and philosophy. In April 1944 they took over the neighbouring Upper Bromdon farm of 165 acres, which, as well as increasing the viability of the farm, gave them extra accommodation and enabled a deep bore-hole to be drilled and an extensive water supply to both farms to be installed. In 1945 the community extended further

*Pictures of the Bruderhof from
Ten Years of Community Living*

still, moving in to Cleeton Court Farm that lay along the southern boundary of Upper and Lower Bromdon and stretching to the foot of Titterstone Clee Hill, on which it carried the rights of common grazing. This brought the total size of the three 'Wheathill' farms to 532 acres. The transformation of the farms in wartime and post-war conditions from class 'C' in 1942 to class 'A' by the late 1940's was a remarkable achievement. The group had ploughed up over 300 acres of old turf, brought several miles of hedges and ditches into order, more than doubled the stock carrying capacity of the three farms and built up the fertility of the soil to a point where, in spite of the altitude, they were achieving good crop yields.

... Our wheat and oats are looking well and promise a good crop. Our hay and silage crops have been most heartening, and we have already cut and stacked nine acres , and ensiled five acres. We have a dairy herd of 30 cows, also 55 young stock, as well as a flock of 214 ewes and 170 lambs, and a few pigs. Other departments of work, besides those in the domestic sphere, are market gardening and fruit-growing, carpentry, engineering and welding, cobbling and poultry-keeping. The surplus of our products, after supplying our household of 120 (including children) is sold...

The Community Broadsheet, Winter 1947/48

At the end of the war the group was able to become more outward looking. They re-established The Plough publishing business and the quarterly publication of *The Plough*, which had stopped at the outbreak of war. They offered to take in orphaned children from war-torn Germany. There was an increase in links with the communities in Paraguay with exchanges of members and supply of machinery and goods. There were also considerable links with other communities in England. Whilst the post-war years were a time of growth and outward activity, the community also faced its own internal struggles. In the late 1940's Llewelyn Harries was sent to take over the spiritual direction as steward of the community. Harries brought with him a strict adherence to ideas of good and evil and began a purge of what he saw as members of the community who had succumbed to the 'lure of evil spirits'.

Evil began to be seen everywhere, and the whole community busied themselves fighting against it. Marriages were separated, and the men sent away. The children were sent to Cleeton Court ... to ponder their sexual sins. Some children were interrogated in such a way that today they have not overcome the abuse. One boy my own age was born before his parents were married, so he was suspected of having inherited an evil, dirty, sexual spirit ... A sister was asked to ring the big bell on the hill to drive away the demons overshadowing the community.

Elizabeth Bohlken-Zumpe – KIT Annual 1991, quoted in *The Other Side of Joy*

Eventually some members stood up to Harries and he himself was exiled in the middle of winter and later had a nervous breakdown. Those members who had been ordered to leave were invited back and the community tried to get back to normal. The episode showed how easy it was in such a hierarchical situation for someone to abuse their position and how many of the group's internal rules could be used against members. This short crisis was to prove a foretaste of things to come a decade later. In the meantime, throughout the 1950's, the community continued to flourish, expand its activities and improve facilities at the farms. Proper toilets and piped water were installed, a generator was purchased to provide the community with electricity and a building program carried out that, with the help of international work camps, saw the erection of ex-army huts for accommodation, the construction of a new dining room, and a new school building all completed by 1956 when the community sold Cleeton Court. As Wheathill was accessible (compared to Paraguay) it attracted many visitors. The violinist Yehudi Menuhin visited several times giving concerts and violin lessons. They also attracted attention in the local press, nearly all of it viewing the community in a positive light.

Life at Wheathill is completely communal in outlook. There is no private property, but instead a common fund into which all the proceeds from the sale of farm produce and gifts are put, and from which the steward draws as necessary to provide the families with clothes and other necessities ...

Article in the Shropshire Magazine, April 1953

At an Interbruderhof conference held in Paraguay in the winter of 1956 it was suggested that the community at Wheathill had reached its optimal size, could not absorb more new members and that a location for a new Bruderhof community in Britain be found. To this end a search for a suitable property was started. The result was the purchase of the abandoned Bulstrode Mansion and 70 acres of adjoining parkland at Gerrards Cross in Buckinghamshire in the summer of 1958.

... The 100-room palace had not been lived in for fifteen years and was in a state of total neglect. The purchase imposed a heavy financial burden on the Bruderhof and appeals to their friends for financial assistance in renovating the building and converting it into suitable housing appeared in the British press. By autumn of the same year there were already some 100 people living there, the majority of whom were members who had come from Wheathill ...

Yaacov Oved, The Witness of the Brothers

At Bulstrode the group struggled to find a source of income that would pay for the massive renovation costs. A British outpost of Community Playthings was set up and a steel fabrication workshop making gates and steel doors. They also sold flowers from the garden and cultivated a piece of land for growing vegetables. In 1959 Pathé Newsreel produced a short film item featuring the Wheathill community under the title 'Communal Village'. The film shows idyllic summer scenes of children gathering hay, boys playing with a telescope, men working making tubular steel gates, herding sheep, packing eggs and a communal meal being served in the garden. It finishes with shots of singing and country dancing. The clipped 'BBC English' of the commentator paints a rosy picture of communal life in the Clee Hills 'This twentieth century has been dubbed the aspirin age, an age of high pressure living with the majority of people under some form of strain, trying to keep up with the Jones's, keep up with the hire purchase payments, with the rent, the butcher, the baker, the milkman the lot. So it's a happy change to find an industrious, cheerful community who have succeeded in eliminating practically all tension from their daily existence ... These people are not just a bunch of escapists turning their backs on life ... they are people with principles and faith and unlike many of us they are doing something constructive about both ...' A number of things strike one in retrospect about the film, including the apparent 'normal' 1950's look and dress of the community members with hardly a beard or headscarf to be seen: by this time the early Hutterite influence had waned. The other is the irony of the portrayal of a successful harmonious community just at the time when the Bruderhof as a whole was entering a period of serious conflict – a period now referred to as the 'Great Crisis'. A crisis that would result in the closure and sale of the Wheathill community within two years and the closure of the Bulstrode community in the middle of the 1960's.

The story of the Bruderhof continues on page 212

Experiments in group living

The 1950's saw a number of small communities set up in and around London. In 1951 a group of professionals and artists purchased a large country house at Underriver just outside Sevenoaks. The idea was in part that by living communally they could provide much needed childcare, enabling the women among them to continue their careers. St Julians' founders and early residents included Doctors Elizabeth Tylden and George Morgan; Leo deSyllas and family; Ian Gibson Smith, a photographer; Margaret Bates, a social worker; Betty Myer; Helena Dennis; Vera Courtney; the film producer John Arnold and family; film director Henry Cornelius and family; artist Rowland Hilder and family; and Charles Sidney McDonald, a musician. Each family had its own separate living area, the children were looked after together and the families had their meals together.

In the Cold War paranoia of the 1950's St Julians became dubbed 'a communist restaurant' and a 'communist co-operative household' and brought them to the attention of the security services. Files released by MI5 show that the group was under surveillance during the years 1951-1953 with the service showing particular interest when Swedish film actress Mai Zetterling, who they considered to be part of a 'coterie of American communist sympathisers in the film and theatre world', moved into one of the units with her family. The MI5 file records that they thought St Julians was somehow run by the 'MacDonald Discussion Group' which they considered to be a 'Marxist study group' and possibly a cover for recruitment to the Communist Party. In 1953 an agent reported: 'The degree of the MacDonald Discussion Group's connection with the Communist Party is not known, but the eminence of some of the Party lecturers, together with other indications, suggests that the Party has sanctioned the formation and continued existence of the group ... Attendance at MacDonald Discussion Group meetings can therefore be taken to signify that the participant is at least regarded by certain members as sympathetically inclined to communism, and as a potential convert.' [21] In the end the spooks concluded that although the group had strong associations with known communists there was nothing subversive about their activities and surveillance was ended although 'an interest was maintained in its members'. It is not clear if the members were aware of the attention from the security services but it did not seem to stop interest in the scheme. In 1956 a members' club was set up to extend the shared facilities with a bar and the communal facilities were started to be used by outside members. In 1963 an outdoor swimming pool was opened which attracted further members to join.

Founder member Dr Elizabeth (Betty) Tylden became an eminent family psychiatrist. She had worked with pioneering psychiatrist William Sargent during the war dealing with people traumatised by the Blitz and soldiers suffering from "shell-shock". Sargent emphasised the use of physical therapies, such as ECT and drugs, rather than the group therapy being pioneered at other hospitals. After the war Tylden developed a particular interest in women's mental health and family relationships and became a regular expert witness in child abuse cases. Later in the 1980's and 1990's she became known for her work with former members of religious and "New Age" cults, including former members of organisations such as the Children of God, some of whom were in secure hospitals or prisons and diagnosed as schizophrenic. '... Betty Tylden regarded conventional psychoanalysis and psychotherapy techniques as worse than useless in such cases, arguing that standard forms of relaxation therapy or hypnotic regression therapy can have a catastrophic effect on people sensitised to group singing, meditation or other group thought-reform patterns of behaviour, sometimes returning them to the mental state they were in when in the cult. She argued that such patients were not suffering from psychosis, but were exhibiting normal 'survival reactions' to the trauma to which they had been subjected ...'

Daily Telegraph **Obituary 25th February 2009**

Over the years St Julians slowly turned from being an experiment in co-operative living into a country club.

The home that she and George built at St Julians was an extraordinary experiment in communal living, its residents the most eclectic collection of artists and free-thinking people that I have ever come across. Over a decade of school holidays spent growing up in and around this island of unconventionality in the stockbroker belt, I learned more about humanity and its variations than I ever did at medical school.

Jonathan Belsey, "Remembering Betty Tylden", *British Medical Journal* **28.10.2009**

Sometime around 1958 a group appears in London called the Communal Living Association. It was started by a John Cooper who had issued a prospectus for a Communal Living Scheme, sending 350 copies out to enquirers after placing adverts in a number of papers. The prospectus declared: 'These pages are addressed to those men and women whose experiences or anthropological studies have already led them to a belief in the superiority of communal living and who now are keen to find by direct participation in a community ways and means of developing to the utmost all its potentialities for enabling the individual to realise a full and happy life.' **22** It went on to invite people to co-operate in launching a 'practical and workable scheme' that would carry the 'seeds of its own expansion' and that through this 'a new form of social evolution will be set in motion; each new group carrying out new experiments of its own and revealing more and more about the pre-requisites of human happiness to the benefit of all participants.' Cooper then outlines what he thinks are the benefits of communal living. The material advantages: 'Bulk buying, mutual co-operation, communal ownership of expensive household machinery, possibly a paid cook-housekeeper, and increased self sufficiency in spare time activities, all help towards a higher standard of living for each participant. Also, there is much more freedom for mothers, less housework, greater ease of obtaining individual privacy, and perhaps eventually, financial security for the individual in case of sickness etc.' And the psychological advantages: '... the sense of belonging and the companionship and security of living with friendly people whom one has the chance to get to know really well; the probable availability at any one moment of someone to share one's mood; the incidental group therapy which improves one's sense of reality in consequence of the fact that neurotic attitudes such as sometimes cause trouble between man and wife are much more difficult to defend seriously against a whole community. When children are included in the group they benefit from the happy atmosphere, numerous playmates and the variety of adult personalities with which they are in frequent contact. There is also the possibility of organising a progressive school catering for several groups.'

Cooper also sent out a questionnaire asking enquirers to state what their interest in communal living was. He received 50 replies and on 17th September 1959 an inaugural meeting of the Community Living Association (CLA) was held in the room above the rear bar of The Swan public house at Cosmo Place in Bloomsbury. The Meeting Started at 8.30pm with an informal discussion introduced by John Cooper with Michael Stack-Dunne in the chair. This included a session of discussion in small groups with subsequent reports to the whole group. A summary of the discussion was given at the next meeting. In general people sought personal freedom (ie own rooms, some personal cooking facilities) with the advantages of living in a group such as: 'possibilities of personal communication, sense of belonging, relief from domestic tyranny, a better environment for children, sharing of domestic facilities, etc.' Fourteen out of sixteen people present wanted to start as soon as possible.

For some months the group met regularly in The Swan to discuss communal living from various angles and to get to know each other. They held a number of social parties in each other's houses and started to search for suitable properties. *The Prospectus* had been deliberately vague on the actual details of any possible communal set-up as Cooper hoped that each group would 'choose its own way.' One person attracted to the meeting was the architect Peter Palmer who had a definite communal project that he put to the group. It was for a simple, well-built block of flats, self-contained with 20% of the space allocated to communal facilities such as laundry, shops, playgroup, communal room etc. He estimated that the flats should cost between £2,500 - £3,000 each. In order to carry out the project the group started the process of registering the Swan Housing Association. While doing this they came into contact with an organisation called Housing Partnership Ltd who were already well underway with their own project on Inner Park Road, Wimbledon. They had well-developed plans for '11 houses, five flats and nine garages' drawn up by Kenneth Capon of the Architects Co-Partnership and hoped to be on site building by September 1959. Members of the CLA who had been interested in the project put forward by Palmer were encouraged to join the Housing Partnership scheme. By this time

> **Community Living Association**
> **CLA Objects**
>
> 1 To assist in forming close-knit communities by all practical means
> 2 To create conditions of continuous expansion in the rate of 'forming' new communities
> 3 To encourage variety in the internal arrangements of the communities
> 4 To maintain contact between the communities for exchange of information and personnel and for various activities of mutual benefit
> 5 To make information on the communities available to anyone interested
> 6 Ultimately to try to reach conclusions about the pre-requisite of human happiness on the basis of the accumulated experience of many communities
> 7 To encourage activities of social value where these were not in conflict with the other aims of the CLA
> 8 To take measures as necessary to ensure the continued survival and activity of CLA whatever difficulties may arise.

Housing Partnership development Inner Park Road, Wimbledon

the group had got the registration of the Swan Housing Association through, and it was decided that as some members were 'too idealistic' to join the HP Ltd scheme, the 'Swan Group' would continue. Those members who either could not afford to join the Wimbledon Park project or who were looking for something more communal continued to meet and early the following year had started a serious property search. Notes from their February 1960 meeting list a number possible properties in north London and in the CLA Bulletin issued in March there are urgent requests from a 'Bought-House Group' who were looking to buy a house in Hornsey Lane Gardens and a 'Rented-House Group' both appealing for people interested in joining them to get in touch. 'We are negotiating for the lease of a house near Madame Tussauds. If successful, most of the tenants will have to move in in May or June. The house has 17 rooms, two communal kitchens, three bathrooms, several lavatories and could house 20 people. It is in good condition and is light. It has no garden, but Regents Park is no distance away.' The Bulletin also lists a series of future meetings and social events through into the summer including: regular Wednesday night gatherings in the Partisan Coffee Bar, trips to the Royal Festival Hall and the Garrick Theatre, a special meeting for "parents with children (of any age) to get to know each other better and to collaborate in practical ways" and a Mayday ramble on the South Downs.

In early summer the 'Madame Tussauds' house at 39 Nottingham Place (also referred to occasionally as the '39 group' and the 'Baker Street group') was leased by CLA secretary Michael Stack-Dunne on a 16-year lease and rooms sub-let to other members. Rents averaged at £170 for the whole year and members were asked to put in £85 'capital' to cover the deposit and a month's rent in advance. A dozen members moved in during the summer months and set about redecorating and planning how to convert the house. In October a story about the group appeared in the *Evening Chronicle* under the headline 'The More The Merrier'.

'I met them in a rambling old house, tucked away in the select neighbourhood surrounding the headquarters of the BBC. It is a house the 12 grown-ups have leased to test their theories that the happiest families are large ones that share everything. Each tenant has separate living accommodation in the home which sprawls over four storeys and a deep, gigantic basement. But cooking, laundry and dining facilities are communal ... Do-it-yourself chaos surrounded the house, during my visit, experienced tenants were decorating their own rooms, building wall shelves and fitments, hanging pelmets and curtains. A young architect and his wife were even making their own furniture. And when they have finished they will all weigh in and help other tenants who are not so handy with the hammer and paint brush.'

The journalist goes on to report that the group had plans to install a laundry, a large party room and a photographic dark room in the basement, a roof-garden and a first-floor 'Big Room', which would have 'Hi-Fi music equipment and a special wall for cine-camera projection.' The article ends on an up-beat note with a quote from one member – 'The modern family unit is too small to provide complete happiness in life. A group of people living together will make for wider horizons and a greater variety of interests' and with the promise of a further visit in a few months time 'to see if everyone is living happily everafter.'

While things had got off to a fairly good start at 39 Nottingham Place things were not all as rosy as painted in the *Chronicle* article. After a house meeting on November 3rd a strongly worded note was issued regarding cleaning, it stated:

1   People leaving a mess should clean it away forthwith! Untidy ones will desist forthwith!
2   People are requested to observe list of house cleaning allocation (areawise)
3   Needless to say, those who are unprepared to clean their own allocated area will be encouraged – nay more than encouraged – to employ a charlady.
4   Women emptying dustbins are advised to do so in pairs -presumably they can agree for that long.
5   Major irritants are:
    a) Bath left dirty
    b) Cookers left greasy
    c) Dustbins left full
    d) Lavatories, including pedestals, which are not cleaned regularly. Haphazard Harpic just will not do.
    e) Undefrosted fridges
NB The alternative to voluntary cleaning would appear to be a Labour Czar, which, it was felt, would be a rather sad innovation.

The cleaning issues seem to have been a manifestation of other underlying conflicts in the group, all centreing around the relationship between Dr Stack-Dunne as the de facto 'landlord' and the rest of the group. By the middle of November the situation had deteriorated to the point that accusations were flying around of 'dictatorship' and call for a vote of confidence in the 'landlord'. At a further house meeting on 15th November the purpose of which was '... to consider Michael's present attitude to ourselves and formulate a basis for the resumption of negotiations, together with a return to more normal relationships' the group expressed its appreciation for all the time and energy that Michael had put into the project, but went on to reaffirm their 'desire and intent' to run the house on CLA principles. By the end of the month both sides had ceased direct communication and started exchanging solicitors' letters. The whole somewhat sorry saga dragged on throughout 1961. While there seemed to be a number of causes of the conflict: personal differences between Dr Stack-Dunne and John Cooper over the running of the CLA and individual decisions that had been taken over exactly how the house was run, the crux of the conflict focussed on the balance of responsibility between the 'official' leaseholder and the group's 'desire and intent' to be a democratically run communal household. The project came to a final end in early 1962 after court cases against some of the tenants for non-payment of rent. Attempts were made to get some sort of 'inquiry' set up through the CLA to establish 'objectively' what had happened so that others might learn from what Michael Stack-Dunne in the end described to another member of the CLA as 'a sad and frightening experience.'

The trials and tribulations of the '39 group' took its toll on the CLA, with members struggling to keep the organisation going. Despite the difficulties, the Association managed to continue and made contact with other groups in London and beyond. A Bulletin was issued in January 1962, which listed a number of groups they were in touch with and contained a report on a visit to Braziers Park by members to attend a weekend entitled 'Community Launching Platform'. It also advertised an open evening at the Community

House at 14 Haslemere Road. The Haslemere Road group were a sort of spin-off or London house for people involved with Braziers. John Woodcock, who had been a regular at meetings of a London-based group that had connections with Braziers Park in Oxfordshire, started discussions in 1959 among the group about acquiring a 'community house' in London to be run along the same lines as Braziers. In 1960 a large house in Haslemere Road, Crouch End was bought by Phyllis Jones and John Woodcock. The little group of Brazierites set to organising their own sensory and executive committees though, being only 8 or 9 in number, everyone had to serve on both committees. A detailed description of the 'theory and practice' of life at Haslemere Road, written by John and Evelyn Woodcock, was printed in two long articles in *Braziers Research Communications* numbers 10 and 11.

'The group at Haslemere Road may be defined as follows: a number (on average, eight to ten) of self-elected adults and their children, not all of one kin, religion or political outlook, sharing many aspects of family life together, on the basis of equality. These aspects include one roof, one household budget, the main meals of the day and public rooms in the house. Household management is shared among members, with regular committee meetings open to all. Other meetings are held to consider mutual and individual concerns and interests apart from those of management.'

The writers go on to explain the pros and cons of experimental group living as opposed to family life.

(i)   The present-day family does not include everybody. We would suggest that the various ways of living at present available to the unmarried, divorced and widowed may be a poor second-best to family life. It is among these individuals, dissociated from any family group, that many problems of social welfare are to be found. The experimental group appears to be a creative answer to their problems.

(ii) Members of the primary family itself often suffer from isolation. The case of the mother with young children confined to the house all day is the most obvious example. The experimental group can provide household shopping, meals, cleaning, baby sitting, etc., together with companionship.

(iii) The physical isolation of individual children is very common in the primary family unit. In the experimental group this is overcome, and the crucial transfer of the young child's interest from his parents to alternative sources of stimulation can be achieved through play activity with the other children who share his home.

(iv) The problem of the isolation of old age is mitigated in the experimental group by the maintenance of an age balance, so that the elderly find an accepted place there.

(v)   Labour mobility, too, would be facilitated if many groups existed in different regions to receive those uprooted from their own locality as the result of economic change.

They also discuss a number of issues connected with group living: 'the problem of leadership' – 'Adults setting up an experiment in group living for the first time will inevitably have been conditioned by their own childhood experiences to accept either the role of leader or the role of being led ... the group offers a wider sphere for personal power and conversely greater protection and security for the timid ...'; 'group size' – '... It must be large enough to give variety yet small enough for all its parts to be in direct communication ... between seven and ten adults is the ideal primary working group ...We would suggest that a larger number than twelve would severely diminish the cohesion of the group.'; and 'Distrust – the Ultimate Obstacle' – 'We keep ourselves to ourselves'. 'She can't stand another woman in the kitchen', 'An Englishman's home is his castle'. 'I like to be able to do just as I please at home'. These are some very common sayings. It would seem that people today have an inbred distrust and suspicion for one another, and this is why they reject all idea of group living, in spite of its many obvious advantages ... Our experience has been that access to a regular forum at which such problems can be discussed is of inestimable value ... In group living, also, it must be admitted that greater self-discipline is necessary; we need to make a conscious effort to foster goodwill and to exercise conscious control over our own worst moods lest others suffer. This is of course very difficult, and we must often fall short of this high standard.'

The Haslemere group would in turn create its own off-shoot with members helping in 1962 to set up a further 'group-house' at 66 Hornsey Rise. The CLA seems to have been supported by the Haslemere Road group. As well as connections with Braziers, the CLA was certainly aware of and had contact with St Julians. Some time around 1963-64 the CLA seems to have faded away with there being no further record of any bulletins being issued or correspondence in the umbrella group's name.

Ever since they moved in a year ago, Muriel (centre) and her house companions have been expecting a first-class row. But so far there hasn't been even a whisper of one

Eight strangers buy a house and beat loneliness
by Isobel Cole

"EVER since we moved into the house a year ago we've been expecting a first-class row," admitted Muriel Jones. "But so far there hasn't been the whisper of one." Muriel, a dark-haired, attractive woman, smiled at me across the sitting room. It was comfortable and warm, like the rest of the house in Crouch End, North London, where Muriel, three other women and four men are trying an experiment loaded with emotional dynamite – an experiment in communal living.

All idealists, they are following out a psychiatrist's theory that people would be happier and mentally healthier if they could live more together, instead of seeking privacy. The theory has certainly worked for Muriel, once a lonely widow. "It's just as if I'd come to life again," she told me. She met her present house companions – Jane, a civil servant, Brian, a public relations officer, Marianne, a secretary, Marguerite and Tom, students, Ian, a carpenter, Bill, a company director – at an adult education course which they all attended in 1959. Their ages, ranging between twenty and sixty, were as widely separated as their temperaments and interests. Yet each had one thing in common. They were living alone in bed-sitters, hostels or flats, and each of them was fed-up with the feeling of being left out.

Muriel told me about herself. "I was brought up with a large family. After losing my husband four years ago the loneliness was awful. When I had put my little boy Ralfe to bed in the evening I felt I was finished. I would be in bed by nine. Now," she said, her face warm and happy, "when we all get together in the evenings there's so much to talk about, we're still up at midnight."

"I was rather scared at first," Muriel admitted. "I thought we would fight over the bathroom, fall over each other in the kitchen, be driven mad by each other's gramophones ..." But the first thing the group did after buying their eight-bedroom house as a limited company on a share basis, was to form a joint management committee to meet monthly and air problems.

Sausage and Mash

Rosters are drawn up for shopping, cooking, washing up. "With eight of us, these chores amount to very little," Muriel said. "At first one of the men was very diffident about cooking. When it came to his first meal we expected to have to make do with sausage and mash. Instead Bill turned out a superlative dinner grilled gammon rashers with pineapple and sweet corn followed by a trifle."

I asked Muriel what would happen financially if anyone suddenly wanted to opt out of this unusual arrangement. "We could sell our share to the others; leave our money invested at six per cent interest or get someone approved by the others to take our place," she said. "Of course, if one of us decided to marry, things could become complicated. But it needn't be the end. We think this scheme can work with married couples too, provided they are not self-centred."

Weekend Cottage

Muriel told me the "family" is thinking of buying a seaside cottage for weekends – again on a share basis. "We could easily afford it," she said. "Here £4.10s. a week from each of us covers everything from building society repayments to a daily." So it seems that idealism can pay dividends. And if that weekend cottage does come off, ten-year-old Ralfe, Muriel's son, can look forward to grand holidays by the sea. "He was a bit upset about moving here at first," said Muriel. "Now he loves it. As the only child, he has so many doting uncles and aunts."

**Article from the *Woman's Mirror*
22nd April 1961**

Post-war Communal Blues: Bibliography & Notes

Allain, R *The Community That Failed*
Carrier Pigeon Press 1992. ISBN: 1882260007

Allsop, K *One and All – Two Years in the Chilterns*
Alan Sutton Publishing 1991 ISBN: 0862999669

Andresen, M *Field of Vision: The Broadcast Life of Kenneth Allsop* Trafford 2005. ISBN: 1412024072

Armatage, W H G *Wheathill Bruderhof 1942-58*
American Journal of Economy XVIII 1959

Arnold, Emmy *A Joyful Pilgrimage: My Life in Community*
Plough Publishing House 1999. ISBN: 0874869560

Baum, M *Against the Wind: Eberhard Arnold and the Bruderhof*
Plough Publishing 1998 ISBN: 0874869536

Bohlken-Zumpe, E *Torches Extinguished*
Carrier Pigeon Press 1993. ASIN: B0006F12R4

Bryant, A *Squatting* in The Illustrated London News
September 28 1946

Burnham, P *The Squatters of 1946* in Socialist History
Journal No 25. ISBN: 185489157X

Bush, R *FAU: The Third Generation* William Sessions York
1998. ISBN 9781850722113

Fretz, J W *Pilgrims in Paraguay* Herald Press 1953

Glaister, D *Braziers: a Personal Story* Braziers Park School
of Integrative Research 1973

Gardner, G *The Bruderhof Communities in Paraguay and England* Libertarian Press 1949

Hinton, J *Self-help and Socialism: the Squatters Movement of 1946*
History Workshop Journal 25, 1988

Larkham, P J *New Suburbs and Post-war Reconstruction: The Fate of Charles Reilly's 'Greens'* Working paper

Mommsen, P *Homage to a Broken Man: The Life of J Heinrich Arnold* Plough Publishing 2004. ISBN 0874869307

Pleil, Nadine Moonje *Free From Bondage* Carrier Pigeon
Press 1997. ISBN: 1882260074

Richmond, Peter *Marketing Modernisms: the Architecture and Influence of Charles Reilly* Liverpool University Press
2001. ISBN 0853237662

Rubin, J *The Other Side of Joy*
OUP USA 2000. ISBN: 0195119436

The Wheathill Bruderhof: Ten Years Of Community Living Bromdon UK, Plough Publishing 1952.

Tyldesley, M *No Heavenly Delusion?* Liverpool University
Press 2003 ISBN: 0853236089

Wagoner, B and S *Community in Paraguay: Visit to the Bruderhof* Plough Pub 1991 ISBN: 0874860334

Ward, C *The People Act: The Post War Squatters' Movement, in Housing: An Anarchist Approach* 1983
Squatters: The Full Story in Labour Research, Nov 1946
The Hidden History of Housing
www.historyandpolicy.org/papers/policy-paper-25.html

Wates, N and Wolmar, C (eds) *Squatting – The Real Story*
Bay Leaf Books 1980. ISBN: 0950725919

Westlake, J *70 Years A-Growing* Hawthorn Press 2000.
ISBN: 186989037X

Wolfe, L *The Reilly Plan* Nicholson & Watson 1945 ASIN:
B0007J1Y7M

Zabloki, B *The Joyful Community* University of Chicago
Press 1971 ISBN: 0226977498

Notes

1   Hansard, House of Commons 1947. 5th series HMSO.
Quoted in Lynn Pearson in *The Architectural and Social History of Co-operative Living* Macmillan

2   The Dudley Report 1944 Central Housing Advisory
Committee. Design of Dwellings Report (1944)

3   *Only Halfway to Paradise* by E Wilson. Quoted in Lynn
Pearson

4   *Who Was Harry Cowley?* Brighton: Queen Spark
Books, 1984

5   *Memories of Superior Camp* Hampshire –
http://www.headley-village.com (22.12.08)

6   Fretz, J W *Pilgrims in Paraguay* Herald Press 1953

7   From PWS document titled *A New Experiment*. Mid
1948 Quoted in *FAU The Third Generation*.

8   Jack Eglon in *The Hants & Sussex News* Oct 1968.
Quoted in *FAU The Third Generation*

9   Addison, Paul *The Road to 1945*

10 Duplicated sheet sent to enquirers, quoted in *One and All*. K Allsop p4

11 Hilde Marchant *Six Families Live as One*. Picture Post
Vol 32 No10, 7 September 1946

12 Andresen, M *Field of Vision: The Broadcast Life of Kenneth Allsop*

13 ibid

14 Allsop, K *One and All: Two Years in the Chilterns*

15 Joy Scott in *Field of Vision* p257

16 http://www.braziers.org.uk/Research%20pdfs/24/
Friends_of_the_Future.pdf (28.3.2012)

17 Dorothy Glaister *Braziers: A Personal Story* 1973

18 Stanley Fletcher, *The Plough* No 31 May/June 1992

19 Derek Wardle *50th Anniversary of the Wheathill Bruderhof* Plough Publishing 1992

20 *The Wheathill Bruderhof: Ten Years Of Community Living*

21 MacDonald Group (KV 5/80) file released 3.3.2009
www.mi5.gov.uk (29.4.2011)

22 Details of the CLA and the 'Madam Tussauds' house
come from papers donated by Michael Stack-
Dunne. This is the 'commune in a box' mentioned in
the Introduction to this book. It was initially given to
Springhill Cohousing group after Michael read about
them in *The Guardian* and later passed to the author.

Communal Therapy

Whilst the First World War had demonstrated that the nation's fittest and bravest could succumb to mental breakdown, this lesson had largely been forgotten by 1939. The principle was re-established during the Second World War that everyone, if subjected to intense stress of combat, would ultimately cease to function. No longer could a line be drawn between those who were regarded as constitutionally inferior and those considered innately healthy. Furthermore, it was recognized that traditional hospital regimes, when applied to psychological disorders, robbed patients of their autonomy and could impede recovery.

Edgar Jones, *War and the Practice of Psychotherapy*

The Second World War saw a transformation in the psychiatric treatment of soldiers that would in turn lead to broader acceptance of psychotherapy within medicine and society at large once peace had returned, and to a whole range of experimental therapeutic communities. This was in sharp contrast to the situation following the First World War when, despite the epidemic of shell-shock and other so-called war neuroses, the limited provision of outpatient clinics set up after the war by the Ministry of Pensions were shut down due to financial pressure and official doubts about their therapeutic value. In 1920 the Tavistock Clinic had opened in Bloomsbury with charitable funding, offering private mental health treatment to war veterans and the general public. But it struggled to secure funding or win official recognition through the inter-war years. On the outbreak of war in 1939 there was a shortage of military staff with any psychiatric background. This led to the appointment of J R Rees, director of the Tavistock Clinic, as consultant psychiatrist to the army. The evacuation of the British Expeditionary Force from Dunkirk in June 1940 brought with it large numbers of troops suffering from psychological disorders. To cope with this, and to try to head off an epidemic of 'shell-shock', Rees recruited a number of colleagues from the Tavistock Clinic including Emanuel Miller, a trained child psychiatrist, Eddie Bennet, a decorated First World War veteran who was also an analytical psychologist and friend of Jung, and Wilfrid Bion. The Sandhill Park Mental Defective Colony at Bishop's Lydeard, near Taunton was taken over as the main Military Psychiatric Hospital. The aim was to treat servicemen suffering from psychological disorders in an attempt to return them to active duty or to useful employment in civilian life. '... Conventional wisdom suggested that after a short period of rest, servicemen should be rapidly re-introduced to military life by graded physical exercise and occupational therapy ...'[1] This basic approach had very little success with not much more than a third of those treated returning to any sort of service. With services under increasing pressure from the growing number of men suffering from war neuroses, Hollymoor Hospital at Northfield was transferred to the military in April 1942. At Hollymoor two pioneering experiments would take place during the war. These became known later as the first and second Northfield Experiments.

Madness in a time of war

As far as treatment is concerned one might well say that everything we do here is treatment.
It is for this reason that our treatment does not consist of bed and rest, or the usual bottle of coloured
medicine. Besides interviews with our Psychiatrist, we spend much of our time in various forms of
exercise and activities.

Introducing you to Northfield (pamphlet)

Hollymoor Military Hospital at Northfield, five miles south west of
Birmingham, was established in the buildings of a Victorian mental
hospital set in extensive grounds isolated from the local community. The
military regime at Northfield was divided into two separate sections, a
200 bed hospital section where daily life was fairly relaxed; soldiers were
tended by nurses and medical staff and slept in beds with mattresses
and sheets. The other section was the training wing, with 660 beds, to
which patients were transferred when sufficiently 'cured'. This was run by
training instructors on much more military lines in order to prepare the
patients to return to their regiments. Men slept on straw filled palliases
with blankets, wore khaki and spent their days doing drill, fatigues and
going on marches. As being 'cured' meant a return to active service men
used whatever means at their disposal to resist 'treatment' and so escape
back to civi-street. Into this fairly conventional military hospital came
two psychoanalysts Wilfred Bion and John Rickman. Bion, a First World
War tank commander who had been one of only three survivors of an
entire regiment had, after the war, studied at both Oxford and University
College London. He met and was impressed by the brain surgeon Wilfred
Trotter, who had written *Instincts of the Herd in Peace and War* on the
horrors of the First World War. After obtaining his medical qualification
he spent seven years at the Tavistock Clinic where he was analyst for the
playwright and poet Samuel Beckett. He met Rickman at the Tavistock
and in 1940 the two set up in practice together. Quaker John Rickman's
pacifist beliefs had stopped him volunteering for active wartime service
and after graduating as a doctor of medicine in 1916 he worked for the
Friends' War Victims Relief Unit for two years in Russia. In 1920 he
travelled to Vienna and worked with Freud who later recommended him
as an Associate Member of the newly formed British Psychoanalytical
Society. When the Second World War broke out Rickman worked as a
psychiatrist first at Haymeads Hospital near Bishops Stortford and later
joined Bion at Wharncliffe Emergency Medical Services near Sheffield.
The Wharncliffe War Hospital, previously known as the Wadsley Asylum,
had been a major military hospital during WWI, during which time a
number of students from the Sheffield School of Art had run painting
classes for the severely injured. Out of this one of the students, Annie
Carter, was inspired to try and set up a business that would be able to
offer the men employment and support when they left hospital. Painted
Fabrics Ltd **2** was formed in 1923 when land and 'hutments' at the old
Women's Auxiliary Army Corps camp at Norton Woodseats were leased.
Over the next 15 years a thriving community developed – initially huts
were converted to homes for some of the men and their families and
others turned into workshops, all adapted to the special needs of the

ex-servicemen. It lasted until 1958. It is not known if Bion and Rickman were aware of the Painted Fabrics project during their short time at Wharncliffe.

Bion and Rickman arrived at Northfield in 1943 and were given charge of a training wing with about 100 men. Issuing what they called the 'Wharncliffe Memorandum' they started the first Northfield experiment. Over the next six weeks a radical and controversial community experiment would unfold. The soldiers were brought together on parade and it was explained to them that the following rules were now in place:

- Every man would do one hour's PT each day.
- Every man was to become a member of one or more groups, designed to study an educational, craft or organisational topic.
- Any man could form a new group which catered for his particular interest.
- A man who felt unable to go to his group must go the rest room. The rest room would be in the charge of a nursing orderly and would be kept quiet for board games and resting.
- In addition there was to be a parade each day at 12.10pm for 30 minutes.

The daily parade was also to function as a group meeting. Bion and Rickman intended to step back and essentially see what happened with very little intervention from themselves as professionals. Very little did happen at first except for much discussion of the new regulations. Then the men started to form the interest groups themselves. On one occasion the men challenged the new scheme by putting forward a request for a group which they expected would be turned down: they proposed forming a dancing class. Instead of rejecting the idea the two psychoanalysts encouraged the men to approach officers and ATS staff for help and to work up a definite proposal. This resulted in the formation of a very lively dance group.

In the space of a few weeks the morale of the training wing was transformed for the better. Men were busily engaged in group activities, even after normal hours of duty, and there was little absenteeism. The soldiers' appearance improved and they became much more responsive. Soldiers from the hospital wing became keen to be transferred.

Brian Nichol, *Bion and Foulkes at Northfield*

The whole tone of the wing was transformed and the men rapidly became self-critical and self-motivated. After complaining about the dirty state of the wing they set up an orderly group responsible for cleanliness. The daily parade meetings became a forum where the men examined relationships among themselves and faced up to the reality of their situation.

The army is primarily a communal living environment, in which each soldier depends on his comrades for survival. By exploring difficulties in relationships in such a direct way they were learning to understand the nature of their obligations, and the responsibilities and pleasures of such mutual reliance.

Bion and Rickman 1943 [3]

Bion and Rickman made one fatal mistake in setting up their experiment in communal therapy: they had gone about it without the support of either medical colleagues in the hospital or the military hierarchy, in fact without even informing them. Other staff at Northfield felt undermined and excluded. Word reached ears in Whitehall who saw nothing positive in the transformation taking place at the hospital but rather a breakdown in both military discipline and the traditional doctor/patient relationship. War Office officials visited one night without warning and 'The chaos in the hospital cinema hall, with newspapers and condom-strewn floors, resulted in the immediate termination of the project.' Bion and Rickman were hastily transferred to other units. The first Northfield Experiment had lasted a mere six weeks.

The second Northfield Experiment came about through a number of other postings to Northfield. Siegfried Foulkes (known as Michael), a psychoanalyst trained in Vienna and Frankfurt, who came to England in 1933 as a refugee, arrived at the hospital in 1942 and started to experiment with small-scale group therapy sessions. He was joined in March 1944 by Dennis Carroll who took over as Commanding Officer. Carroll had previously worked with David Wills at the Hawkspur Camp, a project for the rehabilitation of young men with emotional difficulties established on a few acres of land on Hill Hall Common, near Great Bardfield, Essex by the Grith Frith in May 1936.[4] The third posting was Major Harold Bridger who came as training wing commander at the end of 1944. A maths teacher at Rugby Public School before the War, Bridger had no psychiatric experience. He had commanded an anti-aircraft battery and then worked for the Officer Selection Board carrying out the psychiatric profiling set up by Rees. He was reluctant to take over the post at Northfield and spent months in preparation visiting other military hospitals, talking to Wilfred Bion and reading a recently-published book on the Peckham Experiment.[5] Between the three of them they would change the whole purpose and philosophy of the hospital. This time the initial impetus for the experiment came from the top. On a visit to Northfield, J R Rees noticed the group therapy work Foulkes was doing on one of the wards and that morale there appeared to be much higher than elsewhere. It was Rees who, over the following year, smoothed the way for the military to sanction the change of regime. Foulkes was to carry on with his group therapy sessions and to teach his methods to other sympathetic psychiatrists, whilst Bridger would take over 'rehabilitation'. Clearly the spirit of Bion's and Rickman's work still survived.

There was from the start, though, a tension inherent in this second 'experiment' between the two meanings of the term 'group therapy': between those, like Foulkes, who saw group therapy as the treatment of a number of individuals assembled in a group; and those with experience in the Army, who saw it as a planned endeavour to develop in a group the forces that lead to smoothly running co-operative activity.

Ben Shephard, A War of Nerves

The separation of hospital and training wing was done away with, the whole place operating as one unit. Groups and clubs of all kinds were encouraged. Again, patients were expected to take part in the organisation of the groups and through regular ward meetings with the running of the hospital itself. Each ward also elected a patient to attend a weekly meeting of ward representatives. This was extended beyond the walls of the hospital as links were made with the local community. Some of the men were found jobs with local car manufacturer, Austins, and on neighbouring farms. Trips were also arranged to go ice skating and play golf. A pamphlet, 'Introducing you to Northfield', was produced by one group which was formed to introduce new patients to the hospital. Newcomers were given the pamphlet and a tour by one of the group. 'This magazine has been compiled as clearly and concisely as possible to give you some idea of why you are here, and the facilities and entertainments available during your stay at this Hospital. We are going to try and solve some of your difficulties in the light of those we have experienced.' The group went on to produce their own newspaper, *The Northfield Mercury*, which on occasions acted as a sort of safety valve for patients to vent their opinions about the running of the hospital.

The experience of being at Northfield was an intense one for staff and patients alike. The therapeutic results were beyond expectations. Many of those involved felt they had been introduced into a world where far more was possible in human relationships than they had previously thought. They came to believe that the creativeness and co-operation released might, if replicated on a wide enough scale, provide a means of bringing into existence a more reparative society.

Ben Shephard, A War of Nerves

At the end of the war many of the psychiatrists left Northfield to return to their civilian jobs. The 'experiment' continued for a couple of years into peacetime with others like Dr Tom Main coming in and continuing the work. He tried to extend some of Bridger's ideas including not just the patients and psychiatrists in the running of wards but also the nurses and the civilian staff. Main is one of a number of people credited with coining the name 'therapeutic community'. In an article for a medical journal in 1946 under the heading 'therapeutic community' he wrote;

The Northfield Experiment is an attempt to use a hospital not as an organisation run by doctors in the interests of their own greater technical efficiency, but as a community with the immediate aim of full participation of all its members in its daily life and the eventual aim of the resocialization of the neurotic individual for life in ordinary society. Ideally, it has been conceived as a therapeutic setting with a spontaneous and emotionally structured (rather than medically dictated) organisation in which all staff and patients engage. Any attempt to permit or create such a setting demands tolerance, a willingness to profit by error, and a refusal to jump to conclusions

Dr Tom Main, The Hospital as a Therapeutic Institution

Almost in parallel to the experiments at Northfield similar work was being done at the Mill Hill Emergency Hospital by Dr Maxwell Jones. In 1939 the Mill Hill boarding school had been evacuated en masse to St Bees in Cumbria and the school buildings set in 120 acres of grounds requisitioned for use by the Maudsley Hospital to treat soldiers and civilians suffering from neuroses and shell-shock and the casualties of air-raids. The hospital used a whole range of clinical approaches for treating of the emotional traumas of war, some of which were highly innovative for the time. It used hypnosis, narcosis or semi-narcosis treatment with sodium amytal injections to help patients relive their experiences and was one of the first hospitals in Britain to introduce electroconvulsive therapy (ECT), but it did not use lobotomies or insulin therapy. Psychotherapy was also used. Due to staff shortages this was not done on the usual individual basis but in groups with patients and staff working together as a team. The shortage of nurses also led to the recruitment of 'social therapists', these were female conscriptees, many with arts backgrounds who, as well as teaching crafts, participated in lectures and discussions about the soldiers' conditions. The lectures were part of a programme introduced by Maxwell Jones in the belief that informing the soldiers about their physiology and how to care for themselves would improve their chances for recovery. Later patients themselves took over this role, with those who had been there longer passing on information and advice to newcomers. From an initial question and answer format, these talks broadened out into discussions of problems on the wards and interpersonal relationships with sub-communities forming on the various wards. Some of the social therapists had been drama students and started an early form of drama therapy assisting the patients and staff to act out their dilemmas in 'psychodramas' and in short scripted plays.

The psychodramas were very important in the beginning and the ones they developed became much more sophisticated, eventually written as scripts and produced one day a week. At first, however, the nurses (the drama students) would put them on – hypothetical, but based on material from the case histories. The soldiers would watch the dramatic episode and if they disagreed, would be asked to present the situation the way it should have been – the way it actually happened to them.
You see, they were beginning to dramatize their own case histories.
Dennie Briggs, Maxwell Jones: Photo Highlights from his life and work

As the war went on all sorts of innovations were tried in the wards under Jones' influence. There were Grumbles meetings:

... the Grumbles Meetings concentrated so long on food, draughts, and bad beds and uncomfortable toilets, and all the rest of the things – weeks on end the lavatories would be discussed and it was always the same. The other thing that went on was that each ward had its own meeting, so there was a feedback from the wards into the Grumbles Meetings and the realisation that maybe we should spend more time looking at the here-and-now and so the Grumbles Meetings ceased to be just a gripe session and became a way of looking at the total structure.
Joy Tuxford, Social Therapist in A seminar with Maxwell Jones, 1969

The Misfit family: a theoretical family, with the hysterical mother, psychopathic daughter and so on, that appeared in a series of psychodramas.

... the Misfit Family was really a way of getting patients involved in social problems which were very familiar and it's a kind of crystallized out in our concept of social learning, not that you don't learn by listening – you learn by interacting – if you just listen you're not being taught and you memorize. We make this sharp distinction between learning and teaching. Teaching is what poor kids get at school and learning is what we're trying to develop ...
Maxwell Jones in A seminar with Maxwell Jones, 1969

And Nervy Ned: a humorous cartoon character used to explain symptoms to the patients. As at Northfield these innovative practices were frowned on by those in charge of the hospital and brought Jones into conflict with other staff at the hospital. At the end of the war Jones was transferred to the Southern Hospital at Dartford and put in charge of helping returning prisoners of war. He took along with him 59 members of staff from Mill Hill. The POWs were housed in six sections of 50 soldiers each, which quickly formed into small 'therapeutic' communities. Elements of the programmes devised at Mill Hill were implemented straight away: daily community meetings, weekly discussion groups and psychodrama sessions.

We started psychodramas immediately; this was a perfect opening. Many of the men had developed skills in drama while in the camps, where putting on plays was one of the only forms of recreation in which they could freely participate. In a few camps, theatre had also become a kind of subterfuge through which the prisoners could communicate with each other and the guards couldn't understand it.

Maxwell Jones in Dennie Briggs, *Maxwell Jones: Photo Highlights from his life and work*

Jones also started an early form of occupational therapy at Dartford. He personally canvassed local factories, shops and farms and persuaded them to take on the returning soldiers on short-term, four-hour-a-day placements to help them get back into a work routine. This was made possible by the government provision of three buses to ferry patients to and from work. In the eleven months that the unit operated 1,200 soldiers were 'treated' and prepared for return to civi street. The work Maxwell Jones and his colleagues did at Dartford led on to work in collaboration with the Ministries of Health, Labour and Pensions at Belmont Hospital where an 'Industrial Neurosis Unit' consisting of 100 beds was set up to study and treat the 'hard core chronically unemployed'. It was thought that many people attending outpatient departments in hospitals, as well as having medical complaints, had a 'degree of personality and social disorganisation' that needed a different sort of treatment.

… Many patients are thought to have come from discordant early family situations, from which they developed the type of personality sometimes referred to as the 'affectionless character' generally characterised as a 'lack of sense of belonging', 'rootlessness', or 'social alienation'. The view of the Unit is that the provision of an intensely counteractive environment of the kind the patients missed when children can under suitable conditions, provide a belated 'corrective emotional experience' …

R Rapoport, *Community as a Doctor*

The Unit became independent and was renamed the Social Rehabilitation Unit. It was again set up along what was now becoming a therapeutic community 'method', or system, consisting of a series of small group meetings, workshops and lectures as well as leisure activities, psychodrama sessions and work therapy. In the years following the war the results of the pioneering work carried out at Northfield and Mill Hill would influence not only the 1959 Mental Health Act but would result in an increasing number of therapeutic communities being set up in hospitals across the country. Tom Main would put his ideas into practice again as director of the Cassel Hospital at Richmond. In the 1950's, liberal regimes would be instigated by David Clark at Fulbourn Hospital in Cambridgeshire and at Claybury Hospital in Essex. After working in the USA, where he was influential in the formation of the American Therapeutic communities movement, Maxwell Jones returned in 1962 to take up the post of Physician-Superintendent at Dingleton Hospital in Melrose, Scotland, where he set about transforming a whole hospital along therapeutic

community lines. Social psychiatry received a huge boost by the work carried out in the treatment of soldiers during and after the war, and moved to centre stage in public thinking on mental health for a while. The work laid the foundations for the therapeutic communities movement to be launched and flourish in the following decades. Looking back on impact of those years Maxwell Jones stated that he thought it '... doubtful that this rapid transformation could have occurred in peacetime; hospital traditions are strong. The general tendencies to change were due to the crises of war-time, the temporary nature of the hospital, and nursing staff from other professions. We had evolved a process of growth, without any conscious inkling, spontaneously.'
6

Even the normally level-headed J. R. Rees was infected by this mood. Lecturing in New York in 1944, at a time when the Beveridge Report had thrown the British post-war social order up for discussion, Rees day-dreamed about a future in which 'progressive scientific and health activities [would] pay a positive dividend,' and saw psychiatrists as Platonic Guardians of a Brave New World, vetting politicians for their emotional stability and solving the 'problem of household help' by 'an organisation of women into groups or a service.'

Ben Shephard, A War of Nerves

Distressed children in a time of war

The evacuation was a massive social undertaking, voluntarily carried out in September 1939 in the first days of the Second World War. It affected 47 percent of the country's school children who went with their teachers, and a large number of mothers and younger children who went together. The total amounted to 750,000 schoolchildren, 542,000 mothers with young children, 12,000 expectant mothers and 77,000 other persons, all of whom were transported from cities to the countryside or to smaller towns.

"Family or Familiarity?" J Mitchell & J Goody in What is a Parent?

The experiences of many evacuees was something akin to an extended 'holiday' with strangers in the countryside. The government had been panicked into evacuation by what turned out to be exaggerated military forecasts of mass casualty figures made in the run up to the war. In fact most mothers with young children and getting on for half the unaccompanied schoolchildren had returned home by January 1940. This still left thousands of children taking part in a mass fostering experiment – resulting in some lasting consequences for child welfare and child psychology. Large parts of the country suddenly woke up to child poverty and health issues that had been largely hidden away in inner city slums. Shocked provincial families scrubbed, clothed and fed their charges and after the war let politicians know that they wanted something doing about the state of the nation's children. There were, however, some children who were just too much for any families to handle and these 'unbilletable children' would eventually be placed in evacuation hostels.

From 1936 to the beginning of 1940 an experiment in community rehabilitation, for youths and young men aged 17 to 25, had been being carried out by an organisation known as the Q Camps Committee at Hill

Hall Common, near Great Bardfield, Essex. Known as the Hawkspur Camp, the project set up by the Grith Frith and run by David Wills pioneered therapeutic community ideas and methods. As war approached, and struggling to keep going financially, the Committee accepted an offer from Oxfordshire County Council to move their operations to Market End House, a former poor law workhouse at Bicester. The Committee faced difficulties from the start. There was already a hostel for "unbilletable evacuees" being run by the council in one wing of the workhouse building and the County Council wanted the Committee to take over the running of this and to extend it to cover to the whole region, across Oxfordshire, Berkshire, Buckinghamshire and Surrey, as well as continuing the work with the Hawkspur Camp members (many of them German refugees). All this in an unfurnished, underequipped, 95-room workhouse where nearly all the windows were painted out. David Wills commented at the time: 'It is a dreadful building and everything is at present in a state of chaos.' The difficulty of dealing with two completely different age ranges and different regimes led to conflict between the two groups and damage to the buildings. At the end of 1940 David Wills handed in his resignation and the County Council took back over the running of the Hostel in April 1941. After Bicester Wills was offered a job in Scotland working as a warden for the Religious Society of Friends in Edinburgh at another hostel for the "unbilletable". The Quakers in Edinburgh had started discussions in 1939 with the Scottish Department of Health, Peebleshire County Council and the Edinburgh Education Committee looking into options for boys who were causing trouble with the families they were billeted with and for whom the only alternative was a return to unsuitable home circumstances. The Wemyss Landed Estates Limited offered the use, rent-free of Barns House in the Manor Valley near Peebles and the Barns Hostel School opened to children on July 1st 1940. The project was jointly funded by the County Council who paid the expenses; the Edinburgh Education Committee, who paid the teaching staff and supplied school equipment; and the Society of Friends, who took on responsibility for finding a suitable Warden and the payment of his salary.

David Wills was able to carry on and extend the work that he had started with the Q Camps in Essex with the young boys who were sent to him at Barns House. At the end of the war Wills published details of the work carried out by him and his staff in *The Barns Experiment.*

... They were all difficult boys, hating school, prejudiced against adults in general, punished often but not wisely, fearful, suspicious, aggressive, untruthful, uncared for and, in the main, unloved. During the early days of Barns they were their own worst enemies because they strove hard to compel us to furnish them with the only kind of security they knew – the security of outward compulsion; and we were determined to give them security on a different level – the security that comes from the knowledge of being loved ...

David Wills

Drawing on his experiences at the Hawkspur camp and previously at The Children's Village (in New York State) Wills developed a combination of therapeutic community and libertarian free school modelled very much on the work of Homer Lane at the Little Commonweath in Hampshire. While there was formal teaching during 'school hours' – required by the Education

Committee – the hostel had no punishments and was regulated by a committee made up from the boys who would hear complaints against other boys and staff, and decide on suitable recompense or forfeit of rights. This committee was re-invented a number of times, each time with less involvement of the staff. One incarnation was known as the Citizens' Association.

... The Citizens' Association took over forthwith. They put themselves to bed and supervised themselves in the bathroom. The following morning, Tuesday, my day off, sometimes known as racket day, they got themselves up and did all that was necessary with no adult supervision at all, and May says the dormitories were cleaner than she has ever known them. The Chairman of the Citizens' Association took charge of the Dining Room, ringing the bell for Grace, and so on. And so they continued until bedtime, when they put themselves to bed. Everything did not go smoothly, by any means. There were various contingencies for which they had not legislated in advance; there were conflicting interpretations of such rules as had been made; some boys were jealous of those in office – and so on. But from all accounts it seems to have been as well-ordered and peaceful a Tuesday as we have had for some time ...

David Wills

Others in similar positions were looking to the experience of A S Neil's progressive school at Summerhill for inspiration. Bill Malcolm, who had worked with Neil, found himself during the war in charge of an evacuation hostel at Bryn Conway in North Wales where he was put in charge of thirty-one 'very disturbed children'. Malcolm set up 'self-governing' structures which mirrored those being used at Barns House and so successful were the results that, following a review of the work by the medical officer of health, Malcolm was asked to take over the Regional Evacuation Hostel at Penybrin which was for the most difficult evacuees in the six counties of North Wales. Taking with him the nucleus of staff and children from Bryn Conway Malcolm proceeded to replicate the same regime with children who 'were extremely socially deprived, emotionally disturbed and frequently delinquent.' After the war Malcolm went on to work at a hostel for difficult delinquent boys at Maidenhead and in 1948 to Arlesford Place, a school set up on 'planned environmental therapy' lines. He later set up his own school, Childscourt, at Long Bredy in Dorset. In late 1944, with the end of the wartime evacuation program in sight and with the tenancy at Barn House coming to an end, plans were made to launch Barns on a more permanent basis in new premises. Just before Christmas Barns relocated to Templehall House at Coldingham, Berwickshire and was re-launched as Barns School with Ben Stoddard as headmaster. David Wills went on to be the founding head of Bodenham Manor School for maladjusted children in Herefordshire. A major fire at Templehall House in 1946 forced Barns School to move once again, this time to Ancrum House near Jedburgh where it continued until 1953. From these small-scale wartime experiments in therapeutic community a whole movement of residential communities for children up and down the country would grow. As well as those established by Wills and Malcolm there was Red Hill School and The Caldecott Community (both in Kent), Warleigh Manor near Bath, Peper Harow Therapeutic Community in Surrey and the Mulberry Bush School in Oxfordshire.

Curative community

A small group of Jewish refugees from Vienna arrived in the North of Scotland in 1939 invited by local land owners, Mr & Mrs Houghton, who one of the group had met at a clinic in Germany. In need of a place to escape the march of Nazism across Europe, they had written to the family and been offered a job. The group had made their own individual ways across Europe in search of a safe haven following the Nazi annexation of Austria in 1938. They had met in the years before the war and had formed a Youth Group to study anthroposophy and the works of Rudolf Steiner. The eleven young students in their twenties had gathered around the slightly older figure of Dr Karl König who, along with his wife Tilla, had been studying and putting into practice Steiner's ideas for some time. König had met his future wife while working in Germany in the 1920's. Mathilde 'Tilla' Maasberg had grown up in the Moravian congregation at Gnadenfrei in Silesia. Tilla introduced Dr König to the ideas of Count Nikolaus von Zinzendorf who had inspired the establishment of a whole series of Moravian communities across the globe, starting with the building of the village of Herrnhut – for Moravian refugees fleeing persecution in other part of Europe – on a corner of his estate. Tilla and her sister had been running a small children's home in their family holiday house and had become interested in Steiner's ideas on Curative Education. Tilla had gone on a course on Curative Eurythmy where she met Dr König and invited him back to see the children's home they were running and to meet her family. The young doctor was deeply moved by the Moravian Christian way of life. He and Tilla married in 1929 and were offered a 100-room mansion at Schloss, Pilgramshain to set up a larger home for children with special needs. Karl and Tilla König spent seven years developing and running the home at Pilgramshain along anthroposophical curative education lines. In 1936, because of his Jewish descent, Karl König was stopped from working as a general practitioner and prevented from continuing to work at Pilgramshain. The Königs moved to the doctor's home town of Vienna where he re-established his practice and started to give weekly lectures on zoology, curative education and anthroposophy. It was at these lectures that the members of the youth group would meet. Those making up the youth group in Vienna nearly all came from the local Jewish community and all had the same urge to explore other cultures outside their own Jewish backgrounds. They found themselves drawn to the Christian Community Church founded by Rudolf Steiner and Friedrich Rittelmeyer. As the German threat loomed ever nearer the group discussed what they would do in the event of an actual invasion and started to draw up plans.

We met almost every day. Dr König drew the outlines of the work our group was going to take on. The East was barred for us, we might go to an island: Cyprus perhaps? We would have to take European heritage, culture with us, work on the land, share our lives with handicapped children. We would do all the work ourselves, receive no pay; farmer, teacher, priest, doctor, all would carry the community; our way of life would be simple in Christian brotherhood. We warmed to the idea enthusiastically, connected by an inner will that need not be spoken. Finally a request for entrance as a group was sent to Ireland, which was turned down. But there was no time to be lost, we had to leave Austria individually as soon as possible, especially the men.

Barbara Lipsker quoted in The Builders of Camphill

When the Nazi Army marched into Austria on 11 March 1939, one by one the little group found their way out of the country vowing to meet up once again when a safe refuge was found. Karl König searched for a place in Switzerland and France and finally managed to find safe passage to England and then on to Aberdeenshire where the Haughtons had managed to find a empty Church of Scotland Manse at Kirkton near Insch for the group to move into. The group slowly gathered itself together again in Scotland and started to make plans for setting up a residential community based on curative educational lines. Through a loan from W F MacMillan, of the MacMillan publishing family, who was looking for a place for his handicapped son, they were able to purchase Camphill House and Estate on the banks of the River Dee just outside Aberdeen on June 1st 1940. The group's plans were thrown into confusion when, after the Dunkirk evacuation, all the men in the group were interned as 'enemy aliens', with married men being sent to the Isle of Man and the single men to Canada. The women in the group continued with the group's plans and the men returned to find the community active and flourishing, with about 12 children. The little community thrived and in 1942 Heathcote House across on the south side of the River Dee was rented to provide space for children. In April 1944, again supported by the MacMillan family, another estate with 35 acres of farmland and three houses at Murtle House a few miles closer to Aberdeen at Bieldside was acquired. This was followed a year later by the acquisition of the 170-acre Newton Dee Estate site, almost adjacent to the Murtle Estate, which was to be used as a home and school for delinquent and profoundly handicapped boys. One reason for the rapid expansion of the group's activities was that there was little or no provision at the time for the mentally handicapped and certainly nothing had been seen of the likes of Curative Education.

Rudolf Steiner had developed his ideas about the education and development of handicapped children after he as a young man had responsibility for the education of an apparently subnormal, and supposedly ineducable, hydrocephalic child. Steiner put together a curriculum which addressed the boy's many difficulties and which in the end enabled him to enter university and qualify as a medical practitioner. Towards the end of his life Steiner pulled these ideas together in a short lecture course on 'curative education'. These ideas didn't really provide a blueprint for practice in the new Scottish community, but enabled Dr König and his group to develop a curriculum based on these and other ideas Steiner had for the education of normal children. Karl König claimed not only Steiner as his inspiration for Camphill, but also Count Zindendorf of the Moravians and from closer to home the early utopian socialist Robert Owen – who himself had been inspired by the British Moravian communities.

After the end of the war Camphill continued to expand its activities. In 1947 a small Waldorf School was opened at Murtle and in 1950 a further estate was purchased. The Cairnlee estate was the first accommodation for girls who were severely disturbed. As well as getting private placements, the group was increasingly getting referrals from local councils. In the early 1950's Camphill expanded its activities outside Scotland, opening centres in England at the Sheiling in Ringwood and Thornbury in Bristol in 1951. A group of parents approached Karl König in 1952 asking what could be done for their children with special needs once they reached school-leaving age. They saw them facing a future in hospitals, occupational therapy and training centres when they wanted to see somewhere that they could make meaningful contributions to their community. König had been developing ideas of setting up Camphill village communities for adults with special needs:

... a place where those children, not attaining sufficient improvements to go out into the world could remain and have a sheltered yet useful life. They could do some limited work in the various kitchens and workshops, the houses, the farm and the gardens. They should not live in dormitories , but in small houses in the lap of the family to which they belong and where they feel safe and secure ...

Karl König 1952

The group of parents set out in search of a property suitable for a first village community. Again it was the MacMillan family that came to the group's aid. Peggy MacMillan, whose son Alistair was one of the first children who came to Camphill House, suggested that the family's country estate at Botton Hall in Danby Dale on the edge of the North Yorkshire Moors might be a suitable location. The estate consisted of a Hunting Lodge and three farms with stables and outhouses, and three cottages half way along the eastern side of a rather bleak moorland valley.

On either side of the estate, the moorland rises up to a fair height – typical upland grazing and wide expanses of heather. Trees were sparse and somewhat battered by the inclemencies of the Yorkshire climate, the estate lay towards the head of the dale where life almost seemed to have petered out ... All in all, Botton Hall was a bleak, silent, even forsaken place and with its rough climate and rudimentary amenities, almost a discouraging place, until on occasions, the sun came through and invested the dale with breath-taking beauty ...

Camphill Villages 1988

Botton Village today (Top to Bottom)
Stormy Hall Farm
Chapel and Community Centre
In the Village Café
Martin House

CAMPHILL COMMUNITIES

In September 1955 a small group of eighteen co-workers and young men and women with special needs led by Rev Peter Roth, arrived at Botton from Camphill Schools in Scotland and England. This band of pioneers faced numerous challenges; with very little funds they set about renovating houses and workshops, installing electricity, heating, drainage, telephones. They also faced the challenge of changing the emphasis of the work from being educational, with pupil and teacher relationships, to living together on an equal basis. The co-workers had to learn that '... when people with special needs grow up, they too are adults, with all their obsessions, oddities, deficiencies and streaks of genius ...' and the men and women with special needs had to learn '... to realise that they were no longer going to be 'looked after', but were going to have to take responsibility, not only for themselves, but for the community.'

As they busied themselves with laying paths from house to house, building a system of roads around the estate, planting tree-belts and getting on with establishing bio-dynamic farming practices on the farms, the community also developed its own social life based on the annual Christian festivals on much the same pattern as in the Camphill school communities. In 1966 they celebrated the opening of the village Community Centre with its own hall and stage. The community at Botton provided a model for the Camphill movement to grow in the British Isles and spread to other countries further afield. Camphill adult and training centre communities of varying shapes and sizes were set up from the late 1950's onwards, rapidly expanding across Europe into America and with a small presence in Africa. Today the movement is divided into seven different regions: Scotland, England & Wales, Ireland, Central Europe, Northern Europe, North America and Southern Africa and there are 105 Camphill communities of one sort or another in 23 countries. While each community has its own identity and autonomy, each follows a similar pattern.

Within the Camphill Communities most of us live in large extended families, co-workers (both long-term people with their families, and young temporary volunteers) and villagers (mentally handicapped or otherwise in need of help), sharing our lives, our meals, our living rooms and bathrooms. There may be as many as fifteen people or more gathered round the dining table three times a day. Each house has its own budget, and is run more or less autonomously by a couple of responsible co-workers, the house father and house mother. In the morning and the afternoon everyone goes to work, in a variety of workplaces ... a bio-dynamic farm, extensive vegetable gardens, a bakery, a weavery, a large forest for timber and firewood, herb growing and drying ... Other villages have workshops which produce pottery, candles, dolls or wooden toys. I have eaten meals where the table came from the carpentry shop, the table cloth from the weavery, the plates and cups from the pottery, the candles (which are lit at every meal) from the candle shop, and virtually all the food is produced by the village: bread, milk products, jams, vegetables, herb teas, honey, meat and meat products. This self sufficiency is not an end in itself, but rather a way of saving money, and ensuring that each person is employed doing something that is useful to the village ...

Jan Martin Bang, *Camphill Ecovillages*

Over the years Botton Village has expanded through the purchase of other farms. In the late 1960's Honey Bee Nest Farm and Rodger House were bought and in the 1980's Nook House Farm and Stormy Hall were added, bringing the total holding to 610 acres, making up most of the valley. The villagers also set up a wood workshop, a sawmill, a glass-engraving workshop, doll workshop, weaver, bakery and creamery. A Steiner School was established in 1960. In 1971, a warehouse was built to store finished products from other Camphill villages in Britain and Ireland, creating a Central Sales Department to relieve the individual village workshops of packaging, marketing and distribution. The Camphill Press developed out of a small graphic arts department in 1973 and now prints all stationery requirements for the Camphill Village Trust along with books and leaflets for both Camphill and other organisations. The village today is a thriving little settlement with a population of over 300 people which boasts its own store, bookshop, post office, gift shop and café.

Botton Village having grown so large has divided into 'neighbourhoods' which has helped to decentralise the inevitable amount of organisation necessary in such a community. The neighbourhoods provide a forum for considerations of social and inter-personal contact, of money matters relevant to the households in the respective neighbourhood, and many other problems and potentials more constructively dealt with among neighbours.

Of the Camphill communities in the UK, Botton village in particular has attracted media attention. In 1968 BBC2 broadcast *In Need of Special Care* by film maker Jonathan Steadall and on the 50th anniversary of the Camphill movement in 1990 Steadall was invited back to make a follow-up film, *Candle on the Hill*, also broadcast on BBC2. More recently, in June 2005, Channel 4 screened *The Strangest Village in England*, a strong 'in your face' portrayal of the Village. While the public reaction to Camphill communities has been largely favourable over the years, the movement has had to negotiate the changes in official policy and attitude towards the care of those with specials needs.

... The Camphill Communities of the 1980's and 1990's were under strict residential home, school inspector and health and safety regimes. This usually boiled down to room size, and amenity and fire escape provision, and involved changing physical lay-outs to allow for more space. Amenities were investigated, especially meal choices (every meal had to be recorded) – and why no television?!...
Vivian Griffiths, "From Community to the Individual and Back Again" in *D&D* 08/09

Camphill managed to comply with the raft of regulations and the bureaucratisation of care during this period without too much trouble. At the end of the 1990's when the thrust of social care moved more towards individualisation with 'Supporting People' and 'Care in the Community' polices there was a real danger that Camphill communities would end up being viewed as institutions from which residents needed moving out and into the 'community'. Despite the worries of many people involved that this might threaten the very essence of Camphill, the various communities have proved remarkably adaptable, coming to terms in their own way with 'life learning programmes' and 'individual choice' within a communal context.

The school and college communities seem to survive and even thrive under the new individualising regulations, as much of the Camphill Community ethos can be enshrined in the curriculum. There are many glowing Ofsted reports to verify this statement. It remains to be seen whether the Camphill adult communities can adapt to the changes of managers and management structures which change the emphasis from a group decision approach to a top-down individual support setting
Vivian Griffiths 2012

Camphill offers a challenging antidote to the reductionism that characterises so much residential childcare, affirming the dignity of the 'whole person' and their potential for growth alongside others in community. It provides a lived example of how a coherent philosophy of care can be brought centre stage and owned by well-educated and creative groups of workers.
Mark Smith, *Rethinking Residential Childcare* 2009

All the Lonely People
where do they all go?

Imagine you freak out, come to the end of your tether, can't hold it together anymore. Where would you go?
Imagine you enter a way of being and experiencing the world, which other people call mad,
and your nearest and dearest can't cope with your presence any longer. To whom would you turn?
Imagine you are out of your wits, completely gone over the hill, you've lost it,
plunged into the wild waves of the unknown. What would you need?

Theodor Itten, member of the Philadelphia Association [7]

While the early work on the development of therapeutic communities by the likes of Maxwell Jones, Wilfred Bion and John Rickman had informed some of the thinking behind the 1959 Mental Health Act (effecting a partial liberalisation of the laws around the detention of those with mental illness) one of the major results of the Act was to put large numbers of former mental hospital patients on to the streets with little or no support and precious few places to turn to. A Dutch student of Divinity Elly Jansen rented a house, Lancaster Lodge, in Richmond and simply invited people who had left hospital to move in and share it with her. Jansen ran the house along therapeutic community lines with the aim of helping those who had been in hospital for long periods to reintegrate back into society. Surrey County Council thought Jansen's efforts worth supporting and offered funding for a second house to be set up and in 1960. The Richmond Fellowship was incorporated and registered as a charity. The Richmond Fellowship provided some of the few places where therapeutic community ideas were being put into practice outside of a hospital environment.

Within hospitals a new generation of psychotherapist was emerging, carrying forward the work of the early wartime pioneers. Perhaps the clearest example of a continuation of the work was that done by South African-born Dr David Cooper at Shenley Hospital in Hertfordshire. Cooper was a member of the South African Communist Party and had been sent by them to Poland, Russia and China to be trained as a professional revolutionary. Quite how he then ended up working in a number of London Hospitals is not quite clear, but in 1962 he set up an experimental ward for schizophrenic patients in Villa 21 at Shenley Hospital. The villa had 19 beds for men, mostly in their twenties. Cooper tried to create a situation where the men would have a chance to "discover and explore an authentic relatedness to each other." No distinction was to be made between patients and staff, who wore no uniforms. There were daily 30-minute community meetings, formal therapeutic small group meetings, work groups, staff group meetings and spontaneous group meetings on particular issues. Cooper's view was that patients needed to be allowed to 'go to pieces' before they could be helped to come back together again. The experiment carried on for four years with Cooper having to cope with hostility from the medical hierarchy and from other staff members, in much the same way as Bion and Rickman had at Northfield before. While Cooper was away concerns about the general state of the ward with piles of unwashed plates was used as a pretext to reintroduce staff controls and restore some semblance of order on the ward. On his return Cooper, while accepting the staff's decision, saw it as confirmation that a successful unit could be only developed outside a hospital environment. In 1967 Cooper published an account of his work at Villa 21 in *Psychiatry and Anti-psychiatry*, coining the label that he would come to be most associated with.

Searching for a place to work outside the medical establishment and the hospital environment Cooper teamed up with a small group of other 'Anti-psychiatrists', including R D Laing, Aaron Esterson, Sid Briskin, (a social worker), Leon Redler, Joe Berke, Morton Schatzman and Jerome Liss, in a radical experiment at Kingsley Hall on Powis Road in the East End of London. The Hall had been set up by two pacifist sisters Doris and Muriel Lester in the 1920's and had been the centre of various community activities; it had operated as a shelter and soup kitchen for workers during the 1926 General Strike, Gandhi had stayed there for 12 weeks in 1931 and it housed some of the Jarrow hunger marchers in 1935. In the years after the war the Hall became a Youth Hostel and community centre and by 1965 had become somewhat run-down. The group of Anti-psychiatrists had formed

Kingsley Hall

The Philadelphia Association and approached the Lester sisters and asked if they could use the Hall as a community for themselves and people in a state of psychosis. The group moved in on 1st June 1965 and from the start there was no distinction between 'patient' and 'therapist'; everyone addressed each other by their first names. There was no structured 'therapy', no drugs or other forms of control. All decisions on the running of the house were taken by the whole group. 'Patients' were allowed to experience the full force of their psychotic 'episodes', to live through them. It was described at the time as 'a melting pot, a crucible in which many assumptions about normal-abnormal, conformist-deviant, sane-crazy experience and behaviour were dissolved. No person gave another tranquillisers or sedatives. Behaviour was feasible which would have been intolerable elsewhere. It was a place where people could be together and let each other be'. Most people who came stayed six months, one resident who stayed longer and became something of a cause-célèbre of the anti-psychiatry movement was Mary Barnes, a 45-year-old former nurse who was diagnosed with chronic schizophrenia, who had had repeated admission into psychiatric hospitals.

... Life soon became quite fantastic. Every night at Kingsley Hall I tore off my clothes, feeling I had to be naked. Lay on the floor with my shits and water, smeared the walls with faeces. Was wild and noisy about the house or sitting in a heap on the kitchen floor. Half-aware I was going mad, there was the horror that I might not know what I was doing outside of Kingsley Hall. The tempo was increasing. 'Down, down, oh God, would I never break?' She stopped eating solid foods and had to be fed from a bottle. Various people took turns in feeding her milk. She stopped talking and lay in bed for long periods of time. In bed I kept my eyes shut so I didn't see people but I heard them ... touch was all important ... sometimes my body had seemed apart, a leg or an arm across the room. The wall became hollow and I seemed to go into it as into a big hole. Vividly aware of people, I was physically isolated in my room, my womb ... **Mary Barnes, International Times 55 8th May 1969**

Mary Barnes was an extreme example of what went on at Kingsley Hall and in many ways untypical. Other residents found her hard to live with when she smeared faeces on her body and on the walls of her room, particularly as her room was next to the kitchen and the smell came through the wall. At one point she became so thin that others became worried for her survival and she was nursed back to health by residents taking turns to sit with her and even feed her with a baby's bottle. Only about a third of the residents had previously been in psychiatric hospitals, others had been out-patients and about a third were qualified or trainee therapists who wanted to take part in the experiment. Of the fifteen to twenty-five people living at the Hall at any one time only three or four were actually diagnosed as psychotic. In the end Mary Barnes

came through the other side of her 'madness' and took to painting as a means of expressing herself. She had an exhibition of her paintings at the Camden Arts Centre in 1969 and later wrote a book about her experiences with Joseph Berke which was later turned into a play. The East End local community was largely hostile to the project, and there were regular reports of harassment and vandalism to the building, although most of the windows were broken by the residents from within, not by the neighbours. After five years the project was wound up and Kingsley Hall was boarded up. In the 1980's it was used as one of the sets for the Richard Attenborough film Gandhi. Attenborough joined forces with the Kingsley Hall Action Group and between them raised enough money to carry out an extensive refurbishment and in 1985 the Hall reopened as a local community centre.

Mary Barnes at Kingsley Hall

R D Laing was resident in the hall for the longest time and following its closure he went to Sri Lanka for a year to meditate. Other members of the group carried on the work started at Kingsley Hall throughout the 1970's in a series of condemned houses in Archway, North London, where Leon Redler invited Zen masters to stay at his flat and encouraged the residents to take up all sorts of Eastern practices. In 1971 the film maker Peter Robinson spent six weeks in one of the Archway houses making the film *Asylum*. Joseph Berke and Morton Schatzman started the Arbours Association which ran three community houses and a crisis drop-in centre. The Philadelphia Association carried on with Laing and Cooper in charge and developed further community houses, none with quite the impact that Kingsley Hall had. Through their writings the two anti-psychiatrists influenced the thinking of many in the counter culture, in particular their emphasis on the family being the cradle of much psychosis influenced many in the communes movement. In an interview in *International Times* 59 in July 1969 Laing concluded '... Kingsley Hall is a start but ideally one has to have a place in the country and a number of people who are able to live there permanently and there are all sorts of practical difficulties in achieving that ...'

One resident at Kingsley Hall who found it didn't work for her went on to set up her own therapy-based commune. Originally from America, Carol Anderson had come to the UK having read of Laing's experiment in communal therapy and briefly joined Kingsley Hall but she quickly fell out with the community there and went on to set up her own communal house in Brixton.

... Carol was a woman, an American who was brought up in a very fucked up manner and it ended up that she was more, ended up apparently more fucked up than anyone had ever been in the history of the world to the extent that she started destroying her life-force and was in pain as a result. By facing up to what had happened to her she managed to overcome all this and become totally sane, in fact the first totally sane person in the history of the entire world. But because of what she'd done to herself while she was messed up she couldn't bring back this life-force that she'd destroyed. And she began to realise that what she needed was to form a community around her. The aim was for a growing period of three months with between eight or ten people in it. Which would be very exclusively focussed on her needs and nobody would be going out except to do a bit of shopping. This was what she needed to get well ... [8]

The experiment lasted for four and a half years during which, for a long time, it seemed it was never going to be possible to get to the 'growing period' due to Carol's continuing traumas and her affect on others in the house. These traumas could erupt in any number of ways; something as simple as asking for someone to 'Pass the Salt in a sort of hostile tone of voice' could cause a big scene or Carol could suffer an attack of paranoia and believe that other residents were sub-consciously thwarting her attempts to get well. Anything up to 17 people lived in four rooms and a large kitchen. Tony Haigh – who had responded to an advert in *OZ* magazine and spent two years at the house – recalled:

... it was quite intense. You weren't allowed to have personal visitors. You weren't allowed to have sex in the place – you were allowed to have sex with other community members, but not in the community. Unless it was with Carol who could have sex with whoever she wanted to ... anybody who left was told by everybody else that they were running away from life and they were doomed to be totally unhappy for the rest of their life. And we all believed in it ...

Tony Haigh

Eventually the group managed to get it together to start the three-month growing period and Carol managed to 'grow back this ... whatever she'd lost, whatever it was. The life-force.'

A Community in the Cotswolds (again)

The actual forms of bullying were thus. Firstly, sheer physical force, using fists. Secondly, physical force using boots, usually when the boy was on the ground. Thirdly, the twisting of arms or fingers. Fourthly, the gripping of genitals and twisting them. Fifthly, the strapping of the hand to a hot water pipe, where it comes out of a boiler, and left there until such time as the boy agreed that he would do what the gang wanted him to do. Sixthly, the requirement of other boys to take servant type roles, making beds, cleaning shoes, running errands of all kinds ...

Bill Douglas, chaplain at Cotswold Approved School (1967)

As the last members of the Bruderhof were leaving down the drive of the farm at Ashton Keynes in 1942, it is said that they passed the first members of the Cotswold Approved School arriving. The farm had been bought by the London Police Court Mission, an organisation that had grown out of the Church of England Temperance Society in the mid-nineteenth century and had set up 'court missionaries', early forerunners of the probation service. By the 1940's they were running a number of Approved Schools housing young offenders on approved school orders made by magistrate courts. The idea was that young offenders could be rehabilitated through training, but the schools were in effect junior borstals. After a brief heyday in the 1940's and early 50's they were hit by a number of scandals and the approved school system was abolished in 1969. In 1967 the Rainer Foundation (the new name for the Court Mission) appointed Richard Balbernie as head of the Cotswold school with the task of changing it into a therapeutic community. This was no mean task in the face of opposition from staff, the boys and various bureaucratic authorities. One of the first things that Richard Balbernie had to do was to reduce the number of boys. There were 120 boys in the approved school, living in very large groups. He sent half the boys home very early on, those he regarded as petty criminals, who did not seem particularly disturbed. Just prior to the abolition of Approved Schools the Rainer Foundation came to an agreement with Wiltshire County Council whereby the Council would take some sort of overall 'watching brief', while the Foundation continued to be responsible for the day-to-day management with advice from the Tavistock Institute. This arrangement eventually led to the Council buying the community in 1973 for £400,000 with the aim of seeing how far it was possible to operate a therapeutic community within a local authority. It took Richard Balbernie nearly five years to transform the school into a therapeutic community: from a situation where 85 percent of boys leaving were re-convicted within two years to a figure of only five percent; From a situation where the school was described as being on the brink of collapse, where staff morale was abysmal and 'delinquency was rife not only among the boys but also among the staff ...' to a community that gave "love and understanding, without sloppy permissiveness, and with firmness without repression – a demanding balance to strike.' **9**

The Cotswold Community is a therapeutic community for boys who are seriously disturbed emotionally. It exists specifically to provide an environment for treatment. It recognises that the boys will initially be prone to extreme anxiety and uncertainty, and will be compulsively disruptive ... The community has educational facilities geared to the capacities of individual boys. It is surrounded by countryside, including its own farm, and everything is integrated into a total environment in which the boys' physical, emotional and psychological needs can be met. There is no system of punishment or reward.

From the video *The Recovery of Childhood*

People not Psychiatry

During 1970 a number of strange and intriguing small adverts appeared in *The Times* and *Time Out* inviting readers to join the Psychenautics Institute and embark on a journey into 'inner space'. They were placed by a couple of intrepid counter-culture seekers, Mike Williamson and John O'Shea, who had embarked on a no-holds-barred exploration of their own inner space through, well frankly, anything they came across: meditation, Zen, Krishnamurti, Carlos Castenada, various therapy techniques ... They sold most of the furniture in their rented flat and spent hours sitting in silence '... looking into their experience ...'. It doesn't appear that anyone joined the two of them at the 'institute' as a result of the newspaper ads. The two had been introduced by Michael and Pam Barnett. Michael Barnett felt he was on the borderline of being schizophrenic and had been searching for some years for a therapeutic way forward outside conventional psychiatry. Back in the mid sixties, having read *The Divided Self* and *The Politics of Experience*, he decided to go and seek advice from R D Laing himself.

... I paid my twelve guineas and went. He was reassuringly substantial with his Scots accent and his brown corduroy jacket ... I spilled him out my woes and complaints. Mostly he listened, with an occasional query. Later I listened to him tell me that he thought I had maybe lost touch with myself around the age of four or five, and that perhaps I should try to get back. LSD might help. I listened carefully, though part of me at that time did not want to get well, but to go on as I was ... **10**

Laing recommended other therapists that Barnett could see on a regular basis, he also took a job in a psychiatric hospital to try and learn more about psychotherapy. In May 1969 Barnett spotted a reference in *The Guardian* to a new group that been demonstrating against the use of neurosurgery. The Campaign Against Psychiatric Atrocities, or CAPA, was campaigning against a Harley Street Surgeon who was carrying out psychosurgery. Members had been parading up and down outside his offices with placards that read: Psychiatrists Make Good Butchers, Psychiatry Kills and Ban Legal Murder by Psychiatrists. On each slogan wherever the word 'psychiatry' was used, the 'ch' was replaced by a Nazi swastika. CAPA's mission was to 'topple institutional psychiatry'. It put forward the argument that 'mental illness is a myth'

There are only people with PROBLEMS IN LIVING. Why then are warnings not heeded, and enlightened and humane alternatives disregarded, minimised or discredited? Why the continued mass propagation and fixation of attention upon 'mental illnesses'? Why are an increasing number of types of misbehaviour classified as abnormal and described as illnesses? Why are we being coaxed into psychiatric hospitals with the offer of voluntary treatment and then labelled as 'mentally ill' and violated and degraded? Why are the totally inappropriate or lethal and degrading 'treatments' of electric-shock, brain operations, massive drugging and conditioning techniques being dispensed with such zeal?

CAPA leaflet (undated)

Michael Barnett joined CAPA, went along to further demonstrations and was quickly recruited by the group's leader, Peter Stumbke, as the acting secretary. But Barnett felt ill at ease with some of the other members of the group and the very confrontational language used by the group. About a month after Barnett had joined, a CAPA meeting was attended by Sidney Briskin who had been involved with Laing and Cooper at Kingsley Hall. Briskin persistently questioned the group about its connections with Scientology and despite repeated statements that 'CAPA was a separate organisation', it became clear to Barnett that, whatever its stated aims, it was in fact a front for the East Grinstead group run by Ron Hubbard. Angry that he had been misled by Peter Stumbke, Barnett decided to set up his own organisation. In a fit of activity he penned an article for *International Times* which was printed alongside a feature interview with R D Laing, in July 1969, in an issue entitled Insanity Times. Under the headline The Sick Scene the article set out a critique of psychiatry and mental health services. It asked 'What does this surgery of souls achieve?' and went on to announce the setting up of new group to be called People for a New Psychiatry (PNP) and propose a manifesto for a new vision of mental health provision.

We see the mental hospital as largely an anachronism. And current modes of treatment in all but a very few as medieval and barbaric. The same goes for psychiatric wings. We think the lot should be scrapped. We would like to see State finance provided for the right people to set up sanctuaries in which those in great conflict and distress as a result of what has happened to them, what has been done to them, can take their inner trips, find themselves, work through their living experience in an open environment offering care, understanding and concern. We don't see this as the one answer, or even as necessarily the best answer, but compared with the present ugly scene it's utopian and would do for a start.

International Times 59 July 69

The article ended with an invitation to 'Anyone wanting to join in changing the scene, a revolution no less, contact: Mike Barnett, Operations Room for PNP. 118a Allingham Court, Haverstock Hill, NW3'. The response to the article was almost overwhelming, letters poured in, the phone rang constantly. Barnett set up a series of informal individual talks/interviews with everyone who had responded, sometimes meeting as many as fifteen people a day. From this few hundred people Barnett chose 14 and invited them along to a meeting on 31st July.

... I cannot justify my methods of assessment, but those I picked, whatever they might have satisfied in me, had things like strength and space and life movement. It is also true that those fourteen chose me ... I wrote to the fourteen, suggesting we should all meet. I arranged a time. On the night all fourteen came. I was very excited at this. Time had elapsed, people cool and waver, I had hardly expected a full return ... It was a good meeting, because that is what we did – meet. Needing no pretensions, we could care or go on. The energy level was very high and, though none of the others had previously met, united. The opposition to psychiatry seemed formidable that night ... There was no doubt that we were launched ...

Michael Barnett, People Not Psychiatry

It was through this meeting that the two would-be Psychenauts Mike Williamson and John O'Shea would meet. Another of those invited had somewhat frightened Barnett by the ferocity of her letter, a young woman called Jenny James had written 'Please write to me. I want to help, will do anything, from typing to blowing up psychiatrists.' At the end of the meeting the 15 exchanged contacts and agree to operate as an on-call network that anyone could call at any time. This list was made available to the others who had responded to the original article. In a follow-up report in *IT* at the end August those attending the meeting were described as a mix of '... writers, painters, secretaries, executives, a baker's wife, students ...' The new report asked '... If you are flipping or freaking, or are just hung up high, what's the option? If we discount the whole crazy state structure from beginning to end that is. Well there's Zen, Yoga, the Tibetan monastery; the Marharishi, Kingsley Hall (if you're lucky), turned on therapy (if you're rich), a commune, kingsized friends (if you're lucky). Add what you like to that it still won't add up to that many possibilities ...' The group, now going under the name People Not Psychiatry (PNP), announced that it was now going to meet regularly '... to talk, maybe touch, anything, groove ...' and that if anyone thought they were 'heading hard for the bin' or 'feeling really stewed up inside' they could contact anyone and everyone on the PNP list and expect to get 'acceptance, a bit of understanding, more honesty than from most' and if you were lucky a meal and somewhere to kip. From this small beginning a new radical 'anti-psychiatry' network rapidly began to take shape. From the original group of 15 further little cells of people offering themselves forward as contact points began to spring up across London and beyond. By 1970 there were cells in Leeds, Manchester, Brighton, Birmingham, Nottingham, Bristol, Stoke, Hull, Cardiff, Edinburgh and Glasgow.

What happened? People visited people, explored, found out, moved on. This was therapeutic in any sense. There was much in common and many were glad to learn of each other, and then about each other. There was no credo, not even a cause. It was every man be himself. That's all. Many toured the whole network, sounding out, discovering themselves and others. It was a free tour for interpersonal experimentation. We became important to some, that member, this member, those members, and provided a link where one was wanting ... Here you might get anti-psychiatry, there, politics. There, playing with the children, there astrology, mysticism, or a kind of psychotherapy. There, tea and cakes and a wander through the park. You might well get a smoke too, to the sound of Crosby, Stills and Nash. Who knows what went on?

Michael Barnett, *People Not Psychiatry*

As well as providing a network of contacts for anyone experiencing mental distress, PNP also began to set up a number of 'safe houses' or sanctuaries. The first was instigated by Pam Barnett, during a short separation from Michael, when she invited Jenny James and her daughter Becky who had been living in squats around London to move into her flat in Belsize Park. Jenny remembered '... helping Pam to cope with the influx of cries for help which followed the PNP advertisements, and still trying to deal with my own inner sadness and chaotic relationships.' **11** At first the PNP sanctuaries were little more than crash pads in individuals' houses or flats, but this would change through contact with a Robin Farquharson who wrote to Michael Barnett from a mental hospital in Pretoria, South Africa shortly after PNP had been launched, expressing his support. Farquharson was an academic who had worked on Game Theory and written an influential book the *Theory of Voting*. In 1966 he had dropped out of academia and become involved in the emerging counter-culture in London. In his letter to the PNP, after explaining that he was subject to 'manic upsets two or three times a year, often ending up with him in mental hospital, he mentioned that he was the secretary of something called the Situationist Housing Association which was aiming to set up a house along the lines of Kingsley Hall. Following his letter he turned up at a PNP meeting in the Barnett's flat and then set about resuscitating the Situationist Housing Association. He recruited some new committee members for the Association persuading Rhaune Laslett, linchpin of the Notting Hill Community Trust and Notting Hill Carnival pioneer to join, along with Leon Redler, now with the Philadephia Association. Eventually a short-life house was found at 18 Russell Gardens Mews in Kensington and, although not at all big enough to meet the need that the PNP had created, it was set up as a 'super cell' with six PNP members moving in. These included Jenny and Becky James, Chris Cade, Graham Spowatt and Robin Farquharson who insisted on moving in and, as he had in effect provided the house, there seemed to be no reason to refuse his request. While the house, at Jenny James' insistence, had a completely open door policy, it turned out that tolerance only ran so far and the behaviour of Robin Farquharson very quickly stretched the other members of the household to breaking point. After he had been arrested for punching a police officer who had tried to stop him dancing in the street and had ended up back in mental hospital the group let his room to someone else. For three years the 'Mews' house would act as the fulcrum around which PNP activity would gravitate. After being angered at the rates being charged by the Quaesitor therapy centre for encounter groups, Jenny James instigated free weekly encounter group sessions at the house. The house had its own therapy room (later sound insulated) although it was quite possible to stumble across therapy sessions and encounters happening at any time in the kitchen or elsewhere in the house. As well as encounter sessions the group also became involved in Primal Therapy following the publication in January 1970 of *The Primal Scream* by the American psychotherapist, Arthur Janov. This new radical therapy involved repeatedly descending into childhood memories and expressing long-repressed childhood pain. It quickly became something of a flavour of the month in therapy circles with celebrities such as John Lennon and Yoko Ono heading to California for intensive sessions with Janov.

... Jenny developed her very individual 'confrontational' style of therapy. Nobody at the commune was allowed to get away with any bullshitting or psychological games; if you didn't like what someone was saying or doing, you said so, loudly, forcefully and at length. If you felt bad, miserable or fearful for any reason you were encouraged to get into it and feel worse, so that you would get to the bottom and come out the other side. All psychological (and psychic) defences were battered down; absolute truth and honesty was the goal, to be achieved by any means (including physical violence) and at any costs. These tough methods seemed to work for some, although nobody kept any records of how many people were returned to mental hospitals after a stay at PNP.

Val Dobson, "The Atlantis Commune – a short history" in *Noname* 2, Summer 1988

In his 1973 book about the formation of PNP, Michael Barnet described Jenny James as "queen of PNP house" and the only one of the original group of 15 to remain in the movement throughout its active period. 'Over the years, Jenny has done more in and for PNP than anybody. Many hundreds have graced, or ungraced, PNP house since she moved in – the first tenant. In addition, for two years now, along with her close friend Jerry Rothenberg, she has held free

Encounter groups at the house, of a very high calibre. What's more, beyond her action, she gives to all she knows an honesty and directness as shockingly refreshing as a jet of cold water.' Although by the time the book was published Jenny James herself would describe the view of herself as 'Jenny-who-everyone-depends-on' as already 'strangely out of date.' and she had become less tolerant of people who just took from her and didn't give anything back. Jenny James had come to be involved in the developing alternative psychotherapy scene after years as a political campaigner with the likes of CND.

In 1961 at Easter I was sitting with several hundred other concerned people on the cold tarmac outside Wethersfield American Air Base in England, trying to sing as helicopters intimidated us just a few feet above our heads with a noise and wind so strong we were pressed nearly flat. Early in 1969 I sat, frightened, angry and bitter with 25 other people on the hot tarmac at the American airbase in Udorn, Northern Thailand, watching helplessly as huge bombers took off in pairs every few minutes to bomb peasants in Vietnam.

Jenny James, Green letter from Colombia 17, 3rd April 1997

She turned to therapy after a friend and fellow political campaigner committed suicide in Germany. The years that she lived at the PNP house are captured in her book *Room to Breathe* published in 1983, largely a collection of letters between herself and her Reichian therapist, David Boadella, which catalogue both her own mental struggles and the goings on in the PNP house. In 1973 the house received a demand from the council for 'outrageous back fees for gas, electricity, and rent' and it seems that despite an appeal in the alternative press the house was slowly wound down and closed. Jenny James and some of the residents moved to a rented house in the Lake District to carry on the experiment in communal therapy. Michael Barnett, after working with the Quaesitor therapy centre, became a 'sannyassin' of Bagwan Shree Rajneesh and ran encounter groups in Poona where, under the name Swami Anand Somendra, he became one of the chief Rajneeshi therapists. He left this group in 1982 and set himself up as a spiritual teacher, going on to lead communities in Switzerland, Italy and France and finally in Freiburg, Germany from where he currently runs the OneLife organisation. Robin Farquharson died in a house fire in a squatted house in 1973, two men were later convicted of "unlawful killing". After his death the Mental Patients Union (MPU) in London named a short-life house in Mayola Road, Hackney after him from where they ran a slightly more low-key version of the PNP house. The MPU set up a second house in Derby Road and later two other houses in Woodford. The PNP group in Manchester worked with the TEKLA Housing Association on plans to set up a small residential community. By the end of 1976 there seems to have been little left of the PNP network and individuals had moved on to other groups or activities. The PNP and the MPU were followed by a whole blossoming of self-help and survivors groups that emerged in the late 1970's and early 1980's: COPE (Community Organisation for Psychiatric Emergencies), PROMPT (Protection of the Rights of Mental Patients in Therapy) and CAPO (Campaign Against Psychiatric Oppression) to name a few.

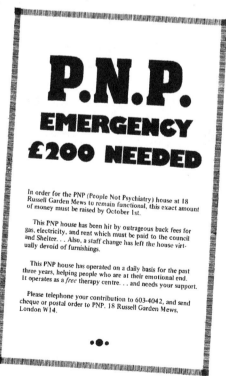

P.N.P.
EMERGENCY
£200 NEEDED

In order for the PNP (People Not Psychiatry) house at 18 Russell Garden Mews to remain functional, this exact amount of money must be raised by October 1st.

This PNP house has been hit by outrageous back fees for gas, electricity, and rent which must be paid to the council and Shelter. . . Also, a staff change has left the house virtually devoid of furnishings.

This PNP house has operated on a daily basis for the past three years, helping people who are at their emotional end. It operates as a *free* therapy centre. . . and needs your support.

Please telephone your contribution to 603-4042, and send cheque or postal order to PNP. 18 Russell Garden Mews, London W14.

•●•

From the 'workhouse' to independent living

Severely physically handicapped people find themselves in isolated, unsuitable institutions, where their views are ignored and they are subject to authoritarian and often cruel regimes. I am proposing the formulation of a consumer group to put forward nationally the views of actual and potential residents of these successors to the workhouse.

Paul Hunt Letter published in *The Guardian* 20 September 1972

The 'authoritarian' and 'cruel' institution that Paul Hunt was referring to in his letter to *The Guardian* in 1972 was none other than the Le Court Cheshire home at Liss in Hampshire where he was a resident. How had the 'Christian Socialist'-based post-war 'Homes' movement, that war hero Leonard Cheshire had started, come by 1970 to be described by a resident as a 'successor to the workhouse'? The Cheshire Foundation Homes for the Sick had grown slowly in the years immediately after the war. From 1955 onwards, when there were five Cheshire Homes in the UK and an overseas project in India, the organisation grew rapidly in the late fifties and throughout the 1960's and by the end of the decade there were some 50 Homes in the UK, five in India and some sort of 'Cheshire' project in 21 other countries. The rapid expansion in the UK had been made possible by the Foundation being able to tap into the newly emerging National Health Service. This changed the emphasis of Cheshire Homes from places where disabled people would come with an expectation that they were going to make a life for themselves and where the residents expected to be involved in the day-to-day management of their home, to institutions working more and more to a medical model and view of disability.

... instead of being a place where they raised money and ran their own lives it rapidly became an institution, and a medical one at that. This was because of the National Health Service's imposition of the nursing criteria in the institution. And so people who had come to find and create a new life for themselves suddenly found themselves being imposed upon and having structures placed upon them which society really wanted because it was a nursing home and nursing homes have to be run along certain lines ...

Phillip Mason, former Le Court Resident

This change away from the original focus of the Foundation set up a fundamental conflict in the organisational structure of the homes which would erupt into out-and-out conflict at Le Court. The tension was between the Management Committee of the Home (who appointed the Warden and the Matron) and the Residents' Association (who appointed a chair and secretary to represent their views). At the end of the fifties Peter Wade and Paul Hunt were the residents reps when a proposal was put forward by the residents to form a "Works Council", made up of staff, residents and Management Committee, as a way of ensuring that residents were properly consulted on day-to-day management issues. This was rejected out of hand by the management committee and resulted in a silent protest by residents who 'sent the staff to Coventry'. A second more serious protest happened in 1962 following the imposition of petty hospital routines and rules by a new Matron. One rule insisted that residents must change into their pyjamas before the Day Staff finished work at 6 o'clock. The residents agreed a united front to resist this rule and on a chosen day all residents refused to co-operate with staff and would not allow themselves to be changed into their pyjamas. This was followed by a showdown one dinner time when the Warden and Matron read out a list of new rules without any prior discussion or consultation. These new rules required all TVs to be switched off by 10.30pm, anyone needing help to be in bed by 11.00pm, those wishing to go out after dark having to ask permission and no public exposure of bodies in hot weather.

... Peter Wade broke the silence that followed this announcement with a loud 'Rubbish!'. The Warden ordered him to leave the room and when he refused a member of staff was instructed to wheel him out. Peter is reputed to have eyed the person indicated and said, 'Lay a finger on me and I'll kill you!' ... **12**

This act of defiance led to threats to have Peter Wade expelled from the Home and following anger from other residents at this move the Management Committee escalated the situation by moving to evict a whole group of "ring leaders". This resulted in widespread protest both within and outside the Home and eventually Leonard Cheshire himself was forced to intervene. After suggesting that the six "ring leaders" should leave and set up their own home in a local town with a gift of £1,000, an offer that was rejected by the residents as an attempt to 'buy them off', Cheshire told the Management Committee that a Cheshire Home was a home for life and that meant that residents could not be evicted. Following this the Management Committee were replaced and a new chairman installed who was charged with working with the residents rather than imposing solutions, although it would take until 1965 before even the smallest of concessions was made to resident participation with two residents then being allowed on to the management committee 'for a trial period'. The small steps taken at Le Court in the mid sixties would lead to it being held up as a 'model' Residential Home. However, a study on living conditions at the Le Court Cheshire Home (and other institutions) in England undertaken at the time by two social scientists Eric Miller and Geraldine Gwynne from the Tavistock Institute reported that 'the crippled' experienced 'social death' in these institutional settings. But much to the disappointment of the likes of Paul Hunt the report failed to lay any blame with the staff or management of the Cheshire Foundation. Hunt left Le Court after marrying a member of staff and following contacts he made after writing *The Guardian* letter set up with others the Union Of The Physically Impaired Against Segregation, UPIAS, with the aim of getting '... all segregated facilities for physically impaired people replaced by arrangements for us to participate fully in society.' The UPIAS would lay the foundations for the Disability Rights movement that would grow and continue to fight for equal treatment in the last quarter of the 20th century.

Back at Le Court, residents would continue to push for changes in the way they were treated and asserting control over the decisions that affected their lives. In 1981, International Year of Disabled Persons, a small group of five residents , later dubbed the 'escape committee' by the late disabled singer Ian Dury, set up what they called Project 81 to pioneer independent living. The pioneers were Philip Mason, John Evans, Philip Scott, Tad Polkowski and Liz Briggs who, following a trip to the USA to see examples of independent living there, successfully negotiated a financial package which enabled them to move out of Le Court and into the community. With support from Hampshire Council and the Cheshire Foundation a way was found of getting around the legal restrictions preventing a direct payment to the residents essentially by 'laundering' the money through Le Court. An arrangement, subsequently copied widely, that persisted from 1983 until direct payments were at last made lawful in 1997. This was the start of Independent Living in the UK that would change the lives of generations of disabled people to come. The Cheshire Home at Le Court played a significant part in the development of both facilities for people with disabilities and the Disability Rights movement. The Foundation is still seen by some as locked into a paternalistic and segregationist model of disability that works counter to disabled people's interests with opposition and protests continuing to the present. In 2002 the Disabled People's Direct Action Network (DAN), in many ways the direct descendent of UPIAS, organised a protest outside a Leonard Cheshire charity fundraising ball.

Community Behind Bars

The therapeutic community model has been used within the UK prison system, most notably at Grendon Underwood. When it opened in 1962 it was the first of its kind in the world and is still the only entire prison in the UK run on therapeutic community lines. Grendon is a medium secure prison with five therapeutic communities in separate wings holding up to a total of 250 adult male prisoners. Mirroring in many ways the military therapy regimes at Northfield, prisoners take part in community meetings and small groups each week and a variety of group activities including other forms of therapy such as psychodrama, art therapy, life skills and practical skills courses. Small groups focus on offence-related behaviour and the community comes together for 'feedback' to the whole community. Each community of 35 to 42 prisoners elects its own officers who represent the community within the wider prison setting. Others take on roles such as food rep or television-video reps. Grendon has provided a template for the other therapeutic communities within the Prison Service.

The Barlinnie Special Unit in Glasgow was set up in 1973 to deal with some of Scotland's most violent prisoners. The Max Glatt Centre at Wormwood Scrubs started in 1975 to provide a service for prisoners with addictive and compulsive behaviour. Gartree Therapeutic Community in Leicestershire opened in 1993 for those serving life sentences. Therapeutic Community units have been set up in a number of Young Offender Institutions and more recently units have been set up in women's prisons and at the Dovegate private prison in Staffordshire.

It would seem that the prison service has finally emerged from the 'nothing works' era of the 1980's ... With its population and pace of growth higher than ever before, the British Prison system has had to re-examine how it can best serve the public. The British Prison system is finding for itself a renewed positive role with its population through the pragmatic use of proven rehabilitative programmes, and at the forefront of this move forward are the therapeutic communities.

Roland Woodward, *The Prison Communities: Therapy within a Custodial Setting*

The Legend of Atlantis

The most scary thing about being first is that everyone hates you. The most scary thing about telling the truth is that no-one believes you. The most scary thing about pushing all your friends to the limit is that eventually they turn against you. The most scary thing about going all the way to get what you want regardless of obstacles is that you grow bigger and wiser and stronger; and the most scary thing about growing big and wise and strong is that people hold you in awe and only a few dare to get close.

Jenny James, *They Call Us the Screamers*

Jenny James left the London PNP house towards the end of 1973 and, together with three other members and their four children, spent a year living in a rented house in the Lake District. This experience led them to decide that they not only needed somewhere more permanent, but also somewhere more remote to establish their Primal Therapy Commune. In the summer of '74 they started a search for property in Ireland eventually finding a large house on the west coast of Donegal in Burtonport. The £12,000 needed to buy the former 'Sweeney's Hotel' was raised by frantic phone calls to friends and supporters. In spring the following year the group moved in and set to transforming the rather drab house, painting it inside and out in bright colours and adorning the walls with astrological symbols, which resulted in a duly ignored letter from the local council asking for it to be repainted a 'monochrome' colour. The house was a large 'double house' that had been converted into a hotel in 1904 by a John Sweeney. It consisted of ten bedrooms, three reception rooms, two bathrooms and kitchens all set in two acres of land with outbuildings and greenhouses. As well as the artistic redecoration the group set about fitting out a therapy room, and getting the garden into shape. At the same time a London Primal Therapy Centre was set up as a base for the group in a row of squatted houses in Villa Road in Brixton.

From the start it seems the new commune, named Atlantis, was a whirlwind of 'therapeutic' activity. Picking up where People Not Psychiatry had left off, and in an extension of the spontaneity and open-door ethos that had been a feature back at Russell Gardens,

encounter and primal therapy sessions abounded. It didn't take long before an irate neighbour was knocking on the door complaining of 'howls, screams and bawls' emanating from the garden driving his mother to the point that she was taking tranquillisers. Burtonport was a somewhat sleepy Catholic Irish fishing and farming village, described by Jenny James as "superconventional". At first the group let contact with local people happened naturally '... buying live yeast from the local bakery; finding out how to cut turf and getting shown the way to our turf bog; buying goats; letting neighbours use the 'phone; repelling after-midnight drunks; going to the occasional dance.' Many of the local population were shocked by 'the types' turning up at the brightly painted house and threats were made that the group would 'cop it'. Jenny James refused to be intimidated. 'All my visions of the locals charging up here with pitchforks and hounding us from town or burning me at the stake were obviously not far removed from reality, but now I don't feel scared in the least, just licking my lips at the thought of battle'. As well as relishing battles with the locals Jenny James relished relationships with visitors who made their way to the primal commune. In July '75 the first Irishman to join arrived and a tempestuous love affair started between Jenny James and the newcomer, Oisin, chronicled in a series of letters between commune members (published as *Atlantis Alive* in 1980).

It seems that quite quickly the group started to look to setting up a base and moving to the partially deserted Island of Inishfree (Inis Fraoigh) in the sheltered bay between Dungloe and Burtonport. In the August 1975 issue of Communes Network an ad appeared stating that the therapy commune was moving house and offering the house to 'people in the therapy/commune movement' for the nearest offer to £29,000. It seems that there were no takers, but Jenny James and Oisin moved into a small cottage that they had purchased with ten acres of land on the island just before Christmas 1975. In the early 20th century Inishfree had been home to a small tightly-knit community who lived in clusters of small cottages complete with school and post office. In the 1960's the numbers slowly dwindled till many of the cottages were empty and derelict. Atlantis acquired a second cottage in early 1976 and in the end would come to occupy six of the fifteen habitable cottages on the island.

Montage picture from cover of Atlantis Is Also opposite. 1980

1975 also saw the publication of *Room to Breathe*, which turned out to be the first of a series of books by

Jenny James on both her own life and times and that of Atlantis. The group attracted a steady flow of visitors from both across Ireland, from England and further afield, and it wasn't long before word of the Primal Commune came to the notice of the Irish Press. The initial coverage was sympathetic towards the group.

I'D PREFER ATLANTIS TO THE MEN IN WHITE COATS! says Patrick Murray

In Burtonport, Co. Donegal, among the white-washed cottages and neatly painted houses, stands Atlantis. Painted all colours of the rainbow, with great red eyes over its windows, Atlantis is an imposing sight in the Donegal fishing town. Inside its multi-coloured doors, Jenny James tries to make people happy. All of the two dozen people in Atlantis have been or are depressed. All have a need for company, a need to talk about their experiences, and most of all, a need to unwind ... Emotional release therapy 'cleans' the subject. They leave Atlantis, or its sister commune in London, with new confidence and self-determination. They come to Atlantis from all over the world. During our visit there, we met Dubliners, Londoners, Glaswegians, an Australian. There have been Swedes and other Scandinavians there ...

Sunday Independent, May 30th 1976

It would not be long though before the press stories would become hostile. One particular incident would cement the name that they would be best known for for years to come. Under the headline 'My Kids and the Screamers' in the *Sunday World* on 24th October 1976 the group were described as a 'sinister cult' and accused of brainwashing members and tantamount to kidnapping children. The story had been taken to the papers by Dara Vallely from Armagh who after visiting 'Atlantis House' in Burtonport with his wife Marietta and kids had been shocked when his wife joined the group. After trying to get his children back, turning up with members of his family and the Gardia, Marietta fled to the group's London house. Things escalated over the next few months with TV crews and reporters turning up to cover the story as windows were broken and threats of kneecapping and bombing were received from the IRA. On 19th December the Gardia raided the group searching through both the house and the cottages on Inishfree, seemingly looking for drugs or evidence of child neglect. Having trashed the house they went away with a collection of henna, lavender, pot-pourri, raspberry leaves, aspirin and hay-fever pills, which was enough for the press to report that police had 'taken pills and some other substances from the house.' In its Christmas Eve edition the Donegal Democrat quoted a member of the Burtonport Residents' Committee as saying that the 'Screamers' were no longer welcome in Donegal. 'People here are living in fear of them and we want them out – we want to live in peace,' he said, adding that telegrams had been 'sent to Government ministers demanding that the sect be asked to leave'. The adverse publicity didn't seem to stifle activity at Atlantis or at the Villa Road Primal Therapy Centre where numbers were on the increase, often reaching 30 or more with talk of expanding into other squatted houses in the street. Villa Road was one of the bigger squatter communities in London with nearly 200 people living there. A whole variety of different sorts of people made up the community from hard left Workers Revolutionary Party members to the Primal Screamers at number 12. This led to sometimes intense disagreements and conflicts.

... in a 'leftwing' street of squats, we are frowned upon, sometimes beaten up, threatened, ostracized, criticized (not directly of course), asked to leave – the revolutionaries can't take us, the conservatives can't take us. Because what we are doing isn't scratching at the surface ...

Left: Atlantis House, Burtonport
Right: Jenny James

In June 1977, in an interview with the therapist John Rowan for *Self and Society, The Primal Issue,* Jenny James expounded the difference between the Primal Therapy as practiced by its originator Arthur Janov and that 'lived' at Atlantis. Asked if Atlantis ran a three-week programme in the same way that Janov did she replied:

Janov's programming makes us sick! You can't programme real growth. Obviously, if you have a clinical set-up, basically a reflection of his own psychiatric, professional, elitist, hierarchical background, then all kinds of unnatural growths occur: like people popping in for daily sessions, crying and yelling in front of a stranger ... No, we have a 3-month intensive, or a 3-year intensive. All living together on the same spot is so intense that there is no artificiality in the therapy, no organisation or special intensives: the encouragement is towards total involvement with one another, and there's nothing like getting close to another human being for bringing up deep feelings ...

She went on to explain that:

...Sometimes intensives do happen as a result of this: anyone who stays here for a few months will go through times when they are having more than one session a day every day for a period, and there are often mini-group intensives when four or five or half a dozen people get deeply involved and their wires cross in good and bad ways and they work together day in, day out. There is also an organic pattern whereby whole-house groups will take three days to come to a closure – with gaps for sleeping, eating and milking the cows, but each group running to 12 and more hours. We've noticed a 'wave' effect in therapy through letting things take their own course.

At the end of 1977 a significant new member came to stay at Atlantis. Described by Jenny as 'the nicest Christmas present anyone could ever receive', her estranged younger sister Snowy came to stay for a week and ended 'staying a lifetime'. Snowy James had been living in various communal set-ups in and around Lancaster including a small group called Badger Gate near Kirby Lonsdale. As described by Jenny in *They Call Us the Screamers*

Snowy had spent years running 'therapeutic groups, participating in communal living situations and helping to organize all kinds of community-based social projects.' After deciding to throw in her lot with her sister in Ireland she sold her house in Lancaster 'and invited her friends – all 129 of them – to join her. Each one refused. So she broke with all of them, kidnapped her two children from their respective fathers and joined the black sheep of Atlantis. Her name and ours are now

Jenny and Snowy James on the steps of Atlantis House Burtonport.

passwords to awe and gossip and horror stories all over Lancaster.' Snowy would become 'Queen of Atlantis' in her own right and along with Jenny's oldest daughter Becky the three women would come to form the core of a 'matriarchal' set-up at the commune. The move to Inishfree brought a shift in the focus of the commune away from therapy and towards a self-sufficient peasant lifestyle.

We used to have a therapy room at Atlantis. Now we have the kitchen, the bathroom, the peatbog and the vegetable garden. We still have a therapy room. But we never use it. We keep it as a kind of showpiece for visitors and reporters. They expect it you know. But the real therapy takes place in our living rooms. What is the use of therapy if you can't live with it?

Jenny James, *Atlantis Is* 1980

1978 was a hive of activity: the group launched the 'Atlantis Road Show' taking 'dressing-up and our fun and dance and antics and cheek and tricks and philosophies' on tour, taking in grey strife-torn Belfast, causing trouble in violence-ridden London and erupting in 'liberal Lancaster'. In September 1978 an RTE film crew arrived to make a documentary about the commune. Directed by Bob Quinn and simply called *The Family* the 27-minute film began with a dramatised sequence showing a traditional 'nuclear' family to provide contrast with what followed. The film showed a fly-on-the-wall view of 'ordinary and extraordinary moments in the lives of an unusual community'. Originally due to be screened in December 1978 it was considered too controversial and was not broadcast until 1991.

The story of these years at the commune can be traced through the series of six books published by Caliban Books. What strikes one reading them through now is that although they all have a similar feel and format – often being made up of letters between Jenny and other commune members,

Atlantis – Top to Bottom
Atlantis Inishfree cover photo
Cottage on Inshfree
Atlantis Adventure

interspersed with newspaper stories and poems – each one appears to be almost a completely different literary genre from the next. Ranging from a fairly straight forward documentary account of the communes early years in *They Call us the Screamers* (1980) to *Atlantis Alive* (1980) which is the unravelling of a love story. *Atlantis Is* (1980) starts as a sort of guidebook for visitors, initially seeing the community through the eyes of a would-be visitor, and then becomes a series of interviews and community diary extracts. These were followed two years later by *Male Sexuality: The Atlantis Position* (1982), a sort of sex therapy manual. *Atlantis Magic* (1982) the tale of the groups' exploration of their latent psychic powers and finally *Atlantis Inishfree* (1985) which tells the story of a year of self-sufficient living on the island which reads in parts like a crazy Irish novel.

I have always written to clear my mind, work out a split in myself (like Atlantis Magic *rational versus psychic), to 'dare' to do something that frightened me (the sex books), or just to tell a good story (the travel book) or share experiences that when I was younger I would have been over the moon to know about (*Room to Breathe, *ie how therapy works). Or sometimes just to annoy all the right people! (the Irish Catholic audience in Ireland) … The 'glut' of books was mainly in my child-bearing years (39, 41, 43) when on Inishfree Island, long winters, pregnancies, a good team to back me up so I had time to write and lots to say.* [13]

Jenny James 2011

What emerges from the books is a story of wild passionate people living to the limits of their emotions, suffering no fools gladly (or at all) and brooking no bullshit from anyone – who also at times are as vulnerable and angst-ridden as the next person, living not only on the very edge of a continent, but at times at the very edge of human emotional endurance. People regularly ran away from Atlantis, members as well as visitors. There are stories of some swimming from Inishfree desperate to escape and one of a visitor trying to call a helicopter to rescue him. What also comes across is a deep political commitment to things such as the campaign against Uranium Mining in Donegal. What the books don't really talk about are the controversies that their actions and writings stirred up in the alternative press at the time. Publications like *Peace News* and *Greenline* carried articles attacking the group from people who had visited. Perhaps the most vitriolic attack was published in *Creative Mind*, a therapy-based magazine whose editor Helen Prescott took a particular dislike to Atlantis, branding it as 'Spiritually lacking ... Having all the makings of a cult ... not interested in anyone else's ideas ...' and going on to criticise the group for worshipping two middle-aged women and having cottages that looked more like a 'Parisian salon' than an island cottage. The article was so over the top that it told you as much if not more about its author than it did about Atlantis and when it was reprinted in *Communes Network* 84, it caused one communard to wonder 'what neurosis Atlantis sparked off in Helen?' The Atlantis books also don't go into any detail of the plans the group had started to formulate from 1980 onwards to escape from what they saw as a corrupt and crumbling western civilisation in Europe. In 1982 the group bought an old 50-foot Norwegian fishing boat, the *Kobben* built in 1910 which had been refitted as a yacht in England in 1945. It was sailed over to Ireland in 1984 and renamed the *Atlantis Adventure*. Long-term plans were to make the boat seaworthy and sail to South America in her. In the meantime the group had been in contact with a former Greenpeace captain and the idea was that the boat should become part of a worldwide 'Flotilla for Peace' to go to trouble spots and political emergencies around the world. An itinerary was draw up that included: a nuclear weapons site on the River Tamar in England; the Indian Ocean island of Diego Garcia, where islanders were campaigning for it to be returned to them and the US Naval Base removed; and the Island of Nauru in the Pacific Ocean to protest at the imprisonment of refugees by the Australian government. The *Atlantis Adventure* spent the summer and later part of 1983 sailing down to the Tamar to protest against Cruise Missiles, but the constant need for repair and lack of resources kept her from sailing to more exotic protest destinations.

In the end the final push to leave Ireland came from outside the commune. Jenny James explains the circumstances leading to their departure in the introduction to her eighth book, *Atlantis Adventure*. 'For a few years, Inishfree spelt Freedom. But during the latter 1970's, a Great Flattening began as the Irish government scrambled ever more to conform to British systems, values and laws. Conformity hit Atlantis through the fashionable concern of social workers for 'children's welfare', the latest name for government intrusion into one's private life ...' The Irish authorities took the two-year-old son of one of the members, Mary Kelly, into care. 'simply because his mother was enlightened enough to admit she had problems and to seek help. The Irish courts decreed the child had to stay in 'care' until he was sixteen. Atlantis decreed the whole system could go to hell.' It would take Mary Kelly years of campaigning and direct action and thousands of pounds of the commune's money to get the court decision squashed, during which time she would become an 'ardent public speaker on the subject of 'parent abuse' and was the scourge of the Irish Social Work Department.' When it appeared that her own children may well be taken away from her Jenny James decided that '... it was time to Move, with a capital M.' An advance party of the commune made up of Jenny James, her three Irish daughters and three men, Fred, Barnsley Bill and Ned, set off in 1987 heading for 'destination unknown' in South America.

I was two weeks short of forty-five when we left Europe for ever. Louise was five, Alice three, and Katie, a year old, was still in nappies. I had never heard of anyone attempting such a journey with three small children before, but other people's precedents had never been a dominant factor in my life. I was nervous, of course, but I figured that a family group, whilst a socially unacceptable unit for rough travelling in Europe, would tune in easily with the Third World societies we were heading for ...

Snowy and other members stayed behind and tidied up affairs, making arrangements to let the cottages on Inishfree to provide finance for the journey and to continue renovation of the *Atlantis Adventure* in preparation for the rest of the group to sail to South America once a base had been established by the advance party. Since 1982, when the group had decamped to Inishfree, the house in Burtonport had been occupied by another group of supposedly 'feminists back-to-the-land, goddess worshipping' women. This new group led by a couple of women, Marianne Scarlett and Priscilla Langridge, became in their own way as notorious as the 'Screamers' before them. The new group went under various names: the Silver Sisters; the Games Mistresses; or the St Brides Academy for Young Ladies. According to one report they started advertising that they were running a 'school' in April 1984.

... This is probably not the sort of school that you'd go to though, because the young ladies of St B's are past the age of compulsory education, from their 20's upwards. And they go there for a week at a time, maybe more, to wear a uniform, sleep in a dorm, to take lessons and obey the rules, all without the creature comforts of 1985. They spend 24 hours a day living in a different time, living a different life. We give people a different experience of living as themselves. Marianne's background is both teaching and humanistic psychology and this is far more than a theme holiday hotel; as an experiment in human behaviour it's fascinating. St Brides works because the pupils are never given the chance to do anything but live the imaginary 1920/30's era ...

Hunter S Minson in "Crash", *ZX Spectrum Magazine* Issue No 26 March 1986

The electrics had been ripped out of most of the house and the house redecorated to turn it from Primal Therapy commune into a fantasy 1930's prep school. The school was advertised widely, in the *Observer*, the *Sunday Times*, *Girl About Town*, and in the theatre programme for Daisy Pulls it Off. News also got around by word of mouth. The girls who attended were reported to be 'Nurses, teachers, office workers, people who are interested in seeing the psychological effect take place on themselves.' The school took up to eight pupils at a time each paying around £120 a week for a supposed week of childhood nostalgia where you could 'spend time in the schoolroom upstairs writing lines for the teacher and catching up on their homework.' But all was not quite as it seemed on the surface at St Brides. While the residents claimed to live as if in the 1930's with no modern conveniences and to not read any book published after 1939 and only then by candle light, down in the basement of the house the group had a printing press and some very early Commodore 64 and ZX Spectrum computers on which they were devising their own computer games with titles such as The Secret of St Bride's, The Snow Queen and Unexpurgated Caves. These were sold mail-order through specialist computer magazines and to the computer world through trade shows such as the Olympia PCW Show. On the printing press the women produced a whole variety of material from labels for the local fishermen's co-operative and posters for the horse races, whimsical publications illustrated with silhouettes of ladies with parasols entitled *The Romantic*, to themed comics to go with their computer games. For ten years the Burtonport 'Ladies' carried on their secret double life appearing in the Irish Press and on television extolling their 'Victorian Values' and claiming never to have heard of George Bush or the exploits of Margaret Thatcher, wanting simply to be "gracious and demure Victorians".

We get on very well with the locals ... Irish people don't think the same as the English, they love people making a splash. They have a phrase, 'to have a bit of crack' which means you're up there at the top. I'm considered the best dressed woman in Burtonport.

Marianne Scarlett in "Crash"
ZX Spectrum Magazine

Marianne Scarlett and wind-up gramophone

The full extent of the double life being lived at St Brides would not come to light until 1992 when, having only received a third of the agreed figure for the house, members of Atlantis decided to forego any legal procedures and reclaim their property themselves by direct action. There had been one or two hints as to extra-curricular school activities taking place at the house in 1991. One member, a Miss Tyrrell, had been found guilty in a local court of caning a girl on the buttocks. But the Secrets of St Brides when they finally came to light would be something of a surprise to nearly everybody. Just before Christmas 1992 the Atlantis 'bailiffs' team headed for Burtonport to reclaim their property.

... we decided on direct action – cheaper, more effective and more fun. We sent a notice that we were going in to do repairs, got refused as usual and went ahead anyway. Mary, Scott and I drove from our boat in Baltimore, Co Cork, in a heaterless car through a deeply frozen Ireland with our ladders and paint brushes. Came here, knocked and knocked and knocked on the door and got no answer. So Scott found a not-exactly-closed window. Mary climbed in and I followed ...

Anne Barr in "The Strange Case of the Burtonport Ladies", *Communes Network* **110**

Inside, after confronting the only inhabitant, who promptly locked herself in the loo for two days, the Atlanteans surveyed the damage to their house; there were ceilings caving in and rising damp throughout. Strewn about the house they found neo-Nazi literature including *National Front News* and the British National Party's *Spearhead* magazine lying alongside anti-Semitic periodicals from all over the world. Mixed in among these fascist papers were sex industry fetish magazines featuring women in gas masks and suspenders and price lists for equipment such as handcuffs and leg-irons. There were printed forms entitled 'Caning Recommendations', indicating that 'education' at St Brides had involved regular beatings with cane, birch and even nettles. After the Gardaí had arrived, had a 'good laugh' at the situation and left the Atlantis members to get on with it, further surprising discoveries were made. In amongst letters from Irish farmers enquiring whether bondage and domination were on offer at the academy was a series of correspondence stretching over a two-year period between the Sisters and the British National Party leader, John Tyndall, who professed admiration for the Ladies and their dislike of the present. He said in one letter 'I admire and respect what you are doing to the point of fascination' and that he agreed entirely that there should be secession from the modern world. He went on to say that he saw himself as 'spiritually with one foot in the 19th century and the other in, perhaps, the 17th and 18th'. Anne Barr takes up the story again 'Then the leader of the group came from Oxford, where she now runs the main part of her spanking business, bringing with her four thugs and trying to intimidate us by lurking around the house all night. Eventually with encouragement from the Gardai and from some local friends of ours, they left Ireland.' The national press in Ireland and Britain picked up on the story, sniffing a salacious scandal, and pursued the ladies of St Brides back to England.

... The sisters have moved to Oxford, where attempts to question them are hampered by their habit of assuming alternative identities. A woman calling herself Laetitia Linden Dorvf, installed in north Oxford in a house she calls The Imperial Embassy ... acknowledged the court case but claimed the girl was caned as part of a disciplinary session to which she quite voluntarily agreed. But she denied that the sisters had links with the publications found in their house. We do not endorse any of them as they are all collaborating with the degeneration of the late 20th century. We simply receive them as part of an exchange subscription ...

The Sunday Telegraph, 3rd January 1993

When Jenny James and her small band of would-be European refugees left Ireland in 1987 they flew first from London down to Lanzarote in the Canary Islands where after a few months island hopping from La Palma, on to Tenerife and to Gran Canaria, living on beaches and in spare rooms in local people's houses, they finally managed to arrange passage first to the Cape Verde Islands and then across the Atlantic arriving in Venezuela just over a year after leaving Ireland. They then headed overland to Columbia where they were able to buy a small farm 30 miles south of the Columbian capital, Bogota.

We have 15 hectares of mostly thick woodland, a small amount of pasture and a small amount of crops which include vegetables, sugar cane, coffee, bananas (it's only just warm enough for these things so they're very slow). Moran, a kind of raspberry, is the local commercial crop and we're planting loads of it. Maize, beans, peas... We have a river for bathing in rock pools and a spring for pure water. Potential interests here include Basketry – easily learned from all locals who make their own, using a creeper that grows in the forest. String and rope making – also easily learned, using a kind of cactus plant that grows locally. We have some on the farm. Pottery, ceramics – there's loads of good pottery clay on our land and unlimited firewood. All kinds of woodwork – there's a huge variety and amount of hardwoods on our land. We have goats, chickens, cats and dogs and a mare – we want to get into breeding horses. They're for riding and for carrying cargo on their backs.

Ned Addis, Lista de Correos, Tolima, Icononzo, Columbia,
in *Communes Network* **99, 1989/90**

Back in Europe, Snowy and the others fought to get Mary Kelly's son released from the clutches of the Irish State and continued working to prepare the group's boat to take the rest of them to South America. An attempt made in October 1991 to sail the *Atlantis Adventure* across the Atlantic nearly ended in tragedy when the boat was caught in a force ten gale in the Bay of Biscay on its way to the Canary Islands and was rescued on the night of 30 October by the Baltimore Lifeboat and taken back to Ireland. It would remain in Baltimore Harbour for many years. Following the episode with the 'neo-Nazi-sadomasochistic ladies of St Brides' there was a fairly short period when a small number of Atlantis members re-inhabited the original house at Burtonport, finally selling it in the early years of the 21st Century. Some of the cottages on Inishfree were for a while a base for some members of the Cartwheel project. More recently the island has been recolonised by locals with some of the cottages being converted into holiday homes.

Barnes, M and Berke, J *Mary Barnes: Two Accounts of a Journey Through Madness* MacGibbon 1971

Bang, J *A Portrait of Camphill* Floris Books 2010. ISBN: 0863157416

Barnett, M *People Not Psychiatry* Allen & Unwin 1973. ISBN: 0046160140

Bierer, J *The Day Hospital: An Experiment in Social Psychiatry and Syntho-Analytic Psychotherapy* 1951

Bloor, M; Neil, P et al *One Foot in Eden: Sociological Study of the Range of Therapeutic Community Practice* Routledge 1988. ISBN: 0415008220

Bock, F *The Builders of Camphill: Lives and Destinies of the Founders* Floris Books 2004. ISBN: 0863154425

Campling, P and Haigh, R *Therapeutic Communities: Past, Present, and Future* Kingsley 1999. ISBN: 1853026263

Clark, D H *The Story of a Mental Hospital: Fulbourn 1853-1983* Process Press 1996. ISBN: 1899209034

Clarke, L *The Time of the Therapeutic Communities: People, Places and Events* Kingsley 2003. ISBN: 1843101289

Farrants, W *Camphill Villages* Camphill Press 1988. ISBN: 0904145298

Grenville, A and Reiter, A (eds) *I Didn't Want to Float; I Wanted to Belong to Something* Rodopi B V 2009. ISBN: 9042025670

Harrison, T *Bion, Rickman, Foulkes and the Northfield Experiments* Kingsley, 2000. ISBN: 1853028371

James, J *They Call Us the Screamers* Caliban Books 1980. ISBN: 0904573273

James, J *Atlantis Is* Caliban Books 1980. ISBN: 0904573265

James, J *Atlantis Alive* Caliban Books 1980. ISBN: 0904573303

James, J *Male Sexuality: The Atlantis Position* Caliban Books. ISBN: 0904573567

James, J *Atlantis Magic* Caliban Books 1982. ISBN: 0904573583

James, J *Room to Breathe* Caliban Books 1983. ISBN: 0904573303

James, J *Atlantis Inishfree* Caliban Books 1985. ISBN: 1850660034

Jones, E *War and the Practice of Psychotherapy: The UK Experience 1939–1960* Published as an article in the Cambridge Medical History Journal, October 2004

Kennard, D *An introduction to Therapeutic Communities* Kingsley 1998. ISBN: 18530260343

Kotowicz, Z *R D Laing and the Paths of Anti psychiatry* Routledge 1997. ISBN: 0415116112

Pullen, G P *Street: The Seventeen Day Community* International Journal of Therapeutic Communities 1982

Rapoport, R N *Community as a Doctor* Tavistock Publications 1960

Rose, J *Half-Way Home: Story of Elly Jansen and the Richmond Fellowship* Religious and Moral Education Press 1986. ISBN: 008031788X

Shephard, B *A War of Nerves: Soldiers and Psychiatrists in the Twentieth Century* Harvard University Press 2001. ISBN: 0674005929

Smartt, U *Grendon Tales: Stories from a Therapeutic Community* Waterside Press 2008. ISBN: 1906534519

Surkamp, J (ed) *The Lives of Camphill: An Anthology of the Pioneers* Floris Books 2007. ISBN: 086315607X

Wills, W D *Spare the Child: The Story of an Experimental Approved School* Penguin 1971. ISBN: 0140802150

Notes

1   Jones, E *War and the Practice of Psychotherapy: The UK Experience 1939–1960.*

2   http://www.utopia-britannica.org.uk/pages/Painted%20fabrics.htm (21.3.2012).

3   Bion and Rickman "Intra-group tensions in Therapy" in *The Lancet* 1943 p678.

4   "The Emotional Vortex" in *Utopia Britannica.* Coates 2000.

5   *The Peckham Experiment* Innes Hope Pearse, Allen & Unwin 1944.

6   *A Life Well Lived: Maxwell Jones - A Memoir* D Briggs.

7   *All the Lonely People Where Do They All Come From? Facts, Feelings and Experience from the Philadelphia Association London* Theodor Itten.

8   Tony Haigh interviewed by the author at Brithdir Mawr, July 2009.

9   John Whitwell staff member and Principal at the Cotswold Community 1977–99.

10   Michael Barnett *People Not Psychiatry.*

11   Jenny James. *Room to Breathe* Caliban Books 1983.

12   The place of Le Court residents in the history of the disability movement in England. http://www.leeds.ac.uk/disability-studies/archiveuk/Mason/le%20court%20-%20philip%20mason.pdf

13   Personal correspondence with the author.

Moved by the Spirit

Angels had actually flown some of the planes
whose pilots sat dead in their cockpits.

Air Chief Marshal Lord Dowding
Quoted by Billy Graham in *Angels: God's Secret Agents*

It has become a widely accepted view that the man who commanded Britain's last line of defence during the summer of 1940, and was the mastermind behind the Battle of Britain, did himself believe that angels had come to the aid of 'the Few' and had helped save the country from Nazi invasion. 'There just wasn't any other way to explain how the RAF outnumbered by planes so much better and outgunned 100 to one, how they won the Battle of Britain.' – or was there?

Air Chief Marshal Hugh 'Stuffy' Dowding, head of Fighter Command, was no ordinary RAF commander. A Royal Flying Corps veteran from the First World War, Dowding had flown at the Battle of the Somme where the Corps had lost 800 aircraft and had 252 aircrew killed. At the end of the battle he clashed with his commanding officer over the need to rest pilots exhausted by non-stop duty – the first of many clashes with his superiors. This time his belligerence may have saved his life as he was promptly sent back to Britain and given a desk job. During the inter-war years he had excelled when in charge of the the RAF training school and in 1933 was promoted to Air Marshal and went on to be knighted the following year.

In the late 1930's Dowding was one of the few high ranking officers in the RAF to argue that it was possible to defend against mass bomber attacks. It was his persistence that led to the development of what became known as the Dowding System, an integrated air defence

Hugh Dowding

system which included radar, raid plotting and radio control of aircraft. He also argued successfully for the introduction of a new generation of fighter planes, the Spitfires and Hurricanes that would win the Battle of Britain. Due to retire in 1939 he was persuaded to stay on as head of Fighter Command. His single-minded dedication to his job continued to bring him into conflict with his superiors. During the Battle of France, it was Dowding who faced down Winston Churchill and, after a heated argument, persuaded the Prime Minister not to send the few remaining fighter aircraft of the RAF to reinforce the British Expeditionary Force at Dunkirk, but to save them to be the country's last line of defence.

Dowding was involved in spiritualism, he travelled up and down the country speaking about his contacts with those in the astral realms. He commissioned a clairvoyant, Margaret Flavell, to help trace missing RAF pilots and worked with what were called Home Rescue Groups who helped the lost souls of those who had suffered violent deaths to find peace. Billy Graham may have made an innocent mistake in attributing the British success in the Battle of Britain to angelic beings – his source for the Dowding quote turns out to be a 1966 work of fiction, *Tell No Man* by Hollywood screenwriter and journalist Adele Rogers St John. The book, a fictional clergyman's memoir, includes a scene where Dowding makes the angels speech at a banquet held in his honour a few months after the Battle of Britain, attended by the King, Churchill and scores of dignitaries; a scene that, in reality, never happened but, given Dowding's reputation, could easily be imagined as having occurred.

Hugh Dowding's beliefs were not as unusual as we might think. The inter-war years had seen something of a revival in spiritualism. Occult groups and evangelical sects had sprung up across the country. Other earlier esoteric groups such as the Theosophical Society saw a renewed interest in their ideas and an increase in membership. The 1930's is now seen as something of a heyday for spiritualism. An investigation by the Church of England into the rise in popularity of esoteric groups at the time heard reports of hundreds of spiritualist groups operating across the country and, in June 1932, a journalist for *Psychic News* estimated that there were in the region of 100,000 home seances operating in Britain. Partly, this was due to neglect by the Church of the mass bereavement that had occurred during the 1914-18 war and partly this was encouraged by a democratising move within Spiritualism at the time that considered psychic power to be latent in everyone and urged people to develop their own powers as well as to consult mediums and clairvoyants.

The period also saw the emergence of a number of Christian revivalist groups. The American Revd Frank Buchman, a sort of peripatetic international evangelist, inspired a number of Oxford undergraduates to form what became known as The Oxford Group – members were exhorted to live up to four ideals of behaviour: Absolute Honesty, Absolute Purity, Absolute Unselfishness and Absolute Love. Joyce Colin-Smyth whose spiritual journey started with The Oxford Group was attracted to them by one particular practice. 'What got me was the 'Quiet Time' concept. This was fundamental to Buchman's ideas. It was a method of prayer that was to be cultivated for half an hour at a time at intervals during the day. The discipline of this – so much more demanding than anything I had encountered in conventional churchgoing, had a certain appeal. ... First, the mind was to be emptied of thought. There was to be a notebook and pencil to hand. In quietness and emptiness, messages would come. These were the words of the Lord and must be written down at once, and when appropriate, acted upon.' [1] This technique, along with public confession of one's sins, led to individuals being 'changed'. The group held summer camps and winter conferences. As war approached Buchman changed the group's name to Moral Re-Armament – he believed that if enough people (especially important influential people) listened to God and could be 'changed', then war could be averted.

Many of these groups were study or worship groups meeting in church halls or private houses, but a number had premises and small residential communities attached to them. The Order of Woodcraft Chivalry, a quasi-pagan version of the Scouts, was running woodcraft and labour camps for the unemployed, along with a Forest School at Godshill in Hampshire. Close by, at Christchurch, George Alexander Sullivan ran the Rosicrucian Order Crotona Fellowship with Mabel Besant-Scott; daughter of the Theosophical Society president Annie Besant. Sullivan's ideas, a combination of various esoteric subjects and positive thinking, were studied by members through lectures, plays and a personal correspondence course. In the garden of a house owned by the group's benefactor, Catherine Chalk, the fellowship built a wooden building called the Ashrama Hall in 1936 as its

Christchurch Garden Theatre, Somerford Road, Christchurch Later used by De Havilland as their Aeronautical Technical School

headquarters. Some of Sullivan's disciples bought up bungalows in the area and a small community grew up. In 1938 the group built the Christchurch Garden Theatre, billed by Sullivan as 'The First Rosicrucian Theatre in England'. It presented mystically themed plays written by Sullivan under the pen-name of Alex Matthews. In 1939 a performance at the theatre based on the life of Pythagoras was attended by a Mr Gardner, a retired civil servant, and his wife. Mrs Gardner thought the whole thing terribly amateurish, badly scripted and poorly acted and refused to go again. Her husband Gerald, however, was intrigued by the group and joined them. Gerald Gardner was in many ways a typical seeker of the time. He had investigated Spiritualist churches and seances, studied native folk magic in Malaya, spent some time on archaeological digs in Egypt and was a member of the Folklore Society. Gardner, whilst sceptical of some of the Rosicrucian group's ideas, participated in many of their rituals and activities. One night in September 1940 the group gathered to take part in what has become known as The Magical Battle of Britain.

We were taken at night to a place in the Forest, where the Great Circle was erected; and that was done which may not be done except in great emergency. And the great cone of power was raised and slowly directed in the general direction of Hitler. The command was given: you cannot cross the sea, you cannot cross the sea, you cannot come, you cannot come. Just as, we were told, was done to Napoleon, when he had his army ready to invade England and never came. And, as was done to the Spanish Armada, mighty forces were used, of which I may not speak.

Quoted by Jack Bracelin (Idries Shah) in *Gerald Gardner: Witch*

This New Forest gathering was not an isolated incident of magical warfare. All along the south coast, if some reports are to be believed, witches and occultists were joining the war effort.

... it was becoming obvious that England was going to be invaded if the German Luftwaffe could get supremacy over the RAF and the witches, all the way around the coast, wanted to make sure that this didn't happen ... a couple of days before this invasion was supposed to happen he, my mother and grandmother and various other old grannies – all went down to the beach right on the tip of Kent. As the tide turned so that it was ebbing, they threw what we call Go Away Powder into the tide with such invocations as 'You can't come here, Go Away, Bugger Off' over and over again. And the invasion never happened ... I know that people might say this is rubbish, sheer imagination, but the powder has this ability to push things away from you.

Paddy Slade interviewed in *Far Out: The Dawning of New Age Britain*

It wasn't just those with pagan and occult beliefs that were coming to the spiritual help of the nation in its hour of need: the spiritualist White Eagle lodge run by the medium Grace Cooke started producing a 'Poster of Light' that they distributed around London and put up in tube station air raid shelters.

There was a very strong sense that we were dealing with the forces of darkness. White Eagle was instructing us then as a group to use that symbol of a cross of light to push back, to protect from those forces of Darkness. We used to visualise the symbol at our Sunday services and our particular work was holding Britain in the light.

Ylana Haywood Grace Cooke's daughter
Interviewed in *Far Out: The Dawning of New Age Britain*

At the end of the war Air Chief Marshal, Lord Dowding took an active part in a variety of spiritualist groups both as a writer and speaker. He wrote a number of books on his beliefs and experiences. He married his second wife Muriel after receiving a 'message' from her dead husband – an RAF bomber pilot – to ask her out to dinner rather than just reply to the letter she had sent and she recognised him as a soldier she had had visions of in her childhood. Through Muriel's influence, her vegetarianism and her concern for animal welfare, Lord Dowding made over thirty speeches in the House of Lords nearly all on animal welfare matters and the plight of laboratory animals. In 1959 Muriel Dowding launched the campaigning charity Beauty Without Cruelty, opening a shop in Bayswater, London, selling cosmetics obtained without mistreating animals. The World Day for Laboratory Animals instigated by the The National Anti-Vivisection Society falls on Lord Dowding's birthday – April 24.

THE FORCES OF DARKNESS ...HALT! BEFORE THE CROSS OF LIGHT

The materialists have had their way with the world, and look where they have led us! We are learning the practical necessity for the Brotherhood of Man, and we are learning the hard way. I believe that by the study of ancient and modern revelation a sufficiently intelligible picture of the scheme of things can be built up so as to serve for a framework for an intelligent man's creed, which in turn can wean his thoughts and actions from the existing almost universal materialism.

Hugh Dowding in *The Dark Star*

Ark builders at Virginia Waters

... an ark is a symbol for a refuge in a time of trouble. Noah was warned of the disasters ahead; we also will require an ark in the time to come, and there is a small group of people now in London that has started building one ... There are great disasters ahead of us and we've got to prepare for them. There will be wars, political unrest, revolutions and all on such a scale that everything that humanity has managed to build up may well fall in ruins.

Maurice Nicoll in conversation with Kenneth Walker 1924
Reported in *Venture with Ideas*

As early as 1923 the Armenian mystic G I Gurdjieff had prophesied that there would be another war and that humanity would fall into ruin. He had spoken to his followers urging them to form arks in the event of a 'flood of evil engulfing the world'. As Neville Chamberlain delivered his message to the British Nation on the 3rd of September 1939 that they were once again at war, the residents of Lyne Place at Virginia Waters in Surrey were escorting their children to a heavily timber-reinforced basement that they had prepared; in the distance the wail of sirens could be heard. Plans for their 'ark' had been in place for some time. In the grounds of the house the group had dug a large underground concrete bunker to store food in, and it was well stocked with provisions of every kind: hams, dried fruit, jars of salted butter, sugar, oatmeal, flour, etc. Arrangements were in place for as many women and children as possible from the London connections of the group to be accommodated in the house and in the various cottages on the small estate. As he checked that the children knew how to put on the 'newfangled gas-masks' Dr Kenneth Walker reflected that he felt 'more like offering the children my apologies than my advice. What a commentary it was on the mis-management of the world by their elders that they should now have to be shown how to adjust their pig-like snouts.' **2**

Lyne Place had been bought in 1936 by Mr and Madame Ouspensky as a base to carry out plans for an esoteric school teaching ideas and practices that both of them had learnt from Gurdjieff. The house and a nearly hundred-acre estate was the third property that the couple and their followers had attempted to set up in. Firstly at 'The Dell' in Sevenoaks and later at 'Little Gaddesden', a large Victorian mansion in seven acres of land that they were 'lent' near Hayes in Kent. But these soon became too small for the group's purposes. The newly acquired property in Surrey came with extensive gardens, rhododendron walks, a small lake with a boathouse, a farm, greenhouses, pigsties, barns, stables and a vegetable garden. It was in a poor state of repair and required three months of repair work before it was fit for the Ouspenskys and other permanent residents to move in. The work was carried out by members of the wider study group that Peter Ouspensky had been running in London for some years. The group included various architects, engineers, electricians and carpenters and, since Gurdjieff's teachings encouraged manual labour, under the direction of the expert members the work was completed without much outside help. The Ouspenskys' plans for the new venture were to, 'so far as was possible', create a self-contained, self-supporting community. With the much larger numbers than they could previously accommodate at Hayes, the permanent residents set about learning how to grow their own fruit and vegetables in the extensive kitchen gardens and orchards. At weekends the numbers were swollen by visitors from London with as many as a hundred people sitting down to meals. By the end of two years in residence the group were growing their own wheat, milling it themselves into flour and baking their own bread. They had constructed a shed containing fruit drying equipment and expanded their work into managing the woodland on the estate; felling timber and converting it in a 'Heath Robinson' sawmill that they had built themselves. Other members were kept busy with sheep and dairy farming. The core of residents of the new community were Russian – the Ouspenskys, the Savitskys, Mme Kadloubovsky, plus a handful of St Petersburg pensioners. Some of Ouspensky's senior English pupils had been drafted in to manage the household and grounds. However some residents were not so sure that this new successful community didn't have its drawbacks.

'Much as we had gained from moving into larger premises, many of us were conscious of having also sustained a loss. One obvious loss was that we saw less and less of Mr and Madame Ouspensky, and as a consequence obtained from them less help. The feeling of belonging to a family had disappeared and been replaced by the feeling of belonging to an institution. Yes, there could be no doubt that some of the things which the older among us greatly valued had been lost by this very rapid increase in the size of our community.'

Kenneth Walker

By the autumn of 1937 the new community was thriving and Oupensky's work was attracting the interest of a younger generation of the English intelligentsia. Aldous Huxley and Gerald Heard visited after having attended one of Ouspensky's lectures with Christopher Isherwood. His works were read by a young Denis Healey, future Chancellor of the Exchequer. With this expanding interest in his work Ouspensky became frustrated with the way things were going, first thinking that he wanted a smaller group that he could work more intensely with, then deciding that he wanted to expand the work further and open the door to more people. To do this a bigger meeting hall in London would be required, and a properly constituted 'society' would be needed, 'so as not to arouse suspicion from the authorities'. In 1938 the somewhat awkwardly named Historico-Psychological Society was set up to study the 'psychological systems of the East which taught the doctrine of metempsychosis, or the perfectibility of man'. Throughout 1938 Ouspensky busied himself with drafting a series of prohibitive rules for the new society which he believed would promote raised consciousness among his followers.

Lyne Place at Virginia Waters

They included: never mentioning Gurdjieff; never addressing each other by Christian names; never talking about the work in front of strangers; and never speaking to anyone who had left the group.

All these plans were thrown into confusion by the outbreak of the war. As the esoteric refugees bunkered down in their Surrey Ark, Ouspensky meditated on the state of the world and came to the erroneous conclusion that Germany would quickly win the war, this would spark a Europe-wide revolution supported by the Soviet Union and that only America would evade the clutches of Communism. London meetings were eventually cancelled due to the frequency of air raids and work at Lyne became harder as members were called up for national service. By 1940, with the Battle of Britain raging in the skies above Lyne and the Blitz having destroyed their London flat, the Ouspenskys decided to emigrate to America, leaving Lyne Place in the hands of trusted senior members of the group. Madame Ouspensky sailed for the States early in 1941 with all those who were able to accompany her and a month or so later she was followed by her husband. With the departure of the two teachers the group's work in England came to an end. In America the Ouspenskys would try to recreate their English set-up at Franklin Farms at Mendham, the former residence of the Governor of New Jersey.

As they sat out the war in the States (Ouspensky spending much of the time in New York writing and lecturing; Madame Ouspensky supervising the new community, teaching 'the movements' and gathering her own group of followers) the health of both of them started to deteriorate. Suffering some sort of existential crisis Ouspensky started to drink heavily, no doubt not helped by his wife's Parkinson's disease diagnosis. Back in Surrey, as the end of the war approached, those who had stayed behind awaited the return of the master with anticipation, seemingly unaware of his declining health and apparent spiritual malaise. While the Historico-Psychological Society negotiated with the Admiralty to get their premises at Collet Gardens de-requisitioned, Ouspensky delayed his return to England until January 1947. He returned to Lyne Place and became almost a recluse: staying in his room and limiting contact to his secretary, a Miss Quinn; Rodney Colin-Smith – who had become a close confidante during the years in America; and a collection of cats. A series of, what turned out to be, final meetings were arranged in London at which Ouspensky shocked his followers by renouncing his own teachings, claiming that there never was any 'system' and that they should all 'begin again, starting from what he or she really wanted'.

Piotr Demianovich Ouspensky died at Lyne Place on 2nd October 1947. He was buried in the churchyard of Holy Trinity Church at Botleys and Lyne and a memorial service was held at the Russian church in Pimlico. Lyne Place was later sold to the nearby Holloway Sanatorium that had become part of the new National Health Service. It was originally intended to be used to house staff, but in 1950 it was adapted for patients' accommodation. It has now been developed into luxury apartments.

Working out the Fourth Way

... the Fourth Way, the Way known to only a few people, although those who follow it go through life in the company of the rest of the world. They do not retire from the world: they simply live in the world but are not of the world. The teaching was carefully guarded in case it should fall into the wrong hands and become distorted, and this was how its original truth had been preserved intact, although it had taken many different outward manifestations, such as Gothic architecture, Alchemy, and the Art of Chivalry.

Maurice Nicoll outlining the ideas of Gurdjieff at a talk at Radcliffe Gardens, 9th September 1931

Dr Maurice Nicoll, a Harley Street psychologist who had studied with Gurdjieff at the Château Du Prieuré at Fontainebleau in France, was given permission to teach the 'system' in England by Ouspensky and for some years ran weekend courses and lectures at a Farmhouse at Rayne, near Braintree in Essex. Lakes Farm was the home of Miss C M Lydall who had also spent time at Le Prieuré in France and was godmother to the Nicolls' daughter Jane. The Nicoll family shared the house with Miss Lydall and from 1931 onwards members of Dr Nicoll's London study group came down for weekends at the farm on an invitation only basis.

The house itself was old and had a delightful atmosphere. Along the back wall a verandah had been built where all meals were served during the summer. A long trestle table covered with gaily coloured cloth and equally gay china looked so delightful that it was a pleasure to sit down and eat the food that Mrs Nicoll provided.[3]

Selene Moxon describing her first weekend at Lakes Farm

Gurdjieff's Work was an esoteric path to enlightenment, supposedly handed down from a mysterious Sarmoung Monastery. Originally shrouded in obscurity, partly due to secrecy surrounding it and partly due to unorthodox teaching methods utilised by Gurdjieff, the Work consisted of various techniques to be practiced by adherents with names such as: self remembering, self observation, conscious labour, intentional suffering. The aim was to wake the person from being constantly asleep.

This work is beautiful when you see why it exists and what it means. It is about liberation. It is as beautiful as if, locked for years in a prison, you see a stranger entering who offers you a key. But you may refuse it because you have acquired prison-habits and have forgotten your origin, which is from the stars.[4]

Maurice Nicoll

Miss Lydall died in February 1934 and bequeathed Lakes Farm to her goddaughter, Jane Nicoll. Soon after, Dr and Mrs Nicoll came up with a plan for building a house on the land next to the Lakes Farmhouse that would be suitable for carrying out the group activities that were by then attracting more and more people down to the farm at weekends. The new house would have large activity rooms on the ground floor with bedrooms above for the weekend guests. Plans for the building were drawn up by young architect George Kadleigh and the 'Work' weekends were transformed into spiritual self-build weekends.

Tyeponds Raynes near
Braintree, Essex

What I recall most clearly is the new feeling of sharing in the building of a house. Energy
was conducted through the single-minded way in which the group worked together,
inspired and directed by Dr Nicoll ... His presence inspired us as Gurdjieff's presence
had been the inspiration at Fontainebleau. The group found themselves discovering new
faculties, that had previously been unsuspected – nothing was impossible.

Beryl Pogson *Maurice Nicoll: A Portrait*

The group tackled pretty much the whole range of building works from digging
the foundations, putting up timber frames, to lath & plastering, carpentry and
even weaving their own stair carpets – almost the only work done by actual
builders was the thatching of the roof and the sinking of a well. The finished
house was named Tyeponds after the name of the field in which it stood. By the
time the house was ready to use, the group found that it wasn't now big enough
to house the numbers of people attending weekend 'Work' gatherings. It was
decided that a further house would be built, this time by a local builder in order
to make sure it was finished 'at the utmost possible speed'. This house, built at
right angles to Tyeponds, had one very large room covering the entire ground
floor with enough space for the group to practice Gurdjieff's Movements

... movements which include the sacred gymnastics of the esoteric schools, the religious ceremonies of the antique
Orient and the ritual movements of monks and dervishes – besides the folk-dances of many a remote community.
The movements are not only bewildering in their complexity, and amazing in the precision of their execution, but
rich in diversity, harmonious in rhythm, and exceedingly beautiful in the gracefulness of the postures, which are quite
unknown to Europe. To the accompaniment of mystical and inspiring music, handed down from remote antiquity, ...

***New York Times* 10 Feb 1924**

In the late 1930's, as well as weekend sessions at Tyeponds studying the Work
and learning the Movements, there were up to four meetings a week in London
for followers of Gurdjieff. Some were taken by Dr Nicoll himself, others were
run by senior members of the group. Occasionally they would join together
with the group run by Ouspensky after which they would at times end up
retiring to the Café Royal where they would talk late into the night. The
Munich crisis of 1938 prompted Maurice Nicoll to start work on a novel, to be
called *The Pelican Hotel*, that he hoped would help to prevent the outbreak of
war. It was the story of a time traveller arriving back in 1913 with knowledge of

the First World War and trying to prevent its outbreak. Before the novel was finished events would overtake Dr Nicoll and the group at Tyeponds. Whilst on holiday in Normandy in August 1939 with a small group of friends, one of the party received and urgent telegram from her husband, a Colonel Humphreys, urging the immediate return of the holidaymakers due to the imminent likelihood of the outbreak of war. The group rushed back to Essex where another military man, Colonel Maffett, had already started organising the digging of trenches in preparation for expected air raids.

We all thought that London would be bombed immediately. Friends came down in crowds and we found room for them all. Some brought their babies, others their dogs. Some came laden, feeling that they had left their homes for ever; others brought no possessions.

Beryl Pogson

Maurice Nicoll had always had in mind that Tyeponds would act as a refuge, or Ark, should Gurdjieff's predictions come to pass. As well as the members of his weekend groups and their families, the farm was allocated a large number of evacuees. These very quickly filled up the accommodation in the houses and further people were crammed in any available space. A group of a dozen or so expectant mothers were put up in the carpentry shed, the music room was turned in to a makeshift school room for the numerous child evacuees. The group rose to the task of looking after these 'guests'. Nicoll spent his own money on whatever was needed; prams for new mothers, extra stoves ... Numbers reached fifty within weeks, children were enrolled in the local school and more suitable accommodation was found for the pregnant women at Frinton. Numbers were further swollen at weekends as the group continued with the group work courses they had run before the outbreak of war. Life settled down for a few months until they were abruptly disturbed on 26th May 1940 by instructions that the area had been declared a military zone and that they had 24 hours to pack and leave the area. The group, who had been celebrating the wedding of two members at Rayne Parish church in the morning, hurriedly phoned friends and relatives trying to find alternative accommodation. The following day, as the group packed to leave, across the Channel the evacuation of the British Expeditionary Force from Dunkirk began.

A member of the group had found a house to rent in the Cotswolds and over the next few days the group made their way to The Knapp at Birdlip, a large Victorian house with grand views out over the Vale of Gloucester. The group settled into the house and within a short period of time the place was up and running pretty much as things had been back in Essex. Weekend group work was started up again and the group took over an empty pub, The King's Head, in the village to put up people coming over from London. Nicoll and the core of the group would remain at The Knapp for the rest of the war; running weekend groups, helping out with the local women's institute and spending evenings in the Royal George Inn talking with soldiers on leave. (Birdlip is only a few miles from the Whiteway Tolstoyan community, but there is no reference to the two groups having been in touch with each other.) At the end of the war Dr Nicoll and the group started to look for a place closer to London where he could set up and start teaching the 'Work' again. The Tyeponds house had been wrecked by the army and was unusable. It would take years of negotiation after the war to agree compensation for the damage caused. A house that seemed suitable was found to the north of London at Ugley near Bishop Stortford. The group didn't like the name of the house, Gauls Croft, and Dr Nicoll suggested

*Great Amwell House,
Great Amwell, near Ware*

that they rename it after a local field as at Tyeponds. A nearby field was known as Square Mead, however following the letter 'S' going astray in a telegram the house was renamed Quare Mead. As well as once again running weekend courses the small number of permanent residents started small-holding.

We were all interested at that time in the idea of keeping pigs and I said I would look after them. We bought four pigs. I liked them. They behaved rather like children and seemed good-tempered and happy. We also had chickens which I looked after, and some ducks. At that stage of the war we were all eager to produce as much food as possible.

Beryl Pogson

Being back close to London increased the number of people attending the weekend courses and after just over a year a decision was made to look for a larger property. The group believed that the universe responded to requests and soon after it had become apparent that they needed more space a friend drew their attention to an advertisement for a suitable house for sale. Great Amwell House was a substantial Georgian house in the little village of Great Amwell, near Ware. The group moved in on 4th September 1946 and continued to run courses until Nicoll's death in August 1953. Beryl Pogson, in her portrait of Nicholl published in the early 1960's, describes the Great Amwell period as 'one of completion', in which Nicoll continued to extend the teaching of the Work to a wider circle of people through running courses and giving lectures. He even found time to set up new groups in London and to concentrate on getting his writings published. Despite being diagnosed with cancer in 1951 he continued holding meetings at Amwell until a fortnight before he died.

He had always believed that groups of people, working together, came into incarnation together in different periods of time to play a part in developing a culture. His group had a part to play in the regeneration of the age. Those who had worked together on Monday would meet more quickly on Tuesday.

Beryl Pogson

*Remember that you are here to contend only with yourself
— thank everyone who gives you the opportunity.*

Written on the wall at Tyeponds

Getting the freedom from inside yourself

John Godolphin Bennett had spent the war years as head of Britain's first industrial research organisation, the British Coal Utilisation Research Association (BCURA). Tasked with finding a coal-based alternative to oil BCURA developed a coal-gas powered car, a coal-based plastic, and more efficient fireplaces that gave more heat for less fuel. The association was based at the seven-acre Coombe Springs estate at Kingston-upon-Thames in Surrey. At weekends the BCURA labs were used by Bennett to pursue his other work – that of exploring the teachings of the mystic G I Gurdjieff. Bennett had met the Armenian Mystic in 1920 in Turkey and had visited Gurdjieff's Institute at Fontainebleau, France and worked with Ouspensky to introduce Gurdjieff's ideas to England. Through running weekend courses Bennett became the focus for many of those interested in Gurdjieff's work and at the end of the war he was able to arrange to buy Coombe Springs with its Edwardian villa and research labs with plans to set up 'a small research community.' To do this he formed the somewhat official and academic sounding "Institute for the Comparative Study of History, Philosophy and the Sciences Ltd"

The aims of the institute: 'To promote research and other scientific work in connection with the factors which influence development and retrogression in man and their operation in individuals and communities; to investigate the origin and elaboration of scientific hypotheses and secular and religious philosophies and their bearing on general theories of Man and his place in the universe; and to study comparative methodology in history, philosophy and natural science.' – sound long-winded and convoluted today, perhaps deliberately so in order to present a respectable face to the outside world or echoing Gurdjieff's own Institute for the Harmonious Development of Man and Ouspensky's Historico-Psychological Society.

Coombe Springs, Kingston-On-Thames, Surrey

Bennett and his wife were joined at Coombe Springs by ten of his closest pupils including Elizabeth Mayall, George and Mary Cornelius and Hylda Field. These formed the core of the new 'research community' whose numbers were swelled at weekends by numerous visitors who came to study the ideas of Gurdjieff – and increasingly the ideas of other spiritual masters. The old BCURA labs were used as dormitories and were known as the 'fishbowl' because of the amount of glass they had. The main house was used for meetings as well as accommodation for the Bennett's. Later, a new building was added to provide 'superior' accommodation for guests. The events at Coombe Springs attracted a wide variety of seekers from spiritual, psychological and scientific backgrounds. Bennett believed that Gurdjieff's 'system' and the 'work' could be reconciled with modern science. His first book, *The Crisis in Human Affairs*, published in 1948, outlined his ideas on 'five-dimensional geometry' that included eternity as a second time dimension. He considered that humanity failed to see or understand the guiding intelligence behind human history because we suffered from what he called "eternity-blindness."

Throughout his life Bennett would be involved in a personal search for a place of 'withdrawal and concentration'. In 1948, fearing the possible collapse of civilisation and a further global war, Bennett and his friends started to look for a 'Noah's Ark', a place where they would be secure from political, economic and social turmoil. Somewhat strangely in retrospect, they looked to South Africa as a possible refuge. Bennett went to Africa to assess the feasibility of moving there and setting up an independent community. In South Africa he met the Prime Minister Jan Smuts, who was in the middle of issuing the *Fagan Report* that proposed relaxing the country's racial segregation laws, the reaction to which would usher in apartheid. Smuts was an intriguing character himself and criticised by many at the time for presiding over racist policies. He had been the architect of the League of Nations and wrote the preamble to the United Nations Charter. He was also the only person to have been a signatory to the charters of both these organisations. In 1926 Smuts had written a book on the concept of holism: the tendency in nature to form wholes that are greater than the sum of the parts through creative evolution. Smuts' pioneering ideas presented in *Holism and Evolution* would later be influential in Bennett's development of the concept of systematics. In the end it was decided that Africa was not 'the right place'. On his travels Bennett also visited Madame Ouspensky in America and after discovering that Gurdjieff had survived the war in Paris he renewed contact with the controversial mystic. In the following months something of a rapprochement occurs between Gurdjieff and many of his former followers. Bennett at this time was prepared to abandon everything, including Coombe Springs and his wife, if Gurdjieff demanded it. He made numerous trips to France introducing as many of his pupils as would come with him to the 'Master'. This led to him being named by Gurdjieff as his 'Representative for England'. He rushed to Paris when Gurdjieff died on October 29, 1949: 'Bennett came, he burst into such sobbing that he had to leave and go outside, where we could still hear him in the distance.' **5**

enneagram

In the following year Bennett was involved in attempts to bring together the different groups and individuals in England who were studying Gurdjieff's work under the direction of Henriette Lannes. He was also falsely accused of harbouring communists on his staff and was forced to resign his job with the mining company Powell Dufryn. Coombe Springs continued to attract visitors and new members, with the number of residents rising to 30. On returning from a trip to the Middle East in 1953 which took in Lebanon, Syria, Israel, Iraq and Turkey, where he made contact with various Sufi sects, Bennett was inspired to build a 'great hall' based on the gathering places of the Sufi Brotherhoods known as Tekke or Khanqahs. Instead of going for a building in any traditional architectural style, either eastern or western, it was decided to base the design of the new building on the mystical geometrical symbol of the enneagram, claimed by Gurdjieff to have great cosmic significance. The unique nine-sided fifty-foot-high hall was designed and built by Bennett and a group of architects led by Robert Whiffen. Construction work began in March 1956 and it would be six years before it was fully complete. In his autobiographical book, *Witness*, Bennett describes the design process '... The team formed itself. In addition to English residents at Coombe, we had Americans, Canadians, Australians, South Africans and a Norwegian. Whenever a specialist was needed, he appeared from somewhere. The work of the architects' group was out of the ordinary. Twelve to fifteen men, with sharply differing tastes and views on architecture, worked together without either pay or personal credit. 'No single feature was incorporated in the building that all did not accept. This sometimes meant waiting for weeks or months before some part of the building could go forward. I took some part in all this, but we were all convinced that no one person could do anything. The building seemed to have a plan and a purpose of its own, and all we could do was to wait until one part after another of the plan was revealed.'

Djamichunatra, Coombe Springs under construction

Money for the project was raised through loans from members of the Institute. The construction work was also carried out utilising the largely amateur building skills of the membership. A small team of residents was swollen at weekends with anything up to forty enthusiastic volunteers. The physical labour was incorporated as part of the spiritual 'Work' of the volunteers.

... As part of The Work Mr B made everything as difficult as possible. We had to dig and screen our own gravel for the concrete from within the grounds. At first he insisted we build a crane instead of hiring one. When this proved dangerous and unworkable, he allowed us to hire one, but only on condition that we erected it ourselves piece by piece. Our trust was exceeded only by our sincerity and commitment. We worked physically until we almost dropped from exhaustion and then continued on with our psychological exercises. We forged a brotherhood through sacrifice and common desperation—the need to remember ourselves. Every detail was constructed with loving care. Scrolls containing information about The Work were sealed into the large redwood frames for posterity.

Raymond van Sommers A life in Subud

The central axis of the hall was laid out so that it pointed to Gurdjieff's grave at Fontainebleau. The hall had three levels: a concrete base, signifying the material world; timber structure and walls, signifying the living world; and a copper roof, signifying the spiritual world. It had a sunken pentagonal floor and three windows designed by stained-glass artist Rosemary Rutherford. A wooden bench seating 80 people ran round the inside walls.

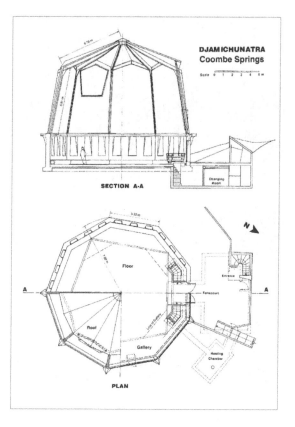

DJAMICHUNATRA
Coombe Springs

SECTION A-A

PLAN

Architects drawing of Djamichunatra, Coombe Springs

The Djamichunatra, or the 'Djamee' as it was affectionately known, was originally designed with the performance of Gurdjieff's movements in mind and was to have had an external staircase leading to a viewing balcony for spectators. However, by the time the building was ready to be used in 1957 Bennett had become interested in Subud. This was a spiritual path 'discovered' by an Indonesian, Bapak Muhammad Subuh, who had developed a following in Jakarta. Through mutual contacts Subuh was invited to Coombe Springs.

The main practice of Subud was the laitihan; Bennett thought that this was very close to what Gurdjieff had been trying to achieve, and the members of Coombe Springs were all offered the chance to be 'opened' – the name given to a person's first laitihan. This new spiritual path led to many of those involved in following Gurdjieff's ideas to come to Coombe Springs to take part in these 'openings'. Interest was further increased when at one event film star Eva Bartok experienced an allegedly miraculous recovery from ovarian cancer, a story that was splashed all over the newspapers. The papers also took an interest when one over enthusiastic participant ignored instructions not to practice the technique too often or on his own and got so carried away that he ended up in a trance-like state and died.

To accommodate use for laitihans. the floor in the Djamee was filled in and use of the building given over to Subud. In August 1959 Coombe Springs hosted the First Subud World Congress. Bennett became something of an international ambassador for Subud travelling to the United States, Australia and Far East with Pak Subuh and family and translating the bestselling *Concerning Subud*. In all, over 300 of Bennett's pupils were opened to Subud and the two years of activity at Coombe Springs would sow the seeds for a UK and Western Subud movement that continues to this day.

During these years the Institute became almost solely concerned with promoting Subud, at one time even proposing to forbid the sale of Gurdjieff's books at Coombe Springs. However, Bennett gradually came to his own conclusion that Subud on its own wasn't enough for him and resumed his Gurdjieffian work. This resulted in increasing conflict among the institute membership over whether you could combine Subud practices with other spiritual paths. The result of this conflict was that in 1962 a separate Subud organisation was formed and Bennett resumed his role as leader of the Coombe Springs Community. The Djamichunatra was finally finished, with its balcony and viewing gallery, and used as originally

envisaged for Gurdjieffian movements. Under Bennett's direction the practices at Coombe Spring would remain a mix drawn from Gurdjieff, Subud and other spiritual teachers such as Shivapuri Baba.

Many people passed through Coombe Springs over the years. If you wanted to join the community you were expected to have attended several 'work Sundays' before the question of becoming a member could be raised at a house meeting. Discussion at the meeting would centre around whether the applicant would benefit from becoming a resident or not; very few applications were turned down. This led to a very 'eclectic' membership.

There were many 'characters' I met at Coombe Springs, as I said, and some of them were near to crazy. I had a friend who had become schizophrenic, possibly through Subud, and spent his time in a hut doing weird paintings. There was a woman who I learned had tried while a teenager to bicycle to Hitler to stop the war, who lived in another building and was wont to scream at night. There was a heroin junkie and labourer who also did strange paintings (I remember him muttering at Bennett during a movements class to 'fuck off'). One day, the men were all agog when a soft porn actress called Dora Doll came to see Bennett about her personal problems! Perhaps the most strange of all was Karl Shaffer, a kind of playboy from America, whom Bennett for some unknown reason regarded as a son. **6**

Anthony Blake

Despite, or perhaps because of, this mix of membership many found their stay rewarding.

Living at Coombe Springs was, for me, a wonderful experience. The rituals of 5.00 am cold water ablutions in winter to midnight saunas only reinforced my zeal. I was young, strong and healthy. We practised sensing exercises – through relaxation and attention; self observation – through acts of self denial, and the movements. All these produced higher quality energies and improved awareness. Not that self-knowledge was always a happy experience.

Raymond van Sommers,
Coombe Spring resident 1956-8

Top to Bottom
Roof structure being built
Half-completed 'Djammee' at night
Completed building
Visit by architect Frank Lloyd Wright to view the
Djamichunatra

According to Angela Barker, who lived there in the early 1960's 'life at Coombe Springs was not quite so arduous as that at the Paris institute.' **7** The daily routine started at 7am with group exercise in the 'Djamee'. Some members worked outside the community while others ran the estate. After work the entire household assembled for dinner which was generally followed by classes in rhythmic movement, or meetings of various sub-groups which might be attended by visitors from London or other nearby groups. By 1966 the community had grown to about 70 members.

The last few years of the Coombe Springs community would be entangled with another self-styled guru who Bennett would take to. This time, however, with drastic consequences for the community. Idries Shah fitted the mould, created by Madam Blavatsky and Gurdjieff before him, of spiritual seeker turned teacher-guru after meetings with masters in the East. Shah's claims, however, have turned out to be harder to substantiate than those who trod the path before him – particularly in an age of increasing communications. Consequently he has attracted much controversy. Prior to his involvement with Bennett he had been working with Gerald Gardner as secretary at the Museum of Magic and Witchcraft on the Isle of Man, where, according to some versions of his life story, he ghost-wrote Gardner's autobiography *Gerald Gardner: Witch*. Shah had also become friends with the writer Robert Graves who had encouraged him to write a book on Sufism. Shah then became interested in Gurdjieffian groups active in England. In a claim reminiscent of those made by Blavatsky and Gurdjieff, Shah claimed that during a period in this early life when he had been travelling he had made direct contact with Sufi Masters at the Sarmoung Monastery in Afghanistan, which was supposedly the source of Gurdjieff's ideas. Shah convinced Bennett that he was a genuine emissary of the 'The Inner Circle of Humanity'. This led to an extraordinary turn of events. At a special meeting of the Institute in October 1965 Bennett persuaded the membership to hand over Coombe Springs lock stock and barrel to Shah. By early the following year the property had been transferred to Shah and all community members were asked to leave. Soon after taking over the estate Shah threw a huge three-day themed fancy dress party (based on his Mullah Nasruddin books) for 500 guests in order to 'deconsecrate' the premises. Windows in the main House were remodelled to allow guests to circulate; pavilions were erected on the lawns; large cartoons of Shah himself hung overhead; there were belly dancers, jugglers and a 'genuine Afghan band'. Shortly after the party Shah sold Coombe Springs, reputedly for £100,000, to a developer who would build luxury homes on the site. The whole estate was flattened: the main house, the 'fishbowl' labs, the amazing Djamichunatra ... everything bar the listed well house. Shah used the proceeds from the sale of Coombe Springs to set up his own spiritual centre at Langton House in Langton Green, near Tunbridge Wells where he continued to run courses for many years.

... we were asked individually to complete a survey which included the question, What do you think Coombe Springs is? I answered that it was a spiritual supermarket, you paid your money and took your choice. Whereas leaders of other groups focussed on a single discipline, Mr Bennett was predisposed to 'try anything', and in later life even became a Catholic. Like me, perhaps, he was always looking for an authoritative and authentic tradition to which he could commit, and never found it. Or perhaps he discovered that no such tradition existed, and that all traditions were equal in efficacy.

Alan Tunbridge, Coombe Spring resident 1966

Bennett continued his spiritual research work through the Institute and following celebrations on the theme of 'The Whole Man', arranged for its

twenty-fifth anniversary in April 1971, Bennett decided that he would attempt to continue Gurdjieff's work and set up his own School of the Fourth Way. To do this he bought the rambling semi-derelict Sherborne House in the Cotswolds that had been used previously as a boys' school and, in October 1971 with the help of his wife and several assistants, he launched the International Academy for Continuous Education. Bennett thought that the old world was likely to disintegrate before the end of the twentieth century, but that the seeds of a new world could be nurtured in experimental communities and that the Academy could be a place where people who were starting to become aware of the coming changes could be 'trained to perceive, to understand, and to withstand the strains of the world process.' To do this, a year-long course was devised utilising Gurdjieffian techniques and ideas alongside material from other sources.

The derelict state of Sherborne House provided plenty of work for the trainees: cooking, washing, and heating facilities were inadequate, and much had to be improvised. Students who had fancied themselves in for a few months of utopian dalliance in agreeable countryside surroundings were rudely awakened. Uncomfortable conditions, hard physical work, lectures, the Gurdjieff movements, discussions, psychological exercises, and conflict were the order of the day. The First Course lasted some ten months; Bennett graduated his first class, whom he encouraged to return home and share what they had learned with small groups.

Eric Tamm in *Robert Fripp – From King Crimson to Crafty Master*

Bennett oversaw two further year-long courses in the following years as part of a five-year program after which his intention was to invite back the best pupils, 'those who have shown themselves capable of transmitting what they have learned', and take the 'next step' with them. It would seem that the next step was to be some kind of self-sufficient community made up of Sherborne graduates. Due to the increasing price of land in England Bennett started to look to the USA as a possible location for a community that could continue his work. At the fourth annual course started at Sherborne in October 1974 an agreement was signed between the Institute and The Claymont Society to lend them $100,000 to enable the purchase of Claymont Court, a farm and mansion on four hundred acres in the Shenandoah Valley, Jefferson County, West Virginia for the foundation of a psychokinetic community. Bennett would see neither the end of the five-year programme at Sherborne nor the development of the community in the States. He died aged 77 on December 13th 1974. Sherborne House continued with the fourth and fifth courses of its five-year programme after its founder's death, but no long-term community was to emerge from its work in the UK. The converted stable block was used from 1978 onwards by the Beshara Trust. A childhood friend of Bennett's, Pierre Elliot, who had also worked with both Gurdjieff and Ouspensky, was chosen to head the American Society for Continuous Education based at Claymont where they would endeavour to carry out Bennett's vision without the help of his guidance. Claymont has published many of Bennett's works, and holds a collection of his taped lectures. The community/school is known today for its distinctive ideas around early childhood development and education. Bennett's ideas have continued to be influential long after his death. Rock guitarist Robert Fripp, who attended the fifth Sherborne course, used Bennett's ideas to set up his 'Guitar Craft' school and samples of Bennett speaking appear on his 1979 solo recording 'Exposure'. Anthony Blake, one of Bennett's leading pupils and editor of his published works, served as a consultant on the 1990 'Biosphere II' project.

Continuous Education is founded on the principle that human beings are capable of unlimited self-perfecting from birth to death and beyond. Self-perfecting is three-fold: bodily, mental and spiritual. It gives meaning to our lives as individuals; but there is also a continuous education of the human race to enable us to become truly human ... It is hoped that the project at Claymont will be the forerunner of similar communities in other parts of the USA and also in Europe, it may also be possible to help in the development of a prosperous village life in the developing countries, nearly all of which are threatened by the flight from the land. If mankind is to have a future, it must be based on respect and love for our Mother Nature

J G Bennett A Call for a New Society, Sherborne House November 1974

A Gurdjieffian Diaspora

In the later post-war years, as those who had had direct contact with Gurdjieff became fewer, a second generation of followers emerged to carry on the Work. Madame Ouspensky would keep the faith in New York, continuing to promote the Movements, and Jane Heap, another pupil of Gurdjieff, would inspire Annie Lou Staveley to set up Two Rivers Farm near Aurora, Oregon. Rodney Colin-Smith and his wife Janet set up their own group in a large house in Tlalpam, Mexico where they gathered a number of friends, mainly from England and began introducing the Work to a South American audience through Colin-Smith's own writing and Spanish translations of Ouspensky's and Nicoll's works. In 1951 the group began building what is now known as the Planetarium of Tetecala on a site in the mountains behind Mexico City. Back in England Beryl Pogson took up the reins after the death of Maurice Nicoll and continued to run regular meetings and quarterly residential groups at a large house, known as 'The Dicker', in the village of Upper Dicker in Sussex. At Collet House in London, Dr Francis Roles held together the small band of Ouspenskyites still active in the Work. This diaspora would transmit the System and the Work on to another generation either through direct contact or through a myriad of publications, some obscure, others highly influential. One 'pupil' who had regularly attended courses at Great Amwell was the economist Fritz Schumacher. He was at the beginning of the spiritual journey that would lead to his concept of Buddhist economics and the publication *Small is Beautiful*. Another was the theatre director Peter Brook who studied with Jane Heap for over a decade and went on to make a film in 1979 based on Gurdjieff's *Meetings With Remarkable Men*. The extent of this influence was seen by Andrew Rigby when interviewing communards in the late 1960's and early 1970's.

... in communes, one finds young people ... who have embarked upon a self-imposed course of study of the writings of mystics of previous ages, such as Gurdjieff, Ouspensky, Blavatsky and Steiner.

Alternative Realities: A study of Communes and their Members

Space guru of East Grinstead

Scientology is basically the explosion of Dianetics (a mental therapy fad of the 50's) into mail order mysticism, spiked with heady overtones of space opera and revolution. Its students find it hard to define. Religion, psychology and philosophy, it claims to 'have the answers' to every timeless query, from the causes of insanity to the life force of tomatoes, with footnotes on flying saucer design and the history of the last 75 trillion years. Much is window dressing of course, but only if you pay £2000 and go the whole route will you know which is not.

Nick Robinson ex-scientologist writing in *International Times* 55 April 1969

The Georgian Saint Hill Manor House on the edge of East Grinstead in Sussex was purchased from the Maharajah of Jaipur in March 1959 by ex-pulp science fiction writer and inventor of Dianetics, Dr L Ron Hubbard. During the war the house had been rented by Elaine Laski, daughter of Simon Marks and heiress to the Marks & Spencer fortune. She was treasurer of the Refugee Children's Movement that helped settle children who came over as part of the Kindertransport. She used part of Saint Hill as a convalescent home for the so-called Guinea Pig Club – badly burned Battle of Britain pilots who were patients of the pioneer plastic surgeon Sir Archibald McIndoe at the nearby Queen Victoria Hospital. The townsfolk of East Grinstead got so used to the 'Guinea Pigs', the strangers with reconstructed faces, that it became known as the 'town that didn't stare.' The reaction to the new owner of Saint Hill was initially positive. The *East Grinstead Courier* referred to Dr Hubbard as a 'man whose work for humanity is known throughout the world' and carried a picture of Hubbard and his family alongside details of his previous career. The estate consisted of fifty acres of grounds, a lake, an outdoor swimming-pool and extensive greenhouses. The house included a marble-columned ballroom, eleven bedrooms and eight bathrooms. By August there was a hint that Dr Hubbard might have plans for more than a family home at Saint Hill. The *Courier* was again invited to cover the story. Utilising the estate's greenhouses 'nuclear scientist, Dr Hubbard' was reported to be carrying out experiments that would revolutionise gardening. He claimed to be growing exceptional tomato plants by treating seeds with 'radioactive rays' and warding off mildew by using infra-red lamps. This news attracted the attention of the magazine *Garden News* who sent a reporter down to Sussex to cover the story – in the ensuing article entitled 'Plants Do Worry and Feel Pain' **8** Dr Hubbard, 'the revolutionary horticultural scientist' told readers that he was convinced that plants felt pain because when he attached an E-meter

Saint Hill

to a geranium with crocodile clips and tore off its leaves the needle on the meter moved. By this time the national press and TV had become interested in the story and pictures of Hubbard poking electrodes into tomatoes appeared. Hubbard later explained that his experiments to produce 'ever-bearing tomato plants and sweetcorn plants' were in order to 'reform the world's food supply'.[9] Quite whether the horticultural experiments were a front for, or at least a diversion from, Hubbard's main purpose for the Saint Hill estate is hard to tell. But certainly the people of East Grinstead were unaware of the 'Doctor's' other plans – to establish the world headquarters of The First Church of Scientology of which Hubbard was the founder and leader. The 'Church' had been formally

Dr L Ron Hubbard – 'the revolutionary hoticultural scientist

established in America in 1954. Becoming a religious organisation bestowed various practical advantages both on the tax and regulation front, both of which Hubbard was keen on. Scientology had grown out of Dianetics, a psychotherapy that Hubbard had devised in the early 1950's. Some of the early claims for the therapy seem now to border on the claims of quack doctors: 'will cure any insanity not due to organic destruction of the brain.' – 'gives any man a perfect, indelible, total memory, and perfect, errorless ability to compute his problems.' – 'a technique for curing – not alleviating – ulcers, arthritis, asthma, and many other non-germ diseases.' – 'A totally new conception of the truly incredible ability and power of the human mind.' But Hubbard had carried out fairly extensive research and the therapy clearly worked for some participants. Hubbard's lack of any medical qualification and the early promotion of Dianetics through *Astounding*, the pulp science fiction magazine, seems to have made it hard for him to be taken seriously by the medical establishment. By the time Hubbard arrived in Britain, Dianetics had evolved a number of techniques or 'processes' that were aimed at making the person receiving the therapy get 'clear', that is clear from unwanted barriers that inhibit a person's natural abilities. The main process was

Hubbard's Electropsychometer or E-meter

called Auditing – this involved sets of questions asked, or directions given, by an auditor to a subject, known as a preclear, during which the subject was connected to a device called the Hubbard Electropsychometer or simply the E-Meter. This was a version of a lie-detector which measured changes in electrical resistance through a pair of tin-plated tubes held by the preclear and attached to the meter by wires.

In March 1960 some of Hubbard's cover was blown in East Grinstead when the publishing of *Have You Lived Before This Life?* (which detailed 'actual case-histories' of reincarnation and past-life histories) caused a storm of controversy in the town. The book contained some forty-one stories that had been collected from participants in auditing sessions at the Church's Fifth London Advanced Clinical Course in 1958. The past-lives recalled in the book range from the ordinary through to the simply odd and strange – a woman who had been a lion who ate its keeper, the historic – a man who was a Roman soldier who had strangled his wife, killed a slave and been killed by a lion in an arena, to the utterly fantastic – the scientologist who fell out of a spaceship 55 trillion years ago and became a manta ray fish.

By now the Hubbards were well settled in at the Manor:

The former billiards room, leading directly from the grand entrance hall, had been re-modelled into Hubbard's private office, with a bench seat upholstered in red leather down one side of the room and a personal teleprinter … Upstairs, Hubbard had his own suite comprising a sitting-room, bedroom and bathroom, adjoining Mary Sue's office, bedroom and bathroom. The children had bedrooms at the other end of the house and the 'Monkey Room', named after the murals painted by John Spencer Churchill, was converted into a school-room and equipped with trampoline. Apart from the kitchen, most of the remaining rooms in the manor were used as offices.

Russell Miller, *The Bare-faced Messiah*

Early in 1961 the launch of the 'Saint Hill Special Briefing Course' was announced, costing £250 per person for auditors who wished to train with Hubbard himself. The course was slow to take off, but as it offered that Hubbard would personally 'discover and assess with the aid of an E-meter each student's goal for this lifetime' students soon started to arrive from around the world – some, like retired businessman Reg Sharpe, were so enamoured by Scientology that he bought a house in the adjoining village of Saint Hill. In order to accommodate the increasing numbers of visitors coming on the Briefing Course Hubbard had the greenhouses demolished to make way for a 'chapel' that was used as a lecture hall and began construction of other buildings on the estate all without any thought to obtaining planning permission from the local authority. Such was the initial success of the Briefing Course that just after Christmas 1961 Hubbard embarked on a speaking tour of America where he did twice-a-night speaking appearances with all the razzmatazz and showbiz glitz that he could muster. Often appearing in a gold lamé jacket, his speaking skill and charisma were such that he could hold an audience for hours. The result of the tour was that hundreds of young Americans headed for the Mecca of Scientology at East Grinstead. This American invasion caused some concern to members of the local Council who urged that the planning situation at the Manor be sorted out. The Scientologists' response was to put in an application to build a seventy-five-room administration centre in the grounds of the manor and Hubbard issued a document entitled a 'Report to the Community' in which he announced that as a result of his experiments on plants and 'living energies' he was able to extend an individual's lifespan by up to 25 years. It is hard to know what anybody in the town made of the increasingly strange pronouncements that were issuing forth from the Manor and many of them were likely to be unaware that the Manor was the centre of an international organisation with branches on three continents. They were probably also unaware that the FBI were paying close attention to the comings and goings in the little Sussex town. As well as being suspicious of Scientology's claims to be a Church, the US authorities may have had cause to be alarmed by instruction from Hubbard to his American branches to do everything they could to prevent Richard Nixon from becoming president and later offers to President Kennedy to help with the space race by putting astronauts through a Scientology training program.

The authorities in England would prove to be as suspicious of Scientology as their American counterparts and Hubbard found it was not as easy to register as a bona-fide church in the UK and so claim the tax and regulation privileges that the group had in the US. He turned his sights on Australia as the candidate to be the first 'clear' continent. The authorities in Australia proved to be even more hostile to the group than those in other countries and fairly quickly a government board of inquiry was set up into the group's activities that pulled no punches when its findings were published in October 1965:

'There are some features of Scientology which are so ludicrous that there may be a tendency to regard Scientology as silly and its practitioners as harmless cranks. To do so would be gravely to misunderstand the tenor of the Board's conclusions ... Scientology is evil; its techniques evil; its practice a serious threat to the community, medically, morally and socially; and its adherents sadly deluded and often mentally ill.'

Australian Board of Inquiry into Scientology

On the back of the damning Government report, Australian states began passing legislation outlawing Scientology and back in England a call was made in the House of Commons for a British Inquiry into the group's activities. Amid what was starting to seem like a witch hunt Hubbard, still searching for a country that would provide a 'safe environment' for Scientology, now turned to Rhodesia. Hubbard had two reasons for choosing the troubled African country: firstly he believed that in a previous life he had been Cecil Rhodes and planned to try to recover gold and diamonds he was convinced Rhodes had buried somewhere in Rhodesia, and secondly he believed that Scientology could provide the answers to Rhodesia's problems. In the spring of 1966 Hubbard travelled out to Rhodesia and started negotiating to buy a large property in Salisbury and a Hotel on the banks of Lake Kariba which he planned to use as a base from which to spread the influence of Scientology in the country. He wrote a new constitution for the country which (whilst maintaining white supremacy) would, he hoped, satisfy the demands of the black majority population. He sent his proposal to both Rhodesian leader Ian Smith and the British Prime Minister Harold Wilson and, after it received a polite but very definite rejection, Hubbard began a series of increasingly desperate attempts to curry favour with the deeply conservative white society. This culminated in an invitation to address the Rotary Club in Bulawayo, which did not go at all well and resulted in him being told in no uncertain terms by the Department of Immigration that he must leave the country. Still expressing surprise that he was not welcome – and putting down his expulsion to a communist plot – Hubbard returned to England where a hurriedly organised Welcome Home party of 600 Scientology students was bussed down to Heathrow to greet their returning leader.

Back in East Grinstead the rapid expansion of the activities at Saint Hill and in the town was causing increasing disquiet among the residents. Through the group's Tottenham Court Road office they were attracting an increasing number of people both from the counter-culture and 'straight' society and Saint Hill started to become an odd combination of extended hippie commune and World Headquarters of what many were starting to see as a dangerous cult. The group also started to expand its activities into the surrounding area. Alan Larcombe of the *East Grinstead Courier* reported that 'There was a lot of resentment and alarm in the town. People felt that Scientology could not be allowed to continue expanding. There was a feeling they were trying to take over – an estate agent; dentist; hairdresser; jeweller; finance company; as well as a couple of doctors; were all Scientology-run. People didn't like it.' Seemingly faced with hostility wherever he turned, Hubbard, in a stroke of real imagination, decided that there was a place where he could be free from government interference, in fact 75 percent of the earth's surface was completely free from the control of any government: the high seas. He started to lay plans to move his operations permanently off-shore.

'Apollo' – one of three ships used to establish The Sea Org
Inset: Commodore Hubbard is on the right

The accounts of the activities of the *Sea Org* read like a strange and slightly surreal combination of Scientology Sea Cadets meet James Bond villains whilst on Indiana Jones-type missions for lost treasure with a bit of Flash Gordon thrown in for good measure. A well-dressed but decidedly motley crew sailed the seas searching variously for a Roman Tax collector's hidden hoard off the coast of Calabria, a Corsican space station, a Carthaginian priest's hidden treasure trove of jewels and gold – all of which Hubbard claimed to have knowledge of from previous lives. The regime aboard the ships would become increasing hierarchical extending Hubbard's control freak tendencies and introducing various levels of Scientologists with the most trusted being 'the messengers' who would go on to control the organisation in later years. The *Sea Org* period continued for nearly a decade with the Commodore and his crew finally coming ashore in 1975 in a return to America.

In 1968 the British Government, growing increasingly nervous about the activities of the Scientologists, started to refuse visas to students wishing to study at Saint Hill and, in effect, refusing to let Hubbard back into the UK.

The group carried on developing the Manor during the *Sea Org* years, constructing a purpose-built student training block in the form of a mock-Norman castle behind the main manor house. They also spread out in East Grinstead, establishing a number of communal houses in the area. Over the years the group has been attacked for some of its more cult-like behaviour and it has reacted with what have appeared like paranoid and ultra defensive tactics: setting up its own 'Guardian office' to defend the group by taking legal action against critics and hounding individual authors and ex-members who have spoken out. In 1980 Hubbard disappeared from public view with, it is rumoured, only a handful of senior Scientologists ever seeing him again. In seclusion he worked on a ten-volume science fiction series entitled *Mission Earth*. With Hubbard officially no longer in charge, the group went through a number of years of turmoil with revelations being made of criminal activities being carried out by the 'Guardian office'.

The Church went through a difficult period. Because of the rigid systems laid down by Hubbard in his literally thousands of bulletins, it was easy for Scientologists to find fault with and inform on each other, and ... many senior people, who had devoted their lives and energies to Scientology, were 'busted' to much lower positions. Many left the Church.

David Barrett The New Believers

Out of this period emerged a new leadership drawn from the Commodore's Messenger Organisation, a trusted grouping within the *Sea Org* who have controlled the organisation ever since. L Ron Hubbard died in January 1986 and the organisation internationally has been run from its American headquarters in California. They have continued to be dogged by controversy. Saint Hill is still a major centre for the Scientologists and they claim close to 100,000 members in the UK[10] (although in the 2001 census for England only 1,781 people answered that they were Scientologists to the voluntary question on religion).

Internationally there are number of organisations run by, or with close links to, Scientology including the Religious Technology Center, ABLE – The Association for Better Living and Education, CCHR – the Citizens Commission on Human Rights and WISE – The World Institute of Scientology Enterprises.

We've been here in East Grinstead for something like 30 years. If there was something sinister or illegal going on, don't you think the police would have done something?

Peter Mansell, director of public affairs at Saint Hill
Evening Argus (Brighton), 28th March 1994

The most complete story of Ron Hubbard's life is told in
Bare Faced Messiah by Russell Miller

From compulsive analysis to best friends

IS there no way out, no escape from the vicious circle,
no way to exorcise the lurking demons of our troubled souls?
Are we shackled forever to these strangers of the dark?
Or is there, somewhere, if we can find the switch,
a light that floods the murky corners of the mind,
reveals the shadowed faces from the pit and casts them out?

From: Handout advertising 'Empathic Sessions' in London circa 1967

In 1963, two Scientology students, Robert de Grimston Moor and Mary Ann McClean, studying to be 'auditors' at L Ron Hubbard's Institute of Scientology on Fitzroy Street in London's West End decided to branch out on their own. Combining Hubbard's ideas with those of breakaway Freudian analyst Alfred Adler, the two created their own therapy system which they named Compulsions Analysis. Robert, a former cavalry officer with the King's Royal Hussars, had been studying to be an architect at Regent Street Polytechnic. After trying their ideas out on some of his college friends they started to run their own sessions, eventually setting themselves up in business in their apartment in Wigmore Street. The two budding new therapists married and Mary Ann persuaded Robert to drop his surname and become Robert De Grimston as she thought this sounded more impressive. The two were very different characters: Robert was 'Tall, handsome, dreamy and charismatic' while Mary Ann, described variously as 'Manipulative, demanding and volatile' and a 'baleful woman', was the power behind the throne, directing operations. Her background was starkly different from Robert's: born in Glasgow in 1931, the story of how she came to be studying Scientology in London in the early 1960's is somewhat hazy. She was said to have been abandoned by her parents and brought up by relatives in poverty: she seems to have emigrated to America in the 1950's where she claimed to have been married for a short while to the boxer Sugar Ray Robinson, a liaison not recorded in any biography

Entrance to 2 Balfour Place, Mayfair, London

of the boxer. She reappears back in London in the early 60's where it is rumoured she was a high-class call-girl with possible connections to the Profumo affair. By 1964 the pair were running a twice-weekly 'Communication Course' and through Robert's network of friends: young architects, artists, scientists, economists and the like, they quite quickly built up a group of some thirty followers who had all gone through what the couple called 'the process'.

New people were signing up for sessions and becoming part of the group. All this gave us the feeling we were onto something big and inevitable. We had come home. We felt part of a special family setting off together on a great inner journey of discovery ...

Timothy Wyllie

This strong group bonding led to the group feeling a sense of shared spirituality and sometime in 1965 the name of the group was changed from Compulsions Analysis to simply The Process. Using one member's inheritance they rented a large house in Mayfair at 2 Balfour Place as their headquarters. Plans were drawn up to convert the interior of Balfour Place as a sort of therapy centre cum luxury residence for Robert and Mary Ann. At some point it became obvious that other members should move in and the group became a communal household. They used the smaller rooms on the upper floors as men's and women's dormitories; all somewhat spartan, with members sleeping six to a room on the floor in sleeping bags. At this time Mary Ann and Robert acquired six large Alsatian dogs. The group started to attract critical attention from the press and from the parents of some of the younger members who were disturbed by what their children might be getting into. One family took the group to court to try and get their son back – at the court hearing R D Laing appeared as a witness for The Process.

Sometime in the next year the De Grimstons decided that they would look for an island retreat for their new group, and in June 1966 Mary, Robert, eighteen Processans and six Alsatian dogs headed out to Nassau in the Bahamas to try and purchase a Caribbean island. When the first deal fell through the group moved on to Mexico, eventually settling on an estate they managed to rent at a place called Xtul near Sisal on the Yucatan coast. The property consisted of four miles of seashore, a palm-tree jungle, a lagoon and the roofless, gutted, stone remains of an old salt works. Word was sent back to England and they were joined by most of the rest of the group. Some of those who thought they were about to leave England forever sold all their personal belongings to pay for the air-fare. In an intense few months on the Mexican coast the group would start to formulate its own alternative theology through a series of meditations during which they were in contact with 'Beings' who would answer questions put to them and give the group guidance. It was through guidance from the 'Beings' that the group had been led to the abandoned salt works.

The Beings in our group meditations or Circles were really what anybody thought their own individual inspiration was. It was a bit nebulous. You also got a sense of this in some poetry in which people are talking to, or relating to an outside being – a disembodied being, a spirit of something.
The great thing about this, I think, is that whatever I might say about it, it made people formulate questions and create dialogue and that was what was interesting ...

Malachi McCormack

The questions and answers from the 'Beings' were written down by Robert and formed The Xtul Dialogues. The questions ranged from 'What is Money?', to which the answer was 'Money is the most solid manifestation of physical responsibility.' (Xtul Dialogue VI) through to 'Is there more than one universe?' – 'Yes. On various levels there are many universes, but they are only part of the One True Universe, which exists on all levels'. (Xtul Dialogue ll). Xtul was a strange, somewhat eerie and magical place for the group, but their time there came to an abrupt end when Hurricane Inez hit the Yucatan on 7th October 1966. The full force of the storm narrowly missed the Xtul area and the little group sheltered under tarpaulins in the ruins of the salt works whilst coconut trees were ripped up and pieces of masonry flew through the air above them. Relieved to have survived, the group helped local villagers to repair

their houses and fed themselves on Mexican Government relief supplies.

We phoned our relieved parents for tickets back to London and returned bronzed, healthy with uncut long hair halfway down our backs and convinced that we had been saved by the Beings for important and mysterious tasks ahead.

Timothy Wyllie

Back at Balfour Place, the group embarked on a new phase of development led by Mary Ann and Robert. They opened a coffee bar in the basement (briefly named 'Satan's Cavern'), adopted a uniform and their own symbol. This was designed by Robert, consisting of four Ps joined in a kind of mandalic wheel, and bearing an uncanny resemblance to a Nazi swastika. They also started to produce their own themed magazine for sale on the streets of London. The first issue on The Common Market was also sent to every Member of Parliament. Through regular street selling sessions, members of The Process would encourage people they met to attend informal meetings, film shows and therapy sessions at Balfour Place. One person who was intrigued enough to go along was the future author of Alternative London: Nicholas Saunders.

It was extremely intense. Everything was very disciplined and punctual. You arrived there early so it could start on the dot of 7am. Then there were three hours of pretty intense exercises done in pairs. Normally you would sit facing someone else in the group, knees touching, looking straight into their eyes. You'd do things like trying to embarrass the other person. The idea was that you should be able to feel hurt but still accept it, feel embarrassed and still accept it. You shouldn't cut yourself off from your feelings.

Nicholas Saunders in *Days in the Life*

The Process also targeted the new celebrities of swinging London, trying to recruit the likes of Paul McCartney, Mick Jagger and Marianne Faithfull.

Because of my father I was quite open to ideas of group mind and power ... I grew up on a commune, so had already been exposed to ideas of this sort. All I did was an interview for their magazine. I was attracted to them at first, mostly because they took me seriously, when nobody else did. The Process people were very admiring of me. They must have recognised that I have got magical powers. All through my life people like this have been trying to get their hands on me. I thought I was being quite sophisticated, but the boys – Mick, Christopher (Gibbs) and the others told me I had made a mistake. On one level it was a bit like The Prisoner – all these handsome young men in turtle necks ...

Marianne Faithfull

The group also held public events and talks with a variety of speakers on what they hoped would be controversial topics. One speaker was Desmond Leslie, cousin to Winston Churchill, Spitfire pilot and co-author of *Flying Saucers have Landed*, who spoke of his contact with extraterrestrial beings. On another night there was a demonstration of self-flagellation and on another a staged theatrical performance in which the Pope debated the pro and cons of Black and White Magic with Aleister Crowley. In the spring of 1967 Mary Ann and Robert embarked on a tour of the Middle East during which Robert wrote two apocalyptic tracts *As It Is* and *A Candle in Hell*. Through these two books and the alternative theology laid out in them the group would complete the journey from therapy-based community to millennial sect. The crux of these ideas was that if God had exhorted us to love thy enemies it followed that we should love Satan as well as Christ. This idea developed into a 'processean theology' in which Jehovah, Lucifer, Satan and Christ are given equal importance. The De Grimstons also developed a strict hierarchy within the group with themselves at the top as the 'Omega' surrounded by a loyal band of initiates who controlled access to the leaders and who issued edicts and orders to the membership. There was also an expansion of the pack of Alsatian dogs; as members of the hierarchy were given their own dog until the group had a pack of over 20 dogs living with them. All money and possessions were handed over to the group when a member joined and all earnings were handed over and 'passed up' to the Omega who started to live a life of considerable luxury. This was justified in the name of 'trickle up' economics.

Only the best for them we would say, encouraged by Robert's trickle-up economic theory that by passing money up to them we would in some way create a vacuum which would suck new money in at the bottom. Thus all would benefit ...

Timothy Wyllie

Towards the end of 1967 plans were afoot to expand the group operations across the Atlantic and a small number of members who had not returned with the rest of the group from Mexico, but had moved up to New Orleans, started the first American 'Chapter' of The Process on Royal Street in the French Quarter. Soon after Mary Ann and Robert moved to New Orleans and by the end of the year a second Chapter was being established in San Francisco. In a move paralleling Ron Hubbard's Church of Scientology the group was incorporated as The Process Church of the Final Judgement.

Process Church ceremony

The new 'church' was then faced with having to justify their official status by creating their own rituals, prayers and church services, or 'Celebrations'. Tabards with a dark red Process symbol on the front were made for 'priests' and 'priestesses' to wear. A room in each Chapter was set aside for services and all members were given new names which began with Father, Mother, Sister or Brother such and such.

THE PROCESS
CHURCH OF THE FINAL JUDGEMENT

The USA proved much more fertile ground for an apocalyptic millennial sect than had swinging London, and throughout 1968 the 'Church' expanded its American operations and ventured into continental Europe, establishing Chapters in Germany and Italy. By the early seventies they had closed Balfour Place and relocated the headquarters to the States. The history of The Process in the US is a tale of an almost classic hippie-era quasi-Christian cult. On the one hand they presented a public face of 'a well-ordered community with a theologically dense but provocative belief system and psychologically well-adjusted and dedicated members' [11] doing good deeds in the wider community. They operated free clothing stores and free food kitchens. Chapters took on a whole variety of community projects and received grants from local and state government agencies. They responded to natural disasters alongside the Red Cross and the Salvation Army, did home visits to the elderly, blind and mentally handicapped and set up prison ministries. Two Chapters formed their own rock groups to take the Process message out to a wider audience. They ordained women as priests, performed wedding ceremonies, baptisms and ordinations, and opposed the Vietnam War.

We were the Foundation Faith of the New Millennium and together, as a microcosm of humanity, we would heal the pain and cruelty of the world. We were archetypes of the human family and as we healed ourselves and served God's will, so the world would be healed ...

Ruth Strassberg (Sister Sarah)

On the other hand they became subject to attack from various anti-cult organisations and were 'exposed' in a number of books. In *The Family*, a book on the Manson murders by Ed Sanders, it was alleged that Charles Manson had been a member of The Process. Despite Manson himself denying it and the sect winning a legal battle and having the chapter that made the allegation removed from later editions of the book, the group have never quite managed to shake off the slur. Other critical books were published on the group in 1978. In *Satan's Power: A Deviant Psychotherapy Cult* sociologist William Bainbridge, who had infiltrated one of the Process Chapters, gave a somewhat more balanced account of the cult, thinly disguised as The Power, with names and places changed. In *Love, Sex, Fear, Death*, written by ex-Process member Timothy Wyllie and published in 2009 with contributions from other ex-members of the sect, there is finally an insider's account of the group through most of the years of its existence. This account shines a light into some of the darker corners of the group's activities and shows that there was much cause for concern, if not quite those things that the more sensationalist headlines would have you believe.

Many lies have been told about The Process over time – that we were murderers and cannibals, that we sacrificed dogs and children in hideous black masses, that we inducted new members by demanding they participate in sexual orgies, that we were 'mindbenders' and 'brainwashers', that we set up and inspired Charles Manson. The list is endless. And none of it is true.

Timothy Wyllie

Wyllie does acknowledge that the leadership manipulated the membership both psychologically and, in some instances, sexually: arranging sexual liaison between members and presiding over compulsory group orgies. He also regrets that at times they treated their dogs better than they did their children.

The final incarnation of The Process had its roots in Mary Ann De Grimston's long held anti-vivisectionist beliefs and love of animals (hence the pack of Alsatians). For some years the group had been taking in strays and unwanted pets and caring for them on a ranch in Arizona. In 1984 the group purchased 2,269 acres in the Kanab Canyon in southern Utah to establish an animal refuge. They named the new home Angel Canyon. Over the years the Best Friends Animal Sanctuary has grown to be the biggest animal refuge in the States, housing some 1500 rescued animals. They acquired additional land in the area and leased a further 30,000 acres from the Bureau of Land Management. Although the group do not deny their colourful pasts, no mention is made of it in any of the Best Friends publicity (see www.bestfriends.org). Mary Ann died on November 14th 2005 at the Best Friends Ranch. Robert De Grimston, who now uses his original name of Moor, works as a business consultant on Staten Island.

We didn't change the world – as of course we had aspired to – but we had a hell of an adventure trying!

Robert De Grimston, 20th April 1990

The Process rediscovered

The Process might have faded into quiet obscurity, living out their days running the Best Friends animal refuge had it not been for the musician and artist Genesis P-Orridge whose Thee Temple ov Psychick Youth (aka TOPY) project drew heavily on ideas from The Process. The TOPY was conceived as a cult-like fanclub for the band Psychic TV. This new interest in the group led to the re-enactment of a Process Church Ceremony to launch the book *Love, Sex, Fear, Death* and the release of a CD in June 2010 of Process Church Hymns by Sabbath Assembly with singer Jex Thoth entitled *Restored To One*.

1001 seekers in search of a guru

Quite why the 'East' has held so much sway over the alternative spiritual landscape of the UK should perhaps not be a mystery: part a legacy of the empire that had inspired an earlier generation to look to the exotic; and part the legacy of groups such as the various branches of the Theosophical Society, the disparate followers of Gurdjieff and other more obscure groups active in the inter-war years such as the Mazdans, who would in effect pave the way for another generation of eastern mystics to travel west. The late fifties and early sixties saw a series of gurus arrive from the Indian subcontinent, each with their own slightly different message based on Hindi teachings, whose followers would go on to form communes and intentional communities. One of the first to arrive was the former Allahabad University physics student Mahesh Prasad Varma who, after studying under his own guru in India and changing his name to Maharishi Mahesh Yogi, was tasked with teaching meditation to as wide an audience as possible. Maharishi set off in 1955 on a two-year tour of India promoting what he called Transcendental Deep Meditation under the banner of the 'Spiritual Regeneration Movement'. The tour of India was followed, in 1958, by a 'world tour' that started in Rangoon and took in Thailand, Malaya, Singapore, Hong Kong and Hawaii, arriving in America in 1959 where a meditation centre was established in San Francisco, followed by a further centre being established at the new Guru's next port of call in London. A communal house was set up at 2 Prince Albert Road near Regents Park as a base for the Maharishi to operate from while he was in the country.

People came and went all day. He liked to have people round him, pressing in on him, sitting at his feet, as pupils crowd in on the master by tradition at home in India. We wrote sitting crosslegged on the floor, interrupted by the perpetually ringing telephone, the arrival of newcomers, or to go and stir the vegetable curry simmering in the kitchen. Once a day he would eat, and all who were at the house at the time would eat with him.

Joyce Colin-Smyth, *Call No Man Master*

The presence of a new guru in town attracted the attention of people in the various spiritual networks in London and soon talks on Transcendental Meditation (TM) were pulling in members and ex-members of Spiritualist groups, Theosophists, Subud followers, Gurdjieffians involved with both J G Bennett and Francis Roles and members of the School of Economic Science. The Maharishi recruited key people from these groups to further his work in London while he continued on his world tour taking in France, Switzerland, Norway, Sweden, Germany, Holland, Italy, India, Singapore, Australia, New Zealand and Africa. Returning to London in 1960, at a meeting at Caxton Hall, he launched a Three-Year Plan to enlighten the whole of mankind. The plan entailed setting up TM Teacher Training Courses, the first being held in an Ashram in Ram Nagar, Rishikesh, India. Over 60 meditators from around the world took part and were then sent out to spread the Maharishi's message. A World Assembly of the Spiritual Regeneration Movement was held in the Royal Albert Hall which some 5,000 attended. The Maharishi believed that if enough people could be persuaded to practice TM then it would be possible to solve all of the world's problems. TM was easy to learn as it involved chanting a personal mantra for 15-20 minutes twice a day, while sitting comfortably with your eyes closed. The rapid expansion of the

TM movement brought its own changes to the easy going early days of life at Albert Road. Dr Francis Roles and his fellow Gurdjieffians from Collet house had become a sort of official wing of TM in London, trying to control what happened and, as Joyce Colin-Smyth recalls, this created two distinct camps at Albert Road. 'I went down to the kitchen where there had always been cheerful noise and chatter. There was silence. About a dozen people seated round the long table jumped guiltily and looked over their shoulders. These were the old inhabitants of the house. Ousted from the upper rooms, deprived of their previous duties, I found they sat and chewed the fat down here in the basement like trolls in the underworld while the Ouspenskyites functioned upstairs.'

Another part of the Maharishi's plan was to recruit initiates amongst the wealthy and famous to help raise the profile of TM. At a planned ten-day conference in Bangor, North Wales in August 1967 all Maharishi's PR dreams came true when John, Paul, George & Ringo accompanied by Mick Jagger, Marianne Faithfull, Cilla Black and Donovan all attended, bringing with them the world's press. The Beatles had met Maharishi on 24 August at a lecture at the London Hilton hotel. Following a private audience with the guru they agreed to travel to Bangor with him and take part in a series of meditation seminars. The Fab Four's introduction to TM was cut short when, two days into the conference, the Beatles' manager, Brian Epstein, was found dead from a cocktail of barbiturates and alcohol in his London flat. The Maharishi's somewhat cold and calculating response when the distraught pop stars turned to him for some sort of solace was 'Now you will be able to come to India with me.' Following Epstein's funeral the four Beatles planned to go out to India in October, a trip that had to be postponed due to their commitments to the *Magical Mystery Tour* film. They eventually travelled to the Maharishi's 'International Academy of Meditation' in Rishikesh, India in February 1968 to take part in a meditation course. They were joined by some sixty people including their wives, Jane Asher, Mia Farrow and her sister Prudence, Donovan, Beach Boy Mike Love and a small group of reporters and photographers. The ashram, set in 14 acres of grounds and surrounded by jungle 150 feet above the River Ganges, was enclosed by barbed wire and the gates were kept locked and guarded. It had been built in 1963 with a $100,000 gift from American heiress Doris Duke and was designed to suit Western habits with stone bungalows equipped with electric heaters, running water, toilets, and English-style furniture. The period in Rishikesh was creative as well as meditative for the musicians. In the afternoons they would gather on the flat roofs of the bungalows to play music.

The long periods spent alone trying to reach pure consciousness put them in touch with previously neglected areas of their minds – long-buried memories of childhood, unresolved problems, lost love, comic books, movies. Paul invented characters such as Martha, Rocky Raccoon, Nancy McGill, and the working girl from the north of England who went to Hollywood. George wrote Animal Farm-style social comments about the bourgeois in Piggies ...

Steve Turner *The Gospel According to the Beatles*

John Lennon wrote 'Dear Prudence', 'The Continuing Story of Bungalow Bill', and the darkly, almost suicidal, 'Yer Blues', while Paul wrote the Beach Boys pastiche 'Back in the USSR' and 'Why Don't We Do It in the Road?', inspired by the mating habits of local monkeys. Overall some 30-plus songs can be attributed to the seven weeks they spent in India; much of the content that would end up on the Beatles' *White Album* as well as songs that would appear on *Abbey Road* and *Let it Be*. The idyllic India journey came to an abrupt end with an incident that has become something of a mystery since. After Ringo and Maureen Starkey had left after just two weeks declaring it was all a bit like a Butlins Holiday camp; and Paul and Jane Asher had returned to deal with some Apple business matters; a rumour started to circulate that the supposedly celibate guru had made a pass at one of the women. In some versions of the story the woman is Mia Farrow, in others, another blonde. Later versions of the story suggest the rumour was either spread by a jealous groupie or a member of the Beatles Apple management, envious of the Maharishi's growing influence. Various participants have both denied and confirmed the substance of the rumour and it did cause Joyce Colin-Smyth to reassess earlier incidents back at Albert Road when the guru 'had first begun locking his door in the afternoons, closeted alone with one young woman or another ... We thought he was giving 'special tuition' to chosen devotees.' Whatever the truth of the rumour, its effect was to bring to an end the Beatles' stay in the Ashram. Lennon and Harrison, after spending the night discussing the alleged incident, decided to leave the following morning. When asked by Maharishi why they were leaving, Lennon replied 'You're the cosmic one, you should know.' The Beatles disillusion with the Maharishi did not turn them away from Eastern religion; they would soon cross paths with another Hindu sect looking to the west for followers.

"More love and joy than 100 bus-loads of archbishops"
John Peel in *IT* 47 January 1969, speaking about Hare Krishna

... To the average man-in-the-street they are inevitably a bunch of weirdos. To those in the hip-scene they are regarded either as freaky-straights or as a groove. Many dig the simplicity of the message and the application of it. However cynical many appear to be about the naiveté of such philosophy, it seems to be working for them. Since they arrived from San Francisco in October '68 they have made their mission widely known, have set up a commune and temple ...

LM in *Gandalf's Garden* 6

In 1968 a small number of American devotees of Abhay Charanaravinda Bhaktivedanta Swami Prabhupada were tasked with establishing a base and temple in London. Prabhupada had left India in 1965 and established the International Society for Krishna Consciousness (ISKCON), better known as the Hare Krishna Movement, in the US. Three couples were sent over to England and they tried to engage young people by handing out leaflets in Oxford Street and attending numerous fashionable venues. They initially relied on members of the local Indian community for support and were offered rooms in an unheated warehouse complex in Covent Garden. After months living in squalid conditions the group got a lucky break. They had been trying to woo members of the Beatles, sending apple pies and clockwork apples with the Hare Krishna mantra on to the Apple Studios. The group had built up a following on the West Coast of the USA and one day one of the devotees, Syamasundar Das, had a call from the manager of the Grateful Dead saying that they were on their way to a function with the Beatles in London and invited him to join them. At this gathering, which included Ken Kesey, and a number of Hell's Angels, the Krishna devotee was slipped through security by Yoko Ono and was eventually greeted by George Harrison with the words 'Where have you been? I've been waiting two years to meet you fellas'. Harrison was already aware of the devotees of Krishna and had purchased copies of the *Happening* album, the first Hare Krishna record. Following this initial meeting Harrison helped the devotees gain the lease on a somewhat run-down seven storey building at 7 Bury Place, which would become the first ISKCON temple in Britain. While the Bloomsbury premises were being renovated, John Lennon invited the devotees to stay at his home in Tittenhurst Park, near Ascot in Berkshire, where they moved into the servants' quarters and set up a temporary temple in a music room. They helped John & Yoko with renovation projects and also spent considerable time at Harrison's Friar Park Mansion in Henley-on-Thames helping with gardening chores. In 1970 the connection with the Beatles led to the recording of *The Radha Krishna Temple* album, produced by George Harrison and with George, Paul and Linda McCartney and drummer Ginger Baker all helping out in the studio. The "Hare Krishna Mantra" track from the record reached the top ten in the British pop charts and resulted in four appearances of the devotees on *Top of the Pops*. The Hare Krishna chant and

some of the devotees appear on later solo recordings by Harrison, notably the hit *My Sweet Lord*. They were also invited by John & Yoko to appear on *Give Peace a Chance*.

The devotees based at the new Radha Krishna Temple at Bury Place lived a strict devotional lifestyle. An article in the hippie magazine *Gandalf's Garden* outlined a typical day at

Bhaktivedanta Manor

the temple. Devotees rose at 5.30am for a cold shower before Atrik, a ritual offering to Krishna of incense, fire and water. They then got stuck into domestic duties, cleaning the house and temple until 7am when, after Krishna had been offered a ritual breakfast of fruit and cereal during the Kirtan ceremony, the devotees themselves ate. The rest of the morning was then spent busy with various duties about the house such as cooking, office work or decorating. At 11.30 there was another Atrik ritual. After lunch the afternoon was spent chanting in public until 4pm. After a further Atrik devotees would have a shower and a meal in preparation for further devotions in the evening. Due not only to their regular trips to chant the Hare Krishna mantra and hand out leaflets in London's West End, but also the celebrity endorsement and publicity from their TV appearances, ISKCON grew rapidly in the first years of the 1970's and the little temple near the British Museum fast became too small for the number of devotees who lived there and the others who wanted to join. Once again George Harrison was asked if he would help out: if they could find suitable premises, he said he would purchase it for them. After looking at several properties, devotees found Piggots Manor with 17 acres of land near Watford. The former nursing home was bought unseen by Harrison in 1973 for £230,000, renamed Bhaktivedanta Manor and given as a gift to ISKCON. In 1974 Roger Middleton spent some time living as a resident at a Hare Krishna temple (almost certainly Bhaktivedanta Manor) doing research for a chapter in Frank Musgrove's book Margins of the Mind. He worked alongside other members cleaning and maintaining the premises, joined in their ceremonies and devotions, accompanied them on a preaching expeditions, and recorded many hours of conversation and discussion with devotees. At the time the commune consisted of 35 men and 15 women, including ten married couples and six children.

... devotees shave their heads (except for a tuft of hair which is a handhold for God), wear saffron robes, take new, Sanskrit names, and live a regulated life of austerity. Their music has strange rhythms. The God Krishna dances on their tongues and his footprint, the 'tilak', shaped like a tuning fork, is stamped on their foreheads in clay. They have an unvarying vegetarian diet of boiled rice, curried vegetables, fruit, yoghurt and milk ... The temple is very sharply marked off from the world: it is separate, contemptuous of 'karmi', the ordinary world in which everyone is uptight, anxious, frantic, 'puffed up', stupid, unclean. It has a strong sense of its superiority and apartness, which is reinforced in daily ritual and routine ...

Middleton found that the commune members considered the local 'suburbanites' to be 'demons' and relations with the local population were such that the grounds of the temple were patrolled at night to ward off attacks. 'We get a lot of intruders ... the villagers. Most of them are demons and they want us out ... They're just demonic, you know. They're frightened of Krishna; and the property values have gone down here, since we came.' This open hostility from some of the villagers seems to have led the devotees to go on the offensive. '... we go out into the village and chant Krishna's name. And the demons can't bear to hear it. So they try and attack us. Prabhupad wants us to take over the entire village. Just think of it ... a whole village of devotees. All for Krishna. So Prabhupad tells us to make our 'kirtan' dancing as loud as possible, so that the demons will not be able to stand it and leave. Then we can start buying up all the houses. Only the devotees will be left ...' Middleton and Musgrove do seem to have started with the assumption that the Hare Krishna community would be full of hippies blissed out on Eastern Mysticism, but by the end of their research they had reached the conclusion that 'It would be wrong to equate membership of a Hare Krishna commune with the 'counter culture' and hippiedom. Devotees are rejecting the basic ground rules of Western society; and they are – often quite explicitly – rejecting hippiedom, too. Many appear to have been 'in the drug scene' a year or two before; their present life is strikingly discontinuous with their hippie days ...' Despite hostility from the outside world ISKCON continued to attract devotees and expand during the mid 70's. By 1977 it had established over 100 temples worldwide along with farms, restaurants, schools, a scientific institute and a book company. They had set up Hare Krishna Food for Life: a network of free food kitchens, cafes, vans, and emergency services inspired by Srila Prabhupada's cry that 'No one within a ten mile radius of our temples should go hungry ...' They had also established annual Ratha Yatra festivals in many major western cities involving huge decorated chariots being pulled through the streets. Hare Krishna founder and guru Srila Prabhupada died in November 1977 and despite trying to prepare for his succession the movement entered a period of flux and uncertainty.

Eleven new 'gurus' had been initiated by Prabhupada each with a regional remit. This contributed to various factions appearing and during this period the movement went through a somewhat apocalyptic phase.

This dose of cold war paranoia was prompted by interpretations of what was known as the World War III tape: a recording of a conversation in 1975 in which Prabhupada discussed tensions between India and Pakistan and said 'Next war will come very soon. Your country, America, is very much eager to kill these Communists and the Communists are also very eager. So very soon there will be war ...' Asked what devotees would do while the war is going on, he replied 'Chant Hare Krishna.'

... most of the eleven gurus embraced the revelation of an apocalyptic world war. According to the widely accepted scenario, only core ISKCON members – a few thousand chosen souls – would survive, with the insiders leading the others into an age of spiritual ; enlightenment ... Leaders implored devotees to stand by their posts on the front lines of preaching, collecting money, and selling books until, upon the Governing Body Commission's command, it would be time to retreat to rural strongholds. They said guns would be necessary to fight off looters and refugees ...

Nori Muster, Betrayal of the Spirit

In the UK, the movement continued to grow and in 1979 the group moved the London Temple to Soho Street, just off Oxford Street and set up new headquarters at Croome Court in Worcestershire, a two-hundred-room stately home with its own church and various outbuildings. Built in 1750 for the Earl of Coventry by Lancelot 'Capability' Brown and set in 40 acres of fields, the group kept Indian cattle and llamas in the landscaped parkland. They renamed it Chaitanya College, transferred all of the British ISKCON administration there, and spent hundreds of thousands of pounds restoring the property, paid for in part through a lucrative business they ran importing oil paintings. More than 150 devotees lived at Croome Court, in cottages in and around the estate and a number of married couples lived in the suburbs of Worcester.

We transformed the old church into a beautiful temple and revamped the school with its many classrooms. I particularly liked the 'long room' which was in the west wing. We used it as a food hall and theatre too. We also set the east wing areas up as a recording and filming facility under 'Metavision'. We also had our mail order and typesetting depts. in the east wing. I helped run a few summer camps over there in the gorgeous grounds up near the entrance arch ... **12**

Steve Hopkins (Sakhyaras Prema Das)

Many members transferred from Bhaktivedanta Manor which was left as a preaching centre from which the group did outreach into the local Indian community. However, the new headquarters were not to last long: the new guru who had initiated the move had not only overstretched the group's finances, but was also suspected of using drugs. At a meeting in 1982 he was expelled from ISKCON for not acting as a 'bona fide spiritual master' and despite Hare Krishna devotees in the UK going on a year-long marathon fundraiser they were still unable to afford the high mortgage payments and eventually had to sell the Croome Court estate. The focus of ISKCON in the UK returned to Bhaktivedanta Manor where, throughout the 80's, numbers of visitors continued to increase. The annual Janmashtami festival held at the Manor was attracting more and more participants year on year. This led the group into increasing conflict with the local Hertsmere Borough Council Planning

Department, culminating in 1988 with the council issuing a planning enforcement notice aimed at preventing all visitors to the Manor. Numbers attending the festival had reached 16,000, resulting in major congestion and traffic jams in the surrounding country lanes and through Letchmore Heath. Other issues contributing to tensions were the fact that a few Indian and western devotee families had moved into the area and devotees were now running the only shop in the village. Adding to this was the group's cultish image, the noise from the festival and elements of underlying racial prejudice. Two public inquiries were held over the use of the Manor in 1988 and 1989 with the then Secretary of State for the Environment, Tory MP Chris Patten, finding in favour of the local council. ISKCON took their case to the Court of Appeal and in the meantime a campaign to save the Manor gathered pace. In 1991 the Hare Krishna Temple Defence Movement was set up and MPs began to receive letters from Hindu communities across the country. As they awaited the result of the appeal, numbers at that year's Janmashtami festival rose to 36,000. As it was, the appeal came to nothing when the judge found against them – giving them two years' grace after which public worship at the Manor would be illegal. As things looked increasingly bleak, devotees staged protests outside British embassies in India, the USA, South Africa and Australia, a youth group, Pandava Sena, was formed to mobilise young Hindus and just before the two years' grace was due to end a campaign march was organised.

... in the middle of March 1994 36,000 people gathered in central London. People came from all over the country, including 150 coaches from Hindu temples. The young and the old, Hindus, Jains, Sikhs and ISKCON devotees marched together in a powerful statement of solidarity ... Outside the House of Parliament many members of the crowd, including the elderly blocked the traffic by sitting in the road ...

The Hare Krishna Movement: Forty Years of Chant and Change

The event was the first large-scale Hindu protest outside India. At the ensuing rally in Trafalgar Square it was announced that the council had bowed to pressure and was prepared to let the temple stay open while they considered an application for a new access road to be built linking the Manor directly with the nearby A41. As it turned out, despite recommendations from local planning experts to support the new access road, local councillors still turned the application down. Furthermore, the group was prosecuted for holding the 1994 festival, becoming the first religious community to be prosecuted for observing a rite of worship in the UK for 300 years. After a further appeal, and public inquiry lasting over six months, planning permission was finally granted for the access road. Today the Manor attracts an astonishing 60,000 visitors during the festival period and relations with the local council and surrounding population have improved considerably. Worldwide, ISKCON has over 400 centres, including 60 farms, 50 schools and 60 Govinda restaurants in India. At the London Ratha Yatra festival 3,000 people join a procession from Hyde Park to Trafalgar Square. Its land holding in Hertfordshire has grown from its original 17 acres to 97 acres and recently they have started producing 'Ahimsa' or 'Karma free' milk.

The farm houses 50 cows and oxen in simple English oak barns. No animal has ever been killed and Hindu principles of cow protection and compassion to all living creatures are neatly transplanted into the modern Western world to successfully run a dairy farm entirely without slaughter or fossil fuels.

www.ahimsamilk.org

Irreversible World Peace

We are working in many directions – dealing with education, community planning, prison rehabilitation, and so on – but our primary focus is on promoting what we call irreversible world peace. We are seeking to establish several permanent groups of 7,000 advanced transcendental meditators in various places around the planet. Their meditations will create a powerful coherent influence in the collective consciousness and neutralize built-up stress and tension in the world, creating an environment of progress and peace. Our goal is to create Heaven on Earth, and we are taking practical steps to accomplish it. **13**

Maharishi Mahesh Yogi

The loss of the support of the Beatles did not prove to be an insurmountable setback for the Maharishi – he would initially continue to promote himself as the 'Beatles' Guru' until they made a legal request for him to stop doing so and would later put out his own version of the falling out in Rishikesh (it was him who threw them out for not giving up drug taking). The Maharishi's Transcendental Meditation movement would go on to be a success around the world and over the years make a number of somewhat fantastical claims. By the mid 1970's the movement had become wealthy and went on a property buying spree in the UK: buying Roydon Hall at Maidstone in Kent; Swythamley Hall in Staffordshire; and a Georgian rectory at Badingham in Suffolk to turn in to Transcendental Meditation training centres. In 1977 they bought Mentmore Towers in Buckinghamshire, the former home of the Rothschilds, for £220,000 as their UK headquarters. Starting off as an administrative centre and venue for meditation courses, the huge mansion went through a number of different incarnations throughout the late 1970's and 1980's. The TM movement began to shed its identity as part of the hippie counter-culture and started to target business and other professionals. Numerous banquets were held to woo influential academic, government and business figures and the movement was restructured more along the lines of a multinational corporation than a hippie cult. In 1979, a hundred young men, all TM teachers, moved into Mentmore in order to maintain continuous group practice of the TM-Sidhi meditation program. A number of TM research labs were set in the former servants' wing under the auspices of the Maharishi European Research University. A number of businesses were run by the movement out of Mentmore including fudge making and a silk dress making business. They also hosted classical music concerts and rented the building out as a film location (it appears in Terry

From Simians to Sapiens to Sidhas

EVOLUTION OF MAN...

Gilliam's *Brazil* (1985), Stanley Kubrick's *Eyes Wide Shut* (1999) and was later used as Wayne Manor in the 2005 film *Batman Returns*).

In 1980 a small band of Maharishi followers founded a community in the Lancashire new town of Skelmersdale. Known as the Maharishi European Sidhaland, or alternatively as Woodley Park, the group has flourished and has slowly built a thriving community based around the Maharishi's ideas and the practice of Transcendental Meditation. As well as a small housing estate the group have built the Maharishi Golden Dome: Britain's first 'custom-designed' building for the practice of Transcendental Meditation, a community centre, an Ayurveda Health Centre and their own school.

In 1992 the movement sponsored a new venture based at Mentmore: its own political party – the Natural Law Party (NLP). They fielded 310 candidates at the 1992 election on a manifesto that included the assertion that if a critical mass of the population practiced Transcendental Meditation there would be overall improvements in society including reduced crime, accidents and hospital admissions, and increased prosperity, national security and quality of life. While this was a serious attempt by the Maharishi's followers to engage in politics in the UK and a number of other countries, the media coverage tended to focus on the more seemingly eccentric aspects of the Party's activities such as Yogic Flying, an advanced TM technique whereby cross-legged meditators, after learning to 'hop' and 'float', went on to full scale levitation or flying. This was the technique that if practiced by enough people would bring about political change. The Party cited studies that they claimed proved the so-called 'Maharishi effect' including a study of crime rates in Merseyside that had found a 60% reduction in crime relative to UK national trends due, according to the NLP, to the presence of a Maharishi Effect group at the Woodley Park community in nearby Skelmersdale. In July 1999 the UK National Yogic Flying competition was held at the Golden Dome in Skelmersdale, as part of an initiative to publicise Maharishi Mahesh Yogi's scientifically proven programme to create world peace. '... The Yogic Flyers will compete in four events: 25-metre hurdles; long jump; high jump; and 50-metre race. All events are performed in the traditional Yogic Flying position, sitting cross-legged. Winners will go on to perform in the International competition ...' [14]

The Maharishi's TM movement has continued to expand worldwide with new initiatives being rolled out on a regular basis: in 2000 the Maharishi launched The Global Country of World Peace, a nation without borders 'to provide a global home for peace-loving people everywhere'. At the same time plans to build Peace Palaces in the 3,000 largest cities around the world were announced. These were to be 'pre-engineered' buildings that resembled 'an Indian temple crossed with a Southern plantation mansion' to be used as multi-purpose TM centres. In 2008 proposals were put forward for a 12-storey Maharishi 'Tower of Invincibility' on a site at Rendlesham in Suffolk that was to form the centrepiece in a 'Maharishi Garden Village'. This followed a failed attempt to buy the Bentwaters RAF base to be used as a TM university campus.

Nuclear Evolution

We have gathered together in a bond of Spirit, Truth and Love, to write in daily living the Constitution of the Universe. By meditation, reflection and perseverance, we struggle to master 'self' and reach the all-seeing, all-knowing centre within from whence comes the vision, inspiration and government of New Age planetary Man.

An Introduction to Centre

In 1966 in a house not far from Holland Park at 10a Airlie Gardens 'self-styled yogi' Christopher Hills set up Centre House, a residential community cum meditation centre and base for both the Commission for Research into the Creative Faculties of Man and the Centre for Education in Spiritual Awareness. The imposing six-storey building housed kitchen, dining and laundry facilities on the ground floor/basement along with meditation rooms. Accommodation for Hills and his wife was on the first floor alongside admin and research offices. The next floor up held a large meeting and seminar room, while the top three floors made up a 'Residential Section' for the other members of the community. The group's introductory pamphlet set out their aims:

To convince mankind once and for all that there is a better alternative to conflict-by-war, we must now discover, orchestrate, and perform the Divine Music, so that all the bugles and drums and flag-waving will seem absurd by comparison. If we can create a single valid community such as the one described below, then children will run away from school to join it, soldiers will desert their regiments to serve it, artists will sacrifice everything but their art to contribute to it, businessmen will topple their money gods to worship it, and the entire world will be at war – but this time all of humanity on the same side – against poverty, famine, disease, hate, fear ...

Centre House

Christopher Hills was something of an enigmatic and exotic character. Having survived the sinking by a U-Boat in the Atlantic of the Merchant Navy ship he was serving on, he ended up after the war in Jamaica where he was not only influential in the Jamaican Art Movement (establishing the Hills Galleries with his wife Norah) but also became a millionaire sugar and spice tycoon. On one hand the Hills rubbed shoulders at cocktail parties with the likes of James Bond creator Ian Fleming, playwright and actor Noel Coward and hotel tycoon Conrad Hilton, whilst at the same time working to protect the country's Rastafarian community from persecution and setting up an exotic wood-carving industry, giving work to dozens of artisan Rastas. A meeting with Indian Congress Party leader Surendra Mohan Ghosh, who was visiting the island, led to Hills being invited to India and being introduced to the newly independent country's first Prime Minister Jawaharlal Nehru. According to Hills, within days of his

Christopher Hills

arrival he was adopted by one of India's most prominent sages Swami Shantanda. He then embarked on a near four year trek around India as a spiritual seeker. His acquaintance with Nehru also led to a project aimed at ending famine. In collaboration with Japanese microbiologist, Dr Hiroshi Nakamura, a project was set up to develop edible algae as a superfood to solve world hunger. Shuttling back and forth between India and Jamaica, Hills built experimental ponds, portable algae stills and a laboratory at his home above Kingston. In 1962 the Commission for Research into the Creative Faculties of Man was formed to 'bring together the work of scientists, psychical researchers, philosophers, holy men, educationalists, and politicians.' In 1965 the Hills decided to move to England to get a better education for their two sons, John and Anthony. Norah and the boys stayed with her father in King's Lynn while Christopher set about setting up Centre House, or 'Center Nucleus', based on ideas that would later be published in his book *Nuclear Evolution: a Guide to Cosmic Enlightenment.* Reviews of the later American edition in *Yoga Journal* describe the book as a "Penetrating insight ... into the next stage of human evolution', in which Hills explores a whole range of esoteric topics from 'Cosmology and consciousness' through 'Life as a Hologram' to the 'mystery of the soul and mind', before going on to introduce techniques that 'deepen and intensify communication on all levels'.

The goal of Hills' holistic approach is to become the 'nuclear self' and evolve consciously by getting rid of all the obsessions, cravings and thoughts which block the functioning of the indwelling creative imagination.

Yoga Journal March 1978

Centre House was an experimental attempt to put these ideas into practice. Daily life sounds, from the various descriptions, to have been a combination of silent meditation and 'continuous encounter situation'. Each day started and finished with a group meditation at 7am and 10pm. It was during these sessions that any important decisions concerning the Centre were taken by a 'Unanimous vote of silence.' Whilst the communal day was topped and tailed by a period of silence it sounds as if the rest of the time could be far from quiet. The group claimed its first and only rule was 'Clean up your own mess (psychological or otherwise) and don't leave it around for others' and that day-to-day decisions were resolved by a process of 'creative conflict'. The group seems to have had no formal constitution and the running of the community relied on the self-discipline of members. One member (Malcolm, aged 32) interviewed by Richard Fairfield in 1970, describing his daily life said 'At Centre we learn to live with conflict creatively. We learn how to recognize our drives and channel them into creative harmony through love. The aim is to create 'spontaneous universities' where knowledge of these drives can be used to enhance the studies of consciousness and its effect on the evolution of government and society.'

The community ran a weekly social and educational program: on Monday you could attend the Homeopathy Study Group; Thursdays had a class in 'extra sensitivity' training giving by Hills himself; on Saturdays a course in Zazen; and on other days there were classes in various forms of Yoga. All these were open to the public and free. On Wednesday evenings there was a residents' only gathering "to examine the building of a bridge of awareness to span the void separating our private inner worlds.'

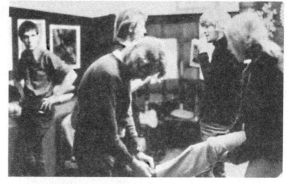

In February 1967 an American, Craig Sams, opened the first macrobiotic restaurant in the UK in the basement of Centre House. He had previously been selling macrobiotic food he prepared at home through a snack bar at the UFO club in Tottenham Court Road. The venture at Airlie Gardens only lasted three months before it was closed down when a solicitor's letter arrived complaining about commercial activity taking place in a residential area, but the short-lived pioneering restaurant had built up a loyal following and would lead to greater things. (Sams went on to set up another little café/restaurant called Seed that in turn led to the creation of Ceres Grain Shop in All Saints Road, Notting Hill. This was followed by the formation of Harmony Foods which finally morphed into Whole Earth Foods in the early 1980's. He co-founded Green & Black's Chocolate in the 1990's and was chair of the Soil Association in the early years of this century.) Hills published details of the Centre's non-constitution

Centre House Community
in the early 1970's

in1970 under the title Christ: Yoga of Peace: 'a practical and demonstrable method of self government.' A member of the group claimed it was not only usable by both individuals and groups 'as a guideline to new age living', but also that the basic principles that underpinned it could be used as 'the foundation stone upon which a new world government could be founded.' Hills left the community in the early 70's and, after some time spent as a lecturer, in 1973 he established the University of the Trees in Boulder Creek, California, an accredited University for the study of Human Potential offering a programme of New Age teachings and granting degrees in consciousness research. Christopher Hills died in 1997, or as the website, www.drhills.com, puts it: 'He left his body'. Towards the end of his life he created a sanctuary dedicated to the goddess on a 50-acre redwood rain forest estate in California with his second wife, Penny Slinger Hills, to 'honor the emergent energy of the Divine Feminine.' Centre House continued as a community until at least the late 1970's.

Only when the old patterns of habit, thinking and behaviour are removed may we discover the inner joy and strength that conquers loneliness. The 'self' may be sought alone, or with a group. At Centre House, we live as a group. We believe that this has much relevance because the world requires constructive alternatives ... a group has further advantages because the other members act as a mirror. They help you to see yourself.

From Centre House entry in *Directory of Alternative Communities* 1977

Where sannyas energy
is the most intense

The world is in such a state of crisis that a single Buddha won't be enough. We need thousands of Buddhas.

Bhagwan – quoted by Ma Satya Bharti in *Death Comes Dancing*

In September 1981 five figures arrived in the small Suffolk village of Herringswell just off the A11 between Newmarket and Mildenhall. They were the advance party of followers of Indian guru Bhagwan Shree Rajneesh who had come to view Herringswell Manor, a large mock tudor house set in 14 acres of grounds that had previously been used as a school for children of servicemen on nearby American bases. The five were incognito, dressed in greens and blues rather than their trademark orange and red clothing, in order not to raise suspicion among local people as to their intentions. They told the agents showing them round that they were looking to set up a school, not that they were looking for a location to establish a UK 'Buddafield'. The group had been living with other followers in a small commune in Oak Village in North London while running the Kalptura meditation centre in Chalk Farm and had been sent instructions from the group's international headquarters in India to find a suitable location for a large commune in England – they went ahead with the purchase of the Suffolk Manor, to be to renamed Medina Rajneesh, for a reputed £290,000. They set about renovating the rundown school premises and by the guru's birthday on 11th December seventy-five adults and twenty-eight children had moved in. A 'grand opening was celebrated with friends who had come from all over Britain ... snow covered grounds were lit by brilliant flashes of fireworks exploding in the night sky, and echoed songs of a joyous family filled the manor'.[15]

Bhagwan Shree Rajneesh, a former lecturer at Jabalpur University, had become a spiritual teacher in his native India in the late 1960's. Initially operating from an apartment in Mumbai in 1974 – he had moved with his followers to establish an Ashram in two adjoining houses on six acres of land in Koregaon Park in the city of Poona, a retreat for wealthy families from Mumbai because of the cooler climate there. The Poona Ashram attracted increasing numbers of western visitors throughout the latter half of the 1970's, many of whom stayed and were initiated as Sannyasins. Bhagwan's teachings and spiritual philosophy proved to chime with the countercultural spiritual pilgrims, being an eclectic mix drawing on many religious sources and western thought as well as including a liberal view on sex. Central to the teaching was the practice of dynamic meditation devised by Bhagwan specifically for Westerners. Dynamic meditation had four distinct stages, each lasting about ten minutes. The first consisted of fast 'chaotic' whole-body breathing to break tension spots and emotional blocks built up from a lifetime of repression. In the second stage the individual was encouraged to let go totally and be spontaneous, expressing any feelings freely, and the energy released often led to fits of laughing, crying, screaming or dancing. Again, this was aimed at releasing pent-up tensions, frustrations and repressions. The third stage involved jumping up and down and yelling the Sufi mantra Hoo!, Hoo!, Hoo! continuously for ten minutes in order to raise the energy level still further. The final stage consisted of total silence and stillness when meditation occurred and 'one feels the emptiness of becoming part of the whole of existence.' The movement attracted a large number of Westerners through links with the human potential and alternative therapy movements. In 1972 Paul and Patricia Lowe, founders of Quaesitor, England's version of the US Esalen Institute, visited Poona after feeling that they had become 'ceilinged and gotten stuck' with their therapy practices and had tried meditation – but found that people couldn't sit still for long enough to get the benefits. The Lowes became disciples and returned to London to turn their centre into a Rajneesh meditation centre. A year later they moved the entire centre to Mumbai. The Lowes were followed by Michael Barnett, author of the book *People Not Psychiatry*, and Leonard Zunin, a member of the American Board of Psychiatry and Neurology who both became key Rajneeshee therapists. Through these contacts ...

... a steady flow of Growth Movement therapists found its way to Rajneesh ... a lot of Californians came, and from Esalen the word spread to various of the other movement circles: to the Reichians, to the group around R D Laing, and so on. Then, as the movement itself spread from England to the Continent, the talk of Rajneesh followed it. Eventually hundreds of therapists and other movement enthusiasts came, many of them to go home in red clothes and malas with new names and new identities. Of these, some stayed permanently with Rajneesh, or went home at his request to found Rajneeshee centers, giving up their independent practices and putting the money they made into the movement.

Frances Fitzgerald, *Cities on a Hill*

In 1975 the Ashram offered encounter groups and Gestalt therapy; by the end of the 70's sixty different therapies were on offer and the ashram was hosting 30,000 visitors per year and looking for larger premises. It was also coming into increasing conflict with the local Indian authorities. After refusing to approve the expansion plans, the government cancelled the tax-exempt status of the ashram and stopped issuing visas to foreign visitors. Amid this mounting hostility, plans were made to move and expand the group's operations and set up communes on other continents and on 1st June 1981 Bhagwan travelled to the United States on a tourist visa, ostensibly for treatment for a slipped disc. By July his personal secretary, Ma Anand Sheela, was negotiating to purchase the 64,000-acre Big Muddy Ranch in Oregon for six million dollars where the group set up the Rajneeshpuram commune which would eventually grow to house nearly 7,000 residents. The plans for the Suffolk commune at Herringswell were not on such a massive scale, although the choice by Bhagwan of the name Medina – meaning 'sacred city' – may have meant that he had envisaged that the group would develop on a much larger scale. Herringswell Manor consisted of a 30-bedroom main house; an oak-panelled hall with a huge fireplace and eight sofas; a communal dining room; a laundry; accounts office; design studio; healing centre; carpenter's and plumber's work-shops; garages; a boutique; a guest cottage; and – in the grounds – an old swimming pool and tennis courts. The group gave Islamic names to the various parts of the property, the main house was called Kabur ('the great one'), the group rooms Hadiq'qa ('the walled garden of truth') and the shop was known as Muti (the provider'). The Rajneesh commune was very quickly a success: attracting members and visitors from among people who had been to the Poona Ashram and other converts who had come through various therapy and spiritual contacts. Within a year they had grown to over a hundred members and were running a number of successful businesses. As well as a therapy and healing centre running courses there was a building company, 'Sun Services', and a Design Studio. Other members went out to work in the local area as doctors, a midwife, computer programmers and cleaners.

As well as the Suffolk commune there was a network of some twenty-two Rajneesh centres across the country ranging from the large to the very small. The Udgatri meditation centre in Bristol had fifteen full-time workers running meditation groups, organising talks and celebrations with the 'Medina Ceilidh Band' and the 'Loose Tights Rock 'n' Roll Band'. In Leeds at the Sangeet meditation centre (where they ran a wholefood business and a Zen Graphics company as well as meditation and T'ai chi groups) you could also attend a 48-hour Star Trek Marathon. The Medina commune was able to tap into this network of clients for courses, for fundraising and to attract new members. They were also the focus for gatherings of sannyasins from across the country.

Brilliant musicians as well as mean DJs lived at Medina. Every Friday was a disco, every Saturday a party. Regularly we would decorate the vast main hall for a summer ball or a winter extravaganza and invite the sannyasins of Britain for a weekend of celebration, meditation, dancing and 'lurve'.

Ma Prem Vismaya/Anne Geraghty

Medina wasn't the only Rajneeshee commune in the UK. Down in Devon just outside the small village of Morchard Bishop was another, not quite on the scale of the Suffolk commune, known as Prempantha. It operated on much the same basis.

Prempantha became this awesome kingdom in the countryside, and the more people knew about it, the more people came. We had wonderful festivals that covered the fields with orange people wearing wooden malas, dancing back and forth from hug to hug in that very stereotypical sannyas way. The kids put on plays, danced, sang, and ran around until their shoes wore out. The festival days were so magical for me. I felt so free to be a child and so loved by those I'd never even met before.

Ma Prem Rupda

There were also smaller communal set-ups such as the Tushita Rajneesh Growth Commune at North Moreton near Didcot in Oxfordshire. Round the country there were also groups of individual followers running meditation centres as well as other 'orange' businesses. They also ran Rajneeshee discos and night clubs to raise funds. The Medina Healing Centre may well have been the first residential alternative therapy centre in the UK offering a wide range of therapies and health treatments as well as its own particular form of therapy.

Rajneesh Therapy is a sharing. There isn't a client and there isn't a therapist, but two people sharing an experience. It's as if the therapist first invites the client to share in that experience, the two come together and there isn't a separation. Then there isn't a client-therapist relationship any more there are simply two people understanding each other. At that moment here is total love, total trust, and total understanding – a glimpse of oneness.

Ma Anand Poonam, Medina Programme Brochure 1982

Bhagwan's teachings had always had an apocalyptic thread running through them. In the late 1970's he predicted that World War Three would start in 1993 in the Middle East, would last six years and would destroy modern civilization except for a few Rajneesh communes which would survive to start the new world. Later this turned into a prophesy of a 'great crisis' that would occur between 1984 and 1999 during which every kind of destruction would be visited on the Earth: floods, earthquakes, volcanic eruptions, nuclear war. In this cyclone of destruction Rajneeshism would create a 'Noah's Ark of consciousness' to save humanity. It appears not to have been clear whether this great crisis was meant to be taken metaphorically or as a reality, although at least one of the group's leading therapists believed that Bhagwan meant that extra-terrestrials would descend in their mother-ships to save them. This doom-laden message was heightened when AIDS broke out in the early 1980's. The reaction of the Rajneeshies to the threat of AIDS was quick and fairly draconian. Bhagwan announced that this was a sign of the great crisis and would wipe out two thirds of mankind. Instructions were sent out from the Oregon headquarters:

... we were told: in order that sannyasins would survive, a radical programme of preventative measures was to be introduced immediately ... all sexual intercourse, with other sannyasins and between sannyasins and non-sannyasins, would take place using protection. Condoms, plastic gloves and dental dams were to be issued to every sexually active sannyasin. Plastic gloves had to be worn for all genital contact. Contaminated waste-bins would be available for disposal in the kitchens, toilets, and dormitories.

Tim Guest *My Life in Orange*

Every member was tested for HIV and a system of coloured beads on members' malas was introduced; a blue bead for those that had not been tested, a yellow bead for those awaiting their test results, and a green bead for those who had tested negative. Anyone who had sex with someone without a green bead was to have their beads confiscated for three months. As it turned out no one at the Medina commune tested positive – had they done so they were to be placed in isolation and cared for by the community. It is hard to imagine the impact that this had on a commune that had been based on ideas of free sexuality and ecstatic meditation.

However, the Medina commune continued to thrive through the early 1980's with a publicly acknowledged 'official' peak of 300 members, although unofficially the numbers were much higher with hidden dormitory rooms housing anything up to another 100 residents. In 1983, the BBC was given access to film the commune during what was perhaps the community's most successful period. The commune had swollen the population of the village of Herringswell to such an extent that it was now of such a size that the village was required to set up a Parish Council. The problem from the villagers' point of view was that with the majority of voters living at the commune the Rajneeshees would end up in control of 'their village'.

British followers of Bhagwan Shree Rajneesh failed recently in an attempt to take control of a newly formed parish that includes the village of Herringswell, site of Medina Rajneesh commune. The Rajneeshees, who now constitute more than half of the voting population in the village, sought to acquire a majority of seats on the local council ... However, the Forest Heath district councillors, under whose authority the village falls, decided that the ward in which the Rajneeshees live will have only four of the nine council seats in order, as councillor Jack Haylock put it, to be fair to the community that has been here for over a thousand years.

Daily Telegraph 19 July 1984

If the residents of Herringswell were worried about the impact that the orange people might be having on their Parish Council, this was nothing to what was happening to the inhabitants of the small town of Antelope in Oregon, the nearest place to the Rajneeshpuram Commune. The Council of Antelope had been taken over, an 'orange' mayor installed and much of the town bought up by Bhagwan's followers. What's more, the Rajneeshees had also set their sights on the Wasco County elections and were bussing in homeless people from all over the United States to try and ensure that they could win the vote. While on the surface Rajneeshpuram was a remarkable physical success, a flowering of the desert, it was rapidly descending into a paranoid authoritarian regime, run by an elite surrounded by armed guards whilst the Guru was driven around in a fleet of Rolls Royces and pampered in isolation from the rest of community. In the end, amid accusations of phone tapping, bugging of members' and visitors' rooms, attempted poisoning of County officials and purges of anyone who challenged the leadership, the commune came apart at the seams. The leadership ran off to Europe with large amounts of the group's money. Bhagwan emerged saying he knew nothing about all these terrible goings on and was promptly arrested for immigration violations as he tried to flee to Mexico. Rajneeshpuram was eventually wound up and Bhagwan returned to Indian and changed his name to Osho. Other Sannyasins were dispersed around the globe. The Medina commune had fallen victim to the power struggles that had beset the movement and was closed in 1985. Osho died on 19th January 1990 of heart failure aged 58. His ashes were placed in one of the main buildings at the Poona ashram. His epitaph reads: 'OSHO. Never Born, Never Died. Only Visited this Planet Earth between December 11 1931 – January 19 1990.'

Following Osho's death in 1990 some Sannyasins started to search for other avenues to spiritual enlightenment. The effect of HIV on the movement had led followers to look for new routes to achieve spiritual ecstasy that did not involve exposing oneself to potentially unsafe sexual liaisons. Some explored the use of the drug MDMA, or ecstasy. Others developed a technique known as Nataraj meditation, outlined by Bhagwan in the book *Meditation: The Art of Ecstasy*. Nataraj was a form of trance dance meditation.

Allow your unconscious to take complete control. Dance as a process. Don't plan nor exercise any control over your movement. Forget onlooking, observation, consciousness – be simply and totally just dance.

Bhagwan 1976

Combining the practice Nataraj and the use of ecstacy the Sannyasins were instrumental in developing and influencing the origins of trance festivals starting in such places as Goa close to Poona. This started at the end of the 1980's, a short while before Osho's death, when, at large Christmas and New Year Sannyasin gatherings in Goa, the DJ Goa Gil essentially invented or developed what would become known as Goa trance or psychedelic trance music. Through Sannyasins this particular form of rave culture was spread to Italy, Germany, Portugal, Spain, Israel, Brazil, Japan and Australia with many of the top trance DJs such as Antaro, Siddhartha, the Banzi and Riktam brothers, and Goa Gil, being either sannyasins, ex-sannyasins or heavily influenced by the ideas of Bhagwan/Osho.

By dancing, the human being activates meditation.
When we dance, we go beyond thoughts, beyond consciousness and
even beyond individuality itself to become just one in the
divine ecstasy of the union with the cosmic spirit

DJ Goa Gil interviewed by Tiago Coutinho 2001

The full story of the rise and fall of Rajneeshpuram is told in *Cities on a Hill* by Frances Fitzgerald

Communes Britannica

The whole world should be an ashram

Another Eastern Guru would come west in the 1970's and establish a network of over 40 communal Ashrams in the UK where his followers lived by a strict Ashram Code. The fourteen-year-old Guru Mahara Ji arrived in Britain and gave his first public address at Conway Hall in London on the 19th June 1971. Two days later he appeared on the pyramid stage at the Glastonbury Fayre where he made a somewhat unintelligible speech late at night to an audience that had been enjoying Brinsley Schwarz. The teenage guru arrived in a flower-bedecked car surrounded by his followers who eventually forced the band to stop playing so the young mystic could address the crowd. He ended his short speech '... to go anywhere you need some money, some pounds to go the picture hall you need some pounds for the ticket or for anywhere you need some pounds. My pounds are the love and the devotion pounds that can only be attained by your bank. You have a bank in yourselves already, the money of love and devotion. Because I have got that Word, I have got that Knowledge, I have got that thing and I can say you all that I can help mankind and everybody of you by giving that Knowledge.' After appealing for money he got back in the car and left.

Mahara Ji had inherited the leadership of his father's Divine Light Mission on his death in 1966. The movement already had a strong following across India and had attracted a number of Westerners searching for spiritual guidance and a few had become initiates or premies (from the Hindi prem, meaning "love"), literally 'love-ies'. These British initiates had invited the young guru to visit the West, and in 1969 he sent one of his closest Indian students, or Mahatmas, to London to teach. In 1970 at a huge gathering known as the Peace Bomb, he announced his intention to spread Knowledge throughout the world. '... Give me your love, I will give you peace. Come to me, I will relieve you of your suffering. I am the source of peace in this world. All I ask of you is your love. All I ask is your trust. And what I can give you is such peace as will never die. I declare I will establish peace in this world.' The teenage peacenik touched a nerve in Britain and the US and the success of Divine Light Mission in the early years of the 1970's is breathtaking. In an article in the *International Times* in October 1971 it was reported that as well as a London base the Mission already had ashrams in Loughborough, Leicester, Nottingham, Inverness, Exeter and Southend. This, despite the fact that the Mission was not officially registered as a Trust until the summer of 1972. By the beginning of the following year the Mission's own magazine *Divine Light* lists a further 22 ashrams spread across the country, with a presence in most major cities in the UK. On top of this the magazine lists a further 28 ashrams in other countries: 15 in the USA, two in Canada, two in Japan and others in Sydney, Johannesburg, Frankfurt, Paris, Rome and Copenhagen. The Mission had also rented a 'Divine Residence' at 3 Woodside Avenue in Haringey as the guru's private accommodation when he was in London. The ashrams, although all relatively independent, were organised along similarly strict guidelines as laid out in *The Ashram Manual*. This document, written by the Maharaji himself, explains that 'Throughout history, all spiritual communities have been structured through adherence to a rule. These rules are not ends in themselves, but simply a means to a goal. Their purpose is to provide for the structuring and smooth functioning of the community. A strong spiritual community, in turn, promotes individual spiritual growth.' Each ashram had an appointed supervisor whose job it was to oversee the personal conduct and activities of all members in the Ashram and to make sure that the Code was being followed 'in order to insure maximum harmony within the Ashram.' The premies who lived in the ashrams were required to stick to a strict daily timetable laid down in the manual and to adhere to a long list of house rules.

1   The Ashram is the shelter of the Renunciate devotees of Guru Maharaj Ji, and should always be kept spotless, honored, and well cared for. It is the responsibility of every Ashram member to keep his personal area and the common areas of the Ashram always neat and clean. The Ashram is for Ashram members only. Hospitality should be accorded to all, although overnight guests cannot be accommodated.
2   The activities and atmosphere of the Ashram should always be conducive to meditation and spiritually uplifting.
3   The kitchen is not a common area for members. It should be considered "off limits" unless the cook permits. Meals must be vegetarian. No meat, fish, eggs, drugs (except prescribed medication), alcohol, or cigarettes should be permitted to be kept in the Ashram

They also had to turn over all income to the Mission and take vows of poverty, celibacy and obedience to Maharaji's organisation. For a decade or more the ashram system proved to be a remarkably successful way for the mission to continue to promote and raise funds for its activities and hundreds of premies lived for years in the ashrams, following the rules stated in the Manual. Despite its initial success in the UK, over the years the Mission became a USA based movement. In 1974, the then 16-year-old guru married 25-year-old Marolyn Johnson, an American airline stewardess who had become a premie. This saw the start of a bitter family feud, with the Guru's mother denouncing her son as a playboy and accusing him of 'drinking alcohol, eating meat and taking too much interest in sex' and ending with a split in the Mission and Maharaji changing his name to Prem Rawat. Despite continued accusations that the Mission was becoming more and more cult-like and that the guru was living an ever more lavish lifestyle, ever more elaborate programmes were devised with stages, thrones, crowns and dancing. All of which required continued fundraising which, by the end of the 70's, was becoming harder and harder as the growth of the movement started to tail off. Prem Rawat appointed a series of 'Initiators' and in 1981 issued a directive that these initiators should 'clean up' the ashrams. While it wasn't at all clear what was meant by this, some initiators took it as permission to psychologically abuse premies in the ashrams under their supervision. Then, in 1983, it was suddenly announced that all the ashrams were going to be closed. 'Many ashram residents were devastated, having dedicated years of their lives to Maharaji and believing, as they had been repeatedly told by Maharaji and the initiators, that it was a life-long commitment. Most had forsaken careers and families to dedicate their lives to him. Now, in their 30's, they suddenly faced having to start their lives over.'[16] No reason was given for the decision, but it seems that financial worries about what financial liability the mission might have for the ashrams residents as they aged, needed medical care, and were unable to work, etc, had led Prem Rawat to view the ashrams as more of a liability than an asset. After the closing of the ashrams most people in the Mission were fired and most of the offices were closed. The Divine Light Mission continued to exist as a charity, but underwent a name change to Elan Vital.

When the ashrams were dissolved, the people who had taken vows to dedicate their whole lives to Maharaji were forced to find new homes, and in many cases, new jobs. Some were deeply in debt since the debts incurred by each ashram were split among the former residents. Many former ashram premies had difficulty adjusting to life in the world after living in the ashram for years, although some of them found jobs as Maharaji's personal servants, or as managers or instructors with Elan Vital. Most of the present managers of Elan Vital are ex-ashram premies.[17]

From the website ex-premie.org

Communes Britannica

Friendly Buddhists

... In Britain today, Buddhist groups and societies seem to be merging overnight and it is sometimes difficult, if not impossible, to gauge the exact number as a whole. The number of actual Buddhists practising and studying the Dharma in Britain is incalculable, and unless a census be taken, the exact number will remain beyond our grasp ... What can be appreciated is that a large number of both old and young people are being attracted to the liberating doctrines of Buddhism.

Christmas Humphreys in foreword to *Buddhism in Britain* 1973

Western gurus like Bhagwan/Osho, Maharaji and the Maharishi can be seen as coming from a clear Hindu lineage that has its own guru and ashram tradition that lent itself to the establishment of communes in the west. Muslim traditions generally lack any sort of comparable monastic practices, although there have been a number of communities in the UK based on Sufi ways. The other religion with a monastic tradition is Buddhism and this has also produced a number of British communities of both lay and ordained members. Again it was very much the work of organisations such as the Theosophical Society in the late 19th and early 20th Century that paved the way for the development of Buddhism in Britain with people like Christmas Humphreys providing a direct link from one generation of seekers to the next. As early as 1926 a British Buddhist Society had been formed and a small community of monks from Ceylon were set up in a house in Ealing by a Mrs Mary Foster. 'Foster House' was the first Buddhist 'missionary' to be founded outside Asia. Soon afterwards they moved to larger premises in Gloucester Road where they continued until the house was requisitioned during the war and the monks returned to Ceylon. After the war, in 1948, some members of the Buddhist Society and others founded the Buddhist Vihara Society in England with the aim of refounding a monastery, or 'Vihara' in London. This would eventually bear fruit when on 17th May 1954 a temple and Vihara opened at 10 Ovington Gardens in Knightsbridge. Around this time societies were also formed in Manchester and Birmingham and in 1962 a second London Vihara was established at 131 Haverstock Hill. The adjoining property was purchased in 1963 and rented out to provide the monastery with an income. That year also saw the establishment of a Buddhist centre in Staffordshire at Biddulph Old Hall.

Buddhism in the British Isles was given a boost in the 1960's and 1970's when a number of lamas exiled from Tibet settled here. Some recreated their own monastic groups, others formed mixed communities. In 1965, a property in the Scottish Borders known

London Vihara

as Johnstone House at Eskdalemuir was purchased by the Johnstone House Trust whose aims were to 'make available to the general public facilities for study and meditation based on Buddhist and other religious teaching leading to mental and spiritual well-being ...' Initially the Trust invited a Canadian Theravada monk to run the centre but this didn't work out and he returned to Canada. In 1967 the Trust offered the centre to two Tibetan refugees, Chögyam Trungpa Rinpoche and Akong Rinpoche. The two young lamas would go on establish the first European Buddhist monastery calling the new community 'Samyé Ling'. Trungpa Rinpoche's interpretation of Buddhism with a Western twist brought him in to conflict with those with more 'traditional' views including Akong Rinpoche. Trungpa drank heavily and slept with his students – the community in the early days gained a reputation locally for 'wild parties, free sex and the use of drugs'. The young lama was eventually banished to a nearby house and stripped of his responsibilities. In 1970 he left for America with Diana Pybus, his 16-year-old bride.

Early visitors to Samyé Ling often had 'New Age' attitudes with only a casual interest in Buddhist teachings. However there gradually emerged 'a more serious application of traditional practice', as Akong Rinpoche 'led the centre through a period of quiet internal spiritual consolidation'.
Robert Bluck *British Buddhism: Teachings, Practice and Development*

Throughout the 1970's a residential community slowly developed, committed to meditation and study, and by 1982 numbers had grown to 50 with 1,000 visitors a year. The 1980's were a period of expansion for the community; work began on a large Tibetan temple, with all the work being done by members of the community, which was opened with a ceremony attended by thousands of visitors on 8th August 1988. By the end of the decade they had grown to 90 members and were receiving getting on for 6,000 visitors each year. Samyé Ling has attracted many famous visitors as well: both David Bowie and Leonard Cohen were students there in the late sixties. The Scottish comedian Billy Connolly has been a regular visitor over the years and former MP and leader of the Liberal Party David Steel, who lives close by is supportive of the community. The temple has been visited by the Dalai Lama and has continued to develop into a unique combination of monastery, nunnery and lay community. A special Buddhist tartan has been designed by Abbot Lama Yeshe Losal Rinpoche: 'we are fortunate to be established as part of the Scottish community and wanted a tartan for our Sangha to show how much appreciation we have for the people, culture and tradition of Scotland.' The Tartan, which is used to line the robes of monks and nuns, is made up from colours representing the five elements in the Tibetan spectrum – Earth, Air, Fire, Water and Space. There have been a number of offshoots from the Samyé Ling community. In 1973 the Kham Tibetan House was established in the village of Ashdon near Saffron Walden as a karma Kagyu Centre. It is now known as Marpa house and is run by the Dharma Trust. In 1989 the premises of the Lothlorien community was donated to the Rockpa Trust to become a Buddhist therapeutic community closely linked with Samyé Ling. The community also has close links with the Holy Isle Project off Arran on the West coast of Scotland, which has been developed through the 1990's into the Centre for World Peace and Health after a Mrs Morris, who owned the island with her husband, offered it to

Lama Yeshe for a knock down price because she felt that its future would be best taken care of by 'the Buddhists from Samyé Ling'.

The different strands of Buddhism have resulted in a number of other centres/monasteries being set up, each with a degree of communal living, but with the focus largely on following a spiritual path. In December 1971, a Buddhist centre was opened at Oaken Holt, a Victorian country mansion at Farmoor, near Oxford by a Burmese businessman called U Myat Saw. Oaken Holt had previous been used as a training centre by the National Provincial Bank who had erected a number of wooden bungalows to the rear of the house as accommodation for trainees. Each bungalow was divided into eighteen cubicles or 'box rooms' and provided accommodation for up to 90 people. Mr Saw had been looking round much of the south of England for a suitable property; his idea was to set up a hotel that would finance a Buddhist Centre out of its own profits. Oaken Holt had obtained planning permission to build a series of permanent buildings to replace the wooden bungalows and this was seen as a way of providing financial support for the project. The Centre also had the backing of the International Meditation Centres, a Trust set up to aid the establishment of Buddhist meditation techniques in the West. The Centre ran meditation courses and provided a home to Theravadin Buddhist monks.

In 1976, what would turn out to become another major British Buddhist monastery, was started just outside the Cumbrian town of Ulverston. Bought for £70,000 at auction, Conishead Priory, the former Durham Miners convalescent home, had been empty for some years and was riddled with dry rot. The group that had bought the huge Victorian mansion had not been aware of the full extent of the damage with some parts about to collapse and having to be propped up with trees from the woods. The group had been formed in 1975 when Peter Kedge and Harvey Horrocks, two students who had been studying at a monastery in Nepal, returned to the UK with the intention of developing a Dharma centre to be called the 'Manjushri Institute'. They gathered a group of people who were interested in Tibetan Buddhism and started looking for a suitable property. Some members of the group moved to the Priory in August 1976 to begin work on transforming the dilapidated building, a project that would take years and involve major structural works, with few of the eighty rooms remaining untouched by renovation. Work carried on throughout the 1980's and in 1991 an appeal was launched to raise £500,000 in order to carry out restoration work on the interior of the building including turning the near derelict top floor into accommodation for the community. The two main teachers and spiritual guides at the Institute were Lama Yeshe and Geshe Kelsang. In the early 1980's the group got into some difficulties over the management and ownership of the Priory. While officially a charitable trust with four trustees the Manjushri Institute was in effect managed by the managers of another organisation, the Foundation for the Preservation of the Mahayana Tradition (FPMT), which the Institute's Spiritual leader, Lama Yeshe, had established at the Kopan Monastery. This confusing situation was further complicated by the fact that the costs of renovation were at the time largely being shouldered by those living there. Following a period of turmoil when the FPMT appeared to be trying to sell the building against the wishes of 'the Priory Group' and intervention by representatives of the Dalai Lama, four new Trustees were appointed, two chosen by FPMT and two by the Manjushri Institute and eventually a new charitable company, the Manjushri

Mahayana Buddhist Centre was incorporated, completely independent of the FPMT. In the 1990's, due to the large numbers attending summer festivals, first a temporary temple was established in a marquee and then plans laid for a permanent temple to be built in the old walled garden of the house. Built by local tradesmen and Buddhist volunteers using local stone, the temple was completed by the end of the decade and dedicated to world peace. The Heritage Lottery recently gave £899,000 towards further restoration work to the outside of the building which will include replacing the main roof and gutters and rebuilding the turrets of the landmark 100-foot towers.

To many of these groups, communal living was somewhat incidental to the spiritual path that its members had chosen. One Buddhist group where living communally was much more central to its being was started in the late 1960's by Dennis Lingwood. During the war Lingwood had served in India, Ceylon and Singapore as a radio engineer with the Royal Signal Corps. In Ceylon he came into contact with swamis at the (Hindu) Ramakrishna Mission and became interested in becoming a monk. Posted to India at the end of the war, one day he handed in his rifle, left the camp where he was stationed and deserted. In May 1949 he was initiated as a novice by the Burmese monk, U Chandramani, then the most senior Theraveda Buddhist monk in India, and given the name Sangharakshita. In 1964, Sangharakshita was invited to help with a dispute at the Hampstead Buddhist Vihara in North London. He had only planned to stay for six months but his somewhat relaxed ecumenical style of teaching made him a popular teacher and he decided to stay and settle in England. His style however brought him into conflict with the stricter 'old school' trustees of the Vihara. There were also suspicions of homosexual relationships between Sangharakshita and a close friend and, amid the homophobic atmosphere of the times, the Vihara's trustees voted to expel the new teacher from the centre while he was out of country on a trip to India seeking out his teachers to ask their advice. On his arrival back in the West in 1967 he decided that a new non-sectarian movement was needed which would revolve around a financially self-sufficient 'monastic' centre. In the basement of a Japanese shop called Sakura in Monmouth Street, London, Sangharakshita set up a small room containing a Triyana Shrine where every Thursday he held meditation classes. From this simple beginning would grow the Friends of the Western Buddhist Order, or FWBO. Summer retreats were organised at a large country house at Haslemere, Surrey.

During the two weeks of the retreat up to eighty people lived a balanced and regular programme of meditation, communication exercises, yoga, lectures, and study. They did the cooking and housework together, and had time to enjoy the surrounding countryside. Each day concluded with a puja, a devotional ceremony of chanting, readings, and recitation. Each retreat quite quickly developed a very happy and friendly atmosphere, light and yet concentrated and purposeful. Many people felt, for the first time, that they knew what it was to live as a Buddhist ... **18**

Some of those attending the retreats felt that they wanted to take things a step further and try to extend the experience of the retreat and live together all the time. So they formed a community at Sarum House in Purley, now known as Aryatara. By trial and error they formulated a way of living that enabled them to try and put their Buddhism into practice in their everyday lives. Towards the end of 1970 a search started for a new base as the lease on the Sakura shop came to an end. Despite a well-organised search, a new centre was not found for over 12 months and in the meantime classes were held at Centre House in Kensington and in the back rooms of SEED macrobiotic restaurant. Eventually, in January 1972, after writing to all London Borough Councils asking for help, Camden Council offered the use of a small disused factory building in Balmore Street, Highgate. Here the group was able to set up on a bigger scale than before. A shrine was set up in an upstairs room, downstairs was a reception room and office. Meditation and study classes were continued at the new centre along with a weekly yoga class, classes in Karate-do, lectures, and festivals. The surrounding area consisted of small and crumbling terraced houses scheduled for demolition to make way for the Highgate Newtown Estate. Many had been left empty and had been squatted by a combination of students, artists, musicians, junkies and drop-outs. This had both drawbacks and advantages for the embryonic new Buddhist movement. On one hand-break-ins and vandalism to the Centre grew so bad that they had to erect barbed wire and bars at every window and at times evening meditation classes were disrupted by flying stones. On the positive side, the abandoned and decaying no-man's-land created by the planning blight on the area provided a temporary social space where the FWBO could formulate and try out ideas of forming an alternative or New Society that was emerging as part of the group's ideology. Friends and Order members squatted a number of the derelict houses in the immediate area and started small community houses. In all, during the FWBO's time in Highgate there were a total of nine assorted communities connected with the Centre. It was during this time that, through experience and experimention, the group established the basic practices and form of FWBO communities and the tenets of its 'New Society' ideas.

It should by now be clear that the only purpose of the FWBO is to encourage and facilitate the growth of real individuals. To that end alone it has created and will continue to create a New Society in the midst of the old. But the purpose of the FWBO is not to find a corner for Buddhists in the midst of the old society. It does not seek to give Buddhism a place in the Establishment so that Buddhists can carry out their own colourful practices and hold their own peculiar beliefs. The FWBO is, to this extent, revolutionary: it wishes to change society – to turn the old society into the new.

Subhuti in Buddhism for Today

In the early 1970's the FWBO expanded rapidly. Looking back at the period, a report from The Third Order Convention in 1976 reports that from just eleven Order Members at the end of 1971 they had grown to 75 active members by 1975. 'Fifty-nine are citizens of the UK, ten are New Zealanders, three are Finns; there's one Malaysian/Chinese; one Order member is American, and one is Dutch.' As well as the Centre and communal household in Archway, Centres sprang up and established themselves in Norwich, Brighton, Surrey, Glasgow and Cornwall. Each Centre became the focus for the new Movement in the area, acting as a meeting place for Order members and community and co-operative members who lived and worked in the area. In 1975 a more permanent London Buddhist Centre was established in a derelict Victorian Fire station in Bethnal Green which was renovated over a number of years by Order members and Friends. Around this base the group developed a network of Buddhist organisations, businesses, and communities. These included 'Right Livelihood' businesses run on Buddhist principles and providing ethical work opportunities for community members. A number of businesses were run by

Bethnal Green Fire Station

The Pure Land Co-operative: The Friends Foods wholefood shop, The Cherry Orchard vegetarian restaurant and a phototypesetting business. There was also a shop selling second-hand goods, clothes, and jewellery. Windhorse Trading was set up importing 'fancy goods' from India and Windhorse Associates was a photographic and design studio. The top floors of the Centre housed a men's community, 'Sukhavati', and there was a flat for Sangharakshita to stay in when he was giving lectures and talks. The details of how communal living was organised in FWBO communities was worked out largely by trial and error in the early days, slowly formulating into a fairly coherent pattern as they found what did and didn't work for them. Almost by chance, separate men's and women's communities evolved – this was a controversial development and while it had started from an informal, somewhat pragmatic basis, it became a sort of official doctrine although not necessarily one subscribed to by all members. Internal arguments were had, some putting forward the view 'that men and women have different spiritual needs and are in a better position to behave as individuals when they are with members of their own sex.' The argument came to a head in 1976 when plans for a women's community at the new London Buddhist Centre were abandoned and the accommodation made men only. A heated debate was had at that year's Order Convention. Many women involved felt marginalised and as a result a women's community, Amaravati, was set up in a large house in Wanstead and also a women-only rural retreat, Mandarava, on a farm near Aslacton, Norfolk.

Not only did separate men's and women's retreat facilities develop, but by the 1980's, communities, businesses, study groups, and Order events were organized on a single-sex basis too. Most people's experience was that this was more helpful, avoiding complex and potentially messy dynamics around sexual attraction and projection. It gave people the opportunity to be with just their own gender, who were likely to understand one another's spiritual needs, and with whom genuine friendship and communication could perhaps more easily develop. Many people's experience was that single-sex activities were just simpler, easier, and more enjoyable.

Vajragupta *The Triratna Story*

This separation along gender lines may have contributed to the biggest crisis to affect the movement. In 1997 an article appeared in *The Guardian* newspaper under the headline 'The Dark Side of Enlightenment'. It alleged that the FWB0 was a manipulative 'cult' whose leader had somehow lured vulnerable young men into sexual relationships with him. The article was followed by revelations on the internet in what were known as the 'The FWBO Files'. The accusations smack of an underlying homophobia and were not helped by the initial silence and denials from Sangharakshita himself. The FWBO Communications Office complained to *The Guardian* that the story had been one-sided, but there was enough substance behind the media hype for the story to carry weight. The FWBO itself was thrown into turmoil by the accusations and a soul searching internal debate ensued. The bigger issue seems to have been not that Sangharakshita was gay, but that he had been sexually active while claiming to be celibate and thus undermining his credibility as a teacher. The internal debate brought out further revelations and eventually the movement was able to come to terms with what had happened.

During the 1980's and 90's the FWBO continued to expand with new communities, retreats and right livelihood businesses being set up across the UK and in other countries. The most successful of the businesses by far is Windhorse Trading, started in 1980 as a market stall. By 1997 it was employing 190 members at its headquarters and warehouse in Cambridge from where it supplied wholesale 'fancy goods' to a network of 18 shops. It had a profit of £1.25 million which was used to support communities and projects in the UK and India. Recently, the biggest growth of membership has been in India itself. This expansion outside the UK led, in 2010, to the movement changing its name to the Triratna Buddhist Community, after deciding that the word 'Western' was no longer really appropriate.

Opinions about the FWBO often remain polarized. Observers may perceive an aggressive approach, a distorted Buddhism and personal misconduct, while insiders may experience a confident inspiration, a link with the essential Dharma and deep spiritual friendship ... The FWBO has overcome its early reputation to become 'a major player in terms of a voice for Buddhism in the UK', and because of its active engagement with the media, it is often found acting as an unofficial representative of UK Buddhism.

Robert Bluck, British Buddhism: Teaching, Practice and Development

The full story of the FWBO/Triratna Community is told in:
Vajragupta, *The Triratna Story: Behind the Scenes of a New Buddhist Movement*

The Essence of Love and Goodwill

My beloved the time will come when people will simply be drawn together in groups and that time is nearer at hand than you can imagine, these groups will not be just those who get together once a week, or fortnight; they will be drawn together to live and work in communities. What you are pioneering here is the prototype for community living all over the world and that is why what you are being shown step by step should be recorded so it can be passed on to help other groups when they start out.

Message to Elixir, 17th August 1968

In 1968 a small booklet entitled *God Spoke To Me* appeared. Several thousand copies were distributed free through the mailing list of a spiritual network called the Universal Link. The booklet contained a selection of messages received 'from God' by a medium, by the name of Elixir, who had recently received guidance instructing her that 'My word is ready now to go out ... Let it go out in hundreds and thousands, The need is very great, withhold nothing ... You will be truly amazed by the response.' [19] The response to the booklet was a prime cause of the expansion of a small group of seekers into what would many years later be called the 'Vatican of the New Age'. The group at the time consisted of a dozen or so spiritual seekers gathered together on a caravan site on the Moray Firth in Scotland, just outside the small village of Findhorn, plus various visitors and fellow travellers dotted around the country. The core of group consisted of the Caddy Family: Peter and Eileen (Elixir) and their three sons; a Canadian: Dorothy Maclean (Divina); Anne Edwards (Naomi/Miriam); Lena Lamont and her children; and Joan Hartnell Beavis. Others involved at the time included: Eileen Keck; Meg Emerson; Kathleen Fleming; Anthony Brooke; Aileen and Ross Stewart; Kathy Sparks; Molly Thompson; and Evelyn Sanford. All had been involved in spiritualist circles for some time, although the group had started to attract a younger generation. Dennis Orme, a psychology student from Hull, had recently joined them along with Janet and John Willoner and a young Scot called Andrew. The Caddys and Dorothy Maclean had been living at the Findhorn Bay Caravan Park since 1962. When left homeless after being sacked from their jobs running a hotel in the Trossachs they had been left no option but to move into their caravan situated in the sand dunes at the end of the runways for RAF Kinloss. The roots of the group that would become the Findhorn Community and then the Findhorn Foundation, or simply just 'Findhorn', go back much further and have been told from their different perspectives in the autobiographies of the main players and condensed and retold in countless publications and articles about the community. These tell the personal stories of the individuals involved, but none really explain where the idea that led to the setting up of an intentional community may have evolved from.

Perhaps the germ of the idea starts in 1948 over a pint of beer in the Carpenters Arms, at Miserden in the Cotswolds, where Peter Caddy (recently promoted to become the Commanding Officer of the RAF School of Cookery at Innsworth) relaxed with his second wife Sheena Govan having parked their caravan on nearby Coombe Hill. The Carpenter's Arms was also the local for the Whiteway Tolstoyan Anarchist Community which at the time was celebrating its 50th anniversary. [20] Or perhaps the seeds were sown earlier, before the war at Christchurch in Dorset in the grounds of a house on Somerford Road belonging to Catherine Chalk. Here in 1939, at the Ashrama Hall of the Rosicrucian Order Crotona Fellowship Peter Caddy married his first wife Nora Meidling – also a Crotona Fellowship initiate – in a 'spiritual marriage' before going on to have a more formal civil ceremony. The teachings of Alexander Sullivan, the group's master, or guru, were a combination of Theosophical and Masonic ideas, mixed with positive thinking and the ideas of the 19th century American New Thought Movement. These ideas were a huge influence on the young Caddy who later described a series of Sullivan's lectures entitled 'Soul Science' as 'the single most important foundation' of his life. A number of the Fellowship's disciples bought bungalows close to the group's headquarters in order to be nearer their leader and a small Rosicrucian community grew up in the area. This would include Nora Caddy who moved to Christchurch with her mother in the early years of the war when her husband was posted overseas. Whether Peter Caddy remembered conversations with members of Whiteway when contemplating the setting up of his own community years later, or thought back to his old spiritual mentor with his group of followers in pre-war Christchurch we shall probably now never know. The 'official' line appears to have been that he was guided to set up a community by the messages that his third wife Eileen/Elixir received from God.

The background of Eileen Jessop does not really give any indication of her later talent as a medium. Her mother had had some involvement with the Christian Science Church and Eileen accompanied her to Bible readings. After both her parents had died, the 19-year-old Eileen ran a pub for a while with her brother in Oxfordshire and just before the outbreak of war married Andrew Combe, an officer from the nearby RAF base. Combe was a keen member of the Moral Re-Armament movement, a keenness bordering on obsession according to his new wife, who accompanied her husband to MRA meetings but found little to attract her in their teachings.

I participated in their 'quiet times', when everyone sat and listened inwardly and then wrote down what they 'heard'. Each person was expected to produce something from these quiet times, and if they didn't the others would help them 'unblock'. I couldn't relate to any of this, particularly as I had no 'guidance' to write down. Although I felt a hypocrite, I pretended to hear something then wrote down the first thing that came into my head to avoid having my inner world investigated.

Eileen Caddy, *Fight into Freedom*

It was her husband who, after the war, introduced Eileen to the dashing young Peter Caddy who he was hoping to recruit as an MRA member. Instead Caddy would declare that he had a vision that Eileen was his other half and persuade her to run away with him. This move seems to have been encouraged by Sheena, Caddy's wife and spiritual mentor at the time. The split would lead to Eileen losing contact with the five children from her first marriage for years to come. Sheena Govan, daughter of evangelist John George Govan, ran a small spiritual group from her flat in Lupus Street, Pimlico, London from where she received inner guidance on behalf of those around her and taught unconditional love and Christ consciousness, an initiatory experience that she called the birth of the Christ within. She was also a somewhat autocratic character and would order her followers to do tasks for her. It would be through the instruction from Govan that Eileen would come to first receive spiritual messages and then later come to trust in them. On a visit to Glastonbury she heard a voice so clear that she turned to see who had spoken. The voice said 'Be still and know that I am God.' Her first thought was that she was going crazy. But the voice went on "You have taken a very big step in your life. But if you follow My voice all will be well.' It would be the guidance from this voice that Eileen Caddy and those around her would follow for the rest of her life. Also part of Govan's group were Dorothy Maclean and Lena Lamont who would later join the Caddys at Findhorn.

Peter Caddy is portrayed in the early literature and reports about the Findhorn Community as a positive thinking man of action, enthusiastically putting into practice the guidance received by the, mostly female, 'sensitives' or mediums that surrounded him. The focus over the years has fallen on Eileen Caddy as the source of this guidance, but in the early days of the group this certainly wasn't the case, nor was Eileen the first medium that Peter had listened to for guidance. After the war, whilst serving as catering manager for British Service personnel who were travelling by military aircraft, he found himself in the Philippines where by chance he met 'a grey haired lady' called Anne Edwards known by her spiritual name as Naomi. Very quickly the two were deep in conversation ranging from discussing Tibetan Masters to the works of Alice Bailey. Excited by meeting an actual medium who was channelling messages from a variety of sources Caddy requested Naomi to ask for guidance as to the purpose of their meeting. The message that came back was that the two of them had been together in past lives and had been brought together to further the development of a 'Network of Light' across the world. Naomi said she had been contacted on numerous occasions by beings from outer space who had instructed her to set up a group that could contact other groups around the world by telepathy and form a psychic network to channel extraterrestrial energies that were being poured down upon the earth by the Space Brothers. She told Peter that her group had been telepathically in touch with 370 other groups around the world. The meeting with Edwards would establish 'an extraordinary bond' between the two of them. For years they would exchange up to two or three letters a week and her revelations sparked a long-term fascination with UFOs in Caddy and their contact would eventually lead to Edwards joining the Caddys at Findhorn in 1964.

Eileen and Peter Caddy

Peter Caddy's interest in UFOs, backed up by the messages from the Space Brothers being received by Naomi, prompted him in 1954 to write a report: *An Introduction to the Nature and Purpose of Unidentified Flying Objects*, explaining what lay behind the increasing numbers of UFO sightings that were being reported at the time. He received guidance to get 26 copies of the 8,000 word report and deliver them to a list of key persons including: Winston Churchill, Clement Atllee, Prince Phillip, President Eisenhower and several other prominent military, scientific and spiritual figures, among them Air Chief Marshal Lord Hugh Dowding. After he had read the report, Dowding wrote back to Caddy saying 'I am personally convinced of the existence of spaceships, and I think it highly probable that they are manned by extraterrestrial crews ... I think that the government ought to take the subject of spaceships very seriously ...' Caddy also got a meeting with the Deputy Director of Intelligence at the Air Ministry who unfortunately was not as forthcoming as Dowding and said that until a UFO landed in front of him and he had the chance to dismantle and examine it he wasn't going to believe in their existence. Messages continued to be received from outer space throughout the late 1950's, becoming increasingly apocalyptic as time went by. In one Eileen Caddy saw the mysterious word LUKANO written in letters of fire. This was quickly confirmed by Naomi as the name of the captain of a spaceship from Venus who was planning a rescue mission to earth should a nuclear holocaust occur. The messages from outer space kept coming, at times on an almost daily basis, with details of the proposed mission. In 1958 Eileen Caddy was told 'this is not the only oasis from which people will be rescued when destruction comes. But it is the only one in this country.' [21] In a story in *The Sunday Pictorial* on 20th September 1960 under the headline 'The Martians Are Coming, He Says' Peter Caddy is reported as declaring that flying saucers from Mars and Venus were on their way to Earth to warn humans that they were on the brink of disaster. 'I believe they will offer people on Earth a chance to leave this planet with them before the catastrophe. They are like us in many ways, but the chief difference is that they have no understanding of such emotions as hatred, greed, jealousy or spite. Their only emotions are love and friendship.' So convinced was he that an extraterrestrial rescue was imminent, Caddy cleared trees from a mound behind the Cluny Hotel in Forres that he was manager of at the time, to create a UFO landing strip and on Christmas Eve and again on New Year's Day a small group kept night-time vigil waiting for the spaceships to land. The little band of watchers were later informed that the landings had been attempted but had failed due to a combination of climatic conditions and the effects of radiation from atomic bomb testing. It is not clear whether it was this instance of UFO enthusiasm that got the Caddys moved by the management from the Cluny Hotel, which he had been successfully managing through a combination of divine guidance channelled through Eileen and his own positive thinking, to the Trossachs Hotel. The little group of 'God's Hoteliers' would not manage to turn round the fortunes of the Trossachs Hotel and with almost no warning they were given notice to leave; there were rumours that they had been sacked for fiddling the books and these would dog them during the following few years.

In October 1962, as the little group moved their caravan firstly on to the Findhorn Sands Caravan Park and then the following month to the Findhorn Bay Caravan Park, the Cuban Missile crisis was unfolding, presumably adding to the bleak outlook and the group's apocalyptic mood. Extra-terrestrial messages kept coming after the group had moved to the caravan park alternating between visions of the Space Brothers:

I have always seen our space brothers and the mothership or a craft, but tonight I seem to be taken to the natural garden with the building carved out of the rock with everything in harmony. It was on Venus. No windows in the building. There were people like us there tonight, but radiant people. I have never been with Lukano or seen him anywhere but on the ship, or flying saucer before. On Venus everything is in harmony.

Eileen Caddy, Elixir 10th May 1963

through apocalyptic scenes of planetary destruction:

I saw a great storm over Washington City, and all the buildings seem to be struck by lightning or thunderbolts as they lay shattered. All the people were dead and an awful darkness seemed to envelope the city. Then I saw thousands of small shadowy forms moving everywhere, and I saw they were black rats swarming everywhere consuming the dead, for there was no one left in the city to bury the dead.

Eileen Caddy, Elixir 23rd November 1963

to the somewhat surreal and dreamlike:

I saw Mr Harold Wilson being sent up in a rocket by the Russians, and it went up and up and when it had reached a certain height it exploded and he rushed down to earth at a tremendous speed. I saw him sitting on the ground rubbing his head and feeling very sorry for himself.

Eileen Caddy, Elixir 8th June 1965

Peter Caddy maintained contact with a network of people interested in UFOs and by 1966 he had set up a telephone tree so that these people could be alerted should a message be received that the spaceships were due to appear. A call went out in May of that year and a band of excited UFO spotters gathered on the beach at Findhorn on the Whit Bank Holiday weekend. As darkness fell the group waited; the spaceship was supposedly going to come in flying low over the North Sea to avoid being spotted by an RAF radar. After a while, and some preparatory channelling, it was declared that the spaceship had been and gone although no-one had noticed anything.

After the failed landing, Eileen Caddy received a channelled message which confirmed contact had almost been made: Let none of you have any feeling of disappointment regarding last night (the landing of our space brothers). All was in preparation for something far, far greater than any of you have ever contemplated. The message went on to advise that what Caddy and his friends believed would be a saucer sent to evacuate supporters as part of the ET plan was in fact merely delivering a message that everything would be OK.

Andy Roberts "Saucers Over Findhorn" in *Fortean Times* December 2006

A fascination with UFOlogy would continue to be part of the ideas that attracted people to visit Findhorn until the early 1970's after which it would slowly fade into the background, warranting little and eventually no mention in any community publications. Later in the same year that saw the publication of *God Spoke to Me* a further booklet was written: *The Findhorn Garden: an experiment in the co-operation between three kingdoms*. It was about the 'magical' garden that the group had been developing and it would be this story – of the Findhorn Garden – that would stick in the popular imagination, even more than the stories of messages from God or communication with UFOs. It became a key part of the founding mythology of the community – with the tale of giant vegetables and talking with nature spirits still being the first thing many people will bring up whenever Findhorn is mentioned (even 40 years after the last giant cabbage was seen). The garden was not started with the intention of carrying out an experiment in co-operating with nature, but out of necessity. In March 1963 being unemployed and not being able to find any work Peter Caddy decided to start growing vegetables on a small 11ft x 6ft plot beside their caravan to supplement the small group's diet. Knowing little or nothing about gardening he read whatever gardening books he could lay his hands on and set about creating compost to improve the sandy soil out of any materials he could find.

I wanted to grow a few radishes and lettuces to supplement our meagre income. There was only about two inches of turf on top – just a tangle of couch grass – and the rest was just sand and gravel held together by the long creeping roots of the couch grass.

Peter Caddy In Perfect Timing

Helped by Eileen and Dorothy, horse manure, greengrocers left-overs, a bale of straw fallen from a passing lorry, seaweed, a dead salmon and a dead swan washed up on the beach were all added to the compost. By May in a letter to Naomi Peter Caddy would describe his compost heap as 'steaming like an ocean liner' and report that his first crops were thriving.

… Peter studied gardening books and gradually brought more bits of land around the caravan into cultivation, which was hard work in which we all joined in. In my daily message on 1st of May 1963 I was told to feel the nature forces, to feel their essence and purpose for god and be positive and harmonise with that essence …

Dorothy Maclean, The Deva Consciousness tape 1973

The message received by Dorothy/Divina instructed her to think about nature spirits and told her that they would be 'overjoyed to help and to find some members of the human race eager for that help.' The message went on to encourage contact with higher nature spirits and said that they were willing to help, but were suspicious of humans. She was at first somewhat sceptical of the whole idea of communicating with plants.

… when I first heard that vegetables had intelligence I thought it was nonsense. How could a cabbage have intelligence it hasn't got a brain. But when I realised that everything that came from that source had validity and I listened and tried to tune in and made the communication with the intelligence. I realised that I was speaking to the soul of the species and that everything has a soul. We have individual souls but the vegetables and the flowers and everything have group souls. And that what I was contacting was the soul level from my own soul level. And that everything that is part of God has got life forms on all levels and naturally intelligence on all levels …

Dorothy Maclean, interviewed by Epiphany Films 2002

The co-operation with the nature spirits was a bit hit and miss to begin with. In *The Magic Garden Workpad*, written during this period, there is mention of early disappointments in the garden in June 1963. But the co-operation soon took off with Dorothy/Divina communicating with what she named devas

Findhorn Garden
circa 1972

from a whole range of plant species and receiving practical advice on how to develop the garden. However, this advice wasn't always taken by Peter the pragmatist, who argued that as he had created the garden he would have the final say and that with the limited resources he had at hand it wasn't always possible or appropriate to follow the devas' advice. Over the following winter the group prepared the earth for the following season and planted fruit trees and bushes. By the following spring the garden was looking in good shape and that summer the combination of hard working humans and helpful devas produced spectacular results.

By May 1964 the fruit trees and bushes were bursting into bud. When the red cabbages matured, one weighed thirty-eight pounds and another forty-two. A sprouting broccoli, mistakenly planted as a cauliflower grew to such enormous proportions that it provided food for weeks; and was almost too heavy to be lifted from the ground.

Peter Tompkins and Christopher Bird, *The Secret Life of Plants*

Caddy and Maclean's belief in the work they were doing with the nature spirits was bolstered by Caddy's acquaintance with Robert Ogilvie Crombie, known as ROC, who he met through his contacts in the Scottish UFO Society in Edinburgh. In his seventies, ROC became something of a mentor to the slightly younger Caddy, being almost the only person that he would listen to and take advice from, other than the guidance received by Eileen/Elixir. As told in Paul Hawken's 1975 book *The Magic of Findhorn*, ROC's story is perhaps the most fantastical of all the Findhorn founders. Although ROC never actually lived as a permanent community member, in all the early community literature he is mentioned alongside the Caddy's and Maclean as one of the group's founding influences. He was a mercurial figure, part natural scientist, part occultist, part modern day Arthurian wizard. 'If Merlin's owl alighted on his shoulder you would hardly be surprised. He seems enwrapped in an amniotic fluid of a world myth which threatens to break at any moment: he is a chrysalis neatly hanging from the old modern reality.' Hawken goes on to tell that, whilst walking in the Edinburgh Royal Botanical Gardens, ROC had met a nature spirit in the form of a classical fawn, called Kurmos, dancing round the trees. This turned out to be the first of many meetings with not only Kurmos, but various nature spirits, elves and the figure of the god Pan himself.

Certainly a reconciliation between man and the nature spirits is now required for the survival of the world. For this reason Pan had to initiate direct contact. It is vital for the future of mankind that belief in the nature spirits and their god Pan is re-established and that they are seen in their true light. In spite of the outrages man has committed against nature, these beings are only too pleased to help him if he will seek and ask for their co-operation.

Robert Ogilvie Crombie *The Findhorn Garden* 1975

The little oasis of green on the caravan park was by now starting to attract interest, firstly among residents in other caravans and then further afield. The garden came to the attention of the County Horticultural Adviser for Morayshire who, after taking a sample of the soil from the garden for analysis, was so impressed by the group's achievements that he invited Peter Caddy to appear in a BBC radio gardening programme. On the programme broadcast in 1965 Caddy steered away from any mention of devas and co-operation with nature as he thought it might sound too much like 'fairies at the bottom of the garden' and instead claimed that their success was entirely due to the use of good organic compost. In October 1965 Peter Caddy managed to get a last minute invite to a conference being held at Attingham Hall in Shropshire, on the subject of 'The Significance of the Group in the New Age', to which a select list New Age movers and shakers had been personally invited. The publicity for the conference announced:

This is an age of conferences, discussion groups, study of 'group dynamics' and the like. The reason is that intense change and pressure in all parts of the social organism demands our learning to absorb new ideas which may have a transforming power. Here the group is a necessary instrument. It is an entity far greater in strength than the sum of its individual members.

Prospectus for *The Significance of the Group in the New Age* conference 1-3 October 1965

The opening address was given by Christopher Hills who called on those gathered there to formulate a charter for a New Age Community. After some discussion as to what this might mean Caddy stood up in frustration and told the crowd that it was nonsense to draw up charters and blueprints. At Findhorn they were already doing what they were all talking about guided step-by-step by God. He sat down to stunned silence. Caddy's outburst led to an invite by the conference organiser, George Trevelyan, to talk about what was happening at Findhorn. This in turn led to Trevelyan visiting Findhorn in 1968 and becoming a lifelong friend and advocate for the community. So impressed was he on his first visit with the Findhorn garden he wrote to Lady Eve Balfour, founder of the Soil Association, describing the garden as '… one of the most vigorous and productive small gardens I have ever seen, with a quality of taste and colour unsurpassed .' This led to a visit from Lady Mary Balfour who too was impressed by the garden '… something important is happening here at Findhorn – something strange and wonderful, hopefully not unique. Gardens like this are needed the world over, desperately needed where deserts flourish and life dies …' Further visits by Soil Association luminaries, Professor Lindsay Robb and Donald Wilson, followed by a visit from Men of the Trees founder Richard St Barbe Baker cemented the reputation of the Findhorn garden. By this time Peter Caddy had dropped the 'It's all done with compost' story and was openly talking about co-operation and co-creation with nature.

No cynic is able to explain away the fact of these flowers. Whatever anyone says, they go on burgeoning. Leading soil experts have declared that, in the initial years, compost and good husbandry alone could not have achieved these sensational results. No artificial fertilisers were ever used and the ground was dead and profitless as imaginable. There must be some other factor.

George Trevelyan in the Foreword to *The Findhorn Garden*

Whether visitors believed in the influence of nature spirits or not, the most remarked upon fact about the success of the Findhorn gardeners was that they had achieved such remarkable results on such poor soil. As the story has been retold countless writers have elaborated on the description. The land is variously described as '… forlorn and arid … no more than sand and gravel … a bleak and windy piece of coastland … extremely poor, being a mixture of sand and gravel and overgrown with couch grass … exposed to high winds and bad weather … desert-like … a barren piece of land … close to the Arctic Circle … constantly swept by gale force winds …' These descriptions have surprised and angered some of the local inhabitants of the area which is generally known for its mild moderate climate, catching as it does the tail end of the Gulf Stream and being sheltered by mountains from the prevailing south-westerly winds.

The area around Findhorn once formed part of the Barony of Culbin, part of the Kinnaird estate, considered at one time to be the 'Granary of Moray'. The estate – consisting of a Laird's House; gardens; orchards; a number of farms and crofts – had, by 1700, 'mysteriously' disappeared; reputedly engulfed overnight by a great sandstorm in the autumn of 1694 which buried the land in places to a depth of 100 feet. The storm also altered the course of the River Findhorn and buried the original village of Findhorn about five miles west of the present village. For the following two hundred years the area resembled a desert landscape with every storm making the sands shift their position, leading to stories of buildings revealed in the dunes: a dovecote, a chapel and parts of the manor house. Local legends tell of the tops of trees from a buried orchard appearing from the sand, blossoming and producing fruit; of smugglers' 'treasure' lost in overnight changes to the sands; of a circus animal's bleached bones appearing thirty years after it was last seen wandering off into the dunes; and of rare Pallas Sandgrouse, desert birds from central Asia, nesting in the area in the late 19th Century. Research has shown that whilst the 1694 storm had indeed devastated the area, the sand had been building up for years, in part due to villagers pulling up marram grass (that stabilised the dunes) to thatch their homes. The influx of sand over previously farmed lands produced an odd patchwork of fertility. Local people knew where peat for burning could be found close to the sand's surface; or where to dig through the sand to plant in the more fertile patches of soil below. An old map in the guard room at Brodie Castle shows where these 'mosses' lay in 1770. A deep trench cut recently into the sands in east Culbin by local scientist and writer Sinclair Ross revealed layers of sand punctuated by thick layers of fertile soil.

Did the little group of magical gardeners' chance upon a buried Culbin moss? Did they get help from nature spirits? Or was it just the result of heaps of good old compost? Or a combination of all three? Whatever the root cause of their initial horticultural successes, the displays of giant plants did not last long and all that remained to convince any sceptics by the time the story was widely reported were a few 'inconclusive photographs' and the testimony of the few people who were there at the time. In the following few years the community saw an influx of both professional and non-professional gardeners each with varying levels of attunement to and belief in the devas and nature spirits which led to heated debates and conflicts. These flared up at a conference titled 'Man, Nature and the New Age' held at Findhorn in the autumn of 1974 where such questions as 'What is the difference between co-operation and manipulation? and 'What is gardening anyway?' were raised.

We saw it as an opportunity to communicate with other lifeforms ... We acknowledged that they had a place but affirmed that the vision for the garden was to grow food for humans to eat. They were welcome if they could be in harmony with that vision. They stayed and so did the vegetables. We had beautiful, healthy and vigorous vegetables. We communicated to the rabbits that they were welcome in the garden if they stayed on the grass banks and ate the clovers and wildflowers there. We asked the moles to leave the garden completely because their presence was too disruptive, but we did suggest an alternative place for them to go ...

Adam, Findhorn Gardener in *Faces of Findhorn*

Despite these conflicts, co-creation and co-operation with nature and nature spirits has continued to be a thread of belief and practice running through the Findhorn community, with one Findhorn gardener stating some 20 years later that:

... My higher self and the garden spirits are the same, we're all energy anyway. I manifested them and co-created them, they are co-workers. Through growing and meditating in the garden, and drawing them, I made contact with the deva of the garden – an energy overlooking it ...

Findhorn Gardener – quoted by David Pepper in *Communes and the Green Vision* **1991**

Findhorn Community circa 1975, Paris Match

Some members have clearly remained sceptical of such views – one reporting in 1992 that 'I never saw any extraordinary growth at Findhorn that was not the result of hard work, lots of compost, expert knowledge and water' **22**. Following repeated incursions into the gardens by deer ('Attunement with nature worked no better with the deer than it did with the moles or the rabbits') the community began erecting deer-proof fencing around its gardens in 1989.

For some time in the late 1960's Eileen Caddy had been receiving messages that told of coming changes; of a 'turning point for every soul', of a 'release of cosmic power into the Universe' and of a time when people would be 'drawn together in groups'. The messages called on the little group to plan to become a 'Centre of Light'.

My beloved, I want you to see this Centre of Light as an ever growing cell of Light. It has started as a family group, is now a community, will grow into a village, then into a town and finally into a vast City of Light. It will progress in stages and expand very rapidly. Expand with the expansion ...

She also received guidance to erect seven prefabricated mobile holiday chalets, one to be used as a sanctuary and the others as guest accommodation. In May 1969 the community published a brief statement of its beliefs and history.

The Findhorn community consists of a group of people pioneering a new way of living. There are no blueprints; we seek and follow God's guidance which comes in different ways. My wife Eileen hears small voices within and receives detailed guidance which we have followed with astonishing results. Our aim is to bring down the Kingdom of Heaven on earth and therefore everything must be as near perfect as possible ... We are pioneering a way for a new age which is gradually unfolding and will require a new type of man.

Peter Caddy *The Findhorn Story* **1969 (Quoted in A Rigby** *Alternative Realities***)**

The growth of the community was boosted considerably by the arrival in June 1970 of two Americans, David Spangler and Myrtle Glinnes. Spangler was a young rising star in the American New Age movement and something of a bridge between the older mystical traditions of the Theosophists and the likes of Alice Bailey and the new wave of 'hippie' spiritual seekers. Since the age of seven he had been having mystical experiences, as a teenager had begun channelling and by 1965 was giving talks and lectures about his experiences. He and Glinnes had been running a small spiritual group together and had received guidance that the "next cycle of work" would be in Europe. They had arrived at Findhorn for a five day visit and ended up staying for three years. The combination of the young charismatic mystic and the older Glinnes, who had counselling and organisational skills, would act as a huge catalyst for growth.

Within six months after David arrived, the community doubled in size to forty-five people, with young people pouring in until they outnumbered all the others. The Lightstone sisters came in through the sound barrier, singing, at the top of their lungs. Jewels Manchester became Peter's 'assistant', and her sister Merrily with husband Jim Bronson, fresh from Outward Bound school, started the photography and outdoor activities departments. Freya Conga joined Merrily in taking over the kitchen from Eileen and Joannie; a flock of artists moved in, starting a weaving studio, a pottery, a candlemaking workshop, and a graphic arts department. Alexis Maxcy began the drama group, while David, along with a Yugoslav artist, Milenko Matanovic, and American singer Lark Batteau started a vocal group called the New Troubadors ...

Paul Hawken, *The Magic of Findhorn*

Spangler began giving lectures to the community in a house next to the caravan site called the 'Park' that had belonged to the caravan site owner and which they were able to buy following a donation of £12,000 by one of the new members. From these lectures grew the idea of a 'College' which by the following year had developed into a full blown programme of courses. A catalogue for the 'Findhorn College' from the time lists classes in such things as Esoteric Wisdom; The Foundations of Findhorn; and Dance & Body Attunement, alongside the more conventional subjects of painting; drawing; choir; and guitar classes. The flurry of new members produced a subsequent surge of activity. Spangler's lectures were reproduced as tapes. Publications started to fly off the group's newly kitted out printing press, audiovisual presentations were put together. The New Troubadors (affectionately known as 'the Troubs'), who had grown out of community 'Fun nights' organised by Peter Caddy, wrote and performed songs with titles such as 'Change Can Come', 'The Love Affirmation', and 'I Dreamed a Dream' and released them on two cassettes entitled *Homeland* and *Love*. Arts and craft studios were set up under the auspices of Findhorn Studios Ltd making and selling a variety of pottery, weaving, jewellery and leatherwork that were sold on site and in shops further afield. All this expansion required more space and an area to the north-east of the caravan park called Pineridge was 'colonised' by the community. The setting up of the 'college' finally enabled the registration of the community as an educational charity, something they had been trying to achieve since 1968. The period also saw a corresponding change in the way the community was organised. Out went the complete open door membership policy and free accommodation for visitors. In came charges for visitors, for publications and for being on the community's mailing list. Various roles were invented and 'departments' set up with department heads, a clerk of works, a domestic bursar and an executive committee that met to decide on policy which was then announced to the community at a monthly meeting (later these distinctly old age titles were replaced with the likes of 'focaliser' and 'core group'). This somewhat hierarchical structure was officially topped off by the new Findhorn Foundation Trustees. However, in reality 'The role of the trustees was seen basically as one of clearing up the legal and financial loose ends' left in the wake of Peter acting under 'guidance', unrestrained by conventional business considerations.' **22**

Findhorn Community Centre extension

The result of all the publicity generated by the group's own publications and stories in various magazines and newspapers was that between 1969 and 1972 numbers visiting and joining the community grew dramatically, with membership rising from 16 in 1969 to 120 in 1972 living in 20 bungalows and 41 caravans.

> *... Findhorn experienced a series of invasions – and crises. Whilst continuing to recruit elderly and relatively moneyed people, especially women, through the networks of spiritist belief. Findhorn was, in effect, discovered by the communes movement. It became almost a centre of pilgrimage for the wandering young, for would-be communards, spiritual leaders and teachers of every description, vegans, vegetarians, craft workers and Americans. The community seemed to flourish in the face of all this.*
>
> **Abrams & McCulloch, Communes, Sociology and Society 1975**

The influx of so many new younger members brought with it conflicts with the older generation of seekers and in particular with Peter Caddy. It was here that Myrtle Glinnes' counselling and interpersonal skills came to the fore, smoothing over ruffled spiritual feathers and helping the different generations to see their common ground. In the middle of all this rapid expansion Eileen Caddy received guidance to stop giving guidance to the community.

> *My beloved, now is the perfect time for a complete change of rhythm for you. It is no longer necessary for you to receive a message from Me each day for the community ... For a very long time I have gone on day after day repeating Myself; it is now time My word was lived and demonstrated ... You cannot spoonfeed a child all its life. The time comes when it has to learn to feed itself and you have to let it do so. Let go and stand back and allow all those in the community to live a life guided and directed by Me.*

This brought to an end the regular sessions in the sanctuary when the guidance for the day would be read out and the group had start to find a way to listen to their own inner voices and a process of group attunement was evolved.

Group attunement became much more important. Having no guidance from an extra source to show us comfortable confirmation we tuned in as best we could and came up with group decisions ...

Raymond Akhurst

In 1973 Spangler and Glinnes returned to the US along with a number of other members, including founder member Dorothy Maclean, to set up the Lorian Association. Shortly before their departure the group was invited to a conference in London for which, inspired by the success of the musical *Godspell*, David Spangler decided to write Findhorn's own musical based on the evolution of the Christ Consciousness called Freedom Man. Written over a three-day period with fellow Troubadour Milenko Matanovic it included songs with titles like 'Let New Worlds Grow' (the Song of the Devas), 'In the Beginning', 'Where There Is A Will', and 'Song Of The Avatars'. In the end the musical never saw the light of day, the songs instead becoming part of the New Troubadours repertoire. David Spangler may have only been at Findhorn for a relatively short period, but his influence and the changes he instigated laid the basis for the community's development over the next decade and has given him the status of the group's fourth founder.

The rapid pace of growth of the community continued throughout the 1970's. In 1973, needing to expand facilities at the caravan site in order to accommodate the increasing numbers of people wanting to visit and come on courses, plans were formulated for a 'University Hall' – guidance from Eileen Caddy stated that it should be a quickly built utilitarian building and that the group should then move on to providing proper housing to replace caravans. However, collective enthusiasm turned the project into something on an altogether grander scale and one that would take ten years to complete. With resonances of the building of the Djamichunatra at Coombe Springs, the 'Universal Hall' was designed and built using a combination of manifestation of materials, money and people, esoteric geometry and hard labour from members and volunteers. It would take a decade and a grant from the Scottish Tourist Board to finish it. 'Ten years later we had the monument, a superb building in stone, beautifully furnished and decorated, with magnificent mural paintings.' **23**

As well as featuring in newspapers, on radio and in TV programmes Findhorn attracted researchers and writers interested in communal living and alternative lifestyles. The result was that sociological studies of the group appeared in a number of books in the mid-seventies. But it would be one book in particular that would really put the group on the New Age map. The *Magic of Findhorn* by Paul Hawken was not some obscure sociological study of communal living published by an academic press. It was a popular account of the founding of the community written to appeal to a wide audience to be brought out by a major publisher, Harper Collins. After an American public relations man pointed out to them that this could bring 'an avalanche' of visitors to their door and 'where were they going to put them?' Peter Caddy's thoughts turned to the Cluny Hill Hotel in Forres to which guidance had said they would one day return. In a special issue of the *Findhorn Open Letter* in November 1975 Billy Sargent tells the story of 'The Return to Cluny Hill'.

Knowing that Findhorn was currently involved in its largest project to date, the building of the University Hall ... Peter's first thought was to call the solicitor Phimister Brown about his original offer to buy Cluny and hire Peter as its manager ... Phimister liked the idea and agreed to contact the managing director of the company. His conversation with the managing director was startling. Phimister expressed an interest in acquiring the hotel and asked if they had ever considered selling it. The managing director replied with surprise that either Phimister had a spy among the board of directors or else he was psychic, for that very day the board of directors had decided to sell the Cluny Hill Hotel. To Peter, this 'coincidence' was God's unmistakable indication that we were to go ahead in faith and purchase the hotel ourselves ...

Caddy presented his idea to the core group and there were some people who instantly felt that the Cluny Hill idea was right, while others reserved judgement. But they decided that a planning group should explore the idea further. This small group arranged to have dinner at the hotel and were able to see the building and grounds for themselves: they returned full of optimism and enthusiasm. Caddy also led small parties of members on trips to see the hotel so that they could 'attune to the situation for themselves' in preparation for a meeting of the whole community to consider the proposal.

The community meeting was on a Friday evening in early August. Peter presented his perspective and read some of the experiences ROC and other sensitives had had at Cluny Hill. He mentioned that David Spangler had once had a dream of Cluny Hill as a college in the University of Light ... Colour slides from the Caddys' years at the hotel were shown then a meditation was held. An open sharing followed. Some queries were discussed and most members offered affirmations about the project ... Michael Shaw ended the evening by saying, I think I've thrown every possibility of a practical nature that I can think of against the planning group over the past three weeks and a solution for every one of them has fallen into place. I've gradually come to the conclusion that despite the apparent illogicality of this decision, it just might be the will of God that we acquire the hotel.

The hotel was large enough to provide extensive accommodation for members and visitors, several lecture and workshop rooms, a laundry, bakery and a large garage. Outside there was a small heated swimming pool (since filled in and turned into a Zen garden); a tennis pavilion with two courts (now a car park); three vegetable gardens; a greenhouse and five acres of grounds; '... there was even a separate billiards room which had a high beamed ceiling, skylights and bay window which seemed perfectly suitable to become a sanctuary ...' With the backing of the group plans were made for expanding the guest programme, cashflows were produced, banks consulted and finally an offer of £60,000 was made to buy the hotel to establish Cluny Hill College. A potential stumbling block to the purchase reared its head; the hotel chain had already accepted bookings from coach parties of holiday makers for the following summer and they insisted Findhorn take on the responsibility of honouring these bookings.

Peter and Eileen were away visiting a light centre in Turkey and had left the decision entirely in the community's hands. The hotel company said that unless we accepted the bookings the deal was off. The community had nowhere to turn but within. The core group met for three hours and from their attunement decided to buy the hotel in the confidence that this was the right thing to do, whether it meant we ourselves would have to accommodate the coach parties or whether we would be able to arrange to have them accommodated elsewhere.

Billy Sargent

Cluny Hill College in 2011

This was the first major decision taken by the community without the involvement or guidance of either of the Caddys. On May 1st the following year the first coach party arrived at Cluny. It was greeted by a crowd of enthusiastic members and excited children all warmly greeting the guests and offering to carry in their luggage. Meanwhile in the upstairs lounge a guest workshop on 'Revelation: The Birth of a New Age' was taking place. While there was serious potential for a huge culture clash and there had been many worries about how they would cope, the first coach party's stay was something of a success. Very quickly there were so many requests from the Yorkshire farmers and old age pensioners who made up the party to see the Findhorn community that group tours were arranged. After a few days the holiday makers were enjoying the novelty of the situation, some even calling in at the bookshop. One man, on being asked how his stay was going, replied 'Lovely. It's a revelation. Really remarkable. Everybody's so happy and giving real smiling service – something we're not used to these days.' Another holidaymaker commenting on his stay remarked that 'We came with a very open mind – I did anyway. Now I've seen what commune life is like in a University of Light. I must admit, and I'll speak for us all, we're thrilled with it really.' **24** Things settled into a pattern for the rest of the summer with a double act going on behind the scenes, Findhorn members one minute serving full English breakfast to holidaymakers and the next minute, after a quick turnaround, serving muesli and toast to guests attending the Transpersonal Psychology event that was the first to be hosted at the new 'college'. Tired and exhausted, the Cluny team made it through the summer. While the holidaymakers may have been 'thrilled' with their stay, Peter Caddy was far from satisfied with the way things were going. Drawing on his oft quoted philosophy of 'Patience, Persistence and Perseverance' and with his best RAF catering corps manager's hat on he explained to a meeting planning the following year's programme how he hoped Cluny was to be run. In so many words he said – pretty much the way it had been when he and Eileen had run it previously as a 4-star hotel. This view was at odds with the more relaxed approach that other members wished to take and it wasn't until one of the members who had been there for some while, Stan Stanfield, stepped in and pointed out to Caddy that 'there may well be more than one way to reach perfection' that a full-scale community conflict was averted.

By the autumn of 1976 the Universal Hall was just about in a state where it could be used and the community hosted its first major conference – 'One Earth: The World Crisis and the Wholeness of Life'. 'We finished the lights in the Hall at 6am on the day of the opening and the Hall was still being built for some time afterwards.' The first and main speaker was Fritz Schumacher of *Small is Beautiful* fame. The Hall would, over the years, develop into a major conference and arts venue, attracting high-profile speakers and well-known artists. Following the 'return to Cluny' a number of other properties in the area were acquired by the community. In 1978 they were given the rather run-down Georgian mansion on the north side of Cluny Hill called Drumduan House. This was followed by the purchase of Station House in Findhorn village for members' accommodation and then Cullerne House and grounds, situated to the north of the Caravan Park. A group of members borrowed money to purchase Newbold House, half mile south of Cluny Hill. The community also became custodians of properties on the west coast of Scotland on the Isles of Iona and Erraid where a retreat house and a sister community was established. The acquisition of these properties and the consequent cost of renovation stretched the Foundation's finances to the point where, by the end of the 1970's, they owed more than £400,000 to private individuals and to the bank. As the 70's ended so did the Caddy's close relationship. Eileen was instructed that she should not give Peter any further guidance and this started to erode his position with the rest of the community and he started to seek guidance from various 'itinerant clairvoyants' which caused some disquiet among members. On a speaking tour of America he started a relationship with Shari Secof, the Findhorn 'contact person' for the Los Angeles area. This would lead to Eileen demanding a divorce. Eventually he was gently nudged into realising it was time to leave. Officially his leaving was '... in accordance with the vision for the community' and he was off to pursue other projects: in reality the process was somewhat more painful.

Following the departure of Peter Caddy, focalisation of the community passed to François Duquesne whose steady hand would guide the group through troubled financial waters. Membership of the Foundation had grown to over 300, income was barely covering expenditure and debts were continuing to mount. Described by one member as a period when the community 'began to wobble – but perhaps needed to wobble to move forward.' **25** Duquesne's time as focalisor would see the transformation from community to village as envisaged in Eileen's guidance. The early 80's were, in some ways, a period of financial retrenchment, with a reduction in membership numbers alongside adoption of a much more businesslike approach to many aspects of community life. But these cultural changes, which included the establishment of independent businesses within the wider Findhorn community framework, did not lead to a reduction in vision; if anything, the vision expanded to include the concept of a 'planetary village'.

A planetary village means more than a multi-cultural, inter-national community. Indeed, to my way of thinking, a planetary village could be made up entirely of people of a particular nationality, or ethnic type. The distinguishing characteristic ... Is the nature of the relationship of the community to the wholeness and life of the earth ... Practicing in microcosm the qualities that make our world a living, evolving entity.
David Spangler, "Stepping into a Planetary Culture", One Earth Magazine 1982

We realise that we are being called upon to root ourselves both into the Earth and into Spirit, and that a new culture and civilisation are not just born overnight. It is the work of several generations. So we can relax somewhat and let go of the sense of urgency and of the missionary impulse; we can get down to earth, get to know our neighbours, give time to raising our children, and think more about how we create culture and less about how we convert people according to our image of change.
François Dusquesne 1983

Various business ventures were set up by community members during this period, or spun-off from existing communal activities: Weatherwise, a solar panel and later a building company; The Game of Transformation, a 'personal development board game'; the Findhorn Press; and Trees for Life, a charity dedicated to reforesting the Scottish highlands. Many of these came under a sort of umbrella organisation called New Findhorn Directions set up in 1979 to co-ordinate and encourage business activities that would, it was hoped, in the end provide an income not just to the individual members themselves but also for the Foundation. Looking back, the single most important development during this period was the opportunity in 1983 to buy the caravan park. While the owner held out for the best price he thought he could get, the chance to be in control of the property on which the community was based and the potential income that would bring was too good to pass up. '... A sustained campaign was launched, in which each member took responsibility for manifesting funds for the cost of a particular area of the Park. This gave individuals a direct stake in fund-raising. Appeals were sent to previous community members and visitors; auctions and fundraising events followed each other in quick succession ...' **26** The owner held out for a further £80,000 above the funds that had been raised and the Park was only purchased by the Foundation taking out a further loan. Writing about this period in an article in the American *Communities* magazine in 1998, Australian academic and long-term Findhorn associate, Bill Metcalf commented:

One of the successes of Findhorn during the 1980's has been to establish a managerial structure which efficiently manages this large, complex organisation without having to create or locate a new charismatic leader to replace Peter Caddy. The apparently bureaucratic structure for decision making which has evolved, however, largely operates through intuitive guidance and divine revelation which is received during meditation. Every meeting whether of the Foundation Trustees or the lunch cooks, will start with an attunement whereby spiritual guidance is invoked. If a consensus is not achieved within the meeting, further meditations will be undertaken in order for everyone to receive further guidance. If a clear decision does not emerge, then this uncertainty is taken as a sign that other issues are not being looked at, and that everything must go on hold until some clear direction emerges.

Bill Metcalf, *Findhorn: The Routinization of Charisma*

In the same article Metcalf gave some statistics that showed that the Foundation had managed to weather the financial crisis of the early 80's. By the end of the decade they had an income in the region of £750,000, 80% coming from the guest programme, the rest coming from a combination of book sales and from members fees and donations. It was spending approximately £100,000 on capital expansion and £50,000 on debt reduction, and had managed to almost eliminate the previously accrued debt of £500,000.

Given its longevity, its success as a community and its high profile in both the national and the alternative press, it is not surprising that the Findhorn Community has been subject to perhaps more than its fair share of criticism. Some were disillusioned when the community didn't match up to their own visions, like hippie poet and painter Neil Oram who hitch-hiked up to Scotland with his young family in 1968 after receiving a letter from guru Meher Baba's secretary telling him about the spiritual pioneers who were '... uniting together Divine Guidance, Alien Intelligence, fairie intelligence and human faith'. Oram found the clash of culture too difficult and years later described the community as feeling '... like Noddyland. Utterly UNREAL ... Like ceramic pixies and gnomes cavorting in the garden. Phoney. 'Croquet on the lawn' type of atmosphere.' His opinion of Peter Caddy didn't mellow over the years: interviewed in 2005 Oram still thought that Caddy was 'the biggest ego-maniac I've ever met. Utterly insensitive. Outlandishly bombastic … He was a total phoney. Con man.' Oram and his family only stayed a short while at Findhorn, shortly after he founded his own spiritual centre at Goshem, high in the mountains above Loch Ness.

Others have attacked the Findhorn take on spirituality: criticism coming from both Christian orthodoxy and from Pagans. In a chapter in her 1985 book *New Age Armageddon* entitled 'Banishing Darkness: Findhorn's Plan of Light', feminist artist and writer Monica Sjöö argued that *The Plan of Light*, a discussion paper circulated by the community, was an attack on neo-pagans 'The conclusion I draw from all this is that pagans and Goddess lovers are seen in relation to the ancient powers that are to fade away in the New Age to give way to messengers of solar male-consciousness.' Sjöö also cited a friend who had written of her experience of living at Findhorn from 1980 to 1983 in an article published in *Spare Rib* – 'Is New Age Spirituality offering anything really new to women?' In this, the community was criticised for not supporting women and for suppressing criticism from women by stressing positive thinking and interpreting anyone who took a stand or disagreed on as issue as being too attached to 'negative emotions' or simply that they were just not 'spiritually advanced'. Coming from a very different spiritual perspective Kevin Logan, Vicar of St John's Church in Great Harwood, wrote of his attendance at a Findhorn Experience week in 1991 in *Close Encounters with the New Age*. Logan, who had written widely in the Christian Press about the dangers of New Age philosophies, was broadly cynical about much of what went on during his week of close encounters at Findhorn. At the end of the week he describes his encounter with Eileen Caddy:

Sign on entrance to Cluny College

The resemblance is uncanny, she looks like Mary Whitehouse, complete with silver-white hair, smile and looks. The style of glasses and the neat well-made flowered suit makes them almost twins. Even the words Eileen Caddy uses might have come from the mouth of the nation's moral grandmother. Some of them at least. I cannot help but warm to Eileen Caddy. She sits in the midst of our group, radiating her own charm and warmth; a seventy-two-year-old grandma with a compelling personality who is to keep the group spellbound. As I warm to her, I listen and then the sadness comes. There is much to agree with, but just as much to query. Questioning Eileen is as daunting as I imagine it could be for a researcher facing her 'twin'. Both know who they are, what they are, what they believe and why they believe. Both are unshakeable.

Findhorn has found itself woven into a number of conspiracy theories. These usually involve connections between the founder members and the intelligence services during the war, suggestions that the actual source of the community's 'guidance' was the CIA who could have been carrying out mind control experiments from RAF Kinloss and that the community's involvement with the United Nations has some sort of sinister sub-plot to take over the world. None of these 'theories' seem to hold much water, based largely on selective reading of second or third-hand reports and consisting of putting two and two together and making five or even seven. Perhaps the strongest criticism has come from ex-members, or those who were refused membership. Perhaps the most pointed case of this surrounds a book entitled *Hypocrisy and Dissent within the Findhorn Foundation*, published in 1996, which catalogues a series of complaints

*Field of Dreams
development
2011*

against the Findhorn Foundation and those in charge at the time. The book sparked off a series of 'reviews' and arguments that have continued on and off for over a decade in various publications and on the internet. Part of the complaint is focussed on the introduction of Holotropic Breathwork to the program of courses on offer at Findhorn. Developed by Stanislav Grof of the Esalen Institute in Big Sur California, out of his initial work on the psychotherapeutic uses of LSD, it involves inducing oxygen deprivation in the brain through hyperventilation. Various therapeutic and spiritual claims are made by practitioners and disputing these claims was part of the attack on Findhorn. The controversy reached such a pitch that in 1993 a report was commissioned by the Scottish Charities Office into the practice. As a result of the negative publicity and the critical report, Holotropic Breathwork was dropped from the course programmes being offered by the Foundation. The thrust of the other complaints in the book surround the way that the Foundation treated those making the complaints. Reviewing the book, former Commune Movement secretary and social inventor, Nicholas Albery commented: 'The main complaint made by this book is about the way that Findhorn has expelled people without giving them the right of appeal and then tried to make them into non-persons, ignoring them whenever confronted by them.' **27** The whole episode is one of the few times that Findhorn has been drawn into defending itself, preferring publically to ignore criticism and try to remain focussed on 'the positive'.

Other areas of criticism have been levelled at the community. One is a resentment from locals over the colonisation of the Findhorn village – both its name and the perceived or actual take-over by members, ex-members and camp followers of property in both Findhorn Village and the nearby town of Forres. This had led to local opposition to plans for expansion put forward by the community. The other regular criticism has been the commercialisation of the community and the high costs of attending events and the experience week programme. Experience Week has been the key way that people have visited the community for over 35 years .

... initially when I came, you just arrived, you got integrated into the work experience. You'd meet with people in the morning, get allocated somewhere to work. There wasn't a lot of people and you could come any day of the week. And then after Paul Hawken's book was published there was a sudden flood of people and the community really just couldn't work because it was constantly dealing with new people coming in with the same questions. So at that point they created what's now called the experience week program ... **28**

Mary Inglis

The details of the experience week programme have stayed remarkably constant over the years and while critics rail at the charges for the week, those members working on the programme express a view that they are performing a service rather than working for a commercial organisation. 'it wouldn't work for us to be serving our paying guests as if we were their support system or paid servants or whatever.' **29**

The final criticism levelled at the community is their general lack of Scottishness. Alastair McIntosh, Scottish writer, academic and activist, has criticised them for having few native-born members and for being 'a community that has parachuted in from all over the world, and in the past has brought with it too much of the Anglo-American colonial arrogance. It has not been good at listening to what Scotland might say to it – particularly about the relation of social justice to spirituality ...' While this may well have been very true in the early days of the community when there was a predominance of American accents among visitors, by the late 1990's there had been a dramatic shift in the demography of visitors and guests with a real shift to a European base with nearly half the guests come from continental Europe, 30% from the UK and a further 20% from USA, Canada, Australia and New Zealand.

Being started on a caravan park has given Findhorn advantages and opportunities not available to other groups set up in less flexible physical surroundings. Simply the flexibility it has given to the expansion (and contraction) of membership and the ability to annex surrounding land and property through purchase and gift over the years has in some ways allowed an organic development to occur, much like any other village but in a compressed time frame. During the late 1980's and 1990's a number of construction projects unfolded in and around the original caravan park. The first to appear were the whiskey 'barrel' houses, an imaginative recycling of whisky vats into small circular homes tucked away on the edge of Pineridge. In 1990 a house called Cornerstone was built for Eileen Caddy designed as a gift by London architect Ekkehard Weisner and built by her son David with community help. These were followed by a cluster of eco-homes called Bag End. This development started to put the community firmly on the eco-building map and led to the publication of *Simply Build Green* by John Talbot. Other environmental improvements were made with the installation of a Living Machine waste-water treatment plant to deal with the sewage for the whole site. This was followed by a single large scale-wind turbine (later three more were added). These developments happened as the global eco-village movement was getting underway and Findhorn became a key player in the development of ideas and practice in the movement, hosting eco-villages conferences and seminars. As the new millennium approached the community moved from growing people to growing community on a large scale. The Field of Dreams project saw the development of a neighbouring meadow as a somewhat suburban style housing development – initially conceived as providing self-build plots for 'modest' eco-homes. Some of these have turned out to be slightly more than modest when they were finished. The year 1997 saw perhaps the final piece of the ecovillage jigsaw with the purchase of over 400 acres of adjoining land by Duneland Ltd, a company set up for the purpose of enabling the continued development of the ecovillage project while at the same time protecting the extensive sand dunes as an undeveloped natural area with public access. Various plans have been developed for the dune lands. After prolonged negotiations a 'historic alliance' was achieved with the local village and 170 acres of the estate was gifted to the Findhorn Dunes Trust, a body made up of representatives of both Findhorn Village and the Findhorn Foundation. This was the first time the village and the Community had come together in a joint project. More recently, a progamme of replacing the stock of old caravans at the Park with more eco-friendly mobile homes has been started.

Alongside the physical expansion, the community has grappled with evolution of its management and governance structures culminating in the setting up. in 1999. of The New Findhorn Association (NFA), an umbrella council that aims to bring together the diverse organisations and people associated with the community within a 50-mile radius. The Association employs two 'Listener Conveners' whose job it is to 'take the pulse of the community, welcome new members, support organisations and businesses, empower grassroots members to take new initiatives and facilitate communication across the community.' [30] The NFA has over 350 individual members and some 32 organisation members. A local currency, the Eko, was launched in 2001, and was estimated to have turned over £150,000 of local trade in its first year. An independent economic impact study commissioned by Moray, Badenoch and Strathspey Enterprise in 2002 concluded that the work of the Foundation generated £4 million and 400 jobs for the region, a factor that may become even more important following the recent announcement of the closure of RAF Kinloss.

I love the Findhorn community. I see it as a high and great endeavour of the human spirit, a birthing ground for a new way of living, so new that the mainstream world still has no frame of reference for it. [31]

Mike Scott

In 2002 rumours circulated of a major movie to be made based on the early years of the Findhorn Community. To be called *The Garden of Angels* it was going to be produced in a new complex of studios planned to be built at Milton of Leys in Inverness. The names of various Hollywood stars were bandied about. It was reported that Meryl Streep and Sam Neill were pencilled in to play the Caddys alongside Glenn Close as Dorothy Maclean and Billy Connolly as the caravan park owner. Julia Roberts, Robin Williams, Sigourney Weaver and Sir Sean Connery were all said to have been approached to appear in the film. The movie project had been in the pipeline for some time. Filmmaker Ian Merrick had been working on the project since the early 1980's when he had concluded an exclusive film rights deal with Peter Caddy. After visiting Findhorn and talking with members, he developed a screenplay. 'This

Old Age style caravans at Findhorn

film is about faith and hope, and that the best of the human race can come out when they have faith and belief in what they're doing.' Neither the movie nor the Inverness Film Studios have materialised as yet.

Peter Caddy died in a car accident in Germany in 1994. In 2001 Eileen Caddy was placed at number 40 in a list of the world's most influential spiritual figures by the BBC TV programme *The God List* and in 2004 was awarded an MBE for 'services to Spiritual Inquiry'. She died at Findhorn on 13th December 2006. Recently Dorothy Maclean has returned and is being cared for by the community.

Looking back at my work at Findhorn I now know it was very important. We have polluted the planet and we are only now realising to what extent. At Findhorn we started dealing with nature in a different way. We've got to change our viewpoint completely and if we recognise that there's an intelligence we can co-operate with, what a difference it will make to the planet.

Dorothy Maclean, Far Out: The Dawning of New Age Britain

New Age style caravans at Findhorn

Annett, S *The Many Ways of Being* Abacus 1976.
ISBN: 0349100713

Caddy, Eileen *Flight into Freedom and Beyond*
Findhorn Press 1988/2002. ISBN: 1899171649

Caddy, Peter *In Perfect Timing* Findhorn Press 1996.
ISBN: 1899171266

Christopher, S *Engaged Buddhism in the West*
Queen Wisdom Publications 2000

Colin-Smith, J *Call No Man Master* Gateway Books 1988.
ISBN: 0946551464

Dwyer, G & Cole, R J *The Hare Krishna Movement: Forty
Years of Chant and Change* 2007. ISBN:1845114078

Findhorn Community *The Findhorn Garden*
Harper Perennial 1976. ISBN: 0060905204

Findhorn Community *Faces of Findhorn*
HarperCollins 1980. ISBN: 0060908513

Geraghty, Anne *In The Dark And Still Moving*
The Tenth Bull 2007. ISBN: 9780955495403

Guest, Tim *My Life in Orange* Granta 2004.
ISBN: 1862076324

Hawken, Paul *The Magic of Findhorn* Fontana 1976.
ISBN: 0006341780

MacLean, Dorothy To *Hear the Angels Sing*
Lindisfarne Books 1994. ISBN:0940262371

Miller, Russell *Bare Faced Messiah* Penguin 1988.
ISBN: 0747403325

Mullan, Bob *Life as Laughter: Following Bhagwan Shree
Rajneesh* Routledge 1983. ASIN: B0026R0YWE

Musgrove, F *Margins of the Mind* Methuen 1977.
ISBN: 0416550509

Musgrove, F *Ecstasy and Holiness; Counter Culture and the
Open Society* IUP 1974. ISBN: 0253319064

Oliver, I P *Buddhism in Britain* Rider & Co 1979.
ISBN: 00981381614

Palmer, S J *Moon Sisters, Krishna Mothers, Rajneesh Lovers*
SUP 1994. ISBN: 0815602979

Riddell, Carol *The Findhorn Community* Findhorn Press 1991.
ISBN: 0905249771

Shine, T *Honour Thy Fathers* 2002
www.buddhanet.net/pdf_file/honourfathers.pdf

Subhiti *Buddhism for Today* Element Books 1983.
ISBN: 0906540321

Sutcliffe, S *Children of the New Age* Routledge 2002.
ISBN: 0415242991

Wyllie, T *Love Sex Fear Death* Feral House 2009.
ISBN: 1932595376

Vajragupta *The Triratna Story* Windhorse 2010.
ISBN: 1899579923

Notes:

1. Joyce Colin-Smith, *Call No Man Master*.
2. Kenneth Walker, *Venture with Ideas*.
3. Quoted in *Maurice Nicoll: A Portrait* by Beryl Pogson.
4. Maurice Nicoll, *Psychological Commentaries on the Teachings of Gurdjieff and Ouspensky (Vol I)*.
5. http://www.gurdjieff-bibliography.com (23.2.2011).
6. http://anthonyblake.co.uk/Meetings.html (3.3.2012).
7. *Diggers & Dreamers 96/97*.
8. *Garden News*, 18 December 1959.
9. *A Piece of Blue Sky*, Jon Atack, 1992.
10. Marianne Rowell quoted as saying that the number of scientologists in the UK is approximately 102,000. *Plymouth Herald*, November 12, 2009.
11. Tim Wyllie, *Love Sex Fear Death*.
12. Comment on BBC website, Croome Court Wartime Memories – http://www.bbc.co.uk (1.1.2011).
13. From: 'Settled Mind, Silent Mind' in *Science of Mind Magazine* November 1993.
14. Natural Law Party Press release 14 July 1999.
15. Bob Mullan in *Life as Laughter: following Bhagwan Shree Rajneesh*.
16. http://www.ex-premie.org/pages/bkgrnd10.htm
17. ibid
18. *The Triratna Story*.
19. Eileen Caddy Guidance quoted by Andrew Rigby in *Communes in Britain*.
20. Personal recollection told to author by Whiteway resident.
21. Eileen Caddy notebook in Findhorn Archive, Scottish National Library.
22. Raymond Akhurst *My Life in the Findhorn Community*, 1992.
23. Carol Riddell *The Findhorn Community: creating a human identity for the 21st century*.
24. Quotes in 'Our First Coach Tour' by Billy Sargent. *Findhorn Open Letter* 10.
25. Richard Coates – Personal interview with the author, May 2011.
26. 'The Sacred Earth and the Heavenly City' in *One Earth Magazine*, Apr/May 1983 p4.
27. Warning signs of 'groupthink' in cults or groups. Nicholas Albery, www.globalideasbank.org (1.10.2004).
28. Mary Inglis – Personal interview with the author, May 2011.
29. Katie – interviewed by Lucy Sargisson in *Utopian Bodies and the Politics of Transgression*.
30. http://www.ecovillagefindhorn.com/findhornecovillage/social.php
31. Mike Scott of The Waterboys – a long time Findhorn associate, quoted in *In search of the Magic of Findhorn*.

New Believers

At the beginning of WWII the RAF selected Blackpool as one of its main training centres due to the ready availability of accommodation in guest houses and on former camping sites. Just to the south of Blackpool, at Squires Gate Camp next to the Aerodrome new recruits lived under canvas, venturing out to do PT and go 'square bashing' along the seafront. All in all they spent some six to eight weeks getting fit and ready for active service. Norman Motley, former curate at the Church of Christchurch in Spitalfields, was posted to the camp as Chaplain in 1941. Two or three times a week he was expected to give 'Chaplain Talks' to hundreds of men at a time. These half-hour lectures took place in the local cinema under the watchful eye of Staff Sergeants and Warrant Officers. The young Chaplain quickly found the claustrophobic lecturing format intolerable and set up his own informal meetings in a room above a shop in the centre of town, inviting all ranks to come and ask questions and enter into discussion and debate on religious and philosophical matters. The meetings, that became known as the 'Answer Back Meeting' or ABM, were regularly attended by forty or so men. This caused something of a stir in both the military and church hierarchies and Motley was 'asked' to at least change the name, if not the format of the meeting as 'answering back' wasn't quite what the RAF wanted to encourage. But the young Chaplain refused to be brow beaten and continued with the meetings.

A strange thing happened! In spite of the constantly changing personnel, the RAF officers and men came as often as possible before their next posting, and though at most the average attendance was two or three days, over a period of six weeks, there grew among some of the participants a sense of belonging, of solidarity; and of caring which made the prospect of breaking the contact painful to contemplate. A demand grew for some visible link which would remind them of their contact with the ABM and also allow the possibility of further contact at a later date. Finally, there was a dream that those who were to survive the war might be able to meet, not simply for an hour or so, but to stay together for a period, in order to think in a similar climate to that realised in that shop room of the problems which would undoubtedly confront the nations and individual Christians in the aftermath of the Second World War. [1]

Norman Motley

It was suggested that each person who wished to make a commitment to Christ should be given an emblem of some sort. It was decided that this should be four nails welded into a cross. Hundreds of these crosses of nails were distributed to those going to fight. Some holders were killed, others simply forgot about them, but there was a strong group of 'nail holders' who wished to keep in touch with each other. In 1943 Norman Motley was released from the RAF and took up a post in the Parish of Stisted in Essex from where he hoped to be able to visit RAF bases in the area and promote the idea of what was becoming known as the Nails Movement with a view to establishing a centre, or centres, where '... interested individuals and parties could come and stay, to think, and play, and work, and if so disposed, to pray.'

Motley started to search for a place near to London, but remote enough for people to be able to feel they were '... apart from the hubbub of subtopia and the technological society ...' In September 1945 he travelled to the Western Isle of Iona in Scotland to discuss his ideas with George Macleod founder of the Iona Community. Macleod was a WWI veteran turned pacifist minister who in 1938 had embarked on an ambitious project from his Govan ministry in Glasgow to rebuild the ruined medieval abbey on Iona. By the time of Norman Motley's visit the project had grown from a simple restoration project – where young men training for the Church would live and work alongside craftsmen and get a sense of community – to a much wider project that was starting to develop a dispersed community of associates and friends and was looking to set up a permanent residential group on the island. After the meeting, Macleod sent a telegram to Motley saying he had dreamt that he should establish his centre at Glastonbury and rebuild the Abbey there. This idea was actually followed up with visits to the Somerset town along with other visits to Lindisfarne and to look at a burnt-out Georgian mansion in Gloucestershire. But Motley felt that they 'did not want to rebuild anywhere but we wanted urgently to be able to link the old and the new, the realities of the distant past with the realities of the present, and to allow ourselves to be led into the future in line with the will of God.' In the end it was a site much closer to his Parish in Essex that would end up as the site for the centre. Prompted by some of his parishioners, Motley went to look at the Chapel of St Peter-on-the-Wall, thirty miles from Stisted on the edge of the Blackwater Estuary near Bradwell-on-Sea. The Chapel originally built by Cedd, the Saxon monk from Lindisfarne, on the foundations of the Roman fort of Othona, had been restored in the 1920's after years being used as a barn. Half a mile away were a collection of army huts that the group were given permission to use. The huts were kitted out from army surplus sales and by July 1946 they were ready to run a summer camp. The participants that first summer were a mix of the International Voluntary Service (IVS), German prisoners awaiting repatriation, some young Russian and Armenian refugees, a few parishioners from Stisted and a number of those 'holding the Nails'. Over the summer they invited a number of speakers to come and join the proceedings, including; Phillip Loyd Bishop of St Albans, Quaker John Hoyland, Father Gilbert Shaw from Glastonbury and pacifist and editor of the *Community Broadsheet* Leslie Stubbings.

After the success of the camp the group were convinced that this was the location for their new centre and having packed the camping equipment away in one of the army huts for the winter, they started to look towards the following summer's camp. In November, a call from the police to Stisted rectory informed them that the huts had been derequisitioned by the army and returned to the farmer, who had then sold the hut that they had been

Early Othona summer camp

using as storage and it had been dismantled and taken away, leaving the equipment exposed to the snow that was now falling. A rescue team was raised and the gear stashed in the attic of a nearby sympathiser. The loss of the huts meant that

the following summer camp had to be held at YMCA accommodation at Chigwell. While this was deemed 'satisfactory', there was a strong desire to return to the Bradwell site and eventually negotiations led to the group being able to secure two acres just to the north of the Chapel on a neighbouring farm. These early camps established a daily pattern of activities that would last for years to come. This began after breakfast, when a short service was held in the chapel taken by a lay member of the group. The rest of the morning was spent in maintenance of the site and preparation of food. The early afternoon was free time, followed by talks and discussions up until suppertime. There was then a candlelit evening chapel service followed by various entertainments '... sometimes bonfires and singing with a barbeque on the beach, sometime music or folk dancing and almost weekly a party.' The camps continued to run for six to eight weeks each summer through the 1950's. Now known as the Othona Community, they were attracting a cross-section of society from local churchgoers to girls from borstals right through to city businessmen.

During the same period, George Macleod's Iona Community continued to develop. Work progressed on the restoration of the abbey itself while the wider network of 'Friends' continued to expand. The group took over a salmon fishing station at Camas on Mull in order to run youth camps where young people could come for a week of outdoor activities, fishing and discussion, and if they so wished they could sail to Iona on the Sunday for communion. The Camas centre became increasingly used for youngsters from borstals, and youth work became an important part of the work of the community. With money from an anonymous donation the group bought 208-214 Clyde Street in Glasgow – two adjoining blocks of office and factory buildings – and set it up as a youth project known as Community House under the auspices of the Iona Youth Trust.

In the immediate postwar years, hope and determination to build a new and more just world were in the air. The Labour government's new health, welfare and housing programmes had the broad consent of the country. The corporate war effort had changed notions of what was or was not possible. The discussion of radical ideas and the quest for knowledge meant that places like Community House had no difficulty in attracting people. The house, with its restaurant, open chapel, library and meeting space, was an ideal base.

Ron Ferguson *Chasing the Wild Goose*

Throughout the 1940's and 50s, Community House played a significant part in the social and political life of Glasgow. The open and unembarrassed talk of religion and politics attracted many people put off by the conventional church. Scottish War on Want, Glasgow Marriage Guidance Council and Gamblers' Anonymous were all founded there. The centre also acted as a base for the Scottish folk music movement. The work at Community House complimented the work being done on Iona and Mull and groups of young people went from Glasgow to camps on the islands. There were those in the Church of Scotland who did not approve of the mixture of radical politics and renewed Christian life that was being explored by the Iona Community, with some accusing Macleod and the community of being heretical. The sheer number of young churchmen passing through the community had a ripple effect throughout Scotland and eventually further afield as the young clergymen tried to put their new found idea into practice. Three members set up a community house in the Gorbals district of Glasgow. A co-operative engineering works – Rowen Engineering – was set up, influenced and supported by the Iona

Community. On Iona work continued on the abbey, while the laying of electric cables to the island under the Sound of Iona and the introduction of a car ferry from Oban to Mull meant an increase in the numbers of students, pilgrims and tourists coming to visit and attend camps and conferences. Speakers who came to talk at the events at this time included; Sir Richard Acland, Martin Niemoller, Paul Oestreicher, Rev Hugh Montefiore and R D Laing. The Iona and Othona groups were not the only Christian-based communities set up in the immediate post-war period. Along similar lines of part retreat, part conference centre and part supporting residential community, there was the Lee Abbey Community, founded by Roger de Pemberton in 1946 in a country house in Devon, Hildenborough Hall in Kent and later Scargill House in the Yorkshire Dales.

In 1958, a Christian community with a slightly different basis was set up at Pilsdon near Bridport in Dorset.

Established since 1958 in a 16th Century Dorset Manor House with a Chapel, out-buildings, separate cottages and nine acres of ground. They are dedicated to the ideas of the Gospel, mainly Anglican and living in what might by many be called poverty. They grow all their own vegetables and fruit, have pigs, cows, chickens and bees, and sell surplus to local markets. They are also developing handicrafts. They attract a lot of visitors with skills who work while there and they receive help from the Church and from official and voluntary organisations, together with gifts from sympathisers all over the world.

Commune Journal 33, June 1970

Pilsdon, circa 1971

During the summer of 1950 the founders of the Pilsdon community, Anglican priest Percy Smith and his wife Gaynor, had been inspired by reading of the 17th-Century community at Little Gidding established by Nicolas Ferrar. On returning to England from Hong Kong in 1954 they searched for a place to establish their own community. Not finding any suitable location, the Rev Smith took a place at a church at Hawkchurch in the Dorset. Three years later he heard that the Jacobean Pilsdon Manor, six miles from his church, was for sale. On October 16th 1958, with the help of friends and relatives, Percy and Gaynor purchased the Manor for £5,000 and proceeded to move in and establish their community. Unlike Othona and Iona, Pilsdon was conceived of as a full-time residential community made up of a core of permanent residents and a whole selection of short- and longer-term visitors in need of respite, care or just somewhere to stay for a short while. The community welcomed drug addicts, alcoholics, homeless families, those suffering mental illness, ex-prisoners, rebellious teenagers and tramps and wayfarers (known as the cowboys) to come and stay and be part of the community. Details of the early years at the community were later recalled by Gaynor Smith in *Pilsdon Morning*:

... we were a family, a large extended family of men, women, and children which had thrown its doors wide open to the questing, the doubting, the troubled, the homeless, the helpless, the unwanted, the unloving and the unloved. We had a patriarchal family structure: meals were family meals with all of us gathered together in one dining-room; prayers were family prayers, however many or few cared to attend; and in a large family there is always plenty of work for everyone, especially if that family lives in the country and runs a small farm, and everyone in a family is expected to help with the work. There was family affection between us and there were also family rows: there were strong bonds of loyalty and also the irritations of too much proximity. But one family feature was noticeably lacking – there was no family likeness between us. Rather we must have been the most heterogeneous collection of people ever to be gathered under one roof. This was perhaps the single most distinctive thing about Pilsdon. We were a very mixed bag and this gave our life a healthy variety and breadth which drew people into its orbit and brought them back time and time again.

Gaynor Smith

Quite quickly local social services started to send people who they could find no place for to Pilsdon. Also, friends and local charities would suggest that people try Pilsdon. The community attracted support both locally and nationally for its somewhat unique brand of low-key rehabilitation through community living. There was a remarkable level of loyalty and appreciation shown by those who had passed through its doors.

Here I can start again. No one knows the things I've done in the past and the distrustful, lonely rebellious young girl who came here a few weeks ago is changing. I still crave like hell, but I'm taking a chance. Like every addict, I still don't want to give up junk, but I will try because I want to live ... Pilsdon is a home. A refuge when there's nowhere else. The people here don't judge. We work, we laugh, we all have our hang-ups, but we have them together. We are a community. We understand each other. We'll come through together. Yes, Pilsdon is a way of life-the best of life. It works and these are the words of a person who never would have thought it possible. I still can't believe it – I still don't know what the end will be, but if I fail it won't be through any fault of Pilsdon.[2]

Su – Young drug addict and resident at Pilsdon 1971

Pilsdon was the forerunner of a wave of Christian communities that developed throughout the 1960's and 70's that focussed on being a respite home for those in need as opposed to a temporary retreat or conference venue. In 1965 David and Monica Horn who had met as students at the Painting School of the Royal College of Art founded the Kingsway community in London. Both had, according to Richard Fairfield who interviewed them in 1970, become Methodists believing Christianity to be the only solution to the world's problems. Their initial experiment in group living lasted for two years, ending because of the disruption from too many 'crashers'. Undeterred, after a break away from London, they returned to establish a second Kingsway house, this time with support from the Methodist Church in a large three-storey house with bedrooms on the second and third floors and a large open first-floor dormitory for 'crashers and transients'. David Horn explained to Richard Fairfeild 'There are two married couples and one couple who intend to get married; there are a few registered 'junkies', there are a few people who like to booze-it-up on the weekends; and there are also quite a few straight people. People in the dormitory were alternately sleeping and shooting dope. Too many junkies in the house is very disruptive. The Community is not very together right now because too few are committed to the Christian way. There are too many people in the house who are destructive, incompetent or disabled.'

The group were later lent Keveral Farm in Cornwall by the Patchwork Housing Association where they set up a workshop to provide employment for members producing fretsawn wooden jigsaws designed by David Horn which were exported all over the world. In 1978 a number of the longer-term residents at Kingsway went on to set up the Crescent Road Community at Kingston in Surrey in three properties owned by Patchwork.

Another community that was a combination of the two models of Christian Community in that it aimed to combine both being a residential respite community and a conference centre also started in 1965 in the ninety-room Bystock Court just outside Exmouth in Devon. Led by Joy and Alastair Jamieson, the group formally known as the Bystock Court Association, planned to operate as an interdenominational conference and community centre aiming to help those suffering from the strains of modern society.

In spite of the wide range of services provided by the Welfare State, and the excellent work performed by the voluntary and charitable organisations, there are many people who are faced with problems which at a particular point in time appear insoluble to them. They do not require professional help, but a temporary respite in a peaceful, secure and friendly atmosphere, away from the source of their trouble where they can find themselves again and reorientate themselves to life ...

Bystock Court leaflet 1969

The house, one of the largest private houses in Devon, standing in 24 acres of grounds, had been used during the war by the Red Cross as a convalescent home for servicemen. By 1965, most of the building had stood empty and unused for two decades and required complete redecoration, new drains and water supply and a new electricity supply, and the grounds had become completely overgrown. With the help of groups from local churches and youth clubs along with work camps sponsored by The World Council of Churches in Geneva, the building and grounds were slowly brought back into use and opened to a wide cross section of people in need of support; from families going through marital difficulties, single parents, men and women coping with homelessness, bereavement, persecution and other crises. Alongside the respite care offered, many youth groups, churches, ecumenical groups and other organisations used the larger rooms within the house and the grounds for camps and conferences. In the 1980's the house was passed to a charity that provided care for people with learning difficulties and finally sold to that charity in 2003 and the proceeds invested in the Jamieson-Bystock Trust which carries on the aims of the original community group by making grants to organisations which help people in need in the Exmouth area.

In the early 1960's the Othona community managed to secure the purchase of East Hall Farm (where their camps were held) and give themselves some security for the future. The 60's would be a period of expansion and consolidation of the group's activities. One of the constraints on the community's activities was the lack of an all-year-round base. In 1964 Norman Motley was pointed in the direction of an empty property on the Dorset coast at Burton Bradstock, just above Chesil Beach. St Bride's farm was in the hands of the trustees of the Contemplative Community who were looking for another group to hand it on to since the original community founded in 1930 by Adele Curtis, and known locally as The White Ladies, had folded. Described by

Aldous Huxley as one of the greatest living mystics, Adela Marion Curtis was a remarkable woman, a prolific writer on mystical subjects, a Christian, vegetarian, tee-totaller, English patriot, pioneer of self-sufficiency, spiritual director, healer, school teacher, economist and ecologist – to give just a few of the titles used to describe her. She had already set up one community (a religious order of silence for women at Coldash, near

Othona Chapel
Burton Bradstock

Newbury in Berkshire) before coming to Burton Bradstock in 1921 in order to retire. But her followers continued to visit her so often that a new community was formed with each member living in a simple wooden hut with a quarter of an acre of fruit and vegetable gardens and trying as a group to be as self-sufficient as possible in clothing, fuel, housing and all other necessities. The women wove their own robes from undyed silk or cotton, hence the White Ladies nickname. Miss Curtis and the White Ladies had built a five-bedroom house in local stone with a common room, dining room and kitchen with a cloister leading to an adjacent chapel. At the outbreak of war, Adela told her 'sisters' that she abhorred pacifism and considered prayer to be the most effective weapon of warfare. The following year in her book, *The Two Edged Sword*, she advised on how to use positive prayer as a weapon against the Nazis '… summon each leader by name. For cumulative effect the message should be spoken three times – Adolph Hitler! Adolph Hitler! Adolph Hitler! Hear the Truth!' The Contemplative Community continued through the 1950's with an aging population of 'white ladies'. Adela Curtis died on 17th September 1960 aged 96 and the trustees of her charity began looking for a suitable organisation to which they could give the house and grounds along with a few of the sisters' huts. When Norman Motley went down to look at the property:

The very first look convinced me that this was for us. Dr Jay had asked if I could let him know the decision of the Executive of our Community within three months. I think I phoned to say that I had decided in three minutes, and that those with me were also hopeful … I felt certain that this was our second home. I went to the next Executive Meeting of the Community and reported what we had found. I explained that there was an enormous amount of work to do and that it was a great distance away. There were no lights except old oil lamps; no heat, no flush lavatories and no drains, but it had great possibilities. I also said I felt so strongly about the need for, and the rightness of, the place that if the Trustees and Executive felt it was too great a risk, I would understand and form another and separate group of Trustees to take responsibility for this new site; but the response was unanimous. 'Let's take it,' they said.

Norman Motley

The house and grounds had been empty and neglected for a number of years and required a huge effort to get it back into use. People from the Othona network travelled down to Dorset and set about cleaning and painting, hacking back brambles and bringing the place back to life. They were now able to offer a year-round programme of events. A warden was appointed to run the place with the help of volunteers and visitors. Over the years money was found to improve the facilities and to connect electricity, gas, water and sewage. Summer camps continued to be run at New Bradwell in Essex throughout the 60's and 70's. Norman Motley died in December 1980 and, although there were some who thought that Othona would fade away after its founder had died, the two centres have continued through to the present day with considerable expansion and new facilities being built at the Essex site in the 1990's.

Othona is an approach to spirituality. The great, intimate mystery we call God surely goes beyond dogma. We all learn from each other, and, without pressure to conform in religious terms, may experience the fellowship of the spirit in everyday life. Othona was founded in 1946 to provide space to explore peace and reconciliation after the Second World War. We still try to face the challenges of our time, spiritual, social and ecological.[3]

The Abode of Fading Love

Skeletons in the family cupboards are one thing — Messiahs quite another.

Kate Barlow

Begun in 1846 in the small Somerset village of Spaxton, Agapemone, or the Abode of Love, must count as one of the longest-surviving intentional communities in the country. By the time Kate Barlow was growing up there in the 1940's the sect had survived two would-be messiahs, the Rev Henry Prince and his successor the Rev Hugh Smyth-Piggot [4], Barlow's grandfather, along with numerous scandals about the two clergymen's 'Soul Brides' or 'Brides of the Week' and the community had settled down to a somewhat genteel, if slightly eccentric country estate, presided over by Ruth Anne Preece, Smyth-Piggot's final Soul Bride and Kate's grandmother.

Basically there were three levels in the Agapemone. There was my mother, her brothers and her mother. They lived mainly in the east end of the house, they ate separately, they had a life entirely of their own. Then there was what are called the residents. These were the people who had money, who'd given their money when they joined the Agapemone, when they joined the community. They lived the life of sort of ladies of leisure, never did a thing unless they had hobbies for their entire lives. And those I would refer to as — I'd just call them by their first names. And then there was the — they were known as The Parlour, the servants, they were actually the servants. They had no money, but they gave their labour instead. The irony is that the older they got the harder they had to work, the less of them there were. I think it's a bit rough, really. And I referred to everyone by their first name and they referred to me by my first name. It was very egalitarian. [5]

The community's colourful past was never mentioned in front of the children and it was not until she was at boarding school that Kate started to learn some of what the outside world thought had gone on behind the high wall that surrounded the estate. It would take years before she would untangle anything near the truth of the group's history. In many ways the Abode of Love was the prototype for the 20th century Christian cult — at least as seen through the eyes of the media. It had charismatic leadership, sex scandals, accusations of kidnapping and brainwashing and a belief in the imminent apocalypse, along with their status as those chosen to survive it. Even a century on from the founding of the group, the elderly female residents still had one eye on the impending rapture and '... would never start a task, darning a sock, or writing a letter, if they didn't think they could finish it say before lunch, or before dinner or before whenever, because you might be swept up. You never knew when you were going to be swept up, so any job you started, you had to finish.' [6]

At the end of the 1950's numbers dwindled due to the deaths of the most elderly ladies, including Kate's grandmother. Due to this and increasing financial difficulties, the community was eventually forced to close. The very final end of the Abode of Love came somewhat appropriately on Valentine's Day 1962, following an auction of the community's furniture and belongings. The estate was broken up, sold off in parcels and renamed Barford Close. In the 1970's the Agapemone Chapel was used as a film studio by Bob Bura and John Hardwick — the makers of the children's animated TV series *Camberwick Green* and *Trumpton*.

The full story of the final years of the Spaxton Sect are told by Kate Barlow in:
Abode of Love: Growing Up in a Messianic Cult

Crisis, Renewal and Keeping In Touch

All we have always wanted is to live this life of brotherhood and love. What have we done? Tell us, what have we done to be sent away? Where shall we go? What shall we do? We gave our word at our baptism to be loyal, and that is what we want to be! Please, please don't send us away! **7**

Elderly couple begging not to be thrown out of a Bruderhof during the 'Great Crisis'

Between 1959 and 1961 over a third of the Bruderhof (adults and children), estimated to be between 500 and 600 members, were expelled and the communities in South America and Europe closed down in what has become known in Bruderhof history as 'The Great Crisis'. This great purge of membership and the accompanying power struggle has reverberated through the ensuing decades and has led to serious argument as to what actually happened. Almost from that point onwards there are contested versions of Bruderhof history with each side accusing the other of distortion and revisionism.

By the late fifties there were ten Bruderhof communities: three in Paraguay, two in England, one each in Germany and Uruguay, and three in the United States. They had reached the point where they were starting to be much more stable economically, with income from the Community Playthings factory (based at the Woodcrest community in the USA) providing an alternative to relying on donations from supporters to supplement their farming activities and subsidise the other projects, such as the hospital in Paraguay. Quite what led from this position of near stability to crisis and turmoil is one of the pieces of the group's history that is hotly disputed. The 'official' version is that the crisis was a renewal or rebirth of the Bruderhof which the founder's second son, Heini, initiated and carried through at great personal cost to himself in order to get the communities back to their original Christ-centered foundations from which they had strayed over the years since his father's death. The alternative narratives are many and layered and range across power struggles within the leadership, economic conflict between the more prosperous American communities and those in Paraguay, through differing temperaments of German and English members and including criticism of fundamental ways that the sect was structured and its rules interpreted and implemented. These ways include, perhaps most controversially, the 'First Law of Sannerz' – commonly known as the 'No Gossip' rule but, in actual fact, much more nuanced in its original form;

There is no law but that of love. Love is joy in others. What then is anger at them? Passing on the joy that the presence of the others brings us means words of love. Thus words of anger and worry about members of the brotherhood are out of the question. In Sannerz there must never be talk, either open or hidden, against a brother or sister, against their individual characteristics – under no circumstances behind their back. Talking in one's own family is no exception to this either.

Extract from First Law of Sannerz

While on the surface of it the 'law' seems a reasonable code of conduct, and strict adherence to it has been cited as the reason for the survival and success of the Bruderhof,**8** the effect of its interpretation and implementation at particular times in the sect's history has led to accusation of it being used to silence dissent among members critical of the leadership. This, along with the practice of excluding individual members for varying periods of time for transgressing group rules seems, whatever the original intentions, to have been clearly open to abuse by those in positions of power. Much has been written on the crisis from both sides and it is hard to unpick the actual story from the accusation and counter accusation. The bones of the story can be gleaned from *The Joyful Community* – a fairly comprehensive and balanced study[9] of the group written by Benjamin Zablocki in the late 1960's after spending six months living at Woodcrest and interviewing various current and ex-members.

Following a break with the Hutterite Church over 'liberal' practices, including smoking, theatre and watching movies, that had become part of the Bruderhof way of life in Paraguay, Zablocki characterises the 1950's as a period of liberalization and expansion when the group moved more towards being a communitarian social movement and away from being an isolated sect. The group showed external signs of liberalisation included beards becoming optional and women's dress becoming more diverse. At the end of the war the group had renewed contact with the outside world, particularly North America where missionary speakers were sent to talk and raise funds among church groups and on college campuses. This in turn led to Americans trekking down to Paraguay and eventually to the establishment of communities in the USA. The mid fifties was the peak of expansion of the sect with communities in five countries spread across three continents.

Community pamphlets of the time proudly catalogued the nationalities represented in the membership: English, German, Swiss, American, Dutch, Swedish, Austrian, Czechoslovakian, French, Italian, Latvian, (Asian) Indian, Spanish, Argentinian, and Paraguayan. Equal pride was taken in the diversity of cultural backgrounds: 'pacifists, anarchists, Moral Rearmers, Communist Party members, vagabonds, Nazis, agnostics, anticlericals, good ordinary establishment church-goers and two native Paraguayan families ...

Benjamin Zablock

In 1957 a two-week-long world conference was held at Primavera where representatives from each of the nine communities reported on progress, and policy matters covering the whole movement were discussed. Almost from this high point onwards it would seem that the movement was on some sort of collision course towards internal conflict. Trying to read between the lines of the differing accounts of the period it is possible to discern an increased polarisation between a liberal, democratic-leaning tendency and an authoritarian, hierarchical, strictly moralistic wing. Things came to a head in 1959 when conflict erupted between the Paraguay and American communities – initially sparked by disagreement over economic issues, but quickly escalating into a full-blown conflict over the behaviour of members at Primavera with accusations of cold-heartedness and straying from the original purpose of the community. This was followed by a bout of inward soul searching that reached near hysteria levels, with an accompanying leadership struggle, the result of which was a mass purge or 'exclusion' of members from Primavera. The crisis then spread, or was deliberately spread – depending on which version of the story you choose – with, in the end, hundreds of members being thrown out, often with little notice and with few or no resources. After over two decades living isolated in South America, many were ill-equipped to cope with outside world. There are reports of at least one family finding themselves stuck in Asuncion, the Paraguay capital, with no knowledge of Spanish, and having to rely on the British Embassy to get back to England. Those members deemed to be 'warm-hearted' and therefore not excluded were dispersed to other communities and the Primavera estate sold to the neighbouring Friesland Mennonite group in 1961. A similar pattern of conflict, exclusions and break-up of the community followed at Wheathill in England, with the remaining members being dispersed (many to Bulstrode in Buckinghamshire) and the Shropshire property sold in October 1962. The whole movement contracted by almost half and by the mid-sixties there were only the American communities left; Bulstrode being disbanded in 1966. While this period of crisis was later looked on by the Bruderhof as a period of renewal, the immediate aftermath was certainly not only traumatic for those who had been expelled, but it was a trauma for the movement itself that would take it some time to recover from. The following years saw very little growth in numbers. Although some of those excluded did return during this period, it appears in general to have been a time of consolidation of a 'new regime'. Overtures were once again made towards joining (rejoining) the Hutterite Brethren and shifting away from the more radical, 'liberal', intentional community world that they had been an intrinsic part of for the best part of three decades.

The great crisis brought about an important shift in Bruderhof values. Before the crisis, the Bruderhof thought of itself as an intentional community among intentional communities. It happened to be a religious community – a church – because its members had found that this was the best way, really the only successful way, of sustaining communal life ... Since the crisis, the Bruderhof has thought of itself more as a church among churches, one that happens to be an intentional community because this is the best expression that its members have found of the true Christian life. Its outside relationships are now mostly with other churches, monastic groups, and religious denominations rather than with other intentional communities.

Benjamin Zablocki, *The Joyful Community* 1971

In the post-war years the Wheathill Bruderhof had played an active part in the British communities' movement, being part of a small network of communities that existed at the time and which people, who would later be involved in the communes movement in the 60's and 70's, recall visiting[10]. The Plough printing press, based at Wheathill, printed a number of issues of the *Community Broadsheet* an occasional publication that tried to keep groups in touch with each other and promote community living. The Shropshire community also provided a positive example to the outside world of what an alternative way of life could be like, through very sympathetic coverage in newspapers and magazine articles and in newsreel film footage.

In 1962 Heini Arnold became the clear overall leader, or 'Elder' of the movement, a position not held by anyone since his father had died over a quarter of a century earlier. This re-established the centrality of the Arnold family within the sect's hierarchy and, depending on your point of view, made him either the saviour of the movement or the chief architect of its slide from thriving community movement towards being a Christian cult. Certainly the new leader was instrumental in brokering a new relationship with the Hutterites, resulting in among other things the reintroduction of beards and a strict dress code for women – long skirts and headscarves – that became distinctive features of the group. By the beginning of the 1970's the group were once again looking towards expanding back in England. According to Heini Arnold the main reason for looking to England at this time was '... to find the way to those who once belonged to us, to find a new relationship. We felt our door should be open to everyone who is really called by God. So we felt we should go to a country where there is more of an open door for all foreigners, and England seemed to be that country ...' [11]

Darvell Hall, a couple of miles from Robertsbridge in Sussex, was a former eighteenth century manor house turned tuberculosis sanatorium in the 1920's and finally declared surplus to use by the NHS in 1970. It was bought by the Bruderhof in 1971 when a few families were transferred from communities in America to re-establish the movement back in Europe. Over the years, Darvell has developed into a small village with a couple of hundred residents. The group developed the estate and, as well as a small farming operation, have built a factory for Community Playthings, a large communal dining room, a school and accommodation for increasing numbers of members.

... typical of most Bruderhof communities: nuclear families each have private living space in which they eat daily breakfast and two evening meals a week; each home also has its own family time in the middle of the day and before the evening meal. Beyond these designated family times most of daily life is communal. Small children receive care in the baby house; children to the age of fourteen attend the Bruderhof school where teachers come from within the community. Older children attend local secondary schools, after which most go on to some further education ... members of all ages have daily tasks. At Darvell the economic engine is a medium-sized industry producing wooden toys and equipment for the handicapped. There is no hesitation about using modern technology: a craftsman in the shop deftly entered instructions into a computerized router that produces intricate wooden parts with speed and precision ... [12]

Nelson Kraybill *A Day with the Hutterian Brethren*

Heini Arnold died in 1982 and his place as Elder was taken by his son Christoph, thus continuing the Arnold dynasty within the sect and further confirming the view among some critics that, despite its protestations to the contrary, the group was controlled by an authoritarian elite. During the three decades following the great crisis, the story of what had happened back in the late 1950's was largely seen through the interpretation (some would say suppression) of information in Bruderhof publications. The voice of those who had been excluded, or who had left, was absent. In some part this was due to the warning given by the Bruderhof that ex-members should not seek to talk to each other or to have contact with those who had stayed. Adherence to this 'rule' was followed by many who had left. This state of play in the telling of the different contested narratives continued until 1989 when one ex-member, Ramon Sender, began contacting and corresponding with other ex-members. Sender had been excluded in 1957 and left behind his wife and daughter at Woodcrest. In 1989 he discovered, five months after the event, that his daughter had died of cancer. Following refusal of his requests to be able to visit and find out about his daughter's life he began to get in touch with former members.

I talked with exiles from the Great Crisis of 1960-1961 ... who were living in dire poverty, and with survivors of various subsequent mass exclusions from the American Bruderhof communities. I discovered that one ex-member, Lee Kleiss, had started a round-robin letter in the early 1960's. I found the so-called Hartford Boys, a group of young men driven away by a Servant of the Word (a Bruderhof elder) who had beaten them severely, and the tightly-knit group of ex-Bruderhof members in England, who had stayed more closely in touch. Like the ex-members in Germany, the English ex-members seemed willing to let bygones be bygones and tried to put a good face on past wrongs, in contrast to the feistier Americans. But they all shared an intense desire to know whom I had found and what these people were doing with their lives. [13]

Ramon Sender Barayon in *The Heart Will Find a Way: Creating a Network of Reunion*

In August '89 Sender began the *Keep In Touch (KIT)* newsletter initially just as a two page round-robin letter to 30 or so names that he had collected. It quickly mushroomed into a monthly ten-thousand-word newsletter being sent to over a hundred people. Such was the interest that the following year a KIT conference was held in Massachusetts attended by 50 'survivors and graduates' for three days of 'shared memories and visiting with old friends and lost relatives'. The conference drafted an open letter to the Bruderhof in which they asked that those wishing to leave be given financial support and the right of continuing contact with family and friends and for a serious dialogue to be had about issues of past abuses. Whilst the reply from Christoph Arnold would state that there was a 'tremendous longing in the brotherhood for reconciliation' this would be the start of almost a decade of escalating conflict. In 1992 KIT was officially incorporated as the non-profit Peregrine Foundation and set up the Carrier Pigeon Press which published a series of accounts, by ex-members, of lives lived in the Bruderhof. From 1992 onwards, regular KIT conferences were held in both America and England and circulation of the newsletter continued to grow. In 1995 a telephone helpline started for 'persons inside and outside of the Bruderhof who wanted information or assistance'. This was done by a small group of those involved with KIT under a separate organisation called the Children of the Bruderhof International (COBI). The helpline number appeared in the New York telephone directory alongside numbers for the Bruderhof who responded by bombarding the helpline number with thousands of calls and issuing fluorescent bumper stickers giving the impression that it was a free telephone sex line. These actions were followed by the filing of a lawsuit charging COBI with trademark infringement and seeking $50,000 damages which, while it was settled out of court, effectively closed down the phone line.

During this period the Bruderhof put out a number of publications in an effort to have their side of the story heard. They also allowed limited access to the communities and their archives by some academics. This resulted in 1996 in the publication of *The Witness of Brothers* by the Israeli and Kibbutz scholar, and founder of the International Communal Studies Association, Yaacov Oved. This has come to be seen as the most authoritative recent academic work on the sect. Oved's book, however, has suffered criticism for being an 'authorised' history and there is suspicion that the Bruderhof exercised considerable editorial control over it. The refusal to allow open access to the group's archives, and the closed nature of the sect has made any study of them problematic. If you are allowed access you are open to accusation of bias in one direction and if you write without it 'How can you possibly know the full story?'

In July 1997 the Bruderhof took further legal action, this time suing Ramon Sender and The Peregrine Foundation for defamation and 'injurious falsehood' over articles published in the *KIT* newsletters claiming damages of over $3 million. While the accusations were potentially very serious the defamation case never made it to a full court hearing, being dismissed on the grounds that the claim had not been made within the one-year-statute-of-limitation period. At the same time, Julius Rubin, a Sociology Professor from Connecticut, was looking to publish a critical book, *The Other Side of Joy: Religious Melancholy Among the Bruderhof*, but was finding difficulty in getting it to press due to the sect writing to his publisher (the Oxford University Press) contesting various issues and pointing to the outstanding defamation case. Rubin did have a paper published in England by the Society for Promoting Christian Knowledge (SPCK) in a collection of conference papers entitled 'Harmful Religion'. When the book appeared in the shops the Bruderhof threatened to sue for libel and the publishers promptly withdrew the book and agreed to sell the entire print run to the Darvell Bruderhof. *The Other Side of Joy* was finally published in 2000.

Despite the internal and external conflicts, the Bruderhof continued to attract new members through the 1990's and in England started the new Beech Grove Community at the former Nonington Physical Education College in Kent in 1995. This has since been followed by new groups in Australia, Germany and a house in Newham in East London. Most recently (2010) there has been a return to Paraguay with the opening of Asuncion House in the capital.

Jesus freaks, basic communities and the coming endtime

On the 11th July 1973 a new multi-media rock musical entitled *Lonesome Stone* opened at The Rainbow Theatre in Finsbury Park, London. Following hot on the heels of other Christian-based rock operas like Godspell and Jesus Christ Superstar, which had opened in London in the previous couple of years. *Lonesome Stone* told the story of a hippie seeker finding God in late 60's San Francisco. The new musical had been written by members of the rock group The Sheep who, since they had arrived from the States in November 1972, had been touring the UK with a stage show called 'The Jesus People Come Alive'.

'Lonesome Stone' is the story of what Jesus is doing now, by his spirit, in thousands of lives. This multi-media rock musical portrays the search of thousands of today's youth surrounded by the darkness of materialism, dead religion, sex, astrology, the occult and drugs. A generation born into the atomic age, confused about God and almost everything else. In protest, they searched to change their destiny ...

Catholic Herald 4th July 1974

The Sheep were the house band for the Milwaukee Jesus People Ministry, set up by Jim and Sue Palosaari from Wisconsin where they had run a coffee-house, newspaper and a communal school called the 'Jesus People Discipleship Training Center' with 200 members. In 1972 the Palosaaris and thirty members flew to Scandinavia at the invitation of the Full Gospel Businessmen's Association where the band recorded – in Finnish – its first record in Helsinki, Finland. From there the group spent the next six months touring through Europe. After spending a month in Berlin in an art deco mansion, the group found themselves with 'No money, no prospects, in someone's house in Holland'. The group received a telegram that said 'Come to England. Money no object'. The invitation was from property developer Kenneth Frampton whose Deo Gloria Trust helped set up the group, now calling itself the Jesus Family, in a large four-storey house in Norwood, south east London. Frampton, a Christian Philanthropist, property developer and member of the Plymouth Brethren, had previously been instrumental in welcoming another American evangelical Christian group to England. In July 1971 he had offered a large factory building that he owned in Sherman Road, Bromley rent-free to the Children of God who used it as the base for their activities in Europe. Frampton's two sons joined this new group, but before the year was out he was having serious misgivings about his generosity having learnt more about the sect's background and leader David Berg. But he was reluctant to evict the group while his sons were still members. His invitation to the Palosaari's was an attempt to promote a rival group and undermine the Children of God's influence.

After a week-long run at The Rainbow, *Lonesome Stone* toured throughout the UK and Europe including many US Air force bases. Over the August bank holiday weekend in '73 The Sheep appeared at the first Greenbelt Christian music festival at Prospect Farm near Woodbridge in Suffolk which had been organised by people inspired by seeing the band's rock musical. The Jesus Family returned to North America in 1974 where members were instrumental in setting up a further commune on Vancouver Island in Canada.

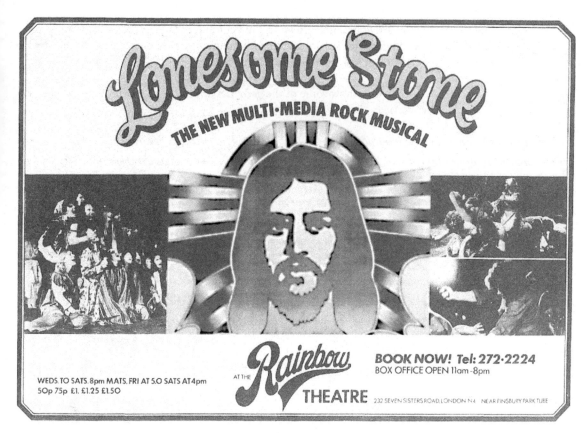

The Children of God were already a remarkably successful sect before they
came to England. Started in the late 1960's on the West Coast of America by
a charismatic preacher David Berg, known at various times to members of the
sect as Moses David, Moses, Mo, King David, Father David – or simply as
Dad! Coming from a strict religious background and following a prophecy by
his mother that he interpreted as meaning that he was the biblical Endtime
Prophet, Berg had started preaching to hippies and young people and recruiting
them as 'revolutionaries for Jesus'. He quickly attracted a group of followers
and set up a commune on a 425-acre colony near the ghost town of Thurber,
in Erath County, Texas from where teams set out on road trips to other cities
to win converts and establish new colonies. They also staged demonstrations
dressed in sackcloth with ashes on their foreheads in Washington DC,
Philadelphia, Times Square in New York, and outside the UN Headquarters.
Dubbed by the media as the 'prophets of doom' for proclaiming the imminent
destruction of America, it was also the media that first called them the
Children of God, a name which stuck, and which the group adopted. Due to
its aggressive preaching and recruitment tactics the sect quickly became the
target of campaigns by worried parents and could almost be 'credited' with
being the root cause of the entire anti-cult movement. Critics accused them
of a whole range cult-like and criminal behaviour from coercion, rape and
orgies, to defrauding the public for donations and evasion of law enforcement.
A group of concerned parents set up a counter-cult movement called Free Our
Children from the Children of God or FreeCOG, enlisting the help of an
African-American, Ted Patrick, who was reportedly experienced in successful
'reverse-brainwashing' of members of cults. This involved kidnapping cult
members, placing them in isolation and using shock tactics to de-programme

*Advertisement for
Lonesome Stone – the
story of a hippie seeker
finding God*

them. Patrick became known to the Children of God as 'Black Lightning' and was charged with several counts of kidnapping and eventually found guilty of conspiracy to kidnap, and false imprisonment.

It is easy to see how some of the activities at the Thurber colony led parents to be worried:

Members now went only by new biblical first names and new tribal identities. They were divided into twelve tribes, inspired by the twelve tribes of Israel, with each tribe assigned different areas of responsibilities; working for several hours a day with camp maintenance, food preparation, procurement of food from neighboring towns, and care of livestock. Berg, at the top with the ultimate authority, assigned members of his immediate family as leaders to some of these tribes. Strict rules were enforced regarding everything in a members life: the "2-sheets rule" decreed the maximum amount of toilet paper a member could use for visits to the latrines; the buddy system decreed that members could not go anywhere without a partner; outgoing mail was checked and censored for "security." Exhausted new members were subjected to relentless Bible classes and indoctrination, their "buddy" helping in the rote memorization of bible passages whenever possible, even during their toilet activities. There was no "idle time" where they could be allowed to gather their thoughts.[14]

By the end of 1970, David Berg was in hiding from angry parents and in danger of being detained by the police. In April 1971, with his partner Karen Zerby, Berg fled to London, initially booking into a boarding house for a couple of months. On the 7th July 1971, BBC2 screened a *Man Alive* documentary 'The Jesus Trip' which featured the Children of God. Realising this was an opportunity to increase the group's profile in the UK, a party of members was hurriedly flown across from the States to appear in a panel discussion chaired by Lord Soper and screened immediately after the programme. The ensuing publicity brought invites from churches up and down the country and an offer from the London City Mission of the use of their premises in Bermondsey, along with a small cottage and the Hop-pickers Medical Mission (both at Horsmonden in Kent). Two of the first English converts to the group were Kenneth Frampton's sons through whom the sect were able to arrange the rent-free use of the factory in Bromley as well as two houses nearby in Chinbrook Road and a Scottish Island that Frampton owned. The Bromley factory rapidly became the new headquarters for the sect with printing and publication operations being run from the Chinbrook houses. More members were brought over from the US and efforts were made to pioneer new groups in the UK and to use London as a 'beachhead'

Children of God bus

for further expansion into Europe. The group acquired two old double-decker buses, painted them bright yellow and emblazoned them with 'The Jesus Revolution' and 'The Children of God' in bright red lettering. These soon became a familiar sight in Trafalgar Square and Piccadilly Circus, and every Sunday in Hyde Park where they would pull up and members would leap out and converge on the crowds, singing 'The Children of God are on Their Way!' and proceed to target members of the counter-culture with their message of the coming apocalypse and the return of Jesus. By 1972 it was reported that the sect had set up ten communes in Britain and a further five elsewhere in Europe.[15]

David Berg and Karen Zerby, now going under the names of Mo and Maria, lived a quiet life out of the public eye in the south east London suburb, issuing instructions and directing the group through a series of letters known as *The MO Letters*. These covered a wide variety of topics and became a form of alternative gospel within the group, seen as on par with the bible itself. In 1972 a letter titled 'The Great Escape' predicted that the appearance of the comet Kohutek in 1973 would herald the destruction of America and that all members back in the US and Canada should prepare to leave and start up new colonies in other parts of the world. This resulted in a mass exodus of the sect from North America. Kohutek came and went invisible to the naked eye and America was not destroyed and, like many who made false prophecy of impending doom before him, Berg gave alternative explanations for the failure. This did not, however, dent the group's belief in their End-time theology, with Berg producing a document called *The 70-Years Prophecy Of The End*, detailing the various stages of the End-time culminating with the return of Jesus in 1993. The idea of the imminent End-time was a key part of Berg's philosophy which underpinned much of the sect's other thinking. This apocalyptic reading of passages from the Bible is not something exclusive to the Children of God, other Christian Sects such as the Mormons and Jehovah's Witnesses and many individual Christians believe in a similar prediction of the end of the world.

In 1973, seeking 'recreation and relaxation', Mo and Maria enrolled at a south London ballroom dancing school. Always on the lookout for new ways to make converts, it would be here that the couple would embark on what would become one of the sect's most controversial activities, known as Flirty Fishing.

... Dad's ploy was to send Maria out on the dance floor as bait to lure unsuspecting men into their lair. The very first person caught through Flirty Fishing was an Englishman named Arthur. After numerous evenings on the dance floor, Arthur and Maria began a sexual relationship ... Maria kept up her new tactic of seducing men into the kingdom. Each night Dad and his team would get a detailed report, record it, and transcribe and edit it for eventual publication. My father boasted that he had found a new method of ministry, but in reality, he had only resurrected the pagan practice of religious prostitution ...

Linda Berg. *The Children of God: The Inside Story By The Daughter Of The Founder*

Arthur joined the sect and was lionised in a later series of Mo Letters entitled *King Arthur's Nights*. Initially, this new way of witnessing for God was kept a secret from all but a few of the top members of the sect. It wouldn't be until over a year later that Flirty Fishing would be introduced to the full membership through a series of graphic and explicit issues of the Mo Letters. In March 1974, Mo, Maria and a small group of disciples moved to the tourist resort of Tenerife in the Canary Islands where 'FFing' was further developed and refined as a honey trap for converts. Frequenting the local bars and dance clubs the group's women met, befriended, and witnessed to the men they encountered and if the situation suggested it, they would have sex with the men. Flirty Fishing didn't come out of the blue as a practice it was part of a philosophy of sexual freedom and experimentation that Berg had been developing for a number of years, using his own interpretation of various passages in the bible to link sexual liberation with spiritual well-being. These ideas were laid out in a 1974 publication *The Law of Love* which encouraged and validated sexual sharing among consenting married couples and single members within the community. While in the early days of the group there had been a strict code for unmarried members with total sexual abstinence and segregation of the sexes, Berg himself had already been practicing a very relaxed version of sexual morality. Having abandoned his first wife and taken Karen Zerby as his mistress, he also began 'sharing' among the members of his immediate household.

The Children of God were not the first Christian based group to embrace a more permissive view of sexual relationships, rather different from that of mainstream Christianity. In America, a number of 19th Century sects broke with society's sexual taboos. In Maine in the early 1820's, the communal Society of Free Brethren and Sisters – or Cochranites – led by Jacob Cochran, practiced what they called Spiritual Wifery in which communal mates were temporarily assigned and reassigned, either by personal preference or religious authority allowing male members to take multiple female partners. Cochran himself spent four years in prison, convicted of gross lewdness, lascivious behaviour, and adultery. A number of his followers went on to join the Mormons and influence that sect's adoption of 'plural marriage' or polygamy which was practiced openly and publicly from 1852 to 1890. In England, the Moravian Church, who established a number of communal settlements in the mid 1700's, had a long held belief in a form of protestant sacred sexuality, based on similar interpretation of biblical passages as those made by Berg, although within a conventional view of marriage. And the Rev Henry Prince used the same justifications at his Abode of Love in Somerset to enable him to take a succession of spiritual brides. So, in a period when society at large was experiencing its own sexual revolution it is not surprising, given the sects recruitment among the counter-culture, that this should reverberate through the Children of God. It has been suggested[16] that Berg's particular take on sexual liberation was heavily influenced by his repressed upbringing and the release from this he felt upon his mother's death. What is clear is that because of the hierarchical set-up and the clear prophetic role that Berg played within the group, the sect was able to codify and ensure implementation of the sexual revolution in a way that could never have happened in the world outside.

The early 70's saw an increase in interest in the founding of communities

with a Christian basis in the UK: not just those imported from across the Atlantic. In the summer of 1970, the then Methodist minister at St Mark's, West Greenwich, David Clark, dropped in 'out of sheer curiosity' at the Communes Festival at the Roundhouse.

... I was fascinated as well as impressed by the idealism and energy of those who attended that event, even though certain aspects of the gathering seemed eccentric and libertarian. Here were groups of young people, including young families, prepared to launch out into the unknown in search of new ways of living and working together. Many of them were setting aside promising careers and material security for a life-style that, though physically very tough, lacking the luxuries of modern life and extremely demanding in terms of relationship building furthered their vision of what an inclusive and open society should be all about. **17**

Convinced that a Christian version of the new budding Commune Movement might be able to contribute to the renewal of the church, in 1971 Clark (with the help of a Roman Catholic Franciscan priest and a Congregational layman) launched a free bulletin simply called *Community*. In its first issue it set out its aims.

... this bulletin is about community. It is not meant to be all things to all men. It is just one attempt to help any today who are concerned about community, and in particular Christian community of an ecumenical and lay nature, to keep in touch and exchange views.

Looking back at its early years when he acted as editor, David Clark explained in more detail the reasoning behind his decision to launch a publication focussed on Christian community.

... Community began because I was searching. For what? As a minister who had just moved to take charge of a church which had once been a cathedral of Methodism, but whose membership was now under fifty, I could see only too clearly that the glory had departed ... The search had to begin again, not only in West Greenwich but across London, indeed across the country, for new forms of Christian community ... That search for 'a new way of being church' brought me immediately into contact with the communes movement which was, in the late sixties and early seventies, exploding onto the North American, and then English, scene, sparked by disillusion with the lethal nature of institutions (VietNam) and an unjust society (civil rights). It was a 'bottom-up' movement driven forward by risk-takers who believed they could turn the world upside down. So why not contract-in not only for the sake of the kingdom, but for the sake of the church? For was it not true that throughout Christian history ... that the small committed group had lain at the heart of Christian renewal? ... **18**

In the next few years Clark toured the length and breadth of the British Isles in search of new forms of Christian community. In addition to calling in at existing Christian based groups such as Pilsdon and Kingsway, he stayed in hostels for the homeless and at schemes for those with severe mental handicaps. He looked at new crofting ventures and witnessed those trying to make reconciliation work in Northern Ireland. He also visited a selection of communities in the Commune Movement, calling in and meeting members from Taena, Laurieston Hall and Findhorn. One group that he came across during his travels provided an interesting link between Christian communities and the emerging counter-culture. The 1971 Glastonbury Fayre (fore-runner of the later festivals), which had attracted a crowd of over 10,000 to see the likes of Hawkwind, the Pink Fairies, David Bowie and Joan Baez perform on the first Pyramid stage, was followed by an informal free festival at Worthy Farm in 1972. In a field just outside Glastonbury itself, a young

Canadian of Mennonite origin, Jim Nagel, set up a summer camp community welcoming those who were attracted by both the music and the mystical aura of the area. The camp would continue to run each summer for a number of years. Named after Jim's van (which was subsequently painted brown and yellow) the Greenbus Community was made up at any one time throughout the summer of both long- and short-term members, some staying for one night, others for longer periods of time with – on average – twenty-five campers each night, although numbers could swell to nearly a hundred for occasions such as the summer solstice. While it wasn't a requirement to be a Christian to stay at the camp, the whole ethos was Christian-based and the pattern of daily life was punctuated by prayers three times a day, before each mealtime. There was also a core of the group known as the Family.

... The Family is a group of people round Jim who in effect take responsibility for the running of the camp. They are not chosen; they simply emerge, commit themselves to the aims of Greenbus and remain. There are no apparent conditions for membership of the Family and members are not always the same. This reflects a genuine openness and lack of definition within the community ... **19**

The group discussed on a number of occasions the idea of setting up a permanent base when 'the right people and the right amount of money will have emerged' hoping to find some land nearby that they could farm. In 1974 the group took on part responsibility for running an unofficial Information Centre in Glastonbury which a member of the camp staffed each afternoon. It was hoped by some that the centre would act as a bridge between 'freaks' and 'straights' while helping visitors with accommodation problems and providing material on the Glastonbury legends and local spiritual happenings. There was also talk of setting up a shop or a coffee-house or maybe a recycling centre.

The Greenbus camp in the shadow of Glastonbury Tor

David Clark's *Community* bulletin facilitated networking between otherwise isolated groups across the country and resulted in a gathering being organised at Harborne Hall in Birmingham in 1975 and a further gathering two years later at Hengrave Hall in Suffolk where, for the first time, older established religious orders met alongside the newer lay communities. The results of David Clark's grand community tour were published in his 1977 book *Basic Communities: Towards an Alternative Society* in which he concluded:

... members of basic communities are so engaged, in a way which at times shames those of us sitting cosily in our armchairs watching the tragedies of the world flash entertainingly by, in colour if we can afford it, on our television screens. They are engaged in communal living, sticking with relationships when most of us regularly escape into less demanding encounters. They are sharing their possessions readily whilst we hoard and covet. They are expending great efforts to conserve the resources and beauty of a world we are busy wasting and polluting. It is they who are challenging us to educate ourselves in a deeper appreciation of the personal and interpersonal dimensions of life when we would rest content with our ignorance and prejudice. They are tending the sick, caring for the lost, supporting the bereaved, and striving to enable men to be free, when we are taken up with ourselves and our trivial ailments and anxieties. They are daring enough to laugh and dance in the presence of the Almighty when we prefer the safe prison of the church pew screwed firmly to the floor ...

There was now something of a head of steam building among Christian-based groups, and in 1980 a five-day Community Congress was held in Birmingham which attracted over 250 people representing some 42 established religious orders and over 50 lay residential communities along with other non-residential lay community groups. Speakers included Jean Vanier of l'Arche; Jim Wallis of the Sojourners Community in Washington DC; and Rosemary Haughton of the Lothlorien Community in Scotland. One outcome of the Congress was the formation of an organisation originally called the National Centre for Christian Communities and Networks, but changed quite quickly to the National Association of Christian Communities and Networks or NACCAN. The Association took over the production of the *Community* bulletin, renaming it *Christian Community*, which would come out three or four times a year throughout the 1980's and 90's. It also published, at irregular intervals, a directory of Christian groups, communities and networks, early editions of which carried entries from some 250 recently established groups and 200 religious orders. In 1981 David Clark became the director/co-ordinator of NACCAN working from 'a modest Community Resources Centre' based at Westhill College in Birmingham, firstly on a voluntary basis then later on a part-time paid basis. He helped to organise further gatherings and two further congresses in 1984 and '87 and edited a series of booklets entitled *New Christian Initiatives*. Another outcome of all this activity was the formation of new Christian-inspired communities. The Neighbours Community was formed in five adjoining terrace houses in Northampton in 1983 by Michael and Anne Jones and Roger and Susan Sawtell, partly inspired by the NACCAN Congresses which they had attended and partly out of concern for the problems encountered by people who had been in-patients in local psychiatric hospitals.

We decided to offer supportive accommodation to a handful of young people living with, or recovering from, mental disorders such as clinical depression, anorexia or schizophrenia. This was a demanding task which could not easily be undertaken by one family on its own, but might be shared between the several adjacent households of a residential community. We knocked down the fences to make all five gardens into one and constructed inter-connecting doorways between the houses, to make a 'community of households' ... Sometimes this restorative task came near to overwhelming us and, after ten years, we laid it down, partly because, by then, several of the community members were working with people with mental disorders issues during the day, and were understandably reluctant to find people with similar problems round the supper table when they returned home from work. The community continued for a further thirteen years but with less emphasis on this supportive task. [20]

Roger Sawtell

In 1987, after funding had started to run out, NACCAN started to change from a resource-centre-based organisation to more of a network or association. In 1988 it moved its base down the hill to the Woodbrooke Quaker Study Centre.

One group noticeable by its absence from the new network and publications during this period was the Children of God. After the media had got wind of the sect's new 'flirty fishing' escapade, Berg had had to flee from Tenerife, although this did not prevent him from rolling out this new technique to the colonies that now existed throughout Europe and in increasing numbers across the globe. While the initial justification for the sexual witnessing was to win souls for Jesus, it is clear that over time, with female members joining escort agencies to meet people, the sect was in effect also selling sex to raise money to keep the organisation going. Between 1974 and 1987, according to the group themselves, members had sexual contact with 223,989 people while Flirty Fishing and by 1981 this practice had resulted in the birth of over 300 children known in the group as 'Jesus Babies'.[21] Berg also instigated a number of changes during the late 70's and early 80's to the way the sect was structured and in 1978 changed the group's name, declaring that the Children of God were no more, and taking the new name of The Family of Love. This was later changed to simply The Family. The group were also seemingly dogged by controversy almost everywhere they went. During the 1980's they were officially banned from several countries and members deported and barred from return. Attacks from the anti-cult movement continued and there was also the start of damaging accounts of life in the sect and of abuse by Berg and others being published by former members. This included, in 1984, a book by one of Berg's own daughters: *The Children of God – The inside story*. In 1987 Flirty Fishing was officially stopped by the sect, largely due to the emergence of AIDS. In the 1990's numerous allegations of child abuse were made against the group in countries around the world including Argentina, Australia, Brazil, Britain, France, Italy, Japan, Norway, Peru, Spain, Sweden, the USA, and Venezuela. Some of these were clearly the result of targeted activity by the anti-cult movement and in nearly all cases it turned out to be very hard to find evidence that would lead to a conviction. In 1994, in the midst of all this controversy, David Berg (who had lived in virtual isolation from the rest of the sect for many years – only communicating with them via *The MO Letters*) died, aged 75, and was buried in Costa de Caparica, Portugal. Through a combination of influences the Family began to change during the 1990's. With Flirty Fishing dropped and, in response to the ageing of David Berg, the leadership passed increasingly to Karen Zerby/ Maria and other senior members in a group known as the World Services. Following the US government attack on the Branch Davidians at Waco in 1993, and nervous that they might also be targeted, The Family contacted a number of academics who studied new religious movements mostly in the USA and gave them considerable access to the group's archives and membership, hoping that favourable reports would help give them a more positive image.

In a child custody case started in 1992 in England and lasting for 75 days spread over three years, the judge, the Rt Hon Lord Justice Sir Alan Hylton Ward spent much of the time investigating the way the sect operated, hearing from current and former members as witnesses, along with testimony from academics and social workers. The court examined thousands of pages of internal Family documents, and ordered social services to investigate and evaluate the conditions in The Family's communities in England. The case finally finished on 26th May 1995 and a 295-page copy of the findings was made public in October 1995.[22] This amounts to perhaps the most detailed available account of the activities of the group in the UK. The report mentions various Family communities, including those at Didcot, Tewkesbury, Rugby, Newcastle, Nottingham, Hendon, Cricklewood, Arkley, Pinner and at least one other in Scotland. There is also mention of a school run by the group in Wantage that was later transferred to Burnt Farm in Hertfordshire. One witness stated that at the time the group in the British Isles consisted of 101 members over 16 and 194 children.

In his conclusion to the report the Judge said in assessment of the group:

To the members of The Family, David Berg was an End-Time Prophet who was revered by his flock as a man of God. He was treated as an icon. Consequently, in the eyes of the members he could do no wrong. Since obedience was a clarion call and since murmuring was a cardinal crime, members faithful to him were unable to articulate criticism of him ... Whilst his Letters were never sacrosanct, they did constitute The Family's theology and they were influential in shaping attitudes and behaviour. Unless they are repudiated, they are likely to continue to hold sway.

He went on to comment on what he considered to be 'Sexually Inappropriate Conduct'.

... Berg freed his flock from the restraints which in society control licentious behaviour. He knew that he was giving his people a dangerous toy, the danger being that lust would be mistaken for love. Having encouraged the sexuality of children, they became, as he must have been aware, objects of the Law of Love when he must have appreciated that by reason of their want of age and understanding they were unable to give full and free consent especially under the pressure of advances made upon them by adults. He also must have realised that harm would be caused to them. I am totally satisfied that a high proportion of children were exposed to the sight or sound of adult sexual activity. I am satisfied that many children and teenagers engaged in sexual activity with other children or teenagers. I am furthermore satisfied that a significant number of children, more within The Family than outside it, had masturbation and even sexual intercourse forced upon them by adults ...

He also made it clear that he considered that those members who had given evidence had not always given 'truth, the whole truth and nothing but the truth' and because they saw themselves as a persecuted minority that they felt free to try and deceive the authorities. But he also recognised that the sect had changed; they had submitted to the jurisdiction of the Court rather than run away and they had 'undoubtedly begun to seek open contact with church, local authorities, academics and society generally.' There was also a call for the group to denounce David Berg:

... They must acknowledge that through his writings he was personally responsible for children in The Family having been subjected to sexually inappropriate behaviour; that it is now recognized that it was not just a mistake to have written as he did but wrong to have done so; and that as a result children have been harmed by their experiences ... The Family must be encouraged honestly to face up to this shameful period in their history so that those harmed by it, victims and perpetrators alike, can seek to come to terms with it. For an honest memorial to be given to David Berg, this dark side to his character must be revealed. By all means, let thanks be given also for the good he did – as I accept he did for many – and for the inspiration he has been to those who through him have devoted their lives to the service of the Lord.

Judge Ward allowed the child at the centre of the case to remain with his mother within The Family. The rather mixed message that came over from the report allowed both the Family and its detractors to claim that they had been vindicated. As the case was in its final months The Family issued a document called *The Love Charter* published in January 1995 (although as it contains a forward by David Berg himself much of it must have been being written in the preceding year). The Charter divided into two sections the 'Charter of Responsibilities and Rights' and the 'Fundamental Family Rules', and running to over 400 pages covered everything from joining and leaving the group, through how communal homes would be organised and run including rules governing: sex and affection; child discipline; marriage; and prophecy. The Charter codified the beliefs, rights, and responsibilities of full-time Family members and individual Family communities have operated according to their own decisions and initiative within this framework since. There have been two further editions of the charter, the last issued in 2009 under the title of *The Family Discipleship Charter*. From the late 90's and into the 21st Century the Family has become less controversial, increasingly concentrating it activities on what might be called conventional Christian mission and humanitarian work worldwide. They still suffer from attacks from the anti-cult movement and in the press, much of it based on decades-old incidents. The sect appear to have moved away and distanced itself from the excesses of the 1970's and 80's to such an extent that one writer on new religious movements commented that '... The impression given by The Family today is that they are sincere and dedicated Evangelical Christians whose only real difference from any others is that they are honest about sleeping with each other ...' [23] In 2004, the sect changed its name once again and is now known as The Family International.

Not all the so-called Jesus People groups during the early 1970's were American imports; the UK produced its own evangelical sect which started in a small village in Northamptonshire, in part inspired by the Jesus freaks from America, but also part of a wider British-based evangelical and charismatic revival that was starting to take place in churches up and down the country. Bugbrooke, seven miles to the south-west of Northampton, was a fairly typical English Midlands village with declining church attendance until the Baptist Chapel in the village appointed Noel Stanton as its minister in 1957. Stanton, a former bank clerk and Navy conscript, who had become a committed Christian after the war, was at the time a fairly conventional young preacher who tried various attempts at outreach in an effort to revive his Baptist congregation, reaching out particularly to young people in the local area. Things started to take off when, at the end of the sixties, some of the people attending the church began speaking in tongues. This attracted further attention to what was happening in this charismatic little Midlands enclave and the congregation continued to grow, attracting those not usually drawn to the church – such as former hippies and bikers. Some of those attracted to the activity going on in the area bought houses in Northampton, quickly dubbed 'Jesus Homes'.

In July 1973 a hundred members of the Bugbrooke Baptist congregation went away together to a hostel in Malhamdale in the Yorkshire Dales. Noel Stanton had taken a copy of the recently published book *A New Way of Living* by Michael Harper with him. The book told the story of the revival of the Church of the Redeemer in a rundown part of Houston, Texas where a network of community houses had grown up to support the work of the Church. Starting from just a few families it had grown to 40 households running a coffee house, medical and law clinics, a shop selling religious books and gifts, and a rehabilitation centre on a ranch in the heart of Texas.

... Perhaps the major contribution that the Church of the Redeemer has made to the Church at large is that it has demonstrated that the practice and experience of community can be easily available to everyone. Community is not easy. But this church has shown that it need no longer be practised by a few dreamy-eyed idealists; nor need it be something special and removed from the rest of the Church. But the local church can become a community of communities, catering for the needs of an entire neighbourhood.

Michael Harper

The Church of the Redeemer reached out to those on the margins of society. As well as hippies, it counted among its members former addicts, alcoholics and prisoners. Those gathered in Malhamdale were inspired and excited by passages that Stanton read out from *A New Way of Living* and over the two weeks they were at the hostel a vision for a similar project centred on Bugbrooke developed.

At Malhamdale we considered how to work the vision out. Many who lived outside Bugbrooke considered moving in to be where the action was. There were schemes for bulk buying, for a second-hand clothes store, and for sharing lists of needs and gifts. A 'Love Community Fund' was also to be set up. As we lived more cheaply, so money would be released to meet needs and buy houses ...

Simon Cooper A Fire in Our Hearts

The group envisaged three types of community homes; extended family houses to be called Jesus Family Homes, frontline evangelical houses to be called Jesus Welcome Homes and, in the Bugbrooke area, Jesus Central Homes, which '... would be at the heart of things to train Christians within community.' Once back at Bugbrooke, the two Jesus Houses in Argyle Street and Harlestone Road in Northampton became a hive of activity as the group worked on putting their vision into practice. The upsurge in religious fervour in one small village attracted the attention of the media. On 16th September 1973 the *Daily Mail* reported that 'Nowhere else in Britain has experienced such a concentrated surge of religious fervour. So many people want to be part of the 'Bugbrooke Miracle' that some travel for miles almost every day to attend prayer sessions'. They quoted one chapel-goer as saying that 'Four years ago the Lord took Bugbrooke by the scruff of its neck and said 'I want you for My own'. Since then the village has been possessed by the love of Jesus.'

The newspaper stories were followed by a Thames Television documentary titled 'The Lord Took Hold Of Bugbrooke' and further press coverage. All this exposure brought more people to Bugbrooke; some moved into houses on a nearby housing estate, with couples sharing their houses with single members. But it was clear that additional accommodation was needed. It was then that Bugbrooke Hall, a Georgian Rectory set in 13 acres of grounds, came up for sale at auction. The group decided this was an opportunity too good to miss and set about raising enough money to pay a deposit. Some members sold rings and jewellery; some pledged their houses; others gave or loaned savings; and come the auction day they were able to outbid others and bought the Hall for £67,000. The Hall, renamed New Creation Hall, needed considerable repair and renovation before it could become the centre of the group's activities.

We were an odd bunch: ex-bikers, hippies and graduates, plus an ex-lay-preacher and her daughter, a pair of village newlyweds, and a Christian family who'd exchanged their council house for a 'mansion'! Life at the Hall was fun, chaotic and rough. We didn't care. If there was any time to lose our comforts, it was now. What we lacked in competence we made up for in enthusiasm. God was real and we were discovering brotherhood and sisterhood.

Simon Cooper A Fire in Our Hearts

Soon after the purchase of the Hall, the group acquired a large farmhouse a couple miles from Bugbrooke with outbuildings and a few acres of orchard and fields, and New Creation Farm was born. A shop was also leased in Northampton and a clothes store and health food shop were set up under the umbrella organisation House of Goodness Ltd.

What was now becoming known as the New Creation Christian Community was not the only communal group to spring up in the UK inspired by the Church of the Redeemer. In 1972, following a visit to the Texas church by the Bishop of Coventry, Graham and Betty Pulkingham and a small group from the Redeemer community came to Britain and established a small informal community in a house on a Coventry housing estate. A year later a trust was formed and they became known as the Community of Celebration. Very quickly it was clear that the new group would need larger premises to accommodate the expanding numbers of people who were interested in their work, and they were able to get the use of a former convent, Yeldall Manor in Berkshire.

The Community at Yeldall Manor was a melting pot of nationalities and churches. The original core of Americans were soon augmented by British members and others from all the English-speaking Commonwealth countries, plus several from Sweden. Churches ranged from Roman Catholic to Plymouth Brethren. Some came for healing; the pastoral ministry was highly effective, gaining the confidence even of the Psychiatric Department of the Royal Berkshire Hospital. Some came for the experience; the Community's policy was to train local church leaders. Some came to offer their gifts in ministry, for which there were many opportunities ranging from children's work to music in worship. **24**

A musical outreach group was established called The Fisherfolk who sang and later recorded Christian folk songs and hymns. The group became in

Fisherfolk

great demand to play at churches up and down the country they also appeared on television and radio. The community set up a mail-order distribution company to deal with production and marketing of the group's recordings. The Fisherfolk were more than just a folk group, David Clark who visited the Community of Celebration on his grand tour of communities described the effect that the group had had on the Christian revival at the time:

... real impact has been made by The Fisherfolk, who in small teams of extremely talented musicians and singers have rapidly moved from local coffee-bar to international fame. The Fisherfolk plan their programme in consultation with local church leaders and give effect to their message through personal testimony, in music and in drama. They sometimes initiate worship workshops around dance, mime, poetry, and the graphic arts with an emphasis on exploring new forms of liturgical expression. Follow-up teaching materials have been designed. Once again the medium is very much the message and, though The Fisherfolk figure as leaders and 'experts', their spontaneity and creative skills can result in active and enthusiastic participation by local people. **25**

In 1975, Graham Pulkingham was appointed as Provost of the Cathedral of the Isles at Millport on the Isle of Cumbrae in the Firth of Clyde. The Cathedral, the smallest in the British Isles, had a former theological college attached to the premises and had been used for a short while in the early 70's by the LSD Guru Michael Hollingshead as the Pure Land Ashram where hippies coming back from the East could 're-enter the west'. For ten years Cumbrae would act as the main base for the Community of Celebration. Here they developed the musical side of the community with much of their income coming from the sales of recordings and songbooks. They developed some small-scale farming and purchased and ran the local bakery. At the same time as the move to Cumbrae, close links were forged with another Christian Community at Post Green House, a Victorian Country house at Lytchett Minster in Dorset. Established by Sir Tom and Lady Faith Lees, the Dorset group had grown from an initial Bible study group that met in the Faith Lees' home in the late 1960's to some 200 people coming weekly for teaching and prayer and running camps and conferences. A small community of linked households in properties on the Post Green Estate had started to develop in 1973 and this was increased after an agreement to join forces and work with the Community of Celebration was made in 1976 and people who had been living at Yeldall and Cumbrae moved to Post Green. This link set a new direction for the Post Green community and it developed a number of business ventures: a publishing business, a local caravan site, garage, fishing lakes and Post Office. The two groups worked closely together until the mid-eighties when, unable to re-negotiate the lease on the Cathedral premises, most of the Cumbrae group moved to the town of Aliquippa, near Pittsburgh (USA). At the same time, the Post Green Community divided, with the communal group moving to Berry House, near Redhill, Surrey at the invitation of the Bishop of Southwark, and Post Green reverting back to its original role.

The late 1970's saw an expansion of the New Creation Community under the broader banner of the Jesus Fellowship. By the end of 1977 they had set up three further community homes; one in Daventry; Sheepfold Grange in Upper Stowe; and Festal Grange in Pattishall. In November the same year they also purchased a builders' yard in Towcester and created Towcester Building Supplies. To this growing collection of property were added Vineyard Farmhouse in Church Stowe; a former vicarage in Flore that was renamed Living Stones; and Cornhill Manor in Pattishall – formerly a hotel that could accommodate 60 people. In 1978 it was decided that the group should spread its wings beyond Northamptonshire and a converted motel (renamed Harvest House) in Leamington Spa was purchased. In 1980 they also acquired Stockton House near Rugby. The Fellowship would eventually grow to include over 60 households of varying sizes. On the business side the original health food shop in Northampton grew to a chain of nine Goodness Foods shops and, in 1981, Goodness Foods Wholesale opened. The group also run Skaino Atmos Ltd a building, plumbing, heating firm; a small timber merchants; an outdoor clothing and equipment shop; and have close links with a firm of solicitors.

With a seemingly ever-expanding empire of property and businesses and an evangelical fervour when it came to recruiting members, the Fellowship was always going to be open to attack from those in the anti-cult movement. The death of two members in slightly unusual circumstances was the hook for the media and anti-cult groups to start to focus on them with the fairly common mix of testimony from ex-members and fantastical accusations ('spy network', a gang of Gestapo heavies bent on 'cracking' the flock! ... force-feeding carrots ... sharing dirty socks, a fanatical colony of brainwashed zombies!). This coverage, and what some saw as the group's aggressive style of evangelising, caused serious consternation among other church groups, and resulted (in the mid eighties) in the group being expelled from both the Baptist Union and the Evangelical Alliance. Being excluded from the more official organisations of the Church may have given the Fellowship more freedom to develop its outreach work. Taking some inspiration from the origins of Salvation Army, in 1987 the new arm of the fellowship was launched under the name of the Jesus Army.

The new venture was planned to give the group a new high-profile public image with deliberate military overtones. Members doing outreach work wore camouflage jacket uniforms emblazoned with flourescent red crosses and, in a move reminiscent of the Children of God sixteen years earlier, double-decker buses were purchased and painted in the new Jesus Army colours. The new name and image were accompanied by a change in

Jesus Army bus

recruitment tactics, moving away from the ex-hippie and biker elements and focusing more on the homeless, drug addicts and alcoholics. There were attempts to target sex workers in Soho and members of the Black and Asian communities for conversion and recruitment, all with little success. The group's *Jesus Lifestyle* magazine quickly changed to a 32-page quarterly publication with a growing circulation. Jesus Centres were established in a number of cities

and plans were developed to extend the 'Jesus Revolution' across the country. Jesus Army buses became a regular presence on many high streets and increasing numbers of people were attracted to the group's regular large evangelical events. Writer William Shaw encountered the groups evangelising while doing undercover research for his book *Spying in Guru Land*. After meeting them at a Wembley Praise Day event in 1993 he was invited back to one of the group's London houses, known as the Battlecentre (in Emanuel Avenue, Acton, West London) which he described as 'halfway between a care home and a spiritual outward bound centre'. After attending a number of meetings in the house he was invited to attend a New Years Day gathering at the Derngate Theatre in Northampton.

> *On stage, hair flopping off his balding pate, the sixty-seven-year-old Noel Stanton fires the crowd, reminds us of the proximity of Satan, berates us for tiring. But then, because it is the start of a new year, he sets targets for 1994, and reviews the achievements of the old. This year the church will seek 600 new converts. Last year 450 new members joined. Deafening cheer. They dedicate the latest household, the first on Tyneside, and the Jesus Army's seventy-second. They name it Flowing Waters. Like the Battlecentre, all the Jesus households have ringing Bible-time names like Bright Flame, Conquering Name, Crown of Life or Living Stones. Back in the Battlecentre there's a map of Britain with pins marking each household. There are eighteen other pins, orange and blue, which mark target towns where the Jesus Army are planning to 'plant' new households ...* **26**

The 'Jesus Army' is the name now most associated with the group, although it still uses the New Creation and Goodness 'brands' for its communal houses and businesses. This multiplication of names has led to some accusations of deceit by anti-cult groups. Despite the group being, in many ways, conservative their enthusiastic street preaching tactics have meant that they have stayed on cult watch organisation lists of groups which they have serious concerns about. The Jesus Army denies that it is a New Religious Movement, instead claiming to be a part of the mainstream church revival. Certainly, compared with the Children of God/Family, the Jesus Army seems ultra-conservative. They put great emphasis on celibacy, encouraging single people to take vows of abstinence and even advising married couples to sleep in single beds and refrain from sex. They also have no women in any positions of authority or power, taking a very traditional view of the roles of men and women to the point of being accused of misogyny. However, there are some similarities between the two sects. Like the Children of God/Family, some members of the Jesus Army are given new names. But these are 'virtue names' rather than biblical, and are usually based on their own name such as John 'Gentle', Steve 'Faithful', Helen 'Pioneering' or Debbie 'Refreshing' and were originally just a way to distinguish between two different members each called Steve or John. Perhaps one of the few areas where the two sects would find any agreement might be in their shared views on the End-time, although the Jesus Army are much less forthcoming about this aspect of their beliefs. The Jesus Army has also had a much improved relationship with the mainstream church, rejoining the Evangelical Alliance in 1999. There is an insider's history of the Jesus Army, *Fire in Our Hearts*, written by a member and first published in 1991 with updated versions bringing the story up to the end of the nineties. At the end of the latest version the author concludes the book with the following statement:

In the late sixties God moved in a remarkable way upon the churches of this land. We were one of many little groups at that time who sprang to life through the Holy Spirit. God took hold of us and opened our eyes. He showed us a people who had been scattered coming together to live for Jesus and his kingdom ... Now, it seems, we stand at the threshold of something bigger. God's movement is among the people and it is spreading daily. We want to be in the thick of it, where Jesus is.

Through the nineties the makeup of NACCAN changed and although the number of member groups remained high, the non-residential groups and networks who had been involved in the early days drifted away and the organisation became increasingly reliant on support from residential communities. Annual assemblies continued to be held, but again with fewer members attending than in the past decade. Roger Sawtell from The Neighbours community was editor of the organisation's magazine during this period. Looking back, he saw NACCAN as 'bringing together people on similar faith journeys, a valuable resource, a place to share our experience and problems, to pray together with like-minded folk, to encourage the faint-hearted and to contribute to widening the opportunities for communal living, as described in the early chapters of Acts of the Apostles.' **27** In 1998 the administration was moved to Newport in Gwent. Due to a continuing struggle with finances and difficulty in recruiting trustees and people to edit the magazine, early in the new millennium a decision was taken to wind up the work of NACCAN, with two final editions of *Christian Community* being published in 2003, celebrating its achievements over the past three decades. More informal networking continued between Christian communities after the demise of NACCAN; The Neighbours Community in Northampton continued to handle enquiries and put out an occasional newsletter called *Touching Place* between 2003 and 2006, and further gatherings of Christian communities were held at Scargill House, in Yorkshire and at Lee Abbey in Devon.,

Though the story of the Christian Community Movement in the UK is ongoing, the hopes of those who believed that it might bring about 'a new reformation' and 'a brave new world' have not yet been realised. One reason for this is the legacy of Christendom that continues to restrict the vision of the institutional church…. the Christian Community Movement encountered an institutional church that failed to recognize that the host of emerging groups and networks might add a new dimension and impetus to its mission. The leading denominational bodies that had welcomed the setting up of NACCAN, failed to follow-up that welcome with any real interest or tangible support…. The conservatism which typified the decades following the social upheavals of the 1960's led to some of the groups involved in the movement being labelled as 'way out'. Who would ever want to choose the uncertainties and stresses of living in an intentional community? And were not some of the causes espoused by those associated with the movement 'Marxist' or even 'anarchic'? A church built on a Christendom model of preservation not transformation was thus very wary of a movement that appeared to it as over idealistic, over enthusiastic and accountable to nobody.

David Clark, *Breaking the Mould of Christendom* 2005

Angerson, J & Shaw, W *Love, Power, Sacrifice: Life with the Jesus Army* 2007 Dewi Lewis. ISBN: 1904587488

Bainbridge, W S *The Endtime Family: Children of God* 2002 New York University Press. ISBN: 0791452638

Barlow, K *The Abode of Love: The Remarkable Tale of Growing Up in a Religious Cult* 2007 Mainstream. ISBN: 1845962133

Barrett, D *The New Believers* 2001 Cassell. ISBN: 1844030407

Bradshaw, P *Following the Spirit: Seeing Christian Faith Through Community Eyes* 2010 O Books. ISBN: 1846942942

Berg, D *Letters from Moses David to the Children of God* 1974 Children of God. ASIN: B0007BF85Y

Berg, D et al *The Mo Letters: A-150 & 151-300 [Vols 1 & 2]* 1976 Children of God. ASIN B0070XKTCE

Bohlken-Zumpe, E *Torches Extinguished* 1993 Carrier Pigeon Press

Chancellor, J *Life in the Family: An Oral History of the Children of God* 2000 Syracuse University Press ISBN: 0815606451

Clark, D *Basic Communities: Towards an Alternative Society* 1977 SPCK. ISBN: 0281029652

Clark, D *Breaking the Mould of Christendom* 2005 Epworth Press. ISBN: 0716205920

Cooper, S & Farrant, M *Fire in Our Hearts: Story of the Jesus Fellowship/Jesus Army* 1991 Jesus Fellowship. ISBN 1900878054

Davis, D *Children of God: Inside Story by the Daughter of the Founder Moses David Berg* 1985 Marshall. ISBN: 0551012137

Duin, J *Days of Fire and Glory: The Rise and Fall of a Charismatic Community* 2009 Crossland Press. ISBN: 0979027977

Ferguson, R *Chasing the Wild Goose: Story of the Iona Community* 1998 Wild Goose. ISBN 1901557006

Ferguson, R *George MacLeod: Founder of the Iona Community* 2004 Wild Goose. ISBN: 1901557537

Hinton, J *Communities: Stories and Spiritualities of Twelve European Communities* 1993 Eagle. ISBN: 086347070X

Holmes, Miriam Arnold *Cast Out In The World: From The Bruderhof To A Life On Her Own* 1997 Carrier Pigeon Press

Jones, Jones & Buhring *Not Without My Sister* 2008 Harper Collins. ISBN: 0007248075

Lockley, A *Christian Communes* 1976 SCM Press. ISBN: 0334019273

MacLeod, G *We Shall Re-Build: The Work of the Iona Community on Mainland and on the Island* 1962. ASIN: B0026W2A44

Manley, Belinda *Through Streets Broad and Narrow* 1996 Carrier Pigeon Press

Melton, J G *The Children of God* 2004 Signature Books. ISBN: 1560851805

Motley, N *Much Ado About Something: A History of the Othona Community* 1985. ASIN: B0007BYA4O

Motley. N *Letters to a community, 1970-1980* 1986. ASIN: B0007BYA4Y

Muir, A *Outside the Safe Place: An Oral History of the Early Years of the Iona Community* Wild Goose 2011. ISBN: 1849520798

Pleil, N M *Free from Bondage* 1994 Carrier Pigeon Press

Sawatsky, J *The Ethic of Traditional Communities and the Spirit of Healing Justice* 2009 Kingsley. ISBN 1843106876

Shaw, W *Spying in Guru Land* 1994 Fourth Estate. ISBN: 1857021525

Shepherd, G *Talking with the Children of God* 2010 Illinois University Press. ISBN: 0252077210

Williams, M *Heaven's Harlots: My Fifteen Years in a Sex Cult* 2000 Morrow. ISBN: 0688170129

Wagerin, R *The Children of God: A Make Believe Eevolution* 1993 Greenwood Publishing. ISBN: 0897893522

1   *Much Ado About Something: A history of the Othona Community*

2   Letter to Richard Fairfield quoted in **Communes Europe**

3   http://www.othona.org (13.5.12)

4   See: The Abode of Love in **Utopia Britannica** Coates, C 2000 for details of early years of the Spaxton Sect.

5   Kate Barlow interview; www.abc.net.au/rn/ spiritofthings/stories/2009/2493474.htm (12.6.11)

6   Kate Barlow **The Abode of Love: The Remarkable Tale of Growing Up in a Religious Cult**

7   Reported by Elizabeth Bohlken-Zumpe in **Torches Extinguished**

8   Benjamin Zablocki **The Joyful Community** 1971 p58

9   The Bruderhof have strictly controlled and often refused access to source material by academics and writers wishing to study them, including this author. This has led to those 'approved' writers granted, in most cases, limited access having the impartiality of their work criticised as being inevitably biased and pro-Bruderhof.

10 Robin Appleby interviewed by the author in 2009

11 Heini Arnold quoted in **Torches Rekindled**

12 Nelson Kraybill A Day with the Hutterian Brethren **Anabaptism Today**, Issue 4, October 1993

13 **Communities** magazine, 1995 Archived at: http:// www.raysender.com/heart.html (20.2.2012)

14 http://www.exfamily.org/children-of-god/history/ index.shtml (23.2.2012)

15 http://www.exfamily.org/hist/ (4.6.2012)

16 Kent, S **A Lustful Prophet** 2000 http://www.arts. ualberta.ca/~skent/Linkedfiles/lustfulprophet.htm (6.6.2012)

17 David Clark 2012, correspondence with the author

18 **Christian Community** No 75 Winter 1996 'Jubilee Edition'

19 The Greenbus Community in **Christian Communes** Lockley, A 1976

20 Roger Sawtell, correspondence with author in 2012

21 Bainbridge, William Sims **The Sociology of Religious Movements** 1996 Routledge. ISBN: 0415912024. p223

22 http://www.xfamily.org/index.php/Complete_ Judgment_of_Lord_Justice_Ward (12.6.2012)

23 David Barrett **The New Believers** p227

24 www.ccct.co.uk/Library/yeldall.html (12.6.2012)

25 David Clark **Basic Communities: Towards an Alternative Society**

26 William Shaw **Spying in Guru Land**

27 Roger Sawtell, correspondence with author in 2012

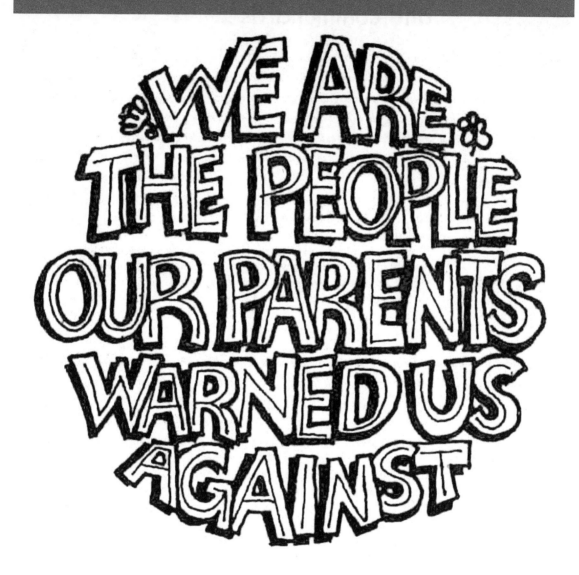

One thing we must always remember is that time is on our side, we have seen the future – we are the future – and we know that it is not only ours, but it likewise belongs to all the people of the planet. The death culture is having ulcers because it's children do not want their values, their morals and the material/consumer society they wish to perpetuate. The death culture expects oppressed groups like blacks to fight them, but it's own kids! Whew! They say the kids will grow out of it, but they know, they have lost their own children, they are losing their replacements, their system is dying.

White Panther statement, *International Times* **127 April 6th 1972**

Hippies, beats, mystics, madmen, freaks, yippies, crazies, crackpots and communards ...

The spread of this disaffection from the 'straightness' of the capitalist society has led many people to believe that a general revolutionary movement is developing, one which has been variously labelled by observers and participants as the counter-culture, the underground, and more recently as 'consciousness III'. This movement lacks any well-defined objectives and goals other than a shared concern on the part of its participants to transform their own lives and that of straight society, to create an alternative social order characterised by values counter to those that appear to dominate present existence ...

Andrew Rigby, Communes in Britain

The seeds of the idea of the counter-culture, of a complete alternative society can be seen in the Situationist inspired writings and activities of some of the early members of the 'underground'. Perhaps one of the first attempts to express this idea was in the *Invisible Insurrection of a Million Minds* by Alexander Trocchi in 1962 and what would grow over time into the Sigma project. This was an attempt to envisage a parallel social society with alternative institutions that would exist alongside the old society until such a point that the new would supersede the old without the need to overthrow it. Trocchi's manifesto included practical suggestions on how this might be achieved.

How to begin? At a chosen moment in a vacant country house (mill, abbey, church or castle) not too far from the City of London, we shall foment a kind of cultural jam session: out of this will evolve the prototype of our spontaneous university

Alexander Trocchi

Trocchi goes on to outline plans for finding a large country house to establish a pilot project where a group of 'astronauts of inner space' would be based along with '... their tools and dream-machines and amazing apparatus and appurtenances ...' The spontaneous university would be no farther from London than Oxford or Cambridge so that the group could maintain contact with the 'cultural phenomena' happening in the metropolis. Trocchi was worried that if the project was too far from the 'centre of power' it would run the risk of being seen as 'a group of utopian escapists, spiritual exiles, hellbent for Shangri-La on the bicycle of our frustration.' The pilot project plan was nothing if not ambitious-looking towards future expansion with a property big enough for outhouses for large workshops that could accommodate light industry and enough space on the entire site to allow for 'spontaneous architecture and eventual town-planning ...'

During the mid sixties Trocchi was one of the participants in the growing counter-culture in London and continued to pursue his sigma project, trying to bring together people from the various strands of underground. By the end of 1965 he thought he had enough support from others to try and convene a conference of like minds to try and kick-start the project. The performance artist/poet/cultural activist Jeff Nutall wrote on the group's behalf to Braziers Park in Oxfordshire asking if it would it be possible to run a weekend conference there. Glynn Faithfull, Marianne Faithfull's father, had recently become a central figure at the Braziers community (following the death of Norman Glaister) and he agreed that the small band of would-be world-changing minds could use Braziers' facilities for their gathering. Recalling the event in his book *Bomb Culture,* Nuttall remembers the community as 'a little colony of quiet, self-sufficient middle-class intellectuals, totally square with heavy overtones of Quakerism and Fabianism' who were 'anxious to extend every kindness and expected in return, good manners and an observation of the minimal regulations they imposed.' Anxious they might be, given the list of people who were invited to attend which included along with Trocchi and Nutall; anti-psychiatrists Ronnie Laing; Sid Briskin; David Cooper; the radical American journalist Clancy Sigal; Beba Lavrin, co-founder of the Centre 42 arts-into-factories movement; the anarchist conceptual artist John Latham; and *International Times* co-founder Tom McGrath; along with their respective buddies, lovers and spouses. According to Nuttal they really had 'no interest of playing guest to the Braziers Park host' and were 'merely wanting to pay their way for a place where they could go a little madder than they already were.'

The weekend seems to have been a chaotic combination of deep political discussion and argument, counter-cultural happening and continuous stoned and drunken party. Tom McGrath recalled 'The basic idea of the conference was that an élite would seize the means of communication and then liberate the working classes. I had been infected by Marxism and thought of myself as a Communist. However, I couldn't stomach this brand of revolutionary talk. I shouted out, 'This room stinks of elitism,' and everyone went quiet.'[1] Over the weekend John Latham created a number of art works – enacting the first of his controversial 'Skoob Tower Ceremonies'. This consisted of building a two to three metre high tower of books (with their pages interleaved), stacked on top of a metal framework which created an improvised chimney that was then set alight and allowed to slowly smoulder. After a couple of hours it burst into a flaming pillar of books. He also created a '3D mural' on the living room wall by gluing a precious book to the wall with polyfilla and spraying wall and book with black aerosol paint to greet the company as they rose on the Sunday morning. This act caused serious distress to some of the older members of the community. The Braziers community members initially tried to be welcoming and get the guests to attend a formal dinner when they arrived on the Friday evening, but by Saturday night had resorted to sitting up all night with a gun at the ready for protection. After a somewhat subdued Sunday morning meeting Ronnie Laing attempted to sum things up. 'It's a question ... Of coming down from the surface of things, from the surface of yourself, down to the core of all things, to the central sphere of being of which all things are emanations.' At midday the group 'fled from one another with colossal relief.'[2] The fallout from the 'conference' saw the participants continue on their own individual trajectories through the rest of the 60's and the sigma project remained an inspirational but somewhat intellectual and academic paper project. The failure of the Spontaneous University to materialise and inspire the 'Insurrection of a Million Minds' did not slow down the continued flowering of the counter-culture.

In July 1967 a two-week-long gathering took place at the Roundhouse in Chalk Farm, London, under the title of the 'Dialectics of Liberation'. Organised by a group of 'anti-psychiatrists' from the Institute for Phenomenological Studies, David Cooper, R D Laing, Joseph Berke and Leon Redler, the aim of the 'international congress' was to 'demystify human violence in all its forms'. The list of speakers now reads like a who's who of the 1960's international counter-culture – as well as Laing and Cooper speaking on alternatives to psychiatry there were talks from Herbert Marcuse, William Burroughs and Marxist economist Paul Sweezy. Cybernetician Gregory Bateson warned of coming environmental disasters and the melting of the polar ice caps. Beat poet Allen Ginsberg was there; Julian Beck from the Living Theatre Group; Emmett Grogan of the San Francisco Diggers; Dutch poet and Situationist Simon Vinkenoog of the Amsterdam Provos; Timothy Leary put in an appearance. Even Jean-Paul Sartre was scheduled to appear but cancelled at the last moment. It is estimated that over the fortnight some 5,000 people attended the lectures, talks and happenings. By far the most controversial speech was that given by Black Panther Stokeley Carmichael who, after talking about the destruction of humanity by racism, berated the gathered throng of long-haired middle class dropouts and would-be Marxist revolutionaries for being advocates of peace-loving-non-violence while revolution came from 'the barrel of a gun'. Carmichael's speech is often quoted as influential in the start of a British black power movement and has overshadowed the contribution of other black speakers at the event, notably the historian C L R James and Black US activist Angela Davis.

In the first days, the theme was mystical, emphasizing the personal experience of LSD, Zen etc, and relating the personal to the political and social liberation movements. Allen Ginsberg, Laing and Cooper guided all the events. It seemed like just another happening, then the Dutch Provos and Emmett Grogan of the San Francisco Diggers – they believe in doing away with money and burn money in public – ran the show and promoted anarchism, questioned the structure. Then Marcuse spoke, and more and more revolutionary theorists and practitioners. Stokely Carmicheal spoke passionately No Vietnamese ever called me nigger! ... The congress went on all day and evening for two weeks non-stop. We ate there, lived there practically. In the evenings, rock groups performed. The only one I'd heard before being Eric Burdon and the Animals ...

Roxanne Dunbar Ortiz Outlaw woman: a Memoir of the War Years 1960-1975

The whole event was recorded and later released on a series of twenty-three LPs. A thirty-minute documentary video about the conference, "Anatomy of Violence" was produced and directed by Peter Davis and an anthology of speeches from the event was published by Penguin. The event also features in *Ah! Sunflower* the film of Allan Ginsberg's visit to London.

I think what our Congress was all about was not the dishing up of solutions to world problems already prepared, but an opportunity to think the thing out together. This is why the 'principal speakers' mixed so freely and spontaneously with the 'audience'. It is why so many young people actually took to living in the Round-house and then took their seminars out into local pubs, cafes and public places.

David Cooper The Dialectics of Liberation

In the September edition of *International Times (IT)* there was a call for another conference to explore the common ground between 'Black Power and Flower Power'. This seems to have led to the 'Ying – Yang Uprising' a 'non conference' held over the weekend of the 3rd, 4th & 5th of November at the Arts Lab in Drury Lane. Billed as three days of 'games, laughter, music, poetry, people, dance, smiles and food' its list of 'hosts' contains most of the movers and shakers of the

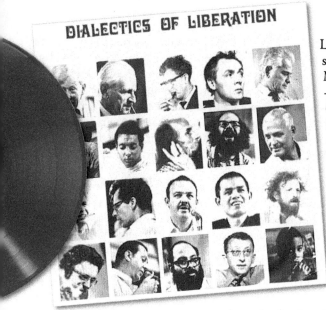

DIALECTICS OF LIBERATION

London alternative scene including: Michael Abdul Mailk – aka Michael X, Caroline Coon, Richard Neville, Sue Miles, Mick Farren, Colin McInnes, Horace Ove, Courtney Tulloch, Alex Trocchi, Bill Burroughs ... 'and surprises Galore'.

In the year of the summer of love you could almost be forgiven for thinking that the counter cultural revolution was about to happen. The 'Dialectics of Liberation' had been closely followed by an 'International Love-In Festival' at Alexandra Palace on July 29th which was itself a follow-up to the '14 Hour Technicolour Dream', held earlier in April as a benefit for the *International Times*. Which had been launched at its own 'Pop/Op/Costume/Masque/Fantasy-Loon/Blowout/ Drag Ball' at the Roundhouse the previous October. An event described by Daevid Allen of Soft Machine & Gong as one of the 'most revolutionary events in the history of English alternative music and thinking.' This was the year of the infamous Rolling Stones arrest and high profile acquittal for possession of drugs. The first issue of *OZ* magazine had come out , Anti-Vietnam War demonstrations in Grosvenor Square had begun, Pink Floyd released their first album *Pipers at the Gates of Dawn*, the second Notting Hill Festival, the forerunner to the Carnival happened ...

1967 also saw the beginnings of a homegrown English Diggers movement. Whether this had anything to do with the presence of Emmett Grogan in the country for the Dialectics conference or whether it was simply the result of large numbers of young people gathering in the capital is hard to tell now as few first hand contemporary accounts exist. In an article entitled 'Where the Diggers are at' in *International Times* 26 February 1968, it was stated that the London Diggers would release their plans for the launching of a new underground movement in the next issue. They were also said to be trying to set up headquarters in the West End to run as a Free school along the lines of the Notting Hill Free School and a free food and clothing store. A Diggers conference and 'open forum on love, freedom and sharing in underground society' was planned for the end of March. They were also planning a summer of fundraising events in order to be able to rent crash pads in Covent Garden and 'to buy land and houses in the country for the formation of tribal living communes, and to support those communes that are already in existence.'

One of those communes referred to may have been the Tribe of the Sacred Mushroom who were featured in a short piece in *IT* 25 February 1968 as 'England's first hippy rural commune'. The story reported that the Tribe had been living in a 'pad' in Notting Hill Gate but had decided that the city wasn't conducive to community living. Lynn Darnton, described as the Tribe's scribe is quoted as saying 'we all had the same vision of a small, isolated village with nature as our garden, populated by organic, rhythmic people, instead of mechanical synthetic ones in it ... we find the combination of beautiful country surroundings and a macrobiotic diet has made the use of acid totally unnecessary.' The Tribe appear to have been a performance group as they are listed as appearing at the '14-Hour Technicolour Dream' and performing a play based on the *Tibetan Book of the Dead* at the Middle Earth club.

'On the Last April Weekend of this year when the parks and gardens were arrayed in the day-glo hues of anemones and tulips, the Diggers and Gardeners of the dawning Age of Aquarius foregathered in London to break new ground for the cultivation of the Digger dharma of love, freedom and sharing.' So began the report on the Diggers Forum on Communal Living in Issue 2 of *Gandalf's Garden*. The Forum, attended by over 100 people, was held under the aegis of the Antiuniversity of London, in a church hall close to their premises at 49 Rivington Street EC2.

... The idea for the Forum germinated in my mind in the winter of last year. It was a sad winter which saw the hopes of the Love Revolution blighted. Expansion of awareness within the Psychedelic Movement had got strung out on chemicals, unable to soar to the heights of total spiritual freedom; and the promise of Flower Power had wilted like the last rose of summer. Dropouts from the system had nowhere to drop into and the socio-economic pressure of the System screwed up many an isolated small group or lone individual trying to do beautiful things. The time was at hand for all love revolutionaries to pool their resources and work closely together to build more free communes within the Alternative Society for their dharma brothers and sisters. The first step was obviously to bring beautiful people into contact with one another. And what better way to do this than bring them face-to-face under one roof at a forum on communal living?

Muz Murray in *Gandalf's Garden*, Issue 2

At the Diggers Forum members of about a dozen urban and rural communes talked informally about various aspects of communal living '... from economies to interpersonal relationships, from the angst of the early budding stages of a commune to the ecstasy of its full flowering.' The forum was addressed by anti-psychiatrists David Cooper and Joe Burke and political theorist Al Krebs. At the end it was stated that 'The prevailing feeling was that the days of airy-fairy speculating and theorizing were past' and that there was an urgent need to create 'a network of economically viable free communes as the soil out of which the Tree of Life of the Alternative Society could grow and bear fruit.' Another report doesn't paint such a positive picture of the forum, saying that the meeting broke up in disorder and was 'terminated by Sid Rawle and Michael Chapman with realism and cups of tea.' Soon after the forum a number of Diggers 'manifestos' appeared both as leaflets and printed in the underground press.

A longer, more comprehensive, manifesto for the Hyde Park Diggers was issued by Sid Rawle, who at the time was living in the basement of a communal house at 101 St Stephen's Gardens in Notting Hill. In it Rawle sets out plans to start an urban community in a large house in Notting Hill Gate '... because it has the largest hip population, and such a community is badly needed.' The house would have workshops in the basement, a free crashpad and a

Dear heads and blown minds,

I am writing this thing out of my own head to try and bring the nice people of the Gate and Grove together. I want our little corner of the Metropolis to find itself in a vision of a new future - of a city fit to live in. We need a consciousness of our own community - and we need our own communication medium - that everyone can share. The Underground press is hung up on producing beautifully designed and printed art works - hence they have to run a bread scene. This little leaf is cheap to make and costs you nothing - because information should be free. Also I want to show you how anyone can do this whenever they want and they should.

Lots of groovy people are digging a rural scene and rushing off to plough the soil and eat the fruits there of. I think this is cool. That is if you want to do it you should do it, if you believe that only the faithful will be saved then get away if you can. That's fine. But I plug a different life - save the world before it's too late - we need the cities. We don't dig Notting Hill because it's crowded, expensive for rent, hot for fuzz, or the carbon monoxide in the air which is poisoning us. We dig it because our people are here - we stop being alone, persecuted freaks, and become a tribe together. The cities must live! We will fill their streets with flowers until they learn to cry.

We will spread our beautiful clothes our beautiful minds until they learn to smile. We want a free food scene - a communal centre - kinetic drama demonstrations to answer hate with love - how could we open the parks for instance? Acid heads are diggers - dig us! Use this sheet to communicate. Because we must learn to live we must live we must make the city fit to live in! NOW!

Love Peace LSD
GRAM.

Excerpt from SCENE W11, a free handout dated 4th May 1968, given away by Interzone, A Digger group

communal kitchen
on the ground floor. On the first floor would be a
communications office and self-contained bedsits for community members
and on the top floor a temple-cum-meeting room '... where people could
have discussions in quiet beautiful and contemplative surroundings.' How the
community would be financed was outlined with plans for sureties, guarantees
and shares to be issued to attract benefactors to invest in the development of
the community. An impression is given that the whole thing will be run on a
business-like basis: 'Proper auditors will handle accounts and issue statements
and our transactions will be guided by professional advice'; and 'Community
members will not be free to doss their lives away ...' Further plans for a farm
community, workshops and industry are hinted at '(this whole question will be
expanded in another pamphlet)'. The manifesto ends with a call for people to
donate materials and tools to get the project started: household goods, tools,
sewing machines, typewriters, duplicators, printing presses ... 'in fact anything
within reason.' Before signing off with 'Greetings love and brotherhood to all
people', Sid Rawle explains his own relationship to the project. After stating
that there will be no leadership, 'When it becomes unnecessary.' and that co-

ordinators have been thrown up for their ability, he goes on to add 'My own position is unique. I am a friend and advisor, and like the state, the group's need for me will wither away in time.'

Soon there were a number of Digger groups springing up, with the Hyde Park Diggers – a group of several hundred who gathered every Sunday at Hyde Park corner to sit, talk and play guitars, being the largest one, with Rawle's Tribe of the Sun being a sort of inner circle. There were the Hapt Diggers down in Hampshire and later in 1968 the Coventry Diggers. A short-lived Diggers Action Movement newsletter DAM was produced by Rawle and Barry Norcott.

We were the Tooting Popular Front of the late 60's. We spent hours writing our Socialist utopian manifesto and even put Bazza up as a local election candidate. Our platform was that the council under our control would nationalise the Slough trading Estate, make the companies there co-operatives in control of the workers, make squatting legal and basically establish a socialist nirvana (in Slough!?). We learnt a lot, had a good time, got pissed, stoned and everything else. Who could want more? [3]

John Gillatt

Sid Rawle leading the Hyde Park Diggers

The Salvation Army and St-Martins-in-the-fields Church worked together to allow St Martins Secondary school building in Trafalgar Square to be used rent-free as a Digger Centre. This functioned as a community centre providing food and shelter for those living rough. Young people were living on the streets in London, sleeping out in the parks in summer or living in derelict buildings – 'Derrys' – a sort of precusor of the later squatting movement. They lived off free fruit and veg scraps from Covent Garden market and bread and cakes from the Wardour Street bakery. Their numbers were regularly swollen by 'weekend ravers'. They congregated in Piccadilly Circus where they were known as the Dilly Dossers and almost inevitably they came into conflict with the authorities. 'The tabloid press suddenly decided that we were fair game with *The News of the World* publishing a centre spread of us sitting on the Dilly steps under the headline: 'Everyone in this picture is a degenerate or a junkie'. ' [4] This publicity brought them to the attention of not only the local authorities and the police, but also to football and skinhead gangs and there were a number of running battles between the gangs and the freaks. There are stories of skirmishes with freaks armed with stolen umbrellas seeing off gangs of skinheads. The local council started sending working men to hose down the steps and 'anything and anyone who got in the way'. The police stepped up harassment. The Piccadilly freaks were joined by Phil Cohen, also known as Dr John, who was one of the Kings Mob situationists, and the idea came about of organising resistance under the banner of the 'London Street Commune'.

... WE are the beats of Piccadilly, a separate society. You may know us. We are the victims of social discrimination. The police bust us for a purely personal reason, they don't like us. The cafes and pubs won't serve us because we wear our hair long. In the last month the campaign to evict us from Piccadilly has hotted up. Every day we are harassed and moved on or searched by the police.

International Times 45 Nov-Dec 1968

On November 9th and 10th 1968, the Street Commune staged demonstrations to protest about the harassment they were getting. Occupying the Pronto Bar in Piccadilly to show that 'though we are beats we are far from beaten.' Despite support from waiters and the public, the company Fortes, who owned the bar, issued a directive not to serve members of the commune and the occupation was broken up by 'the Fuzz'.

The group issued a statement in the next issue of *International Times*.

... we lost the battle – BUT WE HAVE NOT LOST THE WAR. We have decided to use our ready-made community to fight this social apartheid ... The street is our home. It is our kitchen when we eat, our living room when we want to meet and discuss the situation, our bedroom when we sleep.
WE MUST NOT LOSE THE RIGHT TO ABSTAIN FROM 'NORMAL' LIFE.

The Commune

Hippies in Piccadilly on the cover of International Times 62

From AHIMSA to a communes movement

There is a regularly repeated historical chronology of the founding of the communes movement in the UK. In brief, it goes something like this: The Commune Movement was started in the late 1960's by Tony Kelly of the Selene Community in Wales. It had emerged from the Vegan Communities Movement which was itself a breakaway from a group called Ahimsa. After struggling along with small numbers, the movement took off at the beginning of the 1970's with increased sales of the magazine *Communes* ... and the rest, as they say, is history. This story has become the accepted version of communes history by communities and academic commentators alike. From Kenneth Leech in *Youthquake* 1973, Andrew Rigby in *Alternative Realities* 1974, through to Pam Dawling tracing 'Life before Communes Network' in the pages of *Diggers & Dreamers* in 1992. A more complete version of the story is told by Clem Gorman in *Making Communes* (1971) and *People Together* (1975). Rereading these 'given' histories alongside accounts of communes in the underground literature of the time I am struck by the disparity between the orderly narrative created by the later commentators and the much more chaotic, layered feel that you get from the contemporary literature. Almost as if the need for a historic narrative has rounded the story somewhat, neatened up the fuzzy edges and conveniently stopped mentioning those bits that don't quite fit the jigsaw. I'm not saying I think that the story is, in some way, false; rather that there is a richer mosaic-like and somewhat more confusing tale to be told.

It perhaps starts somewhere towards the end of 1963 when a small group of people gathered together by a Stanley Farmer planned to set up a vegan community. This group is mentioned by Gorman in *Making Communes* and may be the same group that involved a Ruth Howard described later by Tony Kelly as a strict vegan. 'She was strict in other ways too. She put that sort of people together and then she had some trouble, and the whole thing fizzled out.' [5] Whatever happened, this group never seems to have set up a community. Sometime in the following year, Ruth Howard joined a group being set up by a Joseph Ledger. This was the Agriculture and Hand-Industries Mutual Support Association, a title chosen because its initial letters made the Sanskrit word ahimsa – meaning to do no harm. Ledger's idea was to be a vegetarian society, to repudiate all mass-produced goods and promote agrarian self-sufficiency. Tony and Betty Kelly also joined this group.

... we joined with Joe Ledger's organisation, and he said people would come together when they thought they'd like to do so. And the idea was that when enough people got together they would take off for an island somewhere which they would buy, preferably a tropical island, and they would then live happily the idyllic life ...

Tony Kelly

The first edition of a planned regular journal, *Ahimsa Progress*, came out in May 1964. In it Ledger explained that Ahimsa was not going to actually be a vegetarian community, but should be seen as a base from which communes could be set up and would act as a support for them once they were established. A conference-cum-AGM was organised and a constitution proposed. But, as the year progressed, the association slipped into debt and members fell out with each other. By the end of the year a split had developed between Tony Kelly and Joe Ledger. Following this, Kelly left with a few others to form The Vegan Communities Movement.

... well, Joe Ledger really threw me out, but he couldn't. I can't quite remember what the details were. Well, I could but it was rather complicated. We had a funny constitution drawn up, it was an enormous thing and there were only 12 people in the group. One of the requirements was that a member had to fill an application form, and of course none of the members ever did. And so he said I wasn't a member because I hadn't filled out the form. Now Joe Ledger had all the names and addresses and he wouldn't let anyone else have them. So the only thing was to split, because it was obviously divided between very radical people like myself, and conservative people.

Tony Kelly

Around the mid sixties another group appeared promoting communal living, Community Experiments Unlimited, set up by a Greek émigré Emmanuel Petrakis who had come to London in 1961. 'My first stay in England was in a community in Hastings where I found out there was something called *The Broadsheet*, a liaison bulletin of communities, but it had become defunct. I read the back issues and was sorry it had become defunct ... So I tried to see if we could adopt this idea to other situations, and decided in 1965 that what was needed was an information service.' **6** Petrakis started his own newsletter called *New Life,* initially based on his own personal correspondence list, but developing over time into a wider network of international contacts interested in communes. 'The next thing I realised was that we badly need a sexual emancipation movement. So I launched this as well.' The two groups were later merged and renamed as the 'New Life Movement' and members were asked to commit themselves to 'actively co-operating with each other to radically transform our sick world into happy, creative communities which assert life and love and which are fulfilling for the individual.' Petrakis set up his own small community in a house on Camden Hill Road in London which only lasted for three months.

We rented this large house for a community but we had people who weren't really suitable. Some people came in as tenants because the house was large and we had to overheads to cover ... We also had people who claimed to be for community, but in fact were destructive and problematic. It was a very interesting experience which included free sexual relationships and so on.

Petrakis carried on producing the *New Life* magazine throughout the late 1960's. He did a tour of universities speaking on libertarian education, community living and sexual emancipation. He did various radio interviews and made an appearance on television. He wrote various articles for the underground press and claimed to have contributed 'in a small way to changing the laws on abortion and the laws on homosexuality.' The *New Life* magazine was described as 'Influential' by Clem Gorman and Petrakis contributed a series of articles on communes to *International Times* showing a wide knowledge of communal living and calling on the counter-culture to get its act together.

To merely protest against the world's evils is not enough. To drop out of the System is not enough. The time has come for the Underground to 'drop into' a constructive scene, to erect the structures of the Alternative Society, to make its own bread without alienation.

Emmanuel Petrakis

Petrakis was a man of many talents; a libertarian poet in both English and French, a teacher of languages; before coming to England he had worked in Egypt as business editor of *The Middle East Observer*. However, some – like Andrew Rigby – doubted whether the New Life Movement was all it was made out to be. 'From my experience this movement was little more than a list of correspondents possessed by Emmanuel Petrakis who always seemed to be asking for funds for some purpose or other.' Later in 1969, those members of the New Life Movement who were interested in communities were merged with the Commune Movement and Petrakis subsequently left England and, after a failed attempt to set up a commune in the West Indies, joined the Domillouse commune in the French Alps.

Another piece of the handed-down history of communes in the sixties is that whilst there was a lot of talk about setting them up actual flesh & blood / bricks & mortar communities were somewhat thin on the ground. This is not born out if one does a bit of delving. A quick trawl through the directory at the end of this book comes up with at least 40 communities of varying types that formed during the sixties. Yes, some were short-lived but many lasted through to the end of the decade and beyond. Add the few communities that had survived through from the immediate post-war period; Braziers Park, St Julians, Othona; the couple of real long-term survivors – Whiteway and the Brotherhood Church; a handful of Camphill communities; and certainly by 1967/8 there were actually, getting on for, something like 50 or 60 clearly recognisable intentional communities dotted around England, Scotland and Wales. It looks as if it was more of a case of there being very little contact between groups that existed, or a lack of any co-ordinating body that had a broad enough definition of communal living to encompass the range of communities that existed, rather than there not being any.

Having split with Joe Ledger and Ahimsa in 1964, Tony Kelly managed to get hold of the Ahimsa address list by a combination of inserting a piece into the final *Ahimsa Progress* newsletter and sending everyone a Christmas card with an invite to join the new Vegan Communities Movement. The aims of the new group were; to establish and support vegan and progressive vegetarian communities, to 'initiate and support humanitarian social experiments and to propagate the principle of non-explotation of all sentient life forms'. A new newsletter was produced called *Ahimsa Communities*, the first copy coming out in March 1965. An initial gathering of members was held in Gloucestershire and Tony Kelly was elected the first secretary of the movement. Things seemed to be going well, membership increased to 22. In issue 3 of the newsletter Kelly wrote an article entitled 'The Need for Urgency' in which he set out his thinking as to why people should join communities and adopt a vegan diet.

This country and Europe are the most densely populated areas in the world, and we are going to feel the effects of world food shortage first ... With food prices claiming an ever greater share of our income, there will be a rush to acquire a stake in our own diminishing acres and land prices will soar out of reach ... At present a few pioneers such as we can still afford to make mistakes and while making them, learn to make our shrinking acres more productive. If groups such as we undertake a hundred experiments and only one succeeds, that one will make the hundred worthwhile and the only viable economy – a vegan one – will be established as a pattern upon which to base future efforts at averting the famine.

In November 1965 Tony & Betty Kelly and Pat Blackmore set up their first communal household in a house at Wheathampstead that would evolve into the Selene commune, the first actual commune to emerge from any of these 'movements'. Unfortunately, after this somewhat promising start, things took a turn for the worse – with something of a repeat of the conflicts that had occurred in Ahimsa. Ruth Howard had become the movement secretary and seems to have taken offence at the open sexual relationships at the Wheathampstead house. Things came to a head after an article by Tony Kelly on group marriage appeared in the newsletter. Howard claimed that she had a letter from the London Vegetarian Society objecting to the article and had replied as secretary guaranteeing that no more such articles could appear in the journal. Kelly took offence to this censorship and the whole thing blew up into a major conflict with Howard tipping off *The News of the World* and *The People* and even handing in copies of the journal to the police. Finally, after trying to get Kelly expelled from the movement, Howard and a number of other members resigned.

Whilst all this was going on, another communities newsletter appeared. In August 1966 the *Sarvodaya Communities Newsletter* was put out by Kate Walters and Peter Twilley who had attended the Vegan Communities Movement gathering the year before. The newsletter seems to have come out for a couple of years and an attempt was made to set up a community, the Tathata Centre, at Botloes Farm near Newent in Gloucestershire. By 1970 this had become a Zen meditation centre.

In 1967 the three members of the Selene group bought 22 acres of land and a caravan near Llanbedr. 'We thought because we know nothing about agriculture, we had better not risk too much. So we bought this bog for £500, and we towed this caravan into this squelch ... There developed a terrible fungus all over the walls of the caravan dripping down the walls and windows in a 22-foot caravan with four people – five at one time. And ice on the floor in winter.' They attempted to grow food on the wet boggy land. 'After a time we realised that you can't grow very much in a bog ... It was horrible. We got discouraged. We'd plant seeds and nothing happened ... About two-thirds of it was very squashy marshy agricultural – no, not agricultural – rushy land. And almost the other whole third of it was stagnant swamp bog.' They tried to keep the Vegan Communities Movement running, continuing to put out bi-monthly newsletters to a dwindling number of members – 'one of our ideals in setting the commune up was to show that we could live on our vegan diet, vegan ecology. But both the Vegan and Vegetarian societies disowned us so we were virtually isolated ... and there were no other communes at the time either, nothing. We had only about twenty members and things got worse and worse, because the membership went down and down, and then there were only seven members left ...'

During this period they were visited by a rather strange character called 'Ticka', who claimed to be a hereditary witch who worked in a scientific lab and was travelling the country, wild camping in a 'tetrahedral tent'. Over two days of discussion and argument, 'Ticka' persuaded the group to stop being vegans. He then disappeared. In the August 1968 issue of the newsletter an account of this discussion was printed under the title 'Vegan Ethic Reappraised'. This radical change resulted in the next issue of the newsletter appearing in October 1968 under the title of *Communes – the journal of the Commune Movement.* Around this time the house in Wheathampstead was sold and Selene moved to a 54-acre hill farm near Ffarmers in Carmarthenshire. The Commune Movement at this stage was almost entirely the creation of the people at Selene, you might actually say it was an ambition rather than an actuality, and its existence relied on them producing issues of the journal, writing most of the material themselves. What happened in the ensuing years has given the Selene pioneers a status as 'founders' of a movement that would seem to somewhat over-emphasise their actual contribution. Yes they were there at the beginning, but things only started to resemble anything like a movement once they had handed the reins over to others.

Dropping the vegan ethic broadened the appeal of the movement and membership started to increase. John Driver, from Taunton in Somerset, took over the 'first secretaryship' in 1969 and for the first time numbers did not drop when subscriptions became due. By the end of the year there were 100 members and the print run of the journal had risen to 700. A federation fund was set up for the purpose of accumulating finance to establish future communes. The following year the fairly disparate bits of the communes world started to link up. This would largely be due to the influence and work of Nicholas Albery who worked for the underground information service 'BIT' in London at the time and who became the communes movement secretary during 1970.

That Nicholas should have been executive officer of the Commune Movement and at the same time a long-serving member of the underground's twenty-four-hour information and co-ordinating service, was significant. With Nicholas Albery taking up the office, it meant that links between the specific Commune Movement and the more general underground scene, centred as it was and is in the Notting Hill - Ladbroke Grove area of West London, were made more firm and tight.

Andrew Rigby

24-hr HELP
FREE INFORMATION SERVICE.
141 Westbourne Park Road,
London W11
01-229 8219
BIT desperately needs crash pads –
we're having to turn people away.
We also need green shield stamps,
cigarette coupons, spare change?

BIT (Binary Information Transfer) information service was something of a lynchpin-hub-cum-clearing house for the growing counter-culture in London. Started by John (Hoppy) Hopkins and friends in May 1968, it had evolved out of *IT* because the paper got far more inquiries for info and help than it could cope with while producing a newspaper at the same time. According to John May, who 'worked' there for a while, BIT 'was a constantly changing collection of drop-outs, misfits, visionaries, deviants, information freaks, students, runaways, travellers, electronics whizz-kids and even 'normal' people from all over the world, none of whom were paid and many of whom worked all hours God sent. Apart from social welfare, info on jobs, housing, squatting, social security, the law and health, BIT could also supply information on anything from geodesic domes and herbal remedies to how to mend your bike when you got stuck on the Yorkshire Moors. It would even mend your television set for you' **7**

BIT received no funding from any official government source for the services it provided. Instead it was financed by a hand-to-mouth combination of income from a highly popular guidebook – *Overland to India & Australia* (Minimum donation 50p.) The odd £500 or £1,000 gift from rock stars with radical leanings and the occasional small grant from the likes of the Gulbenkian Foundation (although in general BIT avoided anything with 'strings attached'). As well as giving the Commune Movement a helping hand, BIT acted as midwife to various other alternative schemes including the Community Levy for Alternative Projects, also known as the CLAP Tax which, during its existence, raised over £30,000 for radical projects throughout Britain by asking readers of alternative magazines to give 1% of their income to projects of their choice from a regularly published list of projects needing money. Through the efforts of Nicholas Albery and helpers at BIT, sales of the *Communes* journal shot up in the first six months of 1970 with 2,500 appearing in the windows of most of the 'head' shops in London alongside *Oz*, *IT*, *Gandalf's Garden* and *Peace News*.

Hells Angels outside Genesis Hall Squat

The year 1969 also saw a new wave of squatting erupt, initially centred on a campaign to house homeless families in Redbridge. The London Squatting Campaign, started the year before by Ron Bailey, helped families to resist heavy-handed action by Redbridge Council who tried to use the courts and then resorted to using hired thugs and strong-arm tactics to evict and deter squatters. The campaign got sympathetic coverage in the press and established precedents which would benefit a whole generation of squatters. The 28th February issue of *IT* carried a story, under the headline 'Squat's Happening: Re-peopling the ghostly empty English houses', covering the news of the campaign in London and places further afield such as Yorkshire, Dublin and Derry. The report also mentioned plans to take over 74 houses on a deserted airfield at North Weald. *IT*'s following issue reported that 'A group of about 20 people from the Arts Lab in Drury Lane stealthily crept out in the black of night a couple of weeks ago to a derelict 100-room hotel just two doors from the Lab. They picked the lock and got inside with spades and brooms and willing elbows and started to shift huge loads of debris from the deserted four-storey shell, which has been empty for at least two years, ready to be knocked down to make way for the Covent Garden Redevelopment Scheme.' The story goes on to say: 'The workers toiled silently for ten nights making the rooms habitable. The intention was to get the scene completely together, move in the 70-80 people that the complex would house and then invite the press, the GLC and the world to come and see what can be done with so-called derelict buildings with a bit of imagination and a revolutionary social consciousness.'

Street view of Genesis Hall

It seems that once the story of a major squat in central London got out, people started to flock to what was now being called Genesis Hall, including people involved in the London Street Commune, Diggers groups and Hells Angels. Various, sometimes conflicting, ideas were put forward as to what the building could be used for: as an Arts Centre – providing cheap accommodation for artists, writers, and visiting theatre groups; as a home for the Arts Lab staff; as accommodation for the many homeless young people who used the Arts Lab as a base; as a hostel to house the 'thousands' of travellers who converged on London in the summer months; as a libertarian Digger commune – for the homeless, social derelicts, drug addicts and unmarried mothers etc. There was serious disagreement on which of the various 'visions' should be put into action. At one point a leader, Kylastron ('a musical cat with obvious organisational abilities'), was appointed to co-ordinate things. Supported by the Hells Angels acting as security he tried to introduce payments and a no drugs policy and ended up expelling several people, leading to accusations of dictatorship. After a 'marathon talk-about' the groups agreed to work together on the Arts Centre project and a co-ordinating committee consisting of Kylastron, Phil Cohen, Jim Haynes and Felix Scorpio was set up to try and unite the factions. All this was to very little avail as on Saturday 22nd March, under the guise of a drugs bust, the squatters were – in effect – evicted. And despite a second attempt to occupy the building the squatters were defeated by the damage done by GLC workmen who had smashed windows and torn up floorboards while the police watched. After the eviction from Genesis Hall the 'Commune of the Streets' found some temporary shelter in some derelict

144 Piccadilly

houses in Lancaster Road and a basement on Tavistock Road. They then, on March 30th, attempted to open up another large squat in an empty student hostel owned by London University at 1 Bedford Way in Bloomsbury. This was raided and broken up by the police the following morning.

The London Street Commune had now taken up squatting as the answer to its needs. '... we heard about the squats out at Redbridge, and that seemed like the answer to our housing problems. But instead of squatting in the leafy suburbs we remembered that we were kids of the Dilly and took for our first squat Broad Court slap bang next to Bow Street Magistrates Court, in fact so close that on several occasions messengers arrived from Number 1 Court asking us if we minded keeping the noise down ... Oh this was kicking authority back in the face all right.' **8** The Broad Court squat led to other Street Commune squats being opened up in the West End. Just round the corner a rambling old church school in Endell Street was occupied and a small group went to secure a property at 144 Piccadilly. What happened next would change the situation drastically and cement the view of squatters in the popular imagination for decades to come. 'Hippydilly' as it became dubbed was huge and on the corner of Hyde Park. Described as an ex-embassy building, or a mansion, it was five stories high, had either 60 or 100 rooms (depending on which report you read) and was surround by a 'dry moat' – some of the early squatters nailed shut the front doors and set up a defendable wooden 'drawbridge' as the main entrance. At the beginning of September 1969, what started off as an attempt to set up a commune for young homeless people developed into what can perhaps best be described as a counter-culture siege. Whilst the Broad Court and Endell Street squats were somewhat off the main roads – 144 was right in the public eye. This not only attracted the attention of the authorities, it also attracted a number of separate groups to come and join, along with a variety of hangers-on and 'weekend ravers'. Reading through the recollections of some of the folks who were there during the occupation it is possible to start to piece together some idea of what went on – or what people thought was going on – the accounts don't always tally with each other and the press reports are so wildly anti the squatters as to be completely unreliable. Quite how long the occupation lasted varies widely. Some press reports talk about a six-day siege, but this may well only refer to the attempts at eviction. Some participants talk of three weeks of occupation. Scrawled on the wall in one of the rooms was graffiti that records the date and time that the first squatters moved in as – 3pm Wed Sept 3rd 1969. As there is no question that the eviction took place on September 21st, I make it that the squatters held the building for the best part of 19 days.

The various groups that gathered together included the core of the London Street Commune or the 'Dilly Dossers' with Dr John, aka Phil Cohen, acting as their spokesperson; Sid Rawle and his group of Hyde Park Diggers; and a group of Hell's Angels, or greasers, who were there as 'security'. One casual visitor commented that 'Many of the leaders were French students from the 1968 demonstrations in Paris.' As well as these 'organised' groups there were many people who just dropped in for a few days and numbers were swollen at the end by people going to the Hyde Park Free Concert that took place on 20th September and where money was collected to support the squat. Fairly early on during the occupation large crowds gathered outside – these were partly sightseers, but it also attracted elements hostile to the squatters. This became more pronounced as stories started to appear in the press.

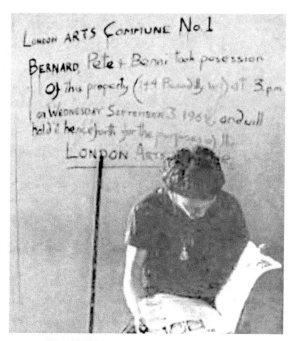

Inside and outside Hippydilly

HIPPIE THUGS; THE SORDID TRUTH. Drug taking, couples making love while others look on, rule by heavy mob armed with iron bars, foul language, filth and stench. THAT is the scene inside the hippies' fortress in London's Piccadilly. These are not rumours, but facts which will shock ordinary decent family loving people.

Front page of *The People*

The squat also attracted the attention of London skinhead gangs who came to give the freaks a beating, but were 'trounced' by a barage of 'hippy canon balls'. '... a smallish room tucked behind the lift well which was full top to bottom with sets of multi coloured boules for some weird reason. There were hundreds of sets, so thousands of heavy, solid, perfect handsize bowls. The fun started with the skinheads making surges towards our railings ... the drawbridge came up and we were impregnable. A balcony ran the length of the building on the first floor with several access points along its run and the entire population of 144 assembled on the battlements for a bit of fun at the coconut shy.' **9**

In later accounts of the squat it is reported that Ron Bailey of the London Squatting Campaign was highly critical of the Street Commune and said that 'squatting was for families, not for single people.' However, in a piece written just after the eviction in October 1969 by Bailey he takes a much more measured view of the Street Commune.

I think therefore that those members of the Squatters Campaign who have said that the activities of the Street Commune have irreparably harmed the Squatters are then jumping the gun. It may be so – or alternatively it may mean that the public may have to face up to their 'if it was families I'd support you' utterances, and indeed do just that. We do not know: we must wait and see – and do all we can to ensure that opinion swings the right way and also to convince people the members of the London Street Commune are human beings.

Ron Bailey in *International Times* 66, October 1969

The accounts of the final hours of Hippydilly are all fairly consistent. Police Chief Inspector Michael Rowling 'tricked' those on sentry duty into lower the drawbridge because somebody inside was either 'in need of a doctor' or 'about to give birth'. At which point 'a hundred' policemen charged over the drawbridge, trampling over the Chief Inspector in the process. A brief fight ensued, but within about five minutes either 100 (or 200) 'Hippies' (depending again on which report you read) were being led away under arrest. Many had been beaten up and most were kept in jail for at least week, some a lot longer. In the hours before the police finally invaded it seems that Sid Rawle and his band of Diggers got wind of the raid, but kept the news to themselves, and quietly slipped out before the cops moved in. After the raid Rawle presented himself to the media as spokesman for the London Street Commune – this led to John Lennon offering the commune Dornish Island off the west coast of Ireland (which he had recently bought) – an offer which Rawle accepted and took up. The actual London Street Commune, whose members were mostly still under arrest, condemned Rawles' action and officially disassociated themselves from his 'Paradise Island' criticising it 'as escapism and political opportunism.' In a final flourish and twist to the story it is said that millionaire property developer Ronald Lyons donated £1,000 (or £1,500) to the Police Benevolent fund as thanks for the police action. 144 Piccadilly stood empty for three years after the siege and was then demolished (despite being listed) to make way for a luxury hotel.

Imagine There's an Island

John Lennon said look Sid I've got an Island off the west coast of Ireland and I will let you use it. If you want to, go and have a look at it, if you want to use it it's yours. Just don't ask me for any money.

Sid Rawle [10]

Lennon, seeking a retreat for himself and first wife Cynthia, had bought the uninhabited Dornish Beg and More islands in Clew Bay in 1967 for £1550 from the Westport Harbour Board. He had plans drawn up to build a house and a recording studio (to be called the Irish Mythical Studios) but abandoned the idea when his marriage broke up. Rawle gathered a group of 20 or so would-be Diggers together and in September 1970 they set off for the 19 bare and windswept acres of what, by then, had become known as 'Beatle Island'. A cargo of tents and camping equipment had been taken to the island ahead of them.

… Slowly we approached Dornish, the island that was to be our home. It is shaped like two wedges of cheese, their low ends at the middle. There are sharp cliffs at the further ends, with gentle slopes down to where they are joined in the middle by a barrier of pebbles and stones that provide a causeway … We gathered driftwood along the beaches and built our fire, in a little nook in the bank of the cliff, above high water mark. Next we struggled to put up a couple of the tents. Then at last it was time to relax and get our evening meal going … I felt wonderful. It was a dream fulfilled and, what is more, a beautiful night. I was really full of myself.

Sid Rawle

The initial plan was to hold a six-week summer camp on the island and see what happened. There was fresh water from an old well, but little else. They lived in tents throughout this time and tried to grow vegetables in the thin, sandy soil – lighting driftwood bonfires to keep warm and storing food in specially built hollows. Once a fortnight local fishermen would ferry them to Westport to buy groceries. An entry in *Making Communes* in 1971 reported that the group had planted potatoes and trees to act as a future windbreak but that 'progress has been slow.' They planned to become economically self-sufficient through a joint lobster-fishing venture with local fishermen. In the meantime the group survived as best they could.

In the second year it was all right because we grew our own crops. In the first year, so many people came and went; it was easy to rob them. By that I mean, say you had someone coming for the night. I'd say, how about a donation? … Well, if he gave us £5, it would feed two people for a week. The usual reaction was Far Out! Can we stay forever? Those usually left after two weeks.

Sid Rawle

Asked later how the commune was run, Rawle replied: 'By dictatorship. Me. Benevolent dictatorship' and that, despite bids by others to take over and turn it into a 'proper commune', 'eventually someone would come in and say "Sid, he's worse than you were. Come back"'. The commune was battered by Atlantic storms that blew away tents unless they were weighed down with rocks – even then they could still be blown over with all belongings getting soaked. Despite feeling like leaving on at least one occasion, the intrepid band of Celtic Diggers stayed on the island for two years, only leaving in 1972 after a fire destroyed the main tent used to store supplies. Yoko Ono sold 'Beatle Island' to a local farmer in 1984 for nearly £30,000 and donated the money to an Irish orphanage. In 2008 RTÉ made a series of television programmes on Irish islands and arranged for Rawle to revisit the island.

Beats, Heads, Freaks or Hippies?

At one point in my research I set myself the task of tracking down the 'first Hippie Commune'. This led very quickly to trying to find out when hippies came into being – which turned out to be somewhat harder than I had imagined. The question should more likely have been when does a beat become a hippie? Or who were the heads or the freaks?

The word 'hippie' is a media invention. It's a diminutive of the word hip. It was meant as a term of derision. It was always a term of derision. It's still a term of derision to this day. According to Richard Neville (of Oz fame) the word was invented by the San Francisco Chronicle as a warning to its readers. Unfortunately its readers refused to heed the warning.

C J Stone, *The Last of the Hippies*

Some, like C J Stone, see 'hippie' as entirely a media invention and doubt whether anyone actually called themselves a hippie. Others trace the word to Jazz slang or African American origins. Malcolm X is quoted as saying that 'hippy' was Harlem slang for white folk who 'acted more Negro than Negroes'. There is also a quite plausible suggestion that the first wave of beatniks that moved to the Haight-Ashbury area of San Francisco in the early 60's used Hippie to refer to the young university student dropouts who came along next and emulated them. One of the first written uses in England appears to have been on the sleeve notes to the 1965 Rolling Stones *Now!* album which refers to the Stones music as being 'Berry-chuck and all the Chicago hippies.' and goes on to mention '... Richmond, with its grass green and hippy scene ...' So it would appear that the term hippie was in use by the mid-sixties. Reading the underground literature from the end of decade, the terms beats, heads, freaks and flower people are all more commonly in use. Beats are generally older - coming from beatniks; heads are beats who smoked dope and 'got into their heads'; freaks are those who took LSD; and flower people appears to be a later, post-1967 summer-of-love term. The only conclusion about the etymology I came to was that it was all fairly interchangeable and what started off as a search for the first hippie commune became more of tour through a continuum of people inhabiting communes – where beats become heads, freaks become flower children, and the media eventually just refers to everyone as a hippies. Whilst many commentators refer to the sixties and seventies as the heyday of the hippie commune, my guess is that for every hippie, freak or head living in a commune there were at least half a dozen communards who would have taken serious offence at being thought of as being a 'hippie'. Perhaps the last word on the search for hippies should go to Ronald Reagan who, when he was Governor of California, defined a hippie as 'a person who dresses like Tarzan, has hair like Jane, and smells like Cheeta.'

None of this musing got me anywhere near finding the first hippie commune. So I decided to look at a sort of generic form of commune for the era and then to find the earliest example. The picture that most people have of a sixties or seventies commune is of a seen-better-days country house with a bunch of long-haired residents on the front lawn surrounded by a posse of unruly kids. If you take this definition, my best guess for a candidate for the first of these classic big house communities is the one established in November 1965 at Crow Hall in Denver just outside Downham Market in Norfolk. The only problem is that the members of Crow Hall denied that they were a 'commune'.

> *We are not a commune - - We are Crow Hall*
> *Our lifestyle is literate, urbane and sophisticated:*
> *We are not, nor do we pretend to be country folk.*
> *We live in the particular, not the abstract,*
> *We have conflicting doctrines, some meetings,*
> *a few rules, always broken.*
> *We have grown into what we are now and*
> *shall continue to grow.*
> *We are not a commune - - We are Crow Hall* [11]

The Hall itself was a big, old country house, Grade II listed, and described as 'Cromwellian' with five acres of land made up of a large garden and a field. The Hall seems to have had something of a varied existence; as a country house and coaching inn, it was used during the war by the Womens' Land Army and for evacuees. After the war it was for some years used as a school. The Crow hall community initially began as an informal group of friends.

> *...We didn't really get started. What happened was we were living in Norfolk doing things together, specifically Allan does up homes. On one occasion Allan was rebuilding a medieval hall. We bought a cheap house in the same area. I came into some money. We bought a house with it and were doing it up in a less ambitious way in the same part of Norfolk and we met Allan. After that we helped Allan and we got closer and closer and particularly with the children being involved, we began to live closely together and out of this developed that it would be more sensible to live entirely together ... if I hadn't been a communist I wouldn't have thought in this sort of direction and if Allan hadn't been what Allan is, he wouldn't have either. When it became a practical possibility we thought we needed more people, so we began to advertise.*

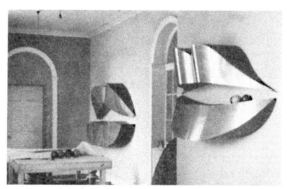

John, interviewed in *Communes Europe*

Crow Hall Top to Bottom

The house and land was purchased in the names of four members, this was the maximum number of individuals who, at the time, could jointly own property. The group, which included a journalist, writer/potter, painter and a builder, converted the house to suit their needs and by 1970 had set up a fully equipped pottery, studios for painting and a gallery, and dark room. They were running a preschool playgroup for their own children and children from the local village. Despite the denial of the title, Crow Hall had many attributes of a commune; a sauna and Buckminster Fuller inspired geodesic dome. On the wall in the dining room for a number of years was a 6ft x 4ft copy of Pieter Bruegel's *The numbering at Bethlehem* – '... it contains so many country activities that we could all identify with, it provided many hours of fun and games ...' They also espoused a definitely libertarian outlook when it came to organisation and decision making. They claimed to have 'No meetings', decisions being made on the spot among individuals involved; or simply by individuals. They encouraged visitors;

... If you want to know, come and see for yourselves – we have no locks on our doors and visitors are welcome. There's no obligation to do anything: all we wish is that you be yourself. Come, come and use your eyes and ears. Those who stay as 'regular' visitors – of whom we have many – or as 'one-timers' benefit from being here and we benefit from having them. Those who speed through give little and receive little. This is the only place in England that I know of where you don't have to please anyone but yourself – and if you have the courage to please yourself – and not simply live up to other people's expectations then you are very welcome. If your only wish is to live up to other people's expectations then you're also welcome.

A picture comes across of a rather relaxed but very practical down-to-earth group whose motto was 'All we can offer you is Yourself' and whose intent was '... to live communally because we like to live that way.' Throughout the 1980's and into the 90's they continued – their time taken up with looking after various animals '... Sunshine our Jersey cow, whose milk we drink. We also have a dog, cats, chickens, ducks, a rabbit and a donkey'. Firing up the Finnish Sauna in the walled garden 'lit every week'; building a floating temple in the pond; on top of their various individual pursuits '... we have a retired member – a photographer – a knitter, two carpenters, a cabinet maker, a sculptor and a nurse, also a porter at Boots ...'

...We're not always on top of each other. I mean you can be on your own if you want to be. Which I think is necessary for the adults who are not used to this type of living. I daresay our children will be able to live much more together. For us, we're asking too much to say that nothings private, it's all everybody's.

Louise Interviewed in Communes Europe

The community was wound up in 1997 and the Hall has been converted into flats.

We are a little corner of sanity in a darkening world. We live for ourselves, but with each other. As separate people we live together and as selfish people we share our lives. We have time for people. At times we tolerate each other and at times we genuinely feel mutual love. We are not a commune, we are Crow Hall.

The Black House

Michael De Freitas, aka Abdul Malik, aka Michael X, arrived in England in 1957 from Jamaica. He was a small-time hustler and became a pimp and drug pusher, eventually working as a rent collector and strongarm for slum landlord Peter Rachmann who was one of the few landlords that would take West Indian tenants at the time. In the1960's, inspired by the likes of Stokely Carmichael, Elijah Muhammad and Malcolm X in the USA, Michael became involved in the early Black Power movement he also became involved with the evolving 60's counter-culture. Sometimes as a drug dealer, at other times providing 'security' at places like the Roundhouse for rock concerts, and at other times as part of the black activists involved with the early days of the Notting Hill Carnival. He was instrumental in setting up the Racial Adjustment Action Society (RAAS) and bizarrely was the first person in Britain to be prosecuted and jailed under the 1965 Race Relations Act for a speech he made at a meeting in Reading in 1967. When he came out of prison, in a move away from party political style politics, he decided to set up a positive project for Black People. With financial support from Nigel Samuel, a key figure and financier of the London Underground, he acquired property at 95-101 Holloway Road, in Islington where he planned to set up a commune and community centre.

At the moment we are building a complex in Holloway Road, Islington, come and see for yourselves what we are doing, our address is 95-101, our floor area covers some 16,000 square feet. We hope to put into what was a run-down empty shell a supermarket, a clothing store, a restaurant and a cultural centre where things like a cinema and a theatre will happen. There we hope to show the people of the host community what we are really like ...

Michael X "Tell It Like It Is" in *IT* 61, August 1-14, 1969

The Black House was a somewhat short-lived project, seemingly always short of funds and functioning more as a crash pad and youth centre than the grand cultural centre that was talked up. The great and good of swinging London were courted for support and money. In a rather strange fundraising stunt Michael X swapped a pair of Muhammad Ali's boxing shorts for a bag of John & Yoko's hair. But the project failed to win support from the local council who refused planning permission for the 'restaurant, mosque, lecture hall, cultural centre and museum' complex. This was officially because they were considered to be 'incompatible' with the surrounding area, but councillors were also concerned about the past reputation of Michael X. In an article headed Problems in the Black House in *International Times* 88 at the end of September 1970 it was reported that the commune was 'chaotic', with no-one knowing what was going on and staff resigning.

... The only real and regular activities the kids know at the Black House is their usual Thursday evening social events. First they are lectured by Brother Herman, the commune Welfare Officer, for an hour on to face the white man with love which often proved very controversial, after which as many as two hundred youths dance to West Indian sounds, the 'Reggae' ...

International Times 88

By the end of the year the Black House had closed its doors. Michael X subsequently moved back to Jamaica where he was involved in an ill-fated attempt to set up a commune there. He was hanged for murder in Trinidad in 1975.

... The Black House was no sinister den of sin. To me and thousands of black people in England it represented a place where black youths could go. Inside the Black House there was a community centre. There were amplifiers and loudspeakers, and the kids – hundreds of kids – used to play records and dance together. There were three kitchens in the Black House where the kids used to experiment with cooking. There was a library where one could go and read ... At the time I respected Michael X ...

Stanley Abbott, *Trinidad Guardian* 11 July 1973

The Story of the Black House is told in: *Michael X A Life in Black & White* by J L Williams.

Eel Pie Island Free Commune

Eel Pie Island Hotel 1971

Perhaps the most oft-cited hippie commune of the late sixties is the Eel Pie Island Free Commune set up in a rented old hotel on an island in the Thames at Richmond. The hotel had been bought in 1952 by Chelsea antique dealer Michael Snapper who had thought it might become the clubhouse for the London River Yacht Club of which he was a founder member and 'First Commodore'. Instead, Athur Chisnall – one of Snapper's associates – was instrumental in creating one of the most enigmatic music venues of the era. Throughout the 1950's and 60's the dancehall attached to the hotel saw the cream of both the British Jazz and Rock/R&B scenes play there. The list of bands that appeared on 'the island' is a veritable who's who of the UK music scene of the time; Ken Colyer, Acker Bilk, Alexis Korner, George Melly, Cyril Davis, Long John Baldry's Hoochie Coochie Men (with Rod Stewart), John Mayall's Bluesbreakers (with Eric Clapton), the Tridents (with Jeff Beck), The Rolling Stones ... Athur Chisnall acted as both amateur promoter and youth leader-cum-surrogate parent to the young people who came to gigs on the island, building up something of a reputation in serious youth work circles for the way he worked. By 1967, however, the hotel was in need of much repair and, short of having a spare £200,000 to buy and modernise the premises, it became obvious that things couldn't carry on as before. A scheme was drawn up by Brian Phillips, a young architect who worked at the Royal College of Art, and a sort of manifesto was produced – but it would all have been too expensive. Added to this was hassle from the local police over licensing and the end of an era eventually came in September 1967 when, after 11 years, Arthur Chisnall shut up shop. These years are detailed in the 2009 book *Eel Pie Island* by Dan Van der Vat and Michele Whitby. Arthur Chisnall went on to be involved in the setting up of BIT. There were a number of attempts to reopen the hotel as a music venue in the following year but apart from a small number of parties, nothing really took off.

In 1969 a small group of local Richmond anarchists, who had been living in a rural commune in Cumbria, persuaded Michael Snapper to let them rent the hotel for £20 a week. The group included the Canadian born writer and poet,

Chris Faiers (who was dodging the US draft) and anarchist cartoonist and illustrator Cliff Harper

... I'd seen the Living Theatre when they were in London, I went to every 'performance'. That was my model. Whereas Living Theatre were mobile, moving round the world, I wanted to start creating static bases to do it from ...

Cliff Harper, *The Education of Desire*

One of the aims was to create a commune of 'politically conscious artists' and for it to be a centre from which 'some sort of revolution could start.' While the little band of anarchists wanted to see a base for revolutionary activity, very quickly the commune attracted members of the Richmond and Twickenham counter-culture, along with US draft resisters and hippies from around the world looking for a crash-pad. This led Harper to decided to just '... let it go the way it wanted to go.' After BIT Information service started giving out the address to those looking for a place to crash in London, the hotel really started to fill up. By 1970 there were somewhere between 100 and 130 people living there. There was no real organisation to speak of and only a limited number of rooms so a 'lot of sharing took place'.

... Some rooms were occupied by couples of lovers, but others were single sex mini-dormitories. The hotel had three floors. The ground floor had big rooms which had formerly been dining areas and bars. The first floor had the most rooms, as well as a small kitchen and a bathroom with the only bath-tub in the building. One room was designated as a sex room for those lovers not shy of making love with other loving couples around them ...

Caroline Porter

Concurrent with the commune, the music venue re-opened for a short while in the derelict ballroom which had been given a psychedelic make-over and opened on Friday and Saturday nights as the strangely titled – Colonel Barefoot's Rock Garden, bringing in six or seven hundred visitors to hear the likes of Hawkwind, The Edgar Broughton Band, Deep Purple, Black Sabbath and The Who. There was an uneasy relationship between the dance-hall and the commune. The commune gave free access through an interconnecting door, but this was later locked. Some commune members made money selling drugs to the punters coming to dances. For a while some people tried to get a coherent community together and make links with other groups. One member sent in a scribbled entry for the 1970 *Communes Directory*.

Eel Pie Commune, 1971

The group was also invited to talk at a 'Communes Seminar' organised by Joan Harvey in Cambridge

The last seminar was at Cambridge Arts Lab, where a couple of invited guests from Eel Pie Island Commune came to talk to us. Actually 40 of them turned up. While we asked them earnestly about their commune structures, their reply was to produce an enormous lump of hash and while Joan went off in a huff, we all got very stoned and spent the evening chanting ...

Tom Bragg *Joan Harvey Memorial Album*

The attempt to get some sort of coherent community together didn't last long. By the time Richard Fairfield, who was doing a tour of European communes, visited in summer 1971 he described it as something of a 'home for stray hippies' and 'the largest and most anarchic hip commune in England' with an estimated 300 people having passed through the place in one year. Fairfield interviewed a number of the people staying there at the time for his book *Communes Europe*.

This is a jumping off point for a lot of people. When I first came here a year ago I used to think it was important for people to have a place to get it together themselves. I still believe that. If people can come here and not have to do too much work like in the regular outside, then in a short space of time they can sort out what they want to do with their lives. They can come here and, over a period of a month or so, slow down; then they can go back into the society but not to a position they were in before ... Some people come here just to crash, some people come because they're looking for a flat and they haven't got enough money and some people come, unfortunately, because they think it's a place where they can do dope.

Frank Howard ('leader' and oldest member (31) of the group)

The Who's Pete Townsend lived across the river opposite the island. 'The so-called 'hippies' actually developed quickly into drug-addicts and thieves. As a rock star I felt quite at home with them, though they often woke me at five in the morning for tea-bags.' Townsend has said that some of the inspiration for The Who's ill-fated Lifehouse project came from observations he made of the Eel Pie Commune, and it has been suggested that the iconic Who anti-anthem 'Won't Get Fooled Again' from the *Who's Next* album was conceived in response to the collapse of the commune. 'At one point there was an amazing scene where the commune was really working, but then the acid started flowing and I got into some psychotic conversations. I just thought, "Oh, fuck it".' **12**

In 1970 the commune was paid a visit by the American Hog Farm Commune founded in the mid 60's by peace activist and clown Wavy Gravy. They were on their way to India (via Stonehenge and Amsterdam) with their 'mobile, hallucination-extended family' and had stopped off to buy two London buses. They were best known for providing security at the Woodstock Festival where they worked under the guise of the 'Please Force' ('please don't do that, please do this instead'). The travelling commune pitched their tents on the banks of the Thames, circled around a large tipi, and proceeded to hold court, bringing an even more carnival like air to proceedings on the island than usual. In the evening the two groups of communards squeezed into the Hog's tipi, sharing hash and stories of commune life. In the night the hippie campers were nearly washed away as the Thames tidal bore swept across the island and the Farmers had to retreat into the hotel. When the travelling hippie convoy moved on they were joined by quite a few of the Eel Pie Island members. Those left behind struggled on but the hotel was now pretty much open house to anyone who fancied moving in.

... There was only a handful of people left who were part of the wonderful early days. The rest had different ideals. There were junkies and speed-freaks, thieves and dossers. And the Angels of course, who had by now, more or less taken over the place ... **13**

Dominic

By the winter of 70/71 we'd had our water, our gas, our electricity – all cut off. It was a very old building, built around 1830, principally of wood. We were heating the building with the building. We started on the ground floor, because the bedrooms were on the first and second floors, ripping it apart for wood to burn. It dawned on me it was getting ridiculous when one night I saw the banisters go from the stairs. That was OK, but when I saw the stairs themselves going, I thought, how the fuck are we going to get to the first floor? There was a lot of that craziness, also a lot of drugs and junkies. **14**

Cliff Harper

The commune finally ended amid chaos at the end of March 1971 when, under threat of eviction, the hotel was damaged by fire while most of the people who were living there were being held by the police following a mass arrest in a nearby pub – it's generally assumed that the two events were not unconnected. Michael Snapper had submitted a planning application earlier in the month to demolish the hotel and build houses on the site.

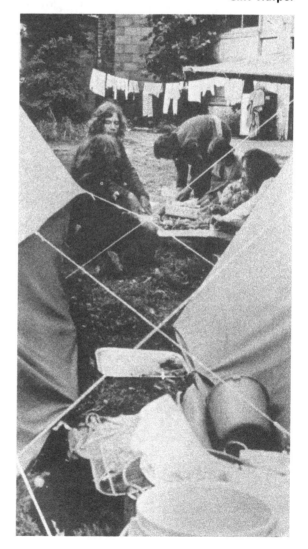

*Hog Farm at
Eel Pie Island, 1971*

Rehearsal for an Alternative Society

We Are All Angry!

The question is not whether the revolution will be violent. Organised militant struggle and organised terrorism go side by side. These are the tactics of the revolutionary class movement. Where two or three revolutionaries use organised violence to attack the class system ... there is the Angry Brigade. Revolutionaries all over England are already using the name to publicise their attacks on the system. No revolution was ever won without violence.

Angry Brigade Communiqué 6

The 60's in Britain would end and the 70's begin with a bang, or more accurately a series of countercultural bangs. No one now seems too keen to claim the Angry Brigade as part of their political heritage. Most histories of the period either ignore the bombing campaign launched against authority figures and symbolic property targets, or else treat it as some sort of slightly comic English sideshow to the serious terror campaigns being waged on the continent by the likes of the Bader-Mienhof group in Germany or the Red Brigades in Italy. Writings about the counter-culture tend to focus more on the 'culture' and gloss over the 'counter'. But the threat posed by the Angry Brigade was taken very seriously by British authorities at the time and that threat was seen as coming from one place – communes. The full story of the extent of the Angry Brigade activities has never been told – partly because no-one was ever convicted of actually planting any bombs and (even fairly recently) Scotland Yard confirmed that it would reopen the case if they came across any new evidence. In the light of this, the continuing vow of (almost) silence from those arrested and convicted for conspiracy to cause explosions seems understandable. What is clear is that there was a far larger campaign of attacks being carried out by a much wider range of people than we would be led to believe by the narrow focus on those brought to trial and dubbed the 'Stoke Newington Eight'. The roots of the counter-culture bombings stem from a combination of the influence of the Situationist writings of Raoul Vaneigen and Guy Debord, connections with the Spanish anarchist First of May group and the perceived failure of the 1968 'revolutionary moment' in Paris and elsewhere. But most of all from the dire state of the world in 1969. It is easy now to forget how bad things seemed then. The spectre of fascism, supposedly defeated in WWII, was still alive and kicking in southern Europe. Military dictators ruled in Spain, Portugal and Greece. Fascist groups were openly active in Italy. The Cold War was raging. American imperialism was at its height in South East Asia and South America. In Britain, Enoch Powell's 'rivers of blood' speech had fanned the flames of racial tension. The National Front were on the rise. Troops had been dispatched to quell the 'Troubles' in Northern Ireland. The new Tory government was about to introduce the Industrial Relations Bill, the latest in a long line of anti-union legislation.

IT, 27 Endell Street, London WC2 (telephone: 01-836-3727) is published by Knullar (Printing, Publishing & Promotions) Ltd from the same address, and is printed by Three Counties Press, Victoria Road, Diss, Norfolk.

it

BOMBERS ZAP LONDON NEWS BLACKOUT ON 30 BLASTS

THERE HAVE BEEN FORTY political bombings in London in the last six months. Three-quarters of these have been kept secret by the authorities.

This discovery was made when Joe, Keith and Tony Swash were picked up for the bombing of a private flat in Hampstead on 26 September. They admitted five other bombings – Clerkenwell County Court on 10 May, Kimber Road Army Depot on 30 June, Norbury

simply referred to as a 'fire'. They've probably done this because they believe they're tracking down a conspiracy and don't want their inquiries confused by bombing becoming fashionable.

Unfortunately for them, there is no conspiracy – except to keep people in the dark. There is, however, an incredible number of revolutionaries intent on bringing pig-Britain to its knees. This being the case, the pigs' next step, probably coinciding with the date of Joe and Keith's trial, is likely to be a saturation coverage of bombings designed to try and scare people into

Perhaps the first politically inspired violent incident of the era in Britain occurred on 1st April 1967 when the Spanish anarchist anti-Franco resistance organisation, the First of May Group, kidnapped and held hostage for a few hours the first secretary and legal attaché at the Spanish Embassy in London in protest at anarchists arrested in Spain being tried by a military court. This was followed by attacks in August by the same group who machined-gunned cars belonging to Spanish Embassy staff and raked the front of the US Embassy with gunfire. Early the following year a mortar was found pointing at the embassy of the Greek military Junta. This pattern of foreign resistance attacks continued through to 1969 with bombs planted at Spanish banks in London and Liverpool. Known anarchists in London were being watched by the police at the time for any connection to the Spanish group. After a powerful bomb exploded at the Covent Garden branch of the Banco de Bilboa two English anarchists, Alan Barlow and Phil Carver, were arrested and in their possession was a letter claiming the action on behalf of First of May. This was followed by attacks on an increasingly diverse set of 'home-grown' targets: the home of Tory MP Duncan Sandys was fire-bombed on 16th August, the following day the Ulster Office in London was hit by a firebomb, a bomb was thrown into an army recruiting office in Brighton on 19th August and the Imperial War Museum gutted by an incendiary device. In the first six months of 1970 there were a further dozen bomb attacks on targets ranging from the US Embassy and Paddington police station; through to Conservative Party offices in Wembley and Brixton; as well as attacks on Spanish Airlines at Heathrow. On 30th August the home of Metropolitan Police Commissioner, Sir John Waldron, was damaged by a blast and on 8th September the Chelsea home of Attorney General Sir Peter Rawlinson was bombed. These bombs were followed by letters claiming responsibility from 'Butch Cassidy and the Sundance Kid' and the 'Wild Bunch'. Neither of these attacks were reported in the national press who had been asked by Scotland Yard not to publish anything until their 'inquiries were complete'. Bombs were now going off at the rate of something like two a week. There were further attacks on Conservative Party offices in Hampstead and Wimbledon and a second attack at the Attorney General's home. On 9th October simultaneous bomb attacks were carried out against Italian State buildings in London, Manchester, Birmingham and Paris. They were claimed on behalf of Italian anarchist Giuseppe Pinelli who 'fell' out of a Milan police station window whilst being interrogated; an incident imortalised in Dario Fo's play *Accidental Death of an Anarchist*.

In November *IT* broke through the press silence. With the headline 'Bombers Zap London' they reported: 'There have been forty political bombings in London in the last six months. Three-quarters of these have been kept secret by the authorities. This discovery was made when Joe Keith and Tony Swash were picked up for the bombing of a private flat in Hampstead on 26th September.' The report goes on to say that police revealed that they were investigating 30 other 'political bombings' while they were interviewing the two men (who admitted five other bomb attacks on targets including Army recruiting offices and Conservative Clubs).

...Very few bombings apart from the ones Joe and Keith were involved in have actually been reported, which suggests that whenever the pigs have been able to get to the press first, the information has been suppressed, or simply referred to as a 'fire'. They've probably done this because they believe they're tracking down a conspiracy and don't want their inquiries confused by bombing becoming fashionable. Unfortunately for them, there is no conspiracy – except to keep people in the dark. There is, however, an incredible number of revolutionaries intent on bringing pig-Britain to its knees.

International Times 5th November 1970

The next target would broaden the scope of the 'political bombings' even further – at 2.30am on 20th November a small bomb wrapped in a copy of *The Times* exploded under a BBC outside broadcast van parked outside the Albert Hall due to cover the following day's *Miss World* contest. The damage did not stop the broadcast, but it was timed to be a prelude to disruption of the event by members of the Women's Liberation Movement who had got tickets to the event. At a pre-arranged signal the women threw flour bombs, stink bombs and smoke bombs, waved rattles, blew whistles, and threw leaflets. The women made it clear that the protest was against the competition not the contestants. One of the leaflets read: 'The competition will soon be over but we have been in the Miss World Contest all our lives, as the judges judge us, living to please men, dividing other women into safe friends and attractive rivals, graded, degraded, humiliated. We have seen through it.' There were an increasing number of attacks on, what now seemed like, a widening set of targets and the police were taking the situation very seriously. Scotland Yard had appointed Chief Superintendent Roy Habershon to lead the investigation and things would now start to unfold at an increasing pace. On 4th December, after a machine gun attack on the Spanish Embassy in Grosvenor Square, a 'communiqué' was issued for the first time to the *International Times* claiming responsibility for the attack in the name of the 'Angry Brigade'. The message contained reference to 'the Miss World farce' and to a series of attacks on branches of Barclays Bank. It ended with the statement:

...We machine gunned the Spanish Embassy last night in solidarity with our Basque brothers and sisters. We were careful not to hit the pigs guarding the building as representatives of British capital in fascist Spain. If Britain co-operates with France over this legal lynching by shutting the truth away we will take more careful aim next time.

SOLIDARITY AND REVOLUTION LOVE.

Angry Brigade Communiqué

The communiqué was printed out using a John Bull children's printing set. Later the same week a second communiqué arrived at the *International Times* office bearing the same stamp, it read: 'Fascism and oppression will be smashed. (Spanish Embassy machine gunned Thursday.) High pigs, Judges, Embassies, Spectacles, Property.' The communiques were the first evidence the police had that confirmed their suspicions that there were connections between the Spanish anarchists and the other 'home-grown' bombings. Police surveillance of known English anarchists with Spanish connections was stepped up. While the urban guerrilla bombings were gathering momentum the TUC was running a 'Kill the Bill' campaign against the Heath government's Industrial Relations Bill, which sought to prohibit wildcat strikes and place limitations on legitimate strike action. On 12th January 1971 a 'day of action' against the bill was held with a march through London. That evening two bombs went off at the home of the Minister for Employment, Robert Carr. A communiqué in tell-tale John Bull print was received simply stating 'Robert Carr got it tonight. We're getting closer'. The targeting of a Cabinet minister seriously worried the establishment and orders were issued by the Cabinet Office that capture of the Angry Brigade was to be given top priority. Full-time guards were provided for all Cabinet members. There followed a concerted effort by the police to flush out suspects from anarchist circles and the counter-culture in general. Raids were carried out at various addresses across London. On all these raids the police were keen to collect any address books they could find in order to try and work out who knew who. Meanwhile explosions were still happening in London and further afield. A bomb went off at the home of the Lord Provost in Glasgow on 25th January and the home of a businessman was fire-bombed on Jersey.

... these were obviously not coming from one group. In fact, even the idea of a 'group' – let alone the idea of a leader – was becoming hazy. People were acting spontaneously, from similar sets of ideas. This drove the police into a confused frenzy – they were trying to find an organisation that increasingly appeared not to exist, but because they lacked any other understanding about how society might work, they were forced to continue searching for a traditional organisation, with a leader, a membership and fixed plans.

And in the end they had to invent one.

Stuart Christie in *Granny made me an anarchist*

Superintendent Habershon was particularly interested in a number of the women who had been arrested at the Albert Hall protests who lived at a commune/squat in a large house at 29 Grosvenor Avenue in Highbury, Islington. 'I learned ... that this four-storied address housed persons who were extremely active full-time in revolutionary politics, and that a large amount of printing in support of various causes in this field was being carried on there, prominent amongst which was opposition to the Industrial Relations Bill and promulgating the more extreme Women's Liberation views.' [15] The Grosvenor Avenue group had come to the fore in the police investigations following the arrest of Jake Prescott for cheque fraud who, following his release on bail, was seen to head straight for the Islington commune. On 11th February, while the women from the commune were attending a hearing into the Miss World protests at Bow Street Magistrates court, the house was raided, searched for explosives and various diaries, address books, newspapers and other articles taken away, despite protests that this did not come into the terms of the police warrants. The police also intervened in the proceedings at Bow Street, taking away for questioning by force four of the women who lived at Grosvenor Avenue who were due to appear as defence witnesses.

The Islington squat, that according to press reports had now become the centre of the 'Angry Brigade conspiracy,' had been set up by, among others, an anarchist printer called Chris Broad and his partner Charlotte Baggins. In the basement there was a well-equipped printshop which printed the anarchist mag *Black Flag* along with a host of other radical pamphlets and leaflets. One of the other eight rooms in the house was set aside for research and writing on the life and death of Italian anarchist Guiseppi Pinnelli. While this was seen as further evidence that the commune was a hotbed of revolutionary activity by the police, Stuart Christie who visited the squat on a number of occasions had his doubts about the communal goings on there. 'The Broads and their friends hoped the 'commune' would provide an alternative model of collective behaviour. That was the theory. The place was an ideological madhouse and as far removed from an anarchist commune as you could get. There was no privacy, no doors on the toilets, no banister on the stairs ...' [16] Christie was also shocked by the way the group looked after the children who lived there. One member of the commune, writing home, described the situation at the commune surrounding the birth of one of the children and, in the letter, he explained that the group believed in collective childcare and that 'the baby's arrival was a time for the practical application of ideals, of alternative ways of living. The mother from the beginning did not want to breast feed the baby so that it did not build a dependence on her, and come to see her as the centre of the universe. The baby, in fact, was looked after by different people all the time. In practice, it means that someone stays the night with her and during the day. There are charts of feeds, changes, steriliser unit changes, so that things don't get overdone.' **17**

Other people who would end up accused of being members of the Angry Brigade also lived in communal households. At 168 Stamford Hill in Hackney a group of mostly students from Essex and Cambridge Universities were involved in the local squatting movement. They included: Hilary Creek, Anna Mendleson, Jim Greenfield and John Barker. Inspired by the revolutionary rhetoric they had picked up in the heady student days of 1968 they saw squatting not just as a solution to the problems of homelessness and slum housing, but also saw in the self-organising, self-help community ethos of the squatters potential for revolutionary confrontation with the authorities. They were also involved in the formation of Claimants Union groups instituted to support the unemployed in getting their rightful benefits. In December 1970 John Barker and Hilary Creek moved their activities to Manchester buying a dilapidated house at 14 Cannock Street in Moss Side with £400 of Hilary Creek's money and setting it up as a communal household. Seven people lived in the house, more or less permanently. It was, according to John Barker, 'a good scene. The joy of being in growing strength of us the people. It was real good there. Very relaxed.' The relaxed times did not last very long. In the middle of February the Manchester house was raided twice by police after the address had turned up in Jake Prescott's address book. The net was slowly closing on the bombers, or so the police thought. The result of all the police raids was that on 7th March two men, Jake Prescott and Ian Purdie were charged with two counts of causing explosions – the two that had been claimed by the Angry Brigade so far. Unfortunately for the police, the arrests did little to halt the bombings. On 18th March, while car workers were on strike, the main offices of the Ford Motor Company at Gants Hill, Ilford (on the outskirts of London) were wrecked by a powerful explosion. This was followed by the issue of communiqué No 7, and by further police raids and further attacks on a whole variety of targets ranging from a booby-trapped incendiary device posted to an MP at the House of Commons; arson attacks on Barclays Bank in Whitechapel, and the Gosport Tory Club; through to acts of sabotage carried out at the Berkeley Nuclear Power Station in Gloucestershire. On the 1st of May a bomb exploded in the Biba boutique in Kensington. It was accompanied by communiqué No 8 which, under the heading 'If you're not busy being born you're busy buying', exhorted its readers to blow up, burn down or simply wreck '... modern slave-houses – called boutiques.' Bomb attacks continued all through the summer of 1971 leading to orders being issued to Scotland Yard by the Prime Minister that 'The Angry Brigade must be found and smashed', *The Sunday Telegraph* reported:

YARD WILL GET THE ANGRY BRIGADE ... A special team of 20 hand-picked detectives from the Flying Squad and Special Branch, working with army bomb disposal experts and Home Office scientists. Their leader, a commander, whose name is being kept secret for his own safety... is known as rough and ready ... The squad is taking a tough line. It will raid hippy communes, question avowed members of the 'underground' and build up a complete file on the sub-culture that threatens the present social order.

The culmination of the police investigation would come at another communal house, the one now most associated with the Angry Brigade, located in a two bedroom top floor flat at 359 Amhurst Road in Stoke Newington. The flat had been rented under false names by John Barker, Hilary Creek and Anna Mendleson. They were joined by Jim Greenfield. Amhurst Road never became a commune along the radical lines of Grosvenor Avenue, nor even the relaxed lines of Cannock

Street. For one thing the group was trying to lie low, being on Scotland Yard's suspect list (as likely members of the Angry Brigade) and were wanted for cheque and credit card fraud. On 21st August, following a tip-off from a police informant, Amhurst Road was raided and the four arrested. Two others, Stuart Christie and Chris Bott, were also arrested when they arrived to visit the flat later. The police announced that they had found a quantity of explosives and firearms in the flat plus two detonators in the back of Christie's car. The police rounded up two other suspects, Angela Weir from a North London address and Kate McClean from the Grosvener Street Commune. There followed one of the longest criminal trials in English history, lasting from 30th May to 6th December 1972. The defendants, known as the Stoke Newington Eight, put in innocent pleas and defended themselves, playing on inconsistencies in the evidence and arguing that the police had been so desperate to convict someone for the Angry Brigade bombings that they had planted evidence. Before the trial started they continually challenged the selection of jurors until they felt it had a more working class make-up. This may well have helped with the final verdicts as the jury was split. Barker, Creek, Mendleson and Greenfield were found guilty of conspiracy to cause explosions and Barker and Creek guilty on a further charge of possession of explosives. They all received ten-year sentences. The other defendants were all acquitted. While the trial got high-profile coverage in both mainstream media and the alternative press and there was an active defence group keeping the trial in the public eye, there is almost no mention that, despite the police's claim to have caught the Angry Brigade, bombings actually continued to occur up to and throughout the court case. Targets included: Edinburgh Castle, Dartmoor prison, Chelsea Bridge, Albany Street Army Barracks, the Post Office Tower, Rhodesia House, Liverpool Army HQ, various Army Recruiting Offices, South African Airways and a railway line near Stranraer.

We are not in a position to say whether any one person is or isn't a member of the Brigade. All we say is: the Brigade is everywhere. Without any Central Committee and no hierarchy to classify our members, we can only know strange faces as friends through their actions ... Let ten men and women meet who are resolved on the lightening of violence rather than the long agony of survival; from this moment despair ends and tactics begin.
POWER TO THE PEOPLE. THE BRIGADE IS ANGRY

The final Angry Brigade communiqué No 13

In the early 1980's there was a brief revival of bombing activity in the north of England by a group calling itself the 'Angry Brigade Resistance Movement'. It carried out at least two attacks, one on the Prison Officers' Training College in Wakefield and another on an electricity pylon north of Maltby – an attempt to disrupt the national grid link from the Midlands to the North East. The bombs got little coverage in the press and one anti-terrorist officer quoted in *Black Flag* considered it was unlikely that the Angry Brigade had reformed. – '... it is not possible for the Angry Brigade to 're-form'. It wasn't an organisation, nor was it a single grouping – but an expression of the anger and contempt many people up and down the country had for the State and its institutions. In this sense the Angry Brigade is with us all the time (the man or the woman sitting next to you?) ...'

The Angry Brigade did not have a monopoly on the sentiments they expressed and they did not change the world, but their methods – effective or ineffective, rightly or wrongly – did give voice to a social conscience and expression to an important libertarian impulse at a time when it felt like huge social change was still possible.

Stuart Christie in preface to *The Angry Brigade*

Abdul Malik, Michael *From Michael de Freitas to Michael X 1968* Andre Deutsch. ASIN: B002G4X1YA

Baron, R W *144 Piccadilly* 1971 Samuel Fuller Publisher. ISBN: 087777033

Berke, Joseph (ed) *Counterculture: Creation of an Alternative Society* 1970 Peter Owen Ltd ISBN 0720614031

Carr, G *The Angry Brigade* 2010 PM Press ISBN: 1604860499

Christie, S *Granny Made Me an Anarchist* 2004 Scribner. ISBN: 0743259181

Dunn, N *Living Like I Do* 1977 Futura. ISBN: 0860075117

Fairfield, Richard *Communes Europe* 1972 Alternatives Foundation. ISBN: 0912976012

Farren, Mick *Give the Anarchist a Cigarette* 2001 Jonathan Cape. ISBN: 0224060740

Fountain, Nigel *Underground: The London Alternative Press 1966-74* 1998 Routledge. ISBN: 0415007275

Gorman, Clem *Making Communes* 1971 Whole Earth Tools *People Together* 1975 Paladin. ISBN: 0586082123

Green, J *All Dressed Up: The Sixties and the Counterculture* 1998 Jonathan Cape. ISBN: 0224043226

Green, J *Days in the Life: Voices from the English Underground 1961-71* 1998 Pimlico. ISBN: 0712666656

Humphry, D & Tindall, D *False Messiah: The Story of Michael X* 1977 Hart-Davis. ISBN: 0246108843

Maitland, Sara (ed) *Very Heaven: Looking Back at the 1960's* 1988 Virago. ISBN: 0860689581

Miles, B *London Calling* 2010 Atlantic Books. ISBN: 1843546140

Neville, Richard *Playpower* 1971 Paladin. ISBN: 0586080422

Neville, Richard *Hippie Hippie Shake* 1996 Bloomsbury. ISBN: 0715637800

Nuttall Jeff *Bomb Culture* 1969 Paladin. ISBN: 0586080015

Phillips, Mike & Charlie *Notting Hill in the 60's* 1991 Lawrence & Wishart. ISBN: 0853157510

Rigby, Andrew *Alternative Realities* 1974 Routledge & Kegan Paul. ISBN: 9780710077158

Rigby, Andrew *Communes in Britain* 1974 Routledge & Kegan Paul. ISBN: 071007915X

Saunders, Nicholas *Alternative London 1970* ISBN 0950162809

Stanshill, P & Mairowitz, D *BAMN (By Any Means Necessary)* 1971 Penguin. ISBN: 0140032673

Van der Vat, D & Whitby, M *Eel Pie Island* 2009 Frances Lincoln. ISBN: 0711230536

Wate, N & Wolmar, C (eds) *Squatting – The Real Story* 1980 Bay Leaf Books. ISBN: 0950725919

Williams, J *Michael X* 2008 Century. ISBN: 1846050952

Notes:

1   *Riverside Interviews 6: Tom McGrath*. Conducted and edited by Gavin Selerie, Binnacle Press 1983

2   Jeff Nuttall in *Bomb Culture*

3   http://www.tribal-living.co.uk/forums/archive/index.php?t-8644.htm

4   http://www.wussu.com/squatting/144_piccadilly_supercrew.htm (30.11.2011)

5   Tony Kelly Interviewed by Richard Fairfield in *Communes Europe*

6   Emmanuel Petrakis Interviewed by Richard Fairfield in *Communes Europe*

7   http://hqinfo.blogspot.com/2006/08/alternative-society-1970s-bit-travel.html (12.2.2012)

8   Recollections of 'London Street Commune' at www.wussu.com/squatting/144_piccadilly_supercrew.htm

9   ibid

10 Sid Rawle Interview *Ledbury Portal* 8th Dec 2007

11 Information on Crow Hall from *Communes Europe* and www.crowhallcommune.com

12 http://www.blender.com/guide/articles.aspx?id=158

13 http://www.eelpie.org/histdm.htm

14 Cliff Harper *The Education of Desire* 1984

15 Superintendent Roy Habershon quoted by Gordon Carr in *The Angry Brigade* p71

16 Stuart Christie *Edward Heath Made Me Angry* 2004

17 Quoted by Gordon Carr in *The Angry Brigade* p37

The Sound of Communal Living

Communal living has always proved attractive to artists. The late nineteenth and early twentieth century saw both artists' colonies in small seaside locations, and communes centred round individual artists. These were echoed in the post-war period at places like Digswell House – a decaying Regency mansion with cottages and outbuildings at Welwyn Garden City. In 1957 the Digswell Arts Trust set up a series of workshops with accommodation for young artists. While the early artist communities were predominantly homes for visual artists, from the 1960's and 70's onwards communal living was taken up by musicians and performance artists. Some were just fascinated by the idea, some tried it and then moved on. But for others it was central to their lives and music. Looking back down the communal musical roll-call of those who dabbled with, or were touched by, the idea of communal living I am struck by the mix of the famous, nearly famous, cult status and the down-right obscure. Of course back then it was less clear which would be which.

Of the now famous who toyed with communal living, Donovan Leitch went the furthest in actually buying a Scottish Estate in 1968 on Skye's Waternish peninsula where he, his manager Gypsy Dave and a group of followers formed a commune. The communal experiment was short-lived and looking back years later Donovan commented. 'It was a romantic return to Bohemia, an antidote to pop stardom. The problem was that it wasn't a proper commune. I ended up having to foot the bill!' [1] Pete Townsend of The Who was a neighbour and occasional visitor to the Eel Pie Island commune. There were The Beatles with their brief flirtation with the Maharishi and later Lennon's connection with Sid Rawle's Diggers as well as Harrison's generosity towards the Hare Krishna community at Bhaktivedanta Manor (see page 157). Quite a few bands lived together for intensive periods to work on particular records, perhaps most notably the Rolling Stones whilst recording *Exile on Main Street*. Other less well-known bands who briefly flirted with periods of communal living include among others: Fairport Convention, Fat Grapple, Barclay James Harvest, Arthur Brown, the Deviants, Hawkwind and Gong. If you search the world of obscure records from the period you come across a number of references of records put out by 'hippie commune' bands with names such as Red Television, Everyone Involved and Sleeping Sun. Sometimes a communal house or flat, home to one musician or manager, became the focus for other musicians. One such house was in Somali Road in London where, at the end of the 60's, folk and blues revivalists The Young Tradition, Davey Graham, Louis Killen, Bert Jansch, John Renbourn, Donovan Leitch, Val Berry and Anne Briggs could be found hanging out. There was also the Hampstead house where the likes of Robert Wyatt, Linda Lewis, Cat Stevens, Marc Bolan and Elton John might be found. Or the flat in Broughton Street, Edinburgh that was home to members of the band Silly Wizard. Others, like folk-rock duo Richard and Linda Thompson, spent some time living in communes for other than musical reasons. They joined a couple of communes in Maida Vale and Suffolk in order to follow the eastern Sufi religion.

There were those within the counter-culture who had a vision or expectation that rock musicians would take some sort of lead in formenting, promoting and financing 'the revolution'. But, while one or two individuals like Paul McCartney and Pete Townsend did give generous donations to keep projects like BIT afloat, and parts of the underground press such as *International Times* relied heavily on advertising from record companies and concert promoters, no real leadership from musicians ever really emerged in the 1970's. Even those who were sympathetic became disillusioned.

I got fed up with people telling me what rock and roll was all about, and what rock musicians were supposed to do now, and how rock and roll musicians were supposed to help overthrow the capitalist regime, and how rock and roll was supposed to sort of finance co-ops and communes and do this and that, and how because you were a rock and roll star and everybody looked to you for guidance and inspiration, that your responsibility was a political responsibility and a liberationist responsibility.

Pete Townsend, interviewed in *Hit Parader* 1975

The Exploding String Band

There were some circumstances more than others that led to those involved in the counter-cultural music scene to form communes. One of these would appear to be the point where rock music overlapped with performance art. Often the line between rock and performance artist was blurred. The Exploding Galaxy 'love-anarchist-dance-company' lived in a communal flat in Islington from where they ventured out to perform at music venues such as the UFO Club, the Arts Lab and the Roundhouse (where they appeared alongside the likes of Arthur Brown and Graham Bond). Originally initiated by Filipino artist David Medalla in 1967, Exploding Galaxy, and its various off-shoots/transformations; Transmedia Exploration and the Stone Monkeys, was a collaboration between a number of multi-media artists who would go on to make their own names as individual artists. These included: Derek Jarman, John Dugger, Hermine Demoriane, Edward Pope and Genesis P-Orridge. Both the Galaxy's performances and living arrangements seem to have been 'challenging':

Their communal flat has been the scene of some of the worst police harrassment to date. They no longer bother to put the door back on the hinges and offer the police tea (unfortunately, there is seldom any tea to be had, but the thought counts). They, like almost all experimental theatre groups, have little or no money and a secure free place to live is what makes life possible for them ... Last Sunday, they gave a performance which must constitute London's most liberated theatrical performance in history. Unfortunately it is impossible to describe the performance without endangering the Galaxy, but let it suffice to say that never have so many been so nude so early and for such good reasons ...

J Henry Moore in *International Times* No17 July 28th 1967

... Every night you had to sleep somewhere else and at another time. Suddenly someone stepped towards you and said: Stop! Why is your hair the same like some hour ago, don't you have imagination? Why do you eat with knife and fork, why don't you use something else? Why do you have the equal name like yesterday? It was a very interesting psychotherapeutical exercise.

Genesis P-Orridge in *Monopol* magazine

A chance meeting between two members of the Galaxy, Malcolm Le Maistre and his partner, Greek-born Rakis (aka John Koumantarakis), and members of The Incredible String Band in June 1968 in the Chelsea Hotel in New York led to further communal artistic ventures. The two dancers proposed to the String Band that there be an extended collaboration between the two groups. Returning to the UK, Le Maistre rented a large disused farmhouse at Penwern (between Newport and Velindre) in Pembrokeshire.

Advertisement for Exploding Galaxy gig at the Roundhouse

Here over the summer and autumn a little artist's colony made up of various members of the Galaxy, Robin Williamson and his fellow band member-cum-girlfriend Christina 'Licorice' McKechnie, the Leonard Halliwell Quartet and an 'ever swirling host of visitors and hangers-on' [2] worked on various ideas for mixed-media experiments. The String Band wrote and recorded a double album, *Wee Tam and The Big Huge*, and the commune was captured on home-made film which was later used in the documentary *Be Glad For the Song Has No Ending*. The String Band toured the UK and America (appearing at Woodstock) throughout much of 1969. At the end of the year they established themselves at a new communal base at Glen Row near Innerleithen, south of Edinburgh. Here the group, mainly under Robin Williamson's direction, developed a multi-media spectacular entitled 'U' which was performed in a ten-night run at the Roundhouse. Described by Williamson as 'a surreal parable in dance and song', it featured the band's music and dance by the Stone Monkey troupe (the latest evolution of Exploding Galaxy). A planned tour of the USA was cancelled after the show was poorly received in New York. Members of the String Band became involved in Scientology and they finally called it a day in 1974.

Another band with performance art tendencies was Principal Edwards Magic Theatre, a loosely-based artistic collective, who began as students at Exeter University in 1968. After University they left Exeter and set up in a large farmhouse outside Kettering. I am told by one of the group that Kettering was chosen because it was 'nice and central for touring'. The group's fourteen members consisted of musicians, poets, dancers, and sound and lighting technicians. Their shows were spectacular combinations of light show, progressive rock, costumed dance and poetry.

It would be nice, perhaps, to talk of Principle Edwards Magic Theater (sic) – a large group of gentle people who would seem to represent what is coming in the boundless universe of music. It is not easy to say exactly how many of them there are because tonight, or tomorrow, you may be part of Principal Edwards. If you are with them in any room as they offer themselves to you then you are indeed part of them – and me too. **3**

John Peel

*Principle Edwards
Magic Theatre*

They released their first single 'The Ballad of a Big Girl Now' in 1969 on John Peel's Dandelion Records label and recorded two albums, *SoundTrack* and *Asmoto Running Band*, the second produced by Nick Mason of Pink Floyd. Peel bought them a van to tour in and some musical instruments. The group toured for two-and-a-half years, opening for an impressive list of headline acts including the likes of: Pink Floyd, Elton John, John Lennon and Yoko Ono, Led Zeppelin, The Who and David Bowie. They broke-up in late 1971 amid business hassles and tensions between fringe theatre and rock priorities. A smaller – just rock music based – group simply called Principal Edwards carried on for a further couple of years with a few of the original musicians.

There were a small number of fringe theatre groups from the period who operated under some sort of communal set-up. In Cornwall, Oliver Foot and John Paul Cook started Footsbarn Theatre in 1971, rehearsing in a barn on the Foot family farm 'Trewen' near Liskeard – hence the name. They toured Cornwall, playing village halls, on beaches, in town halls and car parks, developing a brand of 'rough' or 'raw theatre' based on Cornish myths and legends.

We are as alternative as you can get – no wages, live in a community, grow vegetables, chickens, etc ...
The word 'alternative' alienates the people we play to ... working people.
These working people are not all trade unionists or furry freaks.
A lot of them are conservatives, but what the hell.

Alternative Theatre Handbook 1976

In 1984 the company left 'Thatcher's Britain' after being wooed with financial backing from the French Government. They remained without a base until 1991 when they set up on a farm complex in central France at La Chaussée, where they now have a fully equipped production centre with workshops, rehearsal space, office and studios and from where they continue to tour worldwide.

In the North of England in late 1971 Welfare State Theatre Company were invited by Mid-Pennine Arts to become Theatre Fellows and set up a base on a site on the edge of the council's rubbish tip in Burnley. From there, for the next six years, they would venture out to tour shows across the UK and Europe.

We got a whole mobile village together. Caravans, tents, circus tents, generator ... a travelling terrace street of thirty people ... nine children, 20 married and unmarried men and women who lived on £18 a week each and made a lot of art all over Europe ... and we called it a 'Microcosm of Possibilities' ...

John Fox Engineers of the Imagination

For part of the year they produced shows in Burnley including: Demon Buskers Street Theatre; various seasonal celebrations; a ghost train; and a civic bonfire event 'Parliament in Flames' which attracted an audience of 10,000. In 1975 they started a 'school' for their own children [4]. It was during this period that the company started to develop its own distinctive and highly influential version of community-based theatre and site-specific events. The residence in Burnley came to an end in 1978 – director John Fox and his family went on sabbatical to Australia where they intended to '... research alternative theatre from the Living end rather than the Theatre end.' [5] In Tasmania they met up with Bill Mollison who was in the throes of setting up his Permaculture Institute and they had planned to join forces with him to develop an intentional community. But family ties and illness forced a return to Britain and they landed in the Cumbrian town of Ulverston where they continued to work for the next 25 years.

Listed in the *Alternative Communities Directories* in the late 70's was another communal theatre group – the Rodent Arts Trust, based in Newcastle-under-Lyme in Staffordshire. Described as 'A number of inter-connected communities providing a service' [6] they ran several different projects: RAT Theatre, Mouse Theatre and Squirrel workshops.

Shivering Sands Pirate Commune

Of all the planned locations for a commune, perhaps the strangest was off the Essex coast on a series of Second World War coastal defence forts. By the end of the 1950's the forts, built as the 'Thames Estuary Special Defence Units', had been abandoned by the Ministry of Defence. In the mid 60's there was rumour that a group, said to be backed with money from George Harrison and Mick Jagger amongst others, intended to turn one of the forts into a fun palace and health complex. More likely this was a front for interest in the off-shore platforms as hosts for pirate radio stations. Screaming Lord Sutch was the first to broadcast from the forts, launching Radio Sutch in May 1964, followed by Radio Essex, Radio City, Red Sands Radio and Radio Caroline. After the 1967 *Marine Etc Broadcasting Offences Act* ended the era of pirate radio being broadcast from the forts, the Radio City fort was taken over by a group of squatters led by Alexander Dee (Dennis Swinnerton – a former Radio City DJ) and his girlfriend who planned to set up a commune. They stayed for a period until 1969 when the fort was once again abandoned. This was not, however, the last attempt to populate the forts. Roy Bates from Southend had taken a keen interest in the Forts and made repeated attempts to claim ownership, ultimately declaring the Independent Principality of Sealand – 'the Worlds smallest Country' –
on one of the Forts. Sealand issued its own stamps and coins and a limited number of passports.

The story of the forts is told at: www.bobleroi. co.uk/ScrapBook/ ScrapBook.html

The Globs

When five young men decide to form a pop group they don't usually set up in a remote cottage in the wilds of Norfolk together with all their girlfriends, but the Global Village Trucking Company aren't an ordinary pop group. They're not very worried about making money and they won't take any of the usual short cuts to success. What they are determined to do is make their own way without what they regard as the 'moguls' of the record business, the promoters, the big managers, the professional manipulators.

The Global Village want to do it their way.

Voiceover to *By Way of Change* (BBC 1973)

The fifteen or so members that made up the Global Village Trucking Company based themselves in a ramshackle thatched cottage near Wortham on the Suffolk-Norfolk border. The band, their manager, roadies and girlfriends lived as a commune – venturing out in a battered green bus to play gigs across the country at free festivals, benefit concerts, in prisons and on the backs of lorries in shopping parades. Known to their fans affectionately as 'The Globs', their brand of gritty progressive rock with extended jam sessions and somewhat surreal lyrics and song titles made them favourites of the mid-seventies British festival circuit, drawing comparisons with the likes of the Grateful Dead.

... We decided it's a lot easier to be out in the country which is why we're living out in Norfolk. It creates a much more harmonic feel both within ourselves and with our environment. Like people always think of the country in terms of a place to go away to and do nothing. It doesn't actually work like that with us at all because within this small space under this roof there's incredible energy going on there's incredible determinism to do something which we all believe in. And it gets very hectic at times and tempers get frayed, people say very heavy things to one another but basically it's great. **7**

Jon Owen, Lead Singer 1973

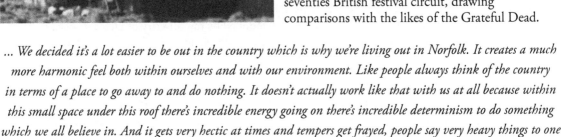

In 1973 the BBC made a documentary about the band's lifestyle, exploring the group's communal life and their philosophy. The group were from a mixed background. Co-founder James Lascelles was second son of the 7th Earl of Harewood and in line to the throne, other members were from less illustrious backgrounds – the programme showed the commune's home life and the band playing gigs. Mixed in were interviews with various commune members about their outlook on life.

We're just one of a lot of people who have felt something about, a new sort of vibration or atmosphere in the air that's affecting everyone really ... It's more a memory, or a flash of something that could really happen. That this world could be a better place and can be a better place if everyone gets down and tries to put something that is only a dream into reality.

Michael Medora 1973

The Global Village Trucking Company's East Anglian commune was featured on their 1975 album cover

Eventually the pressure and tedium of endlessly trooping to gigs up and down the country led to some members of the band leaving and by 1976 the group had split up. Since then members of the Globs have been involved or played with numerous fellow musicians including Bob Dylan, Frank Zappa, Joan Armatrading, Eurythmics, Steve Harley and Cockney Rebel, Steve Hillage; worked and written music for theatre, circus, television and film; run workshops; taught music and produced holograms. In 2007 BBC4 revisited the 1973 documentary as part of their *Whatever Happened to?* series. The new programme ended with a reunion gig which led to further gigs for the band and an appearance at the Glastonbury Festival.

I think the time we were there was such an important moment in time ... I do think the time was morally it was a very good time. I really do believe that it moulded me to some extent ... I think we are hippies, It's in my heart ...
Danielle Cox 2007

Global Village Trucking Company

Endless Acid-Haze Musical Mayhem

Despite one or two high-profile successes, the music scene in and around Bristol never had the caché of Manchester or Liverpool. But for a while in the late 60's and early 70's it was one of the focuses for a South West progressive/psychedelic rock scene involving the likes of Hawkwind, The Pink Fairies, Principal Edwards Magic Theatre, the Crazy World of Arthur Brown, Atomic Rooster, Gryphon, the Third Ear Band ... (to name a few of the better known) ... and Magic Muscle.

Going under the unlikely name of Magic Muscle these boys are gaining a following throughout the country ...
In the great tradition of the British under-ground rock band they don't earn much money, they support a large
family, they take drugs, they play thousands of benefits, they have trouble getting a record deal, they don't get press
coverage, they take more drugs, they ball, they sometimes get the clap.

International Times 18th October 1972

Formed in 1970, the band grew out of, lived at, rehearsed and played in the basement of an anarchic communal house at 49 Cotham Road in Bristol. Other members of the house had set up the Black Dwarf Party (inspired by the Dutch Kabouters) and involved themselves in street politics, campaigning and even standing in local elections on a platform of 'free everything: housing, medicine, love, entertainment and drugs ... we feel that local government needs a fucking good shake-up on all levels.' [8] Magic Muscle started out as a sort of houseband for the Black Dwarf Party, playing benefits and free festivals. The story of the band's evolution is told in detail on guitarist Rod Goodway's website [9]. Sharing stages with the likes of Hawkwind and the Pink Fairies (and sometimes forming an occasional psychedelic jamming supergroup known as MagicPinkWind made up of 'whoever could still stand up and hold an instrument') Magic Muscle built up a following both locally and further afield. Although the latter would seem to have been largely through touring as Hawkwind's warmup band during the era of their successful chart hit – 'Silver Machine'. Magic Muscle never managed to get a recording deal during this period, although one was rumoured to be in the offing with Island Records. Their sound from this period was captured in one of the sessions in the basement at Cotham Road and appeared later on a cassette entitled *Living Weeds From Ancient Seeds*. In 1972, following a particularly crazy period at the Cotham Road commune, Keith Christmas (occasional Muscle guitarist and solo musician) rented a farmhouse between Mells and Radstock in Somerset with money he'd got from his record deals, and the whole Muscle/Black Dwarf gang – some twenty people and sixteen cats – followed him on this exodus from the city, setting up a recording studio and carrying on much as before. The first

Magic Muscle at the Glastonbury Fayre in 1971

incarnation(s) of Magic Muscle lasted until some time in 1973 with their 'last gig' being 800 feet above sea level at the Trentishoe Free Festival in North Devon. By this time operations had been moved to a farmhouse just outside of Bruton, Somerset, where some members of the Magic Muscle commune still live to this day. Various Magic Muscle reunions have taken place over the ensuing years with different variations in the line up – this resulted in 1991 in a series of old and new recordings being released. The Magic Muscle 'tradition' has also continued more recently in various morphed versions of the band under titles such as: The Magic Bevis Muscle Frond, Magic Ethereal Frond Alchemy and Rustic Rod's Ethereal Muscle.

Many bands associated with communes played the free festivals that were starting to be organised in the early 70's. The rhetoric of communal living was often expressed in the publicity for the festivals and some of those involved in organising the festival were, themselves, communards – the manifesto for the 1974 Windsor Free Festival, being written by, amongst others, Sid Rawle and Ubi Dwyer, open with the words:

W*E*L*C*O*M*E: People willing to devote themselves to the work of the Commune (a circle of human love) are most welcome to come and discuss and, if agreed, join ...Communes: The old society is founded on the family which has now grown so small and lonely that it is truly called an emotional gas chamber. Two people smoking dope together don't have half the fun or satisfaction as a group of six or 12. It is TRUE not only of dope but of our whole lives. WE CAN LOVE MORE THAN ONE for before our eyes monogamous love is everywhere failing - far better and from that more generous, peaceful, freer HOME called the COMMUNE we can build a society which will recognise the genius in all of us. In the place of the ripoff employer/employee relationship we can have one of complete co-operation (we can all take part in the decision-making process at work as well as at home). But we have to learn this co-operation in the home and from an early age. It is there-in the COMMUNE-that the Revolution must begin! Here in our commune we aim at practising what we advocate. LOVE! ...

Windsor Free Festival Manifesto 1974

The 1974 Windsor Free Festival has attained something akin to legendary status amongst those chronicling the alternative history of the various strands of the British counter-culture. It has come to be seen as both a high point in the utopian idealism of the period and at the same time the beginning of the end of the hippie dream.[9]

It began as an experiment in a new society of love and mutual co-operation, functioned for six short days as a model world where all differences of creed, colour and politics were non-existent and ended in a nightmare that bore more than a passing resemblance to the Wounded Knee massacre. The third Windsor festival was not a pop music festival, but a gathering of thousands of people, young and old, to experience for nine days the realisation of living what has been termed an alternative society. The creation of a tent city of people who longed to return to the simpler life of tribal concept. While the world outside looked in and saw nothing but the stages from which blared rock music, those who penetrated deeper became aware that by comparison to what was actually taking place, the music was incidental.

Reverend Brian Ferguson in *Maya* 1974

Windsor '74 was broken up by the police in a brutal attack on peaceful festival-goers the like of which wouldn't be seen again until the so-called 'Battle of the Beanfield' in 1985. The government's reaction to the essentially bad press it got from the police actions was to grant organisers an 'official' free festival site at Watchfield and to tolerate a softly-softly approach to policing festivals for the following decade, but for some people things were different after Windsor.

A strange hippie cult calling themselves 'Wallies' claim God told them to camp at Stonehenge. The Wallies of Wiltshire turned up in force at the High Court today. There was Kris Wally, Alan Wally, Fritz Wally, Sir Walter Wally, Wally Egypt and a few other wandering Wallies. The sober calm of the High Court was shattered as the Wallies of Stonehenge sought justice.

The *Times* August 13th 1974

At the end of the first Stonehenge Free festival in 1974, a group of around thirty people stayed on and set up a camp of tents, a rickety polythene-covered geodesic dome and a small fluorescent painted tipi in a field next to the stones. The group lived as an open commune 'Dancing, frolicking, acting out the Gospel of Free using Stonehenge as a cosmic wrist-watch with domes and dogs, and horses, and music, and troub'ador costumes, and giant shirts embroidered with the Eye of Horus.' [10] In order to get an eviction order the Department of the Environment and the National Trust were required to serve a High Court injunction on named individuals. Aware of a potential legal loophole, the group had agreed that they would answer only to the name of Wally. The ludicrous summonses against Phil Wally, Sid Wally, Arthur Wally, Chris Wally, etc set the scene for the somewhat surreal trial that followed.

... A lady Wally called Egypt with bare feet and bells on her ankles blew soap bubbles in the rarefied legal air and knelt to meditate. Sir Walter Wally wore a theatrical Elizabethan doublet with blue jeans and spoke of peace and equality and hot dogs. Kevin Wally chain-smoked through a grotesque mask and gave the victory sign to embarrassed pin-striped lawyers ... [11]

The Wallies of Stonehenge

The Court inevitably found in favour of the 'owners' of the Stones. The Salisbury Journal reported that one Wally Hope saw the defeat as a victory 'We won. We'd have won whatever happened. We were playing with the Ace of Hearts. The judge told us that we were 100 per cent good people We have won because we made friends with him. We made friends with our lawyer. We made friends with you reporters. What more can you want out of life than to make friends?' [12] The Wallies moved their camp, now known as 'Fort Wally', six feet to one side to a piece of common land. The group also set up a 'Wally Squat' in the nearby town of Amesbury. The camp remained in place until after the Winter Solstice. The name 'Wally' has become identified with one man, Phil Russell, who is credited with the idea of having a festival at the Stones and had written and published much of the promotional material for the first festival. Although the Wally camp was run as an open free commune, Russell saw himself as the leader and was said to have marched round issuing orders that no one paid much attention to. Russell died in 1975. He was arrested and drugged in a mental hospital just prior to the '75 Stonehenge Festival, and released after the festival. He died later that summer in circumstances that have never been really fully explained.

Our generation is the best mass movement in history – experimenting with anything in our search for love and peace. Knowledge kicks religion life but even if it leads us to our death at least we're all trying together. Our temple is sound we fight our battles with music drums like thunder cymbals like lighting banks of electronic equipment like nuclear missiles of sound. We have guitars instead of tommy-guns.

Phil Russell, aka Wally Hope 1974

Phil Russell had grown up in Essex near a place called Dial House an 'open door' community started in 1967 in a semi-derelict house as an avant-garde/ anarchist cultural community centre by J J Ratter and Gee Vaucher. It was here that Phil/Wally got support for his Stonehenge plans – other festival organises

had initially opposed his ideas on the grounds that they would distract from
energy going into Windsor and then later Watchfield. The events surrounding
Wally Hope's death led to, or were the catalyst for, the formation at Dial House
of one of the seminal bands of the punk era. Taking Wally Hope's revolutionary
cry on being released after the Wally trial of 'guitars instead of guns', those
living at Dial House at the time changed their names and became CRASS.
(J J Ratter/ Penny Rimbaud, in what turned out to be a piece of counter-
culture myth-making, took the ashes of Wally Hope to be scattered at
Stonehenge during the summer solstice at the 1976 Free Festival.) Between
1967 and the early '70's the rambling sixteenth century cottage on the edge of
the Epping Forest had been renovated to include studios, print-rooms, rehearsal
space workshops and an organic garden. Various art projects were either started
by or involved members of the community; Exit Performance Art Group; ICES
72 – The International Carnival of Experimental Sound – a large avant-garde
art and music festival over the course of two weeks in August of 1972; the
Exitstencil Press; and Ceres Confusion, a free-form music group.

*We had opened up our house at a time when many others were doing the same. The so-called 'commune
movement' was the natural result of people like ourselves wishing to create lives of co-operation, understanding
and sharing Individual housing is one of the most obvious causes for the desperate shortage of homes, communal
living is a practical solution to the problem. If we could learn to share our homes, maybe we could learn to share
our world and that is the first step towards a state of sanity. The house has never been somewhere where people
'drop out', we wanted somewhere where people could 'drop in' and realise that given their own time and space
they could create their own purposes and reasons and, most importantly, their own lives. We wanted to offer a
place where people could be something that the system never allows them to be – themselves. In many respects we
were closer to anarchist traditions than to hippy ones but, inevitably, there was an interaction.*

Crass Collective, A Series of Shock Slogans and Mindless Token Tantrums

Crass drew as much on their background in performance art as the punk DIY
ethos, and with a wide range of influences as diverse as Benjamin Britten, jazz
poetry, and much of the utopian hippie philosophy of the free festivals (that
punk was supposed to be a reaction against). This enabled them to inject an
anarcho-pacifist sensibility into punk which, in the beginning, was more
nihilistic than political. Crass were, perhaps deliberately, politically
contradictory, preferring to challenge people to 'Make your own fucking minds
up!' than to preach a political line. This led to them being accused by both left
and right extremes of the political spectrum of being in the other camp. Fairly
quickly they developed a 'style' and act that included – as well as the
uncompromising lyrics and music – the use of back-projected films and video
collages; detailed sleeve notes on records emblazoned with 'don't pay more than
46p for this'; the wearing of all-black quasi-paramilitary clothes (to undermine
the cult of personality – or to make communal washing easier?); flags and
banners stamped with their own logo/symbols.[13]

*We weren't a band. We never were a band. I don't think we even saw ourselves as a band. I certainly never saw
ourselves as a band. We certainly didn't belong in the sort of pantomime of rock'n'roll, and probably even less in
the pantomime of what became known as punk. It wasn't our interest. I mean, we weren't interested in making
records. We were interested in making statements, and records happened to be a way of making statements* [14]

Penny Rimbaud

Along with other bands that also passed through Dial House at the time (such as the Poison Girls and Flux of Pink Indians – and, perhaps, the northern-based anarcho-punk pranksters Chumbawamba – who started in a communal house in Leeds [15]) Crass took a utopian anarchist sensibility out to a new generation who had never heard of Kropotkin, the Situationists or Ken Kesey's Merry Pranksters. A sensibility that some thought had begun to die at Windsor in 1974. Crass wound up in 1984 – a date deliberately chosen for its dystopian resonance. During some seven years on the road the band gave away thousands of pounds to causes ranging from CND to striking miners; and rejected offers from major record labels who promised to help them 'market revolution'. Crass needed little help with marketing, as they could, at their height, shift 20,000 singles in a week with no advertising and no airplay. They also attracted the attention of the KGB and MI5 along the way for the Thatchergate tapes, a faked conversation between Margaret Thatcher and Ronald Reagan in which they appeared to suggest that Europe would be used as a target for nuclear weapons. Members pursued their own various individual paths after Crass disbanded. In the 1990's, the existence of the Dial House community came under threat from property developers – in the end, with help from supporters and friends, the community was able to buy the house. Recently, there have been performances variously under the names of the Crass Collective, Crass Agenda and Last Amendment.

Following the successful purchase of Dial House, the following statement was issued in October 2001:

Our current plan is that DIAL HOUSE should continue as it always has been, as a 'safe house': a space where there is a welcome, where there is a bed for the night, conversation, food and the possibility of sharing ideas. On this base we will expand on DIAL HOUSE's traditions of radical creativity, offering its facilities to an ever wider public under the new title of THE DIAL HOUSE TRUST – A Centre For Alternative Globalisation. [16]

The true effect of our work is not to be found within the confines of rock'n'roll, but in the radicalized mindset of thousands of young people throughout the world. From the Gates of Greenham to the Berlin Wall, from the Stop The City actions to underground gigs in Poland, our particular brand of anarcho-pacifism, now almost synonymous with punk, has made itself known. [17]

Rockbitch

We play rock. We live together in a commune. We love each other. We have sex together. We're mainly women. We are exactly what we claim to be. We're what you get when strong intelligent women decide to free themselves from the expectations of other people and live closer to the heart to truth to sex. We believe in liberation through sexual freedom and through the evolution of mind and spirit through exactly that. The Rock Bitch side of things was an accident. It's what you get when the sex witches happen to form a band.

Babe Alexandra *This is Rock Bitch*

Formed in the early 1990's, Rockbitch lived on a commune at Metz in France which was envisaged as a feminist, matriarchal, tribal retreat where women could explore their sexuality and psyche. The band had grown out of Cat Genetica and Red Abyss – previous English bands who drew on jazz and funk as well as rock influences. Over time the band's personnel changed, becoming nearly all women, and its music became harder-edged with more punk and metal influences. At what they thought was to be their final gig (they were going to give up playing because of what they saw as the apathy of male-dominated rock audiences) the group decided to put some of the wild orgiastic pagan sex of their home life into the stage act. This went down a storm with some of the audience and they decided to continue touring in order to spread their pro-sex message. The group went on to tour extensively throughout Europe with what became a mutli-media rock/performance art/sex show. The commune/band had been joined by this time by two performance artists who worked together as a sexual performance artist and gonzo-camera team describing themselves as 'Archetypes of the Dark Feminine psyche' and personifying Kali (the Hindu Goddess of Death) and Erzulie (the Voodoo Goddess of Love). The shows included close-ups of stage action projected on to a screen at the rear along with pre-prepared art videos of subject matter relating to the songs. These included graphic and disturbing images of child clitoridectomy, public stonings of adulterous women, binge/vomiting models etc. The most infamous part of the stage act was the so-called 'Golden Condom' contest which involved throwing the golden condom out into the audience. Whoever caught it (man or woman) was then taken backstage for sex with one or more band members.

Illustration from Motor Driven Bimbo booklet

The band and the community have always been inextricably linked – changes in one were reflected by changes in the other ... Our free-sex way of living, our attempts to promote the ancient understanding of sex as a spiritual path, our striving toward a polysexual intimacy within the community, unhindered by jealousy (many persons left, men in particular, who couldn't deal with the level of honesty this required)...all of this was a constant theme within our music and lyrics.[18]

Rockbitch in action

Rockbitch recorded two studio albums: *Motor Driven Bimbo*, which in 1999 received critical acclaim in many countries; and the goth-influenced *Psychic Attack*, which was never released. The group came under increasing attack as their popularity grew. The attacks came from all sides: authorities in the towns and cities where they played increasingly tried to censor the band's act, and when that failed turned to banning them completely. They were attacked by both right-wing Christians and feminists. They were sabotaged by male bands on the same bill and suffered rampant sexism and hypocrisy from the music industry. Following mounting pressure from cancelled gigs and continued attacks from the authorities Rockbitch ceased performing in 2002. Later that year a 30-minute documentary on the band was broadcast on BBC Choice and a further, hour-long documentary was broadcast on Channel 5 in 2003. When they stopped playing the band issued a statement about their future intentions. This included 'The commune is not splitting up, no way. Our lifestyle and craft will continue as it has always done. Rockbitch will be reduced (elevated maybe?) to an internet presence.' They launched their own website www.rockbitch.com. In 2005 they re-emerged under the name MT-TV for a tour of the UK and the USA. This was a 'music-only project – no sex or nudity of the Rockbitch days.'

> *When we first began our show, we were trying to make a visual and musical statement about the way in which women and their sexuality are portrayed in every medium within Western culture We wanted to express our responses to these perceptions, and we wanted to have fun – none of these contradict each other ! It was apparent to us that an extreme double standard regarding male and female sexual stereotypes was still an ongoing, unresolved issue – both within the structure of society, and in the minds of the public and feminist movement alike.*[19]

Exodus: Movement of Jah Luton

On Friday 7th July 1995 more than 250 police officers in riot gear were sent into the Marsh Farm Estate in Luton. This followed two nights of rioting on the estate. The police faced a crowed of up to 500 people who attacked them with bottles, bricks and petrol bombs in five hours of disturbances. A supermarket was ransacked and the windows of the local library shattered. A police spokesman was reported as saying : 'It's hot, it's sticky, people are angry. Anything could happen.' [20] The following night the police braced themselves for a further onslaught, and then a strange thing happened – nothing. No rioters turned up – they had gone to a free gig organised by the Exodus Collective.

Exodus had started back in 1992 when a D J Hazad and some friends using equipment they had reclaimed from a skip organised a free party for 150 people in some woods near Dunstable. Using money donated at this and further parties both the size of the sound system and the audience grew rapidly till by the end of the year they were attracting up to 10,000.

One of the remarkable aspects of Exodus's parties is the broad range of people attracted, from teenagers to middle-agers; employed and unemployed; politically aware, or just wanting a good time; black and white; male and female;' urban and rural youth; old hippies, punks and Hell's Angels; New-Age and traditional travellers; road protesters and squatters. [21]

Tim Malyon

From the beginning, the ethos of the collective was community focussed and there was no interest in the more commercial party and rave scene that was going on at the same time. They set up their speaker stacks and pumped out dance music in a whole variety of warehouses, quarries, barns and landfill sites, away from residential areas. The parties were marshalled by Exodus peace stewards and attended by their own first aid van. They took collections at the parties to fund further events and other local community activities. In January 1993 they supported fourteen homeless people who had squatted the long-empty Oakmore Hotel in Luton. They helped to renovate the derelict property using money from bucket collections taken at the parties. Up until this point some members of the local police force had been taking something of a softly-softly approach to the collective's activities, which were having a knock-on effect of reducing crime and disorder in the town. One senior officer even went as far as calling for a warehouse to be made available for Exodus to hold properly licensed dances. This attitude started to change when the hotel was taken over. On 15th January the police raided the squat on the pretence of being tipped off about criminal damage and charged two people with affray – charges that were later dismissed when the police failed to produce any evidence. Six weeks later the group were evicted by the police and given half an hour to leave during a snow storm. The group promptly squatted the empty St Margaret's Hospital near Streatley, renaming it HAZ Manor (or Housing Action Zone Manor) again raising money to start renovations through collections at the dance parties. The Manor was eventually licensed from Luton Borough Council with Exodus becoming a legal housing co-operative. The group had also taken over Longmeadow Farm, a property purchased by the Department of Transport for an M1 widening scheme and then neglected for years (previously used by the collective as an early free party venue). They planned to renovate the property and turn it into a Community Farm with horses, goats, sheep, ducks and pot-bellied

HAZ Manor

pigs and open it up to the public and local schools.

In many ways Exodus were the 1970's counter-culture reinvented for the 90's generation. Instead of a soundtrack of psychedelic rock, this time the back beat was of dance beats and reggae overlaid by dub DJs and MCs. But all the same ingredients that had fed the counter-cultural explosion the first time round were evident in its latest incarnation on the streets of Luton: there is the emphasis on free events and non-commercialisation (echoes of the Digger groups); the direct action and squatting of empty abandoned property and turning it to community use; even some of Exodus's political stances could have come straight out of a White Panther manifesto circa 1969. And perhaps the most striking similarity, 30 years on, is in the lack of change in the reaction of the authorities. Almost from the beginning, in 1992, Exodus had been under covert police surveillance, trying to prove that they must be a cover for drug dealing as they didn't seem to have any other way of making money from 'free' parties. Once the group moved on to squatting the police harassment stepped up. On the same night that the Oakmore Hotel was raided, 36 members of the collective were arrested before a party at Longmeadow Farm. This prompted a 3,000-strong convoy to surround Luton police station and proceed to party in protest at the detention of members of the collective. Police activity against the group continued throughout 1993 with the police distributing leaflets to local residents asking whether they'd been frightened by Exodus' activities. The response from the community was to tell the police to 'leave them alone'. In 1994 one Exodus member, Paul Taylor, was acquitted of drug charges due to lack of and 'dubious' police evidence. The level of police harassment resulted in a call by Luton Council for a public inquiry into police operations against Exodus. Various reasons have been put forward for the ferocity of the backlash against the group: that there was a Masonic conspiracy to crush them involving police officers; local councillors; the local MP Graham Bright (who sponsored legislation to increase the penalties for people organising unlicensed 'raves'); the local press; and heads of the local brewery – takings in local pubs went down on nights of Exodus parties. Whether the heavy-handed police treatment of Exodus contributed in any way to the rioting in July 1995 is not known. Polly Toynbee, writing in *The Independent*, commented that the rioting was '... blamed by observers variously on one or two commercial television crews, on the SWP, on simple wickedness and the euphoria of mayhem.' **22**

After three nights of escalating disturbances and escalating police responses, the Exodus Collective issued the following statement: 'This collective will stage an all-night party which will serve the following purpose:
1 To demonstrate in a non-violent way against the use of policing methods that have turned a spark into a fire.
2 We also hope to try and alleviate the tension that is in the town and remove the massive and unwelcome police presence from our community.

Communes Britannica

3   To continue by direct peaceful action the campaign for a permanent community and activity centre in order that the youth of this community are able to express themselves positively and build something that belongs to them.' **23**

Exodus statement read out by Glenn Jenkins

The Exodus Free Party on the night of the 8th of July 1995 drew 1,500 young people off the streets of the Marsh Farm Estate. The police tried to claim that 'they had regained control', but it was clear that the real credit went to Exodus. Despite, or perhaps because of, their intervention in 'community policing' the Exodus Collective continued to suffer from increased police harassment. Prominent collective member Paul Taylor was framed on an ABH/murder charge of which he was later acquitted. Glenn Jenkins' mother's public house was targeted by the police and injunctions were served on some members attempting to forbid them '... from holding free parties ... attending unlicensed parties and being held responsible for activities of other Collective members.' This resulted in masked dance parties to hide attendee's identities. Exodus presented a real challenge to the authorities. Not just from the point of the supposed unlawfulness of some of their activities; not just because they were taking business away from commercial enterprises; but from their entire approach and ethos that held up a different vision of what community cohesion and community action might look like. A vision that was a critique and challenge to the ideology of what in the 1970's would have been called the 'straight society'. The collective got publicity for their activities not just in the new alternative press such as *SchNEWS* but also in more academic circles.

... it can just be described as a housing co-operative, or a rave collective, or something like that. But as you look at what it symbolises and what it means it gives you a picture, or a figure, of how things might be ...

Professor John Berrington, Warwick University

In the latter half of the 1990's, Exodus continued to hold large-scale free parties every fortnight 'without fail' as part of a campaign of non-violent civil disobedience with two aims: to get 'a people-owned community centre called The Ark, which would reduce poverty and social exclusion for a large number of 'excluded' people by creating a base for not-for-profit workplaces'; and to get a 'Sanctioned Sites' agreement between landowners, council, police and the community, to allow free use of agreed sites throughout the county for non-commercial outdoor parties. In 2000 the years of harrassment took their toll and the collective splintered over differences in the way things should be organised. Some people stayed on at HAZ Manor while others left to develop their ideas in the wider local community, eventually re-emerging under the name Leviticus, continuing the campaigns that Exodus had started. Ten years later they were able to report that:

After nearly 20 years of building from the grassroots, we are finally moving towards achieving our overall goal, which is to create an alternative way of life in Luton, based on the freedom to work, rest and play in a non-commercial, not-for-private profit environment. **24**

Leviticus 2011

Berger, G *The Story of Crass* 2006 Omnibus Press
Coult, T & Kershaw, B (eds) *Engineers of the Imagination* 1983 Methuen. ISBN: 0413528006
Deakin, R *Keep It Together: Cosmic Boogie with the Deviants and the Pink Fairies* 2008 Headpress. ISBN: 190048661X
Fox, J *Eyes on Stalks* 2003, Methuen. ISBN: 0413761908
Fairfield, R *Communes Europe* 1972 Alternatives Foundation
Kiddle, C *What Shall We Do with the Children?* 1981 Spindlewood. ISBN: 0907349102
McKay, G (ed) *DiY Culture: Party and Protest in Nineties Britain* 1998 Verso. ISBN: 1859842607
   Senseless Acts of Beauty – Cultures of Resistance Since the Sixties 1996 Verso. ISBN: 1859840280
Wainwright, H *Reclaim the State: Experiments in Popular Democracy* 2003 Verso. ISBN: 1859846890
Young, R *Electric Eden: Unearthing Britain's Visionary Music* 2010 Faber. ISBN: 0571237525

Notes:
1 *Time Out*. Interview: John Lewis, http://www.timeout.com/film/features/show-feature/328/ 25.4.2012
2 *Electric Eden*
3 *Disc and Music Echo* – April 5th, 1969
4 *What Shall We Do with the Children?*
5 John Fox *Engineers of the Imagination*
6 *Alternative Communities Directory* (4th edition)
7 Interviewed in *What Happened Next? Global Village Trucking Co*, BBC4 13.05.2008
8 www.achingcellar.co.uk/pages/tree/magic_muscle.htm
9 www.achingcellar.co.uk
10 *Maya: Windsor Free Nation News* No1, Sept 1974
11 *The Times*, August 13th 1974
12 Wally Hope quote from *The Salisbury Journal* http://www.colander.org/gallimaufry/Wally.html 25.4.2012
13 See: *Senseless Acts of Beauty – Cultures of Resistance since the Sixties*. George McKay. Verso. 1996
14 www.furious.com 12.5.2010
15 *Well Done – Now Sod Off!* Video.
16 *The Guardian* – Friday January 5th, 2001
17 www.southern.net/southern/band/CRASS/
18 http://www.rockbitch.com/netpages/playing1.html 26.4.2012
19 http://www.rockbitch.com/netpages/ranting1.html 13.3.2012
20 Extra police sent to riot-hit estate, *The Independent* 8.7.1995
21 Tossed in the fire and they never got burned: the Exodus Collective. Tim Malyon in *DiY Culture*
22 Nothing to do. No jobs. For the buzz. Dunno. Perhaps Luton's three hot nights of rioting defy reason. Polly Toynbee *The Independent* 19.7.1995
23 *Exodus: Movement of Jah People*. Video. Spectacle 1996
24 Leviticus-Timeline-banner-2010-2011.pdf (26.4.2012) http://www.leviticuscollective.co.uk

Networks of Communes

Rehearsal for an Alternative Society
Part 2

Suddenly, everyone is talking about living in communes. And, although there are far more people talking than doing, there is now a fair sprinkling of thriving communities around the country. There is talk of 'the commune movement' ...

Nicholas Saunders *Alternative London* **1970**

As the sixties turned into the seventies, the embryonic Commune Movement issued a manifesto for the creation of *A Federal Society Based on the Free Commune*. Running to thirteen sides of A4 and starting off as an article in *Communes* magazine penned by Tony Kelly, it consisted of a libertarian critique of the 'supermarket society' followed by a call to communal arms with descriptions of various forms of intentional community that readers are urged to aspire to: urban craft-based communities; rural back to the land groups; island communities; self-build country communities; and big house farming groups. Painting a realistic picture of the challenges faced by the 'Movement' it proposed a distinctly anarchist approach and ethic. 'Let us state our ethic as a federation: Everyone shall be free to do whatever he or she wishes provided only that he or she does not transgress the freedom of another. The only morality is to experience and create contentment for all of us – and species not withstanding. Such a federation is the only alternative to present dictatorship by democracy, and the growth of a federation of free communes would eventually render centralised government largely irrelevant.' Showing the movement's vegan roots it encompassed early animal liberation philosophy calling for support for 'free-range farming' and '... the contentment of animals on the same basis that we urge ours because they, like us, are sentient.' The manifesto then details the achievements so far which included the founding of the association with 'no officers, no censorship, no committee'. Decision-making was to be by balloting the whole movement and '... to prevent any possible growth of a power structure, we do not allow rejection or expulsion of any member for any reason whatsoever.' Alongside this the *Communes* magazine was coming out bi-monthly. This was seen as the bare minimum to get the movement going but was seen as still being '... a long way from a realisation of a federation of free communes'. The next step was seen as building up membership and funds and trying '... to do something to keep up morale.'

A small classified ad in the 18th June 1970 issue of *International Times* announced that Implosion was planning to hold a Communes Benefit at the Roundhouse in Chalk Farm on Sunday 2nd August. The bands lined up to play were Stray, Tree Beard, Brett Marvin & the Thunderbolts and Egg (it was also rumoured that Quintessence and the Third Ear Band might play 'Perhaps'). Implosion were also asking for communes to get in touch to let them know whether they could attend and 'set up stalls with literature, home made things.'

The idea was to have a Communes Festival followed by a benefit gig to raise funds for the Commune Movement. Up to a dozen communes responded as well as individuals active in the Commune Movement. The event was publicised as '... a big informal information-exchanging and food sharing Meal and Meeting for Communes and people interested in Communes, plus (perhaps) chanting and other signs of togetherness ...' In the event some 400 people turned up. Richard Fairfield on his tour of European communes was there.

Everything was a little disorganized, and no one knew what was supposed to happen. A free lunch of pilaff for everyone was served on sea shells from the front of the stage in the Roundhouse and from 12:45 to 3pm an impromptu band played repetitive rhythms and people chanted to incessantly pounding tribal drums. Some communes, embryonic and established, had set up stalls in order to explain themselves to the public and to possibly recruit new members. People visited these stalls or sat on the floor trying to talk with friends; others listened to the band and still others got up and danced. Scores of children danced and played on the stage in time to the band. According to the newspaper report one little girl found great joy in taking off her clothes in emulation of a girl who was not quite so little – about 15 – who had taken off hers. [1]

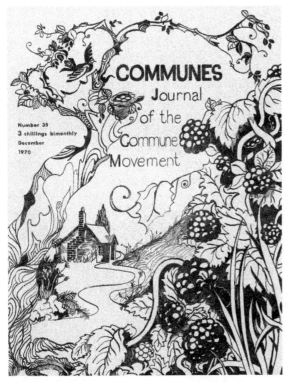

Cover of
Communes Journal No 35
December 1970

Others I have talked to who attended the event claim to recall very little of what happened. Sarah Eno who was taking over as secretary of the Movement from Nic Albery at the time recalls the two of them sitting under a table sorting out magazines, or some other paperwork, while incessant drumming came from the stage and little else. Andrew Rigby who wrote about the event in his book *Alternative Realities* remembered even less of the event today – at the time he wrote; '... Some of us felt that a great opportunity might have been missed that afternoon for groups and individuals genuinely interested in forming or joining communes, and who had never had the opportunity to meet before, to get together, discuss plans, exchange ideas, and so forth. Instead, the information-exchanging function of the Festival had somehow appeared to have been swamped by the 'signs of togetherness' aspect. We had witnessed and participated in a three-hour-long 'happening' dominated by a group around the stage playing an assortment of bongo drums, tambourines, beer cans, sticks, and anything else they could get their hands on ...' Another would-be communard who attended simply remembered seeing John Peel walking round the stalls. Roger Edwards from the Kingsway community later described it as the 'greatest 'organised chaos' ever'.

A report of the Festival appeared afterwards in the *HAPT* magazine:

'We Are Many' were among the opening words spoken at the gathering - we were many more than the representative few hundred meeting at the Roundhouse: You

sensed after the first awkward moments had passed, as the groups quickly merged into a collective of happy, dancing people, that we were not only many but strong. We were there, with our own drum, leading our own dancing ... a very expressive high-energy power which reminded us, irresistibly, that Woodstock grew from the same root of love and service – a people turning outward to each other and turning on to the earth in basic solidarity.

The article went on to report that problems occurred mid way through the afternoon when the time came to change over from the free communes festival to the paying concert that was due to follow at 3:30pm.

The problem was: how to get 400 chanting festive people out of the building and back in again, how to break up such a spontaneous expression and replace it with the benefit-spectator event. Naturally, the vibes got extremely heavy and the high of the moment turned sour. Many people left for the nearby Primrose Hill Park and elsewhere to regroup and play. The benefit concert, however, did continue and was in fact an enjoyable experience for all those who decided to participate.

The event raised £150 for movement funds and while it seems that a good time was had by all at least some of those attending thought it had been a somewhat wasted opportunity.

... It was a marvellous experience of togetherness and an expression of joy in life, movement, song, music and 'Being'; but, at the back of our minds, as we watched the people filing back into the Roundhouse, was the feeling that the whole thing had been a bit too much like some great publicity stunt for the benefit of the mass media of straight society, and to be heralded by the underground press as the Commune Movement's own equivalent to Woodstock.

Andrew Rigby, *Alternative Realities*

Cover of
Communes Journal No 43
Autumn 1973

It was not just in London that people were talking about communes. Cambridge was something of a hotbed of would-be communards as well. Long-time anarchist activist Joan Harvey ran something called the Cambridge Humanists and, in February 1970, she formed something called the Commune Services Agency (CSA). The aim was to create an organisation that would be able to help groups and individuals involved in trying to form new communes by drawing upon an existing pool of practical skills and technical knowledge. She had been running talks in Cambridge for a while, attracting a wide audience to hear the likes of scientists Francis Crick, John Kendrew and Herman Bondi, among others. She was an influence on the young Brian Eno who married her daughter Sarah in 1967 and counted Joan as one of his 'oldest friends'.

Joan, an extremely intelligent woman, said to me, I just don't understand why someone with a brain like yours wants to be an artist, the implication being, what a pointless thing to do. And it set a question going in my mind that has always stayed with me, and motivated a lot of what I've done: what does art do for people, why do people do it, why don't we only do rational things, like design better engines? And because it came from someone I very much respected, that was the foundation of my intellectual life. **2**

Brian Eno

To launch the CSA, Joan Harvey put up notices around Cambridge announcing weekly 'Communes Seminars' to be held at the Arts Lab in Portugal Place.

... Most of us who showed up were starry eyed chaotic idealists who knew that commune life was cool, liked the idea of self-sufficiency and hoped along the way to encounter 'Free Love'. Joan was amazingly quick to understand the depths of our personalities and hangups, she encouraged us to develop visions of our ideal commune and then kept asking penetrating practical and ethical questions ...

Tom Bragg, *Joan Harvey – Memorial Album*

In 1970 Patrick Boase (a young architecture graduate from Cambridge University, who had inherited a sum of money and wanted to do something creative with it), Sarah Eno and Andrew Moffat set out to found '... a rather different kind of food business' – Arjuna Wholefoods. Starting with a market stall they soon moved into premises on Mill Road in Cambridge where they squeezed in, not just a shop, but a restaurant as well.

Arjuna quickly established itself as a modestly successful business and a unique feature of Cambridge life. Pat proved to be an natural organiser, while Andrew looked after the finances. Sarah, as perhaps the most politically orientated of the three, provided much of the ideological direction, and also put considerable energy into developing the cooking. 12 Mill Road became a focus for all kinds of different groups and individuals interested in new social, political or spiritual paths. For instance, Sarah hosted Cambridge's first Women's Lib meetings upstairs, and there were also transcendental meditation classes, and, for many years, meetings of the Strawberry Fair committee. **3**

... while we were running that, it must have been a couple of years, and there was the vegetarian restaurant, there was always that fantasy oh we will get somewhere that we can grow the veg that we sell in the shop and cook in the restaurant. And we were sort of living in that household, well there weren't really very many rooms in that house. So there were probably about four or so of us in the house and Hannah. And the big front room was used a lot by, was a meeting place for everything from all sorts of leftish groups and the yoga meditation type things and women's groups in the middle of Cambridge in Mill road. So it was very much a centre of all that radical kind of thinking, new ideas and new movements ... we weren't really a commune at that stage, we were a shared household that's all and we happened to have the kitchens for the restaurant downstairs ... My mum had done a lot of the decorating at Arjuna and she'd worked there and she'd been running those communes workshops type of things. And then there was her partner Edmund who was looking for a property to start this electronics business. And Edmund and Joan and Pat and us all got on pretty well together. So it seemed sensible to combine forces and we found that place outside Cambridge at Burwell and completely fell for it because it was 15th century you know clunch chalk, just wonderful atmospheric place with a few acres of land. Pat had the money to put down the deposit to buy it ... **4**

Sarah Eno

Along with others who had been attracted to Joan Harvey's Communes Seminars, Parsonage Farm community was established at Burwell just outside Newmarket in 1971. Around this time Sarah Eno took over as Commune Movement Secretary from Nic Albery taking on the central communication role in the budding movement. During the following year she was busy answering numerous inquiries.

I have spent most my time answering letters, phone calls, Putting off the press and doing quite a lot of talks on communal living around England at various education establishments. There have been over 1,400 letters, mostly from people wanting to join a commune; a few from people willing to start one. Most of the time I have been putting people in touch with one another as much as possible. [5]

Sarah Eno

In 1971 a self-published book, *Making Communes*, by Australian theatre director Clem Gorman came out with the stated aim of filling the gap 'that exists between the ideals upon which most British communes are founded and the realities they have to face.' The book was part how-to-do-it manual with everything from maps of nationwide soil types and weather patterns, alongside advice on how to find property and DIY renovation. It also included a brief history of communes since 1965 and a survey of current communes.

It has become painfully evident that too many communal projects in this country have failed because their members expected too much too soon, or were unable to get the practical side together. Under the circumstances, and with so many books already on the market stressing the idealistic aspects of communal life, it seemed sensible to produce a book emphasising the practical.

Clem Gorman

The book was upbeat in tone throughout pointing to successful examples of communes including: the Diggers on Dornish Island; a group of Cambridge graduates sharing a house in Lambeth called the Square Pigeon Community that had been going since 1968; Braziers Park; Selene; and the recently formed Birchwood Hall in Worcestershire.

... Because the communes and communities movements are still in their infancy, their plans and possible future directions are in some ways their most important product. Communards tend to talk of the future, which may be a mistake because communal life can provide here and now what Utopians have always hoped for in the future ... They are laboratories of future ways of living, in which the experimenters are their own guinea pigs. I think they are both a response to, and a part of, the most profound revolution ever to transform society. I also believe that they constitute one of the few hopes that this revolution can be peaceful.

Clem Gorman

Communes Movement Meeting

1971 was a real year of hope for the embryonic communes movement. After the ideological euphoria and eventual dashing of hopes of the 1968 'revolutionary moment' there now seemed to be a realism and pragmatism that would lead to the establishment of a real alternative to mainstream society with communes as a crucial part of that new society. In Tony Kelly's words '... our greatest asset is each other. Let us get together. We have already begun. But we have a federation to build.' **6** The first years of the decade saw a flurry of commune-forming going on across the country. As well as Parsonage Farm and Birchwood Hall; down in Kent there were groups in Ramsgate and Rochester; in Norfolk Shrubb Family had got going on a farm at Larling; in London there were the Street Farmers and the Chapel of Isis (Trans Sex Trip) commune. Further west in Gloucestershire a group had managed to get government funding for 'shared housing' channelled through a sympathetic local authority, and bought a large medieval manor house called Postlip Hall. All these groups were up and running by the end of 1971, joined in the following year by the formation of Hoathly Hill Community, Whitbourne Hall, Trogwell and Laurieston Hall. Despite all this activity and the publishing of an annual directory of communes listing some 30 groups, Sarah Eno opens the editorial to the 1972 Communes Directory in a decidedly pessimistic mood.

"The following words will probably seem very depressing ... the ideas about communes and the interest in them has grown enormously but the actual growth of real communes has been very slow. There are many reasons why this is, but not the least of them are the practical ones of acquiring a property and perhaps some land. The ideas of the Federation Fund although very good, have not taken off very well ... England is a very overpopulated country anyway, so land and housing is in short supply and capitalist methods make hay of such a situation with the quick profits to be made from rapidly rising property prices. It is not easy, either, to build accommodation suitable for communal living since any building land is also an exorbitant price. The difficulty of raising capital, of finding compatible people free enough to make the plunge are the main hindrances to growth ..."

This mood seems to have been more frustration at the slow pace of progress than a reflection that nothing was actually happening on the ground. The steady trickle of communes being formed meant that, by the end of 1972, there was beginning to be something that might actually be called a movement with newsletters being distributed almost every month to a membership of around 200. There were also occasional Bulletins, a 'Commune Services' skills lists of members willing to volunteer their help, the *Communes Journal* was being printed bi-monthly with a staggering 3,000 print run – 600 went to subscribers and the rest were sold in shops. The 1971 *Communes Directory* sold a thousand copies in nine months.

**Fire-Air-Water-Earth Comix
1974**

Squat Now While Stocks Last

A big boost to the counter-culture and increase in communal living came through the growth in the early 1970's of the squatting movement in London and further afield. Growing very quickly from the London Squatters' movement in the late 60's and driven by a mini-boom in house prices (latched onto by developers and landlords who started to realise that they could get more money from selling their properties than they could from renting them). Added to this, a shortage of council housing and, in some boroughs, huge numbers of houses being kept empty by councils because they were 'awaiting redevelopment', it's unsurprising that increasing numbers of people decided to turn to squatting. By the end of 1973 it was estimated that there were 15,000 people squatting in the capital. Many of these were individual families, but often squats were set up as communal households for single people and young couples who would not qualify for council housing anyway. Very quickly some councils started to come to arrangements with various squatter-based organisations to allow buildings to be occupied on short-term licences which permitted the use of a house until the council needed it. This meant that the council avoided getting into confrontation and potentially costly court cases. Nearly half of all London boroughs reached licensing arrangements with local squatting groups. This 'short-life' housing provided some measure of security for the squatters and existed alongside the 'unofficial' squatting movement. This combination of circumstances enabled a mushrooming of squatting in the following couple of years. The estimated peak was reached when between 40,000 and 50,000 people were involved in squatting in one way or another by mid-1975. Squatting solved the problem of the exorbitant price of property which had been identified by the Commune Movement – a whole range of properties now came into use by part of the counter-culture through squatting. There were squatted houses of all shapes and sizes, shops, workshops, music venues, artists' studios, cafes, allotments, city farms, bookshops, women's centres ... There was the infamous 'Ruff Tuff Creem Puff Squatters Estate Agents' who enabled 'viewings' of potential squattable properties. There were repair teams that you could call out who would teach you how to repair services and fix leaks in the roof. There were telephone trees to prevent evictions. In some places whole streets and neighbourhoods were given a new lease of life by squatter communities. One of the first of these was in the streets surrounding Prince of Wales Crescent in Camden, an area awaiting redevelopment and where, by 1972, there were some 280 mainly young people squatting.

... Having been empty for up to seven years the houses were fairly derelict and conditions were primitive. Skills such as wiring or plumbing had to be self-taught and shared with people less able to do it. The increased leisure time available to people who often chose to live on low incomes enabled them to do more for themselves. It also allowed people to experiment and put ideas into practice.

Squatting – The Real Story

The place became a hive of alternative community enterprise. Workshops were set up; electronics, engineering, silk-screening, jewellery and carpentry. One derelict plot was turned into a park with tree-houses, a sand pit, paddling pool and café. All sorts of community activities took place: musical events and barbecues; two community newspapers were started; and a crèche begun. Squatted premises and those licensed by Camden Council provided shelter to a long list of groups

Squatters — Top to Bottom
Bracknell Communal Squat (in Berkshire);
Kingston-on-Thames Squat; Bishops Avenue Squat;
Cornwall Terrace Squat (all in London)

from The London Film Makers Co-op; The Guild of African Master Drummers; The Centre for Advanced Television Studies – a nationwide information centre for video users; right through to Community Supplies – a cheap organic food shop where customers weighed, packed and priced their own goods which was so successful it branched out into bulk supplies.

Almost everyone lived in shared or communal houses, often because the houses couldn't easily be divided into self-contained flats, but sometimes for more positive reasons. One person enthusiastically endorsed communal living as a response to 'the adverse psychological effects of individuals living alone - neurosis, depression, alienation — which can in extreme cases lead to psychosis and general personality breakdown. People in this area have learnt from bitter experience and have set about changing their circumstances – hence the development of community spirit. None of the residents have any desire to return to the isolation of a bedsitter.

Squatting – The Real Story

Leaflets produced at the time talk of the area being a 'decentralised urban self-managed community'; of a 'green revolution in the city'; of finding 'new ways of human interrelationships'; and of building a 'new culture from the pieces of the old'. Day-to-day reality didn't always live up to these grand ideals with the area attracting others who didn't share the same libertarian ideas. There were regular problems with drug addicts, alcoholics and thieves which led the squatters to set up their own forms of self-help community care. A Mental Patients Union was set up that provided a crisis centre for people with mental health problems. There was a group that helped those with drug dependency and an innovative community work directory was established which enabled the unemployed to develop new skills.

In December 1973 the Prince of Wales Residents Association was set up and an attempt made to persuade the Council to shelve its redevelopment plans and let the community stay to retain and reinforce its identity. 'It is a genuine organic community. Planners are searching desperately to produce this phenomenon in new estates, so far without success. Prince of Wales

Crescent is an excellent example of what people can do if left to their own devices.' An alternative plan was drawn up. Houses could be rehabilitated on a self-help basis costing between £300 and £3,000 per dwelling compared with £9,000 for new build – saving £½ million. A further £300,000 could be saved by turning the street into open space instead of knocking down houses to make one. Mixed uses could be allowed to continue instead of providing just housing and 'turning a socially mixed area into another desert like council development where the inhabitants are socially homogeneous.' And more people would be housed because the density could remain at 180 persons per acre instead of being reduced to 125 persons as laid down in government rule books for redevelopment. The squatters suggested that the Council should see the area as an environment for experimenting with ways of living, and that it should actually take a positive interest in its growth. But the Council was not up to the challenge and rejected the squatters plan and eventually the squatters were evicted.

Squatting – The Real Story

There were other counter-culture squatter enclaves dotted around London where similar patterns of community evolved; Elgin Avenue in Maida Vale; Tolmers Village off the Euston Road; St Agnes Place, Kennington and Villa Road in Brixton. People moved from one place to another, from squat to squat, from commune to commune, commune to squat. Some people who had lived at Eel Pie Island commune were involved in squatting houses in Grosvenor Road in Twickenham. Houses on both sides of the street were squatted and between 1972 and 1976 a social and communal network evolved involving at one time some 128 people.

... There was no leadership, only influence. Each house had it's own character. Some were run like conventional households, where one might have to knock on the front door to enter. Some were like blocks of flats where the front door was wide open, and one would have to knock on the door of the room they wanted to enter. Some were just wide open to anyone and everyone. I think most people probably had access, one way or another, to most of the rooms in the street ...

www.grosvenor-road.co.uk

During these years the squatting movement and the counter-culture provided both physical shelter and relatively tolerant spaces for the emerging gay and lesbian liberation movements. Those involved in the Gay Liberation Front (GLF) also found communal living to provide not only a cheap way to live but also a supportive community. The early GLF had its own Communes Group which met weekly at a commune in Penge.

Greetings from Grosvenor Road squat

Communal living was another imported aspect of GLF and a general feature of the counter-culture; the idea was that by living with a number of others who shared everything, the barriers of capitalist society would be broken and new forms of social structure would emerge.

No Bath But Plenty of Bubbles

There were other gay communal set-ups in Colville Terrace in Kensington,

in Railton Road in Brixton (home of the Brixton Fairies Theatre group) and in the old Agitprop bookshop in Bethnal Green where a group calling themselves Bethnal Rouge lived.

The story of squatter communities during the seventies is largely one of resistance and eventual eviction and defeat for the squatters' alternative plans. Except, that is, for one or two instances where the squatters outfoxed councils and developers. One such case is the tale of 'The Free and Independent Republic of Frestonia' – a squatter community which had grown up in the Freston Road, Bramley Road and Shalfleet Drive area. Despite opposition from local residents (as well as the squatters) the GLC proposed to bulldoze the area in order to build a giant industrial estate. As an initial tactic the 120 or so squatters all adopted the same surname – Bramley – in an attempt to have the council rehouse them collectively as one big family. Following a trip to Copenhagen (where he visited Christiania – the 'free city' in a squatted army camp), Nic Albery suggested that the area declare independence from Great Britain. A referendum was carried out and there was a 94% vote in favour. So, on October 27th 1977 a declaration of independence was sent to the Queen and an application made to join the United Nations. Warning that there may well be need for UN peacekeeping troops '... to keep the imperialistic 'GLC' from invading our country.'

It turned out to be a tactic worth recommending to any neighbourhood threatened by bureaucracy. The 'GLC' suddenly started to sit up and take notice. Their spokesman told the press they had a lot of sympathy for us – which was certainly news to us – and that they would talk to us 'in the United Nations or wherever'. The 'GLC' leader, Sir Horace Cutler, wrote a typically quirky letter ending 'if you didn't exist it would be necessary to invent you' ... to which we replied 'since we do exist, why is it necessary to destroy us?' [7]

Nic Albery

The new nation promptly had designed a coat of arms with the motto 'Nos sumus una familia', 'We are one family' emblazoned on it. Everyone who wanted to was invited to become a minister (there was no prime minister). Two-year-old Francesco Bogina-Bramley became the Minister of State for Education; the dwarf actor David Rappaport-Bramley was made the Minister of State for Foreign Affairs (resplendent in a 'Small is Beautiful' t-shirt; the poet playwright Heathcote Williams-Bramley served as the Ambassador to Great Britain; and Nic Albery-Bramley was variously 'British Ambassador', 'Minister of State for Industry' and 'Minister of State for the Environment'. A set of postage stamps was designed (honoured by the post office) and, following an invitation to readers by the London *Evening Standard*, no less than three national anthems were composed. In the first year they established the Frestonian National Theatre in the People's Hall on the corner of Freston Road and held the London premiere of Heathcote William's play *The Immortalist*. This was followed by the Frestonian National Film Institute, which opened with the odd combination of Passport to Pimlico and a film of the Sex Pistols. There was also an art gallery called The Car Breaker Gallery. The world's media beat a path to Frestonia's borders eager to cover the story of the plucky little micro-nation fighting against the goliath of the GLC. Television crews arrived from Japan and New Zealand to film '... nothing much going on in our uneventful communal garden.' The *Daily Mail* printed a report 'from our Foreign

Correspondent in Frestonia'. Tourists started to turn up for a five-minute tour of the country's borders and to have their passports stamped.

We were suddenly transformed in the GLC's eyes from a bunch of squatters, hobos and drug addicts into an international incident that was providing them with an opportunity to show how enlightened they were and threatening them with the prospect of negative media coverage if they carried on with their plans to evict us. A public enquiry was ordered. The GLC had their QC, and I represented Frestonia as the Minister of State for the Environment. We proposed that Frestonia become a mixed used site for houses and craft workshops. We won the enquiry ... **8**

Nic Albery

The Bramleys Housing Co-operative was set up and through the Notting Hill Housing Trust a scheme was developed whereby 'several millions of pounds of foreign aid from Great Britain' could be 'channelled into Frestonia'. The result was a thriving local community being able to have a real say in the redevelopment of its neighbourhood.

Perhaps the most high profile squatting action of the era took place in January 1974 when a group of housing activists from the Family Squatting Advisory Service staged a spectacular publicity coup by squatting one of the best-known empty buildings in Britain. Centre Point Tower at the junction of Oxford Street and Tottenham Court Road had stood empty since it was built in 1963. The occupation had taken months of planning and had involved infiltration of the firm supplying security guards. For two days the squatters held the tower, attracting front page newspaper coverage for their demand that the building be requisitioned by the Council to house the homeless. The protesters received a great deal of support and when they left the building they were greeted by a rally of 3,000 people. Camden Council did later attempt to compulsorily purchase 24 luxury flats at the rear of Centre Point – an action quashed by the Law Lords but most of the building remained empty until 1980.

One of those involved in the organisation of the Centre Point occupation was a young solicitor, Trevor Howell, who had been working for the squatting movement in London. He was concerned that squatting did not offer any long-term solution to the housing crisis and offered no security to those who found themselves homeless. With his partner Cath he decided to try and set up a group that would look to offer people with little or no financial resources a stable, more permanent, self-help solution to the housing problem than could be offered by squatting. Echoing the legal term 'tenants in common' he called the group People In Common. After a number of meetings, which attracted a mixed bunch of squatters and others interested in communal living, a search of the country was carried out by some of the members hitch-hiking from town-to-town looking for areas with cheap housing where they might set up the new community. One lift ended in Burnley in Lancashire where property prices were so low that the group could hardly believe them. They bought a terraced house in a clearance area and the first members moved in. Legally it was still only possible for a maximum of four individuals to own a property and the nearest thing to any sort of communal ownership was either some kind of trust or to use the rather cumbersome and bureaucratic legal structure of a housing association. The 1968 Housing Act had introduced the potential for collective ownership, but the model rules drawn up by housing associations had clauses that were either irrelevant or inappropriate to most communal groups, for instance requiring separate kitchens for the various members and management by committee. Trevor Howell set himself the task of creating a co-operative fully democratic legal structure whereby a group of people could own property on an equal basis with the minimum of legalese and bureaucracy. Starting with basic Housing Association Rules he entered into protracted correspondence with the Registrar of Friendly Societies sending in the most minimal set of rules that he thought might be acceptable to the authorities and having them sent back with comments that this or that wasn't covered, or some other section was still not acceptable. It was Howell's view that the purpose of a legal structure was not only to set out how you wanted to work together, but to protect you from the State taking arbitrary decisions about how it wanted to treat you. There were others concerned about the problems of individual ownership of communal properties. Dave Treanor had been involved in a number of communal projects in London and had seen the problem from both ends of the spectrum. At a communal house in Dartmouth Park Road (DPR) he discovered the insecurity of individual ownership.

... I lived there for a couple of years, and we ran it as a co-operative. We understood that the only reason it was not set up legally as a co-op was that they could not raise a mortgage that way. But after the rapid rise in house prices in the early seventies, the two owners decided to exercise their ownership rights. They declared that the project was no longer the project they originally intended and that consequently they would sell the house and pocket the profits ... **9**

Dave Treanor

He then moved into another house nearby where he found himself on the other end of the stick becoming something of a surrogate landlord:

Dragon was a co-operative set up at 37 Bickerton Road by people who lived at DPR, as a similar communal house that nobody would own. I was one of the nominal owners, and Martin Solity was the other. Martin fell out with his girlfriend at DPR and in a very depressed state moved into the house before the building work commenced, and then invited a load of local squatters to move in there with him. Even though I was the other owner and founder member, I had no say in who had moved in ... I had borrowed the money for the purchase and the building works in my own name from friends and a bank and a building society, but the people squatting it obstructed the builders, who were disturbing their occupation of the house. It was a nightmare. **10**

Dave Treanor

With a new baby daughter Dave and his wife Carol decided that they couldn't move into this chaotic set-up and eventually joined a group who were setting up a commune in south west Scotland with plans for it to become an alternative conference centre – Laurieston Hall. The Bickerton Road property saga would drag on for years involving court cases, dry rot, compulsory purchase orders, and rent tribunals. The experience led to Dave helping to organising a conference on 'Legal Frameworks for Communes and Self-Managed Projects' at Laurieston in May 1974. The result of the conference was the production of a *Legal Frameworks Handbook* put together by several people from Laurieston Hall with advice and contributions from Robin Fielder of Rad-Tech in Sheffield, Trevor Howell and others. The handbook set out the legal options for anyone wanting to set up a 'commune', 'community', 'co-operative' or 'collective'. With a set of case histories as examples it had explanations of the various forms of legal structure available to groups, notes on raising money and a section on 'internal' things that people would probably need to agree. While trying to be a practical handbook and avoid ideological discussions, a statement in the introduction outlines where the authors saw the politics of the frameworks they were advocating:

The world is in a horrible mess. Capitalism is a main culprit. The whole system needs changing. In particular, private ownership of property will have to go. We know all this. You may think (as we do) that each new commune is a helpful, if tiny, step towards change. But as things stand you'll be setting up inside the (state-) capitalist framework – or not at all. Which means that somewhere along the line there'll be a compromise ... we found that there are simple, standard ways to set up, but these have problems for communards; and there are other possibilities, which may overcome the problems, but which aren't tried and tested. If you want to do it the simple way – accepting the known problems – fine. But we hope that more and more groups will experiment with the other possibilities.

Legal Frameworks Handbook 1975

Printed at the back of the booklet were Trevor Howell's newly registered set of minimalist Fully Mutual Housing Co-operative rules that had finally been agreed. Howell had persuaded the Registrar to accept that a small housing co-operative could manage its affairs without a committee, with the membership as a whole taking responsibility, and practically no restrictions on how they structured their living arrangements. People In Common would distribute Gestetnered copies to anyone interested for the price of postage. These rules were used by many groups who set up during the 1970's and 80's, sometimes with minor variations, and groups who had set up under other legal arrangements also used them to transfer from individual to collective ownership of their property. They were later used as the basis of model rules by the National Federation of Housing Co-operatives and by Catalyst Collective. They were also taken by Malcolm Lynch and used to formulate a set of model rules for worker co-operatives for the Industrial Common Ownership Movement (ICOM). Trevor Howell died in a motorbike accident in 1976. At the time he was working on ideas for an alternative building society that would lend to communes.

While some were busy focussing on legal structures for the new emerging alternative, some groups saw themselves as experimenting with both the hard and soft technologies that would be needed in the future, forming a sort of research & development wing for the alternative society. Robin Clarke, editor of the *Science Journal* (later merged with *New Scientist*) had written a proposal in the second issue of *Undercurrents* magazine in May 1972 for a Soft Technology Research Community Project.

... the aim of soft technology is usually stated as follows; to make possible a lifestyle which is compatible with long-term ecological stability. However, the theory can be developed in a way in which an ecologically based and decentralist technology is used as the foundation of an alternative society ... what are needed are centres where all the implications of soft technology can be practised and assessed simultaneously ...

By the following year a definite group of people interested in making the proposal a reality had evolved and by April 1973 they had started sending out reports of progress from Biotechnic Research And Development, known as BRAD for short. The group had bought a 43-acre hill farm, Eithin y Gaer, in Wales and set about building a purpose built 'soft technology' house. This was to include: solar collectors on the roof; a Twin Savonius (oil drum) wind turbine; rainwater recycling; a Jotul woodstove; and a 'swedish' compost loo.

They hoped that for '… about £1,000 per head we shall be occupying and powering, in no mean style, some twenty souls (to be doubled by a later project) on just 43 acres of Min of Ag Grade IV Welsh hillside.' The community consisted of eight adults and three children and it took just over 15 months to build the house. Unfortunately, lack of funds meant that much of the experimental technology had to be put on hold for a while and the group began to focus on self-sufficient farming and the dynamics of communal life. This led to something of a split in the group, resulting in Robin Clarke leaving. He said afterwards that his reason for leaving was a clash of ideas and ideals between those in the commune like himself who thought that the community would be forged by concentrating on the self-sufficiency aspects and the others who considered that the problems of communal living should be tackled first. By the end of 1974 the group had dropped the grand sounding Biotechnic Research & Development tag and were simply calling themselves Eithin y Gaer after the farm and stating that they were 'No longer a soft technology research outfit organised as a commune; we're a commune, not organised, who happen to do some AT research.' The group carried on for another couple of years with a changing but slowly dwindling membership until numbers dropped so low that it was not viable to continue managing a 43-acre hill farm. At this point the remaining members decided to call it a day and the farm was sold for £50,000 to an Ashram of four painters and a potter from Kent. In a final article in *Undercurrents* 16 under the title 'BRAD: The End' members expressed sadness at the final outcome, but reflected that '… everybody seems to have learnt a great deal from the experience and nobody regrets joining.' One member's final comment was 'No flowers, please'.

We each entered the commune with a fantasy; not in the sense of mad delusions, but a well-worked-out scenario of expectations. For a time you project, superimposing your fantasy upon unfolding reality; until the scene diverges dramatically from one's personal script: your wife walks out; the newborn calf dies; the windmill fails to work; your husband sleeps with the woman downstairs; the barley crop rots. Then you either freak out completely, adjust your fantasy, or draw a deep breath and begin to grow up … the essential message from here seems to be that building a solar roof, one's own house even, is child's play compared with close, honest, open communal living.

Philip Brachi in *Undercurrents* 14 Feb/Mar 1976

BRAD were not the only ones trying to pioneer a sustainable alternative. In the autumn of 1972 a charity had been registered under the name of The Society for Environmental Improvement Ltd. Its patrons included Lord Annan provost of University College London; former chairman of National Coal Board, Lord Robens; and Home Secretary Roy Jenkins. Chairman of the directors was Gerard Morgan-Grenville, tasked with carrying out the charity's objectives which were to act as a link organisation between big business and the environmental movement.

… I set about trying to get some funds, and as you know I got some. Then we spent about a year just looking at the whole environmental problem and trying to see what we could do that was not being done by anyone else and which could be done on the sort of money that we had and the sort of skills which we might be able to obtain. Everything fell into place suddenly and this centre was born as an idea and very shortly afterwards in practice as a project.

Gerard Morgan-Grenville in *Undercurrents* 8 1974

With £50,000 from an anonymous backer in his pocket, Morgan-Grenville came across the 40-acre disused Llwyngwern slate quarry a few miles from Machynlleth in central Wales. It was here, amid a collection of derelict buildings surrounded by piles of slate waste and overgrown with birch trees and rhododendrons, that he proposed to set up the 'National Centre for Alternative Technology' as an experimental community working towards a more ecological lifestyle. Things took a while to get going ... after disagreements with Morgan-Grenville the first full-time director of the project quit in 1973 scarcely before they had started. But word spread fast about the project and it was not long before more than 20 people, including ten children, were living on the site busying themselves with rebuilding ruined buildings, getting gardens going on the slate piles with no natural soil and working out ways to generate their own electricity. These early pioneers where described as an amazing mix of 'ecologists, primitivists, disgruntled academics and, most importantly, pragmatists.'

The project attracted casual visitors – interested in the work they were doing – from the start and this grew until it was seen that this could provide an income to support the research and development that they wanted to do. Interest in the work spread not just in alternative circles, but through Morgan-Grenville's contacts to the upper echelons of English society with Prince Phillip being given a tour in 1974. The group's aim was to create a new form of sustainable rural community which would experiment with alternative technologies and ways of life, and to disseminate the results through writing, teaching, and demonstration projects.

There's a crying need for masses of institutions like this one, where people can actually get together and show how you can have a better life, We've had person after person here, people from the entire social spectrum who've said. Thank goodness we've found a place where it's happening – where people are doing things, where they've actually got off their backsides and they're up against real life-sized problems, whether it be knocking nails into a piece of wood or getting on with each other.

Gerard Morgan-Grenville in

Undercurrents 8 1974

Top to Bottom
BRAD under construction,
Members of CAT, Meal at CAT

Communal living was seen as an integral part of this sustainable way of life and the Centre has been consistently listed in community directories throughout its existence.

We all have our own private dwellings – most being renovated slate workers' cottages. These are well insulated and have some form of solar power. We have also recently erected a 'self build' Walter Segal house. We have a community house and meet here for our vegetarian meals. There is a rota for cooking, breadmaking and cleaning. We try to grow as much of our own organic produce as possible and have a few chickens and goats. Our decision-making is done on a consensus basis and we are all paid an equal salary. Our areas of work include engineering, building, gardening, bookshop, restaurant, office and educational work.

Entry in *Diggers & Dreamers* 90-91

From modest beginnings that opened to the public in 1975 (a small permanent exhibition explaining the group's work over the years) the centre has grown to be a major Welsh visitor attraction (it dropped the 'National' tag along the way and is now simply known as the Centre for Alternative Technology or CAT for short). By its 30th anniversary it was attracting in the region of 65,000 visitors a year and was run by 90 permanent staff and volunteers. While the site has been transformed, with new buildings, a shop, ecocabins, a cliff railway and exhibitions revamped on numerous occasions, attracting a wider and possibly less radical audience, the group itself has retained much of its original ethos and ambition.

... premature attempts to create alternative social, economic and technical organisation for production can contribute in a significant way to the achievement of political conditions that will finally allow them to be fully implemented. These premature development projects can both act as motivating 'utopias', thus aiding and stimulating the transition, and also help sort out some of the practical problems, whether at the level of technology or communal organisation.

Peter Harper in *Undercurrents* 6

The influence of CAT on the local area has been significant, not only by providing direct employment, but also incubating a number of spin-off businesses. In recent years CAT has undergone further transformation, culminating with the opening of the Wales Institute for Sustainable Education (WISE), housed in a specially designed eco-building. This provides classrooms, a multi-purpose hall, an auditorium and twenty-odd rooms for students. They have also been instrumental in producing the *Zero Carbon Britain 2030* plan to eliminate the UK's emissions from fossil fuels.

... Dropping out to build a better world has given way to the challenge of developing ideas, tools and technologies which will inspire, inform and enable mainstream society to join the process of sustainable development.

Paul Allen, CAT Director 2010

The Movement is Dead, Long Live the Network

While squatting was booming and some communards were busying themselves with sorting out legal structures and experimenting with appropriate new technologies, the Commune Movement itself was not in very good shape. As early as August 1971 at a Movement gathering at Parsonage Farm there had been discussions on the future structure of the movement and its relationship with the 'alternative society'. Regionalisation had been tried with different secretaries for each region, with little success. By 1972 Bob Matthews had taken over as first secretary and, in an effort to resolve disagreements about the way forward, a 'Commune Movement Reorganisation Committee' was set up. This group issued a first report in the June 1972 *Commune Movement Newsletter,* suggesting partial revisions to the Movement's constitution. This led to further argument and accusations of attempted 'takeovers' of the movement, all played out in the pages of the *Communes Journal* and *Newsletter,* with writers taking radically different views on the subject.

> *... Your course is set and another chance to really alter our way of life is already lost. Wait, be patient. Don't rush into a constitution like rats needing a cage, let a structure, a dynamic relational structure develop. It will, but not if you rush into bureaucracy. Trust those forces of nature you're always talking about. You don't need a constitution: a constitution means we don't trust each other. If anyone tries to 'fine' or 'punish' me I'll kick them in the bum. I'm a free man, I don't need a cage, Fuck constitutions.*

Clem Gorman in Communes Journal 40 December 1972

The row rumbled on into the following year, with accusations of ballot rigging, of the publication of an 'unauthorised' issue of the *Journal* (Issue 42) which was only resolved by Nic Albery stepping in and regularising the 'unofficial' journal with a ballot, but as one newsletter writer put it '... not before considerable bad feeling and chaos had virtually split the movement.' This eventually led to a number of members, including Tony Kelly of Selene, resigning their membership and issuing stark warnings about the Movement's future.

> *... I doubt whether (the Movement) will survive in effective form another year. With ... Bob Matthews' cynical reliance on members' apathy and susceptibility to his 'sales talk' ... when the Movement is pushed aside so blatantly by one entrepreneur, the movement is virtually dead and wishful thinking will not stop Bob's finally killing it ...*

Tony Kelly in Commune Movement Newsletter 90 2nd July 1973

During 1973 problems came to a head. The *Journal* was getting into financial difficulties, proving expensive to produce and was seen as too infrequent to be useful to people seeking a community to join. There were further financial problems in 1974, and the secretary had stopped replying to letters. There seems to have been almost a correlation between the increasing activity in actual formation of communes and a decrease in enthusiasm for the Movement itself with reluctance among communes to host a *Journal* production weekend. A meeting was organised to resolve the situation in Aston, Birmingham at the home of The Gorilla Family on February 15th and 16th 1975. Those attending the meeting decided that the Movement had run its course – at least for them – and that they would set up a looser 'Network' that better suited their needs. Bob Matthews reported back the outcome of the meeting in the next *CM Newsletter*.

CM is dead, Long live CN! – not exactly an accurate statement of the results of our meeting, but likely to be near enough in practice. About 30 of us gathered over the weekend and, we surprised ourselves that so many came to concern themselves with the moribund CM. It was a peculiar meeting and a very fruitful one. No secretaries came, there was no protocol nor tradition to follow. Nobody could have foretold the outcome. But over the course of the weekend we evolved a leaderless consensus style and came to some harmonious decisions. What did CM need? To be revived or buried? We decided to bury; then resurrect ...

Bob Matthews' report of the meeting, *CM Newsletter* 104 14th March 1975

The report went on to outline how the new Communes Network would differ from the Commune Movement. It was to be more modest in its aims; supporting 'the spread of communes generally' and no longer aspiring towards what was referred to as the 'grandiose federal society based on the free commune'. The Network was to have 'no constitution' and decisions were to be taken by consensus. It was intended to stop production of the *Communes Journal* and instead run a bi-monthly supplement in *Peace News* as a 'shop window' for communes and to produce an internal newsletter, with Clive Semmens from Trogwell in Bradford volunteering to be newsletter co-ordinator. A new directory of communes was planned and there was a proposal to create the role of 'Info honk' – a person or group who would run an info-bank collecting, sorting and disseminating info relevant to communes and collectives. Although Bob Matthews did point out that this was 'really another name for the first secretary, although nobody at the meeting said so'. Matthews went on to invite anyone who felt so inclined to 'try to breathe life back into the corpse' of the old Movement.'

The news of the imminent demise of the Commune Movement that he had helped to create so incensed Tony Kelly that he single-handedly attempted to revive it. This was despite the fact that he was no longer a member – having resigned two years before. He put out a further *CM Newsletter* No 105 in July 1975 in which he stated 'I'm not a member of the Commune Movement because there seems no-one willing to accept applications for membership. I've sent no subscription or envelopes to anyone, for who would receive them if the newsletter coordinator would not? I've declared myself secretary because no one else did. And I'm going to rebuild the Commune Movement because no one else could.' He went on to make a passionate plea for the continuation of the Movement saying that somewhere along the way the Movement had degenerated into a centralist structure 'while loudly proclaimed otherwise', and had 'tied itself in a tangle of red tape, and that we must untangle.' He wished the new Network well and there was mutual goodwill between Kelly and Clive Semmens co-ordinating the new *Communes Network Newsletter*, although Kelly could not see that the Communes Network would succeed where the Commune Movement had failed. But the writing was on the wall for the Commune Movement and although Tony Kelly carried on for a few more months, the last *CM Newsletter* appears to have come out on 7th October 1975.

Very quickly the new communes organisation produced its first newsletter, *Network* 1. Right from the very first words the difference in emphasis from the 'old' Movement was clear.

The main aim of this Network is to bring us all closer together as friends. We're trying to get to know each other, so what we're after is not a mammoth effort, once and for all, a condensed, impersonal account of your grand plan: it's an ongoing account of what you're actually doing, newsletter by newsletter, just the bits you'd write in a short note to old friends – which is what it is.

Network 1, 14 March 1975

The aims of the Communes Network were set out as simply to encourage the growth of communes and collectives, and to do this through a monthly newsletter, a directory of communes and other booklets on matters relating to collectives.

The new communes organisation issued a press release:

COMMUNES NETWORK has been set up at a meeting of 30 active members of the Commune Movement. The emphasis of Communes Network will be to serve our own needs as communes and, where we can, to encourage and support people setting up their own living or work collectives. We will all contribute (ideas, activities, or just gossip) to a monthly newsletter so that we keep in closer touch with each other. And we are hoping to write a regular column in Peace News to pass on news of what we're doing to those working for social change in other ways ...

... We feel all of these will give us better communications than the Journal, which had become the main activity of the Commune Movement. The Network has no 'constitution'. Responsibility for making sure it does something useful will stay with each individual member. We expect to meet at least annually to discuss how we're doing – perhaps reorganise – and have a good time.

Communes Network Press Release

The new *Communes Network* newsletter was produced enthusiastically in the early days – initially on a monthly basis but eventually settling down to coming out quarterly. Decisions on direction for the movement, when they were needed, were taken at occasional gatherings – or 'readers meetings' – which were open to all commune members and newsletter subscribers. There were a whole range of different communities that went to make up the network, most of whom had been set up in the first half of the 1970's. Groups both urban and rural inhabiting all sorts of different buildings. Each had its own particular political, spiritual or philosophical emphasis, or none, but despite the differences there was some sense of a broad commonality and a feeling among members that they were part of an emerging alternative. Communes Network became the rather more relaxed organisational core, and semi-public face of communes for the rest of the 70's and beyond. Its loose organisation and 'friendly' ethos being both its strength and sometimes its weakness.

Observers of the Commune Movement, and indeed members,may be forgiven the conclusion that the Movement has at last laid down its weary head to die, and that its function as a catalyst for social change has been taken over by other groups. What in fact has happened is that its original fairies-and-magic-mushrooms pitch has become very frayed at the edges and given way to a much more realistic assessment of its role in society and what it represents to its members.

Geoff Crowther in *International Times* 1st June 1975
reprinted from *BIT Better* 13

The formation of Communes Network gave the communities movement a new lease of life. Instead of what had seemed like endless internal wrangling between fewer and fewer people, regular newsletters were once more appearing; a monthly communities column was coming out in *Peace News;* and there was renewed debate in alternative papers about the role of communes in creating a radical alternative. In a double page spread in *International Times* in June 1975 Geoff Crowther provided both a critique of communes and suggestions for effective ways forward. Against a background of rising fuel prices he called for the movement to be 'realistic about their function as agents of social change', to make common cause with those calling for radical change in the industrial sector and not to retreat into rural isolationism.

Any attempt to construct a modern tribal society must anchor itself in something more realistic than a simple withdraw into the hills, half waiting for the holocaust to destroy modern society. It is just too naive to imagine that a major social and political crisis is going to bypass alternative structures, including rural communes. It may well be that 'self-sufficient' groups will be able to survive intact for a period of months and they might even be in a better position with regard to getting things moving again ...

Geoff Crowther

He went on to call for a wider vision of regional self-sufficiency that would be a 'necessary step in combating the total dependence which most people have on the consumer society.' and ended with a quick tour of the initiatives that were already underway that he saw as steps in the right direction. These included Laurieston Hall who had held a two month 'Alternative University' the previous year and were running adventure holiday breaks for children from Glasgow 'as well as all the usual self-sufficiency activities ...' In Sheffield he pointed to the Rad Tech in Pact group who were publishing *In the Making* – a directory of proposed productive projects in self-management or alternative technology and people who wanted to start or work in them. *In the Making* didn't just cover communal set-ups, but a whole range of projects from worker co-ops, eco-communities, community science projects, through to profiles of would-be alternative engineers and entrepreneurs. Combined with self-funding mechanisms like the Community Levy on Alternative Projects (or CLAP Tax) run by BIT, which asked successful projects to tithe up to 4% of their gross income in order to fund further projects, it was hoped that there was now a springboard for the alternative society to shake off its aura of hippy-dippy idealism and build, as one group put it, a 'reproducable alternative to industrial and agricultural wage slavery.' **11**

In November 1975 the opening film at the British Film Festival at the National Film Theatre was *Winstanley* by Kevin Brownlow and Andrew Mollo. It was the tale of 17th Century social reformer and writer Gerrard Winstanley and the original Diggers who had tried to establish a self-sufficient farming community on common land at St George's Hill near Cobham in Surrey. The film based on the 1961 David Caute novel *Comrade Jacob* was made with a limited budget and with a largely amateur cast – including Sid Rawle and his Hyde Park Diggers in the roles of a band of Civil War libertarian Ranters. Two weeks after the festival on December 2nd there was a free showing of the film for 'the Alternative Society Diggers, Squatters and Communards'.

International Times
June 1975

In many places communal groups made up part of a countercultural jigsaw that consisted of: wholefood shops; cafés and restaurants; radical bookshops; 'head' shops; bands and music venues; local alternative papers and magazines; plus arts, theatre, film and video groups. These were alongside a whole host of different little groups holding meetings about: women's liberation, gay liberation, mental health issues, organic gardening, eastern spirituality, astrology, macrobiotics, animal rights – as well as more conventional political meetings. While looking for imaginative alternatives to what mainstream political groups were offering there was also an emphasis on 'community action' – of getting involved in very local campaigns; and supporting ordinary people in fighting for their rights or against threats to their communities from developers or local councils. A revised and revamped version of Clem Gorman's *Making Communes* book also saw the light of day in 1975 – this time published by a mainstream publisher, Paladin, under the new title *People Together: A Guide to Communal Living*. In the introduction Gorman talked of the 'widening' of the communes movement over the past five years, of the movement being more than just oppositional to mainstream society, of it being 'fused with the movement for popular community development in the large cities.' He went on to put forward the view that with the development of community politics a whole new role for communes could open up as community action centres '... if they will only be aware of it and accept it.'

In Swindon an organisation called The Foundation for Alternatives had put forward a proposal to the local council to rent one of the farms that the council had purchased for the future expansion of the town and to use it as a place to study new approaches to urban development. With a one-year renewable lease and a grant from the Gulbenkian Foundation they took over Lower Shaw Farm and employed Dick Kitto as warden. Kitto had just finished running a joint project between Dartington Hall School (where he had been secretary to the headmaster) and Northcliffe Comprehensive School in south Yorkshire. He had run, what amounted to, a 'free school' within the education system for 15 boys that the school saw as troublemakers, and who had to stay in education for another year due to the pending raising of the school leaving age. 'After three terms of discussions, caring for the buildings and grounds, practical work to make money, frequent expeditions, drama and help with literacy, the boys became confident, responsible and articulate.' **12**

Kitto's work at Northcliffe caught the attention of Stan Windlass – a member of The Foundation for Alternatives – who had been working for a children's rights centre in London. In his work he had become aware of several families who were educating their own children. It was through Windlass that Kitto was recruited for the job in Swindon. One of the first projects instigated at Lower Shaw between 1975 and 1976 was an informal network to support families who were educating their children at home. In 1976 Granada Television made a programme about the group, after which they received around 200 enquiries and the membership expanded to over 50. At a meeting in September 1976 it was decided that a more formal structure for the group was needed and 'Education Otherwise' was formed, taking their name from the Education Act, which states that parents are responsible for their children's education: 'either by regular attendance at school or otherwise'. The following year the group was featured in a BBC2 *Open Door* programme about the ideas behind the organisation. This resulted in a flood of over 2,000 new enquiries and a further increase in membership to around 250. Education Otherwise has evolved from its small beginnings into a large self-help organisation offering support and information to hundreds of families who choose to educate their children outside the formal education system (see: www.education-otherwise.net). Lower Shaw was run for three years or so by Dick Kitto as Warden supported by a group of volunteers. During that time the place was used by various groups as a meeting space. The group that became Working Weekends on Organic Farms or WWOOF, held its early meetings there. After the grant funding ran out Kitto said 'I'll go when I feel there's someone who will take it on'. Various people came and went until a coherent communal group was formed to carry on running the Farm as a small alternative venue running educational and recreational courses. Dick Kitto is perhaps best remembered for the pioneering work he did in promoting organic composting. After Lower Shaw he also founded the Rural Resettlement Group, the Combined Organic Movement for Education and Training, and was closely involved with Tools for Self-Reliance. Lower Shaw continued to be run for many years as a communal group. At the very end of the 1990's it went through a period of turmoil, with the council nearly repossessing the property. It is now run by one of the families who had been part of the community, supported by volunteers.

Lady Macbeth and the Princess

I'm living in a farmhouse with some friends who have nothing to do with the theatre. It's what some people might call a commune, but it's really a sort of artists' colony.

Helen Mirren

While she was playing Lady Macbeth with the Royal Shakespeare Company in Stratford in the late 1960's Helen Mirren spent her spare time relaxing at a house called Parsenn Sally on Ditchford Farm, at Holford, just outside Stratford. Here with other actors, artists and wealthy young aristocrats the young rising theatrical star would hang out, attending wild parties with guests dressed as Marvel comic characters. There was a recording studio that was hired out to bands. Simon Oldfield, brother of *Tubular Bells* creator Mike, was part of the set and used to bring his sound system down to the farm. One of the main movers and shakers in the group was Sarah Ponsonby who, in 1975, moved the commune to Surrendell Farm at Hullavington in Wiltshire – a sprawling Jacobean farmhouse set in 57 acres, which she had bought, with two others, for £37,500. Here the group would continue its combination of artists' colony and back to the land commune. The house was run as a collective, with all residents and visitors helping with renovations and the rearing of livestock. Regular visitors included Mirren's then companion Prince George Galitzine (son of a Russian prince); record producer Simon Heyworth who worked on Mike Oldfield's *Tubular Bells*; tabla player Sam Gopal; photographer Bob Whitaker, famous for his work with The Beatles and Salvador Dali; and Princess Margaret – who came to visit her then boyfriend Roddy Llewellyn who was the community's head gardener. Llewellyn was often be found 'stripped to the waist, swearing at the goats for eating all his strawberries, or moving his prize sow Mah-Jong from one part of the garden to another via an elaborate set-up of electric fences'. The Princess, who according to local villagers, turned up wearing 'old clothes' and 'looking like a farmer's wife' ,was expected to 'muck in' when she visited, doing housework, renovation jobs and looking after livestock. Sean Connery's ex-wife Diane Cilento, who lived nearby, introduced the group to WWOOF and at weekends the bohemian crowd was joined by more 'ordinary folk' who came to dig ditches, paint walls or weed the garden.

The group also set up and ran a restaurant in Bath, called Parsenn Sally (named after the original house). The restaurant ran as a co-operative venture, with Roddy Llewellyn providing vegetables from the gardens at Surrendell. The same artistic vein as found in the community carried over to the restaurant, with ferns hung from the ceiling so it would resembled the 'Hanging Gardens of Babylon'. Later, after the customers had left, there were sing-songs round the piano where Princess Margaret would sing her party piece: Glenn Miller's *Chattanooga Choo Choo*.

Surrendell was a very innocent place. We had fun but it was quite naive and childish ... My clearest memory of Helen is of her playing frisbee in the garden, and our most successful crop was horseradish.

John Rendall

A combination of the press attention that came along with the association with royalty and the discovery of 292 cannabis plants on the farm finally put paid to the commune's days. The Parsenn Sally restaurant went into liquidation later the same year.

"After separating from Lord Snowdon, Princess Margaret, 45, was having a sisterly chat with Queen Elizabeth when Her Majesty waxed curious about the commune near Bath where Meg has weekended with her 28-year-old beau, Roddy Llewellyn. "No one has any money – it's all share and share alike," replied Margaret, in painting a romantic picture of the ramshackle farm. "I should really do something for your commune," declared her beguiled Majesty. "What would you suggest?" Margaret demurred – so the Queen dispatched a dozen brace of pheasants."

People Magazine April 26, 1976

Communes, sociologists
and the alternative society

... in order to understand why such people have resorted to such a strategy in order to create what one commune member described to me as 'a society in which each individual can have the right and the space to exercise their creative autonomy', it is necessary first of all to locate the origins of their estrangement from the existing order, the sources of their discontent with the status quo.

Andrew Rigby *Alternative Realities*

The early seventies saw not only a blossoming movement, or network, of communes but it also saw an increasing interest by academics in the phenomenon of communes. Andrew Rigby was a lecturer in sociology at the University of Aberdeen from 1970 until his resignation in 1974. In some ways he was as much a counter-cultural participant-observer as a detached academic researcher. He was a regular contributor to *Peace News* and to the *Communes Journal*, and was involved with the *Aberdeen People's Press*, a radical not-for-profit printing and publishing company that produced a fortnightly community newspaper. After leaving the University he lived on a croft in Aberdeenshire. He spent much time in the late 60's and early 70's travelling round communes. The results of his research were published in two books in 1974: *Alternative Realities: A Study of Communes and Their Members* and *Communes in Britain*. These oft-quoted publications have come to be seen as the 'seminal' accounts of communes of the period. The first book was a sociological study of the communes movement and its relationship to the alternative society. In it, Rigby attempts to catalogue and categorise the various groups he came across. Identifying a six-fold classification of different types of communities 'based upon the different intentions or motives underpinning the various ventures': Self-Actualising Communes; Activist Communes; Practical Communes; Therapeutic Communes; Communes for Mutual Support; and Religious Communes. Rigby saw the communes of the 1970's as potential agents of real revolutionary social change.

The cover illustration for Clem Gorman's People Together by Sally Kindberg

... the creation of a society where we think of our fellow man's needs rather than exploit him, where an individual can grow and develop his full potential and not live in fear of others, a society where love and co-operation with others are the prime qualities and not the selfishness and power-seeking that appears to characterize the existing social order – the realisation of such a society will never be achieved unless people actively and collectively seek to create such a world through transforming their personal lives and their relationships with others in the here and now, rather than just waiting for the revolution from above at some time in the distant future. This is the lesson that the communitarians have for those of us who share with them the belief in the desirability and attainability of such an age of freedom.

Andrew Rigby *Alternative Realities*

Communes In Britain was a much less academic book, made up primarily of a tour through a number of existing communes, each illustrating one of the types of community classification he had come up with. These included Newhaven in Edinburgh, Shrubb Family, Kingsway Community, Postlip Hall and Findhorn. After detailing these examples of different types of intentional community, the book goes on to put forward various conclusions on lessons that could be learnt from these successful examples of what the alternative society could look like. Rigby concluded that it was not sufficient merely to talk about the alternative society and condemn the straight society and its members. If the counter-culture was serious about creating a real alternative it needed to '... take a leaf out of the communitarians' book and actually get down to the task of creating alternative institutions based on the values of co-operation, personal autonomy and participatory democracy which are sufficiently viable to seduce people away from their straight counterparts.'

... commune members are people who have begun to see through the fictions upon which our social order rests and who have sought to create their own modes of existence. The potential of this movement lies in the fact that through putting their bodies on the line, so to speak, through putting their ideals and beliefs into living practice, they can provide the spark to light the dreams of others and through their example can provide others with the courage to demand the right to decide for themselves the way they should lead their lives. It is this type of demand, crystallised in the stance of many communards, which lies at the heart of any true revolutionary process.

Andrew Rigby Communes in Britain

Another, less well-known, communes observer from the early seventies was Frank Musgrove, Professor of Education at the University of Manchester. Following up on some research he had done in the early sixties, published as *Youth and the Social Order*, he and his colleague Roger Middleton spent the years 1971-73 carrying out a series of interviews with members of the newly emerged counter-culture. Musgrove was interested in the changes that had taken place within youth culture in the decade since his original research. He found that the 'youth' culture of the early 70's was radically different and no longer distinguished purely by age – 'There is now an increasing number of youths aged forty' – rather it was identified by its opposition to mainstream society.

Today in England the counter culture is synonymous neither with student activism nor hippiedom. It has broken from its base. At its core, it is true, there is a relatively small number of people who have rejected work as it is conventionally conceived and leisure which they see as its mirror-image. They are mystics, aesthetes, anarchists, music-makers, community actors, political and social activists, sculptors, painters, potters, wood-carvers, metal-workers, social philosophers, writers and poets, gardeners, poster designers and unpaid social workers. (Many of the

I feel self-conscious now, as I reflect back on that time, but it was a period of messianic hopes. We really did believe that we could remake the world anew, and build Blake's New Jerusalem. And at the forefront of this movement were the communes and the commune dwellers. They were not just weekend drop-outs, they were living the revolution! They were not just talking (or writing) about it, they were doing it! They were the cells of the new world, exemplars of an alternative way of living which, along with all the other alternative institutions, would wean folk away from the old corrupt patterns so that the old world would eventually collapse in on itself for lack of support ...

Andrew Rigby, 'Dig the Old Dreams Man' in Diggers & Dreamers 98-99

'social workers' are, in effect, unpaid and defiantly untrained psychiatric social workers.) They are typically in their late twenties; they are not university students, though many have been to universities.

Frank Musgrove *Ecstasy and Holiness*

Far from the stereotypical view of 'dirty-lazy-hippies' Musgrove found people leading 'a shifting, disorderly, dangerous, and often very courageous life'. Improvising and experimenting with few resources and little money, scraping by on 'meagre and uncertain' social security benefits while often working long and arduous hours on their chosen projects. He concluded that there was a widespread counter-culture that could be conceived of as having a central core of full-time activists and a series of ever widening concentric circles of people involved with varying degrees of attachment and involvement. These circles of counter-culture increasingly interpenetrated and overlapped with 'straight' society. These included people who joined communes and quasi-communes for short periods; attended events and festivals; who went along to encounter and therapy groups; who might 'be vegetarian, eat health-foods, and practice yoga'; or were relatively inactive sympathisers simply reading the 'underground' press, Tolkien's *The Lord of the Rings*, R D Laing, *Gandalf's Garden*, and books about the open family. Musgrove published two accounts of his work *Ecstasy and Holiness* in 1974 based on his early 1970's research and a follow-up *Margins of the Mind* in 1977 which goes into more detailed investigation of a number of different people who had gone through major changes in their lives during this period. These include a resident in a Cheshire Home, a member of a Sufi commune in Dorset and a devotee of Hare Krishna living at Bhaktivadanta Manor.

In February 1972 an article in Issue 2 of *Mother Grumble*, the North East alternative paper, announced that Professor Philip Abrams from Durham University sociology department was about to embarked on a two-year survey of communes in Britain courtesy of a £4,000 grant from the Social Science Research Council. 'The Prof and two trusty assistants intend to knock on doors of various communes all over Britain asking if they can crash awhile to get into the scene, as it were. Prof reckons the family unit has come in for a bit of stick in several post-industrialised societies like our own and so perhaps the commune might teach the nation about alternatives.' The article went on to note that the research team might well have difficulties in actually getting access to some groups '... it is already known that the reaction of some communes to Prof's team of pencil sharpeners has been rather cool, if not cold.' While some communes may well have been unenthusiastic at the prospect of being studied by a bunch of sociologists a reasonable number responded to the approaches made by Abrams and his team, although some of them required that they be referred to by pseudonyms in any publication of the research. Over the two years of the project, the actual 'fieldwork' of visiting communities was undertaken by Andrew McCulloch, Pat Gore and Sheila Abrams, While Phillip Abrams 'studied the literature and tried to maintain a proper academic distance from the real world.' As well as visiting a range of communes across the country and building up files on each group, the team sent out a questionnaire to all members of the Commune Movement and collated their replies. The result of the research was published in 1976 in a book titled *Communes, Sociology and Society*. It featured some communes by name (Findhorn, Postlip Hall, Kingsway Community and Beshara) while others were tantalisingly disguised by evocative names such as Family Farm, Fern Hill, Hillside and Red Dawn. From the point of view of historical research this is somewhat frustrating. I have tried to track down the original research papers with no luck – despite an offer at the end of the book to share data with 'anyone sufficiently interested in the problems of communal living'. I have had a guess at the identity of some of the disguised groups (I think Fern Hill is probably Taena) but, generally, they remain something of a mystery.

During their visits the young sociologists found that communes were not quite what they had expected:

... The communes in which we were staying were in some important ways startlingly unlike the communes we had read about; they were altogether less distant from society, less mysterious, less esoteric, more tied down in everyday practicalities and more interesting.

They quickly concluded that there was something of a 'myth of communes' written about by academic writers, journalists and by members of communes themselves that was not necessarily born out in the everyday reality of communal living. They saw this discrepancy not as some deceit on the part of communes, but a fundamental paradox of what communes were trying to achieve – how to live an imagined ideal in the real world.

Cover illustration for Communes Network 83 by Catriona Stamp

... The special quality of their lives has to be found in their efforts to shift the implicit values of their experiences step by step towards their ideals through such simple, difficult things as forcing themselves to face up to the meaning of quarrels, of demands for privacy or of the failure of some to contribute what others consider their share. What distinguishes them from families is not the absence of such episodes but the effort that is made to treat them as occasions for serious self-questioning and collective change ...

One particular area that they focussed on was the question of sex roles within each community. They published a paper on this aspect of their research in 1976 in *Sexual divisions and Society* – a British Sociological Association publication. In it they reported that they had expected to find within communes deliberate efforts to restructure relationships between the sexes and between adults and children. While there was a lot of rhetoric about communes being an alternative to the family the researchers came to the conclusion from the communes that they had looked at that they were a 'virtual irrelevance' to the problem of sexual equality.

... one might think that the situation of women would be drastically altered in communes. To begin with the home becomes, in principle, the primary scene of value and action for men and women alike ... what commonly occurs is that women in communes broadly go along with everything that femininity, motherhood, and the like ordinarily connote, and seek to alleviate the burdens of their role through essentially passive co-operative female action; for instance, a rota of mothers feed the children. In many communes one sees what is tantamount to a conspiracy to enlarge the value and meaningfulness of conventional women's roles on the basis of more or less elaborate symbolic concessions to participation by men – and the guarantee that 'women's work' will in the end be performed by women ...

They also observed that men often exploited the stated aim of some communes of 'creating a space where people can be more themselves' to their own advantage – '... in effect the male can exploit the female with a lighter conscience in a situation in which she poses as his equal without the strength of real equality to defend herself, and in which he can maintain in the face of emotional havoc that 'she wants it that way'. Femininity was, after all, some protection against this sort of treatment.'

At the end of *Communes, Sociology and Society*, after surveying the highs and lows of communal life in the communes they visited, the sociologists asked whether communes have any relevance to wider social policy. They concluded that while there were real lessons that could be learnt from the likes of therapeutic and squatter communities, the communes movement itself had, in effect, removed itself from the field of public policy with its oppositional stance to much of mainstream society.

We end this book as we began it, as sympathetic outsiders. We have certainly not made light of the ambiguities and shortcomings of communes. But we have tried also to recognise their seriousness as a criticism of the society in which we live, their relevance to the problems of that society and their value, chimerical though they may be, as a tentative statement of how ordinary lives might actually be different. Above all we have tried to recognise their humanity and the enduring, defiant patience with which members of communes go on trying to treat one another as persons. The culture in which we find ourselves is one which in a profound way denies the possibilities of social life. Yet critics of that culture, from Marx onwards, have found it strangely difficult to give an account in any practical depth of what a more authentic existence would be like. By attempting to practice such an existence, communes begin to give us that account

Abrams & McCulloch, Communes, Sociology and Society 1976

While at the end the Durham sociologists were somewhat ambiguous about what they thought were the prospects of the communes to develop into a significant social movement (they saw the change from informal Movement to even more informal Network as a step in the wrong direction) they did see some positive moves being made by individual communities. One in particular, that they thought a 'most remarkable development', was the founding of the Crabapple Community which was modelled on behaviourist psychology and the rational community imagined in the futuristic book *Walden Two*:

... Walden Two was written by the behavioural psychologist B F Skinner. In it he describes a hypothetical community of about one thousand people living to a high degree of self-sufficiency on a large acreage of land. They run their own agriculture, industry and education and have their own doctors, dentists and so on. Each person or couple has their own private room in which they sleep and keep their private possessions. All else is owned communally. eg. Transport, kitchens, dining rooms, workshops, equipment, library etc. Some of the main values put forward in the book are: Co-operation rather than competition as the means of achieving; egality among members, no dominant leaders, elites, heroes etc; people are more important that property or profits; the overall aim of the community being the achievement of the 'Good Life' for its members ...

John Seymour, 'Crabapple' in Undercurrents 12, September October 1975

Crabapple started from a small paragraph put in *Communes Bulletin* No 2 in October 1973 by two part-time teachers, Sally Ross and John Seymour, asking if there was any demand for a meeting to discuss the possibilities of a 'Walden Two type community'. They received four replies and arranged a meeting on their houseboat for the first weekend in November. There had been previous attempts to get a group going along the same lines by two psychologists, Sue Willoughby and Ken Timms, who had both separately duplicated sheets; distributed them at meetings; and tried to get other psychologists interested. Timms' project didn't get anywhere but Sue Willoughby and four others set up an urban commune in Dublin to try and 'live in such an experimental environment'. The houseboat meeting was attended by eight adults and two children. By the end of the weekend a nucleus of four had committed themselves to attempting to set up a Walden Two type community in Britain. The four were Sally and John plus Sarah Eno and Pat Boase from Cambridge. By the end of the month they had put out a newsletter outlining their proposal to others who had expressed an interest. These included: Ken Timms, Pauline and Tim Higgins, Roger Franklin and Lindsay Rawlings. What would later attract the attention of sociologists and psychologists were the proposals for a detailed labour credit system and a rota of 'planners' and 'managers' to make and implement community policy. Over the following two years the group would have a series of meetings, some at Parsonage Farm, to work out the details for the systems. They were inspired by the account of the fictional community in Skinner's book and also by descriptions of progress at Twin Oaks community in the USA. The early editions of its bi-monthly magazine, *The Leaves of Twin Oaks*, had recently been published in book form as the *Journal of a Walden Two Commune*. In February 1975 the group, now consisting of six adults and two children, moved onto a small hill farm in the Welsh borders 17 miles west of Shrewsbury. Middle Ty Brith consisted of a recently rebuilt five-roomed house; along with a series of dilapidated outbuildings; eight acres of fairly flat, potentially cultivatable pasture divided into six small fields; the remains of an old orchard; and about half an acre of 'dingle' – 'a wooded scrubby dell with a small stream running through the bottom'. After a few weeks functioning without any of their systems in place they set about trying to work out how to implement – in a small communal set up – the somewhat elaborate and bureaucratic infrastructure they had gleaned from Skinner and Twin Oaks. They instigated ten 'manager-ships' covering: House / Labour / Finance / Behaviour / Arjuna – running it / Shrewsbury shop – setting it up / Transport / Agriculture / Construction & maintenance / Visitors and information'. And they started to operate a labour credit system.

B.F. Skinner

WAL-DEN TWO

$2.25

MACMILLAN
PAPERBACKS

A controversial novel of morality and immorality in a scientifically-shaped Utopia

MORROW PAPERBACK EDITIONS $3.25

The First Five Years of Twin Oaks Community

A Walden Two Experi-ment

by Kathleen Kinkade
Foreword by B.F. Skinner

Basically a labour credit is a unit of work and all of us must work the same number of credits a week, although a surplus can be carried over to the following week. The credit rate depends on the pleasantness or unpleasantness of the job: pleasant work earns less than one credit an hour and unpleasant more. What is work? Well, to us, it means not only earning money but virtually everything else - all housework, meals, laundry, fire tending, gardening, watering cows (?!) child care, shopping etc, etc. The only things that aren't work are things you do for yourself e.g.; reading books, taking tea breaks, eating meals, lounging about chatting, listening to music and so on. To us the advantages of having a labour credit system outweigh the disadvantages (otherwise we would scrap it.) They go something like this; everybody knows that each person is contributing an equivalent amount of work to the community. The importance of this is two-fold ie. you can take time off to sit in the sun without feeling guilty about not working, and conversely you don't feel that others are loafing if they aren't working when you see them. They have fulfilled their labour credit quota and so have you. A surplus can be built up so that days/weeks etc can be enjoyed as holidays. Another advantage of the labour credit system is that it is actually possible to get the nasty work done ..."

Crabapple Newsletter No 6

After getting somewhat 'bogged down in complexity' they managed to work out a satisfactory and workable system. Each evening the 'labour manager' sat down and worked out a list of the jobs that needed doing the following day and the current rate for each type of job which might be – Washing up breakfast 0.8 credits; Cooking the evening meal 1.2 credits; Shopping 0.9 credits; Firecare 0.5 credits; Construction and Childcare 1.1 credits. Once this was done each member ticked the work they wanted to do the following day. If two or more people signed up for the same job it was given to one of them at random, but the following day the credit rate dropped by 0.1. If nobody signed up for a job it was assigned to the person who had signed up for the least work that day and the rate went up by 0.1. If the average rate for work being done rose above 1.05 then the rate for everything was dropped by 0.1 credits. Apart from the time it took to work all this out the group thought the system worked well, and got the work done (there is no indication as to what rate of credits working out the all the different rates incurred). Although some visitors thought it was all rather 'silly' and that people didn't need systems to allocate work – these were visitors who had failed to meet their daily labour quota.

... Using labour credits made us conscious of lots of things about working collectively that need consideration.... it was important to see that each person pulled their weight and didn't suspect others of not doing so. It was good to be able to get more of the work you preferred (which doesn't happen with a strict rota for each job) without getting trapped in one job (as in nuclear families). It meant we could encourage each other to try new things. We made expectations and commitments clear to each other, we avoided throwing guilt and suspicion around, we avoided the sorts of roles that can pop in when everyone plays the game of waiting to see who cracks first. In which mothers cook dinner because their children are hungry and it would be thought mean to cook only for some people; in which the car owner mends the communally used car before it grinds itself to bits; in which everyone slides back into old culture ideas on ownership and collective responsibility becomes just a theory ...

Pam Dawling, 'Crabapple revisited' in *Undercurrents* 34, June July 1979

Another outside observer interviewing Crabapplers for an article in *Psychology Today* found that while they thought that the labour credit system was really useful, they could take or leave other aspects of behaviourist psychology. With members commenting that '... it just means consciously arranging social conditions so that people can achieve their aims and change their behaviour' or 'the behavioural side was somewhat incidental. I accepted it along with the rest ...' and 'Human motives are so devious'. By the end of the first year differences in emphasis and interpretation of ideas led to the departure of John and Sally Seymour. This led to a reassessment of 'what we were doing and why' and eventually to the decision to look for a larger property to move the community to. In 1977 the group sold Middle Ty Brith and moved to Berrington Hall, a

Farming at
Berrington Hall

rambling, slightly eccentric, Georgian rectory with a two-acre walled fruit and vegetable garden, all set in some 15 acres of farmland. Closer to Shrewsbury, Berrington made it easier to run a wholefood shop in the town and this became one of the main occupations of the community, along with small-scale farming. For a while they retained some 'Walden Two' aspects in the way that the community was run. Instead of 'managers' there were stewards for different areas of work and there was a formal committee of three planners whose task was supposed to be to make long-term decisions, based on 'community opinion and available data'. But, in practice they made decisions using consensus at open meetings of the whole group. And while the more strident behaviourist rhetoric had gone, it could still be seen as a background to many of the ideas that continued to underpin the community.

We favour using rational and organised methods of decision making and problem solving. We expect to work at our interpersonal relationships, altering our behaviour away from adverse conditioning of the past towards something more suitable for a co-operative culture.

Alternative Communities Directory 1977

One other 'habit' that Crabapple became notorious for – and many an exaggerated rumour went round about it – was 'sleeping cards'. In the late 70's members 'moved away from couples to less exclusive relationships, moving very carefully on almost uncharted ground.' This led at one point to there being a series of cards with everyone's name on which were selected at random to decide who slept with who.

The Crabapple shop
in Shrewsbury

... Yes, we had sleeping cards for a few years. We used them once a week at the most. Often weeks went by, of business as usual. There were two envelopes. Everyone got the chance to remove to the Off envelope any cards with a combination of their name and someone else's that they didn't want to deal with at that time. Only the cards in the On envelope were drawn from. And sex wasn't compulsory ... **13**

Pam Dawling

After he left Crabapple, John Seymour along with Nigel Gunton brought out a visionary proposal in 1981 for a large community based on the cybernetic and systems ideas of Stafford Beer. In a self-published paper entitled *Viable Systems and Alternative Realities* they set out to answer the question '... how do we design a viable community that allows freedom for the individual without dissolving into chaos?' In the first part they outline the work and ideas of Stafford Beer who had designed systems for the running of the Chilean economy under the socialist president Salvador Allende. The paper then goes on to imagine what a community based on these ideas might look like, with an imagined tour of the community in 1984 (three years in the future) by Sarah – one of the farm's 'co-alphas' – who was looking after visitors that day:

The site was a 90-acre farm near Orcop in Herefordshire bought about three years ago. Now there are about 100 adults living there and around 20 kids. They say this reflects the national average ration of agricultural land per capita ... the farm was mechanised although the machinery was all quite aged. A pair of Fergusons 35s formed the basis, having advantage of being cheap to buy, run and get parts for. Sarah reckoned the transport co-alphas were secretly in love with them ... Sarah described their labour credits as being a kind of sophisticated barter system. One labour credit was worth one hour's average work. Some people effectively earnt their living in the money economy whilst others, usually in the community core, earned theirs in the labour credit economy. Most people, though, worked part-time in each to suit their particular needs. She described it as a mixed dual economy which allowed people maximum flexibility ... The main community complex had a large meeting hall/eating area – the biggest room in the place – plus kitchen, offices, utility room, laundry, library, kids rooms, lounge and video room, mostly bustling with people. The people were quite an interesting mixture. Most were in the 20-40 age range with far fewer kids and adolescents and fewest of all older people. They seem to be of the mainly 'alternative sub culture' for want of a better classification ...

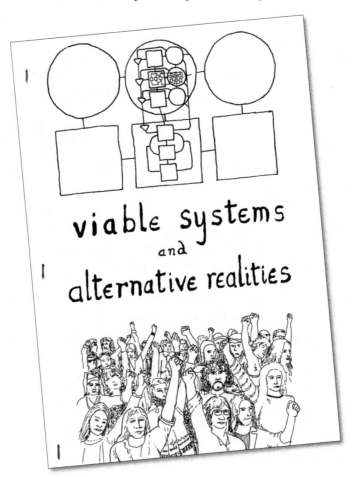

Practicing self-sufficiency

Just as we cannot, for ever, go on keeping hens in wire cages, or pigs in total darkness, or suppressing every species of life on the land except one money-making crop, so we cannot go on for ever ourselves living in human battery cages and more and more distorting our environment. It's all going to collapse. Either the oil will run out, or the grub, or the uranium-235, or the power of man to withstand the unutterable boredom of it all, and Mankind will have to find a different way of life.

John Seymour, *The Complete Book of Self-Sufficiency* 1976

Many people's image of a 1970's commune is of a back-to-the-land farm halfway up some Welsh hillside or hidden at the end of a long trackway in deepest Essex or Suffolk somewhere. But while 'self-sufficiency' was definitely one of the decade's buzz-words, and there was much talk of being more self-reliant, there were very few communes trying to achieve complete self-sufficiency and few actually achieving anything near it. The great guru, and so-called father of self-sufficiency, John Seymour (the same name but a different person from the John Seymour mentioned on preceeding pages) moved with his family from his five-acre small-holding in Suffolk – where he had begun his back-to-the-land exploration – to the 60-acre Fachongle Isaf farm in the Preseli Hills near the small town of Newport in Pembrokeshire in 1963. Here, as well as working the land, he wrote and published a number of books, the most widely known of which was *The Complete Book of Self-Sufficiency* illustrated by his wife Sally. Oddly, it was more of a coffee table book than a practical manual – ask anyone who has tried to butcher a sheep using it as a guide! But the book had the effect of inspiring a whole generation of armchair smallholders to aspire to a return to the country. Seymour separated from his wife Sally who left to run her own small-holding and he slowly started to gather a community of enthusiastic followers keen to try their hand at rural living. Seymour had the idea of establishing a kind of School for Self-Sufficiency and started calling the farm The Centre for Living. Vicky Moller arrived at Fachongle with her three children longing to get back to the countryside and started a relationship with Seymour. The reality of life at the Centre for Living was, however, often a far cry from the one illustrated in the pages of Seymour's books.

... John had just retired to write and had abandoned the things going on here, animals were in a very low state. It would be unfair to describe the whole era of the community in that way. It was a 60-acre farm and there would be between ten and 20 people living here with children. And the farming was not cared for, the vegetables were rotting and the animals were uncared for. But as I say this was a particularly low era and John had sort of escaped into his writing and he used to come down and there was raw chickweed to eat and rancid butter and things like that, it was quite a shock and he used to go to the pub to eat more often than not ... [14]

Vicky Moller

And, despite the considerable success of the books, the farm and Seymour himself were often in debt.

... because he got incredibly famous with his books, bestseller in the hardbacks in Germany along with Hitler or something, we got inundated with letters asking to come. So because he was always broke we tried to have paying guests and we got rooms ready and people to come on courses. Which sometimes they were pretty

disappointed with the standards that they met here. So it wasn't always ideal.
Then other people just came and worked and stayed and lived. And when he did
manage to earn any money John would always give it away and spend it. So it was
impossible to get him back on to the financial rails ...

Vicky Moller

Seymour left Wales and moved to County Wexford in Ireland during the
1980's. There he would later set up another School for Self-Sufficiency with
Will Sutherland. The Fachongle farm was taken over by a group including
Seymour's children who continued to run it along ecological lines.

... we were virtually self-sufficient for food by the end, but there were times when you were sick of beetroot and
leeks as the only vegetable for half the winter, you know as things died out you just used what was left, you got
very creative with presenting them in different ways. But you really really relished the next weeds in early spring
and then the first lettuces. It was good, it was great and also producing all your own cheese, it's very hard to go
back to buying things. It feels like a sort of pollution, to actually bow to having to buy cheese again ...

Vicky Moller

Others were inspired to go back to the country and try self-sufficiency. British
writer, communist, socialite and literary critic for *The Observer* Philip Toynbee
decided in his late 50's to set up a self-sufficient farming community at his family
home Barn House at Brockweir near Chepstow – a house that had been used as a
pacifist commune during the war. Toynbee, the son of historian Arnold Toynbee,
had undergone a personal crisis, and entered into a period of suffering from deep
depression, becoming increasingly concerned about ecological matters.

Our community was established some three years ago with the purpose of exploring a way of life which would
be ecologically sound and which would lead to self-development through shared experience. Thus the people
who came together during our first year were united by their wish to experience community living and by their
common interest in organic gardening and farming.

Barn House Community 'Prospectus' 1977

Nearly all Toynbee's friends regarded the setting up of the commune as 'insane'
and quite quickly Toynbee and his wife decided that they couldn't cope with
living in such close quarters with so many other people and moved to a cottage
a couple of miles away, while still staying involved in the project as 'associate
members'. Within the first year or so a split had also started to develop within
the community between the 'sturdy farming-and-no-nonsense communards' who
had been attracted by the call to be self-sufficient and those, including Toynbee
himself, who were looking for a more spiritual focus for the community and who
saw what they were seeking as '... a love capable of crossing all boundaries and
achieving a level of consciousness on which we can enter into true oneness with
each other'. Toynbee wrote candidly about the commune in his autobiography
Part of a Journey and Jessica Mitford gives a somewhat jaundiced outsiders view
of commune life in her book about Toynbee *Faces of Phillip*.

The split led a number of the original members to leave and made the writing
of the group's Prospectus in 1977 a rather difficult compromise. In the end it
seems the focus drifted more and more towards self-exploration and less and

less work on the farm was done until finally Toynbee had had enough and closed the whole thing down.

Sunday evenings at Barn House ... became eclectic religious and ritual occasions, with group meditation, the chanting of 'Om', spontaneous prayers, and processions with candles. The commune consciously resolved that its object was no longer ecological survival, but shared explorations in spiritual growth, and it subsisted, more or less, by some members taking gardening and agricultural odd jobs around the neighbourhood.

Jessica Mitford

A few of the 'sturdy-farming-and-no-nonsense communards' who had been at Barnhouse in the early days decided that they would try and set up their own self-sufficient community.

... there were two or three people who were interested and I said we really ought to get our own group together and be independent and I said I'll look around and see if there's a suitable house or building where we can start a group ... I went around looking at estate agents, there didn't seem much about in Gloucestershire, so I thought about Wales which I knew was a cheaper area and we came across a place called Glaneirw House through an estate agent in Cardigan ... I told him I wanted a big house for communal living and he said 'Oh I've got just the place for you boy, just the place'. He took me out in the car ... It was an old hotel with sixteen bedrooms. Ideal, big kitchen, living rooms, everything ... **15**

Robin Appleby

The group bought the old hotel, workshops, outbuildings, large walled garden and 44 acres of arable land and moved in in 1975. Their stated aims were: 'to live and maintain a self sufficient community in the country based on organic farming, to live as simple life as possible without reliance on consumer products ... to strive for unity and world peace'. **16** They began improving the land that had been somewhat neglected and started to establish a mixed organic farm, including growing cereals (for bread-making and animal food), milking cows and calf rearing, eggs, vegetable and fruit growing. The farm started to become successful, providing much of the food for the ten adults plus children that lived there. In some of the founding members' eyes, the farm was more of a success than the community side of things.

We were selling vegetables in Cardigan Market. We were growing our own wheat, all our own flour, making bread, making butter and cheese, and milk and everything ... It was a very successful farm. It was a more successful farm than it was a community, relationships that sort of thing ...

Robin Appleby

Appleby left after five or so years. Looking back recently he cited breakdown in relationships, 'people running off with each other's partners, that sort of thing', as one of the main reasons for leaving. Other members came and other small businesses grew to bring in some extra income: one member ran a pottery; others set up repairing and refurbishing Rayburn cookers. Half an acre was developed as a pick-your-own strawberry patch. For well over a decade the community managed to produce virtually all their own vegetables, fruit, milk,

Bim Mason, Robin Appleby, Fred Rees surveying Glaneirw

butter, cheese, eggs and meat and most of the grain needed. The group was income-pooling and had changed from a trust to a co-operative during this period. At this time they, perhaps, got as close as anyone to achieving some balance of what might be called self-sufficiency. However, in a sobering article in *Communes Network* in March 1983 one member wrote about how hard it was to make the finances stack up and how hard the actually reality of what, in effect, was subsistence farming could be.

Organic vegetable growing commercially is really so time consuming that one has to be really dedicated to do it; and to really make a living there would be little time for child-care, relationships, politics, culture, holidays, learning new skills and trying to avoid sex-role stereotyped work, which is a high price to pay for an income I feel. This really seems a pretty bleak picture and one wonders why people own farmland at all ...
Pete West in Communes Network March 1983

In the end it would be the continuing and re-occurring difficulties in relationships between members that would lead to a decline in the farming activity at Glaneirw with a seemingly continual turnover of members leading to a long-term decline of the community.

Others, driven as much by the desire to escape the clutches of what they saw as a confining and oppressive 'straight society' as any rosy view of life in a rural idyll, started off on the path to try to reach self-sufficiency. In 1975 at Leintwardine near Craven Arms in Shropshire, the Wheatstone Community Project bought a large Edwardian house and seven acres of land with the idea that it would be a stepping stone to a larger community.

We knew that it had too little land and was in a soft, rural area where consumerism was rife and where the pressures both social and economic would make it difficult for us to go all the way to realising our ideals. Thus we agreed that Wheatstone was a jumping off ground, a place where we would learn and from which we would, when we felt ready, move to a remote area with more land and more chance of being what we ultimately intended to be. We set ourselves a time limit of five years, intending to move then if not before ...
Mac in Communes Network 52

For a few years the group was successful in growing much of their essential food except only for grain and some animal feed. They claimed no unemployment benefits, bringing in income from casual work for local farmers and odd jobs in the area. Despite the usual communal difficulties of people leaving, struggles with finance and interpersonal hassles, one member looking back on the period said 'We throbbed with vitality and enthusiasm and overflowed with visitors ... the tenor of the place was open and developing and caring.' But almost from the start there was a built-in tension between the various ideals that the community wanted to try and live up to. Between being an open community run on anarchist principles and having a clear direction. Between the practicalities of learning to farm while deschooling children, earning enough to live on and integrating a stream of visitors.

We were into self-sufficiency, we farmed meat really. And because we didn't have this membership structure people could come in with equal rights. There was a little bit of you've only just arrived maybe you should wait a couple of days before you tell us

how many chickens we should have ... I think for me the strongest feeling was I was
trying to do it right, I was trying to live this radical life. I had an idea about what
I should be doing and I should be really open to people ... and anyone could walk
in and have a right to say we should have three cows instead of two, or we should
be vegan or something. It was really extreme to suggest we should be vegan when we
had cows and ducks and chickens and sheep and we were killing sheep and lambing.
And someone would come in and say be vegan. It's like what?! **17**

Gina Heathersprite

On a number of occasions people set off to search for 'new and better places'
which the group could move to, only to find on their return that the group was
unable to agree on whether to move or not. Wheatstone became involved in
both the Fairground and Cartwheel projects in efforts to realise their wider
vision, but still the internal conflicts continued.

... slowly the divisions between those who liked the life here and now and those who wished to develop along the
originally planned lines became more acute. Some kids were dcschooled, some were not; some people wanted more
domestic refinements, some less. And slowly these divisions took their tole (sic) *both in enthusiasm and hope and*
things achieved, and most of all in personal relationships. The classic incestuous hothouse introverted phase had
arrived. So, something had to break ... The stalemate continued and Wheatstone hit the lowest spot in its history.
Everything seemed to be wrong. The financial stress became more than we could deal with and we started a run
on our small and precious capital, people within the group fragmented in an unprecedented way, enthusiasm
disappeared, the winter was somehow darker and more dismal then ever before, and even the hens stopped laying.

Mac in Communes Network 52

The group tried bringing in Red Therapy, a socialist therapy group to help:

Yes, Red Therapy in the form of Jo, Mark and John came and went and left people variously battered, pensive
and elated. I was left both battered and thoughtful and remain so. The methods which were used seemed to be
aiming at bringing out all the shit and putting it on display, rather than to show that there was love as well.
There were problems, communications blocks, pointless resentments to be sure. And it was good that a method
was shown to enable us to express them. But for me the situation somehow often felt out of control and I could
not see how I could find my way to honesty with love rather than the honesty with acrimony which seemed to be
a dominant feature of what we did.

Mac in Communes Network 30

Eventually many of the people who had been there from the start left and the
group's open door membership policy let others in who shared little if any of
the original groups' vision or ethos

... In the early 80's that's when the rot started to set in really. That was when people
came who could never settle. And what I realised was people coming in were looking
for something, but they were coming in with a different way of being somehow.
This was particularly true of the people that destroyed the place and threw me out.
They threatened my life. You know they were troubled people doing a lot of drugs
quite frankly ... Some of them were in vans. Some of them were the travellers. So

there were people who were quite displaced I think. And they came in looking for
something, looking for a place to be. But not coming in with the same values that
we had joined in the 70's. We'd had these very specific idealistic values. You know
the flower power, hippy pippy values and these people that came in didn't have
those values. They were troubled people – so maybe that's what was happening
externally … because we were so open, we weren't protected you see …

Gina Heathersprite

Wheatstone went through a number of years of turmoil with the house being
vandalised and virtually abandoned with a few people continuing to live in the
grounds. In 1989, through Radical Routes, the community was re-colonised
and re-emerged as Earthworm Housing Co-op.

Elsewhere other groups set up in the same period and managed to establish and
run quite extensive small farming and horticultural operations with members
acting as part-time farm hands and with additional labour provided by
WWOOFers. At East Bergholt in Suffolk the Old Hall Community living in
separate units in a former Franciscan friary managed 70 acres with members
putting in a voluntary contribution of 12-15 hours a week to cover domestic
work and work on the land. Started in 1974 as the Unit One Suffolk Housing
Association, the group of 40-plus adults and children has managed over the
years to evolve a successful combination of members working in various outside
jobs while carrying out part-time farming.

As far as we know, the Old Hall land has always been farmed organically … For a good part of each year we are
self-sufficient in vegetables – with just an annual hungry gap around May before Spring-planted crops mature.
We also produce all the meat that we consume: beef, lamb, bacon and the occasional chicken: rabbits are a
perennial pest on the farm and so some are trapped or shot and make welcome addition to winter stews. Through
the time and voluntary effort of those living here it has been estimated that in one year we produce, and consume,
3,525 gallons of milk, 7,500lbs of potatoes and 3,000lbs of tomatoes, 1,000 lettuces, 2,500 leeks, 500 cabbage
and brassica plants, two tons of wheat which is baked into 2,400 wholemeal loaves.

Patricia Mercier, *The Patchwork History of a Community Growing up*

Over in Herefordshire in 1978 a similar set-up was established at Canon Frome
Court – a Georgian manor house and stable block with 40 acres. Like Old
Hall the community was organised as a Housing Association with the house
and stable block divided into self-contained units sold to members on 999-
year leases. The land farmed co-operatively has provided '… a considerable
proportion of our food, including a good deal of our own meat.' These two
communities have combined a larger number of people and a mixed economy,
along with leasehold purchase of units rather than a housing co-op rental set-
up. This model seems to have created more stable communities which have
proved to be more sustainable than the all-out self-sufficiency attempts of
places like Glaneirw and Wheatstone.

An Alternative
Communities Movement

We are a dedicated rationalist teaching order who live in community
We are open to any who will keep our rule
We teach you that you may teach
We learn that we may teach

In the late 70's a kind of rival to Communes Network was instigated by a
community with a base in Bangor in North Wales. They called themselves The
Teachers and published a series of annual directories of *Alternative Communities
in Great Britain & Eire.* The first edition came out in 1977 and contained a
listing of 33 named groups and another five listed anonymously as 'they had
asked not to be listed in the directory'. Each community was categorised by the
compilers on a number of scales that covered such things as: the permanence or
transience of membership, and members social relation – 'celibate or anarchic'.
Each community was also described as either 'Rational' – '... the manner of
functioning of the community implies a latent or active ability to make logical
inferences ...' or 'Non-rational – '... those communities whose members think
and act on an instinctive level ...'

The Teachers were led by two members, Michelle and Kevin, often referred to
as Kevin of the Teachers and Michelle of the Teachers rather than by their
surnames. Kevin O'Byrne had met Michelle in 1967; he was looking to set up a
private school to try out his educational ideas and she was interested in
community living. They decided that the two ideas could be merged and that a
combined school and community 'would be workable'. Kevin was a member of
Mensa and had devised a system of psycho–mathematics that he called 'Choice
Mathematics'. He was also involved in early computer programming which was
how the community financed itself for a number of years. They counted the
start of the community in 1972 when the two of them were joined by a third
member, Christian at their flat in Ealing. In November 1973 they opened a
shop in order to further their educational aims and started to look around for
somewhere big enough to establish a larger community and school. In the
summer of 1975 they bought a large shop at 6/7 Wellfield Court in the centre
of Bangor in North Wales, followed by two derelict cottages '... on which to
learn building techniques.' And later in the year a house nearby, at
18 Garth Road, Bangor.

In the future we intend to obtain land for the school, probably combining the school with a farm and a wildlife
reserve. Also at present work is being done in electronics and we are making a synthesiser for use in a group which
we intend to start. Some of the community occasionally run a mobile disco and some are training in vehicle
mechanics, others are intending to train as teachers and doctors of medicine.
'History of The Teachers' in *Alternative Communities Movement Newsletter* 6, 21.3.80

In the following year the group purchased a new offset-litho printing press and
planned to publish a number of educational books written by members. They
had been working on both a reading scheme and a mathematics scheme based

on 'original work done by one of our members in the field of mathematics art psychology.' On the back of their 1977 directory is a list of titles available from the group including: *The Choice Mathematics – Book One, Aggression* and *I Stalk the Earth A Stranger*, all by Kevin of the Teachers and *Teaching Reading* by Kevin and Lorraine of the Teachers.

Off the back of the new directory the Teachers launched the Alternative Communities Movement (ACM). This was conceived as a campaigning organisation 'To spread knowledge on communal living' and 'to help people get together to build communities'. Their style was more outgoing and brasher than the rather friendly low-key style of Communes Network. The ACM info pack and poster started off with the words: 'Most communes are NOT hippy dope scenes or gurus exploiting innocent babies. That's just the media trying to sell papers to bored suburbia. There are at least 100

Right:
Teachers Community
Below:
Alternative Communities
Movement poster

communities in Britain already – why don't you live in one? Someday most people will live in communes – why are you waiting?' The ACM operated in parallel to Communes Network, producing its own occasional journal and running a mail-order service covering some 100 books relevant to communal living. The Teachers organised ACM camping weekends and courses on a small-holding that they bought close to Bangor. The relationship between the two wings of the British communes during the early 1980's was one of mutual arm's length tolerance. Kevin of the Teachers considered Communes Network to be characterised by a group of communes that had '... yet to define a clear identity for themselves.' and who seemed to him to attract what he referred to as 'immature armchair theorists.' **18** Members of the Network felt that the Teachers were over-rational empire builders. And over a number of years an increasing number of communities who saw themselves as a core part of the Network consistently refused to send in entries for the ACM directory. Which led to the Teachers recycling old entries from previous editions or 'borrowing' them from other publications in order to try and keep their listings comprehensive. This did nothing to improve relations!

The Teachers Community was run along very different lines to other communities. Not only did it clearly have a leadership, it also had what appeared to be (to many communards in Network Communities) a draconian set of membership rules.

We have a code which is enforced (although a member may take some years to reach these standards habitually) as follows:

1   *Members are required to answer any non trivial question put to them by another member to the satisfaction of the person raising the question.*
2   *No member shall own or control another's actions except where those actions are directed against that person.*
3   *No member shall blackmail another emotionally.*
4   *Each member must 'pay their way' emotionally – and otherwise within the limit of their ability.*
5   *Each member will be deemed responsible for their own actions and those of no other person, and shall be accountable on such basis.*
6   *One to one relationships are a matter of negotiation between individuals and are the responsibility – of the individuals where such relationships do not weaken the individuals' rights and duties within the group.*
7   *Competitive status striving will be constantly discouraged within the community, as will aggressive behaviour.*
8   *Intrusion into personal space is only permitted when very necessary or by agreement.*
9   *Triviality and ritual in relationships and conversations will be discouraged.*
10   *Noise levels are to be reduced.*
11   *Smoking is not allowed within community property.*
12   *All income is pooled.*
13   *Members must conform to the law of the land.*
14   *Members are discouraged from getting overweight.*
15   *To live in accord with, not in opposition to, the world at large.*

These codes are a developing charter based on experience, and are open to negotiation and adjustment in the light of experience.

Teachers Entry in *ACM Directory* 1978

Neither did they hold the usual liberal/libertarian views of many of those looking to join communes at the time, drawing decidedly mixed reactions from visitors. Rose Mason who visited in 1980 wrote a letter to *Undercurrents* magazine warning people about the right-wing ideologies she had heard expressed by members of the Teachers. They were in favour of nuclear weapons (on the basis that Britain needed an independent deterrent) and thought Cruise missiles to be a step forward.

... The present government was praised for (among other things) cutting back the Welfare State, which will make everyone learn to stand on their own two feet. Poverty is used as an excuse for laziness and lack of initiative. Unemployment does not really exist, as there is plenty of work for everyone who is prepared to look for it. The person who told me this admitted she had never been to the North of England, but she knew Oxford very well and

there was certainly no lack of work there. People were becoming dependent on the state. Social workers and benefits are undermining the moral fibre of the Nation. All social problems, it seems, will be solved by communal living, although this may take a long time.

'Reactionary Teachers' – a letter in *Undercurrents* 43 Dec/Jan 1981

Kevin replied in typical combative style berating *Undercurrents* and its readers as holding 'softy-lefty' world views and being unable to 'even understand us well enough to 'disagree' with us.' And going on to claim that the Teachers 'run one of the most effective non-marriage, non religious communes in the world. We have built up this from scratch while all around similar efforts flounder. Again we prefer to let the facts 'speak' louder than words or mere theory.'

At the end of the eighties the ACM faded from the limelight and the Teachers went from being one of the most high-profile communes in the country to almost disappearing from view amid rumours that they were beset with internal problems, amidst accusations of mistreatment by ex-members. In 1993 some of what happened came out in a somewhat strange court case at the Old Bailey in which one of Kevin's daughters – a Rebecca Teacher now aged 18 – and her stepfather were cleared of blackmailing her father Kevin O'Byrne for the sum of up to £60,000, threatening to expose the activities of the Teachers commune to newspapers if he did not pay up.

... Miss Teacher admitted demanding the money, but said it was to compensate her for years of suffering. She made the calls after her efforts to sue her father and her attempts to alert the authorities to her plight failed ... The court was also told that children were beaten, whipped, locked up for days without food and made to look after the animals at The Teachers' remote farmhouse commune near Bangor, North Wales ... But David Bate, for the prosecution, said that although the sect was 'weird and bizarre' it was not on trial. The issue was not whether the allegations of abuse were true, but whether the blackmail demands were warranted ... Miss Teacher was born into the sect and the court was told that she was beaten and sexually abused until her mother and Mr Webb left the group when she was aged 11. She was one of at least 12 children fathered by Mr O'Byrne with six women. She said yesterday: 'I did this not just for myself but for the other children.' ...

'Sect Leader's Daughter is Cleared of Blackmail' by W Bennett in *The Independent* 19th August 1993

... The Teachers started the Alternative Communities Movement 'to spread knowledge of communal living, to help people to get together to build communities, and to teach the technology of co-operation and how to live together and deal with the problems caused by alienation, inadequate education and the pressures to conform socially to the stultifying nuclear family' ... Their heyday was the early eighties, and by 1990, although still a commune themselves – they had retired from publicity and stopped answering enquiries about communities. Their valuable contribution of four or five editions of the directory and much national advertising drew many enquiries. Unfortunately their certainty of the superiority of their own model of communal living was off-putting to many people with ideas of their own. Although from time to time efforts were made by individuals within both Communes Network and The Teachers for more co-operation, the main theme was of mutual distaste.

Pam Dawling 'What is Communes Network' in *Diggers & Dreamers* 92-93

Dreaming Big

One of the recurrent themes to emerge from the counter-culture throughout
the period from the mid 1970's through to the end of the 1980's was the desire
to create large village-scale new communities. Back in December 1972 a 'freak
from Dublin' wandered into the BIT office on Great Western Road and handed
over £1,250 to set up an 'Alternative Society Ideas Pool'. The idea was to get
people to send in proposals for projects that they wanted to set up and the best
ones (chosen by a panel of 'Ideas Pool Attendants') would get a share of the
money. Nic Albery, from BIT, organised and ran what was billed as a
'Revolutionary Co-operative Competition' from January through to April 1973
and over 300 entries were sent in. There were various different categories of
entries, ranging from Kids & Freeschools; through Arty-Arty-Crafty-Drama-
Music projects; Religious & other freakishness; to projects for 'the Old, Lonely,
Housewives etc ...' In among these was a section for communes, new villages
and towns, and a section on unusual structures and living spaces. Trogwell
Commune in Bradford sent in a proposal for a 'Floating Island for 30 people
built of scrap', someone called Brown sent in a series of watercolour sketches of
'Live-in-the-sky-balloon-sausages'. A young architect, Will Alsop, sent in
proposals for eight different model communities based on different types of
derelict sites across the country. Each proposal was accompanied by an aerial
photo of the site, a layout map and a futuristic drawing of the proposed
structures and dwellings. There was a commune for 5,000 people in a derelict
china clay works at
St Austell in Cornwall; a
commune in an old
vehicle dumping yard in
Leicester for 250 people;
a community in an old
granite quarry in North
Wales; a 'Lunatic-TV-
Station-Commune' in an
old brickworks in
Bedfordshire; a 'research
commune in the trees' in

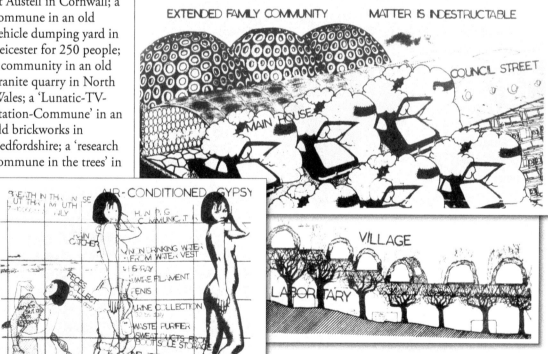

Illustrations for:
Car Dump Commune, Tree Village and
Women's Commune
Will Alsop A Book of Visions

a disused open cast coal mine in the North East; and a futuristic women's commune with computerised body suits and a communal memory stored on the commune's central computer.

The Ideas Pool Attendants met at 11am on April 11th 1973 and the whole day was a farce: first of all, the two most notorious attendants, Richard Neville and Germaine Greer, were both out of the country, which was just as well no doubt. Jim Anderson of (the now-defunct) OZ magazine, stood in for Richard Neville, and after a couple of dozen phone calls to various people, Jenny James of People Not Psychiatry was procured to replace Germaine Greer. BIT worker Bill came along to report the proceedings for Bitman magazine and was promptly roped in as a seventh attendant, to help wade through the huge stack of entries. **19**

Each entry was judged by a number of criteria: Was the money really needed? Would the person(s) do it themselves? Was there activity there already? Was it be likely to become self- supporting? And would it have lasting results? The dedicated 'Pool attendants' ploughed through the piles of entries and then passed them on. 'Double-rejects', were thrown out and only those projects which were unanimously approved of, got considered for money. At 8 o'clock in the evening they had finished and chosen four projects to fund. RadTech in Pact in Sheffield got £500; Aberdeen Peoples Press £350; a free food project near Manchester £300; and a self-help project in the black community in Haringey got £100. None of the grand commune schemes got any funding, but all the entries were put together and published in July '73 as *A Book of Visions*, complete with a cover illustration by Cliff Harper.

a directory of alternative society projects
1973·A BOOK OF VISIONS·£1·00

The main obstacle to setting up a new village-scale community would prove to be finding a suitable site in Britain with enough space and where the planning authority would countenance the establishment of a new community. During the seventies a number of sites were identified and attempts made by a number of different groups to get a large-scale community together. One potential sort of location was abandoned villages. On the north coast of the Llyn Peninsula, in North Wales was the abandoned quarry village of Porth y Nant. Quarrying ceased during World War Two and the village had been empty since. Parts of it were occupied by a group calling themselves the New Atlantis Commune, who had connections with Sid Rawle's Diggers. They caused considerable damage burning much of the timber as firewood. In 1974, while researching his *Alternative England & Wales* book, Nicholas Saunders stumbled across the village and put forward a proposal to buy it. It was eventually purchased in 1978 by the Nant Gwrtheyrn Trust and has been turned into a Welsh Language Centre.

In 1974 a number of people keen to see the formation of new rural communities formed the New Villages Association. Their stated aims were:

> *The New Villages Association was formed as a positive response to the problems facing the world today. As resources and energy become scarce, there is an urgent need to demonstrate the viability and attractiveness of a lower-consumption lifestyle. Village-sized communities, applying labour-intensive methods of co-operative agriculture and small industry to their fair share of the land (in this country, about one acre per head), could provide their basic needs without causing undue exploitation of people or resources. The New Villages Association intends to demonstrate the practicability and desirability of such an alternative, by establishing self-sufficient New Villages to provide the basis for a sustainable and more hopeful society.*

Some of the main movers in the Association were Lin and Don Warren, John Porter, Chris Evans, David Venner and Roger Franklin. They held a number of meetings and started a newsletter and quite quickly developed a network of regional contacts. They initiated a 'New Villages viability study' to work out how much land a village would need to support itself. The newsletters refer to publications such as *The Limits to Growth* and *A Blueprint for Survival* as inspiration and motivation for their efforts.

> *The problems which these and many other studies forecast are now showing themselves quite clearly - in the world situation, in the crisis which this country is facing, and even in our own individual lives. Though many, including the government, refuse to recognise the fact, economic growth will have to end, and the present urbanised and energy-wasting patterns of society will have to face radical alteration. Such changes will be far less disturbing if we begin now to impose voluntary limits on ourselves.*
>
> **New Villages Association Newsletter 4 and Annual Report Autumn 1974**

While the original thrust of the Association had been the establishment of actual self-sufficient village communities, it had been assumed that this could be done by simply finding participants, a site and the necessary capital. Apparently the 'organisation would develop naturally from the participants'. This was easier said than done and the Association turned more and more to being a research organisation. The Warrens moved to a small site at Cleeve Prior near Evesham and set up the Food and Energy Research Centre in order to carry out practical research in self-sufficiency, albeit on a small scale, to test the ideas that were being generated by the viability study. The Association carried on into the early 1980's producing newsletters and carrying out research into planning problems, financial schemes and past co-operative ventures. It had concluded that it was 'clear that no New Village could be set up without some involvement by local, and probably central, government ...' and saw its role as trying to demonstrate that there was a need for new villages and to draw up detailed plans to show that a New Village would actually work and '... that it really is possible for people to supply their needs from a fair share of land without large inputs of resources.'

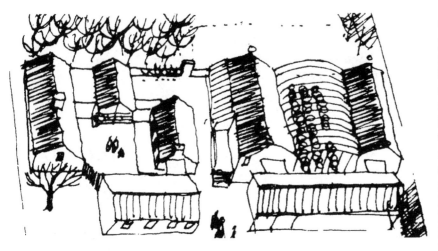

*Sketch of
Park Hall Craft Village*

Others were not so prepared to wait for government involvement and looked round for other sites that might be suitable for setting up new villages; these included run-down holiday camps and surplus military camps. Following a number of Free Festivals, called the Meigan Fayres, held in Pembrokeshire between 1973 and '75, a group hoped to set up a community on the site of Penlan Holiday Village at Cenarth. Their goal was '... To facilitate Harmony. Harmony within man. Harmony between man and his neighbour. Harmony with nature. Planetary Harmony.' Serious proposals were put forward in 1976 by a group called the 'The Association for the Development of a Craft Village and Centre for Charities' to transform over 200 large wooden barrack buildings at the Park Hall Army Camp outside Oswestry in Shropshire into a village-sized community. A planning application was submitted to turn the 260-acre army base in to a craft village with workshops and accommodation for craft workers: '... each having his own living accommodation, workshop and (share of) a retail shop.' While the idea was given support by council meetings at both District and County levels it was turned down at a County planning committee meeting by 13 votes to 11. The participants were left somewhat stoical at coming so close to realising their dream, commenting afterwards:

We have learnt several lessons from this failure: (1) that it's no use sending out a huge well-produced glossy report to councillors, they won't bother to read even the summary. One's time is much better spent going to visit them in their homes. We left this to the last minute, and of the dozen we had time to visit, almost all voted for us. Only by a personal visit can one discover their fears and misconceptions ... on the whole it has been a sobering experience, and makes us realise that without the same sort of pressure that lead to the Garden Cities movement and the New Towns Act – that without some equivalent New Villages Act – we don't stand much of a chance.

Rural Resettlement Handbook

In October and November 1975 one thousand carefully selected individuals and organisations received copies of a prospectus for a new community for 200 people in a location yet to be decided, but possibly in Southern Ireland, Wales, Southern England or New Zealand. The Genesis Community project was the brainchild of Lindsay Rawlings, a former Gurkha, stockbroker and swinging London restaurant owner who had a life-changing moment on reading an article in *The Observer* by Gerald Leach entitled 'Spaceship Earth'.

... It outlined many of the things which he considered likely to go wrong for this planet between now and the turn of the century, and I was astonished. It took me

six months of research and thought to confirm in my own mind the realities of the global situation; and it was during these months that my interest in 'communities' was first aroused ...

Lindsay Rawlings *Genesis Proposal*

Over the next couple of years Rawlings discussed the possibility of setting up a community with a group of his London friends and in January 1974 they started to meet weekly to discuss and plan the project in detail. After spending the summer of '74 touring communities in England, Scotland, France and Belgium, Rawlings spent the rest of the year putting together the first draft of the Genesis Proposal and 'planning how it should be brought to the notice of those who are most likely to contribute to its success'. At the same time he sold his restaurants and on New Year's Day 1975 cropped his hair 'a symbolic clearing of the decks for action,' and set off to scout for a site for the new community. Flying to Australia and on to New Zealand while another member searched among various islands in the Indian Ocean for a suitable location and one of Rawlings' brothers drove the length of South America, from Tierra del Fuego to Mexico, keeping his eye out for a site. Following this grand tour the finishing touches were put to the, nearly, 160-page *Genesis Proposal* and an initial print-run of 1,000 was produced and mailed out to contacts the group had made across Europe, the United States and Australasia. These included some 300 people who the group already knew; several hundred others who had become interested in the project and who had then answered an elaborate questionnaire that the group had sent out; and others who received the document out of the blue. A further 500 copies were printed in December '75 to meet the interest generated by a series of adverts placed in alternative magazines in the UK and USA, newspapers such as the *International Herald Tribune*, *The New Zealand News*, *The Times* and *The Observer*.

The *Genesis Proposal* is a remarkable document. While on the one hand it states that nothing is fixed and how the community functions will be decided by those who eventually live in it ... on the other it sets out, in expansive detail, everything from a community 'behaviour code'; design and construction details; draft community byelaws; policies on pets and working animals; through to community rituals, traditions, routines and celebrations. The proposal sets out to be a visionary document for a new way of living.

The community which we are in the process of creating will be a rural one, with all the land and materials that we need for producing our own food and energy. As far as is possible it will be self-sufficient. It will have a great feeling of privacy, of domain, and yet will be within fairly easy reach of major centres of population. It will provide for considerable interaction with the 'outside world'. It will be simple but comfortable. In some ways it will be very sophisticated. Its members and those passing through it will find in it outstanding opportunities for self-development and spiritual growth. It is likely to appeal to a wide cross-section of people, including many who might not ordinarily have thought of being part of a community. It is going to have to provide cumulatively more of what matters in life to its members than they might find elsewhere, or there will be little point in their being there. It will be a 'light centre' in its particular corner of the globe.

This is set against an almost apocalyptic vision of the future:

... the world situation, already unbelievably serious (unbelievable by some people), will in the foreseeable future reach catastrophic proportions (although I do not regard what is happening as catastrophic). I am not talking about the way that things have always been, extremely tough for some and very tough for most of the others. I am talking about globally inter-related problems so serious that our complete ecosystem, our life-support systems, systems of government, of exchange, of communication will collapse or erupt on a scale never before experienced by humankind. I am talking about destruction and disruption, social and physical, which will make World War II or the great floods or plagues of history look like the limited affairs which by comparison they were.

Genesis Proposal

The appendices of the proposal contained various articles and writings that had influenced and inspired Rawlings to conceive of the project.

A comprehensive timetable is laid out for the setting up of the community. It starts with Phase I the 'Formation Period': to March 1976 which includes the core team meeting with those interested in the project; and concludes with 'The Gathering':

"The Gathering will be a special 14-day 'workshop', carefully designed for Genesis. It is something in which relatively few interested people will be invited to take part. It will provide participants with a very 'safe' space in which to meet themselves and each other and to look at their futures together. We will be working through the proposal, discovering our group consciousness on a host of different issues. We will be working together and playing together. Some of us may be meeting others more closely than they have ever met anybody before. Between us we will be establishing the norms and setting the pace for the future community. The Gathering is likely to be an incomparable experience, not to be missed by anyone who is eligible to be there - to the extent that almost no barrier should stand in the way."

During Phase II, the 'Countdown Period', it was envisaged that members would be 'phasing themselves out of their current work and home situations, liquidating assets and generally preparing themselves for the move into community and for the very different life that lies ahead'. While some would be locating and arranging to purchase the community's land in advance of the group moving in. The hope was that by, perhaps, September 1976 at the earliest, or sometime before 1978 at the latest a site would have been purchased and the community would be ready to start. This would be the trigger for Phase III, the building period, during which the community infrastructure would be realised: renovation of buildings, construction of new buildings 'creating access tracks, laying down services, breaking in new land, not to speak of breaking in ourselves'.

The publication of the proposal elicited responses from the UK and abroad and a date was set for an 18-day Gathering at a large house in Beddgelert in North

Wales. On 25th April 1976 thirty-two would-be participants in the project met for the first time. Some had travelled from the USA, Canada, Australia and New Zealand. Over an intense fortnight the group explored their personal visions of the community and their responses to the proposal. Two of the days were led by Swedish architect-planner Johannes Olivegren and Michael Shaw and Martin Vance from Findhorn. The proceedings were written up and simultaneously projected on to an overhead screen.

There was singing, tears, laughter, sickness, joy and elation and individual times of doubt and sadness. We could hardly have hoped for more. One of the few actual decisions which we felt it necessary to reach was to buy a very large property somewhere in the British Isles as our initial base, one in which to centre ourselves before expanding into further sites in the United Kingdom and abroad.

Genesis Open Letter 1st July 1976

A small group spent a few weeks in the summer of '76 looking at a dozen or so large properties across Britain from a list of 50 they had got the particulars for – 'none with less than 35 bedrooms'. By September they had started negotiating to buy Manderston, a huge 56-bedroom house and grounds in the Borders near the town of Duns. Through their Findhorn connections they were offered a 'winter-let' of the Argyll Hotel on the Scottish Island of Iona and on 11th October twelve adults and two children made their way to Iona, via the first week-long conference at Findhorn. 'The World Crisis and the Wholeness of Life' – with David Spangler and E F Schumacher. While the newly formed Genesis group got busy working out the mechanics of communal living, Lindsay Rawlings spent the last months of 1976 visiting British Colombia to meet with Lord Martin Cecil and his son Michael, leaders of the Emissaries of Divine Light. This meeting would have profound consequences for the future of the Genesis Project. During the months following Rawlings' return to the group on Iona, further links were made with the Emissaries family in England and Genesis members attended a number of meetings and a week-long 'Art of Living' seminar at Findhorn, specially organised by the Emissaries for the Genesis group and 23 of the Findhorn focalisers. As their stay in the hotel on Iona came to an end in the spring, the group made plans to move to Woking in Surrey to help out at The Ockenden Venture, a charity set up to help post-war displaced persons and now helping Vietnamese refugees. The Ockenden Venture were planning an International Youth Festival of Hope for Mankind at which they hoped to get Buckminster Fuller and Mother Teresa to speak. Seemingly gone were the grand plans outlined in the Genesis prospectus.

This step seems a far cry from our original 'vision' of Genesis as a worldwide network of communities, centres and linked individuals, for which the starting point would be a very large and beautiful house somewhere in Britain. That may or may not be so. We rejoice in our increasing willingness to flow in the current of the spirit, releasing whatever images we may have had. We are happy to let the picture for Genesis unfold as it will. We have been very blessed all the way.

Genesis Open Letter 4th March 1977

A few Genesis members seem to have gone on to join the Emissaries, others drifted away from communal living and, apart from copies of the Genesis Proposal which continued to circulate, the project slipped into communal folklore.

Delegates to the 1976 United Nations 'Habitat' conference on human settlement in Vancouver were shown plans for a proposal developed by former Leicester City planner Konrad Smigielski for an 'Evolutionary Village' in the grounds of the Co-operative College at Stanford Hall near Loughborough. The plan for a self-supporting co-operative village with a population of about 2,000 people was being developed by Smigielski and the newly formed Building and Social Housing Foundation based in Coalville. The scheme envisaged utilising 80 acres of 300 acres of parkland surrounding Stanford Hall to build a village of a 1,000 houses with its own industry. 'Parkland trees would be preserved. Carp farming on an existing three-acre lake, a furniture factory and a cheese-making factory are the proposed village industries.' [20] While the local planning authority was opposed to the scheme, Konrad Smigielski was convinced that 'in ten years time there will be such a village! So be it!' The BSHF continued to try and develop the idea for a number of years, but in the end nothing came of the project.

During the latter half of the 1970's some architects and planners would become increasingly interested in the idea of creating new settlements. In 1977 plans were put forward to Devon County Council by the Dartington Hall Trust to create two new hamlets. The plans drawn up by Tom Hancock were for a cluster of houses with communal buildings at the centre; these were to include: 'nursery schools, workshop, meeting halls, etc.' The hamlet would be ringed by a tree belt and the surrounding farmland would be cultivated by the inhabitants. Devon County Council turned the plans down. In May 1978 at the AGM of the Town and Country Planning Association (TCPA), the then chair of the Milton Keynes Development Corporation (MKDC), Lord (Jock) Campbell, suggested that there was a need to reformulate the ideas of the Garden City Pioneer Ebenezer Howard so that they would be '... more directly relevant to the looming problems and aspirations of the 21st century'. He issued a challenge to the Association to create a 'Third Garden City' and invited them to put forward proposals to the Development Corporation in Milton Keynes. Members of the TCPA took up the challenge and set up a series of working parties to look into nine different aspects of setting up a new settlement. These group meetings led to the publication of an *Outline Prospectus for a Third Garden City* which was to initially consist of 100 people on a site of 100 acres, growing eventually to 10,000 people on a site of 500 acres. The prospectus was unveiled at the August Bank holiday Comtek 79 Community Technology Festival held in the Milton Keynes Bowl.

An explosion of interest in the idea of a third Garden City greeted the TCPA's presentation at the Comtek Festival in Milton Keynes. One hundred and seventy people filled a marquee to hear Herbie Girardet, Tom Hancock and David Lock tell the story so far. The interest was such that later the same day a further meeting was held, at which 60 prospective inhabitants of the Garden City discussed what they could do to make the idea a reality. On the spot they formed an action group – the Green Town Group.

Gillian Darley, *Tommorrow's New Communities*

Membership of the Greentown group quickly grew to over 100 people from all over the country. The group worked up their own proposals using the basic principles of the Third Garden City put forward by the TCPA. They wanted the development to be 'a real, village-scaled community, not just a collection of houses'. They also wanted group members to be able to participate in all decisions and for those decisions to be made by consensus. In an attempt to discourage land speculation, the proposal that the group made to the MKDC was for a village where the freehold of the land was held by the Greentown company. It was to be open to anyone who wanted to live there regardless of income. 'The village would grow gradually according to ecologically-sound principles, encouragement would be given to renewable energy sources and energy conservation and the development would include workshops, woodland and horticulture as well as housing and public open space.' **21**

In response, MKDC suggested a 35-acre site in a grid-square called Crownhill. Despite this being much smaller than envisaged in the TCPA proposal, the Greentown group agreed to start working on a detailed proposal for the site. Ideas continued to develop on how the village might operate as work on the proposals progressed through meetings, social events, working groups and a summer camp. Suggestions to raise finance included incorporating a credit union, or establishing their own building society, or even issuing 'Greentown Bonds' tied to the value of land. Various ideas were put forward as to how to get houses actually built: '... Many residents, perhaps most, would self-build their own homes, either individually or as members of housing co-operatives, living cheaply in temporary accommodation over a period of years as they do so ...' **22** The Greentown group went down to Dartington Hall in Devon in August 1980 for a week-long residential event arranged to coincide with an exhibition entitled 'Tomorrow's Village' being put on by the Dartington Hall Trust. The exhibition included other proposals for new village developments. Guy Dauncey and Andrew Page had built a model of their proposal for a 'Community for the Future'.

The conceptual basis for the model is the Protopia papers, a collection of papers and a novella which I have been working on for a number of years. It aims at creative synthesis of the telematic revolution now upon us and the 'green' or ecological movement ... I have tried to combine diverse current ideas of what a sustainable future might be like and to draw on the experience of alternative communities and projects as well as of past failures ...

Andrew Page

The model had been designed in collaboration with Tetra Design Services of Priory Grove and was for a compact community of around 2,000 people that would create a close link between people and the land, facilitating a high degree of self-sufficiency through the appropriate use of high and low technology. The Community for the Future included: high density housing (maximum 4-storeys high); a transport depot, citizen's band radio station; multipurpose village hall; a café-cum-pub; an aquaculture centre; allotments; a constant crèche; and an outlook tower – to give citizens and visitors a view of the whole settlement.

Greentown illustration

Also attending the exhibition at Dartington that August were members of another group who were looking for a 200-acre site to set up their own large-scale alternative community. This group were initially called the Alternative Community Information Exchange, but became better known by the name 'Cartwheel', coined after their imaginative plan to raise their profile and finance by pushing a giant wheel round the country. This group had been formed after a number of people had met and been inspired by Stephen Gaskin, founder of The Farm community in Tennessee when he was on a European tour in the summer of 1978. Hugh Miall, Mike Stanford and Annie Healy, who had met him in Wales, designed a poster which was circulated in magazines and wholefood shops asking people who were interested in setting up a large-scale alternative settlement to get in touch with them with their ideas.

There were about ninety replies, and they were duplicated and recirculated, all being invited to a meeting in the summer of 1979. About thirty people came, from a wide background, both within and outside the Alternative Lifestyle movement. What brought them together was a vision, a fantasy in some ways, of establishing a viable alternative culture, a village where the theories currently circulating could be put into practice and feed off each other to create a new way of life, based upon a series of principles.

Jan Bang 'Cartwheel' in *Diggers & Dreamers* 90-91

The group set out a very ambitious six-month plan that was to start with the writing of a group manifesto and end in the purchase of a 200-acre site. By the end of 1979 a newsletter had been set up and a draft manifesto produced based on four principles of: common ownership of land and houses, income-sharing, non-discrimination and decision-making by consensus. Through the first half of 1980 there was, what one participant described later as, 'feverish activity'. Work groups responsible for different topics held 'countless meetings'. The newsletter was supplemented with a weekly bulletin which was circulated among a core of the most active members. They commissioned a wheelwright to build a giant twelve-foot cartwheel ('the biggest cartwheel in the world') and a three-month-long thousand-mile route was planned for the great 'Wheelroll'. A small group of committed members set off pushing the wheel from Midsomer Norton in June 1980; the first destination was the Free festival at Stonehenge.

Stonehenge. Festival time. We are here, us and the wheel. There is an air of unreality combining with the sense of elation that after so many months of talking and planning, and so much preparatory work we are, at last, on the road ... Today is a rain and sunshine day; tents and tipis, corrugated iron and plastic, wood fires and gas stoves, fluttering flags and wind whipped hair. Today we are resting, repairing ourselves and our things, playing music to others around and collecting a very little money from the more affluent freaks. But really we are here hoping to find a few people who, bored, or enthusiastic for our cause, want to spend a few hours or days or weeks helping to push the wheel.

Mac in a letter in *Communes Network* 52

Despite their small numbers the group continued on their route which took them north through Coventry, Leeds and Scarborough, then back down to London via the Kings Lynn Arts Festival, on to Brighton, Southampton, and down to the West Country. Everywhere they went they managed to get lots of press coverage in local papers and on television and radio. Garnering support from passers-by and getting 'smiles of sympathy for our insanity from butcher and baker alike'. Less successful was the fund-raising aspect of the wheelroll the total collected – after the costs were taken out there was only something in the region of one to two thousand pounds.

In many ways the two groups – whose paths crossed briefly at Dartington in the summer of 1980 – shared very similar visions and ideologies even if they were pursuing them along very different lines. Over the next few years or so the two projects would continue to develop. Cartwheel set up an office in a derelict house in Brighton and continued looking for a suitable site. There was debate among those involved as to the best way forward. Some wanted to create one or more small 'seed sites' where they could get on with building the village immediately while still looking for a main site. Others who had been involved within the commune movement for years were not so keen to join yet another shared household and wanted to wait until the final site was purchased before starting.

This debate was never effectively resolved, and the consensus nature of the decision-making process effectively blocked a great deal of progress. In effect, it was possible for one person, or a small group, to veto any suggestions, and this happened time and time again over the next two years. The question of membership was discussed at great length, but no formal structure was ever set up. This had the effect of giving newcomers as much voice as everyone else immediately, even though they were not familiar with previous discussions and decisions on issues.

Jan Bang

While there was no formal legal structure for the group there was plenty of activity going on. There were seven different working groups, each with its own co-ordinator planning different aspects of the proposed village. There were eight separate regional contacts and the newsletter was being circulated to something like 100 households. Without any fixed location for the new community, Cartwheel members followed up a number of very different possible sites. During the wheelroll contact had been made with Sheffield City Council who invited them to produce an outline draft of how the community was to be set up and organised. A couple of members were offered some land on the west coast of Scotland and moved up there to begin work. Yet other members had identified a number of potential sites in Ireland and set up a Cartwheel Ireland group. Of these Irish sites two came to the fore: one at Glenlough and the other the Inisfree Island in Donegal occupied by the Atlantis community. This multiplying and duplication of possible sites created confusion and led to chaotic organisation and a declining membership. Four or five individuals moved to Inisfree and for a while this became the focus for the project. But in October 1982 a general meeting was held on Inisfree where it was decided that Cartwheel now only existed on Inisfree and that anyone wishing be part of it must move there, that there would be no more newsletters, no more general meetings and that the funds collected would be frozen. This was in fact the final death knell for the Cartwheel project – within a year the group on Inisfree was down to two people, both of whom subsequently moved away.

There is a possibility that had Cartwheel seen itself as an umbrella organisation, encouraging the setting up of several alternative villages, this might have resulted in a number of projects, all working in parallel, and in a position of mutual aid, if not materially, at least morally ... One thing that Cartwheel did prove was that its ideas held currency, and the number of offers that flowed in showed that people were taking these ideas seriously, as an alternative future. Cartwheel's failure in attaining its aims lies not in the impossibility of these aims, but in Cartwheel's failure to take advantage of the possibilities that it was offered.

Jan Bang

In Milton Keynes the Greentown group published their proposals for the Crownhill site and submitted them to the MKDC executive management committee hoping to get approval in principle for Greentown to go ahead. This led to protracted correspondence, with queries flying back and forth between the group and the Corporation. The main difficulty seemed to lie in the fact that while the Greentown group wanted the community to develop organically over time and for the people who lived there to be their own planners, taking perhaps ten years to reach the final completion of the settlement, MKDC wanted to see outline plans for the whole site before it would give approval. To try and get round this impasse the group came up with a style of planning based around clusters of houses.

... Clusters were envisaged as being made up from about eight to 12 households who would act as a group in designing planning and managing part of the Crownhill site: in addition to such clusters there would be planning by all of the village for shared areas such as the network of paths and access roads, services like water, electricity and waste disposal and landscaping and allotments ... the aim was to plan in advance only what was necessary and to leave room for the ideas of residents who joined the group later ...

Hilarie Bowman, *Rural Resettlement Handbook* 3rd ed

The group continued through into 1983, holding meetings and planning workshops trying to refine their plans to meet MKDC's requirements. This involved compromising some of the original ideas that had attracted people to the project but, by working out a plan for the site to be developed in four phases (each of around three to four hectares and each containing several housing 'clusters'), the group thought they had a clear way forward. Members continued to draw up detailed designs and costings for Phase One of the development, but by the following year it was becoming clear that MKDC wanted to treat the group like any other developer and started to demand financial plans. They insisted that the group stop publicising the scheme so as not to cause problems between the Corporation and the relatively newly-formed Milton Keynes Borough Council. Greentown responded by bringing in sympathetic professionals to try and produce proposals that would be more acceptable to MKDC.

... the Corporation's attitude had become one of passive indifference to our project. This shift was probably largely due to changes in the national political climate since the 1970's which had amongst other things resulted in increased pressure on new towns to sell off land as quickly as possible to conventional private developers ... Many of our members left the group because they felt alienated by the apparently endless succession of jargon-ridden meetings with officials. Some suspected that an essentially unsympathetic bureaucracy was simply trying to wear us down. Without a firm commitment by professionals to de-mystify their activities and to facilitate public involvement, community architecture and planning becomes impossible ...

Godfrey Boyle, Carol Barac and David Olivier, *Whatever Happened to Greentown?*

In April 1986 a proposal was made by those who were left in the group to reduce their claim to a 6-acre site for a self-build project. Despite this last-ditch attempt to salvage something from the project, MKDC finally brought an end to negotiations on the pretext that the group had failed to present a 'convincing financial management strategy'. In some seven years the Greentown group had run the whole gamut of emotions from the early idealism when they could state that: 'One Greentown won't save the world. But a million Greentowns, linked in a global community network, may be the only thing that will.' **23** through to final disillusion: 'Our hopes of truly low-cost, low-density housing built by residents in a slow 'organic' process as part of an ecologically self-contained village were increasingly eroded by relentless economic and bureaucratic pressures'. Perhaps in the process they came closer than anyone to realising the dream of a new large-scale community built on the ideas that came out of the 1970's counter-culture.

There was, however, a successful spin-off from the whole Third Garden City proposals. After it had withdrawn from the Greentown scheme, the TCPA teamed up with the Development Corporation at the Telford new town and developed a smaller, more modest, resident-led scheme for 14 self-build houses on what was supposed to be the first phased of a 22-acre scheme. Tony Gibson was appointed as Projects Officer by the TCPA and steered the scheme through to completion. Whilst the Lightmoor project never extended beyond the original houses and was a far cry from the 'Alternative-Lifestyle-ecological-co-operative village' that the Greentown group had envisaged. It was an example of resident-led design, grass roots initiative and co-operation, and was winner of *The Times*/RIBA award for Community Enterprise in 1987. There are signs that in the 21st century it may yet develop further and become something rather larger.

In 1985 a group proposed to set up a 'large-scale/village type community-co-op' in the former Desford Industrial School at Polebrook on the Northamptonshire-Leicestershire border. Polebrook house and 60 acres of land was being offered for sale by Leicestershire County Council for £750,000. A group calling itself the Polebrook Project put together a proposal for accommodation for 150 people, to set up workers co-ops and to run a free-school. Advertising for members in *Communes Network* 85 the group announced 'At the moment there is about 20 of us actively involved in the project, since our advertising campaign last summer we have grown a lot. Apart from larger numbers a wider group of people including coloured people, lesbians and gays are getting involved in the project.' The price proved too high for the group and the school was eventually turned into a retirement village. The group also looked at Murthly Hospital, a former mental asylum and wartime hospital north of Perth.

There was a smaller-scale community that has some marked similarities with some of the 1970's attempts to set up new villages. Actually established in 1964, the 'Far North Project', as it was known, was initiated by Sutherland District Council who had acquired the MoD early warning station at Durness on the remote North Coast of Scotland. They had originally intended to set up small-scale industrial units, but when there was little interest it was decided to try and establish a craft village. Ads were placed in national newspapers offering the buildings for minimal rent to those who had skills and viable business plans.

The buildings were empty concrete shells with no plumbing or electricity. Some had no glazing and were barely habitable. The conversion of the bleak and deserted barracks into homes and workshops was daunting. During the early years there was also help from the International Voluntary Service who erected electricity poles and ran power cables.

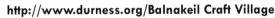

http://www.durness.org/Balnakeil Craft Village

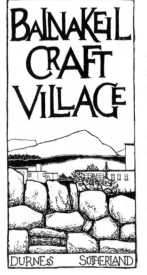

Over the next few years a small craft community started to develop. A coffee shop, pottery and the first commercial transport to Cape Wrath were instigated by founder members and, in 1970, a craft association for the little 'village' was formed. By 1980 numbers had risen to a point where there were 16 independently-owned businesses making up Balnakeil Craft Village and at this point the Highland Regional Council offered to sell the properties to the sitting tenants. The residents took up the offer to buy their houses and workshops. The change in ownership led to the formation in the early eighties of the Balnakeil Craft Village Community Co-operative, set up to provide facilities and services for residents and visitors. A visitor centre was opened and a regular commercial bus service established to Ullapool and Tongue. The community co-operative was wound up in late 1986 but the craft village has continued and by the end of the 1990's had a population of 30 adults and 15 children.

The failures in finding alternative approaches – and there have been quite a number – reflect the fact that while in Britain every housing reformer's interest was in direct provision of housing by local authorities in the mistaken view that this was progressive or socialist, hardly anyone thought it worthwhile to explore the potential of dweller control except in individual ownership. The successful examples of the last decade have all been in spite of, rather than because of, the official system of housing finance, and their endless frustrations and delays have been the result of trying to make adjustments to the official reality and the official way of conceiving loans and subsidies. They have often come into existence in spite of, not because of, the local authorities.

Colin Ward Housing is Theft, Housing is Freedom

Communes Britannica

Going International

The idea grew out of an evening with Alan from Christiania while we had Christian from Germany and Bridget from France staying. We realised how little we knew of other's communities around the world yet together we seemed able to create a great deal of energy, giving each other new perspectives from our different cultural experiences. Since then we've discussed it with people from other groups in this country and abroad who've called by, and it is clear that a lot of people are excited by it.

Dave Treanor of Laurieston Hall in Communes Network 40

During the week of 21st-29th of September 1979 the British network of communes took on a decidedly international flavour with the organisation of an International Communes Festival at Laurieston Hall near Castle Douglas in South West Scotland. Attended by over 100 communards from 14 different countries, a series of newsletters were put out in the run-up to the festival to encourage people to come and let them know what to expect.

Write to us about yourselves, your groups, and what you'd like to do during the week. Bring photographs, slides, film, video, if you can, to give people an idea of what life is like in your community. The week will be full of small gatherings dotted about this enormous house, sometimes on specific scheduled topics, sometime spontaneous; with a few larger meetings with everyone for films or talks about particular groups or topics. And we hope there'll be music and dancing, and walks around the lochs, hills and forests of Galloway.

International Communes Festival Newsletter No 1

Laurieston Hall, set up in 1972, had become a thriving alternative 'conference' and course centre. The large 65-room, somewhat rambling, former tuberculosis isolation hospital and NHS nursing home, set in about 12 acres of grounds with a large walled garden, greenhouses, semi-derelict stables and two cottages had been bought for £25,500 by four families selling their homes in London. Home to about 20 members and children, the group was income- and work-sharing and described itself as having 'Women's Liberation and other tendencies.' **24** After an initial period when members commuted to work elsewhere (some to as far away as London) to support the community, the group realised that the house lent itself to being used as an alternative venue.

... we took on another aspect of our fragmented collective identity: Laurieston Hall as the non-sectarian, libertarian/socialist, personal-is-political revolutionary group. Laurieston as a movement 'base.' Here comes – dah dada dah dah, dada, da dah! – the People Centre ... But 'Conference' wasn't the right word. This was to be a softer, looser, 'tribal gathering', blurring conference with holiday, living together and consciousness-raising. To set the tone, we'd called the whole thing LARFFS: Laurieston's Alternative Revolutionary Fun-Fair & Seminar. 25

Mike Reid

The group settled in to a pattern of alternative courses and gatherings and visits of holiday groups of children from cities during the summer months and quieter winter months when they searched for other sources of income or did jobs around the house and grounds. Alongside growing their own veg in the walled garden and looking after livestock; goats, pigs, chickens and bees.

We support ourselves by working from here, including gardening and tending animals (Smallholding Project), looking after children from cities (Freefall Children's Project), organising conferences or providing space and facilities for others to organise their own (People Centre Project) designing and building farm buildings and housing for local people (Building and Design Project) and selling what we make ourselves (Craft Project, Garden Sales).

Alice Simpson, *Summer Visitor Blurb* 1976

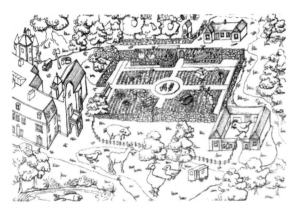

Laurieston Hall from Communes Network Directory 1984

During the late 1970's and into the 1980's Laurieston played a major part in Communes Network – hosting weekend and week-long gatherings on a whole range of themes and topics relevant to communal living and countercultural politics. As well as LARFFS, there were 'conferences' on: Legal Frameworks; Land Issues; Living in the Country; an Alternative University week; and, in 1977, a Gay Men's Week. The group also took on editing, printing and distributing the *Communes Network* newsletter. All of which made them a natural choice as a venue for an international festival of communes. Those arriving at the festival after coming down a long avenue of mature beech trees were greeted by the sight of the word 'WOW' in two-foot-high letters suspended over the main entrance of the hall – courtesy of a salvage excursion to a local Woolworths store. Festival-goers were shown to a variety of fancifully named rooms:

... Some were the original names, taken from the defunct bell-board system for calling servants – Morning Room, Billiard Room. Yes, we are aware that these are ruling class descriptions, thank you, but we've decided to co-opt them. Other bell-board names never stuck: The Big Front Room was never The Ballroom. The Dining Room became Tony's Room then Tony's Old Room then Flight Deck. Some descriptions were the NHS's – Matron's Sitting Room, Nurses' Dining Room. Our own additions came from colour of paint (Passion), existing wallpaper (Roses), what the kids did (Scribble), what visitors did (Seaview - Flick A.'s painting of wavelets), wishful thinking (Warm Room, located over the Old Kitchen) and Patrick's attempt at plumbing (Waterfall). Naming and renaming rooms was part of the, er, fun.

Mike Reid *Mix Café* – unpublished manuscript

The festival was a success and the groups represented at it decided to set up an International Network and organise further annual gatherings.

ICN is a loosely knit global network of communes working on a radical alternative to present day social structures. It carries information and ideological support and gives strength and encouragement through the exchange of communal ideas and experiences.

International Communes Festival Newsletter No2

A second festival was held in Denmark in 1981 – attended by fifty people from communities in eleven different countries who met under canvas at a campsite near Mejlgard Castle. As well as workshops on finance, decision-making and relationships there was discussion of ongoing exchanges between Danish collectives and Tanzanian villages. At the conference were representatives of Danish Bofaellesskaber communities – which by the end of the 1980's would inspire the Cohousing Movement in the USA and other parts of Europe. A bus load of communards from Britain attended the event. The contrast between the Danish communities' movement and that in Britain elicited mixed responses.

Rapid Transformations bus and crew drawn by Charlie Easterfield

There is something unalternative about Danish communes – a response to their affluence. Danish communes seem to be well integrated into the parent culture, and very bound up with the money economy. I found this slightly disturbing.
Clive of Rapid Transformations

Danish alternative projects struck me as much more efficient and business like in their activities, with a greater impact in the fields they work. The publishing side of the castle collective is much better equipped than any similar venture in Britain ... it leaves me with a lot of questions, as to why it has happened more powerfully here than at home ...

Dave Treanor, Laurieston Hall,

In the same year and almost in parallel with the Danish ICN Festival the First International Conference on Communal Living was held in Israel, sponsored by Haifa University and the Tabenkin Institute and organised by the two largest kibbutz federations at Kibbutz Ein-Hashofet. The conference was an altogether more formal and academic affair than the ICN festivals with lectures '... delivered by a kibbutz speaker over a microphone, the 'audience' sitting in a semi-circle on hard chairs. Questions were queued, so the discussion usually became a series of mini-speeches rather than a direct exchange of ideas ...' **26** The conference was attended by 100 people from 16 countries. Although half the attendees were from Israeli universities or kibbutzim it hadn't been intended that the kibbutz movement be the focus of the conference but much time was, inevitably, spent talking about kibbutz history, organisation, ideology and future direction. The proceedings of the conference were published in a small book titled, *The Alternative Way of Life*. The contrast between the two international events was one of emphasis and style and perhaps more fundamentally one of politics both on a personal level and a more conventional political level.

It was in the ICD and ICN newsletters following this conference that the serious conflicts were finally voiced. There were concerns that the First Kibbutz conference in Israel had drawn energy away from the 2nd Communes Festival in Denmark which had happened four months earlier. Also, there was concern that the kibbutz people had ignored the networking which had been going on in Europe. Two

Allen Butcher, An International Network of Communities 1989

The debate around the Kibbutz movement and whether communes should boycott or have constructive engagement with it reared its head in the pages of *Communes Network* now and then throughout the 1980's. A third, more European-focussed, festival was held in Belgium in 1982, and in 1983 a further festival was planned, once again at Laurieston Hall. In the intervening years changes had taken place at Laurieston. In 1980 the legal ownership of the property was transferred to a housing co-op structure and a mortgage taken out with the Housing Corporation to pay back capital lent by early members. In 1981 an opportunity came up to buy a large area of surrounding woodland and farmland; with money raised from loans and donations from members and friends, the group were able to increase their land holding to 130 acres, half of which was woodland.

... As the transfer in 'ownership' of the place began to take effect, several people from the commune took the option of remaining part of the housing co-op but becoming domestically, financially, and to some extent socially, separate from the commune. They moved out of the main house into the cottages, a corner of the stable-block and two caravans. There were tensions then between commune and non-commune members, with the commune being seen as the 'institution' and 'powerful', and non-commune folk as too independent and not accountable to anyone ...

Gilly Fordham, 'Changing and Growing' in *Diggers & Dreamers* 92-93

During this time two of Laurieston's members, Sarah Eno and Dave Treanor, rewrote and updated the Legal Frameworks booklet that had been first produced in 1975. The new *Collective Housing Handbook* ran to 142 pages and was described as 'A practical manual providing all the information you need to set up and run a collective household'. As well as an update on legal structures it included: chapters on raising money through public funding, mortgages and private loans; advice on taxation and accounting; and a whole section entitled 'Being Together' on 'The nuts and bolts of sharing – money, property and work' with sections on how to run meetings, decision making and conflict resolution.

This segment is about new ways of organising, new ways of making and carrying out decisions, of handling conflict, and of eliminating boredom! Boredom is a phony feeling: it covers up other frightening feelings – anger, anxiety, sadness. When we find safe ways to work these feelings out, the 'boredom' disappears – that dreadful Suffocation which many of us have known so intimately for years, and which had the simple function of stilling free expression!

When people first encounter the sorts of new approaches we'll be describing, they often see them as 'artificial', 'unreal'. Living in houses is artificial too; but we've grown accustomed to it. It takes time to get to know new tools; and admittedly, some of these tools are liable to bring up realities we'd rather not face. However, realities are realities; and a trail of bleached bones marks the fate of collective ventures that have tried to ignore the real feelings of members. Women, in particular, have tended to be punished for their better awareness of real feelings - by men who, in pursuit of the highest ideals, have pretended to feel things they don't feel, like universal love and generosity! The techniques we are going to describe act to ground us in solid reality, and to cut through the miasmas of anxiety that often surround quite simple issues. Many of them are also a great deal of fun.

Collective Housing Handbook

When the 100 or so participants at the 1983 ICN Festival arrived they divided into support groups of 7 or 8 people who didn't know each other, each with their own Laurieston resident 'minder'. They took part in various workshops and presentations. Rosemary Randall and Sarah Eno ran a series of workshops throughout the festival on meetings and group decision-making. Everyone mucked in with chores, cooking and cleaning.

… there was plenty of time to … enjoy the commune's sauna and the Turkish bath tent … and get a tan during the few hours of sun. But have you ever tried to conduct a serious discussion on questions of universal importance, on the lawn, with a girl whose only cover is a pair of sunglasses? At my own and some other communards' initiative we held a thorough discussion with most of the leading individuals on the future of the international network of communes. Two trends stood out. One claimed that after five years of links, these should be tightened – and an international center established, at least for the purpose of information and the collation of experiences for the general good. Others argued that the present situation was good enough: we don't have to create more official frameworks so as not to be caught up with problems of decision-making, finances, whom to help, and the like.

Uzi El-Natan of Kibbutz Gesher in *ICD Newsletter*, May 1984

Discussion on the future of the International Network continued the following year when the 1984 festival was held at De Refter, near Nijmegen in Holland. Again the same divided opinions were expressed with some arguing for a central office which could co-ordinate regional or world-wide networks, while others expressed outright opposition to any such formal centralisation. In the end the issue was left unresolved. 1985 saw the founding of a new academic organisation '... to provide a common framework for a scholarly exchange and information on communes, intentional communities, collective settlements and kibbutz throughout the world'. The International Communal Studies Association (ICSA) held its inaugural convention at Yad Tabenkin, the Research and Documentation Centre of the Kibbutz Movement. The emphasis was firmly on the study of communal living and few actual communards other than Kibbutzniks attended. The proceedings and papers were printed in a 758 page book, *Communal Life*. A sixth ICN festival was held at Le Puy in France in 1985 hosted by Collectif Reseau Alternatif in a youth hostel on top of a mountain in central France. Further festivals of mainly European communities were advertised in Denmark and Germany in '86 and '87. But the energy to sustain large annual international gatherings had run out, in part drained by the lack of any resolution of the debate on how, or even if, it was possible to network internationally.

By the time of the second ICSA conference in 1988, most European communitarians were ignoring the ICSA, boycotting, as it were, the academics. Perhaps the sentiment was one of reluctance to continue to debate the networking issue, as though the movement, through hearing years of talk about networking centers and the setting of organisational goals, was tired of competing with the kibbutz movement. An added factor is that after eight years of activism, many communitarian activists were moving on, some of them leaving community, frustrated with the slow rate of progress, others being ready for a lifestyle change.

Allen Butcher, An International Network of Communities 1989

At Laurieston the late 80's saw a major shift in the way the community was organised. This followed a number of years when, at the group's annual 'November Talks', members had expressed dissatisfaction over the way the community was structured. During the winter of 1986/87 circumstances combined to convert the talk into action. The 'changes' were reported in the spring editions of the *Laurieston Hall Newsletter* and in the pages of *Communes Network*.

... many times over the years we've aired, discussed and agonised over big changes here, we always decided it was too too much. There was work to be done and we dropped the ideas, leaving some people relieved and others frustrated. When any change is made it feels sudden. Something different. Not what one usually does. Therefore a risk, we all wanted ways of changing while totally maintaining the status quo! We are a very efficient institution in many ways and are afraid to rock the boat. But never before have we realised we all want to move forward, we all want to change.

The biggest change is that the commune is dissolving. The commune as started in 1972: income and expense, work and home sharing. We are relinquishing control of and responsibility for the house, and gaining more involvement in and responsibility for the wider co-op. The commune has always had the power of the group over the individual. It's been easier for us to communicate, have impromptu meetings, make decisions - which has been fine except that wider co-op members have wanted to take more responsibility, be more involved ... The set-up of commune and co-op perpetuated the very landlord/tenant situation everyone wanted to avoid. The big house – the cottages and caravans ... Now we will all share the same status. People can move to the part of the house and grounds they feel most comfortable with, without having to give up their work, share more than they want to, change status. Some wider co-op people are moving into the house. Some commune people are moving out ...

Jude in Communes Network 90

... we're now a housing co-op within which members can live individually, or in couples, or in families, or in groups. And this is what we already have been for a good number of years, except that there was always the commune at the core of the place – living in the hall, providing most of the resources, looking after

the visitors and running the People Centre. Perhaps it was the very flexibility of
the commune, allowing a degree of individuality not usually found in similar
set-ups – living-spaces for couples and families and people able to make spaces for
themselves outside the house ... But we've done it! With dozens of big meetings and
small meetings, with tears, smiles and sighs, we've achieved a 'revolution' on our
own terms and in our own way.

Gilly in Communes Network 90

Once the new set-up had settled down, and members had got used to a
different way of organising, the group emerged as a more stable, more diverse,
perhaps more sustainable community. One result of the change was that over
the ensuing years Laurieston became less central to the Communes Network.

Laurieston Hall

*I remember thinking through what had happened and reflecting that the change we had made had probably
been inevitable ... perhaps since the housing co-op was formed in 1980, putting all residents on an equal basis as
far as financing the land and buildings was concerned; or perhaps before that, when the first person to leave the
commune (and the main house) stayed within the grounds; or perhaps before that, when the commune split into
separate living-groups. It could even be argued that from the very beginning – because of the house being so huge,
and because of the cottages and the stable-block and the space for caravans – there was a gradual but inexorable
move towards there being a more diverse group here.*

Gilly Fordham 'Changing & Growing' in Diggers & Dreamers 92-93

Abrams, P & McCulloch, A "Men, Women and Communes" in *Sexual Divisions and Society: Process and Change* Editors: Diana Barker & Sheila Allen, 1976 Tavistock Publications

Abrams, P & McCulloch, A *Communes, Sociology and Society* 1976 University of Durham. ISBN: 0521290678

Brownlow Kevin *Winstanley: Warts and All* 2009 UKA Press. ISBN: 1905796226

Eno, S & Treanor, D *The Collective Housing Handbook* 1982 Laurieston Hall. ISBN: 0950831514

Fairfield, R *Communes Europe*

Gamlin, B (ed) *The Patchwork History of a Community Growing up.* ASIN: B005QA1DUK

Hardy, D *From New towns to Green Politics* 2011 Routledge. ISBN: 0415511747

Mitford, Jessica *Faces of Philip, a Memoir of Philip Toynbee* 1984 Heinemann.

Power, Lisa *No Bath but Plenty of Bubbles* 1995 Continuum International. ISBN: 0304332054

Smigielski, Konrad *Self-Supporting Co-operative Village at Stanford Hall* 1978 BSHF. ASIN: B0006D1LC2

Toynbee, Philip *Part of a Journey* 1982 Fount. ISBN: 0006264808

Various Editors *Diggers & Dreamers* Biennial editions:

Ansell, Coates, Dawling, How, Morris & Wood (eds) *Diggers & Dreamers 90/91* 1989 Communes Network. ISBN: 951494503

Coates, Dawling, How, Morris & Wood (eds) *Diggers & Dreamers 92/93* 1991 Communes Network. ISBN: 951494511

Coates, How, Jones, Morris & Wood (eds) *Diggers & Dreamers 94/95* 1993 Communes Network. ISBN: 95149452X

Coates, How, Jones, Morris & Wood (eds) *Diggers & Dreamers 96/97* 1995 D&D Pubs. ISBN: 951494538

Bunker, Coates, How, Jones & Morris (eds) *Diggers & Dreamers 98/99* 1997 D&D Pubs. ISBN: 951494546

Bunker, Coates, Hodgson & How (eds) Diggers & Dreamers 00/01 1999 D&D Pubs. ISBN: 951494554

Bunker, Coates, Hill, Hodgson, How & Watson *Diggers & Dreamers 02/03* 2001 D&D Pubs. ISBN: 951494562

Bunker, Charnock, Coates, Hodgson & How (eds) *Diggers & Dreamers 04/05* 2003 D&D Pubs. ISBN: 951494509

Bunker, Coates & How (eds) *Diggers & Dreamers 06/07* 2005 D&D Pubs. ISBN: 951494517

Bunker, Coates & How (eds) *Diggers & Dreamers 08/09* 2007 D&D Pubs. ISBN: 9780956936721

Notes:

1   *Communes Europe*
2   50 Eno Moments, *Independent on Sunday*, 10th May 1998
3   http://arjunawholefoods.co.uk (26.5.2011)
4   Interview with the author 2008
5   Report on the 'Commune Scene in Britain' in *Communes Europe*
6   *A Federal Society Based on the Free Commune* 1969
7   *Fourth World Review*, Vol 1 No 18, February 1983
8   www.globalideasbank.org (25.12.2011)
9   Personal correspondence with the author
10 ibid
11 Aim of People In Common in original leaflet promoting the group.
12 Information on Lower Shaw Farm from interview with Matt Holland 2010
13 Personal correspondence with the author
14 Vicky Moller interviewed by the author at Fachongle Isaf in 2009
15 Robin Appleby interviewed by the author 2009
16 Entry in *Directory of Alternative Communities 1977*
17 Gina Heathersprite interviewed by the author 2009
18 *ACM Newletter* 6, 21.3.80 Communes Network a review, Kevin of the Teachers
19 *A Book of Visions: A Directory of Alternative Society Projects* 1973
20 *Undercurrents* 19th Dec 1976
21 Godfrey Boyle, *Undercurrents* 43, Dec Jan 1980/81
22 ibid
23 ibid
24 *Communes Network* 21st Jan 1977
25 *Mix Café* – unpublished manuscript
26 June Stratham, Greentown, England, *ICD Newsletter*, August 1982

Towards the New Millennium

Alongside the international networking activity taking place during the 1980's the UK Communes Network was highly active. The network magazine (*CN*) – having changed from a duplicated A4 newsletter to an A5 booklet format in 1982 – came out pretty much quarterly throughout the decade with the editorial role rotating among a number of communities starting at Laurieston and working its way to Lifespan (who also took on responsibility for printing it in the later years). Along the way it was put together by Birchwood Hall, Redfield, Crabapple, People In Common, Wheatstone, Holme Place, Some People In Leicester and Glaneirw. These communities, along with one or two others forming what might be called a core of the network, often contributing much of the content of the issues of the magazine that they produced as well as doing all the practical work of arranging layout, printing, collating and distribution. There was then another layer of communities who regularly appeared in the magazine and in a number of directories that came out during the period, and clearly saw themselves as connected to the network – these included places such as: Atlantis, Beech Hill, Canon Frome and Old Hall. There was then a wider 'diaspora' of communal groups who sent in occasional contributions to the magazine and advertised in it when they were looking for new members. Given its informal nature it is hard to pin down quite how many groups made up the network or considered themselves to be part of it. The 1985 *Communes Network Directory* lists 33 communities, but not all of these groups were subscribers. Although individuals within communities often were, there were many more groups who either did not respond to requests for directory entries or simply did not want to be listed. On top of this there were individual subscribers who ranged from would-be-communards, to academics and ex-community members, to those just interested in what was going on. The *CN* magazine carried adverts for a whole host of communes gatherings that took place during the 1980's – a 'Living in Communities Conference' at Canon Frome; various 'Women in Communities' gatherings; week-long 'Introductions to alternatives' at Lower Shaw Farm and Monkton Wyld; a 'Symposium on Land Use' at Redfield; a 'Relationships in Communities' week at Laurieston; and a series of somewhat occasional *CN* readers' and subscribers' gatherings. From the reports in the pages of the magazine much discussion at the readers' gatherings seemed to have focussed on what was the purpose of the network … the magazine … the gatherings. In some ways the conversation paralleled that which had been going on at an international level. There were those who wanted to see a more outward looking, more organised network with perhaps an office and information exchange actively promoting communal living and supporting new groups that wanted to set up. There were others who wanted a more informal 'sharing' emphasis – with work exchanges and chances to exchange experiences. Like the debate at the International Festivals, it never seems to have reached a conclusion in favour of either approach or to agree that both were equally valid. Time for debate would run out at the particular gathering, there would be a report in the following magazine and the thread of the argument would be left to be picked up at another meeting. Perhaps out of

frustration at this ongoing debate, various slightly more anarchic initiatives were taken by small groups of individuals working outside the auspices of the network itself. In 1981 a small group, made up of members from a number of groups within the network published a prospectus for Fair Ground as a way to establish an alternative financial institution to support communities.

Fair Ground is not just about money. Perhaps most of all it is based on the diggers concept that land and property are the right of all. So Fair Ground seeks to take property out of private exploitative hands, to destroy the concept of bosses and workers and to put common ownership and co-operation in their place.

Fair Ground Prospectus 1981

The idea for Fair Ground had come out of a meeting held in January 1977 where three proposals for funding communes were put forward of which Fair Ground – the so-called 'Maxi Co-op' – was seen to be the most viable. Money collected at Trevor Howell's funeral to be used towards setting up an alternative building society was combined with the £600 collected by the now defunct Commune Movement in its Federation Fund along with the last £30 in CM's current account and passed over to Fair Ground. The idea was to form a secondary co-operative, a co-op of co-ops, made up of communes from all over the country. This 'Maxi-Co-op' would own all the properties belonging to the communities and would rent them back to the individual groups. It was hoped that with the combined capital value of all the properties, Fair Ground would be able to borrow more capital and thus buy more land to establish further communes and co-operatives. It was envisaged that the project would also provide people who had money which they wanted to invest with an opportunity that was 'more consistent with their politics'.

Members from 15 or so communes had met for quarterly two-day meetings for over three years to bring Fair Ground into existence. After protracted negotiations with the Registrar of Friendly Societies and the Inland Revenue the group were finally able to register as a Secondary Housing Co-op under the Industrial and Provident Societies Acts.

Top to Bottom:
Fair Ground logo; Crabapple
Wheatstone; Lifespan

... Fair Ground is just a beginning. It has taken three years of hard talking between the groups involved,

and a long process of negotiation with the Registrar of Friendly Societies, sympathetic lawyers and expensive tax consultants; we have tried to produce a model that can be copied just as so many communes were able to follow the precedents created by People in Common six years ago. [1]

The prospectus set out Fair Ground's aims and objectives. As well as acting as a financial body for communities, the prospectus stated that they also wanted to provide advice and support for member co-ops and to represent the interests of communes in the wider world. The prospectus listed seven groups as the initial members; Lifespan, Laurieston Hall, Glaneirw, Crabapple, Tweed Street, Freeboard boat co-op and Wheatstone. The other groups who had been involved at the beginning had either lost interest or decided that the 'maxi co-op' was not for them. In a way Fair Ground was a descendent of the original Commune Movement's Grand Plan for a 'Federation of Free Communes' – this is what it looked like in the cold legal light of day having been through the threshing machine of registration and tax law. While the Commune Movement manifesto had been high on visionary rhetoric and scant on actual practical detail, the Fair Ground prospectus was pretty much the opposite and therein lay one of its problems. So much time, effort and focus had gone into dealing with the legal and financial issues that the more visionary, idealist and inspirational ideas that lay behind it had somehow been pushed into the background along the way. This was one reason that groups had dropped out, being unconvinced that there was any benefit to them. Of the seven groups listed in the prospectus only two were, ultimately, actually in a position to put their property into the project. It therefore slowly ground to a halt.

By the time Fair Ground was legally established, all but two of the communities involved had no desire to join, or were unable to do so for legal reasons and so the Grand Plan was shelved. One reason was probably that in working so hard to get the scheme accepted by the public bodies, too little attention was paid to its acceptability to the members of the communities involved. Meetings tended to be dominated by the same few men with sufficient legal and financial

Top to Bottom:
Laurieston Hall; Glaneirw;
Freeboard Boat Co-op; Tweed Street

understanding. Many community members were unwilling to risk the autonomy of their commune in the hands of an increasingly small number of individuals, however benign the intentions of those people were. Since those early days, however, secondary housing co-ops and ethical investment funds have become quite common, and there is even the Ecology Building Society, so it can be seen that the ideas have lived on. **2**

Pam Dawling, 'What is Communes Network?' in *Diggers & Dreamers* 92/93

There were other ventures that operated semi-detached from the network. For a number of years in the 80's each summer an old green bus would turn up at a community and out would pour an intrepid band of builders, roofers, their friends and children. They would set up camp, erect their own tent-cum-sauna and set-to, usually tackling a major roofing project for the community which the group on their own didn't have the resources to take on.

In case you haven't heard of Rapid Transformations before, they're an elite anarchistic group (their own description!) who live in communities or are otherwise engaged in alternative activities who choose to take a 'holiday' together each year to do a roofing job for a community in need. In exchange the community offers food and accommodation (in our case a field) and expenses if they can afford it ... **3**

Alison of Crabapple

Each group that was graced by a Rapid Transformations visit provided the materials for the job, fed the crew and, if I remember rightly, provided a bottle of Scotch as payment. The anarcho-builders had a variety of skill levels ranging from willing beginner to construction professional.

... Everyone seemed very keen to share skills however, which I see as one of the most positive aspects of this sort of working. It was also quite incredible to be working with so many people up on the same roof at once, all doing jobs at different stages. No-one seemed to be taking a lead but everyone seemed to find a job and it all went very smoothly and incredibly fast.

Alison of Crabapple

Rapid Transformations helped a number of communities tackle otherwise physically and financially daunting construction projects, even tackling a job at Christiania in Denmark one summer.

Following a network gathering at Lifespan in 1983 where the future focus of the network was discussed, an ad appeared in the next *Communes Network* magazine inviting people to a meeting at Redfield Community to

The COLLECTIVE EXPERIENCE

£1-50

ARTICLES AND POEMS ABOUT COMMUNAL LIVING

SELECTED FROM COMMUNES NETWORK

A Communes Network Information Pack

Communes and Communities

discuss the production of a video and info pack on communes. The idea was to produce a video aimed at 'schools and other groups who want to hire/borrow it' and that 'might also be useful for people in the initial stages of setting up a community'.

... the video to be made for the communities by the communities. Apart from collaborating in the setting up of the project, one possible idea is that each interested community has a 10-minute slot in which to present themselves in whatever manner they wish. We should be able to provide the technical know-how and equipment. It has been suggested that we do an Info-pack at the same time on communities in Britain ...

Redfield, Communes Network 73 October 1983

The video proved harder than anticipated to produce but after a number of meetings at Redfield attended by members of a several different communities it was decided to go ahead and produce a *Communes Network Information Pack*. This was envisaged as a 'general introduction to the nitty-gritty and issues of communal living.' The *Info Pack*, which was published in July 1985, consisted of a folder containing 14 different factsheets covering topics ranging from 'Alternatives to the Nuclear Family' to 'Earning a Living in a Community' and 'Young People and Children in Communities'. There was a copy of the current *CN* magazine; a directory; and a few samples of publicity sheets from individual communes. The group putting it together saw communes as being part of a '... long tradition of socialist and anarchist experiments in lifestyle ...' and hoped that the *Info Pack* would help reach out to a broad cross-section of those who might want to join a commune.

Perhaps you are a school leaver wondering where to start your independent life, a single parent tired of coping with too much work and too many emotional demands, a student facing the choice between unemployment or a career in the armed forces, a single person looking for a friendly and challenging alternative to isolated bedsitter life, someone wanting to move out of a cramping marriage.... perhaps you are wondering if communal life is for you?

Introduction to Communes Network Information Pack, 1985

The pack also included a reading list for those wanting to find out more and a sheet entitled 'What To Do after Reading This?' which encouraged readers to visit a number of communities and '... see for yourself what it's like.'

At the same time as the *Info Pack* group was working, another small group decided to put together a sort of 'best of' compilation of past articles from *Communes Network*. Produced by Bob Matthews, Keith Bailey and Jan Bang, *The Collective Experience* came out in 1984 and complimented the more general approach of the *Info Pack* – the intention was for it to be a celebration and affirmation of communal living. 'We hope this selection will give some insight into the joys, sorrows, humour, theory and practicalities of communal life, as seen through the eyes of communards themselves ...'

Reading through the selection of articles ... I found much with which I could identify, and it consolidated my feelings of being part of a network of groups of people learning in various ways to live and work co-operatively. There is a wealth of contributions – accounts, poems, stories, cartoons – by people wanting to share their experiences and feelings with others. The overall impression I gained was of people facing up to their own shortcomings, people with ideas tempered with realism coming from experience, and with much hope and determination that co-operation and collectivism can succeed.

Martin of Holme Place, 'Review of The Collective Experience' in Communes Network 79

While these two publications were put together by small groups working independently, they were both distributed under the umbrella of the Communes Network. *Collective Experience* was reprinted in 1986, the initial print run of 1,000 having sold out – a copy being included in later sales of the *Info Pack*s. Interest in communal living continued through the second half of the 80's with steady sales of both of these publications but, although this helped raise the profile of communes in general, actual subscriptions to *CN* magazine at the same time saw little or no increase, levelling off at about 200.

As the decade ended, the public profile of communes was given a further boost by a monthly column that appeared in *The Guardian* newspaper. It was written by Bob Fromer who lived at Birchwood Hall. The articles featured an account of the goings-on at a semi-fictitious commune called 'The Lodge'. Each month a different topic of communal living was covered including; visitors – 'Definitely no vegans, no dogs, no God'. The trials of maintenance day – 'Our mansion hath many rooms' and the communal cook's choice of music – 'Hark the errant angels sing ...' The stories, which filled anything up to an eighth of a broadsheet page, struck a careful balance between tongue-in-cheek playful ribbing and cringe-making portrayal of the foibles of those trying to live communally. They were carried off with aplomb because the writer was so clearly speaking from, occasionally bitter, experience.

When the going gets tough in communities, the tough call meetings. And so it was decided to devote a Sunday night Feelings Meeting to the subject of Maintenance. The outstanding feature of Feelings Meetings at The Lodge is that no one ever expresses any. But this time, there were plenty. And the atmosphere could only be described as grim. "I'll tell you the most abhorrent word in the English language," said Bill, bitterly. "It's the word 'just', as in 'You just do this', or 'You just need to do that.' Every time I hear those words, I know I'm a dead man. "That's bad," said Carl, "but what's even worse is starting a job and discovering that some bastard hasn't put the hammer back, or you can't find the chuck key for the drill. Drawing and quartering is the only appropriate response." This latter problem is of course perennial, and there have been attempts to solve it by holding a Tool Amnesty, not unlike the Offensive Weapons Amnesty staged by the Met Police a couple of years back: all knives and guns accepted during the next 30 days, no questions asked. But criminals at The Lodge are a tougher breed: at the end of the 30 days the drill itself was missing ... **4**

Bob Fromer 'Our mansion hath many rooms' in *The Guardian*

The articles first appeared in March 1989 and ran monthly through until December. Each one was eagerly awaited by members living in communes up and down the country and just the presence of these regular stories of everyday commune life – if somewhat spiced up – did much to make the whole idea of communal living seem more 'normal' – Well at least to *Guardian* readers!

... It's not always easy, communal living. Not easy at all. To help us achieve the proper attitude to what is, after all, recreational activity, we have on our a shelves Manuals – nay, Treasuries – of Non-Competitive Games. These books are invariably written by Americans and feature cover photographs of smiling, trusting, blissed-out Californians frolicking on close cropped lawns with enormous Earthballs, or grinning co-operatively at each other as they steer the blindfolded person towards the donkey. We believe implicitly in the philosophy behind these books, in which games are only a means to an end, that being the enhancement of love, trust, caring, and techniques of teamwork. So why do our games go so badly wrong? Why do we fall so spectacularly short of these ideals? Why does a simple game of Spoons result in £75-worth of damaged furniture, two sprained wrists, and a cut requiring six stitches (Spoons is a card game)? **5**

Bob Fromer 'Getting in first with the retaliation' in *The Guardian*

The End of Land Settlement

On 1st December 1982 the then Conservative Minister of Agriculture, Fisheries and Food, Peter Walker, announced to Parliament that the estates of the Land Settlement Association (LSA) would be sold and that all services provided by the Ministry to tenants of the Association would cease on 31st March the following year. The LSA had been set up in 1934 'to carry out an experimental scheme ... for the provision of rural small-holdings for unemployed persons from the industrialised cities'. It was the largest and longest running rural land resettlement scheme carried out in England. In all, 21 estates were set up across the country, mostly on reasonably good quality land, comprising 1,100 small holdings totalling 11,000 acres. Some 2,000 people were set up on their own tenanted small-holdings. The sell-off of the estates was partly ideologically driven – it fitted in with the Thatcher government's right-to-buy ethos. But, in truth, it was largely the result of difficulties with increasingly centralised management by the Ministry.

The settlements had originally been organised at estate level with joint marketing and packaging schemes run locally. But services were increasingly centralised once the running of the LSA was taken over by central government and, over the ensuing years, tenants were encouraged to take part in capital intensive investment schemes. This led to both the Association and some individual tenants getting into debt and struggling to make the small-holdings viable. Despite these difficulties, incomes for tenants on some of the estates had been better than other agricultural workers during the early 1970's. Some of the tenants who had invested in large greenhouses heated by oil were badly hit by the 70's oil crisis and by the end of the decade smallholders were regularly contacting their MPs with complaints about mis-management of the LSA. In his speech to the Commons announcing the sale of the estates, Peter Walker, as well as saying that he hoped that many tenants would take the opportunity to buy their own small-holding, stated he was 'convinced that the tenants of the estates should take over the responsibility for the marketing of their own produce and ... that wherever possible individual estate co-operatives will be formed'. However, this only actually happened in a few instances, such as the Snaith Salad Growers in Yorkshire. On many estates, a majority of tenants did buy their holdings but across the country the following years saw commercial operations moving in. On some estates there was a slow decline with holdings being bought for horse paddocks and other non-horticultural uses.

Following the sell-off, many tenants, who had been left without jobs and potentially without homes, banded together to sue the Ministry on grounds of loss of earnings or profits that they should have made but did not. There were also general damages claims for distress and anxiety caused by the government's decision. The original claim totalled £23.5 million, but the case dragged on for years with successive governments failing to address the issue. The tenants eventually settled for about £7 million in the 1990's.

THE *Healthy Future* FOR YOU AND YOUR FAMILY

LAND SETTLEMENT ASSOCIATION

Radical Work and Housing Opportunities for Everyone

There are plans to set up the beginnings of a new/alternative/green university in Birmingham in the Autumn of this year. It will seek to give its members a holistic world-view and the skills/knowledge to create and live in a peaceful world. We are in the process of buying some property as a housing co-operative to act as a centre for a small radical education community, to promote courses in areas neglected or ignored by conventional universities; eg green economics, non-violence, humanistic psychology, feminism, ecology, the politics of lifestyle, alternative technology, etc. Birmingham will also act as a base for a growing alternative skill/knowledge sharing network. The learning setting will be open to experiment – there will be an emphasis on dialogue rather than one-way instruction. Members will select their own areas of study and design their own courses.

New University article in Communes Network 88 Autumn 1986

In the mid-1980's the New University Project was set up in Birmingham. With echoes of the 1960's Anti-university and even Alexander Trocchi's situationist inspired spontaneous university, it organised skills and knowledge sharing events with the ultimate aim of setting up a rural green college. In1986 the New Education Housing Co-operative was formed and a house in Hockley bought as a stepping stone to establishing a larger centre. However, many of those who came to educational events at the house showed as much interest in how the Co-op had been set up and operated and 'were fascinated by how a bunch of unemployed people had got their hands on an enormous seven-bedroomed terrace!' Gradually, the emphasis of the project changed to promoting social alternatives and their example inspired a number of other co-operative ventures. In October 1988, several of the co-operative projects met at the New Education house in Hockley in order to set up 'a new network' for which they chose the name Radical Routes. The idea of the new network was for co-ops to share skills with each other and to help other groups to set up co-ops.

Radical Routes is a national network of radical co-operatives ... We believe that if radical co-ops are going to get anywhere they have to closely co-operate and Radical Routes is a vehicle with which to organise this support. We are an ambitious organisation – but what's more, we're not about talking about our ideals – we're about getting out there and getting on with it. We're a growing network, we want more set-ups to join us. If you're into our aims and principles and willing to commit yourselves to our criteria for membership, we'd like you to join us.

Radical Routes Co-ops Directory June 1993

After the first few years the group published a booklet written by Roger Hallam, *How to Set Up a Housing Co-op*, written as a toolkit for those wanting to take control of their own housing. This was followed later by *How to Set Up a Workers' Co-op*. As well as producing booklets, Radical Routes hosted events called 'Taking Control of Our Own Lives', where people could come and learn how to set up co-ops.

Any group trying to set up a radical co-op, whether it be to house yourselves, a café or education project, is faced with many difficulties, and most fail because of isolation: believing their problems to be unique, feeling that nobody else is doing anything quite the same as they are, and frustrated by a lack of know-how and finance. The network gives people a feeling of not being alone; of working towards some wider vision than simply keeping their own set-up going. There is great potential for the future ...

Roger Hallam in *Green Line* April 1991

It fairly quickly emerged that raising the finance to set a co-op up was one of the main sticking points for people. In order to overcome this obstacle the network developed a series of ideas and practical examples of ethical and mutual lending. Sometimes this took the form of simply people clubbing together and persuading friends to lend the deposit for a house. This then became more formal with loans being made to Radical Routes, which were then lent on to co-ops. Later, when the exact legal basis for doing this became uncertain they set up their own investors' co-operative called Rootstock which passed the money on to Radical Routes (in the form of shares) to be lent to help new co-operative projects and expand the activities of existing co-ops.

Although Radical Routes is still small and at an early, delicate stage of development, the rapid growth of the member co-ops over the past two years shows the attractiveness and potential of co-operation between radical ventures. Radical Routes has two characteristics which provide the key to the creation of a sustainable and politically radical and independent economic sector. These are its ability to raise ethical investment, and the vision and maturity of member coops which makes them willing to co-operate closely, sometimes putting aside the short-term financial interests of the co-op in order to help another one.

Roger Hallam

The combination of support network with its own source of finance proved to be a real recipe for success, managing to succeed where Fair Ground and the various attempts by the Commune Movement before had failed to get off the ground. Radical Routes operates as a decentralised network with no central headquarters or paid staff except for a single finance worker. Work is carried out through a series of working groups which include finance, publicity, gatherings and co-op support groups by a voluntary work contribution that the people in the member co-ops commit to the network. Quarterly weekend network gatherings are held where member co-ops send representatives to take part in the business meetings where all major decisions are made. Decisions are made by consensus, with voting used only as a last resort on very rare occasions when consensus can't be reached after two gatherings. The gatherings also include skill-sharing sessions where new groups can find out more about such things as meeting facilitation and co-op finances. As well as new ventures, Radical Routes attracted existing co-ops and communities looking for, and able to offer, support to other co-ops. These included Giroscope based in Hull, perhaps the best known and high-profile of the groups to belong to the network.

How to Set Up a Housing Co-operative

Radical Routes

The roots of Giroscope go back to 1985 when a group of young people, fed up with living in sub-standard accommodation decided to take matters into their own hands and buy a communal house. Through various means and some bluffing we raised the money to buy two houses in quick succession, whilst a third (which we eventually bought) was being squatted. The idea of housing ourselves quickly developed into the more purposeful idea of housing other people experiencing housing difficulties in Hull. By August 1986, armed with four houses, Giroscope workers co-op was formed. During the next five-six years Giroscope, through a mixture of hard work, perseverance against the odds, and some good fortune has managed to establish itself. Giroscope undertakes all the renovation work to its houses, although none of its members have received any mainstream training in the building trades. Through the attitude of have a-go, asking friends and talking to workers in the local building yards we've gradually built up our skills and over the last five years or so we felt confident enough to buy and renovate a number of totally derelict houses.

To do this we've had to commit ourselves to working hard, particularly in our early years, although more recently a thirty-hour working week is expected of members without dependents. We've also relied strongly on voluntary workers who have been and continue to be invaluable to us ... Giroscope couldn't be described as a commune but more like a traditional community, developing both housing and working space for people in a local area of Hull. As for the people comprising our community, most of them are vegetarians, some are vegans, some campaign for green politics, some have motor vehicles, some have allotments, some like football, and we all like drinking except Reg. In other words it's a bit of a mixed bag and anybody with a few good ideas and some commitment should be able to find a niche in it.

Radical Routes Co-ops Directory 1993

The network grew quickly, numbering 24 full members after five years. As well as housing co-ops there was also a range of worker co-ops: in Coventry – Green Engineering (building work and car maintenance); in Hull – the Privvy Press (environmentally friendly printing); in Hockley, Birmingham – Zebedees wholefood café and restaurant, Carrot Computer Services, Oddscope (t-shirt screen printers) and Organic Roundabout (supplying cheap organic produce direct from local organic growers). There was also Catalyst Collective, a campaigning co-op:

... a group of people campaigning on a wide range of social and environmental issues. Capitalism is leading us on a path of greed, selfishness and self -destruction, and to change this will involve ALL of us with far-reaching changes in the way we view each other, the planet and other life. To help facilitate these changes we promote all sorts of activities: co-operatives – both workers' and housing; non-hierarchical childcare, particularly de-schooling and home education; products free from animal exploitation and animal rights campaigning groups; groups active in repairing our ecological environment; alternative technology etc.

Catalyst was set up as a sort of co-op registration agency. Helping people who wanted to set up housing or worker co-ops through the legal and financial maze and offering support with the various 'official' roles in a co-op (secretary, treasurer, etc), consensus decision making and conflict resolution. While those involved in Radical Routes were mainly of a new generation of activists radicalised during the Thatcher years they also attracted existing groups whose roots were in the earlier communes movement. One of these was SPIL, Some People In Leicester, a group inspired in part by the involvement of one of its founder members – Woody – with People In Common in Burnley. SPIL evolved as a looser, more diffuse extended community than most other intentional communities, and included people who did not necessarily live in the same houses, but who shared the ethos of the group and wished to co-operate with others. They ran an income pool; car share scheme; Alternative Services workers co-op; as well as providing accommodation as Corani Housing Co-op.

The supportive network of Radical Routes was also able to breathe new life into some groups that had gone into a downward spiral of personal conflict. This happened at Wheatstone where a new group managed to rescue the former self-sufficiency commune and resurrected it as Earthworm Housing Co-op, practising 'organic/veganic Permaculture'. Radical Routes' success has not been without its own problems and disagreements over the years. One major issue was whether member co-ops should be strictly vegan or vegetarian. This was brought into sharp focus at one point after a lamb was killed and eaten at one rural group. It caused a crisis in that co-op, and a wider debate within Radical Routes. The members of the co-op tried and failed to resolve the concerns through consensus and decided by majority voting that they did not want a rigid food policy. Radical Routes itself adopted essentially the same position, but tensions remained between the strictly vegan co-ops within the network and the others.

Another contentious issue has been Radical Routes' rule that requires individual co-op members to have a disposable income no more than twice the state benefit level, with any excess being given away to support radical social change activity. Many co-ops felt that this was an unwarranted intrusion into their internal affairs, whilst the remaining co-ops argued that this voluntary disposable income cap was essential to our collective identity as activist co-ops celebrating low-ecological-impact, low-consumption lifestyles. This was another rare case where consensus could not be reached, and a decision was made by voting that the income rule will be scrapped when 75% of the member co-ops put in place secondary rules on issues like ecological impact and what the co-op, and its members, do with their money.

Patrick Nicholson 'Two decades of grassroots control and social change' in *Diggers & Dreamers* 08/09

A further long-running debate – with echoes of similar debates within the Commune Movement and The New Villages Association before it – centred around regionalisation. Proposals were put forward that co-ops within a geographical region would form a sub-group within the network and be represented at the quarterly gatherings rather than each co-op having to attend.

This idea of local autonomy has only been partially successful. One problem is how diverse views within a region can be effectively represented at the gatherings. Another is that co-ops within a region may not necessarily have a lot in common, or may themselves be geographically distant from each other (for example, the South West region), and so creating an effective regional group can be difficult.

Patrick Nicholson

Radical Routes has proved to be remarkably resilient as an organisation and has managed to overcome many of the problems that dogged earlier attempts to forge more formal networking links between intentional communities and other radical organisations. By its 10th anniversary in 1998 it had grown from the original five groups that had attended the first meeting to a network of nearly 40 co-ops involving some 200 people. It had made over 25 loans to co-ops and had assets of just over £400,000. Perhaps most impressive of all was that they had managed to keep their radical edge intact while never having a single bad debt from a member co-op.

We want to see a world based upon equality and co-operation, where people give according to ability and receive according to their need; where work is fulfilling and creativity encouraged; where there are no hierarchies; where the environment/earth is valued and respected in its own right, rather than polluted and exploited.

Radical Routes Newsletter Special Edition Spring 1998

At the end of the 80's communal living was perhaps enjoying a higher profile in the mainstream media than ever before; a generation of communities that had started off as the Commune Movement and morphed into the Network had survived for over a decade; and there were new initiatives such as Radical Routes that were supporting, what could be seen as, a second wave of communal groups. However, not everyone saw what had developed over the decade in a positive light. November 1989 saw the publication of the 100th edition of *Communes Network* magazine and it carried a letter from Tony Kelly who had been instrumental in the beginnings of the movement 20 years earlier.

It is sad to see the circulation down to 200. You ask, Is it a sign of the times, or is there something we're not doing? I suspect it's both, and I'm pessimistic about a solution to either. Being somewhat of a recluse I'm hardly in a position to offer an opinion, but for what it's worth, I feel that people over the last 20 years or so have lost something. I'd call it 'soul' ... That is, you yourselves aren't taking yourselves seriously; it's as though you're laughing it all off so as not to get hurt too much. But would it even be possible to do otherwise? Just supposing every word in 'CN' was sincere – just suppose slick brush-offs were rejected, and suppose the facade of its all being a huge joke were exchanged for the naked truth. Would that be too painful to accept as reality? To be honest, I think it would. Personally, I'm repelled by the appearance, the layout, the content and the feeling of 'Communes Network'. But at an age of 55, perhaps it's myself who am eccentric, still in love with a world which has gone forever ...

Letter from Tony Kelly in *Communes Network* 100 Autumn 1989

The 1990's would see some quite major changes in the world of communal living in the UK. Some of them an evolution of what had gone before; others driven by changes in the UK property market; others somewhat harder to pin down the reasons for. The decade started with the launch of *Diggers & Dreamers: The Guide to Communal Living*, a 128-page book – part directory, part journal of articles on various aspects of communal living. The book was the idea of members of the group that had come together to produce the *Info Pack*, a few of whom had continued to meet to deal with sales and distribution of the pack. The initial editorial collective consisted of two members from Lifespan, two from Redfield and one each from Rainbow and People in Common. Part of the motivation for the book was entirely practical, the *Info Pack* had sold well over the five years of its 'shelf-life', but one of the major problems had been the reluctance of bookshops and libraries to take a collection of papers in a loose-leaf folder. So when the question was raised as to 'What Next?' a book seemed the obvious step. Also, this was the early days of computer desktop publishing and part of the reason for the Redfield/Lifespan members' involvement was that there was a member of Redfield interested in the layout and design work and Lifespan had developed their own small printing business. The preface of the book explained the group's objectives:

Despite the myth that 'communes' came and went with the 1960's, communal living continues to provide an attractive and viable way of life to many people in Britain today. Part of our objective in producing this book is to dispel the myth and bring the idea of communal living to the attention of more people. If you know little about communalism, then you will find the 'History and Overview' article, and the 'Days in the Lives.' section an illuminating introduction. It is also a practical guide for groups wishing to set up, or individuals looking for a group to join. You will find the sections, 'Getting Started', 'Advice for Newstarts', the 'Communes Directory' itself and the resource section indispensable. Our third objective is to produce a book which is also a journal. You will find articles of general interest reflecting current issues affecting communal living.

The directory listed 57 communities of all types: from communes whose roots were in the early days of the movement in the 1960's and 70's; to newly formed group like the Quaker Community at Bamford in Derbyshire; and some of those involved in the newly emerging Radical Routes network. It also included communal groups with a religious or spiritual focus – be it Buddhist, Christian, Hindu or more general New Age. The directory reflected a whole cross-section of communal life in the UK at the time, running from Ashram to ZAP. The directory entries had been compiled from an extensive mail-out in 1989 to a list of over 400 addresses that the editors had collected from a number of sources including a trawl through past commune directories and *CN* subscribers' lists; other alternative directories both current and historic; and their own personal knowledge. The group brought its experience of producing the *Info pack* and 'vast experience of communal meetings', as well as a wish to produce something that would act as the 'public face' of the communes movement. Together they would produce the first book on communal living in the UK since Clem Gorman's *People Together* back in 1975. The effort proved to be worth it with over half the 1625 copies being sent out to distributors, bookshops and by mail-order in the first three months. Reflecting on the effort it had required in an article in *CN* 102 the following summer, entitled 'The Story Behind the Book', Pam Dawling wondered '... how *D&D* fitted in with *CN* – in some ways it felt like a bit of private enterprise outside the (sluggish?) mainstream of *CN* – I wondered if any *CN* readers were feeling antagonistic or resentful about what we were doing ...'

While sales of the new book showed that there was a thirst for information on communes and communal living (and the book received favourable reviews in the alternative press) there were some people involved in the network who had their reservations. *Diggers & Dreamers* (*D&D*) was launched with an advert in *Communes Network* 100 and the accompanying editorial, on the one hand, encouraged people to go out and buy the book but on the other the CN admin team asked readers whether it should consider undercutting the book 'by giving out information for free, or at low cost?' saying that when people inquired for information on communities they didn't 'always want to tell them that they have to buy D&D!' and would rather be able to send out a low-cost photocopied listing instead. These comments were part of the wider ongoing debate on the future direction of the network that had been trundling on for the latter half of the 1980's. The debate was reignited by a letter from Tony Parker printed in *CN* 100.

... When I first subscribed, I thought I'd get an insight into communities. Ho ho. I'm well informed about kibbutzim. I know

the odd contributor has thoughts about women and kids and stuff like that. But apparently nobody else wants to talk about it ... The simple truth is that nobody gives a shit. The communities that use CN have only one thing in common with each other, they all call themselves communities. They're not particularly interested in each other, let alone the majority of communities somewhere 'out there'. And why would they be? They are interested in advertising for members; and there are people who are looking for places to join. That's a useful function maybe ... The first CNs were four photocopied pages. If you think it's worth doing at all, why not go back to that? You could get all the ads in, and save a succession of editors wasting time and energy on ... Still, whatever turns you on, I suppose.

The letter elicited a flurry of responses in the next issue, some expressing agreement that the magazine was in a sorry state, others defending and even praising it. The issue contained another letter which would spark further controversy. It was written by someone called 'Oisin' from a group calling themselves the Hengistfell Tribe, a neo-pagan survivalist community in the New Forest. The letter may well have been a hoax and no trace of the Tribe has ever been discovered, but the views expressed by 'Oisin' jarred with the general left-green-feminist views of most *CN* readers and got a broadside in the following *CN* accusing the group of being racist, sexist, homophobic neo-fascists, with one reader writing in to say 'This is the sort of crap I'd expect from the NF or BNP not *CN*. Why was this article included? Why was there not even an editorial comment after it? If this is the sort of article *CN* is going to produce in the future it would be better for *CN* not to continue.' **6** It is likely that the hoaxer was trying to provoke a debate on censorship and may well have been a member of Glaneirw who were acting as editors at the time and had been criticised for printing everything they received in the magazine. *CN* 102 carried a request for readers to let the editors know if they wanted *CN* to be 'an open forum for anyone, whatever their views, living in or interested in communities, to share information/opinions/experiences.' or a forum for communities committed to anti-racist, anti-sexist and pro-ecology policies. Pointing out that such policies could as easily result in censorship of articles on the Hutterites or the Bruderhof as much as the likes of the Hengistfell Tribe. The result of the debate was that readers wanted *CN* to remain an open forum for everyone. But it was proposed that each edition carry a brief statement along the lines:

Communes Network Members and Readers are part of a movement for a better society for all, and are opposed to discrimination on grounds of Sex, Race, Sexual Orientation, Age or Physical/mental ability. The views expressed in individual articles/letters are not necessarily those of other members of the network.

This seems to have resolved the debate and a statement appeared in all following issues. After Glaneirw, the editorial role passed to Redfield – a community based in a very large 50-roomed Victorian house with cottages, 17 acres of land and stable block just outside Winslow, Buckinghamshire. In some ways Redfield was one of the most politically out-front of the groups involved in the network, describing itself in its early days as a socialist community. While it may have professed or at least aspired to a socialist agenda, it shared the characteristics of many of the rural big house communes formed in the 1970's. Founded in 1978 in what had been a minor country house that had become used for institutional

purposes after being requisitioned during the war –
in Redfield's case as an old people's nursing home
– they had all the trappings of a back-to-the-land
commune: vegetable garden; orchard; herb garden;
metal and woodwork shops; a blacksmith's forge;
cows and sheep. But instead of being in deepest
Devon or the Scottish borders they were on the edge
of the Vale of Aylesbury and within reasonable
commuting distance of London and easy range of
the new city of Milton Keynes. Writing in 1982,
one member said describing the 'community' bit
was fairly easy; pinning down quite how they were

Redfield members in 1979

socialist was somewhat harder. Redfield had two stints at putting together the
CN magazine (1982/83 & 1991/92). During both periods the issues took on a
more overtly 'political' (with a small 'p'), flavour, with articles and commentary
looking both at the wider political context that communes operated within and
the internal politics of the movement itself.

*On the Redfield kitchen noticeboard, you'll see something of the diversity of our interests and concerns: a
CND poster, a cutting from the Socialist Worker, T'ai Chi classes, a feminist booklist, petitions for the release
of Chilean political prisoners, a list of butterflies seen in the garden. Some of us spend too much time away
from Redfield, working out, others work here solidly with no time for anything else. We're all here for different
reasons, but basically because we've got lots of room, organically-grown food, congenial company and it's great
for the 17 children. What more? Oh yes- we're concerned about social change ... But we represent, like other
communities, merely an alternative. And it's not good enough. To isolate oneself from the political processes
which ensure that the small, rich and powerful bit of the world starves the rest of it to death by perpetuating an
economic system which guarantees that it will become smaller, richer and more powerful, is indefensible. And
when they have trodden on our flowers, killed our dog and stolen everything else to manufacture the weapons
that safeguard their thieving, will we reveal our fear? The choice is simple. Join them – or fight them. There is no
alternative. Alternativeness like silence, is consent.*

Suzanne, Editorial in Communes Network 67 Sept 1982

In the later period, issues edited by members of Redfield covered the politics of
women in communities including hosting two 'Women in Action' gatherings in
the summers of 1991 and '92. These had grown out of a regular fortnightly
Redfield Women's Group.

*What had begun as a group of women living in a community who had decided to meet to discuss ways of
redressing the gender balance in the community had metamorphosed into a group wanting to organise a national
conference for women, How come? ... The group felt that there was so much going on out there involving women's
issues and just as we wanted to share experiences with other women in communities why not try and provide a
forum so that women nationally could talk with other women. So many different strands of interest started to
emerge including, amongst other things, providing a forum for different feminist groups to share their ideas on
the way forward for the movement; exploring health issues together and a commitment to women's art ...*

Penny in Communes Network 106 Spring 1991

The women's gatherings at Redfield turned out to be some of the last large
gatherings that would be held with any connection to something called the

Communes Network. After Redfield, the editorship of the magazine passed to Earthworm and for the next few years there seems to have been little activity actually carried on in the name of the Network. That's not to say that there was no inter-commune activity going on, just that it was of a different type. Less concerned with theory and meetings, more focussed on having fun.

The first volleyball tournament was in 1992, at Birchwood. The motivation was to introduce a fun mechanism for getting communities together at a time when inter-communal gatherings were starting to become less frequent. My day job is as a sports administrator (for softball and baseball), and volleyball was the one sport we all played together at Birchwood, and that was my background for coming up with the idea. The original idea was to combine volleyball with other meetings, but that hasn't often happened. The risk, of course, was trying to institute a sports competition for people and organisations who often like to think of themselves as anti-competitive. As I expected, many people actually get quite competitive during actual play, but the Laurieston Rules prevent the bigger, stronger players from too much domination, and I think it's worked out pretty well over the years.

Bob Fromer 2012

The Inter-Communities Volleyball Championship, complete with a cup for the winning team (and a booby prize for the worst team) turned out to be an inspired piece of network engineering and this unlikely event went on to become a regular summer date in the communal calendar with different groups around the country taking turns to host it. The whole event wasn't quite as competitive and alien to commune culture as it might first sound: the games were played under what were known as 'Laurieston' or 'co-operative' rules – a variation on volleyball rules that makes the game less of a slam-dunk-fest dominated by athletic types. And there were various side-events that took place at these 'sports' weekends, none of them with the same gravitas as the Network meetings. There were slideshows and communal 'gossip' sessions. The atmosphere always tended towards a festival feel rather than a serious sports competition, with some years seeing teams dressed in drag and occasional games that bore more than a slight resemblance to mud wrestling. These weekends were better attended than most of the previous 'serious' gatherings and continued throughout the 90's and beyond.

CN Issue 108, entitled The Winds of Change, contained articles on changes – proposed, actual and envisioned – at a number of groups that had started in the 1970's. These were at People In Common, Wheatstone, Lifespan, Redfield and Old Hall. Some were changes to do with problems that were occurring in the groups. Problems like: how to achieve increased numbers of members; how to cope with the dynamics of increased numbers of members; and how to change when consensus decision-making can take so long (tending to support the status quo and acting, in fact, as a conservative brake on change). Elsewhere the wider political and economic context was changing the way that formation of new communities could be achieved. Increases in property prices meant that the sorts of places that had been available for setting up communes in the 1970's: the large houses in the country; or cheap property in need of renovation in towns and cities, were becoming increasingly scarce. So, during the second half of the 1980's and into the 90's those who might have set up or joined communes previously were forced to look for other options. In many cases they set out on the road in second-hand vehicles – being dubbed by the media as New Age Travellers. The story of the temporary, and often transient communities, formed by the travellers is told in the book *A Time to Travel* by Fiona Earle and Alan Dearling.

There are a multitude of positive ecological and environmental issues which persuaded some people to live nomadically, some political. The opposition to nuclear weaponry and its power, led protesters leaving their homes and moving onto, or around, bases; in particular Greenham Common and Molesworth. Although the cold-war threat has receded, political reasons for living nomadically still exist. The police action of 1985 culminating at the Beanfield, brought many new people onto the scene. Some who believed in anarchy or in the rights to question authority, replaced others who believed stongly in a pacifist role. Legislation, such as the Public Order Act 1986, stirred people to defend basic human rights – as is happening now, with the Criminal Justice Bill. Likewise, the 1990 introduction of the Poll Tax, gave an impetus to some Travellers to try living away from houses ...

A Time to Travel

Communes had a mixed relationship with travellers during the period. Partly based on first-hand experience and partly fuelled by media reports of the 'so-called peace convoy'. Some groups who feared an 'invasion' of travellers went as far as having contingency plans to pull up cattlegrids and prevent access to their land should travellers appear. Other groups were more 'traveller friendly', allowing short-stay stop-overs on their property for small numbers of vehicles. Sometimes this could turn into a problem when the community ended up outnumbered and overwhelmed by people who had little or no commitment to the place or the ideas behind it – this happened at Wheatstone at one stage. The other option open to those looking for a different or alternative way of life during this period was buying a piece of agricultural land or woodland and moving onto it in fairly temporary accommodation: benders, tipis, yurts etc. This had, in reality, been going on at a small scale for years but gathered pace in the 1990's due to both rising property prices and the authorities' clampdown on travellers, some of whom then tried to find or purchase their own stop-over sites. This sort of activity later became known as Low-Impact Development, a phrase coined by Simon Fairlie in his 1996 book of the same name. Perhaps the original low impact intentional community actually dates back to 1974, when a group of free festival tipi-dwellers moved onto land in Carmarthenshire in Wales and started what has become known as Tipi Valley.

The Tipi Village community is dedicated to living lightly upon the Earth and in harmony with the natural environment. We live in native North American style tipis in over 100 acres of Welsh hill land. Each tipi is an individual or family "household", so our community is very much a tribal village rather than a commune, but a village with a high component of communal activity and inter-action. Our land is partly owned by individuals and partly owned in trust on behalf of the community as a whole. We share a large tipi (the "Big Lodge") which functions as a communal space for parties, celebrations, get-togethers and (very rare) meetings ... We regard all of our land as a nature reserve in which humans can live in integrated harmony with nature.

Directory entry in *Diggers & Dreamers* 96/97

Tipi Valley, like many of the later low impact groups over the years, faced local hostility and enforcement action from the nearby planning authority. Much of the debate about such communities has been around planning issues.

... rural communities starting up since the early 1990's have often had to stake out their own dwellings in the face of an uncomprehending planning system. In some cases, such as Keveral Farm and Brithdir Mawr, communards have spilled out of overfull farmhouses into the farmyard and beyond, in converted stables, caravans, wooden shacks, domes or roundhouses. In others, such as Brickhurst, Kings Hill,

Tinkers Bubble and Steward Wood, settlers have simply moved onto the land in makeshift yurts and benders, and fought off enforcement notices until they gained planning consent on the grounds of sustainability and need, a process usually taking about five years. Meanwhile, as derelict cottages and unwanted barns became scarce and expensive, many individuals and families were doing the same thing: moving onto land in low impact dwellings and facing whatever the planners threw at them.

Simon Fairlie 'The Future of Low Impact Development' in *D&D* 08/09

At the summer 1994 inter-communities volleyball gathering held at Redfield, a meeting was called by the editors of *Diggers & Dreamers* to discuss the immediate future of *Communes Network*. The magazine had not come out for a while and the finances had reached a point where the network was pretty much insolvent – owing subscribers more issues of the magazine than it actually had the resources to produce. The *D&D* editors felt that they were becoming by default responsible for the network; answering enquiries and dealing with the media and wanted to propose that the network be wound up. Reactions at the meeting ranged from 'Communes What? ... never heard of it', 'I thought it finished years ago!' to a feeling of sadness for the passing of a once loved friend. It was decided at the meeting to close the Network and either to return subscribers' money or give them a free copy of *D&D*. Despite this decision, taken at perhaps the largest gathering of communes in the country for a decade, there were those who disagreed with the decision to kill off the network. In a move reminiscent of the final days of the Commune Movement back in 1975, members of Lifespan decided to carry on and produced what turned out to be the final issue of the magazine *CN* 115 in the winter of 1995/96. The issue was largely made up of material cribbed from other publications and turned out to be the network's final swansong. After this, *Diggers & Dreamers* became the effective public face of communal living, bringing out a new edition of the book every other year throughout the 90's. Each edition contained a new collection of articles from contributors (including those living in communities but also academics and writers such as Colin Ward) as well as an updated directory listing a growing number of communities from across the UK. Over the years the *D&D* editorial group was made up of members drawn from different communities around the country, always remaining a small task-focussed group of around four or five people. Describing itself as 'a self-appointed-headless-elite-anarchist-editorial-collective with no office, elastic editorial policies, concertina finances and a can-do/why-not attitude problem.' **7**

For a number of years we held our quarterly editorial and production meetings at each others' communities. Then partly out of boredom, but mostly curiosity, we rather cheekily started asking places that we fancied visiting if they would host us. To our pleasant surprise pretty much all the places we have contacted have been more than happy for us to hide away – in one of their spare rooms for a weekend in exchange for our Communities slide show and a bit of inter-commune gossip ...

'Writing, Printing (& Editing)' in *Diggers & Dreamers* 08/09 20th anniversary edition

After it was told it was going to be dropped by its trade distributor, members of the D&D collective set up their own small marketing and distribution co-op, Edge of Time Ltd **8**, to deal with orders and promotion of the book and other small self-published publications and products. The increased public profile that the D&D books gave to communal living attracted the interest of other sections of the press.

The popular image of a commune is of a group of idealistic hippies turning their backs on the world and sharing everything from their brown rice to each other's lovers. But today's commune members – and there are an estimated 10,000 of them in the UK – don't look so way out. The values they espouse – caring, Green living, vegetarianism – are general concerns too. Add on the other benefits of communal living, such as sharing financial and domestic burdens, and is the idea of living with another family or two really such an extreme choice ...

'Is this the Ideal Way to Live?' in *Good Housekeeping* April 1994

The first edition of *D&D* in 1990 had carried a review of an American book, *Cohousing: A Contemporary Approach to Housing Ourselves*. It was by two architects, Kathryn McCammant and Charles Durrett who had been studying the Danish Bofaellesskaber communities (which they translated as 'cohousing') and were busy introducing the model to the USA. Cohousing is a form of communal living whereby members have their own private houses or flats and a share of various communal facilities on a site where the layout has been specifically designed to facilitate and maximise informal social interaction. The communal facilities vary from group to group but centre around a 'common house' where regular communal meals are on offer. This combination of private space linked to communal facilities had proved popular in Scandinavia and had spread into other parts of Europe. It started to take off in the USA following the publication of McCammant & Durrett's book. It is somewhat surprising that the model, which bore similarities to set-ups in some existing communities, struggled for many years to make any headway in the UK. In 1997, following a very positive response to a workshop on Cohousing at a Green Building Fair in Leeds, Mary Roslin (a lecturer in architecture at Sheffield University) got together an informal research group to look into the question of why cohousing was failing to take off in Britain. The group consisted of a number of architects and housing workers and one of the editors of *D&D*. As well as looking at the particular differences in the UK housing market compared to other European countries and the USA, they searched around for examples in the UK that bore some characteristics of the Danish model. In doing so they came across a handful of groups scattered across the country who were trying to set up cohousing projects. In order to support these initiatives the research group registered themselves as The CoHousing Communities Foundation. The aims of this rather grand sounding organisation were to act as a central co-ordinating body that would 'support CoHousing development and enable it to become more accessible and achievable than if groups worked independently in separate parts of the Country.' The Foundation had various ideas on how to do this. It intended to set up a forum or network so groups could get in touch with each other; produce a regular bulletin; a CD-ROM and a website to further publicise cohousing; and to seek funding to carry out research and develop a range of cohousing support services. On November 28th 1998 the Foundation along with Divercity, a London-based would-be cohousing group, held the first UK Cohousing Convention at the Irish Centre in Camden Town. The Convention was attended by 'virtually all' the cohousing groups that the Foundation was aware of, most of whom were in the 'early-ish' stages of development. Some of the groups had been meeting for a number of years and had still to find a suitable site. These included: a group in East Devon; one in Totnes; four groups based in London; one in Edinburgh; one in the Colne Valley in Yorkshire; and a couple of groups who did 'not yet have a firm idea about location'. There were others who were closer to getting something up and running. A group in the

Stroud Valley was looking at two potential sites and The Community Project, just outside Lewes, was about to reach completion of the first phase of construction work on converting the 23-acre former Laughton Lodge Mental Hospital site into 21 individual units with additional communal facilities. The project had been going for six years and had looked at over a dozen potential sites including Chichester Convent; Jago's School in Surrey; Winterbourne Stoke – 'that stripey place next to Stonehenge'; Awebridge Danes in the Test Valley; and Leydene House, the Navy's former HMS Mercury training school at East Meon. Struggling to find a location, the group almost folded before finding the Sussex site. They had not been aware of the cohousing model at the beginning but discovered and adopted it along the way.

We do not want an institutionalised feel, but we do want to be more than simply a housing estate. We want to live next door to people we know and trust and perhaps like.
Whose aspirations we share and with whom we can work and play.
The Community Project Information Pack

One potential cohouser who had attended the convention described the day as being a 'mass of enthusiasm, knowledge and imagination.'

One of the outcomes of the Convention ... was the unanimous support of the CoHousing Communities Foundation to become a membership Network to act as a direct forum for debate and development between individual 'CoHousers' and other groups, individuals and organisations. Whilst the Foundation as a whole focuses on overall research and development, the CoHousing Network is the 'grass roots' membership based part of the Foundation ...
Cohousing Network Bulletin Issue 1, Spring 1999

It was intended for a network bulletin to come out on a regular basis with each issue being edited by a different member of the network with the foundation overseeing the overall production. The first issue contained an advert for a second national gathering to be held on 15/16th May 1999 at Thundercliffe Grange near Rotherham. Thundercliffe was another group which had adopted the cohousing description, having not quite known how to describe themselves since their inception in 1980. Set up by a group of friends and having quite a few members who worked for the Council in Rotherham they had been keen to avoid becoming known as a 'commune'. Once again, like many groups formed in that era, they found a minor country house that had been used for institutional purposes – in this case as a hospital for 'female lunatics' in the late 1800's and then as an NHS home and school for mentally handicapped children. The Thundercliffe Grange gathering attracted similar numbers to the previous one. Following this period of activity on the cohousing front things seemed to stutter for a few years. The Foundation tried to secure grant-funding to set itself up as a support organisation and carry out research. But after a couple of years of applying unsuccessfully to different funding sources it wound itself up. A lack of volunteers to keep the *Bulletin* going saw it stop after a couple of issues. The looser informal Cohousing Network was more successful with a small number of cohousing activists keeping it going on into the 21st century. On the ground, actual groups were also finding it difficult to make progress with only one of the forming groups that had attended the '98 convention actually getting to the point where it had a site and could look towards starting building by the end of 2000. Other groups came and went, often giving up after frustration at the difficulties of finding suitable property that they could afford, or just worn weary by the whole process taking so long. There were a couple of groups who had not been present at either of the national gatherings that had drawn on the cohousing model. A small development of flats in Sheffield and Frankleigh House in Bradford on Avon. The Community Project, Thundercliffe Grange and Frankleigh House all had aspects of cohousing enshrined in the way they were set up: the combination of individual private units and shared communal facilities; and a legal structure that enabled everyone to participate. But none of them reflected the conscious site layout designed to maximise social interaction that characterised the original Danish model. This was either because they had come late in the day to the cohousing model or, perhaps, more because they were all converting existing properties. It wasn't until one of the key people in the setting up of Frankleigh moved on to try and develop a new-build cohousing project in Stroud that this aspect of the model would really get addressed in the UK. David Michael acted as a sort of alternative-developer-cum-cohousing-animateur taking a lead on finding a site, searching for sympathetic architects and putting together a legal and financial package before recruiting a group of people wanting to live there. In doing so he may have managed to short circuit the seemingly long drawn out group process that was one of the factors delaying progress in other groups.

I'd been interested in Kibbutz as a way of life since I was a teenager and stayed on one. I read the cohousing book in about 1994 and it immediately made sense, a sort of kibbutz lite without any economic relationships. In Denmark, I had heard that the early founders of Cohousing had been volunteers on kibbutzim and wanted to re-create something similar in Denmark. I had been interested in communal living all my adult life, lived in squats, student houses, visited Laurieston, Monkton Wyld etc ...

David Michael

In October 1999 an information sheet was sent out to prospective members under the name of Uplands Cohousing Community stating that an offer had been accepted on a site close to the centre of Stroud that had outline planning permission for 29 houses. The sheet went on to say:

Joining now means you will be guaranteed a house in the first new build cohousing community in the UK. You will help to make it possible ... Each householder will be an equal shareholder in Stroud Cohousing Ltd., which will own the land and the communal house. Houses will have 999 year leases. Decision making will be by consensus or failing that 80% majority. An initial Shareholders' Agreement will be drawn up – this will describe how you join(buy) and leave(sell) and how decisions are made. Rules and guidelines will develop and change as the community does.

It also gave details of the proposed Communal House or Cohouse:

This is the hub of the community. The intention is to eat together every evening if possible. Pottery, arts & crafts and meetings will be accommodated in the Cohouse. The size is determined by being able to seat at least 60 people plus kitchen ...

It would take another year of negotiations before the site was eventually purchased for £550,000 by which time the group had recruited some 25 households and, after detailed planning consent was granted, construction of 35 houses, flats and studios started in 2001. The first members moved into, what was now called, Springhill Cohousing during 2003.

The late 90's saw the emergence of another international network of intentional communities; the Global Ecovillage Network (GEN). The network grew out of the Eco-Villages & Sustainable Communities conference held by the Findhorn Foundation in October 1995. The conference had tried to bring together a wide spectrum of participants involved in architecture, design, and building; local and central government; town planning; business and economics; education, the arts and community work; environmental and development NGOs; and 'others working for planetary transformation'. They would look at inspiring examples of sustainable community from around the world with the aim of working towards '... the positive future we all know is possible'. The publicity for the event outlined what eco-villages were:

Eco-Villages represent 'human ecologies' that are sustainable: spiritually, culturally, economically and ecologically. To promote the consciousness of living in balance with the natural world, we must also be in balance with ourselves. The transformation of fundamental human attitudes underlying our destructive impact on Nature requires a deeper look at their causes. In order to solve the environmental crisis we must also look at the social and cultural crisis; we must look at sustainable economics as much as ecological technologies.

The conference had an impressive list of international speakers from intentional communities: Albert Bates from The Farm in Tennessee; Declan Kennedy from Lebensgarten in Germany; and Max Lindegger from the Australian community Crystal Waters. Speakers from the UK included Jonathan Porritt and Peter Russell – it was even rumoured that Prince Charles was to attend. The conference and subsequent launch of GEN resulted in a lot if interest in the ideas and concepts that underpinned eco-villages, but apart from Findhorn there was little engagement from existing groups in the UK. In 1997 a UK branch of the network (EVNUK) was launched which held a number of gatherings and produced a newsletter. But, as in earlier attempts to set up village-scale communities in the UK, proposals for ecovillages faced the – at times – virtually insurmountable vagaries and contradictions of the planning system. This was explored in an article by Chris Reid, a professional planner who lived at Redfield, in the millennium edition of *D&D*.

... It is my perception that an eco-village is many things to many people, ranging from a collection of benders and other low impact structures tucked away on a piece of land to a large group of houses with many modern-day facilities. Such places would and have been described as communities in the past, but the ecological focus and concern for consumption of resources and impact upon the environment has now appeared to have assumed greater importance... The low impact type of eco-village really in my opinion only caters for a minority of people and will not provide a sustainable future for the majority of those interested in finding a more environmentally friendly living situation. It is, I believe, foolish to assume that our cities will depopulate and that people will seek out eco-villages in nice rural settings ...Current planning guidance is that a new settlement should be large enough to cater for a target population of 100,000 people or approximately 40,000 homes (DETR, 1997). This size is suggested with a view to the settlement being reasonably self-contained in terms of employment, social facilities, such as schools, retail, leisure etc. However, when one considers eco-villages, there is a school of thought that, to a certain degree, harks back to the concept of the village, where everybody knows everybody, and works and shops within or around the village ... Such a village may have a population of around 2,000 people or up to 700 homes, but the trend is that such settlements are by their nature becoming less and less sustainable ... **9**

'Eco-Villages – Middle Class Fantasies?'

Reid concluded that it was hard to see how these contradictions could be resolved without changes to both the way that the planning system worked and the way that those promoting eco-villages conceived of them. The interest generated by GEN may have contributed to the Labour government's proposals for Eco-towns but so far – like their predecessors in the New Villages Association, Greentown group and Cartwheel – none of the proposals for eco-villages or eco-towns have actually resulted in any new communities being established.

Townhead

The winds of change that swept through British communes and intentional communities in the 1990's left the movement – if it could be called that still – seemingly more fragmented than at any time in the past 30 years. But there was arguably more communal activity going on at the very end of the 20th Century than there had been in the preceding decades. While the Communes Network had faded away, new networks such as Radical Routes and the Cohousing Network had, in some ways, risen to take its place. Individual communities had weathered the changes with mixed results. Some, like Laurieston, had settled in to a more stable, 'mature', although perhaps less radical, phase. Others had not fared so well. Perhaps the most dramatic of changes had taken place high up on the Pennines at a community called Lifespan. The small hamlet of Townhead, situated just east of Dunford Bridge at 1,200 feet up on the edge of the moors, consisted of two terraces of houses – 19 in all – built in blue engineering brick to house railway workers building the Woodhead Tunnel and later those working in the nearby railway marshalling yard. Numbers of workers living there had slowly dwindled in the late 60's until, by 1974, there was just one retired couple left. The houses and three acres of land were bought for £5,000 by a small group who had previously been at Summerhill – A S Neill's alternative school in Suffolk. They set up Lifespan Community as an Educational Trust, where people could continue to live and learn beyond schooling, very much as a continuation of the Summerhill ethos.

Our aim is to create a lifestyle conducive to the individual's emotional and political liberation. We take the 'small autonomous community' to be the basis of a re-humanised society. In our village we have a degree of freedom from the constraints imposed by the petrified national social order. Out of this freedom a spontaneous social covenant has arisen that weaves together individual personal traits. **10**

'Freedom Rules OK'

LIFESPAN COMMUNITY

The group set to making some of the houses habitable and securing the rest against the winter and, over the next year or so, they created a variety of rooms: library, sitting room, kitchen, dining-room and workshop. A few of the members had building skills and taught them to others – they designed the layouts of the rooms as they went along knocking through from house to house along the terraces as they went.

This method of working has naturally upset the local council, but by a mixture of not taking them too seriously and throwing back at them what they see as 'alternative gobbledygook' (eg: communal living) we have managed to keep them at arm's length. They have no sanctioned categories to slot communes into and they persist in classifying us as separate households, telling us that we don't have this or that amenity. So we have taken to building first and submitting plans later, showing them an example of a new form of life that may come in handy one day ...

Freedom Rules OK

Numbers grew to around 22, including children. Everyone shared living space and ate together. Decisions were made at weekly meetings, by consensus. For the first six years the children were educated at home. All income was pooled, and all expenses met collectively. Several attempts were made to establish home-based industries and bring in a steady income. Casual building work and various crafts were undertaken and, for several years, the community ran a small wholefood shop. They also started to write and publish a series of recipe booklets with titles such as: *Use of Wholefoods*, *Full of Beans* and *Summer Wholefood Recipes*. These were sold through wholefood and health shops and became a major source of income for the group, leading to them setting up their own small printing workshop. In 1978 the group transferred from being an educational trust to a combined housing and workers co-operative which they felt reflected the way that they actually lived. The joint rules took some time to negotiate with the registrar of Friendly Societies and remain unique to this day due to the post-registration intervention of the tax authorities who insisted that no further groups should be able to declare that their entire living expenses were tax deductable. By 1980 the printing business had become a major source of income for the group which did more jobbing printing work for others as well as expanding its range of publications – producing its own *Lunar Tree Calendar*, booklets on *Building Woodstoves* and *Natural Birth Control*. Other sources of income were gradually abandoned.

The stated aim of the community had always been to have somewhere between 25 and 40 people living in the houses once the renovation works were completed. But by 1979 numbers had dropped to a dozen adults and a few children and then fell further – dropping down to six adults and one child for a short period in 1982. During the 1980's the group struggled to find a way to expand numbers while still maintaining close emotional ties between members.

... we had recognised the problem of the 'dozen barrier' – expanding to twelve-14 adults and contracting to seven – nine adults in cycles, rather than managing to sustain growth. To expand the community while retaining a small number of people for each of us to relate closely to, we tried in 1983 and 1985, to divide into small living/ support groups – each of which would have been open to new members – but both times we failed to find a way to choose the small groups. The expansion-and-contraction cycle repeated ... 11

Pam Dawling in 'Changing and Growing'

Despite its changing membership Lifespan played an active part in the Communes Network during this period, hosting gatherings and weekend meetings, printing issues of *CN* and eventually taking over the admin side of dealing with enquiries and subscriptions. They were one of the groups involved in the Fair Ground proposal and members from Lifespan were instrumental in launching both the *Info pack* and *Diggers & Dreamers*. Throughout the decade and on into the early 90's they tried to find an answer to the difficulties of trying to expand. They advertised widely for new members and printed an introductory booklet to the community. None of this activity resolved the fundamental question of how to grow as a community. The debate was still going on into the 1990's with what had in fact been a relatively stable group from some years starting to splinter.

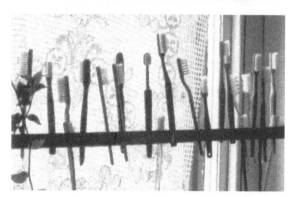

Lifespan is undergoing a period of great flux. Life carries on much as usual but the underlying sense of uncertainty is a relatively new arrival. This time of change is no surprise either – we've been talking about Lifespan's future and possible new living and working scenarios for months – but it appears to no avail. (You notice I'm not happy with the status quo.) Alas in the framework of consensus, new ways struggle to find a handhold. When we can't agree on new directions, we

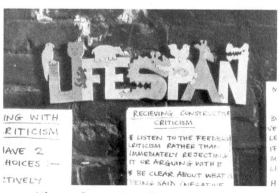

Lifespan Community – One year in the life. During 1987/88 Photographer Howard Davies visited Lifespan, capturing community life in a series of black and white photos that made up a touring exhibition

fall back into our ruts – barren though they seem, they are at least familiar. But the price is high – people leaving, people moving towards leaving, increased uncertainty and disparateness ... **12**

Suzanne

The failure to find a way forward that they could reach consensus on eventually led to a slow downward spiral with long-term members leaving and a high turnover in membership leading to further splintering of the group and eventually serious conflict between members. When the final members with any printing skills decided to leave they negotiated to take the printing presses and equipment with them. This further undermined the viability of the community and the group slipped into an increased reliance on benefits. Eventually by 1996 numbers had dropped to a point where the place was effectively no longer a community and the buildings had been abandoned except for a few squatters. A couple of members who had moved to Leeds tried to work out how they might return and revive the community's fortunes. In the meantime the place was ransacked for building materials leading to calls from local councillors for the place to be requisitioned by Barnsley Council and turned into low-cost homes for local people. In the spring of 1998 a group of road protesters who had been at the Newbury and Honiton Bypass protest camps came across the uninhabited and derelict terraces and, assuming them to be abandoned, moved in. The group took the name the Townhead Collective partly to distance themselves from the former group who had left unpaid debts to local tradesmen and suppliers.

Judging by the condition of the property, we presumed it to have been empty for at least two years. We set to work immediately clearing the debris and making, as many houses as possible inhabitable. Ex-residents, police, media & local people came to visit and in general we attracted quite a lot of interest.

The Townhead Collective – What are we all about

The 25 new inhabitants were in many ways a ready-made community. They had already been living together for some time in fairly extreme conditions at the Trollheim and Fairmile A30 protest camps in Devon.

... Fairmile had been around for a very, very long time, and had in many ways brought into question a lot of what we do. It was the longest community we've had, and at no point did anybody ever think that it was going to be that long. But it meant that, over that two-and-a-half year long period, we had the opportunity to explore community living in a community of resistance ... **13**

Farewell Fairmile

By the end of the year the group had re-roofed five of the Townhead houses, temporarily weather-proofed another two, weather-proofed all the windows (80% of which had either been broken or were completely missing) and repointed an exposed gable wall. The group were contacted by the two former Lifespan members who had moved to Leeds who had been trying to put in place plans to revive the community. They were invited to join with the new inhabitants, but instead chose to try and claim that they were the rightful owners and to serve eviction notices on them. Trying to evict a group of former treetop dwellers and tunnel diggers was perhaps not the best of ideas and the Townhead Collective made links with the wider communes movement to try and raise support. Other communities and former members, who had watched in horror as Lifespan had descended into chaos, chose to rally round the new group and help them fight eviction. When it came to court enough doubt was sown as to the legitimacy of the ownership claim being made that the judge threw the case out. This left the new collective's status in something of a legal limbo-land. But at least they were free to carry on with their plans albeit technically as 'squatters'. Among them they had a whole range of skills – gardening, building, stained glass construction, clothes making, catering, motor mechanics, 12V electrics, computer programming, HGV driving, herbalism, permaculture design, woodland skills, metalwork, community outreach work, drug counselling, self defence ... not to mention tunnel building, treeclimbing and digger diving. They had plans to develop a permaculture programme for the land and established a nature reserve; continue the restoration of the properties and develop small businesses in: metalwork, recycling, 12V electrical systems, clothes making and a tree nursery; as well as running a mobile marine animal rescue service; a recording studio; and a home-based education learning zone. Despite the legal uncertainty hanging over them[14] a decade later they reported in *Diggers and Dreamers*:

... We try to live sustainably with as little impact on the environment as possible. We are into growing our own organic fruit and veg from two large communal gardens containing polytunnels and greenhouses. We also have a medicinal/kitchen herb garden and tree nursery. One of our defining features and strengths is that we produce all of our own electricity from solar and wind. We aim to have hydro-power at some point in the future! ... The atmosphere is informal, friendly and relaxed. A down-to-earth vibe and positive initiative is encouraged. In the recent past, we have been the proud winners of the 'Inter-community Volleyball Golden Bum Award'!

Diggers & Dreamers 08/09 directory entry

Bang, J, Bailey, K & Matthews, B (eds) **The Collective Experience** 1984 Communes Network

Dearling, A & Earle, F A **Time to Travel?** 1994 Enabler Publications. ISBN: 0952331608

Dearling, A & Meltzer, G **Another Kind of Space** Enabler Publications. ISBN: 0952331659

Fairlie, S **Low Impact Development** 1996 Jon Carpenter. ISBN 1897766254

Hetherington, K **New Age Travellers: Vanloads of Uproarious Humanity** 2000 Continuum International. ISBN: 0304339784

McKay, George **Senseless Acts of Beauty: Cultures of Resistance Since the Sixties** 1996 Verso. ISBN: 1859840280

Metcalf, W **Shared Vision Shared Lives** 1999 Findhorn Press. ISBN: 1899171010

Pepper, D **Communes and the Green Vision** 1990 Greenprint. ISBN: 1854250515

Betts, J, Green, J & Wilson, G **An Experiment in Living** 1999 Third Age Press. ISBN: 1898576149

Sargisson, L **Utopian Bodies and the Politics of Transgression** 1999 Routledge. ISBN: 0415214637

Various Editors **Diggers & Dreamers** Biennial editions:

Ansell, Coates, Dawling, How, Morris & Wood (eds) **Diggers & Dreamers 90/91** 1989 Communes Network. ISBN: 951494503

Coates, Dawling, Fordham, How, Morris & Wood (eds) **Diggers & Dreamers 92/93** 1991 Communes Network. ISBN: 951494511

Coates, How, Jones, Morris & Wood (eds) **Diggers & Dreamers 94/95** 1993 Communes Network. ISBN: 95149452X

Coates, How, Jones, Morris & Wood (eds) **Diggers & Dreamers 96/97** 1995 D&D Pubs. ISBN: 951494538

Bunker, Coates, How, Jones & Morris (eds) **Diggers & Dreamers 98/99** 1997 D&D Pubs. ISBN: 951494546

Bunker, Coates, Hodgson & How (eds) Diggers & Dreamers 00/01 1999 D&D Pubs. ISBN: 951494554

Bunker, Coates, Hill, Hodgson, How & Watson **Diggers & Dreamers 02/03** 2001 D&D Pubs. ISBN: 951494562

Bunker, Charnock, Coates, Hodgson & How (eds) **Diggers & Dreamers 04/05** 2003 D&D Pubs. ISBN: 951494509

Bunker, Coates & How (eds) **Diggers & Dreamers 06/07** 2005 D&D Pubs. ISBN: 951494517

Bunker, Coates & How (eds) **Diggers & Dreamers 08/09** 2007 D&D Pubs. ISBN: 9780956936721

Notes:

1   **Fair Ground Prospectus** 1981
2   What is Communes Network? in **Diggers & Dreamers 92/93**
3   **The Collective Experience** 1984
4   **The Guardian** 22 Nov 1989
5   **The Guardian** 25 May 1989
6   Letter in **Communes Network** 101
7   Writing, Printing (& Editing) Diggers & Dreamers **D&D 08/09** 20th anniversary edition
8   www.edgeoftime.co.uk
9   **Diggers & Dreamers 00/01**
10   **Undercurrents** 16 Jun/Jul 1976
11   **Diggers & Dreamers 92/93**
12   **Communes Network** 108 Winter 1991
13   **Do or Die** Issue 6 1997
14   Coda: Despite the obvious presence of a successful new community at Townhead one former member of Lifespan, John Clark, persisted into the 21st Century in trying to repossess the property and sell it to a developer. His tactics included getting official mail redirected from the community's address to his home and continuing to claim that he was acting as the rightful owner. This came to a head when he tried once again to get an eviction order – the case was settled before it got to court with Mr Clark being required to sign a letter relinquishing any claim on the property. The author was due to be called as an expert witness in defence of the Townhead Collective.

Communes come and Communes go

... but communal living goes on forever ...

I hope the previous pages have shown the breadth of what I will call the communal diaspora in Britain in the second half of the 20th century. These final few pages are by way of a conclusion. They are my thoughts as I have wended my way through the stories of a whole myriad of communal groups and tried to make some sense out of a social phenomenon that is as persistent as it is at times elusive and ephemeral. At the end of the journey I have as many questions still as I feel I have found answers. I knew when I started that there would be hidden treasures and untold stories to tease out of piles of papers held in people's attics and dusty filing cabinets – we in the counter-culture have been remiss and slapdash in preserving our stories. Were we too busy 'living in the moment' or 'living the revolution' or just struggling to live, to think about what future generations might want to know about what we were doing? Or perhaps every generation is like that. There is a wealth of information out there waiting for future historians and social researchers to stumble across as I have done – I have tried to give some pointers in *Commune Britannica* that will hopefully help you get there before the papers crumble or the ink fades too much.

One thing that struck me doing research into communal living in the later decades of the 20th Century was the far-reaching and persistent influence on the various communal groups of the Second World War. Some of the influences were obvious, others more subtle. Starting with the pacifist communities set up during the war and stretching right through to the 1970's and 80's communes there are threads that can be traced back to the war. I was very sceptical when I first read anarchist writer George Woodcock's statement that there were 'several hundred' small intentional communities in Britain during the war time period. The written material available seemed to point to only a few dozen groups, not hundreds. Woodcock's own evidence is problematic because he chose not to identify any of the groups he wrote about – referring to them only anonymously as group one, group two, group three etc. It means that it is nigh on impossible to verify the existence of any of the twenty or so groups that he catalogued. However, as I delved into the primary material from the period – I read through every copy of *Peace News* from 1936 to 1950 – I slowly came to believe his estimate. If you

take into account the myriad types of groups: the pacifist farms and training centres; the land and forestry units; the Jewish refugee kibbutz training farms; the urban social centres; the Bruderhof; the Quaker initiatives; the socialist groups; the Christian groups; and then add in the existing pre-war communities like Whiteway and the Brotherhood Church; plus a sprinkling of as yet undiscovered ventures; and there could well have been in the region of several hundred. There was both an organised pacifist network and an overlapping communities movement with their own publications and support networks. Much of the impetus for the growth in communal living in the period was due to the wartime circumstances and the burgeoning number of conscientious objectors searching for both a place to live and to work during the war, and a place where they could attempt to live out their ideals. The roots of this wave of communal experiment, however, can be found in those groups active in the late 1930's who saw communities as a potential way of perhaps avoiding a possible war or at least a preferable way of living should one occur. And even, possibly, a way of rebuilding a society where war would no longer occur.

There was also in the minds of the founders a realisation of the fundamental warlike nature of capitalist society, and an idea that the communities might create an alternative pattern of social organisation which would not be based on acquisitive values and would not lead to war ... They saw their communities as examples from which other people would learn, as the nuclei from which a communal structure could spread through society and take the place of the state. The most pessimistic ... hoped the seeds of freedom and culture could be preserved until the dark ages they foresaw had passed away.

George Woodcock, The Basis of Communal Living

Here are the seeds of the idea of an alternative society that could be brought into being by setting up experimental examples of how the future might be. The period of growth of communities during the war years and the link to the pacifist and peace movements, most notably through the pages of *Peace News,* created an alliance between communal living, peace and non-violence that resonated for decades after, with *Peace News* still carrying articles about and adverts for intentional communities right through until the late 1980's. In the immediate aftermath of the war many of the pacifist land groups were clearly drained by participants leaving to pick up the threads of their interrupted careers and lives and many were disbanded or became more individualised. Andrew Rigby sees this as part of a wider malaise that affected those who had fought for peace in a time of war.

In part the 'death' of many of the ventures has to be located within the general decline in the vitality of the British peace movement in the immediate post-war period ... The end of the war brought severe divisions and disputes within the pacifist movement ... and planting the seeds of a new civilisation through the practice of exemplary non-violent, co-operative lifestyles had little place in the discourse.

Andrew Rigby 'Pacifist Islands in a Martial Sea' in Diggers & Dreamers 94/95

By the end of the 50's it would seem that the peace movement had regrouped and that co-operative lifestyles were once again part of the peace agenda with the Peace Knowledge Foundation's Peace Centre at Langthwaite House near Lancaster and the Garthnewydd Community House in Merthyr both heralding the birth of Peace Studies as an academic subject.

The influence of the War can be seen in the post-war development of the therapeutic communities' movement, and later the anti-psychiatry movement of David Cooper, R D Laing, People Not Psychiatry and the Atlantis commune. Arguably, this was instigated by the changes in views on the psychiatric treatment of troops brought about by the involvement of followers of Freud and Jung, alongside pragmatic hospital staff at places like Northmoor. The ideas that came out of this 'movement' resonated throughout the counter-culture and influenced both the founders of the Camphill Movement and Braziers Park, the followers of Bhagwan Shree Rajneesh at Medina Rajneesh in Suffolk, and communards more generally as witnessed by the efforts of some groups to sort out difficulties by calling in Red Therapy. There is also the strange journey of Leonard Cheshire from decorated Bomber Commander through would-be founder of colonies for ex-servicemen and well known founder of homes for the handicapped to bête-noire of the Disability Rights Movement.

Another far reaching effect of the war can be seen in the vein of apocalyptic thinking that underpins many of the communities in the immediate post-war period and beyond, often characterised by the use of Noah's Ark as a metaphor for the group. This starts during the war with the cluster of groups of followers of Gurdjieff at Lyne Place, Tyeponds, Great Amwell House and Coombe Springs and can be traced through the groups that set up during the 1950's. In some ways it is not surprising that a generation that had grown up in the shadow of one world war and had just lived through a second should be driven by thoughts of impending doom and of founding refuges and 'Arks'. What is perhaps more surprising is that this mood of apocalyptic thinking should be sustained by the cold war through into the 1960's and 70's, casting a shadow over communities that started in that era. Given its reputation as a 'City of Light' and beacon of new age positive thinking, it is hard now to imagine the Findhorn Community to have been influenced by thoughts of impending apocalypse – but in many ways the early flirtation/fixation of the group on the impending rescue by UFO's from some vaguely unspecified (nuclear?) disaster could be seen as a kind of Cold War induced spiritual mass hallucination. It led Peter Caddy to say in his autobiography that in setting up Findhorn he '... felt very much like Noah, building an Ark under God's detailed instruction ...' Findhorn was not the only spiritually based group to have an apocalyptic streak in its history. Both the followers of the Hare Krishna Movement and Bhagwan Shree Rajneesh were subject to pronouncements by their respective gurus that contain more than a hint of Cold War induced paranoia. The Endtime beliefs of the Children of God and to a lesser extent the Jesus Army, whilst coming partly from a more traditional biblical root source, also have similar echoes. The spectre of a Cold War apocalypse both imagined and actual lies behind much of the thinking of the early environmental movement and was a factor in some of the thinking behind the Back to the Land groups in the 1970's and the idea of the need for an alternative society.

The wartime emergence of the Common Wealth party with its vision of a new post-war world – far more radically changed than the Labour Party's welfare statist provisions – provided a catalyst for those with a communal tendency. The roots of ideas that would resurface in the 60's and 70's, such as common ownership and a concern for environmental issues, can be seen in the likes of the Friends of the Future group. The sadly-missed anarchist writer Colin Ward told me that for most of the fifties the Left in England was largely dominated

Communes and Paranoia

One aspect of communal living that I was aware of throughout my research was a strain of communal paranoia that kept popping up – I never quite worked out whether it was justified or not. It is there in George Woodcock's writing in 1944 on the wartime pacifists where he lists 20 or so groups anonymously; my suspicion is that this was to protect the identity of any group that may have been harbouring conscientious objectors who were on the run, but it could have been simply good old anarchist mistrust of the authorities. The Bruderhof, perhaps quite reasonably given their persecution by the Nazis, have a streak of paranoia that I think could be argued may have deeply influenced the way they were constituted with their 'No Gossip' rule and their later reactions to dissent and criticism. There is a serious outbreak of hippie paranoia in the late sixties and seventies. This seems partly drugs related, but clearly also a reaction to wider conflict with the police, authorities and society in general. Much of the contemporary literature simply refers to 'The Pigs', and given the perception by the police – at the time of the Angry Brigade bombings – that communes and the counter-culture in general were a threat to national security, perhaps the antipathy was justified. Add to this a mistrust of the mainstream media, which continues today because of regular misrepresentation and (perceived) sensational reporting of communal living, and it becomes somewhat understandable that when approached by Abrams and McCulloch for their 1972 sociological study of communes many groups chose either not to participate at all or only to do so under the cover of a pseudonym. Repeated government attacks on the civil liberties of those on the margins of society (squatters, new age travellers, ravers ...) by successive governments throughout the 1980's and 90's only reinforced the mistrust and bred a new generation of paranoia-tinged counter-culturists. This instilled an occasional siege mentality in one or two communities and some of their neighbours, despite the fairly obvious fact that communal living was not going to overthrow 'straight society' and that the stereotypical view of communes was in large part a communal bogey-person invented by the media.

Then again I wondered if the paranoia worked both ways. Given the rhetoric of an 'alternative society' that would replace the existing order, perhaps it was the 'straights' who were reacting out of a paranoid fantasy of what might happen should such an alternative come to pass. Maybe we were all just a little bit paranoid?

by the Communist party which had two distinct factions when it came to communal living. Some (the Stalinists) viewed it as a bourgeois distraction from the revolution, while others saw it as 'living the revolution now'. After the suppression of the Hungary uprising by the Soviets in 1956, UK Left politics started to splinter and it is interesting that the late 1950's saw a flurry of communal projects starting and an embryonic network – the Community Living Association – formed.

Taking a broad sweep of communal history over a 60-or-so year period I found myself on the lookout for threads of continuity, whether individuals or groups, that could be said to have passed the communal baton on from one generation of communities to the next. In reality I found little evidence of direct continuity. There are very occasional individuals who bridge the gaps and might be said to have carried a communal flame across the decades. Robin Appleby, who I interviewed, was one of the few people I came across who had started visiting the likes of the Bruderhof in the fifties and then went on to be actively involved in the

1970's wave of communities as a founder member of the Glaneirw Community in Wales. I did think the Bruderhof themselves might have been a continuous influence on the communal movement over the years with their longevity and comparatively significant resources. But after their initial fairly dramatic impact on the pacifist movement (when they first arrived) and a period in the early fifties when Wheathill acted as an example of what a successful communal venture might look like, they no longer had any central role or influence on the communes movement. This was partly due to their geographic dispersal but also the impact of changes brought about by the 'great crisis' when their primary focus moved from communal venture towards a more traditional closed sect. Other long-lived communities such as Whiteway and Braziers have also acted as examples of, well, 'long lived communities', but seem to have remained on the periphery of any later communal movement. Braziers, because of its ethos of social research, had an influence beyond its immediate circle, but this seems to have faded once it had passed the initial inspirational phase of formation. Even Findhorn – perhaps the most widely known of the 1960's and 70's communities has, partly due to its isolation on the Moray Firth, really played only a minor part in the British communes movement over the years, arguably being more influential on an international stage than at home.

So I started to come to the conclusion that my search for some kind of communal continuity was misplaced. It actually seems that individual communities and individual members within communities were remarkably unaware of even many other contemporary groups, let alone groups that had been set up in what may well have seemed like another age. There is also an argument that there is actually real value in re-inventing the communal 'weal' time and time again, that communal living is a journey made in each instance by a particular group of individuals, that it is an experiential experiment and that there is only so much that might be gained from the experience of others who have trodden a similar path before. Although I have a sneaking suspicion that there may well be more to learn from predecessors than we might think.

Rehearsal for What?

I took the idea of the Rehearsal for an Alternative Society from Nic Albery's thinly disguised autobiographical book *Rehearsal for the Year 2000*, written under the pseudonym of Alan Beam back in 1976. In it he charts his involvement in the early 70's underground working for BIT and taking the embryonic Commune Movement from the fringes and, for a while at least, pushing it to a more central place in the burgeoning 'Alternative Scene' of the time. Albery's personal life history mirrors in many ways that of the wider counter-culture. Starting off as a pivotal inspirational character in the formation of many of the key alternative organisations of the time (his book was subtitled: Memoirs of a Male Midwife) he somewhat fades from prominence in the early 80's to re-emerge in a much more mainstream role pushing essentially counter-cultural ideas out to a wider audience under the guise of the Institute for Social Inventions.

... It was a wonderful time when, in a way that it is hard to imagine now, considerable numbers of people enjoyed the space and the opportunity to experiment with their lives. It was a time of enormous creativity which stemmed from the utopian confidence that anything was possible. Moreover, it was during this period that the conception of struggle was deepened beyond a concern with class to embrace issues of identity and patterns of domination in all spheres of life. However hedonistic and self-centred the period and the movement might appear when viewed in retrospect, most of those involved in communes and the wider alternative society movement of that time saw no disjunction between the process of transforming their own life and the wider object of changing the world. It was all part of the same seamless project. And that message is as relevant today as it ever was.

Andrew Rigby 'Dig the Old Dreams, Man' in *Diggers & Dreamers* 98-99

One role that communes played was that of refuge or safe haven (safe house?) for those wanting to explore unconventional paths outside the normal bonds of 'straight' society. Those paths might include exploration of new alternative technologies or farming techniques; or exploration of new relationships; personal, sexual, economic or spiritual. Communes offered a space to carry out these explorations, to see if the 'Hippie Hat' fitted, to see what it might mean to be: liberated, feminist, gay, socialist, communist, anarchist, truly spiritual, Christian, Buddhist, self-sufficient ... what it might mean to try to be 'free'. All of these ideas (and more) found a space to be nurtured, tested, fermented, sometimes pushed to the extreme and communally modified within communes. With, it must be said, sometimes unexpected and personally painful consequences. Communes were not alone in supporting the emergence of new cultural ideas. For a couple of decades in towns and cities across the country there seemed to be – everywhere you looked – overlapping little underground networks of headshops, wholefood shops, macrobiotic or veggie cafés, radical booksellers, music venues, squats, community theatre groups, dope dealers, meetings in rooms above pubs on topics of all political persuasions on the left, meditation retreats, yoga classes, free festivals and retro-mediaeval-style fayres. There were guides published to direct seekers to their nearest 'Underground Station', starting with *Alternative London* and going on to *Alternative England & Wales*, *Alternative Ireland* and right through to *A Pilgrims Guide to Planet Earth*. Various sociologists and commentators at the time proffered their thoughts and sometimes their theories on this parallel society that looked, or at least talked, as if it intended to replace the 'old culture' through a peaceful revolution whereby the old would simply be left to collapse under the weight of its own contradictions while those who had dropped out would emerge with the framework of a new society in the making.

Quite what happened to the alternative society dream is hard to pin down. Did it 'grow up' and drop back in? Well some did. Did it collapse under the weight of its own contradictions? There were plenty of them! Was it defeated by the forces of darkness? – sorry straight society – not really. Was it squeezed out by the combined weight of the individualistic, Thatcherite ('no such thing as society') years of the late eighties and early nineties? Well, maybe. Or was it a victim of its own success?

> *... the seventies communards were not escapist romantics, as witness the strength of their intent to set up educational centres: they wanted to proselytise with their ideas and their example. Since then, with successive waves of newcomers and a fall in the numbers recruited, evangelising zeal and ideological intensity dissipated, while the importance of individual fulfilment through escaping the alienation of mainstream society – especially the nuclear family – increased. In the late eighties there was a further drift towards loss of collectivity and sharing, the rise of private over public domains, and a perceived need to earn a financial surplus, some of which would be spent on increasing creature comforts ...*

David Pepper Communes and the Green Vision 1991

Did the 'underground' go 'overground' and disappear in the process? It is quite uncanny how many of the ideas/social mores that have since become mainstream in the 21st century started or found refuge originally in the counter-culture and in communes. Whether it be the clothes we now wear (I occasionally think the entire remainder stock of all the headshops has migrated to the hangers in Next) or the 'organic hand-pressed fair-trade hummus' that I used to hunt down in my local wholefood shop (which has somehow now made its way on to the shelves of the local supermarket). Glastonbury on the BBC! Virgin Trains! Eileen Caddy MBE! It would seem we are all secret hippies now.

Sociologists and commentators who looked at the counter-culture, communes and the whole idea of an alternative society drew varying conclusions, albeit often as seen through their own particular ideological (often proto-Marxist) filter. They were nearly all in the end dismissive of the potential of the counter-culture to effect real, lasting political change.

> *Communes are an attempt on the part of those who have belatedly and unexpectedly discovered their true situation in market society to follow the example of the working class and construct a little bit of power through combination. But it is an attempt made on distinctively petty bourgeois terms, from within the ethos of individualism and denying the profound contradiction between that ethos and the requirements of effective combination. Hence innumerable 'practical difficulties' constantly frustrate the efforts of the commune movement to generalise and spread the alternative economic relations in which commune members believe. There is an endless watching and checking to make sure that one is not being exploited by the very people with whom one is trying to combine, an endless sad discovery that others cannot or will not give enough.*

Abrams & McCulloch Communes, Sociology and Society 1976

From Abrams & McCulloch in 1976, to David Pepper writing in 1991 academics have looked to communes as a possible agents of change in society, be it in social relations or in relation to the environment. And while they accept in general that communal living has many advantages over 'nuclear living' in offering opportunities for changing individual and group behaviour, they either tend to ignore, or fail to look at, the many attempts to establish structures that might lead to a reproducible alternative. There seems to have been no attempt to look at the repeated attempts, however flawed, to set in motion practical mechanisms that would lead to an alternative society based on a 'Federation of Free Communes'. Whether through the idealistic Commune Movement Fund, the more pragmatic Fair Ground Maxi-Co-op or the later Radical Routes Network, or even the wider CLAP Tax.

Creative responses will be needed to a wide range of social change and the massive 'redundancy' of adults – perhaps, by the end of the century, some 15 to 20 per cent of people between twenty and sixty – may be taken as illustrative. It is increasingly obvious that in industrial democracies human beings will become too expensive for their economies to use on an extensive scale. Non-creative responses include both over-manning and 'job creation'. The problem is less one for social policy than social philosophy: what is at issue is a redefinition of social membership in modern societies and an exploration of new bases of identity and definitions of personal worth. Administrative solutions like retraining schemes, early retirement and short-term contracts instead of tenure for life will doubtless be tried: but the solution lies in a profound modification of consciousness ...

Frank Musgrove *Margins of the Mind* 1977

The communes movement, in so far as there has been anything at anytime that you could call a movement, has not really had any coherent political framework that it fitted into – or identified itself with. Communism never ideologically embraced communal living and you would have to go back to Kropotkin in the late 19th century to find the idea of small-scale communities playing a central role in a political philosophy in his writings. In *Mutual Aid* and, in more detail in *Fields, Factories and Workshops*, he outlined a decentralised anarchist society based on co-operation which bears more than a passing resemblance to the later visions of the late 20th century counter-culture activists and communards – although there is very little evidence that many had actually read Kropotkin. A more recent political philosophy that communes might have found a place in is within the ideas of Murray Bookchin – developed from his 1971 book *Post Scarcity Anarchism* onwards into what became the Social Ecology movement (see: www.social-ecology.org) or even within the ideas of Ecofeminism. But none of these ideologies have embraced communal living as a central, or even peripheral, part of their thinking as a practical transformative social structure that has the potential to bring about radical change in the way that it was envisaged by communards in the 1960's and 70's.

If the idea of the counter-culture as any sort of rehearsal for an alternative way of organising society can be taken seriously then it begs the question – a rehearsal for what? Was it really just a cultural interlude when a generation of the young of the rich western world had the luxury to temporarily opt out and 'do their own thing' before returning to the serious business of running (ruining) the world? Or was it a valuable experiment in a completely different way of looking at the world and organising human activity that we should all take careful note of – just in case? Dr Donald E Pitzer, one of the founder members of the American Communal Studies Association, has put forward the theory that in the past new political regimes had often gone through an early developmental communal phase. So if ... the 19th century Owenite communities begat socialism and the co-operative movement; The Kibbutz were crucial to the development and implementation of Zionism; and Communism required collective organisation for Stalin and Mao to succeed ... then what was the counter-culture a precursor to? The obvious candidate would seem to be the green movement in its various guises. From the early development of alternative, or as we know it now, renewable technology; the use of consensus decision making; the development of organic farming and the idea of self-sufficiency or self-reliance; the exploration of sex role stereotyping; or perhaps more generally: how to live in a sustainable way on the planet. Certainly, lots of those involved in communes and counter-culture politics went on to be involved in the development of many more mainstream groups including the establishment of the Green Party.

If the end result of high capitalist society is alienation, social deprivation and a (classless?) impoverished culture – as the rhetoric of contemporary British politics would have it – then communities may belong to part of a grassroots emergent alternative. A bloc of opposition, perhaps?

Lucy Sargissonn *Utopian Bodies and the Politics of Transgression* 2000

The term 'alternative technology' is rarely used today. An environmental profession has emerged. We have seen a slight greening of some businesses, the rise of environmental consultancies, an expanding portfolio of environmental policies, a growth in official environmental institutions, and a bifurcation between respectable NGOs and radical direct action groups. There are grassroots initiatives that pursue goals reminiscent of AT aspirations, but rarely as a radical package for the self-sufficient, small-scale, communal utopia that originally inspired the movement. Projects in community renewable energy, local organic food economies, and eco-housing may be less strident in their radical rhetoric than AT, and consequently appear less utopian. But their goals for boosting the local economy, raising community participation, and meeting social and economic needs simultaneously occupy similar terrain to AT, though from a more restrained standpoint.

Adrian Smith 'R&D for Utopia' in *Diggers & Dreamers* 08/09

Many of the ideas from the counter-culture have resurfaced in the Transition Network (See: www.transitionnetwork.org). When I first came across the Transition Movement in the flesh my first thought was 'Oh no, not a load of hippie shit all over again' – and I say that as a card-carrying member of the old hippie shit party! Do we really think we are going to save the world by recycling a bit more and putting on an extra jumper instead of turning the central heating on – and this time round without any political analysis of why we have got into the mess in the first place. But then my second thoughts were: 'What if Transition groups could achieve what individual communes struggling to stay afloat in a sea of consumerism were never going to – what if they could spread the counter-cultural gospel wide enough to ... to what? It's called Transition, only one step further on from a rehearsal – but a transition to what?' According to Transition guru Rob Hopkins it would involve '... rebuilding local agriculture and food production, localising energy production, wasting no people, rethinking healthcare, rediscovering local building materials in the context of zero energy building, rethinking how we manage waste – all build resilience and offer the potential of an extraordinary renaissance – economic, cultural and spiritual ...' Sounds dangerously like a federation of free independent communes to me.

The occupations at Sol, Syntagma and Zuccotti Park were like a globally interconnected web of tiny little Utopias. They were a whisper from the future; a reflection of the society we wish to create. A society without parties or leaders – where decisions affecting the community are taken collectively and on the basis of consensus. A society with neither wage slavery nor unemployment – where people choose their own type of work and are rewarded on the basis of need, not greed. A self-organized society based on horizontally-networked federation, without hierarchical structures of power or political representation. A society that does not atomize individuals, but that cherishes the idea of community, providing a sense of belonging and fulfillment while leaving individuals perfectly free to develop themselves physically, mentally and spiritually; to actualize their greatest potential and achieve a sense of internal peace and harmony. A society that cherishes culture and creativity, selflessness and solidarity.

Jerome Roos, 'The meaning and necessity of revolution in the 21st century'
11.5.2012, http://roarmag.org

The recent Occupy movement also bears many countercultural hallmarks and has the political focus that seems to be lacking in Transition thinking. But where are communes in all this? Well, some groups are actively engaged with these movements and individuals from others involved too – but in terms of giving a lead or providing examples of how a new society might look they appear to be hiding their lights under their communal bushels. Or could it be that they are just busy getting on with the day-to-day business of 'living the revolution' which actually takes up a hell of a lot of time and energy, leaving no time or much energy for going out and proselytizing the communal message to the masses. Which may well be one of the reasons that the alternative society never happened the first time round. Deep green commentators like Derrick Jensen would no doubt argue that the main reason that the alternative society never happened is because it never actually posed a serious threat to the old 'straight society' and was therefore tolerated and/or co-opted back into mainstream culture and that it may never happen unless we realise that we need to do more than just wait for the dominant culture to collapse under its own contradictions – waiting that long may be too late.

Whatever questions and criticisms it may attract, New Age is an attempt by people who experience the world as harsh and heartless to bring warmth to that world. As a reaction to modernity, it operates more often than not on the level of feelings, instincts and emotions. Anxiety about an apocalyptic future of economic instability, political uncertainty and climatic change plays a large part in causing people to look for an alternative, resolutely optimistic relationship to the cosmos. There is a search for wholeness and happiness, often on an explicitly spiritual level.

A Christian reflection on the 'New Age'
Pontifical Council for Interreligious Dialogue

Trying to shoehorn communes into a neat political pigeonhole is perhaps something of a pointless exercise; there will always be as many communal exceptions to the rule as examples of communities that seem to fit it. Reasons for the foundation of individual intentional communities differ so much along with the particular circumstances of their founding that to argue that there ever was anything that you could call a movement has been, at times, something of a struggle. But communal living has proved a persistent form of social organisation across the latter half of the 20th century and so while individual communes may come

and others go, it would seem communal living goes on and continues to provide a
viable alternative way to organise living arrangements for a wide variety of people,
be they: peace activists, therapy seekers, spiritual seekers, back-to-the-landers,
musicians, socialists, anarchists, buddhists, feminists, cohousers, low impact livers ...

*Communes contain a lot of people who, having experienced the alienation of work conditions and its
accompaniments in family life, financial security and the rest of it, have got the hell out – very sensibly too.
Normally, in other societies not as civilised, developed, clever, as ours, these are the people who form the frontline of revolutionary change. What happens here? They join bloody communes and wave arriverderci to the rest.
Once people realise we present a viable alternative they say, they'll realise what's what and inevitably flock to
the movement. That hasn't actually happened yet either, and never will. The communes movement has become
divorced from the very mass of people, part of whose ideology it inherits.*

*It is an alternative. An alternative way of coping with a full-frontal attack on people. It operates quite nicely,
thanks, within the system it seems to reject. We'll have our own villages, banks, food, sexual code etc. Alternative
Legoland. It's a neat little get out that has all the gestures and none of the clout, because it doesn't have the
understanding, the knowledge, or the history to make the kinds of connections it should be making with the
experiences and political processes of which change is really made.*

*What will be the position of the communes movement when Tebbitt becomes King and orders the troops in
against the rioting workers in London, Manchester, Liverpool, Leeds? Will it abhor the violence and pity the poor
souls who have failed to come to terms with the destructive urges that exist within each of us? Will it try to get
people on council estates to celebrate the summer solstice as an expression of class solidarity? Will they, WE, build
barricades with herb-flavoured bikes, or make petrol bombs out of re-cycleable bio-degradeable plastic? Or make
truncheons out of rolled-up copies of Resurgence?*

Go on ...!

Paul Coffman, 'Communes Mightwork' in *Communes Network* June 1982

Don't get drowned in the main-stream...

Let your fingers do the talking and join up with like-minded people to turn the tide against corporate capitalism that is killing the planet.

The Author's Tale

Get a big house and share it 197.

I first remember discussing communal living with friends in the early summer of 1975. It was one of those lazy A-Level afternoons after the minimal lessons we had to attend were over and we were round at someone's house (probably with a bottle of wine). Conversation drifted to speculation on each of our future plans. I think there was a realisation that as a group of friends the parting of the ways was going to come once the school term was over. I don't recall who said – "wouldn't it be nice if we could all get a big house and share it" – but we all agreed that it would. In reality we had no idea how to go about it, what it would entail, nor as far as I know did any of us know of any communal household at the time. Looking back, what surprises me is not that a group of school leavers should dream of communal living – were we really suggesting setting up a commune or were we thinking shared student house? I don't know – it was just a collective fantasy. What really surprises me now is that I don't think any of us thought this was an odd or strange idea. Somehow, in the mid 1970's, communal living seemed like a real option.

We all went our separate ways after school – I ended up in London looking for something to do after a summer school at the National Youth Theatre; others went to university, work or whatever and I have mostly lost touch with them (although on my travels I have bumped into two other pupils from the same school, different years, who had joined communes). After the Youth Theatre I got a part-time 'job' – we were only really paid expenses – working for Stirabout, a theatre company that toured prisons. had been living in the basement of a house on the banks of the Thames at Kew – it belonged to friends of friends and I stayed there in exchange for doing some cleaning. But the cost of travelling to Kings Cross for rehearse was rapidly depleting the money I had saved from a job earlier in the summer working in a plastics moulding factory. Jan who also worked for Stirabout was living with an old school friend of hers, Mick, in a 'licenced squat' next to Camden overground station. The house was owned by the council and was waiting to be renovated – which it desperately needed, largely because the whole building shook every time a train pulled into the station! In the meantime it was licensed, along with other properties in the same situation, to Student Community Housing (SCH) which let them out o peppercorn rents. This was the semi-official short-life end of the squatting movement which was growing across London at that time in response to unaffordable rents and huge numbers of empty properties. SCH acted as sort of benign surrogate landlord. I remember that I sneaked in, jumping the 'waiting list', because I knew people in the house. My reward was an attic room with so many leaks in the roof that I had to thread my way through a maze of buckets and assorted pots and pans catching drips in order to get to bed.

It's a short-life   1975/6

Short-life licensed squats turned over pretty quickly and we were re-housed (or should it be re-squatted) by SCH in a property on Camden Park Road. We had by then become a sort of informal communal house — we had a kitty for bread, milk, tea and coffee; an expectation that the cleaning was shared if not actually a rota for doing it; and the occasional communal meal when we were all in. Although, the prospect of having to cook vegetarian wholefood cuisine meant I avoided being cook as much as possible. We also started getting involved with the North London squatters movement, which was remarkably well organised at the time. There was a repairs team you could call on who would sort out basic services and instruct you on how to do your own repairs, lend you ladders etc. There was also the Ruff Tuff Creem Puff squatters estate agents, run by the poet-activist Heathcote Williams, that had a shop (squatted of course) and put out a mag advertising desirable Squats: 'empty 2 years/entry through rear/no roof/suit astronomer.'

We somehow seemed to collect people: theatre friends; Billy and Alan who came through Jan's work at Chiswick Women's Aid ... We clearly needed a bigger house. We talked about doing some 'Real Squatting'. It was Corrina, who ran the prison theatre company, who first discovered the big house set in acres of gardens in Bishops Avenue — known as Millionaires' Row because of the number of mansions and embassy houses on it. As far as we could find out the house had been empty since the 1920's, something to do with an American heiress who had died and left the house in legal-limbo-land. Undercover of night we moved in, changed the locks and pasted the squatters' occupation notice on the door. Half an hour later a blue flashing light approached along the driveway — it sped right past us and further along the drive to a cottage where a caretaker — who had been kept on by the estate — had fallen down the stairs and broken his leg coming to investigate the strange lights in the big house. Next morning the local police inspector turned up, accompanied by the caretaker with his leg in plaster. We exchanged legal pleasantries and they went away. Later in the day the inspector returned on his own. It turned out his daughter was squatting in Streatham and he was remarkably sympathetic — for a police officer. He told us that the estate would get us out, one way or another, probably by declaring the house unfit, or a fire hazard. However, he had just raided three houses further up the road and busted members of the Children of God sect for a rental TV scam they had been running. As far as he knew the houses were empty and we would be alright there. 'Should he catch us breaking and entering of course he would have no option ...' after a month camping in the mansion, with no electric, gas or heating — very romantic, but bloody cold — we decided that he was right and moved to the smallest of the three properties on the corner of Hampstead Lane, opposite Kenwood House. They were actually owned by a property developer supporter of the Children of God who had gone bust.

Not dirty hippie squatters at all

The Hampstead Lane squat turned out to be the most stable address some of us had in London — it lasted over 18 months. Because the houses were owned by a bankrupt developer they were in the hands of the 'official receiver' with whom

LUXURY LIFE ... three of the houses which squatters took over in the Rolls-Royce belt where the famous live

RENT-FREE FOLK DOWN ON MILLIONAIRES' ROW

By ANDREW DRUMMOND

THIRTY squatters are living rent-free in a millionaires' row. They occupy five houses worth about £500,000.

One house alone is worth £200,000. It is one of three belonging to a property company that went bust.

EASY LIVING ... at home with one group of squatters

we came to an arrangement – if we paid the rates and didn't trash the place he wouldn't hassle us until the whole bankruptcy thing was sorted and he had a new buyer for the houses. When we first moved in, the well-to-do neighbours had assumed that we must be rock stars and were subsequently shocked to discover a bunch of squatters had moved into one of London's most exclusive addresses – a story broken to the country by the ITV national news who doorstepped us early one morning with a full camera crew and reporter. Needless to say we didn't look our best at 8am on a monday morning. Having been outed by the press we decided to go on a bit of a charm offensive. We tried to get some more positive press coverage in Time Out and on Radio London. We gave ourselves a name – 'The Golden Spiral Community' and invited the locals round to talk to us. To our surprise a few actually came and we tried to get across to them that we were useful members of society who just couldn't afford London property prices: adventure playground workers; women's refuge staff; running a theatre company that toured prisons (we had Home Office security clearance) ... not dirty hippie squatters at all! I'm not sure many of the neighbours were convinced – and the effect of all the publicity was to attract a motley crew of North London would-be squatters and streetlife to our door. Most of whom moved in to one of the other properties on the site – we had chosen the smallest house (only four bathrooms) partly because we thought it the most 'defendable'. The house nextdoor was so big that people could move in to one end without 'residents' in other parts of the house finding out for a couple of weeks. We paid the rates, a considerable sum at the time, by renting the living room out as a rehearsal space for theatre groups and the triple-garage to a couple of mechanics.

Keeping a communal household together 1976/7

Living on the corner of Hampstead Heath in the summer of '76 now seems somewhat idyllic – we turned over formal flowerbeds to growing organic veg, (not very successfully as there was a drought that summer); had picnics on the lawns of Kenwood House; held parties full of hippies and escaped battered wives; hosted various meetings ... therapy weekends, a Peace News Potlach. A stream of people came and went but we managed to keep the core of a communal household together; Jan, Mick, me, Sheila and the kids, Lorna and her puppets. We had fairly regular communal meals; shared childcare; shared our beds; all went on a brown rice diet to pay the telephone bill; had communal readings of The Hobbit; listened to the Sex Pistols burst forth on the radio; flicked through the collection of Jesus-loves-you propaganda pamphlets the Children of God had left behind in the basement; taught ourselves basic DIY skills to stop the roof leaking and unblock the drains. The gardens – which included an ornamental pond and tennis courts – were taken over, at one point, by folk from Tipi Valley in Wales who had heard that the BIT crashpad in central London had closed and so they had come with a plan to 'rescue' London's homeless hippies and take them back to Wales with them along with a horse saved from the knackers yard. In the meantime they set up their tribal encampment in 'our backyard' and proceeded to demolish the fencing for firewood – progressing later to the staircase in the squat next door!

I don't remember who came home with a copy of John Seymour's Practical Self-Sufficiency but the, now classic, armchair-smallholder's book inspired us to a number of back-to-the-land fantasy plans – I even spent New Year hitching around the Welsh borders sleeping rough at night in barns whilst checking out estate agents and seeing if they had any old farms going for a song. In the end our dreams of rural adventure came to nothing (although years later Lorna did buy half a farm in Devon). Slowly the insecurity of not knowing when we were going to be evicted unsettled us and when we found ourselves acting as surrogate estate agents showing potential buyers around we decide the time had come to go. We said good-bye with one final party and went our separate ways.

I had meant to ... 1978

I spent the summer after leaving London earning enough money working in a bakery to buy a motorbike and then spent the autumn touring round calling on various friends. Somewhere along the way I picked up a copy of the Magic of Findhorn and read it cover-to-cover sitting in the henge at Arbor Low. Whilst I didn't really know what to make of the talking to plant devas and growing giant vegetables, I was inspired by the descriptions of community living. I think in that moment in the sun, in that strange prehistoric landscape I decided that I was going to try and find a commune to live in – I wasn't sure quite how and my biggest worry was that I wouldn't be able to find a place that would 'allow me to be me'. I don't know what I thought would happen ... that I would have to conform to some set of rules or norms prescribed by the community ... or that I would lose my individuality within a group of people who all thought the same? Whilst I had been touring on my motorbike, Lorna (from the Hampstead squat) had done the summer tour of communes around the country and she told me I should visit People in Common in Burnley – because 'You will like them'.

I had meant to do a tour of a few communes (and for years later I always told other people looking for a community that was what they should do) but I never got further than People in Common (PIC). I was seduced by the place, by the people (literally and metaphorically), by the surrounding countryside and by a resonance both politically with what the group were doing and with childhood memories of my grandparents' working-class terraced streets. For a start the group had been set up by ex-squatters, so I felt at home almost immediately. You didn't need any capital to join – I didn't really have any to speak of. They had ended up in Burnley because of the unbelievably cheap house prices and the whole ethos was to create a 'reproducible alternative' that was affordable to those with little or no money. They bought their first house in 1974 for £50 – no that's not a typo! Houses were so cheap in Burnley that people bought and sold houses over the bar in pubs – if your house is only worth a few hundred pounds at the best, why use a solicitor?. Had I not seen it with my own eyes I don't think I would have believed it. And the houses were fine – you could move straight into them. They had an outside loo and no bathrooms but they were sound. Day-to-day the group was funded by a combination of a few people working in outside jobs and others signing on. Those 'out of work' looked after the kids, did building jobs around the eight terraced houses that the group owned, looked after an allotment and got involved in local campaigns. All of which seemed somehow just a natural progression from my squatting days in London. After a couple of visits I signed up for a six month trial membership.

Mill owners out on a stroll   1978/9

A year or so before I joined PIC had bought a derelict cornmill with a three-and-a-half-acre field on the banks of the River Calder some five miles from the houses in Burnley. The Mill was to be the fulfilment of an aim to have a place where 'the group could live together in the country within easy reach of the town ...' Altham Cornmill looked bigger than it was. As an early industrial building it had had a chequered history. Originally a corn mill, possibly dating back to Saxon times, the present building replaced one burnt down by rioting weavers after the introduction of water-powered looms in the early 1800's. It had last been operated as a woodworkshop making spare parts for the weaving industry up until the 1960's. When PIC bought it it had been used for a number of years as a giant chicken house. The word 'derelict' doesn't really do it justice. It still had a roof (just), it was riddled with woodworm, the floors were held together by the three inches of chicken shit which covered them and a small stream trickled through the half-basement. I remember my parents telling me years later of their horror when I first showed them round – wondering what an earth we had taken on and not seeing how, without any money, we were ever going to manage to renovate the place.

In something of a fit of idealistic enthusiasm we set about shovelling chicken shit, propping up roof timbers, waging chemical warfare on woodworms and dreaming wild dreams of what we wanted to do with the place. This wave of somewhat frenetic activity eventually became more measured and whilst some people started working on proposals to apply for planning permission and thought about possible sources of money, others began clearing ground to start growing veg on a small-holding scale. I don't think any of us had any real horticultural experience beyond having an allotment, but what we lacked in skills and practical knowledge we made up for with communal solidarity and WWOOFers. Rod, a gentle Glaswegian, was our main gardener in the early days and I remember the first night we spent at the Mill after a day de-turfing the field. The two of us slept on the concrete floor of a pig-pen in the basement and tried to cook a tin of baked beans for breakfast using a blowlamp! This was the only time I have tried to eat stone-cold beans that tasted burnt. On our way home, walking along the canal towpath, we were stopped and questioned by two police officers who thought we might be 'sheep rustlers' (quite where we could be hiding sheep was a mystery to us). We tried in vain to persuade them that we were in fact local 'Mill Owners' out on a Sunday morning stroll – eventually I think the whole surreal nature of the conversation got the better of them and they left us alone.

During my night lying on the concrete floor of the Mill I had a vivid dream of being part of a sleeping pack of large wolf-like dogs – it was so striking that I looked it up in a dream dictionary which said that it was an archetypal dream of coming home – or being safely at home.

urban myth & magic   Late 1970's

Burnley was an odd place in the late 1970's. A strange combination of industrial decay, spectacular moorland scenery with an undercurrent of left-leaning politics and alternative culture. On the way to nowhere it seemed to be in terminal decline as one after another of its staple industries faded from past glories. First to go was cotton followed by mining and heavy engineering. The population of the valley had been falling since the 1960's, as a whole working generation left to look for employment elsewhere, leaving behind the old, the young and the unemployable. The place did have its up side(s). During the war the country's national theatre companies were evacuated to the town – don't ask me why – but they left behind a thirst for culture that resulted in the setting up of the Mid-Pennine Arts Association (www.midpenninearts.org.uk), an arts development organisation that predates the Arts Council. We went to more theatre/music/art in Burnley than I ever did in London – partly because you couldn't quite believe what was being put on in this post-industrial backwater – the pick of the fringe came through at some point: Monstrous Regiment; 7:84; Gay Sweatshop. It also nurtured an indigenous North East Lancs fringe of its own – in a stroke of inspired arts development, Mid-Pennine invited the mobile fringe art circus that was Welfare State International (WSI) to overwinter its caravans on a section of the local rubbish tip and to put on a series of shows that the town still talks about to this day. Their shows were a mixture of urban-myth-magic and surreal circus with a touch of northern humour. I remember: Parliament in Flames, the everyman epic Icarus Barrabas Quail, a Ghost Train with live ghosts, the Bloodstained Colonial Marching Band and a controversial nativity crib with 'All Power to the People' inscribed in latin above it. Members of People In Common sometimes worked as extra crew on shows, or would answer the call to pack the audience if the culture inspectors from the Arts Council were due to attend. WSI eventually tired of Burnley (or was it the other way round?) and they left the area – leaving behind Horse & Bamboo and IOU theatre companies founded by ex-WSI members and a legacy that would eventually see the corner of the tip they vacated turned into a thriving youth theatre. We got a caravan with a dodgy axel and a picture of an angel painted on the side from them when they left, which became the accommodation for us to start renovating the Mill.

PEOPLE IN COMMON

Fabled days   1980's

There was a regular stream of visitors through PIC, some looking for somewhere to live, some just curious, some on their travels, some members from other communities. We did work-swaps with other places — we had building skills; plastering, plumbing, carpentry, roofing — that were much in demand, and were a passport to staying at other groups. The idea was that it was an exchange of labour and someone would come back to Burnley and work with us in exchange for us doing a building job. But it didn't always work out — other places felt that the exchange was unequal and were embarrassed (I don't know why) and they didn't honour their side of the swap. One group even sent us a visitor in exchange! Sometimes there were good reasons ... shortage of members, goats to milk ... or perhaps Burnley just wasn't picturesque enough. I enjoyed the opportunity to visit other communes as a 'tradesman' without the scrutiny that visitors sometimes came under, or as a sort of communal relative. I remember going to Wheatstone to mix plaster for Laura, roofing at Lifespan and TaC, and a wonderful busman's holiday when all of us decamped for a week's window painting at Laurieston.

These were the fabled days of the Communes Network (CN) which probably existed as much in the informal exchanges that went on between groups, as in the pages of the newsletter or the 'readers' meetings' and organised gatherings. Readers' meetings were an attempt to engage the readership of publications in the editorial policy of a newsletter or magazine — I'm not quite sure where the idea came from — Peace News was the only other publication that I knew that held them. The CN readers' meetings tended to be rather strange affairs, well at least the ones I attended were. Poorly attended by commune members and dominated by one or two subscribers (nearly always men) who didn't live communally and who at some point in the weekend would launch into a session telling us how we were all doing it wrong and if we only did what they suggested how wonderful it would all be. But as the whole network was a wonderful anarchic-jumble-sale-of-a-disorganisation none of the suggestions were ever likely to be taken up. Production of the newsletter depended on the energy of a particular group at any one time, with some groups just producing one or two issues whilst others would get enthused (or stuck?) and end up producing anything up to a dozen. This gave the network an illusive, ephemeral appearance — shifting its location around the country, one moment in SW Scotland, a year later in West Wales, next year coming from an address in the Pennines, popping up a couple of years later in Buckinghamshire. Which was all very well for our anarchistic love of decentralisation, but made the admin a nightmare. In the end, admin and production were separated with, if I remember rightly, the admin being done from Lifespan who also often did the printing. Meanwhile the editorial work continued to hop from group to group.

Voluntary service   1980's

So how do you turn a derelict mill into a thriving community with a handful of semi-skilled enthusiasts and no money at the same time as bringing-up small children (some of them being home schooled)? The answer is slowly. Whilst we had managed to fairly easily get home improvement grants from the council to renovate the terraced houses in Burnley, The Mill was an industrial building and grants were only discretionary. So although we drew up a design for turning it into six flats the council turned us down for grants. The only grant we ever got was £60 towards loft insulation. I recall a meeting where we seriously considered selling the place. But in the end we came up with a somewhat cunning plan, where we would work for six months of the year earning money to pay for the building materials and then spend the rest of the year working on the mill, funded by fortnightly grants from the DHSS called 'giros'. We also tapped into various sources of voluntary labour. Members of other communities came and gave us a hand. Local friends, parents and visitors all contributed. And once a year for a number of years we held an International Voluntary Service (IVS) work camp. The camps gave us a real boost. For two or three weeks we would tackle 'big' projects at the Mill: laying water mains, demolishing pig-pens, laying concrete, landscaping ... We had volunteers from all sorts of places: France, Germany, Scandinavia, Eastern Bloc countries — Poland, Hungary, Yugoslavia and from further afield — India, Nigeria. For me, as someone active in the peace movement, it was a real part of building bridges across cultures at what still felt like the height of the Cold War, with Cruise missiles being deployed at Greenham and Trident being commissioned. IVS had been set up in the inter-war years. Originally growing out of work carried out by a group of French and German volunteers repairing a French village that had been destroyed during the First World War — Service Civil International was set up by Pierre Ceresole, a Swiss national 'To foster peace and understanding between people and nations through voluntary work'. In 1931 the first international project was carried out in Great Britain, to build an outdoor swimming pool for the colliery town of Bryn Mawr, Wales and the International Voluntary Service was born. Without the help of IVS volunteers I'm not sure we would have managed to crack the work at the mill.

VOLUNTEERS Monika Bybzak from Poland, Karolina Neufussoua from Czechoslovakia and Hans Haege from Germany set to work

Volunteers swap desks for rural E Lancs life

A HOUSING co-operative is giving a host of young people from all over the world the chance to experience life in East Lancashire.

The People in Common Housing Co-op is running the latest in a series of voluntary services camps at its old corn mill in Altham.

The young people, who hail from a variety of far-flung places including Poland, Belgium, New Zealand and Hungary, are living and working at the corn mill, which was bought in the late 1970s and provides a permanent home to local housing co-op members.

The ten visitors will stay for weeks at the mill and earn their keep by helping to point walls and level fields.

Co-op member Bob Sproule said: "The camps are organised in different countries by the Civil Service International and governments often pay for young people to take part, giving them a chance to travel and experience life in a different country.

By SHARON DALE

"They don't always come to co-operatives like ours, they sometimes go to help with non-profit making community projects.

Renovations

"We have run quite a few of the camps here at the corn mill and we have had people from all nationalities staying

with us, including people from Africa and Turkey.

"They help us with the renovations and we try to find them some outside work as well.

"In return, we give them food and lodgings.

"It is great for everyone involved and we still keep in touch with some of the people we have met."

For info on IVS see: http://ivsgb.org

Being counted   1980's

We took the dictat that the 'personal is political' very seriously at PIC. I think we were viewed by other local politicos as 'Person Centred Troublemakers' because in our dealings with local groups ... if the political wasn't seen as personal then we were the people who were going to make damn sure that it was. We were active in many local campaigns over the years, sometimes as key players other times just as peripheral members. I remember: baby sitting for Reclaim the Night Marches; occupying the public inquiry into the M65; singing as part of the BANANA band for Anti-nuclear events, NELCAR, CND; building a fallout shelter from a kitchen table in the Market Square in Burnley; running a weekend crèche for a local women's conference; supporting a sacked lesbian bus driver; smashing up war toys donated by our kids in protest at a military march past;

Pendle Witches Against the Bomb; scaling the Town Hall to unfurl a 'War is No Game!' banner during a civil defence exercise; producing our own Stop the Poll Tax leaflet ... Looking back I can see it was incredibly empowering, the collective support that we had, the ability to take time out from whatever we were doing to 'Protest & Survive'. Just coming home to supportive people after a hard day 'at the front'. For many years we had a political fund which funded personal political activity. We also had resources that we could use for political activity – we built a

scaffolding stage for Arthur Scargill to use at a local rally during the Miners' Strike (it rained and he went inside the local Labour Club – but it was the thought (or sweat) that counted). One year we took on the full might of the state and refused to fill in the census – we objected to being classed as separate households (there being no way to fill the census return in as a communal household living at different addresses). We argued that the only way we could fill in the form was by all of us lying. Which freaked them out – 'No you mustn't lie!' – in the end I think we fudged it and filled it in as if we all lived in the same house.

The price of free love   1980's

The barmaid at the local pub once told me that she 'knew' that we 'must be in and out of each others' beds all the time'. I have a feeling that there were far more sexual shenanigans going on amongst the locals she was serving than were going on at PIC. That's not to say we were chaste or puritanical when it came to sex – far from it. Its just that serial monogamy was pretty much the norm and its hard to hide anything that is going on when you live in the pockets of a dozen other people all the time. I didn't really discover sex until I discovered communal living – or rather until I discovered older women who lived communally. I don't know what it was about women my own age or younger – largely just that their (and I guess my) inexperience – meant that I could never really get it together with anyone who wasn't older than me. I had spent my teenage years reading about sex and everyone else assumed that I was getting some because I could talk about it in a relatively knowledgeable way. I somehow lost my virginity in stages whilst I was in London looking for love and finding loneliness in the metropolis. I realise now that there was nothing really wrong with coming fairly late to sex, and once I got there I took to it like a duck to massage oil. Communes can work as a sort of informal laid-back dating agency. A place to meet like-minded people and get to know them, all without the pressure usually associated with dating.

I was part of a multiple relationship which lasted for three years or so. Me and two women. It happened partly due to circumstances: one started as a long-distance relationship with Catriona at Laurieston; the other an on-off relationship with Barbara at PIC that developed into something more meaningful over time. It was also due to ideas around at the time about non-possessiveness, sharing your love etc etc ... easier to say than do most of the time and very easy to cynically misrepresent when it all goes wrong. Somehow, we made it work for us for what, looking back now, seems like a decent length of time for a relationship. We had mini-meetings to talk about how it was going for each of us, rotas for spending time together, had holidays, babysat for each other. The relationships coped with David (Barbara's son from another relationship), Finn being born and brief encounters with others. If you want the salacious details — hard luck — Yes I did and no we didn't! In the end perhaps there were just not enough hours in the week or enough love or commitment to go round. It ended slowly and without fireworks. None of us left the group at the time. We are all still friends and I have fond memories of that time.

There was a place in Leeds called The Future Studies Centre which ran a course on Alternatives, funded by the Workers Education Association, I think. We used to go and talk about living together along with a few people from Lifespan. Someone would inevitably ask 'Are you a Free Love commune?' The best answer I can remember anyone giving was a woman from Lifespan who, after explaining that she had been seen as somewhat unusual in that when she first joined she had sexual encounters with several of the men who lived there, answered 'Do we have Free Love? No — it costs just as much as it does anywhere else'.

Your children are not your children ...   1980/90's

In my late teens I had a dream that I would fall in love with a red-haired woman and bring up a child that was not my own — and in a way that's what happened — but not in the way I had thought from the dream. Catriona (with hennaed hair) came to PIC for a week from Laurieston on a work-swap and ended up spending summers in Scotland running conferences and flying (or was it fleeing) south for winters with us in Burnley doing building work. And so our relationship started as a long-distance on-off affair. While she was away one winter there was talk at Laurieston of forming a baby group to support new babies and establishing a baby 'house' in one of the cottages. I think the idea somehow came from Pat and Sarah's trip to Twin Oaks and was originally conceived to support Linda who wanted to have a child. In the meantime, down in Nottingham in the offices of Peace News, where we were doing a building job, Catriona and I were busy conceiving a child of our own. Finn was born as part of the 'baby group' at Laurieston with five or six of us taking turns to do childcare in one of the cottages. I lived at Laurieston for six months — not joining but becoming a sort of communal relative. I returned to Burnley the following spring and Catriona followed with Finn for her winter season later in the year. Looking back it seems a somewhat crazy way to be bringing up a new baby; but it worked and felt incredibly supportive at times. Finn slotted almost seamlessly in to the shared childcare/crêche that we ran at PIC and then back into the baby group on return to Laurieston (by this time Linda's daughter Josie had been born). I think it was the support from others: other parents; single members; and visitors who would help out with looking after the kids that gave me and us the confidence to keep Finn out of school and teach him ourselves. I think it also helped that all Finn's grandparents were either teachers or school secretaries or school librarians. Home schooling had been a feature both at PIC and Laurieston over the years with various kids being taught at home. It was a challenge at times and we often wondered if we were doing the 'right thing' – we often thought we were as well. Finn decided to go to school of his own accord aged nine just after we had moved to the Mill.

When I had first arrived in Burnley one of the things that had attracted me to the group was the chance to sort of try out being a parent: to be allowed to build a relationship with some kids that was more meaningful than just kicking a ball about or reading them a story now and again. When I joined there were a few kids around: Leigh, Simon, Katie and Sammy, David, Eleanor and Max. I enjoyed getting to know them, and later Nicky, Toby, Jim and Alex as well. At one point we tried to somehow categorise the relationship of non-parents to some

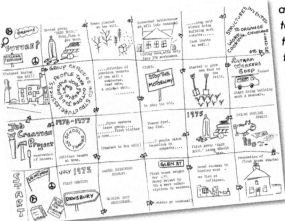

of the children with a system of what we referred to as 'ones, twos and threes' – Ones were equivalent to biological parents, two like aunts and uncles and threes just friends – I think for a while I was a one to Leigh (12) who I shared a house with; and a two to David (2) who I did childcare for and regularly babysat; and I was probably a three for Simon. It didn't last long as an experiment, but highlighted some things around responsibility and commitment – for both non-parents and parents, I think.

Your children are not your children.
They are the sons and daughters of
Life's longing for itself ...

Kahlil Gibran

Social entrepreneurs   1980/90's

You never know quite how the outside world sees you. Local opinion suddenly changed to us when we put a painted sign in the window of our main communal house advertising that we were a Building Co-operative and were looking for work. Talking to neighbours later they told me that the sign explained why our front room looked like an office and why we seemed to be running a playgroup. It also helped no end in dispelling the view that we were dirty hippie DHSS scroungers. Building work sort of grew on us: a natural progression in many ways from squatting through DIY renovation; doing up our own houses on improvement grants; to more official work on a job creation scheme. A couple of us: Pete and Laura, went on TOPS training courses to learn carpentry and plastering. And when no local building company would employ Laura afterwards (saying 'We don't have toilet facilities for a woman!' despite the fact that they didn't have any for men either ...) we set up Altham Workers Co-op and set off on something of an adventure in running our own business. There was an element of making it up as we went along. I do remember sitting on a roof with a copy of the Squatter's Handbook working out how to replace slates. We taught each other whatever skills we had picked up. Derek became 'the plumber' because he seemed to understand things like that. I did general labouring and then became the carpenter when the real carpenter left. Plastering became a woman's job – due to Laura having done the training and passing it on to Barbara and then Jackie. We nearly always had a couple of women working on site at any one time. This caused quite a stir, not only among the people we worked for, but also with delivery men (I think they were all men, although I have a memory of a concrete truck arriving one day driven by a woman – much to our pleasant surprise). It wasn't long before the local paper got wind of a good story ... We were part of the Women in Manual Trades Network – well the women were – and every Christmas we did our little bit to undermine the rampant sexism in the building industry by sending all our suppliers a calendar with pictures of women actually doing manual work – as opposed to posing scantily clad with power tools between their legs.

Girls build history

By Richard Catlow

PEOPLE tend to sit up when they see Barbara Sanders humping bricks, or when Laura Campbell knocks at their doors and announces she's come to do the plastering.

But it's not just the fact that they're women in a man's world which makes them unusual.

For Barbara and Laura.

I once had a conversation with a Lancashire Co-op Development Agency worker in which we both bemoaned the lack of entrepreneurs – whereupon she said that they had always seen us at PIC as entrepreneurs – which sort of caught me off guard – my picture of an 'entrepreneur' was of some smart guy in a suit who could wheel-and-deal and make loads of money. I then started to think of us as social entrepreneurs. Rather than taking risks and experimenting in a financial sense – as in conventional entrepreneurship – we were pushing the boundaries of what was possible in social organisation, taking risks with each others' lives and lifestyles. And like all entrepreneurs, sometimes we hit on something that worked, sometimes we didn't and for most of the time we got by much like everybody else.

Digging & Dreaming & Editing & Writing 1990's

I failed my English O-level the first time round and would probably have been diagnosed as mildly dyslexic had such a thing been around when I was at school. So how I ended up being a writer is something of a mystery to me. I started off sending in short pieces to Communes Network: letters; responses to other people's writing; the odd cartoon or joke piece – to my surprise this qualified me to be described years later as 'a regular contributor'. When the Info Pack group was advertised I was looking for some way to contribute something to the Communes Network in a way that was more than just 'living it'. I saw what we were doing as a viable way to live and wanted to encourage more people to give it a try. PIC supported me in attending meetings – paying my travel expenses. I think it was really the idea of a video that had attracted me in the first place, having worked for a community video project in London in the 70's. When the video didn't materialise I sort of drifted into writing a few short bits for the Info pack – book reviews etc. As the group morphed into the D&D collective I gradually found myself writing the odd longer article, usually based on my own experience. Never did I imagine I would end up writing a book on my own. What ended up as Utopia Britannica started off as the D&D history project. A book in search of an author – until eventually someone said why don't you write it? You seem to know as much as anyone about the subject! To which I actually had no answer. So I thought 'OK, I'll give it a go'. Writing a book was a daunting task and ironically I don't think I could have found the time to write a book (two books!) about communal living whilst actually living communally. I also couldn't have done it without the backing of other D&D editors and others in the communes movement.

Swimming in the income pool   1980's/90's

In one way or another for nearly all of my life I have been part of an income pool. As a child, my parents pooled their income to bring me up, and, like many families, have continued to occasionally help out financially through the years. Today I do the same with my partner and for the best part of 20 years or so at PIC I pooled income with other members. The big difference was that there were no 'blood ties' to motivate the sharing of income — income pooling was ideological. Or so I thought.

My relationship with money has been undermined by years in an income pool — for me it bears no relation to the work I have done. I have 'earned' 50p an hour for serious hard labour on a building site and been paid well for work I consider to have been easy. Neither of which made any difference to my standard of living or the amount of money that I had in my pocket — it all went into the pool and was used for collective projects or distributed on an agreed equal basis. This can seriously mess with your head — on balance I think mostly in positive ways. It blurs the differences in income earning power between the sexes, between those with qualifications and those without, between the young and the old. It challenges some fairly deep psychological assumption that we carry round in our heads about money. I recall Woody from SPIL struggling to come terms with the idea of not being a 'breadwinner' at the point where he was taking more out of the pool than he was putting in.

For many years pooling income was seen as a sort of ideological litmus test for joining PIC — it sifted out the economically compatible wheat from the chaff before they even applied to join. In the late 1990's the system unravelled and we stopped income-pooling, though we maintained some cross-subsidy around paying utility bills and rent. It was a momentous event at the time and felt like a betrayal of all we had stood for over two decades. One way of looking at why it happened is that we had too much money. We had reached the point where we had a surplus over and above what was needed to meet our basic needs, and we failed to find a way to agree how to spend it. Talking to some founder members afterwards who had been around when income-pooling had been started I discovered that it had been largely a pragmatic measure to cope with extreme poverty within the group. Some people had been worried that it would handicap the group by making it too big a deal to join — condemning the group to a limited membership — but couldn't at the time see any other way of the group surviving. Only later did it evolve into an integral part of the group's ideology.

People in Common – 20 years of Co-operation.
1973-93

"All That Way For This!"

Leaving

In some twenty years at PIC I think I nearly left three or four times before we finally moved on. The first time was fairly early on when I considered moving to Laurieston Hall. The other times were when things got difficult between me and other members or I felt completely at odds with the way the group was going. What kept me there? Mostly I thought that the group was there to meet individuals' needs and should change to accommodate them – even as those needs changed. Also, I refused to leave and go to a situation that was worse than the one I found myself in. I saw too many people leave and end up in much worse situations materially, and I felt that this was a failure on the group's part. In the end it seemed to boil down to a fairly hard-nosed assessment on my part that there was no way in the 'outside world' I would have access to the resources, tools, land and money that I had collectively in the group, and I didn't want to give all that up – I wanted to make it work. So why did we leave? Mostly because we reached a position where we could. Too long living in cheap co-operative affordable rented housing means that you end up stuck in a poverty trap of your own making – something of a stark realisation when it came. The longer you stayed, the harder it was to get out as you had no collateral to feed into the housing market and you had got used to living a low-income lifestyle. In my case it was the Welfare State that came to the rescue. No, not the DHSS – the International one. Working for performance company Welfare State International on their ambitious Lanternhouse building project in Ulverston was the steadiest income I had ever had and I think allowed us to imagine that we could afford to rent a place somewhere else. On top of that, Finn was almost at the stage where we felt he could be leaving home soon.

Looking back, I can see that I had been frustrated for a few years before over the lack of any progress on any expansion of the community – or any real opportunity for growth. Despite repeated times when we looked to become a bigger group – it never happened. Why? Perhaps because the people who joined were attracted by what we were, not what we might be. I don't know – all I can recall is thinking that our visions were just too big for our resources and all the things we had dreamed of were never going to happen if left to such a small bunch of people. I'm not sure I gave up on the dream – just decided that it wasn't going to happen there and then with those people. And I gave up trying to push people in directions that they didn't seem to want to go. Leaving came much quicker than I had expected or had really wanted. We looked around for a suitable smallish city to move to, thinking it would take a long time to find somewhere – but very soon it narrowed down to Lancaster and on about our second trip house hunting we ticked all the boxes on our list and suddenly we were on the move. Before we left we had one last look through the PIC communal archives and made an attempt to put the communal history in some sort of order; names on photos, papers in some sort of order, that sort of thing. To me it felt like the end of an era – what it felt like to anyone else I don't know.

Living in an unintentional community   1999

After so long living communally the outside world was both somewhat strange and a little scary. The realisation that I had become alternatively institutionalised – it was ten years since I had actually paid a gas or electric bill

— shopping for three of us was a bit of a novelty and cooking for such small numbers ... well ... seemed like a waste of time. We also weren't quite sure how to relate to our neighbours — we decided that the normal-done-thing must be to organise a house-warming and invite the street. Turned out we were the first newcomers to do such a thing since anyone could remember. The neighbours who came decided we had done it because we were 'communal' — and there was us thinking we were being normal! Finn never did manage to adjust to the new situation — a lifetime of living with others, the alien experience of living 'just with your mum and dad' and the wrench away from his friends all led him to go back to PIC and spend a further 18 months there.

Did I miss communal life? Yes and no. I didn't miss meetings about the minutiae of everyday life, I didn't miss cleaning rotas or waiting for someone to get back with the shared car so I could go out ... I did miss the easy socialisation, the conversations over dinner, the chats in the corridor. I did miss the camaraderie of working closely with others on a project. I guess I'm saying that I missed the people not the 'institution'. We had wondered about looking to join another community, but were not sure whether that was what we really wanted — we liked the Danish idea of cohousing, but there wasn't anything really like that in the North of England — and anyway we wanted to see whether we really liked 'nuclear living' once the novelty had worn off.

Doing it all again   2005 - 12

In 2003 some friends in Lancaster looked at buying an old Victorian school to convert to flats or apartments with some shared facilities. They got me to look round it with my builder's hat on and when I said 'So you want to set up a cohousing project' ... they looked somewhat blank, needed an explantation of what I was talking about but ... the seed of an idea was sown. The school project fell through, but a small group of us kept talking about doing something along cohousing lines in Lancaster and after a good few 'pub' discussions we embarked on what would eventually become Forgebank Cohousing. I know it has been said before by many others — but if we had known what we were letting ourselves in for we may well have thought more than twice before we started. And I say that from the perspective of someone whom you would have thought ought to have known what it would entail. But I had never been involved in the process of trying to set up a group before and — while twenty odd-years of communal living had given me lots of useful experience and skills that were relevant to setting up a group — I set off on this new adventure with a little trepidation and if I am honest a little excitement. When we finally settled on a location for our cohousing project there was a moment of déjà vu when we found ourselves buying a derelict industrial site on the banks of a river ...

Chris Coates

COMMUNES BRITANNICA

Directory of Communal Groups 1939 – 2000

Listed in this section are the communities that I have come across during my research arranged chronologically county-by-county in England and then with separate sections for Wales, Scotland and Ireland. If the group is featured in the main text of the book I have kept the details in this section to a minimum and, vice-versa, if they don't feature then there is a more lengthy description here. Entries shaded in grey are those groups where either I have only sketchy information from a single possibly unreliable source which has led me to be cautious about the actual existence of a community on the ground or the information was in the form of an advert for a group which may never have got beyond the embryonic forming stage. I have given dates for the forming and winding up of groups. All information is from publicly available records and publications or directly from information provided by the groups themselves.

If you wish to visit a community please do not rely on the information in these pages – for up to date details of existing groups open to visitors and contact details see: **www.diggersanddreamers.org.uk**

ENGLAND

BEDFORDSHIRE

TINGRITH MANOR FARM   circa 1939
Training farm for Jewish refugees.
Location: Tingrith (on Bucks/Beds border)
Ref: Bedfordshire Archive

CPFLU LAND UNITS   1940 - 1946
Christian Pacifist land-based units organised for conscientious objectors.
Location: Bolnhurst, Shillington.
Ref: M Maclachlan **CPLFU**

BARWYTHE HALL   1946 - 1949
Community set up by members of the Common Wealth Party who aimed *"to live in real country, but near enough to 'belong' to a village. About an hour from a London terminus ..."* Featured

as Berewode House in Kenneth Alsop's autobiographical *One and All*.
Location: Pedley Hill, Studham, Dunstable
Ref: K Alsop **One and All: Two years in the Chilterns**

AMPTHILL PARK HOUSE   1954 - 1977
Early Cheshire Home for the disabled in mansion that had been requisitioned during the war. Moved in 1977 to new premises in Woburn Road Ampthill.
Location: Ampthill
Ref: L Cheshire **The Hidden World**

ARARAT   circa 1971
Small commune in a village eight people involved at the start *"It has no especial reason for its existence except the stimulus and happiness of living together ..."*
Location: South Bedfordshire
Ref: **Directory of Communes** 1971

EXODUS

1992 -

Dance music collective that organised free parties in the Luton area where they raised funds that supported further parties and various community projects inc: housing for homeless people, HAZ Manor, a community farm on MOT land and campaigned for a permanent community owned centre for the people on the Marsh Farm estate and for a legal venue for outside dance parties.

Location: Luton

Ref: *DiY Culture: Party and Protest in Nineties' Britain*

BERKSHIRE

WINTERBOURNE

1940 - 1946

CPFLU land unit site.

Ref: M Maclachlan *CPLFU*

NORTHUMBERLAND ROAD SQUAT

1946

Squat in Anti-Aircraft Battery camp.

Location: Reading

Ref: www.arborfieldhistory.org.uk (23.12.08)

ARBORFIELD HALL CAMP

1946

Nissen huts in grounds of hall used by RAF and US troops, squatted by local families at end of war.

Location: near Reading

Ref: www.arborfieldhistory.org.uk (23.12.08)

RANIKHET CAMP

1946 - 1950

Squatted Army camp. There were so many squatters in the Reading area that efforts were made to form a Berkshire Federation of Squatters. Delegates from eight camps representing 250 families met on the parade ground at Ranikhet Camp on 8th Sep 1946. Apart from the two Reading camps, there were squatters from Theale, Upper Culham, Chaddleworth and Bucklebury Common.

Location: Tilehurst, Reading

Ref: www.arborfieldhistory.org.uk (23.12.08)

BARKHAM MANOR

1946

Eight families – all Barkham ex-Service men squatting in empty manor house formerly used as offices by Berkshire War Agricultural Committee. They were evicted within a few months, but were offered accommodation in huts at Arborfield Hall Camp.

Location: Barkham

Ref: www.arborfieldhistory.org.uk (23.12.08)

WESTWICK CAMP

1946

Squatted officers mess and Nissen huts.

Location: Bagshot Road, Bracknell

Ref: *Reading Mercury*, 17 Aug 1946

GREENHAM COMMON

1946

Abortive attempt by five families to squat base.

Location: near Newbury

Ref: www.arborfieldhistory.org.uk (23.12.08)

CIVIL REHABILITATION UNIT

1946

Several families squatting in huts.

Location: Hermitage

Ref: *Reading Mercury*, 31 Aug 1946

WELFORD PARK CAMP

1946

Several huts squatted at USAF base whilst other still occupied by US airmen.

Location: Chaddleworth

Ref: *Reading Mercury*, 31 Aug 1946

WOODLANDS PARK

1946

Families squatting in Army Nissen huts.

Location: near Maidenhead

Ref: *Reading Mercury*, 31 Aug 1946.

COOKHAM COMMON

1946

Four families squatting in huts alongside Royal Engineers.

Location: Hermitage

Ref: *Reading Mercury*, 31 Aug 1946

TOUTLEY CAMP

1946

Camp originally squatted by three families – then taken over by local council who moved a further ten families in.

Location: Wokingham

Ref: *Reading Standard*, 21 Sep 1946

THEALE CAMP

1946 - 1950's

'Squatter' colony of 1200, mostly ex-munitions factory workers, living in wartime army huts.

Location: near Reading

Ref: D Thomas *Villains' Paradise*

WOODLEY AIRFIELD

1946

Following the departure of American airmen keys to Nissen huts were handed to men who worked in the Miles Aircraft Company factory they lived there in a '*village like*' atmosphere. A plan to rehouse the men was drawn up by architect Charles Reilly based on his 'Reilly Greens' layouts. The factory closed before the houses were built.

Location: near Reading

Ref: P Richmond *Marketing Modernisms*

SWALLOWFIELD PARK
1950's - 2003

Country house 'saved' by the Mutual Households Association. The house was used in 1972 as a set for filming of the Doctor Who episode "The Time Monster"
Location: near Reading
Ref: *SAVE Casework News*, Jun 2004

DIVINE LIGHT MISSION
circa 1970 - 1983

Ashram lived in by Divine Light devotees.
Location: 6 Devon Avenue, Slough
Ref: www.prem-rawat-bio.org (31.7.2011)

YELDALL MANOR
1973 - 1976

Almost defunct convent used by the Community of Celebration Christian Trust. Housed some 120 people at its peak. *"The Community at Yeldall Manor was a melting pot of nationalities and churches ... Outreach ministry from Yeldall was extensive. The Community's teams, known as the Fisherfolk, were in huge demand for conferences, cathedral and church ministry, on radio and even TV. Teams travelled throughout Britain and overseas."*
Location: Bear Lane, Hare Hatch, Reading
Ref: www.ccct.co.uk/Library/yeldall.html (4.12.10)

COMMUNITY VENTURE
circa 1977

Community Venture between Reading and London. *"Families purchasing large country house seek others with £10,000 cash ... Objectives co-operation, conservation, appropriate technology and greater access to tools."*
Ref: Ad in *Undercurrents* 22 (Apr May 1977)

NEW VILLAGES COMMUNE
circa 1976

Short-lived commune set up by a loose group of people from the New Villages Association.
Location: Reading
Ref: *Communes Network* 18

CHURCH FARM
circa 1980 - 1984

Community of five adults and five children farming 16 acres with cows, pigs, sheep, goats, chickens, geese and bees. Also ran Newbury wholefood shop.
Location: Ashmansworth, Newbury
Ref: *Alternative Communities* 3rd ed;
J Mercer *Communes*

ELMORE ABBEY
1987 - 2010

Small group of Benedictine monks who moved from Nashdom Abbey. Created a timber frame chapel with windblown timber from 1987 'hurricane'.
Location: Church Lane, Speen
Ref: www.newburytoday.co.uk (14.6.2011)

BUCKINGHAM SHIRE

NASHDOM ABBEY
1929 - 1987

Anglican Order of Benedictine Monks living as a monastic community in Nashdom House built by Edwin Lutyens as summer mansion for wife of Russian Prince Dolgorouki. Combination of tightly disciplined monasticism and *"slightly racy country club."* Moved to Elmore near Newbury in 1987.
Location: Taplow, Slough
Ref: *Alternative Communities* 3rd ed

CPFLU LAND UNITS
1940 - 1946

Christian Pacifist land-based units organised for conscientious objectors.
Location: Chesham, Slough and Winslow
Ref: M Maclachlan *CPLFU*

VACHE CAMP
1946 -

Army camp that Ministry earmarked for Italian women who married Polish soldiers taken over by 100 squatters.
Location: Chalfont St Giles
Ref: D Thomas *Villains' Paradise*

BEECH BARN CAMPS
1946 - 1950

Post-war squatter camps at Beech Barn "Top" and "Bottom" Army Camps.
Location: near Amersham
Ref: www.amersham.org.uk (22.12.08)

GROVE PARK CAMP
1946 - 1957

Camp occupied by squatters and families of Polish soldiers with nowhere else to go.
Location: Iver
Ref: northwickparkpolishdpcamp.co.uk (24.12.08)

TUNMERS
1955 - 1959

House used by the Friends Ambulance Post War Service as headquarters, provided alternative service for conscientious objectors.
Location: Chalfont St Peter
Ref: R Bush *FAU: The Third Generation*

BULSTRODE BRUDERHOF
1958 - 1966

Second Bruderhof community set up in the empty Bulstrode Mansion and 70 acres of parkland when the Wheathill community in Shropshire became overcrowded. From here the group ran a metal fabrication business and established the children's

play equipment business, Community Playthings.
Location: Bulstrode Park, Gerrards Cross
Ref: Y Oved *Witness of Brothers*

HMP GRENDON   1962 - present
Prison run as Therapeutic Community with
235 places for Category B men. Consists of five
separate communities and an assessment unit.
Location: Grendon Underwood
Ref: *Therapeutic Communities Past Present & Future*

BROTHERHOOD OF THE CHRIST LIGHT
circa 1971
Two married couples living a 'Christian based life'
in large house with garden. Produced their own
pamphlets and free leaflets.
Location: Sanctuary of the Christ Light,
Sunbeamends, Latimer Road, Chesham
Ref: *Communes Journal* 42 (April 1973)

PIETALS   1975 - 1983
Co-operatively worked organic small-holding
based at Springhill Organic Farm, set up to
provide an opportunity for unskilled people to get
a year or two's experience of running a small-
holding. *"There are no tutors here and people are
encouraged to learn what they want to know at their
own pace. There are usually four to six people living
here – in a small cottage, caravan, and converted
barn."* People's desire for longer term employment
led to a wholefood shop (Tantadlin) plus trucking
and flour milling businesses. The increasing scale
of the operation meant the creation of the Tipi
Co-operative in nearby Aylesbury and Pietals
ultimately came within this umbrella organisation.
Location: East Cottage, Springhill Farm, Dinton.
Ref: *Alternative Communities* 4th edition

MENTMORE TOWERS   1977 - 1997
Huge country house and former Rothschild
home used by the Maharishi Mahesh Yogi's
Transcendental Meditation movement as its
headquarters. Used variously as a Meditation
training centre, banqueting suite, film location and
finally as the base for the Natural Law Party.
Location: Mentmore
Ref: B Oates *Celebrating the Dawn*

RAINBOW HOUSING CO-OP   1977 - present
Began when aspiring communal group found two
rows of railway cottages saved by preservation
order. Milton Keynes Development Corporation

renovated the cottages in consultation with the
group. Rainbow has since purchased the terraces.
Location: Spencer Street, New Bradwell, MK
Ref: *D&D 90-91*;
www.rainbowhousingcoop.org.uk (31.8.2012)

REDFIELD   1978 - present
Large Victorian house and stable block with 17 acres
of land run by the Redley Housing Co-op. Ground
floor in the main house used communally for cooking,
eating, entertaining, meetings and courses. Upstairs
members each have a private room. Originally set
out to be a 'Socialist' based community has become
more 'sustainability focussed over the years. Home to
LILI – Low Impact Living Initiative. Run regular 'Living
in Communities' Weekends.
Location: Winslow
Ref: *D&D 90-91*; www.lowimpact.org;
www.redfieldcommunity.org.uk (23.8.2011)

GREENTOWN   circa 1979 - 1990's
Plan to establish a 'third Garden City' on
land owned by Milton Keynes Development
Corporation. The Greentown group, with at one
time over 100 members, drew up proposals for
an 'ecological village' and spent seven years
negotiating with the Corporation. In the end the
project faltered and was wound up.
Location: Crownhill, Milton Keynes
Ref: "Whatever happened to Greentown?" in
D&D 92-93

CAMPHILL MILTON KEYNES   1981 - present
Willen Park village houses over 50 residents
together with volunteer staff and their families in
ten separate households. Together the households
along with associated workshops, café and 'The
Chrysalis', a multi-function venue which serves as a
theatre, concert hall and meeting place, make up
Camphill Milton Keynes.
Location: Japonica Lane, Willen Park, MK
Ref: www.camphillmk.co.uk (21.4.2011)

THE LAURELS   1982 - 2011
Small communal household set up as a housing co-op renting house from Milton Keynes Development Corporation. Each tenant had private room and shared kitchen, dining and living rooms. Plus workshop and Laundry.
Location: 64 High Street, New Bradwell, MK
Ref: *D&D 90-91*

SUNNYSIDE   1983 - 1997
"Fairly derelict" 18th Century farmhouse bought by five friends and extensively rebuilt and renovated.
Location: Gawcott
Ref: *D&D 92-93*

LITTLE GROVE   1983 - 2002
Small community in house and five acres of gardens and fields formerly used as school. *"About half of us work partly or wholly from home: there is plenty of space for offices, studios and workshops, plus a thriving education centre. Some of us use the latter to run a programme of personal development courses and it is also used extensively by visiting groups."* Group dwindled in numbers in the late 1990's and the community later closed.
Location: near Chesham
Ref: *D&D 92-93*

COBWEB   1985 - 1987
Small co-operative in five terraced houses owned by Milton Keynes Development Corporation. *"The group operates on a co-operative rather than a communal basis – sharing cars, washing machines, tools – as well as trying to give each other practical support around childcare and emotional support in our lives."*
Location: Penryn Avenue, Fishermead, MK
Ref: *D&D 90-91*

SOLARIS   1993
Proposal for a Cohousing scheme in Milton Keynes.
Location: care of address in Milton Keynes
Ref: *D&D 94-95*

THE WELL AT WILLEN   1997 - present
Faith based community of families, couples and single people attempting *"to live a shared expression of life through our values of spirituality, hospitality, inclusivity, peace and justice and sustainability."* Each family/individual has own living space as well as sharing in the communal areas (a work of the Society of the Sacred Mission).
Location: Newport Road, Willen, Milton Keynes
Ref: *D&D 08-09*; www.diggersanddreamers.org.uk

CENTRE FOR SUSTAINABLE LIVING   circa 1994
Proposal for a loose-knit *"living-apart-together"* community to explore the practicalities of sustainable living.
Location: Dinton
Ref: *D&D 96-97*

THE CHILTERN UNIT   1997 -
Therapeutic Community at Young Offenders Institution.
Location: Aylesbury
Ref: *Therapeutic Communities Past Present & Future*

CAMBRIDGE SHIRE

MAVIS HOUSE   circa 1940
Christian income pooling community conceived as a *"communal guest house, convalescent home, settlement and propaganda unit."* Numbers increased during wartime by evacuees and refugees. Also known as 'the Cambridge Group'.
Location: 163 Hills Road, Cambridge
Ref: *Community in Britain* 1940

CPFLU LAND UNITS   1940 - 1946
Christian Pacifist land-based units organised for conscientious objectors.
Location: Caldecote; Swaffam Prior; Towlers Farm Upware
Ref: M Maclachlan *CPLFU*

MILTON PARK CAMP   1946 -
Army huts on Milton Park estate used to accommodate 'squatter' families.
Location: Near Peterborough
Ref: D Thomas *Villains' Paradise*

WIMPOLE PARK CAMP   1946
American wartime hospital taken over by squatters situated just inside the Wimpole Estate.
Location: Wimpole
Ref: www.wimpole.info (11.01.09)

WINSTON HOUSE   1958 - ?
Psychiatric halfway house.
Location: Brooklands Avenue, Cambridge
Ref: www.archive.pettrust.org.uk (30.6.2010)

GLEBE HOUSE   1969 - present

An internationally recognised therapeutic community for children. *"We see ourselves as an extended family, living and working together in a beautiful rural village."* Set up by a group of Quaker trustees as a children's home for up to fifteen young people, who for one reason or another could not live at home.
Location: Shudy Camps
Ref: www.rd29.net/cc/sc/newsjuly2003.htm (13.12.2010)

CAMBRIDGE CYRENIANS   circa 1970

A group of people living and working in a disused public house in the centre of Cambridge helping members of the vagrant population suffering from mental problems and personality disorders. *"The house we use is not run as a hostel or as a clinic, with a marked division between staff and patients, but as a home and community in which the vagrants and the Community workers live side by side, sharing the tasks and responsibilities as a group. ... our object is not to 'cure' people and return them to 'normal life'. Society has rejected them and they society – we offer them an alternative way in which to live."*
Location: 19 Mill Road, Cambridge
Ref: *Directory of Communes* 1972;
Alternative London

DIVINE LIGHT MISSION   circa 1970 - 1983

Ashrams lived in by Divine Light devotees.
Location: 14 Pretoria Road, Cambridge
Ref: *Alternative Communities* 3rd ed

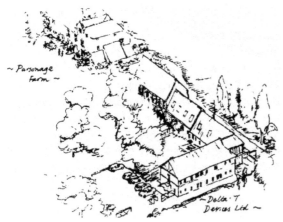
~ Parsonage Farm ~
~ Delta-T Devices Ltd ~

PARSONAGE FARM   1971 - present

Community that grew out of meetings run in Cambridge by Joan Harvey. House and outbuildings including shell of a medieval barn, and worm-riddled Tudor barn, used for storage and workshops. Three and a half acres of vegetables plots, fruit, trees and grass for hay and goat pasture. Some original members ran Arjuna wholefood shop and were involved in setting up Crabapple community. In parallel to the community a co-operative business making scientific instruments for agricultural and environmental research, Delta-T Devices, has grown alongside the community and many residents over the years have worked in Delta-T. Also known in early days as The Old Priory.
Location: Burwell
Ref: *Directory of Communes* 1972; *D&D 91-92*;
www.parsonage1.plus.com; www.delta-t.co.uk (23.8.2011)

STREET WARD   1975 - 1979

Attempt made to run an orthodox acute admission ward within a Mental Hospital as a therapeutic community. It tried to run as a therapeutic community whilst still using both drugs and electroconvulsive therapy (ECT). *"Even though the average length of admission was only 17 days there was often a powerful sense of community and shared purpose. Reality confrontation was usually vigorous and an emphasis was placed upon democratisation and permissiveness ..."*
Location: Fulbourn Hospital, Cambridge
Ref: *Therapeutic Communities: Past, Present and Future*; www.tc-of.org.uk/wiki/index. (20.2.09)

ARGYLE STREET   circa 1981 -

Fully mutual housing co-op funded by the Housing Corporation, to house 96 tenants. Individual houses with shared living rooms and kitchens. Each with *"their own level of communal living"* Also shared communal gardens and allotment on a three acre site.
Location: Fletchers Terrace, Cambridge
Ref: *D&D 92-93*

CAMBRIDGE BUDDHIST CNTRE circa 1987-?

Four FWBO communal houses three for men and one women's house.
Location: 19 Newmarket Road, Cambridge
Ref: *D&D 92-93*

QUAKER COMMUNITY   circa 1991

Proposal to set up small 'village style' community following the success of Bamford Quaker community.
Location: c/o address in Dry Drayton
Ref: *D&D 92-93*

CHESHIRE

PLUMBLEY EXPERIMENT circa 1940

Part-time communal experiment on five acres of land.
Location: Wash Lane, Plumbley
Ref: **Community in Britain** 1940

CPFLU LAND UNITS 1940 - 1946?

Christian Pacifist land-based units organised for conscientious objectors
Location: Delamare Forest; Nantwich
Ref: M Maclachlan **CPLFU**

**CHEADLE HULME
COMMUNITY FELLOWSHIP** 1941

Income pooling community of three families and woman teacher who gave up their homes and rented a large house. "*Each member has a small annual dress allowance and a very small weekly allowance. – The community has devoted some of its resources to social service and the members have given service for a nearby refugee hostel.*"
Location: 4 Queens Road, Cheadle Hulme
Ref: **Peace News Community Supplement** 14.3.41

'REILLY GREENS' 1946

The Reilly Plan was an alternative report on post-war reconstruction of Birkenhead by Professor of Architecture at the University of Liverpool Sir Charles Reilly's. The plan included Reilly Greens, small village greens which most houses adjoined. With groups of three to five greens around a community centre containing a restaurant, bar, sports and hobbies areas, library and hall. Family houses around the greens would not have kitchens, as the community centre's restaurant was to provide a low cost catering service to be managed by residents. Houses would be provided with small electric cookers for emergencies. This would leave women free to undertake paid work. None of the proposals were taken up by the Council.
Location: Birkenhead'
Ref: P Richmond *Marketing Modernisms; The Architectural & Social History of Co-operative Living*

OAKCROFT GARDENS 1962 - ?

Organic market garden on four acres set up by Mehr Fardoonji who had worked for six years in Gandhi's Ashram in India. During the 1970's links were made with the communes movement and a small community of people who came to work on the small-holding grew up."... *We aim to be a first step in real community living. Giving people a taste for manual work, fresh air, tolerance of each other and time to rethink a way of living away from busy urban life. We hope to grow in every sense of the word.*" Still operates today as an organic market garden.
Location: Cross'o'the Hill, Malpas
Ref: **Directory of Communes** 1972; **Alternative London**; www.oakcroft.org.uk (30.1.2011)

CORNWALL

ST IVES ARTISTS COLONY 1885 -

The best known of the English artists colonies. Originally known for its mainly foreign landscape painters. Was always more cosmopolitan than its sister colony at Newlyn. Enjoyed a renaissance when discovered by a new generation of modern artists in WWII, becoming home to Barbara Hepworth and Ben Nicholson. The older generation of artists gave some support to the new beatnik and hippie 'blow ins' in the 1960's.
Location: St Ives
Ref: **Stanhope Forbes & the Newlyn School; The Good and Simple Life**

'NANCLEDRA' circa 1940 - 1942

Community of pacifists that grew from a single small-holding to a number of households farming 42 acres. Went on to form the core of the Taena community.
Location: near Penzance.
Ref: **Utopian England; Community Journey**

CARCLEW MANSION 1940

Workcamp with pacifists and refugees from eight nations renovating mansion. Run by IVS and Society of Friends. "*The camp gives to men and women of goodwill a sound system of training in mutual help, voluntary discipline and comradeship.*"
Location: Perron-ar-Worthal near Truro
Ref: **Community in Britain** 1940

NEW LIFE MOVEMENT 1941

Temp office of organisation hoping to form a Collegiate house in large property.
Location: Tintagel
Ref: **Peace News Community Supplement** 14.3.1941

ST TERESA'S   1949 -
Cheshire Home set up in disused buildings on RAF base.
Location: RAF Predannack
Ref: L Cheshire *Hidden World*

HOLY CROSS   1950 -
Cheshire Home set up close to St Teresa's.
Location: near Predannack
Ref: L Cheshire *Hidden World*

HELIGAN WOODS CMNTY   circa 1962-1965
Adhoc Summer 'beatnik' community. "We discovered a clearing deep in the middle of Heligan woods and built the sort of wood cabin you used to see in western movies, ... Gradually a community of a dozen or so grew up around our encampment, old army tents were pitched and other beats would turn up from all over the country after we met up with them at festivals and demos. These newcomers had long flowing hair and exotic names – several of them really were 'on the road' and we held them in great awe. We ourselves, still in our late teens, were considered a rather inferior breed, 'ravers' which in those days meant week-end beatniks who could always run home to mum and dad if things really did get tough. I remember that we seemed to live almost exclusively on mackerel and porridge which we cooked over the camp fire whilst we listened to Jonathan and others with guitars play the songs of the Kingston Trio, Leadbelly and Woody Guthrie."
Location: Heligan
Ref: www.rainydaygallery.co.uk/musicarchive (13.12.2010)

THE MONKEY SANCTUARY   1964 -
Group looking after a colony of Amazonian woolly monkeys rescued from the pet trade in the 1960's and 70's. "recently became a charity but has always been run in a co-operative spirit (and was a co-operative for many years), and about 12 keepers live on site all year round caring for the monkeys."
Location: Murrayton, Looe
Ref: www.monkeysanctuary.org
www.diggersanddreamers.org.uk (23.8.2011)

ST IVES STREET COMMUNE   1967 - 1969
In the spring of 1967 a group of 20 or so beats had gone down to St Ives to help with the clean-up of the Torrey Canyon oil disaster. Because of the oil they could not sleep on the beaches and were allowed to sleep in a disused army lookout post. This carried on for the next couple of years – Just after Easter 1969 a member of the Street Commune in London went to St Ives in Cornwall and formed a 'branch' – the St Ives Street Commune. "For the first month this was about the most beautiful scene possible. There were only about 14 beats in Ives but these lived as a perfect community, everyone shared everything they had, everyone lived for everyone else without thoughts for themselves". Members of St Ives' older artists' colony seem to have offered some support to the members of the Street Commune. Things came to a head with the local council who, egged on by reactionary pressure groups decided to try and clamp down on the 'undesirable visitors' who were now taking up residence in assorted shacks, railway huts, army lookouts, air raid shelters and derelict buildings. When the combination of civic vandalism and special security beach patrols with guard dogs failed to deter this latest bohemian invasion a group of self-styled vigilantes calling themselves the Final Solution got up a petition to the Home Secretary calling for the police to remove the beatniks under the vagrancy act.
Location: St Ives
Ref: *International Times* 63 (Aug 1969)

GREAT PILCHARDS SQUAT   circa 1969
"We chose a building known by us as the Pilchards, and officially as the Huers Hut. It was out of the centre of town, big enough to hold at least 30 on its two floors, and if we occupied it very little annoyance could be caused to anyone It was an old lookout used by fishermen when Ives was a big fishing port ... The next evening one fuzz turned up and told us to move out. We had made every effort to see that all taking part understood the situation – particularly that we could not be moved without a court order ... The battle lasted more than four hours, the council using sulpherous bombs and generators, pickaxes, crowbars, boots and fists. We fought the whole way, once with a bucketful of piss and though the council have now bricked up all windows, doors and holes, smashed the whole first floor and stairs, and poured pitch over the floor, the Great Pilchards Squat was the turning point of the St Ives scene."
Location: St Ives
Ref: *International Times* 63 (Aug 1969)

MEVAGISSEY COMMUNE early 1970's

"After a period of bumming around Britain, I learned blues harp crossed style while in a commune in Mevagissey in the early 70's."

Location: Mevagissey
Ref: www.boblove.co.uk/html/roger_strange (13.12.2010)

FOOTSBARN THEATRE 1971 - 1975/84

Communal touring theatre who toured Cornwall, playing village halls, on beaches, in town halls and car parks with shows based on Cornish myths and legends. In 1984 the company left 'Thatcher's Britain' to tour Europe. Settling in 1991 on a farm complex in central France.

Location: Trewen, near Trewidland
Ref: www.footsbarn.com (22.1.2011)

GODOLGAN COMMUNITY circa 1972

Farmhouse with 12 acres being converted into craft workshops and meditation centre *"We live according to the Eternal Tao, a timeless, unhurried, natural and harmonious existence."*

Location: near Helston
Ref: **Communes Journal** 40 (Dec 1972)

KEVERAL FARM 1973 - present

Thirty acre small-holding with farmhouse and outbuilding originally established by members of the Kingsway Community in Chiswick. *"We had many ideas, including one of becoming self sufficient overnight, and another, more realistic perhaps, of providing holidays, working weekends and workshops for those who needed relief from the demands city life made on them."* Later became a separate independent community. Now set up as a housing co-op and farm is run by a workers co-op who rent the land from Keveral Sustainable Landholdings Ltd. *"... members have their own veg plots, and some of this supplies restaurants and our privately run veggie box scheme. We also produce organic preserves, and have a small campsite in our orchard. Our members also do tree-work, joinery, ecological consultancy, and medical herbalism."*

Location: St Martin-by-Looe
Ref: www.keveral.org; www.diggersanddreamers. org.uk (23.8.2011); **Alternative Communities** 4th ed

POLTESGUE FARM circa 1975/6

Farm on Bodmin Moor occupied by group of Diggers with plans to work the land. *"... widespread and misleading publicity given to the farm encouraged the unacceptable face of the alternative society to descend in strength, ravaging communal food supplies, though not in any way contributing to production. This eventually culminated in a two-day running battle, and the community was at an end."*

Location: Bodmin Moor
Ref: **Undercurrents** 19 (Dec Jan 1976/77)

TREMBRAZE COMMUNITY circa 1975

Craft based community for post-cure drug addicts.
Location: St Keverne near Helston
Ref: CLAP 7 in **Peace News** 2.3.75

THE ECO-OP circa 1979

Proposal by a David Stringer for the *"Creation of a Kibbutz for survival"*. To include Housing co-op and aim for partial self-sufficiency.
Location: West Cornwall?
Ref: *Communes Network* 42

BUDDHIST CENTRE circa 1976

FWBO Community of 12 residents planning to be self-supporting living off their land.
Location: Emprill Farm, Beacon, Cambourne
Ref: **The Many Ways of Being**

CAER 1978 - 2004

Personal development centre set up by former actor and psychotherapist Jo May *"to provide innovative workshops for personal and spiritual development, and training."*
Location: Rosemerryn, Lamorna
Ref: www.developing-people.co.uk (22.1.2011)

TRURO COMMONWEALTH 1978/1984

A spin off from local branch of the 'Diggers of Albion'. *"... to enable members, friends and followers to follow more closely the way of life they desire."* Started a number of ventures; catering in local markets, experimental manufacture of beekeeping equipment, agricultural contracting. Turned a house one of them owned into a Housing Association. Some members also farmed four acres of land and ran a small printing and publishing co-op.
Location: 8 Tabernacle Street, Truro
Ref: **In The Making** 5 Supp; J Mercer **Communes**

TRETHILL COMMUNITY   circa 1984

Group listed in back of Communes book.
Location: Sheviock, near Torpoint.
Ref: J Mercer *Communes*

A VILLAGE COMMUNITY   circa 1984

Group that met at Hood Fair with vision of a
network of co-operative villages.
Location: *"a particular area in Cornwall."*
Ref: *Alternative Communities Movement Magazine*
18 (Dec 1984)

HARMONY COMMUNITY TRUST   1992

Group being helped by Devon CDA to realise their
vision of a 'non-hierarchical sustainable community'
in Cornwall.
Location: c/o CDA address in Plymouth
Ref: *D&D 94-95*

CUMBRIA

CPFLU LAND UNITS   1940 - 1946

Christian Pacifist land-based units organised for
conscientious objectors.
Location: Grizebeck; Greenod; Russland
Ref: M Maclachlan *CPLFU*

WALNEY AIRFIELD   1955

Late post-war squatter camp occupied as
soon as the RAF moved out by people made
homeless by bombing of Barrow. Remained
until Council re-housed them. Buildings then
demolished to stop others moving in.
Location: Barrow in Furness
Ref: www.cumbria-industries.org.uk (24.12..08)

FRODDLE CROOK COMMUNITY OF
CHRISTIAN LOVE   circa 1965 - 1984

Small residential community running Ecumenical
conference and retreat centre.
Location: Froddle Crook, Armathwaite
Ref: J Mercer *Communes*;
D Clark *Basic Communities*

MIDDLE FARM   circa 1971 - 1972

Nine people, house in 'sorry state'. Sold pottery
and rings to pay the bills"*We're a bunch of
idiots trying to survive the harsh winters in the far
north ...*"
Location: Cumberland
Ref: *Directory of Communes* 1972

DALSTON GROUP   circa 1972

Group living in old house with small veg garden.
Made clothes and candles. *"in fairly isolated part
of Cumberland."*
Location: Dalston
Ref: *Directory of Communes* 1972

'ATLANTIS'   circa 1974

Lake District farm rented by the group that would
go on to become Atlantis in Ireland.
Location: Whinfell Hall, Lorton, near Cockermouth
Ref: Jenny James *They Call us the Screamers*

BADGER GATE   early 1970's - ?

Loose communal group.
Location: near Lupton
Ref: Personal contacts

MOORLANDS   circa 1974

*"At present nine of us in a 400 year old farmhouse.
We hope to start various projects; Large vegetable
garden, planting a wood ... hope to built a wind
generator possibly a solar heat collector ... Beautiful
country, very powerful, but the wind makes excessive
demands at times."*
Location: Nenthead
Ref: *In The Making* 2

CASTERTON GRANGE   circa 1975 - ?

Small communal group formed by some ex-
residents of the Langtwhaite House group and
others from something called the March 29th
Group. Large house and outbuildings with six acres
of pasture, orchard and woodland.
Location: Casterton, Kirby Lonsdale
Ref: *Communes Network* 8

MANJUSHRI INSTITUTE   1976 - present

Tibetan Buddhist centre in large Victorian Gothic
house formerly used as; Hydropathic hotel, WWII
military hospital and Durham Miners Welfare
Committee convalescent home. Over the years
the community has restored the house and built a
Kadampa Temple for World Peace in the grounds.
Location: Conishead Priory, near Ulverston
Ref: *D&D 90-91;*
www.newkadampatruth.org (6.2.2011)

HIGH HOUSE FARM COTTAGE   circa 1976

"Winter Let commune"
Location: near Kendal
Ref: *Communes Network* 13

BRACKENBER TRUST circa 1978 - 1984

11 adults and children running an educational charity "... concerned with the spiritual nature of man and the universe." Connected to the Society of Emissaries. Also ran holiday accommodation.
Location: Brakenber Hall, Brakenber
Ref: *Communes Network* 41 and 42

SANDRIGGS FARM circa 1984

Group listed in Communes book.
Location: Thrimby, Penrith
Ref: J Mercer *Communes*

HIGH CARLEY late 1990's

Plan to turn disused hospital into eco-village.
Location: near Ulverston
Ref: Personal contact

DERBYSHIRE

J.I.F. ENTERPRISES 1941

J.I.F. Enterprises and J.I.F. Club (Jiffy Cult)
"After a hard 12 months in Derby I am now able to take others into this, the only genuine mutualist co-operative scheme in existence. We prefer socialists and materialists, but do not place any bar on religionists — we have land (and more available cheap) greenhouses, rabbits and newsagency."
Location: 37 Leopold Street, Derby
Ref: *Peace News* Community Supplement 25.4.41

BEIGHTON CAMP 1946

Post-war squatter camp on army base.
Location: Beighton
Ref: D Thomas *Villains' Paradise*

KINGSWAY CAMP 1946 -

Army camp taken over by squatters.
Location: near Derby
Ref: D Thomas *Villains' Paradise*

EATON HILL HOUSE 1948 - 2004

Childrens home run by the Church of England childrens society along Therapeutic community lines.
Location: Alfreton Road, Little Eaton
Ref: www.tc-of.org.uk (2.8.2011)

STAUNTON HAROLD CHESHIRE HME 1954-85

Early Cheshire Home for the disabled. The Hall became a Cheshire Home in 1954, and in 1985 was sold to the Ryder-Cheshire Mission. It was a

palliative Care Home until 2002.
Location: Ashby-de-la-Zouch
Ref: L Cheshire *Hidden World*

DERBYSHIRE MYSTICAL COMMUNE circa 1970

"Well a year has passed, a year of sitting plotting in flake-walled working mens clubs throughout the midlands little huddled clod groups of people gathered around the communal half pint — and yet high hopes and nice people are dashed to the ground and winter creeps on."
Location: c/o Male Nurses Home, Kingsway Hospital, Kingsway, Derby
Ref: *Commune Movement Newsletter* 7.12.70

THE RED HOUSE 1975 - 1990's

White Meadows Villa bought by Corin Redgrave used by the Workers Revolutionary Party used the house as a venue for training, under the name 'Red House', run by television producer Roy Battersby. Was later squatted by new age travellers.
Location: White Meadows Villa, Parwich
Ref: www.nw4u.co.uk; *Time Magazine* (13.12.2010)

SWYTHAMLEY HALL 1977 - 1987

Hall and parkland bought by the World Government for the Age of Enlightenment, followers of Maharishi Mahesh Yogi, as Transcendental Meditation training centre.
Location: Swythamley
Ref: www.nationalarchives.gov.uk (29.12011)

COMMUNITY OF THE KING OF LOVE 1979 -

Ecumenical group running retreat and conference centre
Location: Whaley Hall, Whaley Bridge
Ref: *D&D 98-99*

QUAKER COMMUNITY 1988 - present

Community set up following responses to an article in The Friend in 1985 entitled "Quaker Kibbutz Anyone?". After three years of meetings and negotiations the group bought the former Derwent Valley Water Board offices and ten acres of land in Bamford following the receipt of a substantial Quaker legacy. 12-16 people live in a combination of self-contained living space, flats and several bed-sits, with shared use of a large communal kitchen, The group host regular Quaker meetings.
Location: Bamford
Ref: *D&D 90-91*

TARA CENTRE
1996 - present

"Tara KMC's community includes people of all ages and from all walks of life, who live, work and study together ... Some work, or meditate and study, full time at the Centre, others work in the local area." Linked to the Manjushri group in Ulverston.
Location: Ashe Hall, Etwall
Ref: www.taracentre.org.uk (6.2.2011)

DEVON

BUCKFAST ABBEY
1882 - present

New monastic order originally set up by French Benedictine monks fleeing persecution. The self-sufficient community rebuilt the original Abbey church and produce their own successful tonic wine and range of arts and crafts. Through selective breeding the monks created a docile and disease resistant 'Buckfast' Bee featured in the 1986 BBC documentary, The Monk and the Honey Bee.
Location: Buckfastleigh
Ref: *Utopian England*;
www.buckfast.org.uk (29.1.2011)

WEST MILL CO-OPERATIVE FM
1939-1943

Farm set up by pacifist poet Ronald Duncan.
Location: West Mill, near Welcombe, Devon
Ref: R Duncan *All Men are Islands*;
R Duncan *Journal of a Husbandman*;
www.brionylawson.com (29.1.2011)

BYDOWN HOUSE
1939 - 1941

House taken over by the Jewish Refugee Committee. Housed between 80-90 young Jewish refugees from central and eastern Europe.
Location: near Swimbridge
Ref: www.britishlocalhistory.co.uk (9.5.09)

AGRICULTURAL TRAINING CENTRE
1940

30 Jewish refugees engaged in farm work as part of a joint project between Youth Aliyah, Hechaluz and the British Council of the Young Pioneer Movement for Palestine. Offshoot of the Bydown House group. Existed between Mar and Dec 1940.
Location: South Street, Braunton
Ref: www.britishlocalhistory.co.uk (9.5.09)

ASHBURTON COMMUNITY
1940

Community for conscientious objectors doing land work on six acres neighbouring market garden.

Set up by Deryck Bazalgette with the help of the Society of Friends.
Location: St Bridget, West Street, Ashburton
Ref: Ad in *Peace News* 13.9.40

SPICELANDS CAMP
circa 1941

Address listed in *Community in a Changing World*.
Location: near Collumpton
Ref: *Community in a Changing World*

WITHYMEAD
1941 - 1954

Georgian house beside the River Exe outside Exeter in Devon. Home of Gilbert and Irene Champernowne who during the Second World War turned it into residential therapeutic community for people in mental distress know as 'The Jungian Community for the Healing Arts'. Withymead pioneered the use of art therapy and Jungian analysis in a family setting. Treated some 240 adults between 1942/1954 supported by the Elmhurst's of Dartington Hall.
Location: Exeter
Ref: A Stevens *Withymead*

SOUTH WEST CO-OP HOUSING SOC
1944-?

Pioneer housing association set up by L Elmhirst of Dartington Hall, A E Malbon of Staverton Builders and Dr A Mansbridge. Built properties at Yate, Totnes and Bridgewater.
Ref: Eric Stafford *Brick Upon Brick* 1994

ALPHINGTON CAMP
circa 1946

Squatter camp in empty Army Nissen huts.
Location: Matford Lane, Alphington
Ref: www.livinghere.org.uk (24.12.08)

BURNSHILL CAMP
1946

Army camp taken over by squatters at the end of the war – the squatters were evicted but they promptly occupied two other sites in the area.
Location: near Taunton
Ref: D Thomas *Villains' Paradise*

LIPSON FARM
circa 1947/8

"Lipson folk have been co-operating with two neighbouring farms in haymaking. Two trainees have been working out on other farms during the summer: both intend to stick to the land. Following the bad winter and the late spring there is a great deal of work to be done demanding all the available time and attention of those concerned."
Location: Lipson Farm, Ashwater, Beaworthy
Ref: Report in *Community Broadsheet* 1947/48

LEE ABBEY
1946 - present

Christian conference, retreat and holiday centre on 280-acre coastal estate Run by a residential community of around 80-90 people of all ages and 20 nationalities. Basically Anglican, but ecumenical ministry. Hostel for 150 overseas students was opened in London in 1964.
Location: Lee Abbey, Lynton.
Ref: *Directory of Communes* 1972;
Community News

FLETE
1950's - 2003

Country house 'saved' by the Mutual Households Association.
Location: near Ermington
Ref: *SAVE Casework News* June 2004

KILWORTHY HOUSE
1963 - 1997

Originally started as small boys school as the Kilworthy House Tuition Centre by Rev John Lyon. In the early 1970's became an alternative school run as a therapeutic community.
Location: Tavistock
Ref: www.astro.columbia.edu (4.8.2011)

SHILAY COMMUNITY
mid 1960's - 1984

Group providing shelter for homeless men.
Location: St Nicolas School, Holloway St, Exeter
Ref: J Mercer *Communes; Basic Communities*

BYSTOCK COURT
1965 - 1984?

Interdenominational Christian Therapeutic community house supporting women and children in acute need through marital or other relationship problems.
Location: Whithycombe, Exmouth
Ref: *Directory of Christian Communities & Groups*

MARJORIES COTTAGE
circa 1971

Group listed as affiliated to Commune Movement.
Location: Yealampton, South Devon
Ref: *Commune Movement Newsletter* 30.7.71

NORTH DEVON SNAILS
circa 1972

Couple living in a flat in a large house producing local mag The North Devon Snail. *"... we can only put up two or three people at a time. If anyone likes vegetarian food, some home made bread and the beautiful harmony of the countryside and does not mind Geronimo (our dog) jumping on them come and see us; we cannot offer practical help on finding your own place, except for the local paper and if we*

happen to hear of anywhere, but we can offer a hell of a lot of peace from the cities."
Location: near Barnstaple
Ref: *Directory of Communes* 1972

COMBE MARTIN ASHRAM
1972 - 1980

Group that was focus for psychotherapy, personal growth and yoga in the South West.
Location: King St Combe Martin
Ref: *A Pilgrims Guide to Planet Earth* 1981

EARTH WORKSHOP HOUSE
circa 1975

"TO PROSPECTIVE URBAN COMMUNITY: Earth Workshop Community (+C.A.G.E.) moving out to country would like to sell Its Exeter house to a Craft/ AT/organic based group wishing to move West. Detached Georgian house, walled organic garden, semi-basement workshop, display possibilities ... Central heating from Baxi Burnall; house Insulated for low energy living. Reasonable price."
Location: Exeter
Ref: Ad in *Undercurrents* 10 (1976);
In The Making 2

'ECO COMMUNITY FARM'
circa 1975

Plans for community on six acre site.
Location: Chudleigh
Ref: Ads in *Peace News* 7.3.75

HAMLET TRUST
circa 1976 - ?

Small group of vegetarian families and individuals working towards building an earth, crafts, arts based hamletPlanned to build 11 *"ecologically balanced houses with natural sustainable energy and food supply systems."* from local materials with walled gardens, workshops and a communal centre (Social-cum-dining room, kitchen, crèche, small library, meditation room and laundry) in about 25 acres.
Location: Holme Cross near Ashburton
Ref: *Undercurrents* 22 (Apr 1977);
Alternative Communities 2nd ed

'TWO HAMLETS'
circa 1977

Proposal for two hamlets that the Dartington Hall Trust wanted to build. Each 'cluster' of houses was to have a number of communal buildings, including nursery schools, workshop meeting halls, etc in the centre. Surrounded by kitchen gardens a tree belt and farmland, which was be cultivated by the inhabitants. Devon County Council refused the schemes planning permission.
Ref: *Undercurrents* 20 (Feb Mar 1977)

THE CULVERLANDS   circa 1980

"We are the Culverland family, a new commune at present comprising five adults and a dog. We live at the moment in a Victorian terrace in Exeter but our long-term aim is a semi-self sufficient community based in a large country property, maybe in the West Country. There are houses in this road for sale or to let, where others could live as the first steps to the joint purchase of a large house in the country ... a place to live as one large family and co-operate in child-raising, farming, publishing and other projects. We are non-couple based, our average age is 29, we have no group politics, and are not particularly religious."

Location: 15 Culverland Road, Pennsylvania, Exeter
Ref: *Alternative Communities* 3rd ed

HOLME PLACE   1980 - ?

Small group living in former Victorian rectory with coach-house and stable block and seven acres. Growing veg organically and keeping goats and chickens. *"We are involved in personal growth and therefore in a changing society, enjoy our own personal space as well as sharing with others."*

Location: Holme Place, Oakford Tiverton.
Ref: *Alternative Communities* 4th ed;
Communes Network Directory 1985

HAPSTEAD CAMPHILL   1980 -

Village community with 68 acres. Emphasis on therapeutic activity rather than production.
Location: Buckfastleigh
Ref: *D&D 90-91*; www.camphill.org.uk (21.4.2011)

SHARPHAM HOUSE   circa 1983 - late 1990's

100-acre farm and large Palladian house bought in 1962 by Maurice Ash, chairman of the Town and Country Planning Association and the Dartington Trust and his wife Ruth, daughter of Dartington Hall founders Leonard and Dorothy Elmhirst. The farm was run on biodynamic principles, and hosted the Robert Owen Foundation, a charity providing agricultural experience for people with mental disabilities. In 1983 a Buddhist-based group, The Sharpham Community, was set up at the house. *"It was a nonsectarian Buddhist community with no leader, no guru and no tradition that they were attached to. That community — small and idyllic as it was — ran into the shadow stuff, entrenched positions, personality conflicts and irresolvable this and that.*

Mediators were brought in to facilitate conversation but in the end it could not be sorted, so it was wound up." Guy Claxton
Location: Ashprington
Ref: www.sharphamtrust.org (21.2.2011)

PREMPANTHA   circa 1979 - 1983

Sister Rajneesh community to Medina commune in Suffolk. Large house with outbuildings and walled garden.
Location: Beech Hill House Morchard Bishop
Ref: www.sannyasnews.com (23.8.2011)

BEECH HILL   1983 - present

Originally eight adults and three children from a 'variety of different backgrounds' living in 25 roomed house set in seven acres with outbuildings. *"... there is no absolutely rigid philosophy. However, supporters of the status quo are unlikely to fit; the group seeks people who wish to go beyond narrow definitions of party, creed, class, cult or whatever."*
Location: Beech Hill House, Morchard Bishop
Ref: *Communes Network Directory* 1987;
D&D 90-91

NETHERLEIGH   circa 1984

Group listed in Communes book.
Location: Cocks Lane, Axminster
Ref: J Mercer *Communes*

TAPELEY PARK   circa 1990's - ?

Aristocratic estate inherited by Hector Christie maverick son of Glyndebourne opera founder Sir George Christie. Dabbled with New Age mysticism and in late 1990's started running the estate as an autocratic commune.
Location: Westleigh, Bideford
Ref: "An opera family's dissenting voice" in
Daily Telegraph 30.3.2002

GRIMSTONE MANOR   1990 - 2007

Manor house and mews set in 27 acres of land with large walled vegetable garden, a formal garden and several acres of paddock and grazing. On the edge of Dartmoor — home

to group running residential group training centre, hosting or running over 50 workshops a year, involving a wide range of spiritual paths, disciplines and techniques.
Location: Horrabridge, Yelverton
Ref: *D&D 92-93*

ARK 2000   circa 1991
Proposal to set up large (30-50 people) community that would be an *"educational and research facility for the study and practical application of alternative technology."*
Location: near Tavistock?
Ref: *D&D 92-93*

AMADEA COHOUSING   circa late 1990's
Proposed Cohousing project mainly for older people.
Location: Devon (but other parts of south west considered)
Ref: *D&D 92-93*

DORSET

THE WHITE LADIES   1921 - 1965
Christian commune of 'celibate and contemplative vegetarian ladies' formed by Miss Adela Curtis at St Brides Farm to prove *"... on a small scale, that they could not only be self supporting in food, clothing, fuel, housing and all other necessities but that they could provide for a larger healthier and happier home ..."* Over the years a little colony gradually grew up of wooden cottages each with a quarter of an acre of fruit and vegetable gardens known locally as the Christian Contemplative Community or 'The White Ladies' They built a large chapel completed in 1938. Miss Curtis died in Sept 1960 and The Othona Community took over Street, Bride's farm in 1965.
Location: Burton Bradstock
Ref: C Rudd *The Rustic Mystic of Burton Bradstock*; www.burtonbradstock.org.uk (30.12011)

ST FRANCIS FARM   circa 1947/48?
"A farm whose members, and those who join them may learn how to live in dedication, not only of spiritual faculties but of those of mind and body too ... No vows are taken and there is no Common fund ; each may have his or her rule of life and each may share a simple corporate rule. By ownership ultimately of small holdings on the land – it is
intended that members learn stewardship but they will co-operate in such things as ownership and use of agricultural machinery ..."
Location: Flowers Farm, Dorchester
Ref: *The Community Broadsheet* Winter 47-48; The International Review of Missions xi 47

SOUTH LYTCHETT MANOR   circa 1954
'Christian commune' set up by Lady Madeline Lees whose purpose was *"World Peace Through Religious Drama."* Members of the group took part in the making of Voice In The Wilderness a film about the life of John the Baptist made by Lady Rees and shot glorious Technicolor on location in the local sandpits and heathland.
Location: Dorchester Road, Lytchett Minster
Ref: www.south-central-media.co.uk (29.4.2011)

PILSDON COMMUNITY   1958 - present
Inspired by reading about Little Gidding the Rev Percy Smith and his wife Gaynor bought Pilsdon Manor in 1958, for £5,000 and set up a Christian community as a place for people who'd been through a hard time, wayfarers, and volunteers who want to support them. *"... a school for sinners and not a museum of saints."*
Location: Pilsdon Manor, Pilsdon, Bridport
Ref: *Communes Europe*; www.pilsdon.org.uk (27.8.2011)

OTHONA COMMUNITY   1965 - present
Following the death of Adela Curtis St Brides Farm was offered to the group running the Othona community in Essex. They took it on as a Christian centre which could operate and welcome visitors all the year round.
Location: Coast Road, Burton Bradstock, Bridport
Ref: www.othona-bb.org.uk (27.8.2011)

POST GREEN COMMUNITY   circa 1968 - ?
Centre of Christian ministry since the 1960's. Established a residential community in the early 1970's. Joined with the Community of Celebration in 1975
Location: 57 Dorchester Road, Lytchett Minster, Poole
Ref: *Directory of Christian Communities & Groups* 1980; www.ccct.co.uk

SUFI COMMUNE   1970 - 1975?
Community featured in sociologists Frank Musgrove's book under the title Dervishes in

Dorsetshire. Members described as 'Somewhat upperclass' "... *short-stay members typically have full-time jobs (as teachers, government scientists, secretaries, journalists) or are self-employed (as potters, writers and painters). Many come back again and again. They pay two pounds a day. Most of the twenty to thirty short-stay members, both men and women, are married, but none brings a spouse (though women bring their small children). None of the inner core members is married. The commune lives in an ancient and very beautiful stone farmhouse which stands by a trout stream a mile off a minor road, nine miles from the nearest small market town, forty miles from a (cathedral and university) city. The commune has a telephone and an old van. There is no television or radio. No-one brings a transistor. No-one is quite sure how mail is collected or despatched ...*"

Location: Address unknown
Ref: F Musgrove *Margins of the Mind*

STURTS FARM COMMUNITY   1981 -

Camphill community working with people with learning disabilities. 100 acres of land, market garden and plan nursery for bedding plans, herbs and cuttings. Farm shop sells bio-dynamic produce.
Location: Three Cross Road, West Moors
Ref: www.sturtsfarm.com (21.4.2011)

BOWHAY CENTRE   circa 1981

New Age Centre listed in international guidebook..
Location: Shillingford Abbott
Ref: *A Pilgrims Guide to Planet Earth* 1981

MIDDLE PICCADILLY   circa 1983 - 1986

Small group living in this 'new age centre' in a 17th Century thatched farmhouse. Interested in alternative therapies and crafts. Became the Middle Piccadilly Spa Retreat and Wellness Centre.
Location: Holwell, Sherborne
Ref: *Alternative Communities* 4th ed; www.middlepiccadilly.com; *The New Times Network*

MONKTON WYLD COURT   1983 - present

Victorian Gothic Rectory run as co-educational school from 1940 – 1982 – from 1967 onwards run by a staff collective. Closed by impact of 1981 education Act, after a short occupation by pupils and parents. Evolved into education centre run by residential community Continue to develop courses in sustainable living and run 'Steiner-Focused' Kindergarten.
Location: near Charmouth
Ref: *No Master High or Low*; J Shotton *Libertarian Education in Britain 1890 -1990*; *D&D 90-91*; www.monktonwyldcourt.co.uk (19.10.11)

GAUNTS HOUSE   1990 - ?

Group running country house estate. "... *home to the Community of Profound Learning a spiritually based holistically minded group of free thinkers committed to exploring and supporting the evolution of consciousness and the awakening of their inner selves.*"
Location: Wimbourne.
Ref: *D&D 94-95*; www.gauntshouse.com (20.10.11)

OSHO LEELA   mid 1990's

School house and cottages used as base for Osho Leela.
Location: Wimborne
Ref: www.osholeela.co.uk (21.4.2011)

HOLTON LEE   1996 - present

Off shoot of the Post Green Community set up to provide "*an empowering holistic space to all people, but particularly disabled people and carers.*"
Location: East Holton
Ref: www.holtonlee.co.uk (27.8.11)

OSHO LEELA   2000 - present

"*In 2000 Osho Leela moved to its present address in Gillingham, Dorset. Close to a mainline railway station and having the benefit of a caravan park and fifteen acres of land, everyone was excited by the move. The programmes offered expanded to include introductory weekends, singles weekends, healing workshops, massage groups and theatre and comedy gatherings. The Therapist Training grows from strength to strength and the community has expanded from ten to over 20 people, including four children.*"
Location: Thorngrove House, Gillingham
Ref: www.osholeela.co.uk (21.4.2011)

DURHAM

MOOR CLOSE   1944 - 1945

Large detached suburban house on the edge of Middlesborough where the Max Lock Group Architecture practice set up as a communal

household. "... *many specialist professionals and helpers passed through this household sharing their ideas as well as their rations. This mixed collection of single and married women and children with not so many men (who were either exempt from military service for one reason or another or on leave) was not entirely understood by their suburban neighbours.*"
Location: Moor Close, Middlesborough
Ref: University of Westminster archive

TUNSTALL GRANGE   1946 - 1949
Second Co-operative house of the Max Lock Group. "*Living and working as a Group we have found that the co-operative principle has extended itself throughout the official departments and into the town itself ...*" Max Lock
Location: Grange Road. Middlesborough
Ref: University of Westminster archive

JARROW CAMP   1946 -
Camp occupied by post-war squatters.
Location: Jarrow
Ref: D Thomas *Villains' Paradise*

KIORA HALL CAMP   circa 1946
Anti-Aircraft battery, barrage-balloon site and German
POW camp squatted by ex service men.
Location: Kiora Hall near Blakeston School, Stockton
Ref: picture.stockton.gov.uk (24.12.08)

COXHOE HALL CAMP   1946 -
Army huts in the grounds of Coxhoe Hall occupied by 33 families of squatters from surrounding villages.
Location: near Durham
Ref: Paul Addison *Now the War is Over*

ASHRAM COMMUNITY HOUSE circa 1967/84
One of a network of Christian Community households (others in Rochdale, London and Sheffield) Aiming to "*discover new implications of the way of Jesus for today's world ... through a contemporary Christian lifestyle.*"
Location: 56 Woodlands Road, Middlesborough
Ref: J Mercer *Communes*

RAILWAY STREET   circa 1974 -
Group living in row of terraced houses. Ran café/bookshop in Durham that doubled as cheap fruit and veg shop every friday. "*... We are not an*

outgoing 'group' trying to turn the world on to living communally ... we are just onto living our own way ...*"
Location: Langley Park Durham
Ref: *Alternative Communities* 4th ed; *Communes Network* 21

LARCHFIELD COMMUNITY   1986 -
Camphill community in five newly built houses spread out across 160-acre mixed organic farm. Also have; horticultural unit, organic butchers shop, organic bakery; textile and wooden toy craft workshops Wheelhouse Farm Shop & Coffee Bar. Community was established after requests from the Middlesborough Borough Council to the Camphill Village Trust to set up a community within the town's boundary following a visit by a group of officers and councillors to Botton Village.
Location: Stokesley Road, Hemlington
Ref: www.camphillfamily.com (21.4.2011)

ESSEX

LAKES FARM / TYEPONDS   1931 - 1940
Farmhouse used by group studying the 'Work' of Russian mystic Gurdjieff run by Dr Maurice Nicoll. Initially used as a venue for weekend gatherings. In 1935 the group started self-building 'Tyeponds' a house and workshop space in an adjacent field. At the outbreak of the war Nicoll gathered the members of the group at Tyeponds. In early 1940 the buildings were requisitioned by the military.
Location: Rayne near Braintree
Ref: B Pogson *Maurice Nicoll: A portrait*

ADELPHI CENTRE   1934 - 37
Socialist communitarian 'training centre' set up by John Middleton-Murry at 'The Oaks'. A market garden was set up in the old kitchen garden and paddocks. The house was used during WWII for East End evacuees.
Location: Langham
Ref: *Utopian England*

FRATING HALL   late 1930's - 1950's?
Group that was connected to Adephi Centre in it's early days. Continued after the war.
Location: Frating
Ref: *Valiant for Peace*; Personal contact

FORDSON FARMS
1931 - 1956
On a trip through England in 1930, Henry Ford noticed dilapidated buildings, obsolete farming methods, and the resultant poor crops. He planned a venture to improve British agricultural production through the application of American farming methods and technology. In 1931 he purchased Boreham House and either bought or leased some 7,000 acres of adjoining land. He financed a joint company called Fordson Estates Limited, consisting of several co-operative societies. Fordson Estates was an agricultural experiment using modern farming methods and equipment, relying heavily on Fordson tractors. Two years were spent repairing buildings and readying the land. Farming operations began in 1933 and continued through World War II. In 1937 Boreham House became home to the Henry Ford Institute of Agricultural Engineering, offering training courses to farm workers, mechanics, and agricultural students.
Location: Boreham House
Ref: www.perryfoundation.co.uk (30.1.2011)

SOUTHEND COMMUNITY
1939
Wartime community listed in the Community Life Journal issued by the British Llano Circle.
Location: 34 Retreat Road, Westcliffe-on-sea and Oakwood Brook Hill, Wickford
Ref: *Heavens Below* p415

MOORE PLACE
1939 - 45
Fifteen acre small-holding worked by 12 pacifists.
Location: Stanford le Hope
Ref: A Rigby *Pacifist Islands in a Martial Sea*; *D&D 94-95*

BACHAD TRAINING FARM
circa 1940's
Hachsharah training centre for would be Kibbutznics. Grew into a successful agricultural venture. *"winning 1st prize for having the best milk yielding cow in Essex."*
Location: Thaxted
Ref: www.bauk.org (25.6.09)

CPFLU LAND UNITS
1940 - 1946
Christian Pacifist land-based units organised for conscientious objectors.
Location: Epping; Dagenham; Ilford
Ref: M Maclachlan *CPLFU*

RUNWELL HOSPITAL
circa 1940's - ?
Early therapeutic community set up by Joshua Bierer as a Patient's Social Club.
Location: Wickford
Ref: L Clarke *The Time of the Therapeutic Communities*

WRI COMMUNITY SETTLEMENT
1941
Fifty acre mixed farm being run by five men and two women from War Resisters International.
Location: Lower Ford End Farm, Clavering
Ref: *Peace News* Community Supplement 25.5.41

FRANCISCAN COMMUNITY
circa 1940's - ?
Group seeking members for land work and book and vestment business. (Possibly same group as on page 436.
Location: "near Essex coast"
Ref: Ad in *Peace News* 15.11.44

GREAT SALING CAMP
1946 -
Post-war squatter camp on US Air Force base.
Location: RAF Andrews Field (or Great Saling)
Ref: www.grahamstevenson.me.uk (20.12.08)

SIBLE HEDINGHAM CAMP
1946 -
Post-war squatter camp on army base.
Location: Rectory Army Camp Sible Hedingham
Ref: www.grahamstevenson.me.uk (20.12.08)

OTHONA COMMUNITY
1946 - present
Founded in an attempt to establish *"some form of meaningful Christian living in the aftermath of the Second World War."* Started as a summer camp in two fields behind the seawall next to the ancient Chapel of St Peter's. Extended into some semi-permanent 'huts' with large dining area, common rooms, and bedrooms. Facilities have been upgraded and modernised over the years. Sister community in Dorset started in 1965
Location: East Hall Farm, East End Road, Bradwell on Sea
Ref: *Community News*; www.othona.org (11.6.2011); www.bos.othona.org (11.6.2011); *D&D 90-91*

GOSFIELD HALL
1946 - 2003
Country house 'saved' by the Mutual Households Association.
Location: near Halstead
Ref: *An Experiment in Co-operation*

INGREBOURNE CENTRE
circa 1950's - 1990's
Therapeutic community based in acute psychiatric

Ward 3G – renamed the Ingrebourne Centre after a stream that ran nearby. Patients ran their own Ingrebourne Society with it's own funds, committee and newsletter. Some ex-patients went on to form the Mental Patients Union.
Location: St George's Hospital, Hornchurch
Ref: archive.pettrust.org.uk (2.8.2011)

PRESTED HALL   1956 -
First National Spastics Society's residential centre.
Location: Witham
Ref: British Journal of Nursing April 1956

CLAYBURY HOSPITAL   circa 1960's -
Mental hospital reorganised as therapeutic community.
Location: Woodford Bridge, Woodford Green
Ref: Adventure in Psychiatry; A Hospital Looks at Itself

CROSS END COTTAGES   circa 1962
'Small community house' advertising for members in Community Living Association newsletter.
Location: Pebmarsh, Halstead.
Ref: CLA Bulletin Jan 1962

DIAL HOUSE   1967 - present
Anarcho-pacifist open house and cultural community centre base for a number of cultural, artistic and political projects. Best-known as the home of anarcho-punk band Crass. Came under threat from developers in the late 1990's, but was bought at auction from BT and community continues.
Location: Dial House, Ongar Park Hall, North Weald
Ref: G Berger The Story of Crass;
G Mckay Senseless Acts of Beauty

DESMOND JEFFERY GROUP   circa 1969
"... group is somewhat scattered, but it has good potential. It has two houses, a bookshop and a printing workshop, Geographically separated ..."
Location: Burnt Oak, East Bergholt
Ref: Gandalf's Garden 2

PORTAL CHRISTIAN REHAB CNTRS 1970-?
Therapeutic community helping residents become self-reliant and move from institutional care to independence.
Location: 50 Geoffrey Avenue, Romford
Ref: D&D 92-93

SMALL COMMUNE IN ESSEX   circa 1970
"WE ARE A small commune in Essex forming a local commercial band and need a vocalist/guitarist or organist ..."
Location: Stanford le Hope
Ref: Ad in International Times 91 (Nov 1970)

PLIMSOL SANDWICH   early 1970's
"Plimsoll Sandwich evolved as the part-time project of musicians assembled from the hippie communes of Essex."
Location: Essex
Ref: www.licoricesoul.co.uk/lsd014-plimsoll.php (1.1.2011)

KHAM TIBETAN HOUSE   1972 - present
Also Marpa House. Small residential community running Buddhist retreat and meditation centre dedicated to the advancement of Tibetan Buddhism. Now run by the Dharma Trust.
Location: Rectory Lane, Ashdon
Ref: Buddhism in Britain;
www.marpahouse.org.uk (21.12.10)

OLD HALL   1974 - present
"Old Hall was set up as a housing association and is fairly informal in its day to day running with a weekly decision making meeting open to all members. With 70 acres of farmland we grow as much of our own food as possible and keep cows, goats, sheep and chickens, all are kept organically. The building has served many purposes over the years (including being a Friary) before becoming our home – it requires a lot of maintenance. We all have our private rooms but most of our activities are communal, including our meals which are cooked on a voluntary rota basis."
Location: East Bergholt
Ref: D&D 90-91

GLOUCESTER SHIRE

WHITEWAY   1898 - present
Tolstoyan anarchist colony on 42 acres in the Cotswolds Original communal group in Whiteway House surrounded by open fields the colony became a thriving anarchist community over the years developing into a patchwork of small-holdings with people living in a variety of homemade sheds, huts, houses and railway carriages etc. In 1924 a colony hall was erected to house social activities and a school house. During WWII Freedom Press was run from the colony. Over the years the community has continued to develop with some of the original shacks and chalets now replaced with substantial houses. Still operating under their original constitution they are the longest surviving secular community in the country.
Location: Whiteway
Ref: Joy Thacker **Whiteway Colony**

PRINKNASH ABBEY   1928 -
Prinknash house and 28 acres given to Benedictine Monks from Caldey Island by the Earl of Rothes. Buildings were converted and more land acquired creating a self-contained community given abbey status in 1937. Further offshoots were set up in 1947 at Farnborough and Pluscarden. In 1951 the Taena Community were encouraged to move to nearby Whitley Court by the then Abbot to create a lay community alongside the Abbey.
Location: near Upton St Leonards
Ref: www.prinknashabbey.org (30.1.2011); **Utopian England**

GLOUCESTER LAND SCHEME   1939 - 1945
Land loaned by local Quaker for a pacifist land scheme. Conscientious objectors lived in an old sports pavilion whilst growing vegetables and dreaming of self-sufficiency.
Location: near Hempsted
Ref: A Rigby **Pacifist Islands in a Martial Sea; D&D 94-95**

RICHMOND GROUP   1939/41
Community set up by Richmond PPU after visiting Albery group. Originally on nine acres in Garsley later moved to six acres and small cottage in Yaton.

Location: Brook Cottage, Garsley; Yaton, Forest of Dean
Ref: *Peace News* Supp. 25.5.41; **Utopian England**

CPFLU LAND UNITS   1940 - 1946?
Christian Pacifist land-based units organised for conscientious objectors.
Location: Saintbury Hill and Norton Grounds Farm, Mickleton; Parkend, Longhope, Dymock, Cinderford and Sedbury in the Forest of Dean
Ref: M Maclachlan **CPLFU**

THE ALBERY GROUP   1940/41
Land-based group with chickens, ducks, goats and bees. Did knitting to earn income and ran WEA classes. Took in Bruderhof members when others went to Paraguay.
Location: The High Houses, Bromash, Ross-on-Wye
Ref: **Peace News Community Supp.** 25.5.41

THE KNAPP   1941 - 1944
Rented house used by group run by Dr Maurice Nicoll after they were forced to move from Lakes Farm in Essex. The group also rented the King's Head – an old inn – to house members and carry on their studies of Gurdjieff's 'Work' throughout the war.
Location: Birdlip
Ref: B Pogson **Maurice Nicoll: A portrait**

ADAMS COT   circa 1942
Small community who helped the 'Taena group' when they were homeless. Members went and joined the Wheathill Bruderhof.
Location: near Ross-on-Wye
Ref: G Ineson **Community Journey**

THE BARN HOUSE   1940/41
Small pacifist community of craft workers. "*Since the war the group has been working on a full sharing basis and it is hoped to prepare eight acres of ground for a market garden.*"
Location: Brockweir near Chepstow
Ref: *Peace News* Community Supp. 25.5.41; **Community in Britain** 1940

STEANBRIDGE   1941
Country household offshoot of Michael House Christian Community NW London. 20 people.
Location: Slad near Stroud
Ref: **Peace News Community Supp.** 25.5.41

TAENA FARM
1942 - 1952

Small pacifist based community on 55-acre wooded farm on sloping rocky site. Initially highly organised with consensus decision making, communal meals and plans for home education. Later became more informal. When lease ran out moved to Whitley Court.
Location: Warren Farm, Forest of Dean
Ref: *Utopian England*

WHITLEY COURT
1951 - 1980's

135-acre dairy farm bought by the Taena Community after they converted to Catholicism. The group lived in six separate houses on the estate. Taena Pottery still runs from Whitley. One of the few wartime pacifist groups to last through to and make connections with the late counter-culture communes movement.
Location: near Upton St Leonards
Ref: *Communes, Sociology & Society;*
www.taena pottery.co.uk (30.1.2011)

GRANGE VILLAGE
1957 -

Camphill community on the edge of the Forest of Dean made up of a number of supported living households in a variety of old and new buildings. Inc: *"Wayside, an adventurously-designed building incorporating circular and spiral themes."* Home for around 80 people, half of whom have special needs. Run a farm, bakery, pottery, basket workshop and wood workshop.
Location: Littledean Road, Newnham-on-Severn
Ref: www.cvt.org.uk; www.grangevillage.org
(21.4.2011)

TATHATA CENTRE
circa 1966 - 70

Meditation and retreat centre set up by Peter Twilley and Kate Walters. *"... there has been an attempt to build an intentional community here, but our efforts to date have been more of the nature of experimental explorations of what is involved rather than in the realm of actual achievement ..."* Produced the short-lived *Sarvodaya Communities Newsletter.*
Location: Botloes Farm, near Newent
Ref: *People Together; International Times* 36 (Jul Aug 1968); *The Ecologist* Vol 1 no3 (Sep 1970); *Gandalf's Garden* 6

'FERNA ROSA'
early 1970's

Abandoned small-holding on hillside where three different groups tried to establish a commune.
Location: Forest of Dean
Ref: *Communes, Sociology and Society* p47

POSTLIP HALL
1970 - present

Eight families living in an imposing Jacobean manor house with fourteen acres of land in the Cotswold hills. Set up as a Co-ownership Housing Association and originally funded mostly by a mortgage from the local council who insisted that they divide the building into separate unit – which they did themselves with help from professional builders. Each family own the leasehold of its private part of the Hall. All families communally own the freehold. The grounds, outbuildings and some part of the Hall itself are shared. Also two acre organic vegetable garden. Pigs, sheep, goats, hens, geese, rabbits, cats and various other animals. The group run the Gloucestershire Beer Festival in the Hall, the grounds and the Tythe barn each year.
Location: Winchcombe
Ref: *People Together; Legal Frameworks Handbook; D&D 91-92*

JOLLY WATERMAN COMMUNE
circa 1971

Small craft based group named after nearby pub. *"They live in a run-down cottage on a small piece of ground. They bought a car after their first selling trip, but it's not easy to get it up to the cottage because of the rutted condition of the track. When they've sold enough candles, they hope to be able to move to another cottage nearby, not so primitive."*
Location: Longford
Ref: *Making Communes*

SHERBOURNE HOUSE
circa 1971 - 1976

Large stately home surrounded by gardens and meadows in the Cotswolds bought by J G Bennett as a base for his International Academy for Continuous Education. Ran a series of year long courses loosely based on Gurdjieffian ideas. The derelict state of house provided plenty of work for the students.
Location: Sherbourne House, Sherbourne
Ref: *Alternative Communities* 1st, 2nd & 3rd eds

BESHARA   1971 - 1978
Residential group running spiritual retreat, meditation and conference centre. Also from 1976 ran courses at Sherbourne house where they moved to in 1978.
Location: Swyre Farmhouse, Aldsworth
Ref: *Alternative Communities* 1st & 2nd eds

HAYDEN FARM   1972 - 1982?
Commune set up by I Ching scholar Nigel Richmond on farmhouse with a few acres. *"Marijuana seeds were sown in the hedgerows, bees were kept in hives and the honey collected, and chickens roamed freely about the place. They baked bread, brewed beer, and planted a large vegetable garden. One year they bottled 80lb of tomatoes. They experimented in growing tobacco, but it went mouldy at the curing stage. A tree surgery business sprang up. There was a large workshop where Nigel and others did woodturning and carpentry."*
Location: Rodley, Westbury-on-Severn
Ref: www.biroco.com (21.12.2010)

BLACKBERRY HILL   circa 1974 - 1983?
Community set up by Musician Keld Liengaard and his wife Anja (the daughter of Ove Arup).
Location: Horley, Nailsworth
Ref: *Alternative Communities* 4th ed;
Communes Network 65

PARADISE COMMUNITY   1976 - ?
Christian and Steiner based community offering residential care for adults with learning disabilities.
Location: Paradise, Painswick
Ref: www.paradise-house.org.uk (20.10.11);
D&D 96-97

OAKLANDS PARK   1977 -
Camphill community offering supported living for around 100 people, about 50 with special needs. nine households, five in a converted Victorian mansion, which also houses a library, games room, meeting room, health centre, hall and coffee bar. As well as land-based work on 120-acre estate, they have developed a cafe, art gallery, weaving studio and bookshop.
Location: Newnham-on-Severn
Ref: www.cvt.org.uk (21.4.2011)

TAURUS CRAFTS   1981 -
Camphill Crafts centre, created as a social enterprise, includes a restaurant, pottery, craft gift shop, gallery, artist-in-residence studio, craft units, organic food and wine shop and organic market garden. Also have two community houses and a number of town houses and purpose-built flats providing supported living.
Location: The Old Park, Lydney
Ref: www.cvt.org.uk; www.tauruscrafts.co.uk (21.4.2011)

GANNICOX CAMPHILL   circa 1980 -
Camphill community made up of two houses. Between 1950 and 1980 Gannicox House was a nursing home, incorporated one of the first anthroposophical medical NHS practices in the country. Then the Medical Centre moved next door into new purpose-build premises and Gannicox developed into a Camphill life-sharing community. Also incorporates the Sunlands Waldorf Kindergarten. Whittington House built in the 1980's by a housing association as a retirement home was closed in 2006 and converted into seven self-contained flats providing a home with a social support network for elderly individuals and couples.
Location: 57 Cainscross Road, Stroud
Ref: www.camphill.org.uk (21.4.2011)

MICKLETON EMISSARY   1980 -
Community of up to 50+ members of the Emmisaries of the Divine Light living in Mickleton House and in communal and family houses around the village, Held public meetings and ran seminars on *"The Art of Living"*. Aim to *"magnify the finest qualities of character in every field of human endeavour"*.
Location: Mickleton
Ref: *D&D 90-91*; www.emissaries.org (19.10.11)

WILLIAM MORRIS HOUSE   1981 -
Camphill college offering further education, training and social therapy for young people with learning disabilities. Five households, teaching facilities, craft workshops, a hall and a library set in three acres of gardens.
Location: Eastington, Stonehouse
Ref: www.camphill.org.uk (21.4.2011)

ORCHARD LEIGH COMMUNITY   1981 -
Small Camphill community for adults with learning disabilities. Do gardening, felt-making, and run a bakery.
Location: Bath Road, Eastington, Stonehouse
Ref: www.camphill.org.uk (21.4.2011)

VIVIDUS circa 1983 -
Group listed with 'partial entry' in Teachers directory.
Location: Buck Farm, Corse, Hartpury
Ref: *Alternative Communities* 4th ed

STROUD SUSTAINABLE VILLAGE circa 1994
Proposed village based on Permaculture principles.
Location: c/o PO Box in Stroud
Ref: *D&D 94-95*

STEPPING STONES 1999 - ?
Thirty acre farm in the Wye Valley members of
Radical Route Network "*We are a group of people
who have come together to live low impact lifestyles,
with a variety of living spaces (house, benders,
caravans, etc ...). We are committed to working the
land, and would like to turn this farm into a small
prototype organic ecovillage.*"
Location: Highbury Farm, Redbrook
Ref: *D&D 00-01*

SPRINGHILL COHOUSING 1999 - present
First new build cohousing community in the UK.
Pedestrianised estate of 35 houses, flats and studios,
plus large common house for shared evening meals.
Location: Springfield Road, Stroud
Ref: www.springhillcohousing.com (16.9.12)

HAMPSHIRE

SANDY BALLS 1919 - 1980's
Estate on the northern edge of the New Forest
bought as a base for the Code of Woodcraft
Chivalry. Ernest Westlake and his family drew up
a plan for a forest park stocked with the surviving
fauna of the Old Stone Age. During the 1930's the
estate served as a home for the Grith Fyrd. Annual
Woodcraft folkmoots were held there until 1934
and Westlake is buried there in a replica Bronze
Age burial mound. After Ernest Westlake's death his
son Aubrey carried on his ideas and established the
forerunner of Forest School Camps. In the 1940's a
dozen simply furnished camping huts were built and
the estate slowly developed into a holiday camp.
Aubrey's daughter Jean Westlake had links with
Braziers Park community near Oxford. Site is now
run as a commercial campsite.
Location: Fordingbridge
Ref: *The Triumph of the Moon; 70 years a growng;
The Story of Godshill*; www.sandyballs.co.uk
(21.12.2010)

PACIFIST LAND SCHEME circa 1940
Twelve acre Christian based land-scheme
advertised in Fellowship of Reconcillation circular
at the outbreak of war.
Location: near Alton
Ref: *Valiant for Peace*

ROPLEY PEACE SERVICE circa 1940
25-acre Pacifist land settlement. Four acres
ploughed for potato growing plus more land to
be worked as market garden. Members lived in
caravans with a wooden hut for a kitchen and
common room.
Location: Gascoigne Lane, Ropley
Ref: *Community in Britain* 1940; *Utopian England;
Valiant for Peace*

CHEESECOMBE FARM 1941
Small community settlement started by East Hants
and West Surrey Peace Pledge Union. Advertising
vacancies for unmarried conscientious objectors
who "*want to make a serious attempt towards a new
way of life.*"
Location: Hawkley, Liss
Ref: Ad in *Peace News* 3.1.41

CPFLU LAND UNITS 1940 - 1946?
Christian Pacifist land-based units organised
for conscientious objectors.
Location: Burriton; Micheldever; Falklands
Farm Newbury; Norley Wood; Allington
Manor, Fair Oak; Hook; Sadlers Farm; Sway
and Beaulieu; Lymington; Headcorn; Burley,
Brokenhurst, Lyndhurst and Ringwood in the
New Forest.
Ref: M Maclachlan *CPLFU*

ALBERY HOUSE circa 1940
Group of 10-12 pacifists and refugees trying by
living communally "*to eliminate competition, which
it believes to be one of the major causes of war.*"
Albery house was one of four chalk house built on
Hugh's Settlement.
Location: Quarley near Andover
Ref: *Community in Britain* 1940

V.I.P / LE COURT 1945 - ?
VIP stands for 'Vade in Pacem'. Colony of ex-
servicemen set up by Leonard Cheshire which later
became first of the Cheshire Homes for the disabled.
Location: Greatham, Liss
Ref: *Cheshire VC: The story of war and Peace*

SUPERIOR ESTATE — 1946 - 1962
Post-war squatter camp.
Location: near Gratshott
Ref: www.headley-village.com (21.12.2010)

FOXDOWN CAMP — circa 1946
Families squatting in chalets originally put up to house evacuated Bank of England staff.
Location: Overton
Ref: www.arborfieldhistory.org.uk (23.12.08)

OAKRIDGE FARM SQUAT — 1946
Families squatting on US 'coloured' troops base.
Location: near Basingstoke
Ref: *Reading Mercury* 17.8.46

HECKFIELD CAMP — 1946
25 families take over huts.
Location: Heckfield, Hook
Ref: *Reading Mercury* 17.8.46

'SOLENT HOUSE' — 1946 - 1949
Third and last co-operative house of the Max Lock Group. A large house facing directly onto the Solent was made available for the team to live in.
Location: Exact location unknown
Ref: University of Westminster archive

DUNANNIE — 1948 - 1951
Headquarters of the Friends Ambulance Unit providing alternative National Service. Large victorian house and grounds next to the Bedales progressive school. Moved to Lavender Farm, Wiltshire in 1951.
Location: Steep
Ref: R Bush *FAU: The Third Generation*

THE SHEILING COMMUNITY — 1951 - present
Camphill school and community. Part of a wider local network under the Sheiling Trust.
Location: Horton Road, Ashley, Ringwood
Ref: www.sheilingschool.co.uk (12.5.2011

HAPT (DIGGERS) TRIBE — 1967 - 1971?
"Decentralised mobile printing collective" with plans to set up rural commune.
Location: West Howe, Bournemouth (also Butterrow, Gloucestershire)
Ref: *Directory of Communes* 1970

ALPHA HOUSE — 1968 - ?
A residential community, on a self-help basis, for the social rehabilitation of ex-drug users.
Location: Alpha House Wickham Road, Droxford
Ref: *Basic Communities*;
www.phoenix-futures.org.uk (12.5.11)

DIVINE LIGHT MISSION — circa 1970 - 1983
Ashram lived in by 'Premies' or devotees of Guru Maharaj Ji (now Prem Rawat).
Location: 116 Dean Road, Bitterne, Southampton
Ref: www.prem-rawat-bio.org (31.7.2011)

ANDMOREAGAIN — circa 1971/72
"We hope to live and communicate on the basis of love and to spread this idea of society by all the best means possible." Ten month commune with eight people. Started in Brighton.
Location: 172 Derby Road, Southampton
Ref: *Directory of Communes* 1972 & 1972

STONEYMARSH COMMUNE — 1972 - ?
Group of 5-8 living in two adjacent cottages looking for a hill farm in Wales or Northern England while working on local farms to pick up basic farming skills. *"We are a pretty close knit group, and having got to know each other very well during the last few months; breaking down barriers in relationships with honesty and sharing; working out fears and hangups by confronting them. We all feel that we have grown tremendously from this, and if we have a communal direction, it is to keep travelling on this path towards the unknown and thereby realise a greater spiritual harmony with each other and our environment."*
Location: Exact location not known.
Ref: *Directory of Communes* 1972

THEDDEN GRANGE — 1975 -
Group of 13 adults (all architects, except for a structural engineer and a psychotherapist) and 14 kids living in large country house and cottages with 40 acres of land. *"... We decided to take things slowly and not involve ourselves in more sharing than we were able to handle. There was an initial idea that we should work for a balance between privacy and communality, and this has persisted, We have our own houses but there are many projects in common: most of the animals are run on a shared basis by those interested, and the maintenance of the estate is our common*

commitment. We have Jersey cows, Jacob sheep, a pig, a goat, two ponies, chickens and bees; we grow some fodder crops and produce a lot of food from our kitchen garden."

Location: near Alton
Ref: **Alternative Communities** 2nd & 3rd eds; "Communards of the Nineties" by Lesley Gillilan in **The Independent** 6.6.1996

ORION CENTRE   1979 - 1984?
Communal group involved in music scene. Ran eight-track recording studio and provided arranging service as well as sessions. Money from studio went to fund school for children. *"... Music is an integral part of our lifestyle, both as our bread and butter and also as a way of communicating our ideas and beliefs in a non verbal medium ..."*

Location: 57 St Denys Road, Portswood, Southampton
Ref: **Alternative Communities** 3rd ed;
J Mercer **Communes**

WHITEHILL CHASE   circa 1980
Retreat Community house in 19th century hunting lodge set in several acres of woods and gardens. Base for the Acorn Christian Healing Trust.
Location: Bordon
Ref: **Directory of Christian Communities & Groups** 1980; www.acornchristian.org (21.12.2010)

LANTERN COMMUNITY   circa 2000 -
Ten houses for children and adolescents with a learning disability.Part of the Sheiling Trust which also runs the Sheiling School and Sturts Biodynamic Farm.
Location: Folly Farm Lane, Ringwood
Ref: www.lanterncommunity.org.uk (21.4.2011)

HEREFORD SHIRE

BODENHAM MANOR   1950 - 1987
Residential School established by the Birmingham Society for the Care of Invalid and Nervous Children David Wills who had run Barns House near Peebles during the war was appointed as warden The Society also set up a hostel for ex pupils to live in.
Location: Bodenham, Hereford
Ref: www.archive.pettrust.org.uk (3.8.2011)

CANON FROME COURT   1978 - present
Fifty (adults and children) living in Georgian manor house and stable-block divided into 19 self-contained homes, also run 40-acre organic farm. *"In addition to working together ... other community activities currently include supper on Saturday nights (Pot Luck), trips to the pub, a house band, involvement in HArt, as well as celebrations – Bonfire Night, Christmas, Easter, the Summer Party, solstice celebrations, children's birthdays – and the agricultural rituals of haymaking, harvesting, potato-lifting, fruit picking."*
Location: near Ledbury
Ref: **D&D 90-91**; www.canonfromecourt.org.uk (19.10.11)

BLUE FROG HOUSE / MEDWELL circa 1978/84
"Established communal household in Welsh – Hereford border town seeks members. Possible involvement in café, wholefood shop on premises. Some workshop space available."
Location: 4 Church Street, Knighton
Ref: Ad in **Undercurrents** 45;
Alternative Communities 4th ed

HERTFORD SHIRE

MEADOW WAY GREEN   1914 - 1960's
Co-operative housekeeping scheme set up by Ruth Pym and Miss S. Dewe for 'single business women'. Ran as semi-communal scheme through the war and into the 1960's.
Location: Meadow Way Green, Letchworth
Ref: L F Pearson **The Architectural & Social History of Co-operative Living**

SPIELPLATZ   1929 - present
Residential nudist camp. Up to 35 families renting plots in an area of woodland.
Location: Bricket Wood
Ref: I Richardson **No Shadows Fall** 1994

HOLWELL HYDE — 1939 - 1942

11-acre farm with a house, a cottage and a separate recreation facility operated by the Friends Committee for Refugees and Aliens under the eye of three *"older and experienced"* refugees. Offered training in agriculture, horticulture, stock and poultry keeping, and periodically organised lectures on those subjects. The combined influences of safe haven ,productive work, training and *"agreeable camaraderie"* helped and it soon became noticeable that *"without exception"* the trainees *"greatly improved in health and physique during their stay ..."*
Location: near Hatfield
Ref: www.traces.org/quakerrefugeeprojects.html (21.12.2010)

DOWER HOUSE FARM — circa 1940's - 1950's

Training farm owned by the Jewish Agency.
Location: Hatfield Heath
Ref: www.marblearch.org.uk (25.6.09)

HITCHEN COMMUNITY HOUSE — 1940's

House of the Guild of the Second Order of the Brotherhood of the Way. 22 residents ran small bakery, market garden, reared poultry and ran a printing press.
Location: The Priory, Little Wymondley. Hitchen
Ref: *Community in Britain* 1940

TRING YOUTH HOUSE — circa 1940

Attempt to convert Refugee Centre into communal experiment for young people.
Location: Tring
Ref: *Community in Britain* 1940

THE WHITE HOUSE — 1941

A Gerard Reilly attempt to found a self supporting agricultural and crafts community.
Location: Muswell Lane, Tring
Ref: *Peace News Community Supplement* 14.3.41

QUARE MEAD — 1944/46

Half-timbered house used by Maurice Nicoll's Gurdjeiffian group just after the war when they moved from Birdlip to be closer to London. The group kept pigs, chickens and ducks.
Location: Ugley
Ref: B Pogson *Maurice Nicoll: A portrait*

GREAT AMWELL HOUSE — 1946 - 1953

Large Georgian house with walled garden and large grounds used by Maurice Nicoll and his group of followers/students to run courses. Continued as a community running courses until Nicoll's death.
Location: Great Amwell, near Ware
Ref: B Pogson *Maurice Nicoll: A portrait*

US AIR FORCE BASE CAMP — 1946 -

Base taken over by squatters.
Location: Watford
Ref: D Thomas *Villains' Paradise*

THE HOUSE IN THE SUN — 1947 - 1997

School set up by Lisa and Alfred Gobell, inspired by a German book called *The House in the Sun*, to meet the needs of children with behaviour and learning problems.
Location: Hengrove, Chivery
Ref: http: //cholesbury.com/pdf/htn-200712.pdf (3.8.2011)

THE ABBEY ARTS CENTRE — 1947 - 1951

Arts centre and artists' commune set up by art collector and Berkeley Gallery owner William Ohly. Attracted many expatriate Australian artists to its doors during the post-war years. Became a base for artists, trying to gain a foothold in London's contemporary art scene.
Location: 89 Park Road, New Barnet
Ref: http: //web.ukonline.co.uk/mr.king/pek/ (9.5.09)

DIGSWELL HOUSE — circa 1957 -

Regency mansion with cottages and outbuildings on the edge of Welwyn Garden City home of the Digswell Arts Trust. The Development Corporation agreed to restore the house for artists' accommodation, studios and workshops and lease it to the Trust at affordable rents for 'Fellows'. The first six artists and their families moved in in 1957. Over the next 27 years nearly 150 artists were accommodated by the Trust, some became internationally famous: Hans Coper, Michael Andrews, John Mills ,John Brunsden, James Butler, Ralph Brown, Peter Collingwood, Liz Fritsch, Lol Coxhill. In the early 1980's the House was sold and divided into apartments. The Trust continued in Attimore Hall Barn and in 1993 leased Fairlands Valley Farmhouse from Stevenage Council as further studio space.
Location: Monks Rise, Welwyn
Ref: www.digswellartstrust.com (29.4.2006)

VILLA 21   1962 - 1966
Experimental 'anti-psychiatry' ward at Shenley Hospital.
Location: Radlett near St Albans
Ref: *Therapeutic Communities: Past, Present and Future*

'SELENE COMMUNITY'   1965 - 67
Small communal vegan house that formed the basis of the Selene community in Wales.
Location: Wheathampstead
Ref: Andrew Rigby *Alternative Realities*

BHAKTIVEDANTA MANOR circa 1966 - present
Large house and grounds bought by George Harrison as a UK base for ISKCON, the Hari Krishna movement.
Location: Letchmore Heath
Ref: *D&D 90-91*

POTTERS BAR COMMUNE   circa 1969
Group listed as UK centre for the Diggers International Co-ordination. *"For streaming information – manifestos, publications, posters, leaflets, ephemera, etc – put out by radical Digger groups in this country and abroad."*
Location: 216 Mutton Lane, Potters Bar
Ref: *Gandalf's Garden* 5

THE JESUS LIBERATION ARMY   1971 - ?
Group of 'Jesus People' living in two semi-detached houses; collected and circulated tracts, books, posters and cassettes. With names such as 'Little Green Book' and 'The Permanent Revolution' Membership of the JLF was free to all who had been *'born of the Spirit'*. The group ran its own 'Jesus Bus'. Featured in 1973 BBC2 documentary *By Way of Change*.
Location: Sunnyhill, Hemel Hempstead
Ref: *Jesus Bubble; Youthquake*

OPTIKINETICS   circa 1970's?
"Optikinetics' response was to move from its Hatfield farmhouse commune to business premises in Luton."
Location: Hatfield?
Ref: www.tpimagazine.com (3.4.2009)

'LARGE HOUSE'   circa 1974
Project set up by Roger Franklin as an 'Intermediate stage' towards a self-sufficient village community. Linked to the New Villages Association.
Location: 36 Loom Lane, Radlett
Ref: *In The Making* 2

SHANTOCK STUDIO   mid 1970's
Small group linked by experience of J G Bennett's 'International Academy for Continuous Education' at Sherbourne House. Also had a connection with the Genesis Project. Held *"weekend 'programmes for achievement' which include Gurdjieff music and movement"*.
Location: near Bovingdon
Ref: *Alternative England & Wales*

CALDECOTE FAMILY COMMUNITY   1981 - ?
Small group running Childrens Theatre Club and children areas for festivals and events. *"Our original group of eight has now been cut down to three, mostly due to emotional upheavals of individuals who want to live in community but haven't the resilience or energy to start from the beginning! These problems have drained us somewhat ... we're learning from our mistakes, and though a little depleted, we're still working on ourselves, and keeping our gentle energy moving."* Held Free Festival at farm in August 1983.
Location: Caldecote Manor, Caldecote
Ref: *Alternative Communities* 4th ed

DELROW COMMUNITY   1980 -
Camphill community based in 300-year-old Tudor mansion and surrounding estate. Households and flats in Delrow House plus purpose-built houses and apartments in the grounds and houses and cottages in the adjacent lanes. Run workshops including; basketry, needlecraft, pottery, woodwork and weaving.
Location: Hilfield Lane, Aldenham
Ref: www.camphillfamily.com (21.4.2011)

CAMPHILL ST ALBANS   1980 -

Urban community with two houses for shared living in small groups and a number of smaller houses and apartments for couples and single occupants. Provide support and social network for over 20 adults with learning disabilities and mental health problems. *"We encourage independence in the wider community while offering a secure network of support that our community members can rely upon. People are supported in working towards individual aims and coping with challenges in their lives in their own way and in their own time ..."*
Location: 76 Sandridge Road, St Albans
Ref: www.cvt.org.uk (21.4.2011)

HUNTINGDON SHIRE

LITTLE GIDDING   mid 1970's - 1998

Site of 17th Century Christian lay community founded by Nicholas Ferrar. In the 1970's the property was home to the Little Gidding Community and subsequently in 1977 the Community of Christ the Sower, which included Anglican, Catholic and Free Church members, worshipping together and sharing Communion. Later a second branch formed at Leighton Bromswold. Now run as retreat centre.
Location: Ferrar House, Little Gidding
Ref: *D&D 92-93*; www.ferrarhouse.co.uk (19.10.11)

ISLE OF MAN

UPPER BISHOPS COURT FARM   circa 1983

Group listed with 'partial entry' in Teachers Directory.
Location: Ballaugh
Ref: *Alternative Communities* 4th ed

ISLE OF WIGHT

QUARR MONASTERY   1908 -

Established by French Benedictines fleeing persecution. As well as farming the monks are known for their music, painting, weaving, and carpentry.
Location: Ryde
Ref: *Utopian England*; www.quarrabbey.co.uk (19.10.11)

KENT

FINCHDEN MANOR   1930 - ?

"Finchden Manor is a community consisting of between 50-60 boys and young men, and some ten members of staff. The boys have always been known as The House; the staff are called by first or nicknames ..." Started on a farm called the Guildables, in Edenbridge, Kent it moved to Finchden Manor in 1935.
Location: near Tetterden
Ref: http://finchdenfellowship.com (20.2.09)

PACIFIST FRIARY   1939

"Anyone interested in establishment of a Pacifist Friary — a community living under pacifist principles. Run otherwise on Franciscan lines."
Location: c/o H M Jones, Kelham, Kent
Ref: Ad in *Peace News* 24.11.39

GREAT ENGEHAM FARM   June - Nov 1939

Agricultural training camp for Jewish refugees. Housed in tents or old railway carriages. They worked the farm and also dug trenches for defence at sites around Kent. A total of 134 children and 30 chalutzim lived there rent-free. It served mainly as a transit camp for the Kindertransport. Closed in November 1939 when Kent was designated off-limits to aliens.
Location: Woodchurch, Ashford
Ref: www.britishlocalhistory.co.uk (21.5.09)

DAVID EDER FARM   1935 -

Training farm for Jewish refugees which prepared idealistic Jewish youngsters for farm work and life on the Habonim kibbutz, Kfar Nanassi.
Location: Harrietsham
Ref: http://community.thejc.com (25.6.09)

CPFLU LAND UNITS   1940 - 1946?

Christian Pacifist land-based units organised for conscientious objectors.
Location: Hemstead Forest, Dockenden and Bedgebury Forest, Flimwell.
Ref: M Maclachlan *CPLFU*

REDGATE COMMUNITY   1940/41

Community venture sponsored by Tunbridge Wells PPU to provide accommodation and work for conscientious objectors running ½ acre kitchen

garden. "Proposal for income pooling and purchase of land being considered."
Location: Wadhurst
Ref: **Peace News Community Supplement** 25.4.41

HIGH HALDEN   1944 - 1948?
281-acre farm purchased by London Region Youth Hostels Ltd "as an experiment in furthering the Association's objects by relating hostel life to Agriculture." Members worked in the mornings, afternoons being spent in visiting other farms and evenings in talks. "Farmers in the locality assist in the evening events and genuine contact is made with country people."
Location: Turk's Head Farm, High Halden.
Ref: The Community Broadsheet Winter 47/48

SOUTHERN HOSPITAL   1945 - 1946
Continuation of development of therapeutic community ideas by Maxwell Jones at hospital set up for returning war-weary prisoners of war.
Location: Dartford
Ref: Stijn Vandevelde **Maxwell Jones and his work in the therapeutic community** 1999

THE CALDECOTT COMMUNITY   1945/6 -
Originally a day nursery in Street, Pancras, London, providing care for low income families founded in 1911 by Leila Rendel. Moved to Mersham-le-Hatch, Kent, at the end of World War II. Became group home providing residential care for vulnerable children.
Location: Mersham-le-Hatch
Ref: www.otherpeopleschildren.org.uk (2.8.2011)

SQUATTERBURY   1946 -
Large wartime training camps for D-Day infantry commanders. Covering 165 acres with 800-plus huts, concrete roads and walkways. Squatters moved in, in August 1946, the local authorities accepted responsibility for them and acknowledged the new community, which became known as Squatterbury. The estate was later developed as a series of woodland enclaves comprising 780 homes. Advertised as 'a new concept for living'.
Location: Now the village of Vigo
Ref: www.visitoruk.com (23.12.08)

HARVEL   1946 -
"A squatters' camp at Harvel was a constant topic of discussion at Meopham Parish Council and Strood Rural District Council meetings over health and rehousing problems."
Location: Harvel
Ref: www.discovergravesham.co.uk (23.12.08)

OTTERDEN PLACE   1946 - 2003
Country house 'saved' by the Mutual Households Ass.
Location: Eastling
Ref: **An Experiment in Co-operation**

GREAT MAYTHAM HALL   1950's - 2003
Country house 'saved' by the Mutual Households Ass.
Location: near Cranbrook
Ref: **SAVE Casework News** June 2004

ST JULIANS   1951 -
Experiment in co-operative living set up by a group of professionals and artists in a large country house. Families had separate units but provided shared childcare enabling the women among them to continue their careers. Slowly morphed over the years into a country club with restaurant, swimming pool etc.
Location: Sevenoaks
Ref: www.stjulians.co.uk (26.5.2011)

HILDENBOROUGH HALL   1963 - ?
Interdenominational Christian House community of some 25 people used as a base for the communication of the Gospel amongst young people. Held 'Open House' weekends. Sent musical teams into schools.
Location: Hildenborough Hall, Oxford Hills, Sevenoaks
Ref: **Basic Communities**

SIMONWELL FARM   1965 - ?
Well Farm bought by theSimon Community who "used it for a strange combination of purposes — experimental commune, rest centre for workers in the various 'units' and, in fact, the national headquarters." Used by American Vietnam deserters as one of a network of UK 'safe houses'
Location: Well Farm, Crundale
Ref: www.coughtrey.me.uk (22.8.08)

CO-OPERATIVE HOSTEL FOR THE HOMELESS   circa 1966

Proposal outlined by Brian Richardson in an article in Anarchy magazine following publicity about conditions at King Hill hostel in West Malling. There would be a furniture store to help families who had been evicted with nothing. A shared workshop as well as accommodation. It would be set up as a housing association and funded through local authority subsidy. *"Most important of all the hostel would be run by and for the residents, calling on such outside help as they require. Rather than being run as an obligation by an authority somewhat remote from the problem of homelessness ..."*
Location: Kent
Ref: *Anarchy* 67 (Sep 1966)

KENWARD TRUST   1968 - present

Christian based drug and alcohol rehabilitation and supported housing project.
Location: Highgate Hall, Hawkhurst; Kenward House and Kenward Barn Yalding; Upper Fant Road, Maidstone; Portland Road, Gravesend; Springfield Road, Southborough; Tunbridge Wells
Ref: **NACCAN Directory** 4th ed;
www.kenwardtrust.org.uk (17.6.2011)

'COMMUNITY HOPEFULS'   circa 1969

"We're getting one started In North Kent."
Location: write to 120 Mill Street, East Mailing.
Ref: Ad in *International Times* 68 (Nov 69)

ROCHESTER COMMUNE   1970?

"Our main aim, we all agree, is to get as far away from the plastic society as we can. To slow down into a large farmhouse somewhere in the woods, meadows and rivers of the countryside where we can remould our lives and live uninhibited by the hustles of straight life."
Location: Rochester
Ref: **Communes Europe**

RAMSGATE COMMUNE   1971 - 79

"There are three of us aged 25 to 35 and a boy of six in a large Regency terraced house, the proverbial stones throw away from the sea. We think there is space for about three or four more adults and children and we look forward to having more people so that our energie can be put together to get going on the various projects we plan, in the house and the locality ... As well as living space we have an office, a room for jewellery making, another work

room and a projected pottery. In fact there would be space for almost any craft. We have had fantasies about renting a small shop for handmade goods, books and radical literature. There is nothing of the kind anywhere in this area. We are anarchists, very concerned with education. A free school has been a recurring idea but it wouldn't be possible in this house and of course it will not get off the around until we are a larger, stronger, more established ..."*
Location: 22 Royal Road, Ramsgate
Ref: **Directory of Communes** 1972; *Living Like I Do*; **Communes Network** 42; **People Together**

STAINMOSS   1973 - 1975?

Large house and outbuildings bought with money from the sale of members original homes. Started with a combination of outside teaching work and homebased craft projects, pooling income. *"Within a year a split developed due to differences in lifestyles and philosophies, so much so that one side stopped talking to the other ..."* Things improved to the point where they were able *"to discuss arrangements for splitting up."*
Location: Exact location unknown
Ref: **Legal Frameworks Handbook**

KENT COMMUNE   circa 1974

"Some "good friends" of BIT − trying to set up a commune in Kent that would absorb the occasional emotionally disturbed person from BIT COPE"
Ref: *BITMAN* 11 May 1974

L'ARCHE KENT   1970's - present

Six community houses for International L'Arche movement.
Location: Little Ewell, Barfrestone, Dover
Ref: www.larchekent.org.uk/

WESTBERE COMMUNITY   circa 1975

Group listed in back of *Communes Network*.
Location: Westbere Court, Hersden, Canterbury
Ref: *Communes Network* 8

ROYDON HALL   1977 - 2003

Transcendental Meditation Centre.
Location: Roydon Hall Road, East Peckham
Ref: http://globalcountry.org.uk (1.1.2011)

SOLEIL CO-OP   circa 1980 -

"Easy going communal household"
Location: 7 Burnt Ash Lane, Bromley
Ref: **Communes Network** 64; **Alternative Communities** 4th ed

GILLETTS COMMUNITY   circa 1984 -

11 adults living in large house with a couple of acres *"Interests include peace work and organic gardening."*
Location: The Street, Smarde near Ashford
Ref: **Communes Network Directory** 1985

BEECH GROVE BRUDERHOF   1995 -

Sister community to Darvell Bruderhof on site of a former sports college.
Location: Sandwich Road, Nonington
Ref: www.bruderhof.com (16.9.12)

LANCASHIRE

STONE BOWER FELLOWSHIP   circa 1939

Peace Pledge Union sponsored communal scheme for elderly WWII evacuees supported by Canadian Red Cross and Mennonites at Stone Bower House, Burton in Lonsdale. After the war became independent old peoples home, becoming a housing society in 1949 and moving to the Cove, Silverdale in 1950. Merged with large housing association in 1995.
Location: Silverdale
Ref: R Douglas Young **The Stone Bower Fellowship**

YEALAND MANOR   circa 1939

Experiment in communal living for evacuated children set up by the Manchester Friends' monthly meeting. Up to 50 children lived together in *'an atmosphere of service, love and peace.'*
Location: Yealand Conyers
Ref: Pat Starky **Pacifism in Lancashire**

THORNHAM FOLD FARM   circa 1939

Refugee training farm set up by Bachad.
Location: Middleton
Ref: Bill Williams **Jewish Manchester**

KIBBUTZ HAKORIM   1943 -

Group of 20 young Zionists living together communally. The men worked as 'Bevin Boy' miners while the women worked in the local town.
Location: Stalybridge
Ref: Bill Williams **Jewish Manchester**

SE LANCS COMMUNAL CENTRE   circa 1940

Proposal by Oldham and Crumpsall PPU and Oldham Friends Service Committee for an income pooling community house with sufficient land for kitchen garden and poultry.
Ref: *Community in Britain* 1940

REGENT STREET   1940

Carl Wragg writes in Community Notes in *Peace News* *"Early in July last four of us came together to live in community. It is only a beginning. We have our little plot of ground which we work in our spare time for we are continuing in our own jobs for the present; but we hope to increase our numbers and then increase our acreage. Eventually starting a small farm to be run in conjunction with the town house. We welcome inquiries from people of like mind to ourselves, whatever their financial circumstances."*
Location: 6 Regent Street, Lancaster
Ref: **Peace News** 15.11.40

CPFLU LAND UNITS   1940 - 1946?

Christian Pacifist land-based units organised for conscientious objectors.
Location: Ormskirk and Quernmore
Ref: M Maclachlan **CPLFU**

LIVERPOOL PSU   1940 - 1944?

Large Victorian house base for Pacifist Service Unit.
Location: 56 Grove Street, Liverpool, L7
Ref: **The Revolution in Post-War Family Casework**

WENNINGTON SCHOOL   1940 - 1945

Progressive school set up by two former Bedales teachers Kenneth and Frances Barnes to house and educate evacuees. Became a 'community' growing food and small-holding with chickens, pigs, goats and bees. Moved to Ingmanthorpe Hall near Wetherby at the end of the war.
Location: Wennington Hall, Wennington
Ref: www.wenningtonschool.org.uk (4.8.11);
K Barnes **Energy Unbound**

ANTI-AIRCRAFT CAMP   1946 -

Camp occupied by post-war squatters.
Location: near West Derby
Ref: D Thomas **Villains' Paradise**

WINSTANLEY PARK   1946/7

Nissen huts in mansion grounds used by WAAFs. Squatted by 20 families of local homeless people, many of whom were ex-servicemen.
Location: Wigan
Ref: www.wlct.org/Culture/Heritage/pf40.pdf (22.12.08)

BURSCOUGH CAMP   1946 - 1950's

Huts at Royal Naval Air Station Burscough occupied by squatters, mainly families from Liverpool who had lost their homes in the bombing. During the Fifties the huts were replaced by council houses.
Location: Burscough
Ref: www.wartimememories.co.uk (23.12.08)

LANGTHWAITE HOUSE   1960/62

Home of the Peace Knowledge Foundation set up by among other Paul Smoker and Vivienne Cooper. In 1961 there were "... a team of seven peace researchers at Langthwaite, some being part-time long-termers and others being full-time short-termers, but at present none is a full-time long-termer." Eventually became the Richardson Institute for Peace Studies and part of Lancaster University.
Location: Langthwaite Road, Lancaster
Ref: *Peace News* 26.11.68; *Peace Knowledge Foundation Broadsheet* May 1961

GREAT GEORGES COMMUNITY
CULTURAL PROJECT   circa 1963 - present

Centre for experimental work in contemporary arts, education and youth work housed in an old church Known locally as the 'Blackie'.
Location: Great George Street, Liverpool
Ref: *Alternative Communities* 4th ed; www.theblack-e.co.uk (19.10.11)

ASHRAM COMMUNITY HOUSE   1967 -

One of a network of Christian Community households (others in Middlesborough, London and Sheffield) Aiming to "discover new implications of the way of Jesus for today's world ... through a contemporary Christian life-style." Originally mainly Methodist, but other denominations also represented. Put out a periodical: ACT.
Location: 17 King Street South, Rochdale
Ref: *Basic Communities*

COLLEGE 6   circa 1968 - 1970

Plan formulated by a group of young lecturers who formed "College 6", which they envisaged as a commune style building where students could exercise their own influence on the direction of the college.
Location: Lancaster University
Ref: (accessed 2.6.09)
www.lancs.ac.uk/users/fylde/allabout/abouthistory.htm

WELFARE STATE
INTERNATIONAL   1968-2006

Fringe theatre/community arts group offered 'winter quarters' for their touring cavalcade of caravans on council tip in Burnley by Mid-Pennine Arts. Established little enclave of artists in various sheds, huts and caravans. Did shows locally and internationally. Home educated children. Left East Lancs in late 70's and reappeared in Ulverston. Where they settled as a more integrated part of the wider community. Burnley site became youth theatre base. "Welfare State is not an experimental theatre company as usually understood, but rather a journey into unknown and undiscovered ways of living and creative communication ..." Dave Cunliffe PN 15.6.73
Location: Burnley then Ulverston
Ref: *Engineers of the Imagination; What Shall we Do with the Children?;* www.welfare-state.org (19.10.11)

LIVERPOOL COMMUNE   circa 1970

"Commune forming. Aims, self-awareness, companionship, involvement and sensory re-awakening through encounter groups, sensitivity training, meditation, etc ..."
Location: Liverpool
Ref: Ad in *International Times* 81 (Jun 1970)

CANNOCK STREET   1970 - ?

Dilapidated house bought by John Barker and Hilary Creek, who would later be convicted for conspiracy in the Angry Brigade trial. A small group of seven people lived there. John Barker described it as "a good scene. The joy of being in growing strength of us the people. It was real good there. Very relaxed."
Location: 14 Cannock Street, Moss Side, Manchester
Ref: Gordon Carr *The Angry Brigade*

DIVINE LIGHT MISSION   circa 1970 - 1983

Ashram lived in by 'Premies' or devotees of Guru Maharaj Ji (now Prem Rawat).
Location: 4 Chester Road, Tuebrook, Liverpool and 66 Derby Road, Fallowfield, Manchester
Ref: www.prem-rawat-bio.org (31.7.2011)

MANCHESTER COMMUNE PROJECT circa 1970

Group of three living in suburban semi – went on to set up Latham Farm commune near Hebden Bridge
Location: 1 Hawthorn Drive, Burnage, Manchester
Ref: *Communes Journal* 35 (Dec 1970)

FORMBY UN-TIED WORKSHOP   circa 1971 -
"Our aim is to establish a working example of an alternative to the present economic system – an alternative based on love and mutual aid rather than the profit-motive and status seeking individuals. Thus we work for nothing and our products and services will be free ..."
Location: Formby Hall, Formby
Ref: *Directory of Communes* 1971

TRANQUILLITY TEA SERVICE   circa 1972
"Tranquillity Tea Service is to be a sort of mobile Gandalf's Garden cum info-service, loosely commune-ish, in a converted single deck bus. They're going to travel round Britain rapping with people about the alternative services."
Location: c/o 7 Summer Terrace, Rusholme
Ref: Ad in *International Times* 124 (Feb Mar 1972)

THE ROADRUNNERS   circa 1973 - ?
A small group of young adults living in a community house. Produced the Catonsville Roadrunner (radical Christian magazine) for a period amongst other activities.
Location: 8 Brundetts Road, Manchester
Ref: *Communes Network*

SPIRITUAL COMMUNE   circa 1973
"SPIRITUAL and philosophical commune into Yoga, Zen, Wicca, Magick, Leary, Watts, Crowley, Hesse ..."
Location: Merseyside
Ref: Ad in *International Times* 156 (1973)

SOMEWHERE   circa 1974
Proposed scheme to coax freaks away from London to declining East Lancs town of Colne. Plans included; cleaning up local areas, setting up a Housing association – *"Our initial target is 85 houses in the Colne area and some other property ie – a farm and a mill ..."* Also had plan for a free shop, food co-op and craft industries.
Location: "Ask for Rik" 14 Patten Street, Colne
Ref: *BITMAN* 11 (May 1974)

ASHTON MOSS COLLECTIVE   circa 1974
Self-sufficiency project started on 2 acres of land that was then purchased by BBC as site for a transmitter. *"This doesn't mean the project is dead ... The aims will be as before; to create a non-capitalist world from the ground up, finding alternatives to just about everything that isn't*

good enough in this system." Simon & Bob
Location: c/o 32 Parkfield Street, Rusholme
Ref: *In The Making* 2

ANANDA MARGA   circa 1974 - 1980?
'Social spiritual group' of 15 adults running wholefood shop, bakery, veggie restaurant, art gallery and theatre group. Believe in liberation of the self through service to humanity.
Location: 8 Ullet Road, Liverpool, L8 3SR
Ref: *Alternative Communities* 3rd ed

THE CHILDREN OF GOD   mid 1970's
Communal house of Christian sect.
Location: 90 Ullet Road, Liverpool 8
Ref: *Jesus Bubble*

PEOPLE IN COMMON   1974 - present
"Flexible-living-working-Co-operative" that emerged from the early 70's squatting movement. Bought a number of cheap terraced houses in Burnley. Ran job creation program to renovate central communal house and used skills learnt to set up building co-operative. Bought derelict mill building and three acres on banks of the river Calder at Altham in 1977. Took over ten years to complete first phase of conversion of mill to large communal building with workshop and large market garden. Group was involved in local community politics, ran a food co-op, home-educated some of the children and was income pooling until the late 1990's. Some members established successful timber business using local oak for building. (See: www.oak-beams.co.uk) Community continues on housing co-operative basis. *"We see ourselves as a fifth column within capitalism and hope that just as the 'workers friendly societies' could be said to be the forerunners of the welfare state so the 'workers co-operative living group' could be the forerunners of a new social creation."* 1975
Location: Burnley and Altham Cornmill (Accrington)
Ref: *Communes Network Directory* (various); *D&D 90-91*

OLDHAM ROAD COMMUNE circa 1976

Group involved with Tractor Music a hippie music shop, rehearsal rooms and PA hire company. Also involved with the 1976 Rivington and Deeply Vale Free Festivals.
Location: Oldham Road, Balderstone, Rochdale
Ref: www.ukrockfestivals.com (20.5.09)

NORMAN ROAD circa 1970's

Group that started living together as students and continued after they all left university.
Location: Longsight
Ref: Personal contact

BARN HOUSE 1977 - 1980

Address listed in *NACCAN directory*.
Location: Little Crosby, Liverpool
Ref: *Directory of Christian Communities & Groups*

STACKSTEADS COMMUNITY
circa 1977 - 1984?

Small group in three cottages started a number of community ventures.
Location: 308 Newchurch Road, Bacup
Ref: *Alternative Communities* 3rd ed

FIRS CHRISTIAN COMMUNITY
circa 1979 - 1983?

Group from *"a variety of Christian traditions"* living in big house.
Location: 18 Firs Avenue, Ashton-under-Lyme
Ref: *Alternative Communities* 4th ed

47 COMMUNITY circa 1979 -

Small communal household, six adults and two kids. *"... Four of us who live here are Christian although this isn't nay kind of a division in the household ... We're all fairly libertarian in outlook, and "spare time interests' include Trade Union work, 'Troops Out'. digging a garden and allotment, various women's movement activities etc"*
Location: Manchester
Ref: *Communes Network* 46

MAHARISHI EUROPEAN SIDHALAND
circa 1980 - present

Transcendental Meditation community with 300 members including children. Facilities include the Maharishi Golden Dome, where Transcendental Meditation and Yogic Flying™ are practiced, the Maharishi School, a business centre, an Ayurveda Health Centre and a Sports and Arts Centre.
Location: Woodley Park Road, Skelmersdale
Ref: www.maharishi-european-sidhaland.org.uk (31.7.11)

ALEXANDRA PARK CO-OPERATIVE
circa 1980

Small group living in large Victorian house with 'enormous garden' overlooking Alexandra Park. *"... trying to improve the quality of life for ourselves and other single-parent families ..."* planned to set up 24 hour childcare service and build a small adventure playground.
Location: 62, Demesne Road, Whalley Range.
Ref: *Alternative Communities* 3rd ed

CRDRAKUTA circa 1980-

FWBO House.
Location: 9 Aycliffe Grove, Longsight Manchester
Ref: *Alternative Communities* 3rd ed

ULLET GRANGE 1982 - 2006?

30 plus room Victorian mansion on edge of Sefton Park bought from Council. Residents shared costs and communal chores. Held "famous parties" that attracted hundreds from across the city., where local bands would take to the stage in the garden led to being nicknamed 'Grangestock'. *"At first it was full of Socialists and vegetarians, then professionals such as psychologists, lawyers and teachers, and then artists and sculptors."*
Location: Sefton Park, Liverpool
Ref: *Liverpool Daily Post* (3.5.07); Personal contact

TOWN & COUNTRY circa 1983 -

Small communal group in Longsight.
Location: 2 Mentor Street and 19 Duncan Road, Manchester
Ref: *Alternative Communities* 4th ed

BOAT CO-OP circa 1983 -

"We aim to build a canal based community earning its living by canal carrying an other canal based activities"
Location: 15 Greenheys Road, Liverpool
Ref: *Communes Network Directory* 83

BURNLEYWOOD HOUSING CO-OP late 1980's

Offshoot of People In Common in original houses after PIC moved into converted Mill.
Location: Burnley
Ref: *D&D 94-95*

RIVENDELL circa 1986 -
Victorian farmhouse in Lune Valley seeking to be a *"safe place in the wilderness"*. Core family of three plus three volunteers who stayed for varying periods. Offered short breaks for people who came from *"all sorts of stressful situations."* The 'therapy' offered consisted of" ... *interaction with country things: care of goats, hens and pony, walking, riding, sailing, gardening, music, reading and (not least) people with time to talk and listen."* Christian but not denominational.
Location: Mansergh, Carnforth
Ref: *D&D 92-93*

INCOGNITO 1989 - ?
'Loose' communal household.
Location: 26 Hawarden Avenue, Liverpool, L17
Ref: *D&D 90-91*

LOSANG DRAGPA CENTRE 1995 - 2007
19th Century mansion house built by local mill owner John Fielden. Used after the war as an approved school. Had been empty for six years before it was turned into a Buddhist Centre by the New Kadampa Buddhist Tradition whose "Mother Centre" is at the Manjushri Centre near Ulverston. Sold in 2007.
Location: Dobroyd Castle, Todmorden
Ref: www.newkadampatruth.wordpress.com (31.7.2011)

LEICESTER SHIRE

V.I.P. 1945/6
Vade in Pacem ... colony of ex-servicemen set up by Leonard Cheshire.
Location: near Market Harborough
Ref: *Cheshire VC: The story of war and Peace.*

BITTERSWELL 1945/6
Co-operative for returning soldiers set up by craftsman Michael Murray who had been born at Whiteway Colony and apprenticed at both Eric Gill's communities at Piggots and Ditchling.
Location: Bitterswell
Ref: R Braddon *Cheshire VC: A Story Of War And Peace*, Companion Book Club, 1956

ELLISTOWN CAMP 1946 -
Post-war squatter camp.
Location: Ellistown
Ref: D Thomas *Villains' Paradise*

BRAUNSTONE PARK CAMP 1946 -
Military units were moved from Braunstone Park to accommodate 'squatter' families.
Location: Leicester
Ref: D Thomas *Villains' Paradise*

DIVINE LIGHT MISSION circa 1970 - 1983
Ashram lived in by 'Premies' or devotees of Guru Maharaj Ji (now Prem Rawat).
Location: 157 Mere Road, Leicester
Ref: www.prem-rawat-bio.org (31.7.2011)

EVOLUTIONARY VILLAGE circa 1976/7
Proposal by Konrad Smigielski — former Leicester City planner — and the Building and Social Housing Foundation for a new village in the grounds of Stanford Hall.
Ref: *Undercurrents* 19 (Dec 1976); *In the Making 5*

GLEN PARVA THERAPEUTIC COMMUNITY 1979 -
Therapeutic Community in HM Young Offenders Institution.
Location: Glen Parva
Ref: *Therapeutic Communities: Past Present & Future*

SOME PEOPLE IN LEICESTER 1979 - present
Urban group with two levels of membership; core residential group and looser network of people co-operating on different levels. Ran wholefood shop, electricians co-op, Rusty Car Pool and income sharing scheme. In part inspired by one member's stay at People in Common. Had a number of houses in the Highfields area. Later became part of Radical Routes network.
Location: Evington Road and Bartholomew Street, Leicester
Ref: *D&D 91-92*; www.corani.org (20.10.11)

COUNTESTHORPE COMMUNE   circa 1981

Small group of women planning commune "...
want members ... to be interested in or have
experience of personal growth/therapy/co-
counselling/Rajneesh."
Location: Countesthorpe
Ref: *Communes Network* 56

POLEBROOK PROJECT   circa 1984/5

Attempt to set up large scale communal project
for 150+ people. Looked at Polebrook House,
former industrial school and children's home with
60 acres of good farmland. Planned to set up
different co-ops; farming, woodwork etc, and
a free school. Site bought by developers for
retirement village.
Location: Desford
Ref: *Communes Network* 85; *Communes Network
Directory* 1985

GARTREE THERAPEUTIC COMMUNITY 1993

Therapeutic Community at Gartree Maximum
security prison with 23 places for Category B
lifers.
Location: near Market Harborough
Ref: *Therapeutic Communities Past Present & Future*

LINCOLN SHIRE

CPFLU LAND UNITS   1940 - 1946

Christian Pacifist land-based units organised for
conscientious objectors.
Location: Lissington; Chambers Farm; Bardney
Forest, Hatton Sykes; Willingham Forest, Market
Rasen
Ref: M Maclachlan *CPLFU*

LAURELS FARM   1941 - 1948

Wartime pacifist land settlement set up under
the auspices of the Community Land Training
Association. (CLTA) Also a CPFLU unit site
Location: Holton-Cum-Beckering.
Ref: J Makin *Pacifist Farming Communities*

HOLTON GRANGE   1941 - 1947

Neighbouring farm to Laurels farm bought by
supporter and let rent-free to the CLTA.
Location: Holton-Cum-Beckering.
Ref: J Makin *Pacifist Farming Communities*

COLLOW ABBEY FARM   1940 - 46/7

Lincolnshire Farm Training Scheme (LFTS) set up
by Peace Pledge Union to train conscientious
objectors.
Location: Collow Abbey Farm, East Torrington
Ref: *Community in a Changing World*; J Makin
Pacifist Farming Communities

BLEASBY GRANGE   1941 - 1946/7

Second farm bought by the LFTS used as base with
Collow Abbey becoming sleeping quarters.
Location: Legsby, Market Rasen
Ref: *Community in a Changing World*; J Makin
Pacifist Farming Communities

HOLTON RECTORY/GLEBE   1943 - 1947

House and Ivy Lodge Farm bought by a 'Splinter
group' from Bleasby Grange after one of them
inherited some money.
Location: Holton-Cum-Beckering.
Ref: J Makin *Pacifist Farming Communities*

MID FARM   1942 - ?

Farm rented by CLTA as extra accommodation.
Location: Lissington
Ref: J Makin *Pacifist Farming Communities*

HOLTON HALL   1943 - 1947

Bought by the Community Farming Association
(formerly the CLTA) from the army for
accomadation for single men. In the evenings
the men met for music, singing and play reading
inviting local people to come and join in or watch.
This group evolved into the Holton Players who
after the war converted an abandoned nissen hut
into a theatre. This was burnt down in 1960 after
which The Players continued to meet in the drawing
room of Holton Hall finally moving to the Methodist
Chapel at Wickenby in 1970 and changing their
name to the Lindsey Rural Players. One of the
prime-movers of the theatre was Roy Broadbent,
father of the current president actor Jim Broadbent.
Location: Holton-Cum-Beckering.
Ref: J Makin *Pacifist Farming Communities*;
www.broadbent.org (10.4.2011)

SCUNTHORPE SQUATTERS CAMP   1946

First recorded instance of a post-war squat in
officers' mess of an unoccupied anti-aircraft camp
Location: Outside Scunthorpe – exact location
unknown
Ref: Colin Ward *The hidden history of housing*

SANDTOFT SQUATTERS CAMP circa 1946

"Twenty families of squatters have moved into the RAF Station at Sandtoft, and occupied huts on a dispersal site ... The site which the squatters have taken over has a guardroom close by, but this has been closed down. No attempt has been made by the RAF To move the squatters who are families from Thorne and Moorends, and have already christened their new community 'The New Village.' The men are nearly all colliers and cycle daily to and from their work at Thorne Pit some eight miles away." Article in the Epworth Bell's. 23.8.46
Location: Sandtoft
Ref: www.pwilmot.freeserve.co.uk (23.12.08)

GRIMSBY SQUATTER CAMP 1946 -
Squatter camp on military site support by local council who reconnected water and electric.
Location: Grimsby
Ref: D Thomas *Villains' Paradise*

BELTON PARK CAMP 1946 -
The RAF Regiment was moved from Belton Park to make way for housing 'squatter' families.
Location: Grantham
Ref: D Thomas *Villains' Paradise*

ACACIA HALL circa 1960's -
Therapeutic Community for children.
Location: Friesthorpe, Lincoln
Ref: www.tc-of.org.uk (2.8.2011)

NEW LIFE FOUNDATION mid 1960's
Two houses run by Interdenominational Christian ministry set up to reach and help drug addicts.
Location: The Red House, Kelham, Newark
Ref: *Basic Communities*

PURELAND circa 1973 -
Meditation centre set up by Buddha Maitreya.
Location: North Clifton near Newark
Ref: *Alternative Communities* 3rd ed

OLD FARMHOUSE circa 1983
Proposed Wimin's Peace Farm.
Location: Old Church Lane, Great Steeping.
Ref: *Communes Network Directory* 1983

TRUE VILLAGE ASSOCIATION circa 1983
Group listed with 'partial entry' in Teachers Directory.
Location: 71 Waterloo Street, Lincoln
Ref: *Alternative Communities* 4th ed

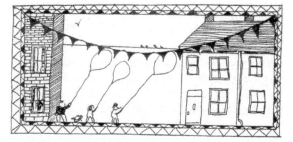

LONDON

WATERLOW COURT 1909 - 1960's
50 flats arranged as a cloistered quadrangle designed by M H Baille Scott as a women's home for the Improved Industrial Dwellings Company. Run on Co-op Housekeeping lines until 1960's.
Location: Hampstead Garden Suburb
Ref: L F Pearson *The Architectural & Social History of Co-operative Living*

THE GRAIL COMMUNITY 1932 -
Community of Catholic women living in large rambling house involved in craft work, social work and publishing.
Location: 125 Waxwell Lane, Pinner
Ref: *Directory of Communes* 1972; *Alternative London; Communes Europe*

HINDUSTAN COMMUNITY HOUSE circa 1938
Project to try to meet needs of East End Indian immigrants. *"The household welcomes Buddhists, Christians, Hindus, Jews, Muslims and Sikhs."*
Location: 5 Rupert Street, Aldgate, E1
Ref: *Community in Britain* 1940

TIMBER HOMES COMMUNITY late 1930's
Proposal to by architecture students to establish a residential community of self-build timber houses.
Location: "Outskirts of London"
Ref: G Ineson *Community Journey*

PACIFIST COMMUNITY circa 1939 - 1945
Writer Denys Val Baker was secretary of this group.
Location: Camden Town
Ref: Denys Val Baker *The More We are Together*

MILL HILL 1940 - 1946
Early Therapeutic Community set up in military psychiatric hospital by Maxwell Jones. Part of the Maudsley Hospital evacuated to Mill Hill.
Location: The Ridgeway, Mill Hill, NW7
Ref: *Psychiatric Quarterly*, Vol 75, No 3 (2004)

COMMUNITY OF THE WAY
circa 1940

Group carrying out an experiment in *"Christian love, community, brotherhood and adventurous giving and sharing."* Made handspun and handwoven woollen goods to 'Old English Designs'.
Location: 22 Raverley Street, Bow, E3
Ref: *Community in Britain* 1940

CHRISTIAN PACIFIST
COMMUNITY
circa 1940

Group running community shop selling *"all kinds of jumble"*. Gave shelter to unemployed pacifists.
Location: 95 Leighton Road, NW5
Ref: Ad in *Peace News* 19.1.40

KINGSWAY HALL
1940 - 1946

West London Mission of the Methodist Church where Donald Soper was minister, used as headquarters for the CPLFU and as base for the Kingsway service unit.
Location: 75 Kingsway, London, WC2.
Ref: M Maclachlan *CPLFU*

PACIFIST SERVICE UNIT
circa 1940

Unit operated by members of the Fellowship of Reconciliation and the Peace Pledge Union carried out various activities including fire-watching at hospitals and community centres, mobile canteen to air raid shelters and an advice service for bombed out families.
Location: Glenhouse Road, SE7
Ref: *Valiant for Peace*

A COMMUNITY FOR ARCHITECTS circa 1940
Proposal to set up a communal living group practice inspired by Frank Lloyd Wright.
Location: c/o 16 Abbey Road, Herne Hill
Ref: *Community in Britain* 1940

MENNONITE HOUSE
1940 - 1945

Large house used by North American Mennonite relief workers during WWII, distributed food, clothing and blankets. At the end of the war the relief workers moved to the continent.
Location: 80 Shepherds Hill, Highgate
Ref: www.menno.org.uk (27.2.2011); *Anabaptism Today* Issue 32 Feb 2003

ONSLOW SQUARE
1941 - 1942

House of Primrose Cordington with almost an acre of ground from where a group of J G Bennett's pupils grew veg and kept chickens in bombed out gardens.

Location: Exact location unknown
Ref: *Madame Blavatsky's Baboon*

PACIFIST COMMUNITY
circa 1941

Small income pooling group advertising for women to join to assist with social work.
Location: 17 Wellesley Road, Chiswick
Ref: Ad in *Peace News* 14.2.41

WEST LONDON SOCIAL SERVICE
COMMUNITY
circa 1941

Small income pooling community with large house - local gardens taken over for cultivation. *"Surplus money and energy devoted to social and cultural service."*
Location: 39 Blenheim Road, W4
Ref: *Peace News Community Supplement* 25.4.41

MICHAEL HOUSE
circa 1941 - ?

Christian Community. Also had country house at Steanbridge, Slad near Stroud.
Location: North West London
Ref: *Peace News Community Supplement* 25.4.41

CASSEL HOSPITAL
1945 -

Hospital where Tom Main put into practice his thinking about the therapeutic community way of working and it continues to operate a residential therapeutic community within the National Health Service.
Location: Ham, Richmond
Ref: D Kennard *Introduction to Therapeutic Communities*

DUCHESS OF BEDFORD HOUSE
1946

400 homeless families squatted 7-storey block of flats owned by the Prudential Assurance Company who were waiting for it to be handed back to them by the Ministry of Works.
Location: High Street Kensington
Ref: Andrew Friend *The Post War Squatters*

FOUNTAIN COURT
1946

60 homeless families housed in well organised squat.
Location: Pimlico
Ref: Andrew Friend *The Post War Squatters*

IVANHOE HOTEL
1946

Small group squatting 630 room Ivanhoe Hotel.
Location: Bloomsbury
Ref: Andrew Friend *The Post War Squatters*

ABBEY LODGE   1946

Flats occupied by small group of squatters.
Location: Regents Park.
Ref: Andrew Friend *The Post War Squatters*

SOUTHWARK PARK CAMP   1946

29 displaced families squatting huts in Anti-aircraft
battery in Southwark Park.
Location: Southwark
Ref: www.glias.org.uk (24.12.08)

MARLBOROUGH DAY HOSPITAL   1946 - 47

Hospital where Tom Main put into practice his
thinking about therapeutic communities.
Location: Ham, Richmond
Ref: D Kennard *Introduction to Therapeutic
Communities*

ST CELIA'S CHESHIRE HOME   1951

Early Cheshire Home for the disabled.
Location: Bromley
Ref: R Braddon *Cheshire VC: A Story Of War And
Peace*

STRATFORD EAST   1953

Home of Theatre Workshop run by Joan
Littlewood. In early days lived as a commune
sharing the tasks of running a theatre.
Location: Theatre Square, Newham, E15
Ref: www.stratfordeast.com (21.12.2010)

RAVENSWOOD VILLAGE   1953 -

Scheme that grew out of the work of the Jewish
Orphanage society. Established initially as
Ravenswood residential school in a house in
Crowthorne Berkshire purchased by four families
to provide care and education for four 11 year
old boys. This sowed the seeds for the Ravenswood
Village a second house and a farm outside
Crowthorne were purchased in 1958. By 1961
they had acquired a nine houses in Norwood
and 100 children were accommodated in family
homes. The parents founded the Jewish Association
of Parents of Backward Children which later
became known as The Ravenswood Foundation. In
the following years a number of separate services
were set up including Norwood Jewish Adoption
Society. In 1996 a merger created Norwood
Ravenswood, the largest Jewish organisation in
Europe specialising in children and family care.
Location: Norwood
Ref: www.norwood.org.uk (21.12.2010)

LONDON VIHARA   1954 - ?

Buddhist Centre and monastery initially in a small
rented building just behind Harrods.
Location: 10 Ovington Gardens. In 1964 moved
to 5 Heathfield Gardens Chiswick and then to The
Avenue, Chiswick in 1994
Ref: T Shine *Honour Thy Fathers*

MUTUAL HOUSEHOLD ASSOCIATION.
circa 1955

Head office of MHA running co-operative schemes
for retired people in country houses.
Location: 23 Haymarket, SW1
Ref: *An experiment in co-operation*

PACIFIST COMMUNITY   circa 1950's

"A group of us started a small pacifist community
in Tulse Hill, which consisted mainly of people
involved directly or indirectly in "direct action"
against the nuclear bombs/deterrents. From time
to time we also took in people in need and it was
one of these people, a former barge boy living
rough who motivated us to do something with
our pacifist principles. He was very good for us,
asking basic questions which made us think about
our assumptions, and he was also puzzled that
we did not spend more time helping people. The
outcome was that we felt that we should help
troubled children as, if difficulties are not resolved
in childhood, they can lead to conflict in later life."
Cynthia Cross
Location: Tulse Hill
Ref: news.pettarchiv.org.uk (6.11.08)

RICHMOND FELLOWSHIP   1959 - present

"The Richmond Fellowship runs eighteen halfway
houses for people discharged from psychiatric
institutions and for others as a preventive measure
if breakdown seems imminent. Residents age
between 16 and 65 and the average length of
stay is approximately twelve months. Residents
are encouraged to work outside the community of
the house and are helped to cope with whatever
problems they encounter by both the staff and the
residents."
Location: Main contact address: 8 Addison
Road, Kensington. Also had community houses in
Richmond, Manchester, Oxford, Hatfield, Romford,
Purley and Southampton.
Ref: *Directory of Communes* 1972;
Alternative London;
www.richmondfellowship.org.uk (12.2.2011)

THE YELLOW DOOR   circa 1956
A *"sort of pre-hippie Beatnik commune"* called The
Yellow Door next to The Cave café
Location: Waterloo Road
Ref: www.nickelinthemachine.com (21.12.2010)

MAHARISHI HOUSE   1959 - ?
Communal house used as base by Maharishi
Mahesh Yogi when he first arrived in UK.
Location: 2 Prince Albert Road
Ref: J Collin-Smith *Call No Man Master*

THE SWAN GROUP   circa 1959/60
Group that planned to set up a housing
partnership that met in the Swan Pub – the
Community Living Association also came out of
these meetings.
Location: The Swan, Cosmo Place, WC1N
Ref: Private correspondence

HOUSING PARTNERSHIP LTD   1959 - 1961
Group planning to build 11 houses and five flats
as a non-profit housing association.
Location: Wimbledon Park, Inner Park Road,
SW19
Ref: *CLA Memorandum*

THE POLYARCHY   1960 - 1983
Communal house set up by members of earlier
'travelling commune. Also ran Escapade Fancy
dress joke and magic shop in Camden High Street
Location: North London
Ref: *Alternative Communities* 3rd ed

39 NOTTINGHAM PLACE   1960 - 1961
Community Living Association rented house.
Location: 39 Nottingham Place, W1
Ref: Private correspondence

HASLEMERE ROAD COMMUNITY   1960 - 67
Group-house with connections to Braziers Park.
Location: 14 Haslemere Road, N8
Ref: www.braziers.org.uk (12.3.2009)

CROUCH END COMMUNAL HOUSE   circa 1961
Eight people sharing a house as part of *"an
experiment in communal living."* Trying to follow a
psychiatrist's theory *"that people would be happier
and mentally healthier if they could live more
together, instead of seeking privacy."*
Location: Crouch End
Ref: Article in *Woman's Mirror* 22.5.61

'A SMALL COMMUNITY'   early 1960's
Group mentioned by Evelyn Woodcock in tribute
to her husband. *"a second London community,
nearby, was started by John and Ann Murrell and
Gailean Davidson ..."*
Location: 66 Hornsey Rise, N19
Ref: www.braziers.org.uk (12.3.2009)

MAX GLATT CENTRE   1962 - ?
Therapeutic Community within Wormwood Scrubs
Prison.
Location: Du Cane Road, W12
Ref: *Therapeutic Communities Past Present & Future*

LONDON VIHARA   1962 - 1979
Buddhist Centre and monastery
Location: 131 Haverstock Hill
Ref: T Shine *Honour Thy Fathers*

HOUSING ASSOCIATION   circa 1962
*"A Housing Association is in the process of
being formed for the purpose of providing self-
contained, or partially self-contained flats, flatlets
and single rooms by converting existing freehold
property. The area being considered is in or around
NW3 ..."*
Location: c/o 74 Clarence Road, Teddington
Ref: *CLA Bulletin* Jan 1962

FAMILIES BY CHOICE   1963 -
Four Victorian terrace houses knocked together to
create accommodation for a community of about
100 parents and children. Had a combination of
private space and shared communal living areas.
Location: Kew
Ref: www.guardian.co.uk (9.5.09)

KINGSLEY HALL COMMUNITY   1965 - 1970
Radical psychotherapy commune set up by
'anti-psychiatrists: R D Laing, David Cooper and
Joseph Berke in community centre set up in 1928
by two sisters Doris and Muriel Lester. Run by the
Philadelphia Association the idea was to create
a model for non-restraining, non-drug therapies
for seriously affected schizophrenics. Was used
as the set for the film "Gandhi". During the filming
Richard Attenborough and the Kingsley Hall
Action Group raised enough funds to carry out
refurbishment to the centre which reopened in
1985 as a community centre.
Location: Powis Road, E3
Ref: www.kingsleyhall.co.uk (20.10.11)

CND / Jazz Flat
circa 1964

"I soon teamed up with a group of friends who I had met through CND and Colyers Jazz Club to rent a large unfurnished flat in Fulham Road. A mixed bunch we were, Julian and Anne were anarchists as was Roy ... Wyn Gardener was, like Julian, a member of the Committee of 100 ... a hot bed of politics ... Almost certainly our phone was tapped and probably the mail was opened."

Location: 744 Fulham Road, Hammersmith
Ref: www.rainydaygallery.co.uk (21.12.2010)

Camden Hill Community
1965

Small short-lived community set up by Emmanuel Petrakis as part of New Life Movement. Experimented with *"free sexual relationships"* – only lasted three months. Also had a community house at Gypsy Hill SE19.
Location: 15 Camden Hill Road
Ref: *Communes Europe*

Cranley Mansions
circa 1965

Early hippie commune. Residents included Thom Keyes, Johnny Byrne, Spike Hawkins, Jenny Fabian and Brian Patten. *"There was an otter that lived in one of the bath tubs."*
Location: Gloucester Road, SW7
Ref: *Days in the Life*

Lee Abbey
1964 - present

Started as a *"home from home"* for students studying in London. Housing up to 150 students from many ethnic backgrounds run by a Christian Community of some 40 people.
Location: 26-27 Courtfield Gardens.
Ref: www.leeabbeylondon.com (29.1.2011)

Square Pigeon Community
1965 - 71

Group of Cambridge graduates sharing a house. *"All of them were working at outside jobs, and most of them were architects or designers."*
Location: 128 Westminster Bridge Road, Lambeth
Ref: *Making Communes; People Together*

The Process
1965 - early 1970's

London base of group that started off as an offshoot of Scientology and developed into a quasi Christian cult. Produced their own magazine that was sold on the streets of 'swinging London'. Spent a short time in Mexico before relocating to the USA.
Location: 2 Balfour Place
Ref: *Alternative London; Love Sex Fear & Death*

The Kingsway Community
1965 -

Series of Christian communal households started by David and Monica Horn. *"... we intend to create a society, moved and sustained by the example of Christ, in which we deal with each other as brothers and sisters ..."*
Location: Chiswick, Hackney (and Devon?)
Ref: The Community Voice; *Directory of Communes 1972; Alternative London; Communes Europe*

Centre Nucleus / Centre House
1966 – ?

Residential community cum mediation centre set up by Christopher Hills as base for various projects. The six-storey building housed kitchen, dining and laundry, admin and research offices. A large meeting and seminar room. With the top three floors used as a 'Residential Section'.
Location: 10a Airlie Gardens, W8
Ref: *Directory of Communes 1972; Alternative London; Communes Europe;* Andrew Rigby *Alternative Realities*

Pace Developments
mid 1960's

Seven brick, concrete and glass-walled houses on the edge of Blackheath designed by architect Royston Summers and 'self-built' by six families. Inc: Writer Michael Frayn who used the experience as the basis of his 1984 play Benefactors. *"We all had children, we were living in flats and we had no money ... so the only way to afford more space was to do it ourselves. One of the group was the architect, one the solicitor, another the builder. I didn't really offer any professional contribution. It took about four years, because every time there was a credit squeeze the bank would pull the loan in and work stopped. There was an idealistic element in that we wanted a shared garden particularly for the children. But living like that can be difficult."*
Location: Blackheath
Ref: www.guardian.co.uk (21.10.11)

Hyde Park Diggers
circa 1967

Name given to 'several hundred' young people who would gather at Hyde Park Corner every sunday to *"... sit, talk and play guitars."* Were given access to St Martins secondary school rent-free by Salvation Army to use as community centre. A sort of inner group known as the Tribe of the Sun was led by Sid Rawle.
Location: Various central London
Ref: *People Together*

NW4 — 1967 - ?

Group living in large suburban house. "*Decisions are reached through talking and finding out feelings. It isn't possible for something to happen if someone feels strongly that it shouldn't. Somehow this strength of emotion is communicated without stress. Talking and soul-searching, always with regard to the idiosyncrasies of others. We share very little in common other than a desire to make personal relationships ... Some of us are single, some are coupled with other inmates, some with people from outside, one married couple (now separated), with two girls of 9 and 10½ years ... We don't want our address commonly known because we have found through experience that a continual stream of crashers who have no commitment to the house can be destructive in certain circumstances. There is nearly always someone going through a paranoid or isolation scene*"

Location: NW4?
Ref: *Directory of Communes* 1970;
Communes Europe

MONTAGUE ROAD — late 1960's

Communal household.
Location: 12 Montague Road, Hackney
Ref: S Rowbotham *Promise of a Dream*

EXPLODING GALAXY — late 1960's - 1972

Communal flat that was home to London's love-anarchist dance company run by David Medella. "*Last Sunday, they gave a performance which must constitute London's most liberated theatrical performance in history. Unfortunately it is impossible to describe the performance without endangering the Galaxy, but let it suffice to say that never have so many been so nude so early and for such good reasons.*" Later became Kinetic/Mixed Media Performance group — Transmedia Exploration with Derek Jarman, John Dugger, Hermine Demoriane, Edward Pope and others.
Location: 99 Balls Pond Road and Islington Park St
Ref: *Directory of Communes* 1972

ASHRAM COMMUNITY HOUSE — 1967 - ?

One of a network of Christian Community households (others in Rochdale, Middlesborough and Sheffield) Aiming to "*discover new implications of the way of Jesus for today's world ... through a contemporary Christian life-style.*"
Location: 36 Key House, Bowling Green Street
Ref: *Basic Communities*

(SOUTH LONDON GROUP) — 1967 - 70

Group listed anonymously in first issue of *Alternative London*. "*A group of five girls, five men (mainly couples) ... we have a place to live, friendship, eating, books, some clothes and records in common.*"
Ref: *Alternative London* 1970

SARUM HOUSE — 1968 -

First FWBO community by 1972 had 11 members.
Location: 3 Plough Lane, Purley
Ref: *Directory of Communes* 1972; British Buddhism

SIMON COMMUNITY — circa 1968

"*... addiction unit which is very sympathetic to junkies.*"
Location: 154, Malden Road, NW5
Ref: Ad in *International Times* 29 (Apr May 1968)

TRIBE OF THE SACRED MUSHROOM — circa 1968

Original 'pad' of England's "*first hippie rural commune*". They decided that the city "*wasn't conducive to community living*" and moved to Wales.
Location: Notting Hill
Ref: *International Times* 25 (Feb 1968)

ST JOSEPH'S HOUSE — circa 1968

"*... part of the Simon Community this offers hospitality to the homeless and restless.*"
Location: 129 Malden Road, NW5
Ref: Ad in *International Times* 45 (Nov Dec 1968)

INTERACTION — 1968 - ?

Umbrella organisation covering wide range of community and self-help projects including City Farm, fun Art Bus, Professor Dogg's Theatre Troupe, community film and video projects and the Almost Free Theatre — lunchtime plays where the audience paid what they could afford. Set up by social entrepreneur Ed Berman. In the 1970's architect Cedric Price designed an innovative home for the group in Kentish Town based on ideas he had developed for a Fun Palace for Joan Littlewood's Theatre Workshop that was never built, but did inspired Richard Rogers and Renzo Piano's Centre Georges Pompidou in Paris. The InterAction Centre was made up of a variety of modular elements such as shipping containers that could be slid in and out of

place as needed. Later moved to Hampstead Town Hall. Also had 'country' outreach in Milton Keynes.
Location: 15 Wilkin Street, NW5
Ref: *People Together;*
Alternative Communities 4th ed

CINEMA ACTION   1968 - 1986?
Left-wing film collective whose core members lived together as a commune in its early years. Produced such films as: *Not a Penny on the Rents, Arise Ye Workers* and *The Miners' Film.* Later made films for Channel 4.
Location: Exact location unknown
Ref: www.screenonline.org.uk (5.2.2011)

DPR   1968 - 1973
Communal house run on co-operative lines, although two members actually owned the property. Broke up when – after house price increases – the 'owners' sold up.
Location: 127 Dartmouth Park Road NW5
Ref: *Legal Frameworks Handbook*

'MIXED COMMUNITY'   circa 1969
"Mixed community starting in beautiful house by river – few minutes Putney tube ..."
Ref: Ad in *International Times* 66 (Oct 1969)

'LARGE COLLECTIVE HOUSE'   circa 1969
"A large house collectively rented by people Interested In non-violent revolution. Potential for idea development and action, as well as a cheap roof. No queers or freeloaders."
Ref: Ad in *International Times* 52 (March 1969)

RADHA KRISHNA TEMPLE   1969 - 1979
Hare Krishna London Base set up with the help of George Harrison. In 1979 the Temple moved to Soho Street.
Location: 7 Bury Place, WC1
Ref: *People Together;*
Alternative Communities 2nd ed

'AND' COMMUNE   circa 1969
"CRICKLEWOOD may soon be on the map, if and when the members of the 'AND' Commune successfully negotiate their intended house purchase. The first issue of their 'AND' poetry magazine will be on sale soon ..."
Location: Cricklewood.
Ref: Ad in *International Times* 55 (Apr 25th 1969)

GENESIS HALL   1969
Large Squat involving the London Street Commune, Diggers groups and Hells Angels. Various ideas were put forward for its use; as an Arts Lab, accommodation for homeless young people and a libertarian Digger commune. Came to an end when it was raided by the police.
Location: 78 Drury Lane, the former Bell Hotel
Ref: *International Times* 53

AGIT PROP   circa 1969
Anarchist Bookshop and commune – raided during Angry Brigade arrests. Later taken over by GLF members.
Location: Bethnal Green Road
Ref: Gordon Carr *The Angry Brigade*

BLACKHEATH COMMUNE   1969 - ?
Group with eight regular members who *"Aimed to establish a Christian yet open community to be a base for radical political activity in the surrounding neighbourhood."* Grew out of the Student Christian Movement
Location: Blackheath Rise
Ref: *Communes Europe;*
Directory of Christian Communities & Groups 1980;
Directory of Communes 1970

BROMLEY ARTS COMMUNE   circa 1969
"ANYONE INTERESTED In helping to start a Bromley Arts Commune ... Advice, encouragement and help in finding premises urgently needed."
Location: Bromley?
Ref: Ad in International Times 69 (Dec 1969)

STAMFORD HILL   circa 1969
Group heavily involved in the squatting movement. Included Jim Greenfield and Anna Mendelson who would be convicted of conspiracy in the Angry Brigade trial.
Location: 168 Stamford Hill
Ref: Gordon Carr *The Angry Brigade*

'SAFEHOUSE' COMMUNE   late 1960's
Safehouse for American 'draft dodgers' during the Vietnam war run by Harry Pincus and Clancy Sigal who had been 'barefoot doctors' at Kingsley Hall.
Location: 56 Queen Anne Street
Ref: London Review of Books 9.10.2008

PLACES

THE BLACK HOUSE   1969 - 1971
Communal project set up by Michael X under the
banner of the Racial Adjustment Action Society
(RAAS). Had grand plans for a supermarket, a
clothing store, a restaurant and a cultural centre
run by black people for black people. Functioned
more as a crashpad and youth centre. Planning
permission was refused for the other parts of the
plan. Came to a somewhat chaotic end.
Location: 95-101 Holloway Road, Islington
Ref: *International Times* 88 (Sep Oct 1970);
A life in Black and White

GROSVENOR AVE COMMUNE   circa 1969 - ?
Squatted large four-storey house base for various
radical activists. Had printing press in basement.
Was involved in womens movement activities.
Came under suspicion during the police harassment
of counter-culture communes and squats during the
Angry Brigade bombings. Later was part of the
Wild Children Network.
Location: 29 Grosvenor Avenue, Islington
Ref: Stuart Christie *Edward Heath made me Angry*

LONDON STREET COMMUNE   circa 1969-71
Group of homeless young people who lived in a
series of squats in abandoned buildings around
Soho and Covent Garden. Consisted of young
mothers who did not want to be separated from
their babies, young addicts who could not find
work, or young working class boys just come
down from the North. In 1970 they issued a
Street Peoples manifesto, exposing landlords who
left perfectly good buildings empty to force up
prices and make a larger profit, and expressed a
desire for total revolution to end capitalism. Later
involved squatting 144 Piccadilly.
Location: Soho, Covent Garden and elsewhere
Ref: Making Communes; International Times 112
(Sep 1971)

HIPPYDILLY   Sep 1969
Squat of large property on corner of Hyde Park
that attracted much media attention.
Location: 144 Piccadilly
Ref: www.wussu.com/squatting/144_piccadilly.htm
(16.9.12)

BROOMHILLS   circa 1970's
Therapeutic community managed by Bexley health
authority in the grounds of Bexley hospital.
Location: Bexley
Ref: yourdemocracy.newstatesman.com (3.6.2011)

AMHURST ROAD COMMUNE   1970?
'Angry Brigade commune' – two couples wanted
for cheque fraud who were living in the top floor
flat were arrested and charged with some of the
bombings that had been taking place in the late
60's. The Stoke Newington Four plus four other
libertarian and anarchist activists entered the
dock at the Old Bailey for what proved to be the
longest criminal trial in Britain.
Location: Amhurst Road, Stoke Newington
Ref: Gordon Carr *The Angry Brigade*

DIVINE LIGHT MISSION   circa 1970 - 1983
Ashrams lived in by Divine Light devotees.
Location: 206 Acre Lane, Brixton;
5 College Mansions, Winchester Avenue, Kilburn;
5 The Avenue, Muswell Hill
Ref: www.prem-rawat-bio.org (31.7.2011)

PNP HOUSE   circa 1970 - 1973?
'Sanctuary' house provide for People Not
Psychiatry by the Situationist Housing Association.
Location: 18 Russell Gardens Mews, W14
Ref: *Directory of Communes* 1972;
Communes Europe

NASHERIF COMMUNE   1970 - ?
Group set up after 2 members inherited house. "*...* We
*are subdivided into three couples and three individual
males. Ages range from 20 to 27, three women, six
men, no children (yet) but one dog and six cats. Finances
on a very ad hoc basis ... we do not welcome visitors.*"
Location: Exact location unknown
Ref: *Directory of Communes* 1972;
Communes Europe

SACRED SEED COMMUNE   circa 1970?
*"Ideas for a free shop may be put into practice in
the near future, but we will be much in need of help*

by way of unwanted books, clothes, records, etc. We will probably start by using a garage in W11/W2 area. If anyone has any ideas or any help they can give with suitable premises."
Location: 50a Princedale Road, WI
Ref: Ad in *International Times* 90 (Oct Nov 1970)

DRAGON HOUSING CO-OP   1970's - 1990's
Attempt by some members of DPR to set up a communal house *"that nobody would own"*. There were two 'nominal' owners and a housing co-op was set up, but the house suffered from squatters moving in and never got fully refurbished. Two members (inc. one of the 'owners') left and went to set up Laurieston Hall. The co-op continued renting the house from the 'owners' until after dry rot was found the house was wound up and sold after a lengthy legal battle – the co-op moved into some short-life housing offered by Islington Council. Also known as Junction Housing Association.
Location: 37 Bickerton Road, N19
Ref: *Legal Frameworks Handbook*

CLEARWATER PRODUCTIONS   circa 1970
A management company/commune operating out of a Notting Hill bedsit. *"a clearing house for stoned-out musicians"*. Among them were Silver Hawkwind who were *"training to become fully qualified space cadets"*.
Location: Notting Hill
Ref: www.kissingspell.com (9.5.09)

ISLINGTON COMMUNITY HOUSE 1970 - 1984
Small Roman Catholic group, six adults and two children living communally *"... in order more effectively to carry out their everyday work."*
Location: 157 Copenhagen Street, N1
Ref: J Mercer *Communes; Basic Communities*

GURU RAM DAS ASHRAM   circa 1970's
Sikh Ashram run by the 3HO Foundation.
Location: 22 All Saint Road, W11
Ref: *The Many Ways of Being*

COMMUNITY HOUSE   circa 1970 -
"... terraced house in West London inhabited by five girls and five men in their twenties who stay from six months to three years. All have full-time jobs and give a percentage of their earnings to the Community. They are all committed Christians, meeting for prayer and discussion at the beginning and end of each day. There is no leader: each takes turn to be chairman of the month. The community

runs childrens' playgroups, old peoples' clubs and youth clubs locally."
Location: West London
Ref: *Alternative London* 1970

HARAMBEE PROJECT   circa 1970
Project set up by Antigua born builder Brother Herman (Edwards) to help young black people who had missed out on education, got in trouble, or faced unemployment. Harambee is Swahili for *"pulling together"* Worked helping those who had been in trouble with the police or been released from prison or remand centres with nowhere to go. One of the earliest Afro-Caribbean community projects aimed at the rehabilitation and support of its young people.
Location: Holloway Road, Islington
Ref: www.irr.org.uk (21.12.2010)

SOMALI ROAD COMMUNE   circa 1970
A 'sort of commune' where various members of the folk revival could be found hanging out including any or all of the following: the Young Tradition, Davey Graham, Louis Killen, Bert Jansch, John Renbourn, Donovan Leitch, Val Berry or Anne Briggs. *"... the house in Somali Road was acting as a mixing pot, a forcing house for the hybrid that was later to find its flowering in electric folk."*
Location: Somali Road, Hampstead
Ref: www.karldallas.com (21.12.2010)

MESSENGER HOUSE TRUST   1970 - 1987
Accommodation for single young mothers and their babies set up by Dr Lomax-Simpson to help them establish bonding in a stable environment prior to being re-housed in society. Project grew from having a single house to having at one time nine houses.
Location: 17 Malcolm Road, London, SW19
Ref: archive.pettrust.org.uk (20.8.11);
Peace News 23.1.73

PYE BARN TRUST   circa 1970 - 1984
Therapeutic Community
Location: 16 The Chase, Clapham Common, SW4
Ref: *Directory of Christian Cmnties & Groups* 1980

SYRINX CO-OP HOUSING ASS.   circa 1970 -
Non-profit company whose aim was to house members *"with tastes and temperaments sufficiently in common to benefit from a degree of sharing some aspects of living."*
Location: North London
Ref: *Alternative London* 1970

CHAPEL OF ISIS COMMUNE   1970 - ?
Trans Sex Trip. Five members brought together by a common interest in transvestism and trans-sexual freedom *"... not fixed in a strict male or female sex or work role ... within the commune structure everything is shared, including clothes, car and food. They practice a loose form of group marriage ... they prefer not to hold meetings or make decisions, but to let matters work themselves out."*
Location: Exact location unknown
Ref: *Directory of Communes* 1972;
Making Communes

SHAFTESBURY AVENUE   circa 1970
Communal flat over the Shaftesbury Theatre occupied by members of the Deviants rock band whilst Hair was showing in the theatre.
Location: Flat above 210 Shaftesbury Avenue
Ref: *Days in a Life*

LAMBETH COMMUNE   circa 1970
Group listed in Communes Journal.
Location: 23 Newport Street, London SE11
Ref: *Communes Journal* 35 (Dec 1970)

'MUSWELL HILLBILLIES'   1970 - 72
"... in 1970 when I was a physics student at Imperial College. London University. I met a group of people gathered around a space age box that emitted strange noises. They were the Electronic Music Society, and the box was a synthesizer ... I fell in love with it and the sixties finally caught up with me. I played guitar and twelve-bass accordion and moved into a house in Muswell Hill, London, which became a two-year experiment in communal living, technology and psychedelic sound."
Location: Muswell Hill
Ref: T Pinch, F Trocco *Analog Days: The Invention and Impact of the Moog Synthesizer* 2004

FAMILY EMBRYO   circa 1970 -
Group living together *"sparingly, overcrowded and communally and even happily"* saving to buy a farm *"somewhere in these islands"*.

Location: 21 Drylands Road, London N8
Ref: *Communes Journal* 35 Dec 1970

THE STREET FARMERS   circa 1971/2
Group of architects from the Architectural Association formed as a radical eco response to the technological supremacism of Archigram. Street Farmer, Graham Caine, built a full size experimental 'eco house' on some playing fields in Eltham, where he lived for a year.
Location: Eltham,
Ref: www.stefan-szczelkun.org.uk (31.7.2011);
Mother *Earth News* 20 (March 1973)

GENTLE GHOST COMMUNE   circa 1971 - ?
Group that came together in response to an ad in Time Out seeking people interested in making a communal film of the Bath Festival. After the film had been completed some of the people stayed together. To make a living they advertised, through leaflets and the alternative Press, all the things they could do between them. Gradually they built up a pool of over three hundred skilled and semi-skilled people on their lists. *"... Our ultimate aim is to work together, live together, help people do the things they like doing and generally to improve the quality of life in a sick world."*
Location: 99 Addison Road, Holland Park
Ref: *Making Communes*;
International Times 96 (Jan Feb 1971)

LADBROKE COMMUNITY   circa 1971
Group of young people working in "professional or media jobs" living in large rented house.
Location: Ladbroke Grove
Ref: *Making Communes*

KNIGHTSBRIDGE COMMUNITY   circa 1971
Group mentioned in description of Ladbroke community in *Making Communes* as 'similar group'.
Location: Knightsbridge
Ref: *Making Communes*.

COMMUNITY HOUSE   circa 1971
Christian community of up to ten people who stay for periods six months to three years. *"Using the community as a base, members have attempted in various ways to serve some social needs of the local neighbourhood."*
Location: West London
Ref: *Directory of Communes* 1971

HIGHBURY RENT COMMUNITY   circa 1971
"This is my name for a group of young people occupying flats and bedsitters in a big old house ... who began sharing things. They shared records and record players, clothes, telephone, a car and finally rent."
Location: Highbury Park
Ref: *Making Communes*

SIDCUP COMMUNE   early 1970's
Group mentioned by Clem Gorman.
Location: Sidcup?
Ref: *People Together*

'SMILEY' COMMUNE   early 1970's
Basement flat off Caledonian Road with a 'whack off' size smiley face painted on the door. Home of Bill 'Ubi' Dwyer one of the Windsor Free Festivals organisers
Location: 52 Winford Road
Ref: www.ukrockfestivals.com/UBI-DWYER.htm (31.7.11)

HAMPSTEAD 'COMMUNE'   early 1970's
House full of various musicians run *'on the lines of a hippie commune'*. Included; Soft Machine drummer Robert Wyatt, DJ/concert promoter Jeff Dexter and Singer Linda Lewis. Cat Stevens, Marc Bolan and Elton John were frequent visitors.
Location: Hampstead
Ref: www.newhamstory.com (21.12.2010)

CUMBERLOW COMMUNITY   1970's - 2005
Therapeutic community providing residential care and education for 15-19 year olds.
Location: 24 Chalfont Road, South Norwood Croydon
Ref: www.tc-of.org.uk (2.8.2011)

COLVILLIA   circa 1970 - 1973?
Commune of drag queens and radical feminists in squatted film studio involved with GLF protests including disruption of the Festival of Light in 1971
"The commune was absolutely wonderful, something none of us had experienced before; it was bliss ... We were starting to explore sexism and did it through drag. We weren't pretending to be women — we were men in frocks, working out what it meant to be gay men: no fake breasts. I found people's liberalism went out the window when actually confronted by a man in drag. It was very empowering." Stuart Feather

Location: 42 Colville Terrace and 7a Colville Houses, Powis Square
Ref: Lisa Power *No Bath But Plenty of Bubbles*

PENGE GLF COMMUNE   early 1970's
Gay Liberation Front commune — base for GLF communes group. Mentioned in oral history of GLF.
Location: Exact address unknown
Ref: Lisa Power *No Bath But Plenty of Bubbles*

TULSE HILL GLF COMMUNE   early 1970's
Group mentioned in oral history of GLF.
Location: Athlone Road, Lambeth
Ref: Lisa Power *No Bath But Plenty of Bubbles*

BOUNDS GREEN COMMUNE   early 1970's
Group mentioned in oral history of GLF.
Location: Exact address unknown
Ref: Lisa Power *No Bath But Plenty of Bubbles*

FARADAY ROAD COMMUNE   early 1970's
Group mentioned in oral history of GLF
Location: Exact address unknown
Ref: Lisa Power *No Bath But Plenty of Bubbles*

GROSVENOR AVENUE   early 1970's
Women's Collective mentioned in oral history of GLF.
Location: Grosvenor Avenue
Ref: Lisa Power *No Bath But Plenty of Bubbles*

ST CHARLES HOUSE   early 1970's
Richmond Fellowship halfway house for those recovering from mental health problems.
Location: North Kensington
Ref: *People Together*; www.richmondfellowship.org.uk (21.2.2011)

EAST COMMUNITY   circa 1971 - ?
Group running East End Abbreviated Soapbox Theatre.
Location: 17 Woodford Road, E7
Ref: *Alternative Communities* 3rd ed

Notting Hill Commune   1972
"felt they were less of a commune, more a loose group."
Location: Notting Hill
Ref: *Directory of Communes* 1972; Lisa Power *No Bath But Plenty of Bubbles*

'Womens Commune'   early 1970's
"The members of London's first women's commune in Notting Hill first made contact through a local consciousness raising group. Living together communally was for them a natural development of their collective ideals and the process of selfrealisation. They found a suitable empty house and squatted in it."
Location: Notting Hill
Ref: *People Together*

St Mungos Trust   1970's -
Trust running a house for rough sleepers in Battersea. Expanded during the 1970's opening large hostels in disused buildings and smaller supported houses.
Location: Various
Ref: *People Together*

'Actors Community'   early 1970's
"An actors' community in east London developed a close relationship by repeated weekend party and encounter groups in a Gloucestershire cottage. When they came to live together it wasn't a new experience. They had already had a sort of communal trial marriage."
Location: East London
Ref: *People Together*

Kentish Town Squatter Commune
                                early 1970's
Group mentioned by Clem Gorman in *People Together* as having "... squatted without hassle and succeed fairly well in old terraces."
Location: near Tufnell Park
Ref: *People Together*

The Children of God   1971 - 1976
Christian sect started by David Berg in the USA. Moved headquarters to the UK after they became the target of newly formed anti-cult groups. Had various houses around London and further afield. Believe in the 'Endtime' and that only they would survive. In the mid 70's and 80's used the controversial honey trap technique of 'flirty fishing'

to attract new members and financial supporters. Expanded with communal houses in Europe and worldwide. Were targeted by authorities working with anti-cult groups over allegations of child abuse – none of which have been proven.
Location: 112 Mayall Road, Brixton, SE24; 3 Walterton Road, W9; Hampstead Lane; and Bishops Avenue
Ref: www.one-way.org; *Jesus Bubble*

First of May Commune   early 1970's
Group mentioned by Clem Gorman in *People Together* as living in rented house.
Location: Forest Gate
Ref: *People Together*

81 Thicket Road   1970's
Legal squat run by a group of architectural students as communal house with the agreement of the local council. Group consisted of around ten adults and four children sharing resources, childcare, cooking, and chores. *"They wanted to support each other's growth, experiment with pushing the boundaries taken for granted within conventional relationships, deal with conflicts creatively."*
Location: Penge
Ref: www.growingupinthenewage.org (8.8.2011)

Laurie Park Road   1970's
Communal squat in *"Enormous, decrepit Victorian villa with weed-ridden gardens, a huge wooden staircase, large rooms and a rambling summerhouse."*
Location: Sydenham
Ref: www.marjolaineryley.co.uk (22.7.2011)

Bethnal Rouge   early 1970's
Anarchist Agitprop bookshop/commune taken over by drag queen members of GLF and became a Gay commune. *"Their motivation is as much political as sexual. They do not differentiate between political liberation and the liberation of sexuality. They run a small Left bookshop in the house where they live, and they relate to activities in the local area through community groups, and to the public through the bookshop."*
Location: 248 Bethnal Green Road
Ref: *People Together*

Philadelphia Association   1972 - ?
Set up by some of those who had been involved with R D Laing and David Cooper in the 'anti

psychiatry' movement. Ran half-way houses for
those with mental problems.
Location: 20 Fitzroy Square, WI
Ref: **Directory of Communes** 1972; **Communes
Europe**

CRACKER CO-OP   1972 - ?
Group of mostly students that came together
through *"love and luck and an ad, in Time Out."*
Inspired by the 'Institute for the Study of Non-
violence' set up by Joan Baez in Colorado. Planned
to set up a play centre in the garden, and a
tenants association and claimants union to make
links with the local community *"... we have been (and
will be) using encounter/sensitivity groups to get to
know each other better and sort out group frictions
as they arise. We are all (in varying degrees) into
Yoga, wholefoods, film (we'll build a darkroom in a
cupboard) and street theatre and other arts."*
Location: 33 Tredegar Square, E3
Ref: **Directory of Communes** 1972

EVERYONE INVOLVED   early 1970's
Gay rockband sometimes referred to as being a
'hippie commune', although they planned to they
never actually set one up. Gave away 1,000
copies of their only album.
Ref: www.awakeman.co.uk (21.12.2010)

ARCHWAY CENTRE   1972 -
Disused factory owned by Camden Council used
by the FWBO as a centre for activities.
Location: Blamore Street, Highgate
Ref: **Buddhism for Today; The Triratna story**

JESUS FAMILY   circa 1972
American Christian rock group cum commune who
staged the Lonesome Stone rock musical and
founded the annual Greenbelt Music Festival.
Location: The Living Room, 41 Westow Street,
Upper Norwood, SE19 and 56 Beulah Hill Road,
Upper Norwood
Ref: **Jesus Bubble; Basic Communities**

PSYCHEDELIC COMMUNE   1972
*"We are a psychedelic based commune which at
the moment has rather a sexual imbalance. We
need more chicks at this stage but as we have been
together for some time and a strong collective
consciousness has evolved, anyone joining will not
have an easy time ... We believe in group marriage
and the expanding of the conscious etc and also live*

*on a vegetarian/health food basis. All resources and
knowledge are obviously shared and any commitment
would be expected to be for life. Any chicks
interested please contact us at the address below.
Love and peace. ROGER and THE GANG"*
Location: 86 Sandringham Rd, Hackney Downs, E8
Ref: Letter in International Times 132 (19.6.72)

SHEPHERDS BUSH HOUSE   circa 1972 -
Large ten-bedroom house due to be knocked down
rented by two workers at BIT. Ground floor was
used as a crashpad while upper floors were used
either by BIT workers or *"... those in acute need eg:
destitute and pregnant or something like that."*
Location: Exact address unknown
Ref: **Directory of Communes** 1972; CM Newsletter
1.10.72

RANDOM ASSOCIATION   circa 1972 -
Ten adults and five children for some years.
*"quite ambitious until '79. Then more modest aims
(eg incomes not shared) and changeover of many
original members."*
Location: 51 Buckingham Road, N1
Ref: **Communes Network Directory** 1982;
Alternative Communities 4th ed

TOLMERS VILLAGE   1973 - 1980
Many communal houses amongst the numerous
squats in this area. Students from nearby UCL
joined with squatters and trade unionists in resisting
evictions. Camden Council eventually compulsorily
purchased the site, office space development plans
were abandoned and the area was rebuilt with
council flats. *"An elderly lady commented 'I think the
squatters have introduced the only communal element
we have ever had in this district.'"*
Location: area between Euston Station and
Hampstead Road, NW1
Ref: Nick Wates **The Battle for Tolmers Square**

SOME FRIENDS   1973 - 2011
*"Our community house is large, full of character and
provides us with individual rooms, two bathrooms,
shower, laundry room, television lounge, two large
kitchens and a roof garden. We eat vegetarian/
vegan food and aim to eat communally each
evening, house meetings occur twice a month and
decision-making is by consensus — reflecting our
Quaker origins."*
Location: 128 Bethnal Green Road, E8
Ref: **D&D 90-91**

ROBIN FARQUHARSON HOUSE   1973 - 1976
House run by the Mental Patients Union. Individuals had their own rooms. House was base and office for the MPU.
Location: 37 Mayola Road, Hackney. Also in Derby Road
Ref: www.studymore.org.uk/mpu.htm (10.8.2011)

PUNDARIKA   circa 1973 - 1976
Large building used as temporary centre for future FWBO developments. In the surrounding area a total of nine community houses were set in squatted houses.
Location: Balmore Street, Archway
Ref: *Moving Against the Stream*

PEOPLE NOT PSYCHIATRY   circa 1973
Squatted communal house set up by Jenny James under the banner of People Not Psychiatry. Acted as a London base for the Atlantis commune in Ireland. "Nobody at the commune was allowed to get away with any bullshitting or psychological games; if you didn't like what someone was saying or doing, you said so, loudly, forcefully and at length. if you felt bad, miserable or fearful for any reason you were encouraged to "get into it" and feel worse, so that you would "get to the bottom and come out the other side"."
Location: Villa Road
Ref: *Lefties: Property is Theft* BBC4; **Communes Network** 4

SLEEPING SUN COMMUNE   circa 1973
"BASS PLAYERS! Are you tired of the rock scene? Are groupies getting you down? Well, here is a real fun way to get stoned. Come and play bass for Sleeping Sun, the improvisationally insane commune band. Spacious mattress filled rooms await your tired and weary soul to live and work in harmonious flow. If you think this is your kind of scene ... call us! The Sleeping Sun Commune."
Location: 88 Adeney Road, London W6
Ref: Ad in *International Times* 163 (Sep 1973)

WORD OF GOD COMMUNITY   1973
Anglican group of some ten adults living in three houses aiming "to integrate the concept of the religious life and the covenant community in the service of Church and society."
Location: 74 Elderfield Road, Clapton, E5
Ref: *Basic Communities*; J Mercer **Communes**

EARTH EXCHANGE   circa 1973 - ?
"What we are today has grown from many people's ideas, contributions and enthusiasm. At the start money was short, yet a derelict four floor building was obtained at low rent and rebuilt and slowly established as a craft and wholefood shop Several ideas flourished and wilted before the cafe was started. Crafts were discontinued, being replaced by a book and herb shop and the limited company changed to a collective. During these formative years, those involved had lived in small groups in flats and houses ... We are a group of people who have come together out of a common interest in communal living, vegetarianism, co-operatives and health. We are also interested in self-awareness, ecology, alternative technology, the third world etc. We are developing an alternative lifestyle to mainstream society by working in a non-exploitive collective situation and living together communally. We have no set philosophy but do believe that many of the problems in society, are rooted at the individual level. Living and working together continually reveals and challenges our individualistic attitudes and assumptions and in their place comes more honesty ..."
Location: 213 Archway Road, Highgate
Ref: *Alternative Communities* 3rd ed

BRIDGE   1974 - 1975
Mainly Anglican community house aimed to provide a point of contact between the traditional Church and those 'outside' who shared its concerns.
Location: The Vicarage, Follett Street, E14
Ref: *Basic Communities*; J Mercer **Communes**

THE 101'ERS SQUAT   1974 - ?
Squat where the band the 101'ers was formed and named after. The band were originally called 'El Huaso and The 101 All Stars. They played

regularly at The Charlie Pigdog club and The Elgin on Ladbroke Grove. The band included Joe Strummer who would go on to form the iconic punk band the Clash. Strummer said *"I wouldn't say squatting was a political act, but politics came into it in the sense that it was necessary to know your legal position, your rights as an occupant, standing up to the police, the authorities, getting the electricity connected, etc."*
Location: 101 Walterton Road, Maida Vale
Ref: www.101ers.co.uk (2.4.2001)

CORNWALL TERRACE   circa 1974/5
"These desirable Nash residences, up til four weeks ago mismanaged by the Crown Estates Commissioners, premise to be a thriving example of how the homeless, particularly young and single, can make use of vast empty properties. It is also proof of how well organised the London squatters are that such a large building comprising same 150-200 rooms could be taken so quickly and effectively. Despite all the hustles of setting up home the squatters have still found time to relate with the outside community. They have set up a food kitchen, bulkbuy, and a communal evening meal. Workshops are being set up, and several kinds of yoga meditation and dance are being taught. They have set up their own committee to negotiate with the Crown Commissioners and are playing host to the forthcoming Windsor conference. We hope to print a much longer article in the next Maya as this is certainly a prototype community for many properties at present waiting to be re-cycled."
Location: Cornwall Terrace NW1
Ref: *Maya News* 4 (Feb Mar 1975)

ARBOURS ASSOCIATION   circa 1974 - ?
Radical 'Anti Psychiatry' Association set up by two US psychiatrists who came over to work with R D Laing. Set up a crisis centre and community houses at Norbury and near Tufnell Park.
Location: 55 Dartmouth Park Road, London NW5
Ref: *Maya Free Nation News* Oct Dec 1974

BEGINNING NOW   1974
Community experiment based at residential conference centre belonging to the Diocese of Southwark. Small group formed to discover *"ways in which a traditional conference centre might become a working model of an institution in transition, making decisions about the use of*

facilities and resources appropriate to a world facing ecological and economic crisis." Project fell apart after objections from the Bishop over proposed non-meat diet and *"fear of more wide-ranging inovations."*
Location: Dartmouth House, Dartmouth Row, SE10
Ref: *Basic Communities*

CAMBODIAN EMBASSY SQUAT 1975 - 90?
15 year long squat of Embassy property during Kymer Rouge period. Run as Arts Centre sometimes under the banner of the Guild of Transcultural studies. The Third Ear Band rehearhed here and Poet Harry Fainlight gave a series of lectures/ readings.
Location: 64 Brondesbury Park, NW6
Ref: www.scriptconsultancy.com (21.12.2010)

CHAMBERLAYNE COMMUNE   circa 1975
Commune that started out in a rented flat in kensal Green while negotiating to purchase a house in Kilburn Park. *"... People share some of their lives, but not all."*
Location: Kensal Rise and Kilburn Park
Ref: *People Together*

LANCASTER GATE   1975 - ?
UK headquarters of the Unification Church or Moonies. For a number of years there were a network of communal houses that members lived in going out to sell flowers on the streets to raise money for the church and recruit new members.
Location: 43-44 Lancaster Gate
Ref: D Barrett *The New Believers*

SUFI COMMUNE   mid 1970's
Commune lived in by Richard and Linda Thompson.
Location: Bristol Gardens, Maida Vale
Ref: *Electric Eden*

COMMUNITY   circa 1976
Group of eight or so people living as a commune running a therapy centre.
Location: 15 Highbury Grange, N5
Ref: *The Many Ways of Being*

GOLDEN SPIRAL COMMUNITY   1976/77
Name taken by squatters in large house on corner of 'millionares row' previously occupied by Children of God.
Location: Hampstead Ln and Bishops Ave junction
Ref: Authors personal contact.

THE TEACHERS
1976 -
Base of Teachers group later moved to Bangor
North Wales.
Location: 27 Bloomsbury Close and
1 Charlbury Grove, Ealing
Ref: **Communes Network** 25

AMARAVATI
1977 -
FWBO women's community "Most of the people who
moved into the house had previously been associated
with the Archway Centre a few years earlier and
were well orientated to communal life. After a year
of renovating and decorating, the community have
now got down to Right Livelihood activities. Presently,
the community are involved in their 'Kusa Cushions'
business which is being expanded to accommodate
clothes, upholstery and curtain-making."
Location: 30 Cambridge Park, E11
Ref: **Buddhism in Britain**

L'ARCHE LAMBETH
1977 -
Ecumenical Christian community with five houses for
adults with learning difficulties.
Location: 15 Norwood High Street, SE27
Ref: **D&D 98-99**

BEULAH
1977 -
Small FWBO women's community set up for women
who wished to lead a spiritual life as well as
holding down a full-time job.
Location: 95 Bishops Way, Bethnal Green, E2
Ref: **Buddhism in Britain; Alt Communities** 3rd ed

WHOLE THING COMMUNITY   circa 1978 - 80
Group living above shop running vegi snack bar,
arts and crafts, bookshop and meeting space.
Location: 53 West Ham Lane, E15
Ref: **Alternative Communities** 3rd ed

ENCLAVE EX
circa 1978 - ?
Group living in large Victorian House in Tufnell
Park owned by Dutch musician, painter, astrologist
and author Freya Aswynn. The house had an
Odinic Temple in the basement and the various
residents had connection to 'neo-folk' bands such
as Current 93 and Sol Invictus .
Location: 43 St Georges Avenue, N7
Ref: **Alternative Communities** 4th ed

DOUBLE HELIX
1978 - ?
Housing co-op with four large houses with private
rooms and shared communal space. "Each household

decides autonomously on its own income sharing
and domestic arrangements. We all eat together
every Sunday and we have formal meetings monthly.
We co-operate across the houses on building and
maintenance, sharing skills and various facilities."
Location: Josephine Avenue, SW2
Ref: **D&D 90-91**

LONDON BUDDHIST CENTRE   1978 - present
Former Bethnal Green Fire station converted
by FWBO and opened as the London Buddhist
Centre with meditation and yoga classes. They
also set up a co-operative which involved 'printing,
building and decorating, wholefood distribution
and catering alongside a residential community,
Sukhavati, for 25 men.
Location: 61 Leswin Road
Ref: British Buddhism

THE LEARNERS
circa 1978 - 1983?
"5 bedroomed house, nice garden, fluctuating
enthusiasm for forming some kind of group family.
Feminist/anarchist leanings. Group still young and
small children planned."
Location: 7 St Pauls Road, N17
Ref: **Communes Network Directory** 1982;
Alternative Communities 4th ed

COMMERCIAL ROAD
circa 1978
Communal Squat.
Location: 527 Commercial Road, E1
Ref: **Communes Network** 34

KOLLONTAI
late 1970's
Communal household set up by ex-Laurieston Hall
members.
Location: Tufnell Park Road
Ref: Personal contact

OAK VILLAGE
1979 - 1982?
Group of ten followers of Bhagwan Shree Rajneesh
living in three-bedroom house while working at
Kalptura Meditation Centre in Chalk Farm and
planning to set up a British 'Buddafield' – went on
to set up the Medina commune in Suffolk.
Location: 10 Oak Village, NW3
Ref: A Geraghty **In the Dark and Still Moving;**
T Guest **My Life in Orange; Communes Network** 37

CAUSEWAY COMMUNITY   circa 1979/80
Group looking for "large house with outbuildings
and 2-5 acres of land north of London" to set up

community based on democracy, egalitarianism and polyfidelity.
Location: 201 Wightman Road, North London
Ref: *Alternative Communities* 3rd ed

LONDON EMISSARY CENTRE   circa 1980
Address listed in Teachers directory.
Location: 1 Augustine Road, W14
Ref: *Alternative Communities* 3rd ed

FRIENDS OF THE WESTERN BUDDHISTS COMMUNAL HOUSES   circa 1980
Communal houses across East London set up by members of Buddhist sect.
Location: Arunachala, 29-31 Old Ford E2; Colgonooza, 119 Roman Road, E2; Ratnadvipa 34 Daventry Street NW1; Sukhavati, 51 Roman Road, Bethnal Green E2; Vajrasamanya, 30 Cambridge Park, Wanstead E11; Kalpdruma, 3 St Michaels Road, Croydon
Ref: *In The Making* 5;
Alternative Communities 3rd ed

CINTRA PARK COMMUNITY   circa 1980/84
Four Adults and two children living in large south London house. "... *we are trying to create a supportive living environment for exploring and developing ourselves through therapy and through working with improvised theatre, dance, music, painting and drawing ...*"
Location: 87-95 Lawrie Park Gardens, SE26
Ref: *Alternative Communities* 4th ed;
Communes Network Directory 1982

LAMERS   circa 1980
Polygamous family.
Location: 7 St Pauls Road, N17
Ref: *Alternative Communities* 3rd ed

FAMILY TREE   1980
Small Christian group providing accommodation and care for adults with learning difficulties.
Location: 10 Queensdown Road, Hackney
Ref: *D&D 94-95*

FREE SEXUALITY COMMUNE   circa 1981 - 1984
Group inspired by the Austrian Friedrichshof commune. The group was helped to get on its feet by Norwegian performance artist Wencke Mulheisen. "*What kind of sexual freedom? First of all, freedom from the limitations of the couple relationship. When we started, the group agreed that anyone could enter into sexual relationships with anyone else regardless of existing partner relationships. But sexuality should also be set free internally. One should be free from guilt, fear and jealousy.*" W Mulheisen
Location: Finsbury Park, N4
Ref: *Undercurrents* 48 (Nov 1981)

FEETS TOO BIG   circa 1981 -
Group of eight adults inspired by the Austrian Friedrichschof commune. "*What has interested us the most has been the process of living together and confronting all the emotional and practical questions which stem from this – such as, how can people live together creatively without endless discussions?*"
Location: 201 Wightman Road, N8
Ref: *Alternative Communities* 4th ed

MORNINGTON GROVE   1982 -
Mixed community of 16 people living in two large Victorian houses with a large garden. "*We organise mainly through fortnightly meetings where consensus decisions are made. These are either "business" meetings to discuss issues like rent, food, finances, repairs etc. "Relationship" meetings are very variable meetings. They range from working on relationship difficulties, to a time for people to 'share things'. Each house has meetings to discuss the practicalities of day to day living.*"
Location: 13/14 Mornington Grove, Bow, E3
Ref: *D&D 90-91*

GREEN KITE   circa 1982 -
Group of single parents looking for property
Location: c/o Gypsy Hill, SE10
Ref: *Communes Network Directory* 1982

BRIDGE AVENUE COMMUNITY   circa 1983 -
Group "*orientated towards natural healing*" looking for members and buildings with land.
Location: 11 Bridge Avenue, W6
Ref: *Alternative Communities* 4th ed

VEGAN COMMUNE   circa 1983 -
Group listed with 'partial entry' in Teachers directory.
Location: 12 Wray Cresent, Finsbury Park, N4
Ref: *Alternative Communities* 4th ed

GUILDFORD ROAD COMMUNITY circa 1983 -
"Small community looking for new member to focus on children within the community, involving non-conventional hours and the possibility of psychosynthesis training."
Location: 50 Guildford Road, SW8
Ref: ***Alternative Communities*** 4th ed

THE GRAIGIAN ORDER   1983 - ?
The 'first New Age monastic community' consisted of three 'green monks' who produced a seasonal newsletter which circulated to 200 lay members of the Graigian Society. Also had small cottage in North Wales. House had a meeting room, dark room, studios, a shrine room and a pottery in the garden. Went in to decline after founder, Anelog, died.
Location: 10 Lady Somerset Road, Kentish Town
Ref: ***D&D 92-93***

COMMUNITY OF ST PETER   1983 - ?
Redundant church and vicarage run as ecumenical centre of prayer and an experiment in urban monasticism by monks from Worth Abbey near Crawley. In 1990 the monks handed over to a lay community following a Benedictine lifestyle.
Location: 522 Lordship Lane, East Dulwich.
Ref: ***D&D 96-97***

ASHRAM COMMUNITY HOUSE   circa 1984
Group listed in back of Communes book.
Location: 36 Key House, Bowling Green St, SE11
Ref: J Mercer **Communes**

CATH-CO   circa 1984
Group listed in back of Communes book.
Location:14 Littles Road, NW3
Ref: J Mercer **Communes**

FOCOLARE HOUSE   circa 1984
Christian house part of Italian based movement.
Location: 57 Twyford Avenue, W3
Ref: J Mercer **Communes**

SIMON COMMUNITY   circa 1984
Community house for the homeless.
Location: Challenge Hse,118 Grove Green Rd, E11
Ref: J Mercer **Communes**

SERVANTS OF CHRIST THE KING circa 1984
Group listed in back of Communes book.
Location: 16 Coppice Walk, N20
Ref: J Mercer **Communes**

CLAYS LANE HOUSING CO-OP   1984 - 2007
Co-op with 107 houses arranged around courtyards, 57 purpose built as shared houses. Entire estate was later subject of compulsory purchase order and all 430 residents were issued with orders to leave. Buildings were demolished to make way for 2012 Olympic Park.
Location: Clays Lane, Stratford
Ref: ***D&D 00-01***

RITHERDON ROAD   1987 - ?
Group of seven gay men living communally. Were inspired by Wild Lavender in Leeds. *"Our intention is to provide mutual support for ourselves in a caring environment and to reach out to the brotherhood of gay men around us."*
Location: 37 Ritherdon Road, Tooting Bec
Ref: ***D&D 92-93***

DOLE HOUSE CREW   1990's
Large squat in disused DHSS building. Squatters adopted the name Dole House Crew and held impromptu parties on the ground floor of the building whilst living on the upper floor.
Location: Peckham High Street
Ref: www.the-halls.org.uk (22.12.2008)

NEW AGE TRUST   circa 1990
Charity involved in *"development of small scale village community lifestyles."*
Location: Maitland Park Villas, NW3
Ref: *D&D 90-91*

MARLOWE HOUSE   1990's
Around 350 Spaniards, Italians, French, Polish, Japanese and English squatters occupying 93 flats in two tower blocks due for demolition. A Polish website even advertised for people to come to the blocks.
Location: Lewisham
Ref: "My place or yours?" in **The Independent** (3.2.2005)

NEW CHRISTIAN COMMUNITY   1996
Proposal to set up a new Christian community in a large empty house owned by Notting Hill Methodist Church and Ecumenical Society.
Location: North Kensington
Ref: *Christian Community 75*

LIVING GREEN
1996

Group who met regularly in central London to plan the development of a spiritually focussed, environmentally sustainable village. *"We aim to buy land in a rural area and develop accommodation for a residential group of between 100 and 150 people."*
Location: c/o address in NW1
Ref: *D&D 96-97*

MIDDLESEX

POTTERS BAR
1940 - 1946?

CPFLU Land unit site.
Ref: M Maclachlan *CPLFU*

UNIVERSAL BROTHERHOOD
1941

Spiritual Community. Seven adults, four children.
Location: Potters Bar
Ref: Ad in *Peace News* 14.3.41

EEL PIE ISLAND COMMUNE
1967 - 1971

Best known of the 1960's 'hippie communes' in an old hotel on an island in the Thames. Before it became a commune it was a jazz and early rock music venue. Was described as *"the largest and most anarchic hip commune in England"* with an estimated 300 people having passed through in one year. The high turnover and anarchic set up led to conflict. The owner repossessed the property after it somewhat mysteriously burnt down.
Location: Eel Pie Island, Twickenham
Ref: *Directory of Communes* 1972; *Alternative London* 1970; *Communes Europe; Making Communes;* Who Needs Eel Pie (Rank, "Look at Life" series, 1967); documentary on the commune (BBC2 TV, 1970 – Open University)

HARROW COMMUNE
circa 1969

"HARROW COMMUNE urgently need bread to open a shop and are holding regular Saturday night benefit dances in a hall in Rayners Lane. They would welcome support, especially from groups willing to play for expenses. If you think you can help or want more information, contact Nuts Cockersell"
Location: 74 Harrow View, Harrow
Ref: Ad in *International Times* 55 (Apr 25th 1969)

EVOLUTIONARY COMMUNE
circa 1971

Report in *Commune Movement Directory "members went their own ways"*
Location: c/o 57 Otterburn Gardens, Isleworth
Ref: *Commune Movement Directory* 1971

GROSVENOR ROAD SQUATS
1972 - 1976

"There was no leadership, only influence. Each house had it's own character. Some were run like conventional households, were one might have to knock on the front door to enter. Some were like blocks of flats where the front door was wide open, and one would have to knock on the door of the room they wanted to enter. Some were just wide open to anyone and everyone. I think most people probably had access, one way or another, to most of the rooms in the street."
Location: Grosvenor Road, Twickenham
Ref: www.wussu.com/squatting/grosroad.htm (2.4.2011)

NORFOLK

JEWISH CHRISTIAN COMMUNITY
1939

Group in old country house with six acres of land was broken up when most members were interned on the Isle of Man at the outbreak of war.
Location: 'Zion', Archway House, Kenninghall
Ref: *Community in Britain* 1940

CPFLU LAND UNITS
1940 - 1946?

Christian Pacifist land-based units organised for conscientious objectors
Location: Two Mile Bottom, Thetford Chase and Kings Lynn.
Ref: M Maclachlan *CPLFU*

RACKHEATH LAND SETTLEMENT
1941

Land scheme for conscientious objectors.
Location: near Norwich
Ref: *Peace News Community Supplement* 25.4.41

OULTON SQUATTERS CAMP
circa 1946

Squatter camp on RAF base.
Location: Oulton RAF Base
Ref: Norfolk Sound Archive: Blickling Hall oral history project

SUBUD HOUSE

circa 1960's

Group of followers of Guru Pak Subuh mentioned in Joyce Collin-Smiths autobiography. *"... a collection of mildly creative people live with one another in harmony, practising the Latihan together daily."*
Location: The Close, Norwich
Ref: J Collin-Smith *Call No Man Master*

CROW HALL

1965 - 1997

Small group living in 18th century house with five acres of land. Plus geodesic dome, sauna, swimming pool, as well as various workshops, playrooms, cellars, sheds. *"We are not really structured at all – only having one rota and that's for cooking. We have separate incomes and pay a daily rate all in, sharing food etc. There is no 'entry fee'."*
Location: Denver, Downham Market
Ref: *Directory of Communes* 1972; *D&D 90-91*; *Alternative London* 1970; *Communes Europe*; www.crowhallcommune.com (21.9.2011)

LARLING COMMUNITY/SHRUBB FAMILY

1969 - present

About six adults and several children who renovated old practically derelict farmhouse with about an acre of land and established small commune. *"We aim to be as self-sufficient as possible – we grow most of our own vegetables and have two goats and 40 chickens. We are beginning to establish home industries, primarily wood turning. But at this stage we still have much work to do outside – building work, fruit and vegetable picking, farmwork and etc. We pool all our income; individuals take what they need, as we can afford, although the majority of things are bought communally anyway. We also run a bulk distribution service, buying food and things in bulk and selling them at cost price to individuals/couples/groups in the area around."* One of the longest surviving late 60's communes. *"We are not a farm, don't live in a cottage and if the 'family' brings images of Californian style cults ... we're not a family! We have tended to be a practical, secular, dirty-handed, music-playing, screaming kids community"*
Location: Larling
Ref: *Directory of Communes* 1972; *Communes Europe*

NORWICH HOUSING CO-OP

1970's

Housing co-op involving members from Braziers – George Ropley, Stephen Field and Bonnie Russell. Mentioned in Braziers newsletter.
Location: Norwich
Ref: *The Outside Bell* Christmas 1988, Braziers Publication

CASTLE ACRE

1970's

Cottage bought as personal retreat for FWBO founder Sangharakshita. Now used as Retreat Centre.
Location: Castle Acre
Ref: www.norwichbuddhistcentre.com (22.7.2011)

PADMALOKA

1976 -

FWBO men's retreat centre and community of 12 or so members. Also housed the office of the Western Buddhist Order and the archives of the FWBO movement. Ran a right livelihood candle-making 'factory' distributing candles to FWBO branches and craft shops up and down the country.
Location: Lesingham House, Surlingham, Norwich
Ref: *Alternative Communities* 3rd ed; *Buddhism in Britain*; www.padmaloka.org.uk (3.4.2011)

VAJRAKULA

1977 -

FWBO men's community next door to the Norwich Meditation Centre. First community in the movement's history to refuse entry of women onto its premises. Set up the Rainbow Vegetarian Restaurant as a Right Livelihood business. Also ran Buddhist arts workshop in Queens Road.
Location: 41b All Saints Green, Norwich
Ref: *Alternative Communities* 3rd ed; *Buddhism in Britain*

MANDARAVA

1977 -

FWBO women's community and retreat centre in farmhouse with outhouses and barns.
Location: Aslacton
Ref: *Buddhism in Britain*

ZANZIBARIANS   circa 1980/84

"Wanted men to form Christian community, based on liturgy, aiming at reasonable self-sufficiency. Advertisers current businesses (metal, woodwork, textiles, books) can be used as foundation. State your abilities and interests".
Location: 45 Sandringham Road, Norwich
Ref: J Mercer **Communes; Undercurrents** 39 (Apr May 1980)

THORNAGE HALL   1987 -

Former grange of the Bishops of Norwich donated to Camphill Community by Lord and Lady Hastings. Community of 20 adults with learning disabilities and 12 co-workers run a 70-acre biodynamic farm growing vegetables, flowers, herbs, soft and top fruit. Also have a herd of Red Poll cows, some pigs, sheep and chickens.
Location: Thornage, Holt
Ref: **Camphill International Directory**

NORTHAMPTON SHIRE

LAXTON DISTRIBUTISTS   1935 - 1980?

Catholic land community where five families worked the land together on a 77-acre holding attempting the *'restoration of Christian rural life.'*.
Location: Laxton
Ref: **Utopian England; Directory of Christian Communities & Groups** 1980

WOLLASTON HALL   1940 -

Base for Scott Bader Commonwealth
Location: Wollaston
Ref: **The Man who gave his company away**

CPFLU LAND UNITS   1940 - 1946?

Christian Pacifist land-based units organised for conscientious objectors.
Location: Denton Wood; Kings Cliff; Grendon; Barnwell; Oundle
Ref: M Maclachlan **CPLFU**

PRINCIPAL EDWARDS
MAGIC THEATRE   circa 1968 - 1971

Rock band and performance art troupe signed to John Peel's Dandelion label. Lived together in large house.
Location: Kettering
Ref: **People Together**

NEW CREATION/JESUS ARMY   1974 -

New Creation Hall (formerly Bugbrooke Hall) in Bugbrooke and New Creation Farm at Nether Heyford, form the original home and headquarters of the evangelical sect commonly known as the Jesus Army. The group has expanded hugely and now has communal houses as well as farms, various businesses and a cinema. Property includes Vineyard Farmhouse in Church Stowe; Plough Hall Farm in Warwickshire; Cornhill Manor in Pattishall (formerly a hotel); Honeycombe Grange near Weedon; Sheepfold Grange in nearby Upper Stowe; a former vicarage in Flore; Festal Grange in Pattishall; and Cornerstone Hall in Birmingham. In addition the group also owns a large number of houses in the villages surrounding their headquarters, and many sizeable houses scattered within towns and cities throughout the country, in some cases adjoining properties have been purchased to create larger community houses.
Location: Nether Heyford
Ref: **D&D 90-91**

LIVING STONES   1978 -

Jesus Fellowship Church household also several other houses linked with Living Stones.
Location: Flore
Ref: www.livstones.freeserve.co.uk (19.4.09)

THE NEIGHBOURS   1984 - 2010

Small ecumenical Christian Community in five adjoining terraced houses, with some interconnecting doors and shared gardens. *"Maybe we are searching for a life-style a little nearer to what we know of the early Church in Jerusalem. There, small groups met daily to pray together and support one another in trying to live-out the Gospel values."*
Location: 140-148 Ardington Road, Northampton
Ref: **D&D 90-91; NACCAN Directory** 4th ed

BLACKCURRENT   1988 -

Small communal housing co-op, part of Radical Routes network.
Location: 24 St Michaels Avenue, Northampton
Ref: **D&D 92-93**

NORTHUMBER LAND

CPFLU LAND UNITS   1940 - 1946
Christian Pacifist land-based units organised for conscientious objectors.
Location: Redesland, Otterburn; Keilder.
Ref: M Maclachlan **CPLFU**

HIGH SPEN CAMP   1946 - 1952
Post-war squatter camp on old POW Camp. Four families occupying the premises known as 1, 2, 3 and 4 Rickless Bank. The Council took over the premises, accepted the occupants as tenants, and made extensive modifications including the provision of a new toilet block, separate male and female bathing facilities, new drains and water supply, electric lighting and power points. The camp was eventually demolished after the occupants had found alternative accommodation.
Location: Rickless Bank, High Spen
Ref: www.bpears.org.uk (22.12.08)

WHICKHAM ACK ACK CAMP   1946 -
Anti-Aircraft Gun and Research camp squatted by local families after the war.
Location: Milfield
Ref: www.webwanderers.org (22.12.08)

SEAHAM SQUATTERS HUTS   1946 -
Wooden huts erected to provide holidays for disadvantaged school-children in the 1930's. Used during the War by the army, and after the War occupied by 'squatters' awaiting rehousing. *"Men and women chalked their names on the doors of huts, elected camp committees to see that no damage was done and put seven shillings a week into a 'rent pool' to show that they were willing to pay the owners of the accommodation."*
Location: Seaham
Ref: www.seaham.i12.com (23.12.08)

MILFIELD CAMP   1947 - 1954
Squatter camp on RAF base. In May 1950 the Ministry of Health approved the conversion of huts into fifty six dwellings. An old WAAF dining room was used as a school and a picket hut at the entrance to the site was used as an Infant Welfare Centre.
Location: Milfield
Ref: www.milfield.org.uk (22.12.08)

THE BLACK HAND GANG   circa 1968
"Recently according to rumours, a kind of commune in the West End (ghetto) area of town has set itself up and goes under the name of THE BLACK HAND GANG. It seems it is made up of college/university drop outs and professional 'working' entrepreneurs of the N.A.B. and is oriented in an unusual political direction. Some very peculiar small crudely printed stick-on labels have been appearing on boards and walls exhorting people to extreme acts of vandalism like SMASH THIS WINDOW, TEAR UP SEATS, DYNAMITE IN A HOLE together with more even tempered statements like FUCK THIS FOR A LIVING and PREPARE NOW FOR THE NEWCASTLE COMMUNE."
Location: Newcastle
Ref: *International Times* 30 (May 1968)

LARKSPUR COMMUNITY   1970 -
"... ideas as to what we are about vary. Music, food growing, the way of liberation, laughter, cats, revolution love and the divine game ..."
Location: Newcastle
Ref: **Directory of Communes** 1972

DIVINE LIGHT MISSION   circa 1970 - 1983
Ashram lived in by 'Premies' or devotees of Guru Maharaj Ji (now Prem Rawat).
Location: 18 Holly Avenue, Desmond, Newcastle
Ref: www.prem-rawat-bio.org (31.7.2011)

THROSSEL HOLE PRIORY   1972 -
Converted farmhouse and barn set up as Zen Buddhist monastary. Sister community to Shasta Abbey, California.
Location: Limestone, Brae House, Carrshield
Ref: **Buddhism in Britain**; www.shastaabbey.org; www.throssel.org.uk (6.2.2011)

NORTHERN RURAL COMMUNITIES   circa 1976
Group of dozen people doing research into communal living *"all interested in communes, working towards self-sufficiency etc (some actually doing it!)"*
Location: Newcastle
Ref: **Communes Network** 12

WOOLEY HOSPITAL   circa 1976/78
Former tuberculosis sanatorium and geriatric hospital consisting of 17-acres and a series of wooden huts considered for an alternative technology demonstration centre by New Age

Access – a group researching post-industrial society.
Location: Four miles south of Hexham
Ref: *Undercurrents* 25 and 26 (1978)

JESMOND TERRACE   circa 1970's?
"We lived in a commune for a time in the one time highly residential Jesmond Terrace. It became for a period the Anarchist Embassy flying the red and black flag."
Location: Whitley Bay
Ref: www.sandyford.techie.org.uk (1.2.2009)

SUMMERHILL HOUSING CO-OP 1980-present
Two shared houses in city centre. "We are very "ordinary people" with a variety of "ordinary' jobs. The shared house we live in is our home, with many advantages such as warmth, good food, washing machines, rented video etc that would be difficult or impossible if we were all living singly."
Location: 6 & 11 Summerhill Terrace, Newcastle
Ref: *D&D 90-91*

MARYGATE HOUSE   circa 1984 - present
Ecumenical Retreat Centre home of a small community who run it under a board of Trustees as an independent Charitable trust.
Location: Marygate & Cambridge Hse, Lindisfarne
Ref: www.marygatehouse.org.uk (14.6.2011)

NOTTINGHAM SHIRE

LANGAR AIRFIELD SQUAT   circa 1946 - 1960
Post-war squatter camp in deserted Nissen huts on RAF airfield. The local council improved some of the accommodation there for the 40 to 50 families there and decided to re-house them in the villages from which they originally came. Those in the worst accommodation were re-housed first; others followed throughout the fifties and early sixties.
Location: Langar
Ref: www.binghamheritage.org.uk (11.9.08)

ST ANNS COMMUNITY CRAFT CENTRE
                              circa 1970's - ?
Group involved in community action in St Anns area.
Location: 90 Bluebell Hill Road, Nottingham
Ref: *Peace News* 28.1.72; *A Completely Different Way of Life,* ITV Feb, Mar 1971

BEESTON COMMUNITY   1975 - present
Ecumenical Christian house founded with four aims: "to live together as an extended family, to live a life centred on prayer and worship, to work for unity in Christ among the local churches, to have outreach into the wider local community."
Location: 4 Grange Avenue, Beeston
Ref: *D&D 90-91; NACCAN Directory* 4th ed

GROVE ROAD HOUSING SCHEME   1976 -
Three flats for disabled families linked to three for non-disabled 'supporting families', set up at the instigation of disabled people between 1972 – 76. Built by a Housing Association using Local Authority finance and the disabled people concerned worked closely with the architects on the design of the scheme. Britain's first integrated co-operative housing complex.
Location: Grove Road, Sutton-in-Ashfield
Ref: Ken Davis ***The Emergence of the "Seven Needs"***

COMMUNITY OF HOPE   circa 1977
"In the process of being set up. A dozen members intending to serve the local church and neighbourhood and eventually to live communally in an extended household. Ecumenical ..."
Location: St Francis' Vicarage, Southchurch Drive, Clifton, Nottingham
Ref: *Basic Communities*

RADFORD COMMUNITY HOUSE   1977 -
Christian shared house.
Location: 33 Radford Boulevard, Radford
Ref: *NACCAN Directory* 4th ed

OXFORD SHIRE

KINGSTON COMMUNITY FARM   1939 - 45
Three acre small-holding set up by a group of pacifists from Kingston on Thames.
Location: Rectory Farm, Charney Basset
Ref: Pacifist Islands in a Martial Sea in ***D&D 94-95***

TYTHROP HSE AGRICULTURAL EST circa 1939-
Formed by Jewish refugees. Listed in the journal *Community Life*. Basque children's colony.
Location: Kingsey (on border with Bucks)
Ref: *Heavens Below*

NORTHMOOR   1940 - 1946?
CPFLU Land Unit site
Location: Eynesham Banbury area
Ref: M Maclachlan *CPLFU*

MARKET END HOUSE   1940 - 1941
Workhouse taken over by Q Camps committee where
they transferred the work they had been doing at the
Hawkspur camp in Essex. Expanded their work to include
running an evacuation hostel for *"unbilletable evacuees"*.
Location: Bicester
Ref: www.childrenwebmag.com (21.8.2011);
C Fees *A Fearless Frankness*

FIELD FARM CAMP   1946 - 1958/9
A hundred families occupied an MOD camp
stayed together for over ten years. In the late
1950's were re-housed in the new village of
Berinsfield on the same site.
Location: Berinsfield
Ref: Colin Ward *The hidden history of housing*

DRY LEES CAMP   circa 1946
Squatters camp supported by Henley Council who
arranged for troops to clear 42 'Elephant' Nissen
huts and get services connected.
Location: Henley
Ref: www.arborfieldhistory.org.uk (23.12.08)

WHEATSHEAF MEADOW   Aug 1946
12 huts occupied by squatters.
Location: Henley
Ref: *Reading Mercury* 17.8.46

MOUNT FARM CAMP   Aug 1946
Squatted War Dept huts *"These huts are
considerably superior to the 'nissen' type, some
having been officers quarters."*
Location: Dorchester, Oxfordshire
Ref: *Reading Mercury* 24.8.46

EAST HENDRED   Aug 1946
Five huts in the grounds of Orchard House. *"The present
owner Mrs Lionel Fox-Pitt has welcomed the squatters,
promising to help in making the huts more habitable."*
Location: near Didcot
Ref: *Reading Mercury* 24.8.46

KINGSWOOD COMMON   1946
US Red Cross huts occupied by squatters.
Location: Henley
Ref: *Reading Mercury* 31.8.46

COWLEY MARSH CAMP   Aug 1946
Rocket battery occupied by squatters.
Location: near Oxford
Ref: D Thomas *Villains' Paradise*

BALLIOL COLLEGE SQUAT   Aug 1946
Short-lived squat in Admiralty huts on Balliol
college playing field by group previously at
Cowley Marsh.
Location: Jowett Walk Oxford
Ref: D Thomas *Villains' Paradise*

AYNHOE PARK   1950's - 2003
Country house 'saved' by the Mutual Households
Association.
Location: near Banbury
Ref: *SAVE Casework News* June 2004

COMMUNITY OF ST CLARE   1950 - ?
Small Anglican closed contemplative womens
community.
Location: St Mary's Convent, Freeland, Oxford
Ref: *D&D 92-93*

OXFORD SIMON   1967
Community for homeless men.
Location: Oxford
Ref: *Directory of Communes* 1972;
Alternative London 1970

BRAZIERS PARK   1950 - present
Community set up as 'The School of Integrative
Social Research' in 'Strawberry Hill Gothic'
style mansion near Goring. Also farm with many
outbuildings and estate cottages. Developed
into an independent conference and adult
education centre.
Location: Ipsden
Ref: *People Together*

ROWLANE FARM   1970 - ?
Rented farm-house that became the
headquarters of the Unification Church or
Moonies. Transferred to Lancaster Gate in
London in 1975.
Location: Rowlane Farmhouse, Dunsden
Ref: *Alternative Communities* 3rd ed

HOWARD CHENEY GROUP   circa 1970
Group listed as having *"... a farm in Oxford."*
Location: Oxford
Ref: *Gandalf's Garden* 2

OAKEN HOLT — 1971 - 1983/4?

Large Victorian country house bought by a Myanmar businessman to turn into Buddhist meditation centre.
Location: Farmoor
Ref: *Buddhism in Britain*

THE LEY COMMUNITY — 1971 -

Therapeutic community for drug and alcohol addicts set up by Dr Bertram Mandelbrote and Dr Peter Agulnik following a visit to Phoenix House in New York. Originally located in a ward at Littlemore Hospital moved to a house in Oxford in 1974 and then to Yarnton in 1979. *"... This is no holiday camp. Many residents arrive after a long period of chaotic living: the Ley Community provides a rigid structure for them to rebuild their lives."*
Location: Sandy Lane, Yarnton
Ref: www.ley.co.uk (17.01.09)

DIVINE LIGHT MISSION — circa 1970 - 1983

Ashram lived in by Divine Light devotees.
Location: 56b Abingdon Road, Oxford
Ref: www.prem-rawat-bio.org (31.7.2011)

'COMMUNE' — circa 1975

"COMMUNE at present saving money to buy smallholding and evolve towards self-sufficiency seeks new members".
Location: c/o Fipp, 28B Polstead Road, Oxford
Ref: Ad in *Undercurrents* 11 (May Jun 1975)

TUSHITA RAJNEESH GROWTH COMMUNE — circa 1975 - 1984

7 Adults living in large farmhouse running various therapy and meditation courses.
Location: North Moreton, Didcot
Ref: *Alternative Communities* 2nd & 3rd ed

'ALTERNATIVE SOCIETY' — circa 1975

Group mentioned by Clem Gorman.
Location: Oxford
Ref: *People Together*

ERIC BURDEN COMMUNITY — circa 1980's

Young Adult Unit supporting young men and women living in Oxfordshire with disabling and often dangerous psychotic disorders.
Location: Littlemore Hospital, Oxford
Ref: *Therapeutic Communities Past, Present and Future*

THE ABBEY — 1981 - present

Christian community and retreat centre.
Location: The Green, Sutton Courtney
Ref: *D&D 98-99*

WALTONS OF WOOLF TERRACE — circa 1985

Lesbian feminist community in large Victorian house.
Location: Oxford
Ref: *D&D 92-93*

BESHARA — 1988 - 1990

Home of the Beshara Trust after Sherbourne Hse.
Location: Frilford Grange, Frilford.
Ref: www.beshara.org (21.2.2011)

SHROPSHIRE

PACIFIST LAND SCHEME — circa 1940

Land Scheme operated by members of the Fellowship of Reconciliation.
Location: Shrewsbury
Ref: *Valiant for Peace*

MYDDLE PARK LAND SETTLEMENT — 1941

Thirty-five acres of rough land being cleared by members of Levenshulme, Oswestry and Shrewsbury Peace Pledge Union. Two small huts erected to house conscientious objectors.
Location: Myddle
Ref: *Peace News Community Supplement* 25.4.41

WHEATHILL BRUDERHOF — 1942 - 1960

Farm bought by the Bruderhof for their English members when the main German group went to Paraguay. Served as a refuge for pacifists and had grown to 200 members by 1950.
Location: Lower Bromden, near Ludlow
Ref: *Utopian England*

PEPLOW CAMP — circa 1946

Possible squatter camp on RAF base.
Location: RAF Peplow
Ref: www.wartimememories.co.uk (23.12.08)

WHEATSTONE/EARTHWORM — 1974 - 89

Commune aiming for self-sufficiency. After an initial period when the community was fairly stable they ran into difficulties due to a radical open door policy. House became largely abandoned at one point with a few members living in the grounds. Taken over by new group and renamed Earthworm in the late 1980's part of Radical Routes network.
Location: Leintwardine
Ref: Various *Communes Network*; *D&D 90-91*

CRABAPPLE 1975

Large Georgian house that was second home of group trying to establish a 'Walden Two' type community in the UK. Original behaviourist ideas mellowed over time. Group ran 20-acre small-holding and wholefood shop in Shrewsbury for a number of years.
Location: Berrington Hall, Berrington.
Ref: *D&D 90-91*

THE OMEGA POINT circa 1977

Attempt to set up a monastic style community in former workhouse under the auspices of the Omega Point Trust that ran hostels for 'inadequate men'.
Location: Morda, Oswestry
Ref: *Alternative Communities* 3rd ed; *Communes Network* 39 and 40

PARK HALL CRAFT VILLAGE circa 1977

Proposal to set up a village sized community on 260-acre army base. Idea was to transform old wooden barracks into houses and craft workshops
Location: near Oswestry
c/o 48 Abingdon Villas, London
Ref: CN 29; *Rural Resettlement Handbook*

YARBOROUGH HOUSE circa 1977 - 1984?

Small group making home made wooden toys, candles and furniture to sell in craft shop.
Location: The Square, Bishops Castle
Ref: *Communes Network* 42

TARALOKA BUDDHIST CENTRE 1985 - ?

FWBO women's community and retreat in large farm house and converted outbuildings.
Location: Cornhill Farm, Bettisfield, Whitchurch
Ref: *D&D 92-93*; www.taraloka.org.uk (28.4.2012)

SOMERSET

AGAPEMONE (ABODE OF LOVE) 1856 - 1962

19th Century cult on large estate bought with money given by wealthy converts with house, cottages and chapel surrounded by high wall. By the mid 20th century the group had outlasted two gurus and become a strange extended family of descendents of the founders and their servants. Numbers dwindled and the estate was finally sold in 1962.
Location: Spaxton
Ref: Charles Mander *The Reverend Prince and his Abode of Love*; Kate Barlow *Abode of Love: Growing Up in a Messianic Cult*

COMMUNITY OF ST FRANCIS 1905 - ?

Community of Franciscan Sisters.
Location: Compton Durville, South Petherton.
Ref: *D&D 96-97*;
www.franciscans.org.uk (28.4.2012)

PACIFIST LAND SCHEME circa 1940

Nine acre Land Scheme run by the Fellowship of Reconciliation who went on to establish Goose Green Fm.
Location: Glastonbury
Ref: *Valiant for Peace*

CPFLU LAND UNITS 1940 - 1946

Christian Pacifist land-based units organised for conscientious objectors.
Location: Bruton; Rowberrow
Ref: M Maclachlan *CPLFU*

GOOSE GREEN FARM 1940 - 1943

Bought by company that had been set up to purchase the Bruderhof farms in Wiltshire when they emigrated to Paraguay. Training centre for COs.
Location: Sutton Mallet
Ref: *Peace News* 14.2.41

'ANARCHO-TROTSKYIST' COMMUNE 1944

"Commune of Anarchists and Trotskyists" in which Jewish photographer/artist Gustav Metzger lived in.
Location: Bristol
Ref: www.ucl.ac.uk (23.12.08)

BRISTOL SQUATTER CAMPS 1946 -

20 vacant army camps around the city occupied by squatters at the end of the war.
Location: Bristol
Ref: D Thomas *Villains' Paradise*

MOUNT AVALON circa 1970's -

House used by composer Rutland Boughton when he tried to set up an artistic community after WWI while running the early Glastonbury festivals. Later became a nursing home and was then sold to the British Israelite Trust for a conference centre. Was finally a large squat before it burnt down and was finally demolished.
Location: Bove Town, Glastonbury
Ref: *Utopia Britannica*

DIVINE LIGHT MISSION circa 1970 - 1983

Ashram lived in by 'Divine Light devotees.
Location: 103 Belmont Road, St Andrews, Bristol
Ref: www.prem-rawat-bio.org (31.7.2011)

49 COTHAM ROAD   circa 1970

Large 'shambling' house.owned by beatnik and artist, John Osborne, who lived with his family on the top floor, the rest of the house was *"inhabited by a variety of students, madcaps and misfits. Anarchy ruled and, almost as in some profound artistic statement, old fridges and a chaise lounge' lay entangled in the overgrown garden ..."*
Location: Bristol
Ref: www.achingcellar.co.uk (3.10.2009

MAGIC MUSCLE COMMUNE   circa 1970's -

Home of members of 70's rock band Magic Muscle.
Location: Bruton, Somerset
Ref: www.achingcellar.co.uk (3.10.2009)

GREENBUS COMMUNE   early 1970's - 1974

Christian Summer camp community.
Location: Wick, Glastonbury
Ref: *Christian Directory, Christian Communes*

GLASTONBURY GREEN TRUST   circa 1971 -

Possible continuation of Greenbus community.
Location: c/o Abbey Gatehouse, Glastonbury
Ref: *Directory of Christian Cmnities & Groups* 1980

HARVEST   circa 1971 -

Macrobiotic commune and shop. Expanded to include a wholesale warehouse and second shop in Bristol.
Location: Bath
Ref: www.essential-trading.co.uk (2.8.2011)

DOVE CENTRE OF CREATIVITY   1972 - 1977

"A centre to practise and teach crafts within the context of community living. No religious connections. Community emphasis declined and craftwork and teaching predominated after the first year or two."
Location: Butleigh, Glastonbury
Ref: *Communes Network* 29

SOMEWHERE HOUSING CO-OP   circa 1972 -

Communal group living in 2 houses, one flat and a caravan. Helped to set up Bristol federation of Housing Co-ops.
Location: 124 Coronation Road, Bristol 3
Ref: *Alternative Communities* 4th ed

BATH GROUP   circa 1974

Project proposed by New Age guru Michael Riddell looked at various places to set up a community including Victorian castle owned by the Wills (cigarette) family, St Catherine's Court near Bath and Castle Pub at Keinton Mandeville.
Ref: www.rjstewart.org/heaver.html (21.12.09)

WICK COURT   circa 1976

Headquarters of Student Christian Movement.
Location: near Bristol
Ref: *Christian Communes*

FLORENCE PARK   circa 1977

"Small urban community of at present six members, Some in full-time employment working with mentally handicapped. Interested in hand printing and weaving."
Location: 33 Florence Park, Bristol 6
Ref: *Communes Network* 22

RADFORD MILL   1970's?

Community on organic farm.
Location: Timsbury, Bath
Ref: www.radfordmill.com

ROCK BAND COMMUNITY   circa 1978

"The two entities will be equal; the community nurtures the band and the band motivates the community ... We must do anything we can to counteract the product orientated approach of the record companies, to discredit the technological overkill and to debunk the superstar myth. We believe that despite the present dire state, rock music can still be a valid form of communication, a positive social force and a hell of a lot of fun as well."
Location: c/o 27 Grove Road, Bristol
Ref: *In The Making* 5 Supplement

BINDON AGRICULTURAL COLLECTIVE
                                   circa 1980 -

"We make a living growing organic produce (vegetables, wholewheat flour) on a rented 30-acre farm, which holds the Soil Association's symbol of organic standards. This is not easy! We all have varying degrees of commitment to organic practice in agriculture, skill-sharing, political activity for a society where each individual has responsibility for her/his life. At present, we are trying to put the collective on a more sound financial base while not working so hard, so that we have time and energy for other interests"
Location: Bindon Home Farm, Landford Budville, Wellington
Ref: *Alternative Communities* 4th ed

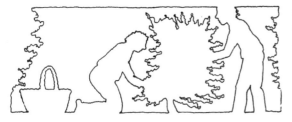

DURDHAM PARK COMMUNITY   circa 1980

Huge old house in beautiful grounds owned by the Dartington Hall Trust squatted by a group of single mothers and their children. *"Throughout the two years of its existence, it was a centre for all kinds of grassroots activities involving a large number of people, and was a welcoming place for travellers and tipi-dwellers. We shared cooking and cleaning on a rota basis; the children took decisions at their own meetings and were very free. We ran workshops and arts events. Many homeless people came to us ..."* Monica Sjoo. They were threatened with eviction by the Trust who wanted to convert it into luxury flats. The group suggested that they be allowed to set up a 'mutual aid' centre, but the trustees including Maurice Ash, Lord Michael Young and Satish Kumar refused to speak with the squatters. After an attempt to negotiate with the Trustees by squatting in the toilets of the Elmhurst Centre at Dartington Hall the group were evicted by bailiffs sent by the Trustees.
Location: Durdham Park Clifton Bristol
Ref: M Sjoo **New Age & Armageddon** 1992

COMMON PROPERTY
HOUSING CO-OP   1981 - ?

Communal Housing Co-op in large mock gothic Victorian Town House.
Location: Trinity Road, Old Market, Bristol.
Ref: **D&D 96-97**

LOWER ROCKES   circa 1983

Small community running weekend therapy workshops.
Location: Compton Street, Butleigh, Glastonbury
Ref: **Alternative Communities** 4th ed; The New Times Network

CHERRY ORCHARDS   circa 1989 -

Therapeutic Camphill community, set in 18-acres of land. Offers residential care to help adults recovering from the debilitating effects of any life crisis.
Location: Canford Lane, Westbury-on-Trym
Ref: www.cherryorchards.co.uk (21.4.2011)

THE HATCH   ? - ?

Therapeutic community for young adults living in four households run as independent family units.
Location: Kington Lane, Thornbury
Ref: www.camphill.org.uk (21.4.2011)

CROYDON HALL   circa 1990's

Sannyas community
Location: Felons Oak, Minehead
Ref: www.croydonhall.co.uk

BRISTOL BUDDHIST CENTRE   circa 1991

Small FWBO men's community.
Location: 9 Cromwell Road, St Andrews, Bristol
Ref: **D&D 92-93**

TWO MULES HOUSING CO-OP   circa 1991

Small inner city communal housing co-op part of Radical Routes network
Location: 34 Bellvue Road, Easton, Bristol.
Ref: **D&D 92-93**

SPIRITUAL FAMILY COMMUNITY   circa 1994

Existing network-cum-spiritually based community group looking to establish residential base.
Location: c/o address in Bristol.
Ref: **D&D 94-95**

STAFFORD SHIRE

THE WOODLANDS   1941 - present

Hostel run by the Friends War Victims Relief Committee for elderly bombed out evacuees. In 1945 became a home for the elderly with a quarter of the residents Quakers.
Location: Penn Road, Wolverhampton
Ref: C Jones **Wolverhampton Quakers 1704-1988**

'REILLY GREENS'   circa 1946

Innovative post-war reconstruction proposal for housing estates with extensive communal facilities.
Location: Bilston
Ref: P Richmond **Marketing Modernisms**

BIDDULPH OLD HALL   1963 - 1969

Buddhist meditation centre.
Location: Biddulph
Ref: T Shine **Honour Thy Fathers**

DIVINE LIGHT MISSION circa 1970 - 1983
Ashram lived in by 'Premies' or devotees of Guru Maharaj Ji (now Prem Rawat).
Location: 7 Howson Street, Hanley
Ref: www.prem-rawat-bio.org (31.7.2011)

R.A.T. circa 1972 - 84
Short for Rodent Art Trust. Theatre group listed in *Alternative Communities* directory.
Location: The Jam Factory, 35a North Street, Newcastle Under Lyme and also 108 Ashmore Terrace, Chesterton
Ref: *Alternative Communities* 4th ed

SWYTHAMLEY HALL 1977 - 1987
Hall and parkland bought by the World Government for the Age of Enlightenment, followers of Maharishi Mahesh Yogi. Run as a Transcendental Meditation training centre.
Location: Swythamley near Leek
Ref: www.nationalarchives.gov.uk (29.12011)

HMP DOVEGATE circa 1990's
Therapeutic Community Unit in privately run prison. 200 places for Category B men (four communities, an assessment unit, and a High Intensity Programme Unit)
Location: near Uttoxeter
Ref: www.therapeuticcommunities.org (12.3.09)

SUFFOLK

HAWSTEAD PLACE circa 1940
Planned pacifist land community.
Location: Hawstead Place farm Bury St Edmunds
Ref: *Community in Britain* 1940

PACIFIST LAND SCHEME circa 1940
Fellowship of Reconciliation Land Scheme.
Location: Ipswich
Ref: *Valiant for Peace*

CPFLU LAND UNITS 1940 - 1946
Christian Pacifist land-based units organised for conscientious objectors.
Location: Santon Downham; Brandon; Rendlesham
Ref: M Maclachlan *CPLFU*

THELNETHAM 1942 - 45
Run-down farm bought by *Peace News* editor John Middleton Murray in a last attempt at forming a community. Acted as a refuge for conscientious objectors.
Location: Lodge Farm, High Street, Thelnetham
Ref: J M Murray *Community Farm* 1952

ELMSETT COMMUNITY 1939 - 45
Ambitious wartime venture based on 41-acre mixed farm. Aim was to *"lay the foundations of a new order"* whilst restoring buildings, running study groups, setting up a community library, holding peace Pledge Union meetings, Sunday services and selling *Peace News* in Ipswich market each Saturday. Decisions were made by consensus, links were made with neighbours and the local retail co-op. The group hoped that by example they could demonstrate *"the soundness of community as a new order of voluntary and non-violent communism."*
Location: near Ipswich
Ref: A Rigby *Pacifist Islands in a Martial Sea; D&D 94-95; Heavens Below; Far Out*

ABBEY FARM circa 1943
Base for the Brotherhood of the Way tramp preachers.
Location: Hoxne
Ref: Rev Stimson *The Price to be Paid*

RINGSFIELD HALL 1972 -
Small interdenominational Christian Community running residential centre and small-holding, to which groups from schools and churches come for study and recreation.
Location: Ringsfield Hall, Beccles
Ref: *Basic Communities; Directory of Christian Communities & Groups* 1980; www.ringsfield-hall.co.uk (21.12.2010)

'DEADHEADS WANTED' 1973
"ANYBODY INTO GRATEFUL DEAD type or Brinsley type music (it doesn't matter how good or bad you are) who would like to form a chaotic commune type band in Norfolk or Suffolk ..."
Location: The Haven, Yaxley, Eye
Ref: Ad in *International Times* 162 (Sep 1973)

MANOR FARM 1974 - 1978
Commune on derelict farm where David Van Edwards made lutes in a converted pig sty.
Location: Bramfield
Ref: www.vanedwards.co.uk (12.3.2006)

HENGRAVE COMMUNITY
OF RECONCILIATION   1974 - 2005
Conference and retreat centre in Tudor Hengrave
Hall, with 44-acres of grounds. Originally
consisted of a group of families of different
Christian denominations. aiming to *"renew the
Church by community witness ..."* Later, they became
a mix of long-term members, who remained in
the Community for up to seven years, and short-
term members, many who came from Central and
Eastern Europe for periods ranging from one year
to three months. The Community was dissolved
in 2005 after failing to find £250,000 to fund
improvements.
Location: Bury St Edmunds
Ref: *D&D 90-91; Bury Free Press* 20.5.2005

SUFI COMMUNE   circa 1970's
Community of the Sufi Sect the Creed of Love.
Folk duo Richard and Linda Thompson lived there
for a while.
Location: Hoxne
Ref: *Electric Eden; The Great Valerio*

LOWESTOFT CRAFT SOCIETY   circa 1975 -
Group listed in *Communes Network*.
Location: Lowestoft
Ref: *Communes Network* 2

BADINGHAM RECTORY   1977 - 2003
Transcendental Meditation Centre.
Location: Old Rectory Road, Badingham
Ref: www.globalcountry.org.uk (1.1.2011)

INNER GARDEN   1977 - 1984?
Country cottage retreat centre. *"The centre
continues the spirit of the original Gandalf's Garden
mystical community ... and grows in the same
vibration."*
Location: 14 Bury Road, Hengrave,
Bury St Edmunds
Ref: *Alternative Communities* 3rd ed

MEDINA RAJNEESH   1980 - 1985
Main UK commune for followers of Bhagwan Shree
Rajneesh with up to 300 members living in the
30 bedroom Herringswell Manor and converted
outbuildings. Group ran a number of successful
businesses and a healing centre.
Location: Herringswell, Bury St Edmunds
Ref: *My Life in Orange;*
Alternative Communities 4th ed

SIMPSON HOUSE   circa 1984
Group listed in Communes book.
Location: 52 Queen Street, Bury St Edmunds
Ref: J Mercer *Communes*

THELNETHAM HOUSING CO-OP   circa 1986 -
Rural community of seven adults and eight
children living in individual units with two acres
of land. *"No specific philosophy except to live co-
operatively."*
Location: Manor House, Thelnetham, Diss
Ref: *Communes Network Directory* 1986

SURREY

LYNE PLACE   1935 - 1947
Country house and farm set up as a base for the
Historico-Psychological Society by P D Ouspensky.
Location: Virginia Waters
Ref: *The Strange Life of P D Ouspensky;
Madame Blavatsky's Baboon; Venture with ideas*

QUAKER COMMUNITY SCHEME   1941
Plan for Educational community 'somewhere near
London'
Location: Fredly Lodge, Mickleham, Dorking
Ref: *Peace News Community Supplement* 14.3.41

BUREAU OF COSMOTHERAPY   1941
*"An experimental small-holding is being
established where the aim will be to provide
for a specified number of persons sufficient
fruit, vegetables, eggs, milk products and,
later grain to assure a diet in harmony
with the most recent findings of nutritional
science."*
Location: Lawrence Weaver House, Leatherhead
Ref: Peace News Community Supp. 25.4.41

PACIFIST LAND SCHEME   circa 1940
Fellowship of Reconciliation Land Scheme.
Location: Hindhead
Ref: *Valiant for Peace*

CPFLU LAND UNITS   1940 - 1946
Christian Pacifist land-based units organised for
conscientious objectors
Location: Chidding Fold; Plaistow; Egham;
Banstead; Titsey; Riegate; Guildford; Holmewood;
Bear Green; Heath Farm; Godalming; Godstone
Ref: M Maclachlan *CPLFU*

AGRICULTURAL COMMUNITIES TRUST 1941
Address listed in *Community in a Changing World*
Location: Rainbow Dell, Little Sandhurst, Camberley
Ref: *Community in a Changing World*

SHERWOOD SCHOOL COMMUNITY 1942
Group inviting inquiries from *"those wishing to accept a simple standard of living, pooling incomes, probably sharing large house with one or 2 other families and sending children to progressive co-educational school."*
Location: Epsom
Ref: Ad in *Peace News* 20.11.42

CAMBERLEY NAAFI 1946
Several families of squatters living in NAAFI Institute on a communal basis.
Location: Portland Road, Camberley
Ref: *Reading Mercury* 31.8.46

COS DEPOT SQUAT 1946
Central Ordinance Supply depot where 17 families were squatting using communal cookhouse and laundry.
Location: Between Steventon and Hanney
Ref: *Reading Mercury* 31.8.46

BLACKBUSHE AIRFIELD CAMP 1946 - 1950
Squatter camp at the newly renamed RAF Blackbushe. Was base for the 1948 Berlin Airlift. Also hosted 'The Picnic at Blackbushe' festival in 1978.
Location: Between Camberley and Basingstoke
Ref: D Thomas *Villains' Paradise*

COOMBE SPRINGS 1946 - 1965
A small 'research community' in an Edwardian villa founded by J G Bennett to explore the mystical ideas of Gurdjieff. Bennett gave the property away to self-styled Sufi guru Idries Shah who then sold it on to a property developer.
Location: Kingston-upon-Thames
Ref: *D&D 96-97; Madame Blavatsky's Baboon*

GREATHED MANOR 1946 - 2003
Country house 'saved' by the Mutual Households Association.
Location: near Lingfield
Ref: *An Experiment in Co-operation*

IPSLEY LODGE circa 1946/48
Venture to form a self-supporting community for youths of 16-21 with no homes, unsatisfactory homes, or maladjusted lives. *"The object was to make a home ; to turn each lad into an essential member of society and to give him individual study and attention."*
Location: Ipsley Lodge, Hogs Back, Farnham
Ref: *Community Broadsheet* Winter 1947 – 48

BELMONT INDUSTRIAL NEUROSIS UNIT 1947
Established by Ministry of Health and the Ministry of Work and Pensions for the treatment of *"chronic unemployed victims of the industrial society"* with Maxwell Jones in charge. Run along therapeutic community lines. Renamed the Henderson Hospital in 1959.
Location: Sutton
Ref: Stijn Vandevelde *Maxwell Jones and his work in the therapeutic community* 1999

ALBURY PARK 1950's - 2003
Country house 'saved' by the Mutual Households Association.
Location: near Guildford
Ref: *SAVE Casework News* June 2004

BEVERLY LODGE circa 1956
Offshoot of Coombe Springs Community. Five families living in a large Edwardian house converted into apartments.
Location: Coombe Lane, Kingston upon Thames
Ref: Raymond van Sommers *A Life in Subud*

FRIMHURST RECUPERATIVE HOME 1957 -
"... a kind of therapeutic community for 'problem families'"
Location: Frimley Green, Camberley
Ref: *The International Journal for Therapeutic and Supportive Organizations* Vol 19, No 2

THE FARNCOMBE COMMUNITY 1964 - 1984
Community of five sisters with a wider circle of Companions and a Fellowship of Prayer.
Location: 5 Wolsely Road, Farncombe, Godalming
Ref: J Mercer *Communes; Basic Communities*

UNIFIED FAMILY (MOONIES) 1970
Address listed in *Alternative London.*
Location: 305 Commonside East, Mitcham
Ref: *Alternative London* 1970

Peper Harow House   1970 - 1990's
Approved School turned into Therapeutic Community by Melvyn Rose and gained international reputation for pioneering work with disturbed adolescents. Closed in the 1990's. Work contiunues under the Childhood First charity who run residential communities at Thornby Hall, Greenfields, Earthsea House and Merrywood House.
Location: Peper Harow, Godalming
Ref: www.childhoodfirst.org.uk (31.7.2011); M Rose *Healing Hurt Minds: The Peper Harow Experience*

Divine Light Mission   circa 1974 - 1983
House used by Guru Maharaj Ji (now Prem Rawat).
Location: Swiss Cottage, Reigate, Surrey
Ref: www.prem-rawat-bio.org (31.7.2011)

Zorch   1970's - ?
Communal set up for rock band Zorch. "*... working, and R&D'ing in a cottage commune lost in the Surrey pine forests.*"
Location: Churt House Cottage
Ref: www.planetgong.co.uk/gas/archives/zorch.shtml

Bridge Trust   1976
"*GROUP PLANNING to purchase 100-acres to farm organically and create a co-operative community endeavour for all to work together and find common purpose for the future, need someone to help with an interest free loan to enable start.*"
Location: Bridge Trust, 20 The Chase, Reigate
Ref: Small ad in *Undercurrents* 15 (1976)

'Allways'   1976
"*A GROUP OF MATURE New Age workers are planning to buy a large property with at least four acres of land to form a mainly self supporting Light centre for retreat, healing and teaching of all kinds. Also art and craft work and animal care.*"
Location: Write: 21 St Pauls Road West, Dorking
Ref: Small ad in *Undercurrents* 15 (1976)

Moorhurst   1976 - 1984?
Group of three families running a centre for healing "*in the broadest harmony on all levels*" in Elizabethan farmhouse.
Location: South Holmewood, Dorking
Ref: *Alternative Communities* 4th ed

Crescent Road Community   circa 1983 -
Group listed with 'partial entry' in Teachers directory.
Location: 4-8 Crescent Road, Kingston
Ref: *Alternative Communities* 4th ed

Berry House Community   circa 1986 - 1998
Small community established at the invitation of the Bishop of Southwark, Ronnie Bowlby part of the CCCT network.
Location: near Redhill
Ref: www.ccct.co.uk/Library/bhouse.html

Centre For Holistic Living   circa 1993
Proposal to set up a holistic green spiritual community.
Location: c/o Address in Croydon
Ref: *D&D 94-95*

Zacchaeus Community   circa 1998
Christian community looking for members and property.
Location: Croydon
Ref: *D&D 98-99*

SUSSEX

St Hughs Charterhouse   1873 - ?
Carthusian monastary listed in *Diggers & Dreamers*.
Location: Partridge Green, Horsham.
Ref: *D&D 96-97*

The Community Of St Hilda   1937 - 38
Small community linked to Mission of St Hilda in Camberwell at the outbreak of war took in families of evacuees.
Location: Micklepage Farm, Nuthurst
Ref: *Community in Britain* 1940

Battle Botanic Garden   circa 1940
House and five-acre estate growing vegetables, salad and fruit. Also goats and poultry. Quaker horticultural training centre training pacifists and refugees.
Location: Battle
Ref: *Community in Britain* 1940

Pacifist Land Scheme   circa 1940
Land Scheme operated by members of the Fellowship of Reconciliation.
Location: Lewes
Ref: *Valiant for Peace*

CPFLU Land Units   1940 - 1946
Christian Pacifist land-based units organised for conscientious objectors.
Location: Arundel; Brinsbury; Field; Jevington; East Marden; Graffham
Ref: M Maclachlan *CPLFU*

East Grinstead   circa 1940
Small group raising and marketing food on two acres for the assistance of 'conscience victims.'
Location: 200 Hartye Road, East Grinstead
Ref: *Community in Britain* 1940

St Julians   1941 - ?
Community founded by Florence Allshorn. Moved to house and farm near Horsham in 1950. Core of about a dozen women providing a retreat. Also had a house in Kenya. Had their own publication – Community Review.
Location: Coolham, Horsham, RH13 8QL
Ref: D Clark *Basic Communities*

The Vigilantes   1945
Group of local war veterans who began breaking into empty property to house the unemployed and returning servicemen's families. *"By the first week in July, the Vigilantes (or 'the Secret Committee of Ex-Servicemen') were claiming a membership of 1,000 and squatting was beginning to spread along the coast to other resorts ..."*
Location: Brighton (First squat in Roundhill Crescent)
Ref: Andrew Friend 'The Post War Squatters' in Nick Anning et al (eds) *Squatting: the Real Story*; Jackie Blackwell (ed) *Who Was Harry Cowley?* QueenSpark Books, 1984

Bernhard Baron Cottage Homes   1945 -
Quaker cottage homes scheme.
Location: Polegate
Ref: *Fifty Years On – Bernhard Baron Cottage Homes*

Kibbutz Training Farm   circa 1949 -
Eder farm used from as a centre for the training of young Jews intending to work in kibbutzim in Israel.
Location: West Grinstead
Ref: *A History of the County of Sussex* Volume 6

St Bridget's Cheshire Home 1951 -
Early Cheshire Home for the disabled.
Location: East Preston
Ref: L Cheshire *Hidden World*

'Polish Commune'   circa 1956
Short-lived commune set up by a group Polish ex-servicemen at Combe Farm on the Wadhurst Park estate.
Location: Wadhurst Park
Ref: www.wadhurst.info/whs/newsletters (8.11.08)

Danny House   1950's - 2003
Country house 'saved' by the Mutual Households Association.
Location: near Hassocks
Ref: *SAVE Casework News* June 2004

Saint Hill Manor   1959 - present
UK headquarters of the Church of Scientology.
Location: East Grinstead
Ref: *The New Believers*; *Alternative Communities* 3rd ed

The Dicker   1961 - 1973?
Large house used by small residential group studying Gurdjeiffian ideas led by Beryl Pogson.
Location: Upper Dicker
Ref: B Hunter and B Pogson *A Pupil's Postscript*

STONELANDS   1960's -
Large ramshackle country mansion used by the
Church of Scientology as a hostel for the nearby
UK headquarters at Saint Hill Manor.
Location: Selsfield Road, West Hoathly
Ref: *The New Believers*

ARCHWAYS VENTURE   circa 1967
In the wake of the mods v. rockers riots on Brighton
beach the Archways team persuaded Brighton
Corporation to allow the use of Arches 141 and
167 on the front for government funded research
project into why young people behaved like that.
*"The idea was that young people could drift into
either arch, help themselves to as many free coffees
as they liked, and hang around chatting. One of
the people they were chatting to would in fact be
an undercover researcher, paid to memorize all
conversations of the day, write them up in the evening
and send them to a government sociological research
centre in Leicester."* Became a hangout for all sorts of
misfits, dossers, 'beachniks' and mental cases.
Location: Archway 141
Ref: www.coughtrey.me.uk/ (22.8.08)

BRIGHTON HOSTEL   1968/9
Illegal hostel for the homeless set up by former
dosser and beachnick V T Coughtrey – modelled
on Simon communities.
Location: 105 Islingword Road
Ref: www.coughtrey.me.uk/ (22.8.08)

W.O.R.M.   circa 1970
*The Worthing Overground Revolutionary Movement!
"Political? Could be. Arts Lab? Could be. Workshop?
Proposed projects: Getting own duplicator/ own
mag. (Drug) Information service (informing straights)
Premises (Commune) Getting People Together. Can
you help? Ideas, practical help, love people needed."*
Location: Write/Come and see Rod, Flat 6,
Corporation Buildings, Brougham Road, Worthing
Ref: Ad in *International Times* 76 (Mar Apr 1970)

BRIGHTON ANARCHIC HOUSE   early 1970's
Group featured in Nell Dunn's book.
Location: Brighton 'Stones throw from sea'
Ref: Nell Dunn *Living Like I Do*

DIVINE LIGHT MISSION   circa 1970 - 1983
Ashram lived in by Divine Light devotees.
Location: 20 York Villas, Brighton
Ref: www.prem-rawat-bio.org (31.7.2011)

CROWBOROUGH HALL   circa 1970's - 1980's
Hippie commune where filmmaker Sam Taylor-
Wood grew up. *"... the inhabitants wore orange
robes and the cats ate out of the chip pan ..."*
Location: Crowborough
Ref: www.independent.co.uk/news/people
(21.8.2011)

WORTH ABBEY LAY COMMUNITY   1971 - ?
Lay community connected to Benedictine
Monastary.
Location: Turners Hill, Crawley
Ref: *D&D 96-97*

DARVELL BRUDERHOF   1971 - present
*"Voluntarily pooling money, talents and energy,
we base our life on the revolutionary vision
and teachings of Jesus: Love each other, and
your enemies. Make peace. Don't judge. Don't
worry about tomorrow. We try to connect
with people the world over who struggle for
justice, community and the value of all life.
Our children are our primary concern. Babies
are cared for at the community nursery while
parents work; children attend Bruderhof schools.
Young adults go to local secondary schools, then
are encouraged to leave the community for at
least a year – to live independently and make
decisions about their future ... To put bread on
our table, we manufacture classroom equipment
and furniture, and aids for physically disabled
people. But our work is more than a business
venture: from washing laundry to assembling
wooden products, work is 'love made visible'".*
D&D Entry 2001
Location: Robertsbridge
Ref: *D&D 90-91*

HOATHLY HILL COMMUNITY   1972 - present
Steiner based community comprising of
about 70 people living in 27 properties set
in some 22 acres of gardens and fields. Also
community facilities including: Two meeting
halls, Saturday cafe, formal communal
garden, playing field for children, Biodynamic
gardening area and area for communal
bonfires and camping for the children in the
summer.
Location: West Hoathly
Ref: home.btconnect.com/hoathlyhill/
hhr/2006/10/welcome-to-hoathly-hill-community.
html (1.1.2011)

AMITAYUS   1975 - ?
FWBO communal houses and meditation centre. Right
Livelihood activities include a vegetarian restaurant
called 'Sunrise', and 'The Windhorse Bookshop'.
Location: 15 Park Crescent Place and
13 George Street, Brighton
Ref: *Alternative Communities* 3rd ed;
Buddhism in Britain

S.C.R.U.   circa 1978
Small Communities Research Association. Formed
after unsuccessful attempt to set up rural
community of a dozen houses on 240-acre site.
Location: 13 The Rose Walk, Newhaven
Ref: *Communes Network* 40

L'ARCHE BOGNOR REGIS   1978 - ?
Community house for International L'Arche
movement.
Location: 51a Aldwick Road, Bognor Regis
Ref: *D&D 00-01*; www.larche.org.uk (30.4.12)

CHITHURST MONASTERY   1979 - present
20-25 monks, nuns and novices following the Thai
Forest Tradition of Theravada Buddhism.
Location: Chithurst House, Petersfield
Ref: *Alternative Communities* 4th ed;
www.cittaviveka.org (17.6.11)

LIVING STONES   1980's? -
Jesus Fellowship Church household.
Location: Abundant Grace House, Firle Rd, Seaford
Ref: www.ukchurch.org (19.4.09)

MOUNT CAMPHILL COMMUNITY   1980 -
Set in 20 acres of land in the heart of the Sussex
Weald the community consists of five households
offering formal courses for students. Largest household
was once a monastery and chapel is now used as
hall for cultural and social events Purpose-designed
buildings house Bakery, Pottery, Weavery, Wood
workshop, Horticulture classroom and Gymnasium.
Location: Faircrouch Lane, Wadhurst
Ref: www.mountcamphill.org (21.4.2011)

'OAKLEA'   circa 1980 -
Community of four one-parent families and
six single people with 11 kids between them.
Appealing for help to buy the house they were
living in which was due to be sold.
Location: Hawfield
Ref: *Communes Network* 50

CHALVINGTON SCHOOL   1980 - 1992
Therapeutic community for disturbed children
aged 11-16.
Location: Firle Road, Seaford
Ref: The Independent 16.6.1994

RIVENDELL RETREAT CENTRE   1985 -
FWBO retreat in large Victorian rectory.
Location: Chillies Lane, High Hurstwood
Ref: www.rivendellretreatcentre.com (22.7.2011)

ST ANNE'S CONVENT   late 1990's
Large communal squat in a disused 100-room
Nunnery. Group set up a crèche, a gallery,
a meditation room, rehearsal spaces and
meeting rooms for a host of local groups. Were
eventually evicted by an Order of Catholic
nuns who took the squatters to the High Court
after selling the property to boxer Chris
Eubank.
Location: Hove
Ref: *SchNews* 41 22.9.95

THE COMMUNITY PROJECT   1996 - present
Community in converted former 1930's mental
hospital set in 23 acres who adopted the
Cohousing model during the process of setting up.
Location: Laughton Lodge, Laughton near Lewes
Ref: *D&D 00-01*; www.laughtonlodge.org
(20.10.11)

WARWICK SHIRE

ST GEORGES COURT   1923/4 - 1957
Quadrangle of 32 flats for single professional
women at Bournville model village developed
along Co-operative Housekeeping lines.
Communal facilities included: dining room,
kitchen and 'shared servants', with groups
of flats sharing bathrooms and living rooms.
The communal facilities declined and were
wound up in 1957. Flats were used by social
services for a number of years and in 1999
the complex was refurbished by the Bournville
Trust providing 28 one and two bedroom
apartments
Location: Bournville
Ref: *The Architectural & Social History of
Co-operative Living*

THE COMMUNITY GROUP circa 1937

A group of seven people in an urban commune with contacts with the Cotswold Bruderhof who they later joined. The community was used by the Bruderhof as a centre and meeting-place for doing outreach work.
Location: Birmingham
Ref: Y Oved **Witness of Brothers**

BACHAD TRAINING FARM circa 1940's

Training Farm for Jewish refugees.
Location: Bromsgrove
Ref: www.bauk.org (25.6.09)

LAND & INDUSTRIAL GROUP circa 1940

Three acre small holding being shared by group as first step to community co-operative.
Location: c/o 117 Lower Hill Marten Road, Rugby
Ref: **Community in Britain** 1940

SPRINGHURST COMMUNITY circa 1940

Experimental 'sharing group' in community house with 11 rooms, outhouses, small workshop and 2 acres of land. Trying to open a shop.
Location: Springhurst, Bubbenhall, Coventry
Ref: **Community in Britain** 1940

THE GRANGE CENTRE 1940/41

Centre with room for 20 people. Had ten acres market garden also hoped to covert outbuilding to workshops. Rented another 36 acres for livestock. Sheltered evacuees from London.
Location: Wythall
Ref: **Peace News** 6.9.40 and 25.4.41

COVENTRY DIGGERS circa 1967/68

Joined Sid Rawle's group on Dorinish Island.
Location: Coventry?
Ref: **Directory of Communes** 1972

HERONBROOK HOUSE circa 1968 - 1990's?

International therapeutic centre treating priests and members of religious orders suffering from stress disorders following trauma, e.g. those who have been working in war or famine zones.
Location: Knowle
Ref: www.tc-of.org.uk (2.8.2011)

PARSENN SALLY late 1960's - 1975

"Life at Parsenn Sally, near Stratford, was drugs and Rock and Roll and also dressing for dinner and backgammon. It was called a commune by journalists, but in reality it was far from that. More a house shared by friends, a cross between a travellers' encampment and a posh country house"
Helen Mirren
Location: near Stratford,
Ref: Helen Mirren **In the Frame**

SHENLEY HOUSE COMMUNITY 1969 - 1976

Small group of four to seven young people trying to develop a sense of community on a suburban council estate.
Location: 126 Oak Tree Lane, Selly Oak
Ref: **Christian Communes;**
D Clark **Basic Communities**

LINDLEY LODGE circa 1970 - 1984

Interdenominational community of 20 people set up to "provide an opportunity for young people in their early years of employment to examine and develop their attitudes towards work and society, and to give them a greater understanding of other people and their problems."
Location: Watling Street, Nuneaton
Ref: J Mercer **Communes;**
D Clark **Basic Communities**

DIVINE LIGHT MISSION circa 1970 - 1983

Ashram lived in by Divine Light devotees.
Location: 10 Dovey Road, Moseley, Birmingham
Ref: www.prem-rawat-bio.org (31.7.2011)

DIVINE LIGHT MISSION circa 1970 - 1983

Ashram lived in by Divine Light devotees.
Location: 181 Staverley Road, Wolverhampton
Ref: www.prem-rawat-bio.org (31.7.2011)

DIVINE LIGHT MISSION circa 1970 - 1983

Ashram lived in by Divine Light devotees.
Location: 52 Windsor Street, Rugby
Ref: www.prem-rawat-bio.org (31.7.2011)

THE CHILDREN OF GOD circa 1971 - 76

House used by Christian Sect.
Location: 91 Heathfield, Handsworth
Ref: **Jesus Bubble**

COMMUNITY OF CELEBRATION CHRISTIAN TRUST circa 1973

Early attempt by CCCT to set up a community prior to Yeldall Manor.
Location: Coventry
Ref: **Christian Communes**

REDBRICKS
circa 1973 - ?

Urban collective. *"Large garden; vegetarians but sometimes eat bacon. Income from outside jobs. Communal meals daily. No capital needed."*
Location: 36 Anderton Park Road, Moseley
Ref: *Alternative Communities* 3rd ed, *Communes Network Directory* 1985

GWERIN HOUSING ASSOCIATION
circa 1974 -

Group with five large Victorian terraced houses supporting people with special needs.
Location: Stourbridge
Ref: *Alternative Communities* 4th ed; *D&D 94-95*

LOVE OF GOD COMMUNITY
1974 - 1977?

Christian Fellowship house established to *"build a model of the Church based on the communal style of life characteristic of early Christians."* Interdenominational. Six extended households.
Location: 6 Willow Avenue, Edgebaston
Ref: D Clark *Basic Communities*

BRANDHALL BAPTIST HOUSEHOLDS
circa 1974

Six extended households established to provide communities of fellowship and caring within the life of a local Baptist church.
Location: 53 Kings Way, Oldbury, Warley
Ref: D Clark *Basic Communities*

SPARKBROOK COMMUNITY HOUSE
1974 -

Methodist venture to link communal living with local neighbourhood and church. Ashram Community house.
Location: 1 Anderton Road and 23/25 Grantham Road, Sparkbrook, Birmingham
Ref: D Clark *Basic Communities*; *D&D 90-91*

GOUGH ROAD COMMUNITY
circa 1975 -

Ashram Community house with *'Young single committed Christians'*
Location: 115 Gough Road, Birmingham
Ref: *Directory of Christian Communities & Groups* 1980; *D&D 90-91*

BIRMINGHAM BUDDHIST VIHARA
circa 1978

Monastary, or Vihara, for both Tibetan and Theravadin traditions.
Location: 41 & 47 Carlyle Road and Osler Street, Ladywood
Ref: www.bbvt.org.uk (5.2.2011)

PROMISE HOUSE(S)
1979 -

Jesus Fellowship Church (Jesus Army) households in various locations in and around Coventry. First city where they did any large scale outreach.
Location: Harvest House, Eathorpe; Kings House Rugby Road, Stockton, Southam; 45 St Pauls Road, Coventry; White Stone house Leamington Road Coventry; Bright Flame, Stoke area of Coventry; 453 Foleshill Road, Coventry. Also rented house in Leamington.
Ref: www.promisehouse.org.uk (19.4.09)

ALBERT ROAD COMMUNITY
circa 1980

Group listed in Christian communities directory
Location: 213/5 Albert Road, Aston, Birmingham
Ref: *Directory of Christian Communities & Groups* 1980

BIRMINGHAM SETTLEMENT
circa 1980

Group listed in Christian communities directory.
Location: 318 Summer Lane, Newtown, Birmingham
Ref: *Directory of Christian Communities & Groups* 1980

DIVINE LIGHT MISSION
circa 1980

Ashrams lived in by Divine Light devotees.
Location: 40 Broad Road, Birmingham
Ref: *Alternative Communities* 3rd ed

ZAP
1986 - ?

Housing co-op spin off from a radical education project called the New University, set up to provide a space for informal skill sharing. The 'Z to A Project' is based in a seven bedroom Victorian terraced house. Also heavily involved in running a vegan cafe. *"Our house is available for use by groups sympathetic to our aims, and we hold occasional courses (eg Lesbian and Gay History, Massage) and skills sharing events."* Part of Radical Routes Network.
Location: 24 South Road, Hockley, Birmingham
Ref: *D&D 90-91*

ASTON LEE ABBEY HOUSEHOLD
1986 -

Small Christian community *"We live and work, learn and serve in a multi-cultural, multi-faith inner city area, aiming to be open and responsive to the many opportunities we have of sharing the Gospel."*
Location: 121 Albert Road, Aston
Ref: www.leeabbey.org.uk (14.6.2011)

THAT COMMUNITY   1988 -
Therapeutic community for emotionally and
psychologically disturbed adults.
Location: Birmingham
Ref: **D&D 94-95**

PARKDALE YOGA CENTRE   circa 1996
Group running Yoga courses and classes.
Location: 10 Parkdale West, Wolverhampton
Ref: www.heartyoga.co.uk (14.6.2011)

WILTSHIRE

ASHTON KEYNES   1936 - 1940
Bruderhof community set up on the 200-acre
Ashton Fields Farm after the sect was forced to
leave Europe by Nazi persecution. Grew to some
250 members attracting English followers. The
group developed the farm, renovating buildings
and cultivating the land; adding 103 adjoining
acres in 1937 and running a successful mixed farm
and large market garden. They also set up craft
and publishing ventures. Following anti-German
harassment at the outset of the War they sold up
and moved to Paraguay.
Location: Ashton Keynes
Ref: **Utopian England**

OAKSEY PARK   1938 - 1940
320 estate bought by the Bruderhof as their
community at Ashton Keynes expanded. The
purchase was referred to the Home Office when
local landowners complained about the sale of
land to Germans. The Home Office supported the
Bruderhof, but following further harassment the
community moved to Paraguay.
Location: Oaksey
Ref: **Utopian England**

SELLS GREEN   1938
*"One-man farm hopes to develop along communal
lines. Wanted two war resisters capable of looking
after nine acres of land, three goats and two sheep
– it is hoped to rebuild a ruined cottage."*
Location: Sells Green, Seend
Ref: Ad in *Peace News* 1.1.38

CPFLU LAND UNITS   1940 - 1946?
Christian Pacifist land-based units organised for
conscientious objectors.
Location: Collingbourne Ducis; West Woods,

Lockeridge; Seend; Mere; East Knowle; Bowden
Park Farm, Laycock; Downton
Ref: M Maclachlan **CPLFU**

HARNHAM CAMP   1946
Post-war squatter camp on army base.
Location: Harham
Ref: D Thomas *Villains' Paradise*

PYTHOUSE   1950's - 2003
Country house 'saved' by the Mutual Households
Association.
Location: Tisbury
Ref: **An Experiment in Co-operation**

LAVENDER FARM   1951 - 1955
Headquarters of the Friends Ambulance Unit
providing alternative to National Service for
conscientious objectors. Small farm with pigs,
poultry and market garden. Previously the home
of Beltane progressive school.
Location: Shaw Hill Road, Melksham
Ref: R Bush *FAU: The Third Generation*

THE COTSWOLD COMMUNITY   1967 - ?
Therapeutic community for emotionally disturbed
boys created out of a failing Approved School
that was set up on the site of a former Bruderhof
community. Consisted of five households; The
Cottage, Springfield, Northstead, Larkrise and the
Long Barn.
Location: Former Bruderhof Farm, Ashton Keynes
Ref: www.johnwhitwell.co.uk (1.1.2011)

SOUTH FARM – MOONIES   circa 1972 -
Six-hundred acre farm given to the
Unification Church by Henry Masters after
his daughter had joined them. The Moonies
renovated the farm and initially ran it as a
fairly conventionally farm. Later it became
a training centre for the Church hosting
seminars and workshops.
Location: Stanton Fitzwarren
Ref: *A New Tomorrow* – a 1974 documentary now
posted on YouTube (22.1.2011)

CLOUDWATER COMMUNITY   circa 1974
Seven couples proposing to set up a Centre for
*"stimulating potential through organic farming; arts
and crafts; alternative technology and therapy ..."*
Location: 'Compton', London Road, Devises
Ref: *In The Making* 2 Supplement A

FORT WALLY
1974

Thirty or so people who stayed on after the 1974 Stonehenge Free festival living communally in tents, in a field next to the stones. *"It was an open camp, inspired by a diversity of wild ideas, but with the common purpose of discovering the relevance of this ancient mysterious place by the physical experience of spending a lot of time there."* When the National Trust took them to court they all gave their names as 'Wally'. When they were evicted the Wallies moved their camp six feet away to a stretch of common land and stayed until the winter solstice.
Location: Stonehenge
Ref: www.earthlydelights.co.uk/netnews/wally.html (1.1.2011)

SURRENDELL FARM
1975 - ?

'Aristocratic' commune residents included Lady Sarah Ponsonby, Roddy Llewellyn, Helen Mirren and occasionally Princess Margaret. Llewellyn had a restaurant in Bath, Parsenn Sally, and the commune was supposed to provide vegetables for the restaurant.
Location: Hullavington, near Chippenham
Ref: www.telegraph.co.uk/arts/main.jhtml?xml=/arts/2003/08/23/bfmirren23.xml (3.6.11)

LOWER SHAW FARM
1975 - present

Farm rented from local council by Centre for Alternatives in Urban Development with Dick Kitto as warden. Birth place of Education Otherwise. Became communal household running variety of courses. Still run as course centre – also base for co-ordination of Swindon Literature Festival.
Location: Shaw near Swindon
Ref: *In The Making* 3; *D&D 90-91*

EAST LEAZE FARM
circa 1976 -

Small communal group renting farmhouse and garden.
Location: near Swindon
Ref: *Communes Network* 11

BARTON FARM
circa 1982 - ?

Sufi community, followers of the Sufi Order. Published local mag 'The Flute'
Location: Pound Lane, Bradford on Avon
Ref: *Alternative Communities* 4th ed; *The New Times Network*

GROUNDWELL FARM
circa 1984 -

"Performing arts/crafts community. Have goats, poultry, and a large garden. Excellent environment for children. Non-smokers; vegetarian in diet; prefer peace activists ..."
Location: Cricklade Road, Swindon
Ref: *Communes Network Directory* 1985

FRANKLEIGH HOUSE
1995 - present

Victorian Mansion with shared grounds of about seven acres, inc: open air swimming pool and rose garden. Bought after being used as school and turned into self contained flats along cohousing lines.
Location: Bradford on Avon
Ref: *D&D 96-97*

WORCESTER SHIRE

SUNFIELD
circa 1930 -

Steiner based 250-acre residential home with 80 to 90 pupils. Took in 20 refugees during war. Started in Birmingham in 1930 as home for 'backward children'.
Location: Clent Grove, Clent, Stourbridge
Ref: *Community in Britain* 1940

CPFLU LAND UNITS
1940 - 1946

Christian Pacifist land-based units organised for conscientious objectors.
Location: Charlton, Evesham and Harvington.
Ref: M Maclachlan *CPLFU*

CROSSWAYS FARM
1940 -

Farm bought by Quaker John Jenkins to assist conscientious objectors and who were being discriminated against by employers. The farm was little more than a peasant holding with a cottage and a number of out-houses in need of repair. *"We had four cows, one sow, three piglets, thirty three hens and a horse. Many prominent people were our house guests including the popular radio philosopher Dr C E M Joad, who used to visit us for weekends. There were four of us and I gave the others ten shillings a week pocket money but nothing for myself. We lost money. Sending one boy to buy a cow he came back with a car and a radio. I threw them out and I worked the farm by myself for some months in order to make a profit to pay back John Jenkins."* Cliff Holden
Location: Cradley
Ref: www.cliffholden.co.uk (18.9.08)

LAVERTON VILLAGE GROUP
1941

Address listed in *Community in a Changing World*.
Location: Thatched Cottage, Laverton, Broadway
Ref: *Community in a Changing World* 1941

WAC COMMUNITY SETTLEMENT
1941

Farm run by Worcester War Agricultural Committee for conscientious objectors. Housed 24 conscientious objectors plus four staff.
Location: Woodhouse farm, Wichenford
Ref: *Peace News Community Supplement* 25.4.41

WOLVERLEY CAMP
1941

20 families from Wolverley and Kidderminster squatted the former American hutted camp.
Location: Wolverley
Ref: www.wolverleycamp.org.uk (23.12.08)

OLD PARK FARM ESTATE
1946 - 1950's

Post-war estate developed by Dudley Town Corporation along plans drawn up by Charles Reilly incorporating his Reilly Greens concept. Included; two, three, and four-bedroomed houses and flats and, as basic essentials, a community centre or Club house and nursery school and a district heating scheme. The estate is known locally as "The Greens" as most of the roads on it are called "Green"; ie Ash Green, Oak Green ...
Location: Dudley
Ref: P Richmond *Marketing Modernisms*

CAMPHILL HOUSES
1969 -

Four community houses close to the centre of Stourbridge, and one just outside town. Households include community members with disabilities and support co-workers and their families.
Location: 19 South Road, Stourbridge,
Ref: *Camphill Villages*; www.cvt.org.uk (21.4.2011)

BIRCHWOOD HALL
1970/1 - present

Large house set in nine acres of mostly woodland. Started as a Trust and later became a co-op. Communal kitchen, sitting room, TV room, laundry, workshop, games/music room and vegetable garden. *"We are quite a structured group having meetings, either business or feelings, once a week; we also aim to stay in touch with each other at an individual level as well as within the group. Decisions are made by consensus. We all value harmony within the group, perhaps sometimes to the extent of pushing things underneath the carpet rather than dealing with them, and live with each other because we like each other most of the time."*
Location: Storridge, Malvern
Ref: *Directory of Communes* 1972;
Legal Frameworks Handbook; D&D 90-91

WHITBOURNE HALL
1977 -

Victorian mansion built by Edward Evans from profits from vinegar works and English wine making. Run as family house till 1970's when it became too expensive to pay servants and maintenance bills. Eldest son, Bill Evans, persuaded his father to let him have the Hall on licence for two years to start an experimental community of six families who would *"make the Hall their home, and keep it running with their combined labour."* The experiment was a success with the group evolving over the two years and working hard *"to eradicate the damp and dry rot which had also taken up residence."* In 1980 Whitbourne Hall Community Limited obtained planning permission to convert the Hall into apartments, and purchased the Hall from the Evans family.
Location: Whitbourne
Ref: *Alternative Communities* 4th ed; D&D 94-95;
www.whitbournehall.com

NEW VILLAGES ASSOCIATION
circa 1974 - 1980's

Set up to *"establish land-based villages where people can live and produce as much as possible of their own food, clothing, and other necessities*

locally, and recycle their wastes." Became a
research project and loose network.
Location: Food and Energy Research Centre,
Evesham Road, Cleeve Prior, Evesham
Ref: *In The Making* 2; *BITMAN* No 6 (May 1974)

HARMONY   circa 1975
Proposal for large scale community 40-100
people that would aim for 'near self-sufficiency'.
Planned both communal and independent living
Location: c/o 'Greenways', 200 Wells Road,
Malvern Wells
Ref: *In The Making* 3

CROOME COURT   1979 - 1985
Two-hundred-room mansion set in 40 acres of fields
and landscaped park land built in 1750 for the Earl
of Coventry by Lancelot "Capability" Brown. Bought
by the Hare Krishna movement who renamed it the
Chaitanya College. They set up a novice training
programme and a school. More than 150 devotees
lived at the Court, some in cottages on the estate and
a number of married couples lived in the Worcester
suburbs. The group kept llamas and Indian cattle.
Location: Croome D'Abitot
Ref: *The Hare Krishna Movement*

COMMUNITY FOR RECONCILIATION   1986 -
Small residential Christian community serving as
resource for wider community network spread
through the United Kingdom and overseas.
Location: Barnes Close, Bromsgrove
Ref: www.cfrbarnesclose.co.uk (14.6.2001)

YORKSHIRE

AMPLEFORTH ABBEY   circa 1802 -
Benedictine monastery often listed in communes
directories.
Location: York.
Ref: J Mercer *Communes*;
Alternative Communities 2nd ed

PAINTED FABRIC LTD   1918 - 1959
Small community of disabled ex-servicemen based
on the old Women's Auxiliary Army Corps camp.
They made high quality fabric goods whilst living
in converted huts and ten houses. Also worked
gardens and allotments.
Location: Norton Woodseats
Ref: Exhibition Leaflet

BROTHERHOOD CHURCH
STAPLETON COLONY   1921 - present
Christian anarchist land colony set up by
group from Leeds. They live by the precepts
of the Sermon on the Mount, recognising no
authority other than that of God, a stance
that has brought them into repeated conflicts
with the authorities, for erecting dwellings
without permission (the group rebuilt the houses
everytime the council demolished them!), failing
to register children's births, keeping their
children out of state schools, refusing to fill
in census forms and to pay the poll tax. They
have close links with the Peace Pledge Union
(PPU) and War Resisters International holding
a 'Strawberry Tea Party' each summer to raise
funds for them. During the 1960's they ran a film
van for the PPU, showing back-projection peace
films in town centres up and down the country.
The colony consists of a series of small cottages
dotted about a large small-holding. Over the
years they have run a market garden, carried
out knitting, sold honey and Christmas trees
to support themselves as well as running their
own small printing business publishing booklets,
recipe books and calendars. Over the years
the community has developed into a network
of extended 'families' that extend beyond the
geographic bounds of the colony.
Location: Stapleton
Ref: John Quail *Slow Burning Fuse*;
A G Higgins *A History of the Brotherhood Church*;
D&D 94-95; *Utopian England*;
www.thebrotherhoodchurch.org (14.6.2011)

CPFLU LAND UNITS   1940 - 1946?
Christian Pacifist land-based units organised for
conscientious objectors.
Location: Selby; Allerston
Ref: M Maclachlan *CPLFU*

TRANS-PENNINE CHRISTIANS   1940
Plan to create a community on 70 acres.
Location: near Wakefield
Ref: Ad in *Peace News* 19.1.40

HOLLINGTHORPE COMMUNITY   1941
Land-based community five adults three
children. (Possibly same as Trans-Pennine
group.)
Location: Hollingthorpe Farm, Chapelthorpe
Ref: *Peace News Community Supplement* 25.4.41

SORBY RESEARCH INSTITUTE   1941

Suburban house used by Dr Kenneth Mellanby as a research base for experiments to find a cure for scabies. Mellanby came up with the idea of using conscientious objectors as guinea pigs because they were unlikely to be suddenly called up into war service.
Location: 18 Oakholme Road, Sheffield
Ref: *Community in a Changing World*; www.ppu.org.uk (21.9.2011)

SQUATTERS PROTECTION SOCIETY   1946

Group formed by squatters of several Ministry of Works camps around Sheffield.
Ref: Colin Ward *The hidden history of housing*

MANOR LANE SQUATTERS   1946

Around 15 homeless families squatting in disused military huts in grounds of Manor Lodge
Location: Manor Lane, Sheffield
Ref: www.manorlodge.org.uk/mcv_squatters (17.6.2011); *Sheffield Telegraph* 26.8.1946

CAULMS WOOD CAMP   1946 -

Post-war squatter camp *"Within hours of the soldiers leaving, families from all over the area descended on the camp, breaking the padlock on the iron gates to get in. Nobody had foreseen this, and it took the council, who had ownership of the huts, some time before they could sort out the situation. Some families were eventually evicted, especially those who had come over from Ossett, but others were allowed to stay ... However, a settled community was quickly established there, much to the dismay of people living nearby, who complained that the camp was spoiling the area. One local councillor visiting the site disagreed and said some of those living in the huts had converted them into 'little palaces' and begged people not to tar everyone with the same brush."*
Location: near Dewsbury
Ref: *Dewsbury Reporter* 11.9.2008

BOTTON CAMPHILL VILLAGE 1955 - present

Around 150 'Villagers' with learning difficulties and the same Co-workers living in 28 households on 610 acres including extensive forest and six bio-dynamic farms. Workshops and services include bakery, cheese making, glass engraving, wood workshop, doll making, weaving, candle making, post office, cafe and shops. There is also a Waldorf School for children from the area and a

retirement home for the elderly.
Location: Danby, North Yorkshire
Ref: *D&D 90-91*; www.cvt.org.uk (11.6.2011)

PASHBY HOUSE   circa 1950's -

Built originally as the Reckitts Girls Hostel as part of the Hull Garden Village, later became a therapeutic community, and then a Social Services office.
Location: 69 James Reckitt Avenue, Hull
Ref: www.tc-of.org.uk (2.8.201)

SCARGILL HOUSE   1959 -

Christian community serving holiday and conference centre.
Location: Kettlewell
Ref: *D&D 96-97*; *NACCAN Directory* 4th ed

COMMUNITY GROUP   circa 1962

"Community group beginning in village ten miles from Leeds, offers gracious living in a Georgian house to anyone of either sex and any age, who is interested in philosophy, psychology and art in any form."
Location: '10 miles from Leeds'
Ref: *CLA Bulletin* Jan 1962

ASHRAM COMMUNITY TRUST 1967 - present

Radical Christian ecumenical community with individual members, regional groups and community houses/ projects in urban neighbourhoods.
Location: 178 Abbeyfield Rd; Burngreave Rd; 75-77 Rock St; 84 Andover St, Sheffield
Ref: *NACCAN Directory* 4th ed; www.ashram.org.uk (17.6.2011); D Clark *Basic Communities*

WESLEY COMMUNITY   circa 1968 -

Christian Community House.
Location: Barnsley
Ref: *Directory of Christian Communities & Groups* 1980

LEEDS COMMUNE(S)   circa 1970

"... there's a couple of communes at 2, Carberry Place and 2 Springfield Mount"
Location: Leeds
Ref: *International Times* 82 (July 1970)

OUTSIDER COMMUNITY
   PROJECTS TRUST   circa 1970

Charity set up by a group of young people who wanted to tackle the problems of the vagrant,

alcoholic and the mentally ill. Offer help to up to 12 residents at a time. Basic aims were: *"(a) to provide shelter to those who have none. (b) to provide some sort of alternative employment activity for those termed socially inadequate and (c) to provide community living for those people who are unable to form emotionally satisfying relationships."*
Location: 71/2 Princes Avenue, 9 Leonard St, Hull
Ref: *International Times* 92 (Nov 1970); *Peace News* 23.2.73

LATHAM FARM COMMUNE   circa 1970/71
Two men and one woman trying to establish small commune based on group marriage and self-sufficiency on Pennine farm — Ex Manchester commune project.
Location: "an hour's drive from Manchester", Wadsworth near Hebden Bridge.
Ref: *Making Communes*; CM Newsletter 7.12.70

LINDLEY LODGE   circa 1970's
Sister household to Lindley Lodge Nuneaton.
Location: Masham House, Masham, near Ripon
Ref: J Mercer *Communes*

DIVINE LIGHT MISSION   circa 1970 - 1983
Ashram lived in by Divine Light devotees.
Location: 67 Otley Old Road, Leeds
Ref: www.prem-rawat-bio.org (31.7.2011)

ANARCHIST COMMUNE   1970 - 1980
"We've had a very varied existence over the years. Resident numbers are usually low about three to six adults. All understandings are reached by mutual agreement, which leads to a certain fluidity. We function as a 'crashpad' for visitors to Sheffield. Advance notice is not necessary, but is useful ... We believe, as anarchists, that our venture is a valid and reasonable reaction against the authoritative, chaotic shambles which is accepted as being the social and economic norm of modern society."
Location: 4 Havebrook Square, Sheffield 10
Ref: *Alternative Communities* 3rd ed; Andrew Rigby *Alternative Realities*

FLUFF COMMUNE   circa 1971
"'Fluff' a rural commune near Bradford recently got busted. They're organising a benefit featuring Hawkwind and others in St Georges Hall ..."
Location: near Bradford
Ref: *International Times* 112 (Sep 1971)

TROGWELL   circa 1972 - 1984
Pronounced 'Troggle' — a loose communal household. Involved in early days of **Communes Network**.
Location: 31 Woodview, Bradford
Ref: **Communes Network** 1

THE ELMS   circa 1970 - 1972
Group renting large dilapidated farmhouse for £1 a week.
Location: near Roos
Ref: **Communes Journal** 40, Dec 1972

ABBEY ROAD COLLECTIVE   1972 - 1977
Group featured in Nell Dunn's book.
Location: Leeds
Ref: Nell Dunn *Living Like I Do*

FOLD FARM   circa 1975
Small group living on a third of an acre small-holding.
Location: near Sowerby Bridge?
Ref: **Communes Network** 10

LIFESPAN   1973 - late 1990's
Community in two terraces of empty railway workers houses on top of the Pennines set up by former Summerhill pupils as educational trust where people could learn by "living and doing." Early years spent renovating houses and running wholefood shop for a while before setting up printing business. Published own series of wholefood recipe booklets and printed *Communes Network* and *Diggers & Dreamers*. Planted trees as wind breaks and cultivated large vegetable garden. Struggled to find a way to expand numbers to fill the 19 houses. In the 1990's many long-term members left and the group had high turnover of members. Numbers dwindled and the community was eventually all but abandoned.
Location: Townhead, Dunford Bridge nr Holmfirth
Ref: **Communes Network** (various); *In The Making* 2 Supp A

RADTECH

circa 1977

Collective interested in radical science and self-management based in two communal houses in working class area of Sheffield. Had large workshop which they planned to set up 'productive project' in.

Location: 71 Thirlwell Road and 12-14 Goodwin Road, Sheffield

Ref: **Communes Network** 21

RURALLY BASED COMMON OWNERSHIP PROJECT

circa 1974

"We aim to buy sufficient acreage and accommodation probably north of Birmingham for obvious economic reasons to allow for the production of as much of our own food as possible ... The primary aim is self-sufficiency and a better life for us and the kids."

Location: Eden House Nursery, Westgate, Pickering

Ref: In The Making 2 Supplement A

LEGRAMS LANE

circa 1975

"COMMUNE – Are you interested in joining an established group to form a ten people unit who are planning to buy a farmhouse in order to progress from the present five person urban commune. Main outline of commune, non nuclear, progressive self manufactive, communards retain "straight" occupations, radical, communards to contribute aprox. £200 initially."

Location: 257 Legrams Lane, Bradford

Ref: Ad in **Undercurrents** 12 (Sep Oct 1975)

L'ARCHE

1975 - ?

Community house for International L'Arche movement.

Location: 10 Briggate, Silsden

Ref: **D&D 94-95**

ADDISON HOUSE COMMUNITY

circa 1976

Group involved in local youth and playgroups

Location: Hull

Ref: **Christian Communes**

EXPERIMENTAL COMMUNITY WORKSHOPS

circa 1976 - ?

Small co-operative group renovating derelict buildings and running craft project.

Location: Moor Cote, Ellingstring near Ripon

Ref: **Alternative Communities** 2nd ed

BOWES COMMUNITY

circa 1976

"WE ARE IN the process of renovating a farm house on the bleak Pennines four miles west of Bowes. The house backs on to a main road but looks south over miles of field and moorland. We have ½ acre of garden and some grazing. We have gradually been moving towards self sufficiency in food for some time, but the land we now have increases our potential enormously, At the moment we have hens, bees and a cow. The climate is not ideal but is all we can afford. We would like some one (or two) to share this place with us, sharing lives, work etc in fact everything baring actual ownership ..."

Location: near Bowes

Ref: Small ad in **Undercurrents** 16 (1976)

THE CROFT COMMUNITY

1976 -

Camphill community of 70 people living in six community houses in different areas of Malton, Norton and Old Malton, ranging from a large Grade II listed Georgian townhouse to small modern cottage. Run Kingfisher Café, Gift and Bookshop. Have large market garden and craft workshops.

Location: 4 Old Maltongate, Malton

Ref: www.cvt.org.uk (21.4.2011)

DUMB TOM'S

circa 1977 - ?

Communal house bought by group of friends. Some with close links to Lancaster University. "A kind of hippie commune and focal point of the alternative scene in Bentham."

Location: Ingleton

Ref: **Communes Network** 22

PENNINE CAMPHILL COMMUNITY

1977 -

Community supporting specialist college providing further education and support for young people with learning difficulties. Five households where students live in extended family groups together with vocational co-workers and their families. Small farm covers about 25 acres of grassland plus three acres fruit and vegetable gardens "we are almost 50% self-sufficient in terms of garden produce for about 75 people on site."

Location: Wood Lane, Chapelthorpe, Wakefield

Ref: www.pennine.org.uk (21.4.2011); **D&D 92-93**; **NACCAN Directory** 4th ed

TANGRAM HOUSING CO-OP

1977 - present

Group of squatters from London intending to set a community up in the rural North stopped off in

Leeds and set up initially in short life housing. Later developed into housing co-op with 40 units.
Location: 76 Bankside Street, Leeds.
Ref: *D&D 00-01*

BECKONING MOLE   late 1970's
Small housing co-op with house on moors.
Location: near High Bentham
Ref: *Communes Network*

CRACKS HOUSING CO-OP   circa 1978 - ?
Small communal group renovating terraced house.
Location: 4 South View, High Bentham
Ref: *Alternative Communities* 4th ed

HOLT LAITHE   1976 - 1979
Three couples co-operatively owning and working a small farm. Had goats and working horses.
Location: Holt Head, Slaithwaite
Ref: *Communes Network* 22; *Alternative Communities* 4th ed

HAREHILLS COMMUNE   circa 1978 -
"Inspired during our stay at Laurieston Hall, a plan for a commune organised on neo-Reichian socialist-feminist principles, where every decision was made by consensus, ... To break down bourgeois individualism, everything would be owned collectively. Even T-shirts and knickers would be kept in a communal drawer. We would write a manifesto to explain to the rest of humanity why what we were doing was better than what they were doing, and if they did it our way, they too could share toothbrushes and total orgasms."
Location: Leeds
Ref: In the Dark and Still Moving

TWEED STREET HOUSING CO-OP   1980 -
Small group renovating a couple of terraced houses – also large garden.
Location: Tweed Street, High Bentham
Ref: *Alternative Communities* 4th ed

THUNDERCLIFFE GRANGE   1980 - present
Former country house, hospital for "female lunatics" and NHS residential school for severely mentally handicapped children a stone's throw from the M1 motorway acquired by a group largely made up of local authority officers who were interested in developing a co-operative lifestyle. The buildings were converted on a mainly self build basis into 12 flats in a sort of prototype cohousing set up.

Location: Grange Lane, Rotherham
Ref: *Alternative Communities* 4th ed; Publicity leaflet; www.cohousing.org.uk (25.7.2011)

WILD LAVENDER   1981 -
Housing Co-op established by group of gay men who met up at an anti sexist men's conference in 1980. Moved to two communal houses in London.
Location: 27 Sholebrook Avenue, Leeds
Ref: *Communes Network Directory* 1983; *D&D 90-91*

WARREN COURT   circa 1983 -
"... interested in alternative technology, pacifism, vegetarianism, self-sufficiency, direct action. Looking for new members."
Location: Park Lodge Lane, Wakefield
Ref: *Alternative Communities* 4th ed

UNSTONE GRANGE   circa 1983 -
Small group of five adults, two young people running a conference centre.
Location: Unstone, near Sheffield.
Ref: *Alternative Communities* 4th ed

CHUMBAWUMBA   1980's
Communal house lived in by anarcho-punk band.
Location: Leeds
Ref: "Well Done, Now Sod Off" – Video

GIROSCOPE   1985 - present
Co-operative set up by students and unemployed young people to house themselves. Renovated houses and set up work projects including print co-op and crèche. *"Ideologically Giroscope is more about 'taking control' and 'working for change' than it is about the usual cosmic self(ish) development of some right on schemes."*
Location: 8 Glencoe Street, Anlaby Road, Hull
Ref: *D&D 92-93*; www.giroscope.co.uk (22.5.12)

MADHYAMAKA CENTRE   1986 -
Buddhist college in Georgian Mansion.
Location: Kilnwick Percy
Ref: *D&D 00-01*

WELLSPRING   circa 1991
Group looking at old hospital and 60-acre wooded site *"on the edge of moors"* with plan to set up a *"Living working community college along ecological lines."*
Location: Leeds/Bradford area
Ref: *D&D 92-93*

WOMENS COLLECTIVE HOUSING PROJECT

circa 1991 -

Four self-contained flats with communal areas as an integral part of the design.
Location: Sheffield
Ref: **D&D 92-93**

BRAMBLES

1992 - ?

Housing Co-op and resource centre. Part of Radical Routes network.
Location: 82 Andover Street, Sheffield.
Ref: **D&D 94-95**

CORNERSTONE

1993 - ?

Small housing co-op set up to provide base for people involved in social and environmental issues. *"... try to live communal, low consumption lifestyles ... United in at least eight different visions (so far)... evening meal is often the setting for a lively debate over the 1001 different ways to define 'social change'."* Part of Radical Routes network.
Location: 16 Sholebrook Ave, Chapeltown, Leeds.
Ref: **D&D 96-97**

SPACE HOUSE

1994 - ?

Communal household in large renovated Victorian terraced house.
Location: 8 Beaufort Road, Sheffield
Ref: **D&D 96-97**

CONNECTIONS

1996

"A small nucleus is growing but is, as yet, unstructured. We are seeking an opportunity to live with others where we will connect; with ourselves (through personal growth work),with others (through community living) ... with nature, seen and unseen (in our organic gardens, woods and meadows),with the Universe (through our meditation and healing work) ... offering love, harmony and joy to ourselves and others. we will acknowledge the oneness of all."
Location: c/o address at Kirbymoorside, York
Ref: **D&D 96-97**

WALES

THE ISLAND FARMERS

1939 - 1946

Co-farming experiment set up by Welsh naturalist Ronald Lockley on two coastal farms.
Location: Dinas Cross, Pembrokeshire
Ref: **The Island Farmers**

LLANDOUGH CASTLE

circa 1940's

Youth Aliyah Hostel housing Jewish refugees in ex-YMCA training centre for unemployed boys.
Location: Cowbridge
Ref: **The History of the YMCA in Wales;**
www.ajr.org.uk (KinderTransport Survey) (1.1.2011)

RUTHIN CASTLE

circa 1940's

Base for Bachad Zionist youth movement from where they set up training farms across the UK.
Location: Denbighshire
Ref: www.bauk.org (21.3.2009)

GWRYCH CASTLE

1940 - 1945

Camp run 'like a Kibbutz' housing 200 Kindertransport refugees. *"facilities were extremely basic, with no running water or electricity, as the castle was not connected to the main water and*

electricity supplies, and no fuel was available for the generators."
Location: Denbighshire
Ref: www.gwrychtrust.co.uk (21.3.2009)

ELLERSLIE COMMUNITY

1940 - 1941

Small Pacifist Community in six-bedroom house with an acre of land who hoped to acquire the property as a permanent communal centre. Also called Cardiff Community Peace centre and had links to the Cardiff Homecroft scheme.
Location: Sully Road, Penarth.
Ref: **Community in Britain**; Peace News 3.1.41

CARDIFF HOMECROFT

circa 1940

House and ½ acre of land donated by local pacifist to Cardiff Peace pledge Union who attempted to run home-crofting scheme with six refugees.
Location: Cardiff
Ref: **Community in Britain** 1940

CPFLU LAND UNITS

1940 - 1946

Christian Pacifist land-based units organised for conscientious objectors.

Location: Caio, Llanwrda; Halfway, Llandovery; Ryhdfedw, Pencader; Margam; Michaelston; Tintern; Trellech; Monmouth
Ref: M Maclachlan **CPLFU**

LLANISHEN HOUSE COMMUNITY   1941
Eight members working eight acres giving produce and hospitality to local homeless dockworkers.
Location: Llanishen, Cardiff
Ref: **Peace News Community Supplement** 25.4.41

BRYN CONWAY HOSTEL   circa 1942 - 1945
Childrens Evacuation Childrens Hostel.
Location: Conwy
Ref: J Coleman **Childscourt**

PENYBRIN HOSTEL   circa 1942 - 1945
Regional Evacuation Children's Hostel which was for the most difficult evacuees in the six counties of North Wales. Run by Bill Malcolm became a forerunner of post-war therapeutic communities.
Location: Penybrin
Ref: J Coleman **Childscourt**;
www.pettarchiv.org.uk (17.01.09)

MALPAS ARMY CAMP   circa 1946
Army camp taken over by squatters.
Location: Malpas near Newport
Ref: www.bbc.co.uk/wales/southeast (3.1.09)

BARRY ARMY CAMP   circa 1946
Army camp taken over by squatters at the end of the war despite efforts by the local authorities and police to stop them. *"A former tenant of the camp said that when they heard that there was a five to seven year waiting list for council houses, her husband, an ex-serviceman, decided to move into the camp. He approached one of the police manning the barrier and asked if he could pass, whereupon the officer said that he was sorry, but his orders were to let no one through the barrier. He then added that there was nothing to stop him carrying his furniture and other belongings across the fields ... to the camp, but that he could not allow him to pass the barrier."*
Location: Barry
Ref: www.barrywales.co.uk (23.12.08)

MAES PADARN ARMY CAMP   circa 1946
Army camp taken over by squatters.
Location: Maes Padarn Estate, Llanberis
Ref: www.geograph.org.uk (3.1.09)

GARTH NEWYDD HOUSE   1958 - ?
Small Gandhian inspired community that was established after the 1957 Fellowship of Friends of Truth Conference in Bristol. They were offered an old house in Merthyr Tydfil that had been given to the town during the Depression. Members had links with the Direct Action Committee Against Nuclear War, International Voluntary Service, Plaid Cymru, Servas and Peacemakers. *"... we have established a community house. It will be based on service, primarily with the local community. We are prepared to accept the greater self-discipline that this living together implies, and will endeavour to make ourselves better instruments of service through individual and group study. Income will be pooled, and decisions taken on the basis of unanimity. We envisage the possibility of non-violent action in the face of social and other wrongs."* The house later became something of Welsh Nationalist commune with clandestine broadcasts from the pirate radio station Radio Free Wales being made from the attic. The Commonweal library collection, now housed at Bradford University School of Peace Studies, started life as the library at Garth Newydd.
Location: Merthyr Tydfil
Ref: Bradford Peace Studies

'SELENE COMMUNITY'   1967 - 68
20 acres of boggy land where members of the Selene group lived before moving to the farm near Llanbedr.
Location: Exact location unknown
Ref: Andrew Rigby **Alternative Realities**

'SELENE COMMUNITY'   1968 - ?
Forty four acre hill farm.
Location: Rhydcymerau, Llandelio, Sir Gaerfyrddin
Ref: Andrew Rigby **Alternative Realities**; Ad in International Times 35 (July 1968)

INCREDIBLE STRING BAND COMMUNE   circa 1968
Commune in a farmhouse near Newport set up by members of the The Incredible String Band and the Exploding Galaxy dance troupe.
Location: Penwern, Pembrokeshire
Ref: www.makingtime.co.uk/isb.html (5.7.11);
Electric Eden; Be Glad For the Song Has No Ending

SELENE COMMUNITY 1970 - ?

Fifty-four acre farm in the Cambrian mountains bought for £5,000 by three members of Selene. *"... between the coldness of the nation and the rigidness of the family is the commune, a group of people living and working together, with a shared ethos, providing each other with varied stimulation, helping each other in times of need and sharing with each other a love which is rare in the nuclear family ..."* Very involved in establishing the Commune Movement and Pagan goddess worship.

Location: Cymdeithas Selene, Can-y-lloef Ffarmers, Llanwrda, Dyfed
Ref: **Directory of Communes** 1972; **Alternative London** 1970; **Communes Europe**

LLANERCHWEN RETREAT 1970 - present

Core group of three adults and two children on an eight-acre hill property with cottages Running an Anglican retreat getting some 200 visitors a year. *"... there is space to discover security, meaning, and purpose and to grow in maturity and union with God."* In 1979 was sold to The Society of the Sacred Heart who continue to run it as a retreat There is a small resident community of Roman Catholic sisters who are assisted by an ecumenical team of visiting retreat guides (women and men, lay and religious).

Location: Llanerchwen, Llandefaelog, Brecon
'Ref: D Clark **Basic Communities**; www.llannerchwen.org.uk (1.1.2011)

NANT GWRYTHEYRN circa 1970's

Deserted granite quarry village taken over by the 'New Atlantis Commune'. *"They lived without either a water supply, an electricity supply or a sewerage system. The hippies were responsible for creating great damage to The Nant as floorboards and doors were burnt, roofing slates were smashed and walls were covered with graffiti."* Nicholas Saunders who came across the village in 1974 whilst researching his Alternative England & Wales book put forward a proposal to buy the village. It was purchased in 1978 by the Nant Gwrtheyrn Trust and has been turned into a Welsh Language centre.

Location: LLynn Peninsula
Ref: **BITMAN** 11; www.nantgwrtheyrn.org (21.12.10)

PANT-Y-POWYSI circa 1970's

Couple living in semi-derelict farm wanting to set up a co-operative venture making and selling craft products.
Location: Talerddig, Powys
Ref: www.coughtrey.me.uk (1.1.2011)

CREATIVE AID TRUST 1970 - 72

"COMMUNE WEEKEND COURSE. Creative Aid Trust (CAT) at the MAGI performing group have decided to open their place at weekends for invited visitors. The course offers music, poetry, walks, picnics and talks on meditation, creation and commune living. Visitors will bring sleeping bag, some cash or provisions sharing and a donation – gift to help extend the work of the commune ..."

Location: Chapel Coll Kerry, Newtown, Montgomeryshire
Ref: **Directory of Communes** 1972; **Alternative London** 1970; ad in **International Times** 103 (May 1971)

DIVINE LIGHT MISSION circa 1970 - 1983

Ashram lived in by Divine Light devotees.
Location: 31 Summerfield Avenue, Cardiff
Ref: www.prem-rawat-bio.org (31.7.2011)

FACHONGLE ISAF circa 1970 - present

Farm of self-sufficiency guru John Seymour and his wife Sally. After the couple split up was turned into 'The Centre for Living' a School for Self-Sufficiency – after Seymour left in the 1980's became a loose informal community.

Location: Porth Newydd, Dyfed
Ref: **Alternative Communities** 4th ed; J Mercer **Communes**

STUDENT COMMUNITY circa 1971 - ?

Group of about a dozen students living on the top floor of 18th century mansion turned museum owned by the National Trust. *"The property is beautiful, with a lake, a stream, woods and hills."*
Location: Aberstwyth (possibly Llanerchaeron)
Ref: **Making Communes**

THE CHILDREN OF GOD circa 1971 - 1976

Hotel bought for £50 by Christian sect.
Location: 3 Ystrad Road, Pentre, Glamorgan
Ref: **Jesus Bubble**

FRED 1971 - 2

Rented a flat in Merthyr in Aug 1971 prior to buying a row of derelict cottages. Sold the cottages and set off back to *"the smoke; not to talk*

about setting up a rural commune, but to set up an urban one" after members failed to materialise.
Location: Merthyr Tydfil (moved to Bradford 1972)
Ref: *Directory of Communes* 1972

CATMAGI   circa 1971
Group listed as affiliated to Commune Movement.
Location: Chapel cottage, Kerry, Newtown, Monmouthshire
Ref: *Commune Movement Newsletter* 30.7.71

CRAFT COMMUNE   circa 1972
"CRAFT commune developing at large farmhouse in North Wales."
Location: North Wales (Possibly same as Pant-y-Powysi)
Ref: Ad in *International Times* 123 (Feb 1972)

– NO NAME AS YET- COMMUNE –   1972
"We are trying to establish what is by popular definition a craft commune, but in effect a functional alternative to existing codes of living ... we wish to maintain all the outward signs of self-sufficiency, viability and functionalism ... Also all the usual crap about ecology, pollution and organicals – freedom, spirit and oneness – man, myth or magic ... dogma, stigma etc etc, blah, blah ..."
Location: Unknown
Ref: *Directory of Communes* 1972

OERLE COMMUNE   1972
"OUR commune is faced with extinction unless we find £2,000 within the next two months, we are trying to get loans etc, but without much success. Please help. Any financial support, however small, will help to keep us going. Love and Peace. Gilly and all at Oerle Commune."
Location: Trefeglwys, Caersws, Monmouthshire
Ref: Ad in *International Times* 132 (Jun 1972)

'LOVING COMMUNE'   1972
"IF anyone who would like to be part of a loving commune with an interest in mysticism, personal freedom etc, based at the moment in a small primitive but beautiful and isolated cottage (children very welcome)..."
Location: Maesmynach, Cilcennin, Lampeter
Ref: Ad in *International Times* 138 (Sep 1972)

MILLER FAMILY COMMUNE circa 1972 - 1975
8 people living in old farmhouse with ½ acre of land, others living in caravans – hoping to grow to 25.

Location: Waun Lwyd, Carmarthen
Ref: Communes Journal 40 Dec 1972; *Directory of Communes* 1972; **Communes Network** 4

SERENDIPITY COMMUNE   1972
Two couples in small rented house *"... on the lookout/hoping for capital to buy larger place (or two or three smaller ones close together, or preferably a privately owned village for sale ...)"*
Location: Nant-y-Llyn, Ffarmers, Llanwrda, Carmarthenshire
Ref: Entry in *Directory of Communes* 1972

B.R.A.D.   1972 - 1976
Biotechnic Research and Development project known as BRAD for short. Built early eco-home on 43-acre hill farm with solar collectors, oil drum wind turbine, rainwater recycling, Jotul woodstove and compost loo.
Location: Eithiny Gaer, Churchstoke, Montgomeryshire
Ref: *Undercurrents* May 72

THE TEACHERS   circa 1972 - late 1980's
Ambitious group set up by Mensa member Kevin O'Byrne – known as 'Kevin of the Teachers' – and his partner Michelle. Had houses, toy shop and ran a disco in Bangor and farm nearby. Produced a series of *Alternative Communities* directories in the late 70's and early 80's and tried to set up an Alternative Communities Movement with regional reps and its own magazine.
Location: 18 Garth Road, Bangor and Carreg Y Fedwen, Sling, Tregarth, Bangor
Ref: *Alternative Communities* 1st ed; *CN* 21

CENTRE FOR ALTERNATIVE TECHNOLOGY
1972 - present

Project set up by Gerard Morgan-Grenville in 40-acre disused Llwyngwern slate quarry an experimental ecological community. Attracted visitors from the start and has developed over the years into a major tourist attraction. Residential group running the centre has always had a communal component although living in separate houses. *"We have a community house and meet here for our vegetarian meals. There is a rota for cooking, breadmaking and cleaning. We try to grow as much of our own organic produce as possible and have a few chickens and goats."*
Location: Machynlleth
Ref: **D&D 90-91**

TOWY COMMUNITY WORKSHOP
circa 1972 - 78

Craft based community with potters, weavers and gardeners in large house with 22 acres of land. *"Pretty well everything is shared – money, possessions (no compulsion) household chores, decisions etc ... the future is so promising and any hardships and difficulties seem small when set against the chance of living in a place of such beauty, peace and neighbourly friendlyness."* The house was advertised for sale in **Communes Network** 30 in 1977.
Location: Natymwyn House, Rhandirmwyn, Dyfed
Ref: **Communes Network** 5, 13 and 30; **In The Making** 3

BARN HOUSE
circa 1973 - 79?

Community set up by Phillip Toynbee in a 5-bedroom former pottery at Brockweir Common on the southern edge of the Forest of Dean.
Location: Brockweir near Chepstow, Gwent
Ref: **Communes Network** 21; **Part of a Journey**

MOUNTAIN OF LIGHT LLWYN ARFON FARM
circa 1973 -

13 adults and 2 children on 40-acre organic farm; cows, goats, bees, chicken and sheep. Committed to spiritual growth. Hold Tai Chi and Shiatsu weekend courses.
Location: Hollybush, Blackwood, Gwent
Ref: **Alternative Wales** 1982; **Alt Communities** 3rd ed

EARTH WORKSHOP
circa 1973

A seven strong eco-commune formed by among others the artist Eric Raven; architect and Street Farmer Peter Crump; Peter Harper; and Stefan Szczelkun author of the Survival Scrapbooks. *"We occupied an Old Vicarage built within a Neolithic circle in Llandeussant, an ancient settlement on the west end of the Brecon Beacons which was to have been paid for by the proceeds from the sale of Peter Crump's London house."* Suffered set back when vicarage fell through, but project continued to look for somewhere to set up research centre open to visitors. *"We intend to use our background experience from the broad based disciplines of art, architecture and literature to explore possibilities of life support systems that may be developed and controlled on a small scale and that will integrate most fully with the existing support systems of nature."*
Location: Llandeussant
Ref: www.stefan-szczelkun.org.uk (1.1.2011)

SKANDA VALE
1973 - present

The Community of the Many Names of God – an ashram.
Location: Llanpumsaint, Carmarthen
Ref: www.skandavale.org (2.12.2012); **A Pilgrims Guide to Planet Earth** 1981

COLEG ELIDYR
1973 - present

Camphill Community and specialist college for further education and training for young people with moderate to severe learning disabilities. Young adults live in eight community houses in an extended family setting.
Location: Rhandirwmyn, Llandovery
Ref: www.colegelidyr.com (21.4.11)

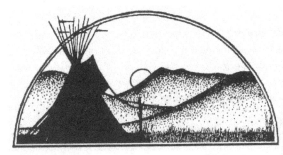

TIPI VALLEY
1974 - present

Village of tipis, yurts, domes and other low-impact dwellings on 200 acres high in the Welsh hills. Fought long battle with planning authorities for right to live on land. *"To be honest, we're a bunch of hippies."*
Location: Machogwyn Fawr, Llanfynnyd, Carmarthen
Ref: **Alternative Communities** 3rd ed; www.tipivalley.co.uk

CWM MEIGAN COMMUNE circa 1974 -
Group mentioned as involved with organising the Meigan Fayre free festivals.
Location: Boncath, Dyfed
Ref: www.meiganfayre.co.uk (6.8.11)

GLANERIEW 1975 - present
Communal organic farm set up by some members of the Barn House group in old hotel with 44 acres on Pembrokeshire coast. Initial group managed high degree of self-sufficiency including growing cereals, milking cows and calf rearing, eggs, vegetable and fruit growing. Also ran pottery and plumbing business. Later struggled to get stable membership.
Location: Blaenporth, Cardigan, Dyfed
Ref: *D&D 90-91*

CRABAPPLE 1975 - 1977
Small group inspired by B F Skinner's book *Walden Two*. Moved to Berrington Hall in Shropshire in 1977.
Location: Middle Ty Brith, Llansantffrald, Powys
Ref: *Communes Network* 2

MACDONALD'S FARM circa 1975/78
Group planning to set up large organic farm. Finally manged to buy farm in 1978.
Location: Llwyncelyn, Ffynongroes. Aberteifi
Ref: *Communes Network* 12, 21 and 34

ASLAN COMMUNE circa 1975
Commune of members of celtic-folk rock band Aslan.
Location: Anglesey
Ref: www.clubska.com (20.5.09)

CARDIFF FOE GROUP 1976
"The local FOE group are at the fore of environmental action in Cardiff ... Their attitude to the use of AT appears to be very positive. Amongst other things, they are in the throes of trying to obtain a house to convert to an eco house, to be run as an 'environmental commune' ..."
Location: c/o 2 Manor Street, Cardiff
Ref: Small ad in *Undercurrents* 14 (1976)

SPIRIT OF MEIGAN COMMUNITY TRUST circa 1976
Group set up after Meigan Fayre free festival in 1975. Planned to set up a community on the site of Penlan holiday village. *"GOAL: To facilitate Harmony. Harmony within man. Harmony between man and his neighbour. Harmony with nature. Planetary Harmony."*
Location: Penlan Holiday Village, Cenarth
Ref: www.meiganfayre.co.uk (6.8.2011)

LLWYN PIOD circa 1976 -
Small group of six adults and two kids living in two domes, a showman's caravan and a bender
Location: Benderville, Dodowlod, Llandrindodwells
Ref: *Alternative Communities* 3rd ed

THE LLAITHDDU circa 1976/77 - ?
Small group renovating cottages planning craft village.
Location: Llaithddu Hamlet, Llandrindod Wells
Ref: *Communes Network* 21

'BOMA' circa 1977/78
"We live communally pooling income and are working towards self-sufficiency using organic principles."
Location: Slade Acre, West Lane, Templeton, Narberth
Ref: *Communes Network* 21;
Ad in *Undercurrents* 28 (Jun Jul 1978)

ZENZILE circa 1977/8 -
Group of ten adults and five kids who after a year searching for a place to set up a community moved to the 12 bedroom Rhiewport Hall set in seven acres with cottage and coach house.
Location: 28 Tonteg Close, Tonteg, near Pontyprid. Mid Glamorgan; Rhiewport Hall, Berriew, Powys
Ref: *Communes Network* 32;
Alternative Communities 1st ed

OAKLANDS WOMENS CENTRE circa 1977 - ?
Centre offering space for women and children for retreats, holidays and study groups.
Location: Welsh Borders
Ref: *Communes Network* 22

BLAEN CWM circa 1977
Small group, some land, kept goats – described as having an *"anything goes atmosphere."*
Location: Porthyrhyd, Llanwrds, Dyfed
Ref: *Communes Network* 32

VILLAGE CO-OPERATIVE   circa 1977

"People are wanted to develop a rural village co-operative on the Welsh Borders. A group of cottages and some land are available. Anyone interested should be concerned to relate personal growth to a wider political perspective of alternative feminist and socialist ideas. Long-term aims would be to develop local community ties, build more houses, be relatively self-supporting with a mixed workshop — agricultural economy. Capital not essential, willingness to work hard is."

Location: Welsh Borders
Ref: Ad in *Undercurrents* 20 (Feb Mar 1977)

COMMERCE HOUSE   late 1970's

Commune *"occupied by London hippies"* used as a rehearsal space by Welsh Punk band the Predictors.
Location: Corwen
Ref: http://link2wales.co.uk (28.5.2011)

CIL-YR-CHAIN   circa 1978

Small community on eight-acre small-holding advertising for new members in **Communes Network**. *"Open to any ideas towards further growth towards political and spiritual fulfilment in an alternative lifestyle."*
Location: Cwn-Ann Lampeter, Dyfed
Ref: **Communes Network** 37

PORTHRHIW   circa 1978 -

Group in *"Rambling old white house about ten miles inside Wales"* mentioned in **Communes Network**.
Location: Welsh Borders
Ref: **Communes Network** 34

L'ARCHE BRECON   1970's - present

Community house for International L'Arche movement.
Location: Glasfryn House, Bailihelig Road, Brecon
Ref: www.larchebrecon.org.uk (30.4.12)

GWELEDIGAETH COMMUNITY   circa 1978 -

Group listed in Teachers directory as in a *"state of flux"* living in former workhouse. Up to 12 members *"Focus on education, psychology and healing."*
Location: Albro Castle, St Dogmaels
Ref: **Alternative Communities** 4th ed

COMMUNITY OF DESIGNERS   circa 1979 -

"Rural community of designers and crafts people in mid-Wales seeks people with commitment, capital (and children) to buy parts of a complex of self-contained houses (converted, un-converted and unbuilt) plus share in communal spaces, workshops and land ..."
Location: Caecoedifor, Newtown, Powys
Ref: Ad in **Undercurrents** 32 (Feb Mar 1979)

ECO LIFESTYLES   circa 1980

"ELS has just bought its first farm, near Carmarthen in South Wales. This will be mainly for part time members who like to do some practical farming, and ecological improvement. The farm was bought with subscription towards Ecological Land Bonds. ELS is planning to build ecological villages. The next part of the project will probably be a large country house in the South West, near Taunton with plenty of land to serve as an ecological centre."
Location: c/o Radlett, Hertfordshire
Ref: **In The Making** 7

GLYN COCH   circa 1980?

Small group *"More a community than a commune."* living in a small house and caravan on 73-acre farm with two acre market garden and two large greenhouses. Growing 25 acres cereals plus potatoes, hay,grazing *"Organic bias — Self sufficient in several foods."*
Location: Glyn Coch Farm, Bancyfford, Llandyssul
Ref: **Alternative Communities** 3rd ed;
Communes Network 12

VICTORIA HOUSE   1981 -

Large house with courtyard and large garden offering independent living for students from Coleg Elidyr.
Location: Church St, Llangadog
Ref: www.colegelidyr.com/vichouse/index.htm (21.4.11)

CASPER HAUSER COLLEGE   circa 1982 -

Twelve adults and nine children living in large mansion and cottages running courses and lectures.
Location: Dynevor Castle Llandeilo, Dyfed
Ref: **Alternative Wales** 1982; **Alternative Communities** 4th ed

WARDEN COURT   circa 1982

New Age Centre exploring alternative medicine and new age economics.
Location: Presteigne, Powys
Ref: **The New Times Network**

CARDIFF HOUSING CO-OP   circa 1982

Co-op renovating property not suitable for families for single people to live in on a communal basis.
Location: 109 Connaught Road, Cardiff
Ref: *Alternative Wales* 1982

GLYNHYNOD   circa 1981 -

Communal Organic Farming school set up by three people from De Kleine Aarde in Holland.
Location: Ffostrasol, Llandysul
Ref: *International Communes Network Newsletter* Feb 1983

GALACTIC FEDERATION   circa 1983

"Esoteric/Occult type community."
Location: Gwynfryn, Roscoloyn, Holyhead
Ref: *Alternative Communities* 4th ed

GLANYRAFON   circa 1983 -

"Findhorn type community."
Location: Foel, near Welshpool, Powys
Ref: *Alternative Communities* 4th ed

KAMPO GANGRA DECHEN LING BUDDHIST CENTRE   circa 1983

Group listed with 'partial entry' in Teachers directory.
Location: 11 Montpelier Terrace, Mount Pleasant, Swansea
Ref: *Alternative Communities* 4th ed

KARMA NARO   circa 1983 -

Buddhist meditation centre and retreat
Location: Middle Wenallt, Hay-on-Wye
Ref: *Alternative Communities* 4th ed

LAM RIM BUDDHIST CENTRE   circa 1983 -

Group listed with 'partial entry' in Teachers directory.
Location: Pentwyn Manor Penrhos, Raglan, Gwent
Ref: *Alternative Communities* 4th ed

MORFA CO-OP   circa 1983 -

Rural living collective of six adults and four children with four acres of land. "Generate income with some difficulty, allocate income with even greater difficulty. We're very individualistic, a group which takes as its reality the actions and preferences of its individual members rather than trying to impose a group identity on the process."
Location: Blaenffos, Boncath, Dyfed
Ref: *Alternative Communities* 4th ed; *Communes Network Directory* 1985

PLASDWBL   circa 1983 -

Group listed with 'partial entry' in Teachers directory.
Location: Mynachlogddu, Clynderwen, Dyfed
Ref: *Alternative Communities* 4th ed

THE TIPI'S   circa 1983 -

Group listed with 'partial entry' in Teachers directory.
Location: Blaenllyn, Llangolman, Clynderwen, Dyfed
Ref: *Alternative Communities* 4th ed

GLASALLT FAWR CAMPHILL   circa 1984

Five households living on 90-acre farm offering adults with learning disabilities the opportunity to live and work together. Extensive gardens and grounds.
Location: Llangadog, Carmarthenshire
Ref: www.glasallt-fawr.com (21.4.2011)

CYNLAS   1986 - 1992

Small communal group in three bedroom house with five acres of land and a variety of outbuildings and caravans. "We live together for fun and to learn. We share a belief system based around self-responsibility, thought is creative, personal freedom, emotional expression and support, and spiritual growth ..."
Location: Rhos Isaf, Caernarfon
Ref: *D&D 90-91*

TWR GWYN   1985 -

Small group on ten acre small holding living in chalet and caravans. Main income from goat herd.
Location: Twr Gwyn, Penuwch, Tregaron Dyfed
Ref: *Communes Network Directory* 1988

UNDERGROWTH HOUSING CO-OP   circa 1988 -

Group of three women, three men, with one child "sometimes", living in isolated, semi-derelict farmhouse with no Mains services with 15 acres of land. Planned to renovate house, build a water turbine "... to have nuclear free electricity by next winter" and plant 11 acres of trees.
Location: Dynyn, Eglwys-Fach, Machynlleth
Ref: *Communes Network Directory* 1988

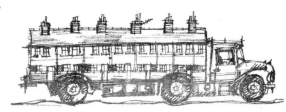

VEGAN COMMUNITY HOUSING COLLECTIVE
circa 1988/91 -
Attempt to set up vegan community in large terraced house. Later became known as Prometheus Project.
Location: 31 Caerau Road, Maestag, Bridgend
Ref: *D&D 90-91*

BRITHDIR MAWR
1994 - present
'Low-impact' group living on 165-acre farm in farmhouse, outbuildings and series of eco-buildings built around the farm. Became notorious in the press when they were 'discovered' by the Pembrokeshire National Park Planning Authority. There ensued a long protracted battle with the authorities over their planning status. Became something of a cause célèbre among low impact enthusiasts and was in no small part responsible for changes to planning designation of sustainable living in Wales. "We milk goats and keep ducks and chickens. Gardens are large and organic. We use horse power for cart, harrowing and snedding. Fuel is wood. Energy is all from renewable sources."
Location: Cilgwyn Road, Newport
Ref: *D&D 00-01*

CHICKEN SHACK HOUSING CO-OP
1995 -
Group with house and four acres in Snowdonia National Park. Planned to design *"the land, the organisation of the community and our individual lifestyles."* using Permaculture principles. Part of Radical Routes network.
Location: Brynllwyn, Rhoslefain, Tywyn, Gwynedd
Ref: *D&D 96-97*

COED HILLS
1997 -
Low-impact arts based project living in range of benders, tipis and self-built homes in woodland.
Location: St Hilary, Cowbridge
Ref: *D&D 00-01*

HEARTWOOD
circa 1997 -
Farm with 35 acres of land: woods, pasture, wetland, streams, orchards and gardens. "Our practice of permaculture and sustainability includes maintaining sustainable relationships with each other as well as with the land we live on; this forms the basis of our community."
Location: Blaen Y Wern, Llangyndeyrn, Kidwelly
Ref: *D&D 00-01*

CWRT Y CYLCHAU
1998 -
Small group that grew out of the Amadea project with Farmhouse, cottage, barn and five acres.
Location: near Lampeter
Ref: *D&D 00-01*

FOX HOUSING CO-OP
1998 -
Group on 53-acre former dairy farm. "We are committed to home education, simple healthy living, freedom from addiction. Our members have a variety of interests and vocations; running an organic box scheme on site, land art and sculpture, counselling, working with children, paganism, eco-building, bee keeping, permaculture, painting ..."
Location: Werndolau, Gali Aur, Carmarthen
Ref: *D&D 00-01;*
www.foxhousingcoop.blogspot.co.uk

SCOTLAND

IONA COMMUNITY 1938 - present
Community set up by WWI veteran turned pacifist minister George MacLeod with aim of restoring the Abbey on the Isle of Iona. Developed into a wider dispersed community network running retreats and doing youth work. Also had base at Community House Glasgow.
Location: Isle of Iona;
208-214 Clyde Street, Glasgow
Ref: R Fergusson *Chasing the Wild Goose*; www.iona.org.uk (23.6.09); *Community News*

'CAMPHILL HOUSE' 1939 -
Series of residential communities set up by Karl König and a small group of Austrian refugees. First at Kirkton House, a 25-acre estate near Insch. Then in the larger Camphill House on Royal Deeside with 170 acres. Murtle House and 35 acres were added in 1942 as the scheme expanded. They were the only educational provision for the mentally handicapped at the time and were supported by the Macmillan family. The Camphill Movement went on to found communities worldwide.
Location: near Aberdeen
Ref: C Pietzner *Candle on the Hill: Images of Camphill Life* Floris Books

'IONA' HOUSE circa 1939
House of Rev Dr R.Selby Wright used as an early base for the Iona Community.
Location: Canongate Kirk Edinburgh
Ref: R Fergusson *Chasing the Wildgoose; the story of the Iona Community*

EDINBURGH PEACE GROUP circa 1940
"Some members of EPG are planning to work ten acres of land outside the city as a training in community work and preperation for more comprehensive activities."
Location: Edinburgh
Ref: *Community in Britain* 1940

CPFLU LAND UNITS 1940 - 1946?
Christian Pacifist land-based units organised for conscientious objectors.
Location: Ardentinny; Tarbert; Twiglees,
Eskdalemuir; Invergarry; Leanachan; Corrie-doo; Clatteringshaws; Laurieston; Strathyre; Durris; Garve; Poyntzfield; Bonchester Bridge
Ref: M Maclachlan *CPLFU*

BARNS HOSTEL 1940 - 1953
Residential hostel and school for 'unbilletable' boys run by David Wills.
Location: Barns House, Manor Valley near Peebles; later moved to Templehall House, Coldingham in 1944 and then to Ancrum House, Teviotdale in 1946
Ref: D Wills *The Barns Experiment*; www.pettarchiv.org.uk (17.01.09)

MILHEUGH HOUSE 1945
First recorded instance of post-war squatting. The men of seven families were arrested after occupying an empty mansion. They were fined after being convicted of trespass which, differently from England and Wales, was a criminal offence (having been so since the Highland clearances).
Location: Blantyre
Ref: Andrew Friend *The Post War Squatters*; www.blantyre.biz (1.1.2011)

NEWTON DEE CAMPHILL 1945 -
173-acre estate with mansion house, several cottages and home farm acquired by Camphill Schools in Aberdeen, and run first for delinquent boys, and later for older boys with special needs. Developed into village community and became part of the Camphill Village Trust in 1960. 200 people live in twenty households of varying sizes including Francis House built to provide a home for those who are elderly or frail and need extra care. Two farms and gardens supply the community with meat, dairy produce and vegetables. There are also a number of craft workshops – joinery, weaving, batik, metal, soft dolls, textile printing and wooden toys – producing high quality goods. In 1977 Newton Dee became the base for Camphill Architects.
Location: Bieldside, Aberdeen
Ref: *Camphill Villages*; www.newtondee.co.uk; www.camphillarchitects.co.uk (2.9.2011)

LOCHINVAR CAMP 1946 - 1956

Naval training establishment taken over by Edinburgh Council used to house homeless families that did not qualify for council housing. In 1951 there were 168 families living at the camp, in a barrack block, Nissen huts and new wooden huts, with communal kitchens and washhouses. The council ran other emergency housing camps at Duddingston, Craigentinny and Sighthill.
Location: Wardie Primary School playing fields, Granton Road, Edinburgh
Ref: www.edinphoto.org.uk (16.6.08)

CRAIGENTINNY CAMP 1946 -

Camp commandeered by squatters in an 'after darkness' raid by 60 or so families, comprising nearly 300 people, including children.
Location: Edinburgh
Ref: Paul Addison *Now the War is Over*

TORRY BATTERY CAMP 1946 - 1950's

40 families squatting in the nissen huts at Torry Battery and Balnagask. Squatters also took over Balnagask Golf club house and an unoccupied house at 63 Albury Road.
Location: Aberdeen
Ref: www.leopardmag.co.uk (23.12.08)

POLKEMMET ARMY CAMP circa 1947 - 1949

Army camp taken over by squatter families.
Location: West Lothian
Ref: *West Lothian Courier* 29 Aug 1947

PRESTWICK AERODROME CAMP 1946 -

Messages were flashed on local cinema screens and telephoned to dance halls in the area summoning RAF personnel back to guard the aerodrome from an invasion of squatters. After fifteen huts were occupied by homeless families following the departure of the Royal Canadian Air Force.
Location: Prestwick
Ref: D Thomas *Villains' Paradise*

CAMAS circa 1946 - present

Off shoot of the Iona community set up in a Salmon fishing station on remote bay on the Isle of Mull as a base for residential work with young people.
Location: Mull
Ref: *Chasing the Wildgoose* R Fergusson.

COMMUNITY HOUSE circa 1946 - ?

Urban base of the Iona Community.
Location: 214 Clyde Street, Glasgow
Ref: R Fergusson *Chasing the Wildgoose*

HIGHLAND COMMUNITIES circa 1947/48

"Highland Communities' has been formed having as its object the reviving of the national life of Scotland by settling young people in depopulated areas in the Highlands. The scheme is, briefly, that at first one empty glen with an outlet to the sea will be acquired by gift or purchase, and by concentrating mainly on farming a community almost self-supporting will be built up. Attention will be paid to forestry, sea-fishing, trout-farming, sheep-raising, weaving and other pursuits, and it is hoped that there will be a re-interest in and development of Scottish Art. Later, more communities will be organised in the same way ..."
Location: Highland Communities, c/o Scottish Youth Association, 181, Pitt Street, Glasgow
Ref: *The Community Broadsheet* Winter 47/48

MORTON HALL 1949 - ?

House requisitioned during war as an officer's mess and later leased to Edinburgh University for a *'Marxist experiment in communal living'*.
Location: near Edinburgh
Ref: hsewsf.sedsh.gov.uk (8.5.09)

CALA SONA 1958 -

Refugee community set up by Muriel Gofton a Red Cross worker who was one of the first people into the Belsen concentration camp after it was liberated. After the war, she lobbied the British Government to accept disabled or ill people who had been displaced by the conflict. Ten families from Serbia, Latvia, Poland, Russia and Ukraine were housed in flats within a mansion house and lodge, together with six prefabricated bungalows, built in the grounds. The site was redeveloped in 1979 and is now run by the MBHA.
Location: Wishaw, Lanarkshire
Ref: www.mbha.org.uk (1.1.2011)

PARKNEUK circa 1960's

House fostering children run on therapuetic community lines.
Location: Parkneuk
Ref: *One foot in Eden*

DINGLETON HOSPITAL   1962 -
Mental Hospital transformed into a therapeutic
community when Maxwell Jones becomes head.
Location: Melrose
Ref: Stijn Vandevelde *Maxwell Jones and his work*
in the therapeutic community 1999

LOCHBAY / STIEN COMMUNE   1960's?
Loch Bay House built in the 18th century as part
of a model fishing village by the British Fisheries
Society was bought by Donovan in the 1960's and
used for a short while as a commune.
Location: Loch Bay House, Stien
Ref: www.users.globalnet.co.uk/-gboote/stien.html
(3.5.10)

FINDHORN   1962 - present
Spiritual community founded by Peter and
Eileen Caddy and a small band of followers
on a caravan site on the edge of the Moray
Firth at the end of an RAF base runway.
Became known in early years for growing
of giant vegetable through communication
with plant Devas. Has developed into an
extensive village with a wider community
living in nearby towns and surrounding
countryside. Run a wide variety of New Age
conferences.
Location: Findhorn near Forres
Ref: *Directory of Communes* 1972;
www.findhorn.org (24.5.12)

BALNAKEIL CRAFT VILLAGE   1964 - present
Craft Village set up by local authority
in former nuclear attack early warning
station "... *buildings are typical military*
structures: single-storey, flat-roofed and of
concrete block construction. They vary in
size, but are mostly roomy enough to contain
a shop, workshop and ample family living
accommodation."
Location: Durness
Ref: www.durness.org/Balnakeil Craft Village.htm
(24.5.12); *D&D 92-93*

SCORAIG   1964 -
"*A traditional crofting community spread over two*
miles of coast, gradually changed since 1945
from native crofters to 'incomers'. Some people
make a living from crofting (small holding),
others from fishing, winkle picking, making violins,
boats, furniture, welding, art, knitwear or working
outside Scoraig ... There is limited co-operation
between households for hay making, peat cutting,
sharing machinery, a communally owned boat and
the school ... Many people are on various spiritual
paths, one house is run as a centre for spiritual/
New Age activities. We are fairly involved in
local politics, a CND group (although this is fairly
dormant), and active on environmental issues. We
are a windmill powered community — TV's grid
computers ..."
Location: Scoraig Pennisula, Dundonnell,
Wester Ross
Ref: *D&D 90-91*

THE ROSLIN COMMUNITY   1965 -
Community of the Transfiguration, an ecumenical
monastic community set up by Father Roland Walls
in an abandoned Miners' Institute.
Location: 23 Manse Road, Roslin, Midlothian
Ref: D Clark *Basic Communities*;
R Ferguson *Mole under the Fence*

'THE ONES'   circa 1965
Group mentioned in Peter Caddy's autobiography.
They claimed to be receiving messages from the
Archangel Michael. The 'Recorder of the One'
claimed that Findhorn's messages were "*from the*
darkside".
Location: Glen Rossal
Ref: P Caddy *In Perfect Timing*

PLUSCARDEN PRIORY   circa 1966
Benedictine monastery founded in 1230
restoration of priory started by monks from
Prinknash Abbey in Gloucestershire in 1948.
Became independent from Prinknash in 1966.
Location: near Elgin, Moray
Ref: www.pluscardenabbey.org (25.5.12)

JOHNSTONE HOUSE CONTEMPLATIVE
COMMUNITY   1967 - 1969
Therevadin Buddhist Centre was sold to form
Samye Ling when original group dwindled.
Location: Eskdalemuir near Langholm
Ref: *Meditation in Action*

SAMYE LING
TIBETAN CENTRE   1969 - present
25 room mansion set in 23 acres of grounds.
Location: Eskdalemuir near Langholm
Ref: *Directory of Communes* 1972;
www.samyeling.org (1.1.2010)

STUDENT CHRISTIAN MOVEMENT   1969

Group with eight regular members who aimed to establish a Christian yet open community to be a base for radical political activity in the surrounding neighbourhood.

Location: House in Newhaven, Edinburgh (also at house in Blackheath)

Ref: D Clark *Basic Communities*

RAINBOW LIGHTHOUSE   1969 - 74

Nucleus of three couples with children living communally, simply, and 'near to nature'.

Location: One of the northern Orkney islands

Ref: D Clark *Basic Communities*

GLEN ROW   1969 - ?

Artistic community gathered around members of the Incredible String Band: Mike Heron and Robin Williamson. Also Stone Monkey dance troupe (Formerly Exploding Galaxy)

Location: Glen Row near Innerleithen

Ref: R Young *Electric Eden*

GLASGOW ARTISTS COMMUNE   circa 1969

"POETS, musicians, artists, writers, etc and lots of ideas and suggestions are required for an artists' commune in Glasgow. As yet there is no definite site, but the following has evolved: The idea of the commune is to enable the artists to have the required time and environment to execute their ideas. At present there are three writers and lots of ideas. We intend to work on a basis of pooling each member's national assistance money and augmenting it with each member's abilities, and then to proceed by existing on our own earning powers."

"NUMEROUS PERSONS and organisations have written to me in connection with a Glasgow Artists Commune. I would like it to be known that my proposed commune barely left ground and does not exist in any shape or form at present nor do I have any intentions of participating in such a venture again. Love WILLY BAKER"

Location: Glasgow

Ref: Ad in *International Times* 54 (Apr 1969); *International Times* 77 (Apr 1970)

CROFT COMMUNE   circa 1969?

"A group of young Edinburgh New-Agers interested in experimental group-living are hoping to set up a Croft-Commune somewhere in the Highlands. They plan to survive by making tourist crafts from natural

resources such as polished sea stones and the like ..."

Location: The Highlands and Edinburgh

Ref: Ad in *Gandalf's Garden* 5

PURE LAND ASHRAM   circa 1970

Short-lived commune set up in one of the ancillary buildings to the Cathedral of the Isles by LSD Guru Michael Hollingshead who wanted to create a space where those coming back from the hippie trail in the East could *"re-enter the west"*. Closed due to pressure from church authorities over drug taking. The group renamed itself The Free High Church of Cumbrae and had a brief existence in Edinburgh and London.

Location: Greater Cumbrae

Ref: *Albion Dreaming; Shoot Out the Lights*

BALLIVICAR FARM   circa 1971

"There have now been four Scottish commune busts since the beginning of the year, including one in the Orkneys which was raided by helicopter. The latest bust took place at Ballivicar Farm (Isle of Islay) where a young Glaswegian had been staying. One night he felt like a swim with his clothes on — a local farmer saw him and decided to rescue him from his apparent suicide bid. Being stoned out of his head the cat didn't know what was going on and let himself be taken to the police station. There he was examined and the doctor said he was "suffering from hallucinations" and that "cannabis could be detected on his breath"! Knowing this to be impossible the young Glaswegian retorted that the doctor must be suffering from hallucinations, whereupon he was jumped upon by two pigs who began picking out wet strands of tobacco from his pockets. The pigs decided to take the — opportunity to use their newly acquired shining white car to visit Ballivicar Farm, where they found three roaches, not to mention a small Buddha (leading to the News of the World headline — 'Buddha Temple in Highland Farmhouse'!). The local magistrate, finding the whole thing totally outside his experience, fined three of the communards £100 each."

Location: Islay

Ref: *International Times* 99 (Mar 1971)

GOSHEM   early 1970's

Commune set up by beat poet and painter Neil Oram in farm. Group known as the 'The Psychonauts' were parodied in Oram's 24 hour play *The Warp*

Location: Goshem, Bunlight, Drumnadrochit

Ref: *Flying Saucerers: A Social History of UFOlogy*

DIVINE LIGHT MISSION   circa 1970 - 1983
Ashram lived in by Divine Light devotees.
Location: 2 Marine Place and 16 Ferryhill Place, Aberdeen
Ref: www.prem-rawat-bio.org (31.7.2011)

DIVINE LIGHT MISSION   circa 1970 - 1983
Ashram lived in by Divine Light devotees.
Location: 79 Overdale Drive, Langside, Glasgow
Ref: www.prem-rawat-bio.org (31.7.2011)

DIVINE LIGHT MISSION   circa 1970 - 1983
Ashram lived in by Divine Light devotees.
Location: 37 Forrest Road, Edinburgh
Ref: www.prem-rawat-bio.org (31.7.2011)

DIVINE LIGHT MISSION   circa 1970 - 1983
Ashram lived in by Divine Light devotees.
Location: Achnacloich, Kiltarlity, Inverness
Ref: www.prem-rawat-bio.org (31.7.2011)

LAURIESTON HALL   1972 - present
Begun as a radical 1970's commune and alternative conference centre in former grand house turned TB Hospital. Was involved in early days of Communes Network and International Communes Movement (ICM) — hosted two international communities conferences in early 1980's. Later became looser co-op with members living in cottages and caravans as well as in the main house. "... members ... *spend half of each working week gathering wood, working in the garden, milking cows etc, while the other half is often spent in outside employment. Work is organised via members' committees and a weekly meeting makes decisions by consensus. Members have use of numerous common rooms, such as a TV room, computer room, and wood workshop. The co-op hosts events for the public (harmony singing, dancing, also work-based events to help with maintenance ...*"
Location: Laurieston, Kirkudbrightshire
Ref: *Legal Frameworks Handbook; Collective Housing Handbook; Communes Network* (various); Laurieston Hall Newsletter (various); *D&D 90-91*

OCHIL TOWER   1972 - present
Small residential School founded in 1966 by C R Lewers became part of the Camphill Movement in 1972.
Location: Auchterarder
Ref: *D&D 90-91;*
www.ochiltowerschool.org.uk (24.5.12)

SALISBURY CENTRE   1973 - present
Large Georgian house and gardens that provides "... *a peaceful haven in the middle of the city*". Half the house is residential the rest forms a Holistic centre running educational courses, workshops and therapies for spiritual, emotional and physical well-being.
Location: 2 Salibury Road, Edinburgh
Ref: *D&D 90-91;*
www.salisburycentre.org (12.6.2011)

BARLINNIE SPECIAL UNIT   1973 - 1995
Small Unit established as a therapeutic community to deal with difficult and violent prisoners.
Location: Barlinnie Prison Glasgow
Ref: *Therapeutic Communities Past Present & Future*

HERUKA   1973 -
FWBO Community and meditation centre set up in 1973 in Bath Street. In 1976, owing to financial difficulties, the group left Bath Street and took up temporary residence in a Glasgow Council House in Nithsdale Road. Due to generous donations and loans, the group was in 1977 able to buy a spacious flat at Kelvinside Terrace South. In 1983 a Buddhist Centre was opened in Sauchiehall Street.
Location: 246 Bath Street; Nithsdale Road; 13 Kelvinside Terrace South, Glasgow
Ref: *Alternative Communities* 3rd ed

CHISHOLME HOUSE   circa 1973 - present
"... in 1973 work started on restoring the then derelict Chisholme House in the Borders of Scotland, and the Beshara School ran its first course of Intensive Esoteric Education there in 1975, with 36 students."
Location: Roberton near Hawick
Ref: www.beshara.org (21.2.2011)

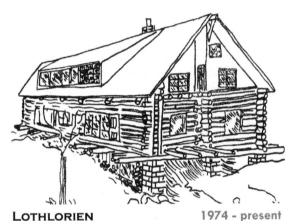

LOTHLORIEN   1974 - present
Originally started by the Haughton family, *"... inspiration was the creation of a warm simple lifestyle based on Christian values."* Built a 13 bedroomed log house, one of the largest in its kind in Britain, from locally hewn larch and pine trees. Became a Charity in 1978 and developed into a Therapeutic community. Run since 1989 by the Rokpa Trust a charity set up by the Samye Ling Tibetan Centre.
Location: Corsock
Ref: *Alternative Communities* 4th ed; www.lothlorien.tc (1.1.11)

'ECOLOGICAL COMMUNE'   circa 1974
Group living on croft seeking funds.
Location: 3 Cairnleith Croft, Ythanbank, Elton
Ref: CLAP 3 in *Peace News* 21.6.74

QUAKER GROUP   circa 1974
Six quakers living in large flat on a 'communal basis'.
Location: Central Glasgow
Ref: *Basic Communities*

TEMPLEHILL COMMUNITY   circa 1975
16 people living in farmhouse with some land who *"... cannot or will not live within the confines of normal society."* Living and working together in a *"... compassionate and therapeutic way."*
Location: Milltown, Arbuthnott
Ref: CLAP 7 in *Peace News*

L'ARCHE INVERNESS   1975 - present
Community house for International L'Arche movement.
Location: Braerannoch, 13 Drummond Crescent, Inverness
Ref: www.larcheinvernessblog.blogspot.co.uk/

ISLE OF CUMBRAE   circa 1975 - 1985
Former theological college attached to the Cathedral of the Isles, situated on the Isle of Cumbrae in the Firth of Clyde. Became the primary base for the Community of Celebration Christian Trust for a number of years. Carried out experiments in farming and ran the local bakery. In 1985. When they were unable to re-negotiate the lease of the Cathedral premises, the bulk of the Community moved to new premises in the town of Aliquippa, a few miles from Pittsburgh (USA).
Location: Forth of Clyde
Ref: www.ccct.co.uk/Library/cumbrae.html (25.5.12)

'GENESIS'   Oct 1976 - Mar 1977
Temporary home of ambitious community project whist negotiating to buy Manderston House.
Location: Argyll Hotel, Iona
Ref: *Communes Network* 18; Genesis Open Letter 2.9.1976

OPUS GROUP   circa 1976
Group mentioned in book on Christian communities
Location: Glasgow
Ref: *Christian Communes*

EDENBANK COTTAGES   circa 1976
"YOUNG rural community aiming for self-sufficiency, experimenting with alternative technology and co-operation needs people. Those with building skills especially welcome, as we're about to start a major renovation job on part of the property ..."
Location: Dairsie, Fife
Ref: *Communes Network* 16 and 21; Ad in *Undercurrents* 15 (1976)

TUARACH   circa 1976 - ?
"... fairly lean lifestyle as a response to society. We don't consume much treading lightly. Still learning the skills to live 'self-sufficient' whatever that means."
Location: Perthshire
Ref: *Alternative Communities* 3rd ed

SIRIUS
circa 1977

"Sirius is a project on going onto Highland land as from 1st July — as yet only two participants and lots of energy and plans to form a healing centre incorporating Pyramids, Solar Dome and magical plantation of herbs and flowers planted in accordance with celestial influences, (see Bio-Dynamics and Findhorn.) We need money to finance 2 goats, bees — as much experimenting to be done in search of flowers to produce edibles and elixic honey, books for research, building tools for healing chambers, and weaving equipment. The landscape surrounding cottage to be used for camping for willing helpers through out the summer — cooking with herbs to produce tonics and elixirs. Could eventually act as prototype for others similar as will be info centre if successful ..."

Location: write to Claire Sataqua, The Cottage, Glenrath near Meemsdale, Sutherland
Ref: *International Times* 11 (Jul 1977)

COMHLA COLLECTIVE
circa 1977

Group mentioned in **Communes Network**.
Location: via 157 Bellfield Street, Glasgow
Ref: *Communes Network* 22

THE ERRAID COMMUNITY
1978 - present

Five acre walled settlement with cottages, outbuildings and gardens built by the Northern Lighthouse Board as a shore station on the Isle of Erraid on the southern tip of Mull. Now the home to a community linked with Findhorn. *"We see ourselves as caretakers of the island and the planet. We are a spiritual community, which flourishes as an independent, self supporting and yet integral part of the Findhorn Foundation." "The resident group on the island usually consists of between six and ten members, including single people, couples and families. Turnover is gradual with most members staying for three years or more ... Each member has an area of focus for which they are responsible, for example, the gardens, kitchen, homecare, animals or candle making. Daily work for both members and guests revolves around these areas."*
Location: Isle of Mull
Ref: *D&D 90-91*; www.erraid.com (24.5.12)

CORBENIC CAMPHILL
circa 1978 - present

Property was bought from Murthly Estate as a College for Further Education for young adults who had outgrown the Camphill Schools. In 1990 they bought some more land from a neighbouring farmer and with care of the land and animals became a more prominent part of the work. In 1994, due to a shortage of places for adults and students wishing of many stay on it changed its aim and became an Adult Community.
Location: Trochry, Dunkeld, Perthshire
Ref: www.corbeniccamphill.co.uk (21.4.2011)

CRAIGMYLE CAMPHILL
circa 1978 - ?

Small community with places for five adults with special needs. Have shop and small-holding.
Location: Tornaveen, Torphins, Banchory
Ref: *Camphill Villages*

NEWBOLD HOUSE
1979 - present

Victorian mansion former family home and hotel rented by the Findhorn Foundation in 1979 as additional workshop space for their educational programmes. Resident group gradually took over running of house and in 1982 a separate Charitable Trust was set up to take over and run the house. Has extensive organic gardens and woodlands.
Location: St Leonards Road, Forres
Ref: *D&D 90-91*;
www.newboldhouse.org (24.5.12)

VAGRASANA
circa 1980

FWBO House
Location: 10a Atholl Place, Edinburgh 3
Ref: *Alternative Communities* 3rd ed

SCHIEHALLION
circa 1980

FWBO mens community.
Location: 329 Sauchiehall Street, Glasgow
Ref: *D&D 92/93*

OPEN SKY COMMUNITY
circa 1983 -

Small community of two household with focus on home education.
Location: Barrackan, Adfern by Lockgilphead
Ref: *Alternative Communities* 4th ed;
J Mercer **Communes**

MONQUHANNY
circa 1983 -

Group of independent family units working co-operatively towards 'total self-sufficiency'.
Location: Shapinskay, Orkney KW17 2DZ
Ref: *Alternative Communities* 4th ed

ELTRICK SHAWS CENTRE
circa 1984

Group mentioned in **Communes** book.
Location: Eltrick Bridge, Selkirk
Ref: J Mercer **Communes**

FALKLAND
COMMUNITY VILLAGE   circa 1984
Attempt to set up a community within an existing
village context by people from Glasgow and
Edinburgh. Two households moved to the village and
hope to form the nucleus of a bigger community.
*"Within the village context we aim to be reasonably
self supporting (skill-sharing/growing most food) but
not isolationist. On a wider scale we see the rural/
urban link as an important one ... We hope to offer a
welcome and long-term therapeutic support to a number
of marginalised people. An organic small holding might
be a way of creating work for those not in ordinary
employment, or there are plenty of local outlets for some
forms of craftwork. Any such ventures would probably
be small scale and probably co-operatively run."*
Location: Falkland, Fife
Ref: **Alt Cmnties Movement Newsletter** 18, Dec '84

LOCH ARTHUR CAMPHILL   circa 1984 -
500 acres of farm and woodland home to around
75 people, some 30 of whom have special needs.
The community produce fine cheeses, hand-churned
butter, yoghurt, bread, biscuits, fresh vegetables,
fruit and farm-reared meat for sale in farm
shop. *"... our farming activities and creamery have
inspired others in the region where agriculture is still
the mainstay of the local economy ... Our cheeses
are medal winners in the British Cheese Awards."*
Location: Beeswing, Dumfries
Ref: **D&D 92-93**;
www.locharthur.org.uk (21.4.2011)

MILLTOWN COMMUNITY   circa 1984
Big old farmhouse home to six people with
learning disabilities, a family of three and a
co-worker. With other coming in to work in Day
Workshop. Built new six bedrooms self-build
timber kit house, named Peesies Knapp. Part of the
Camphill Movement.
Location: Milltown, Arbuthnott, Kincardinshire
Ref: www.milltowncommunity.org.uk (21.4.2011)

TIPHERETH   circa 1984
Three residential Camphill homes Torphin house,
Kitezh and The Hollies.
Location: Edinburgh
Ref: www.tiphereth.org.uk (21.4.2011)

SHINDIG   circa 1984 -
Six adults living in a two-storey flat in an
Edinburgh tenement. *"... committed to living a*
*responsible lifestyle and action for social change,
living together and supporting one another as a
community."*
Location: 26 Glen Street, Edinburgh
Ref: **Communes Network Directory** 1985;
J Mercer **Communes**

MONIMAIL TOWER PROJECT   1985 - present
Small community living in a walled garden and
orchard set around a medieval tower that was
formerly part of the Monimail Palace. Originally
lived in various huts around the garden. Built
'Segal' low-energy timber framed house. Aim
to provide a supportive environment for those
undergoing mental stress.
Location: Letham, Cupar, Fife
Ref: **D&D 92-93**; www.monimail.org (25.5.12)

EDGEWISE   1988 - ?
Converted stable block round courtyard plus a
mill and three acres of land. Home to small group
publishing New Cyclist and Permaculture News as
well as running a bike hire business.
Location: The Lees Stables, Kelso Rd, Coldstream
Ref: **D&D 90-91**

KARUNA BHAVAN   19??
Hari Krishna community consisting of a number
of houses set on a hill, with a small temple, an
asrama, an orchard and gardens. 'Famous' for
their 'GOURANGA!' campaign.
Location: Bankhouse Road, Lesmahagow
Ref: www.iskconuk.com (21.12.2010)

OPEN CLOSE   1988 - ?
Ecumenical Christian community in inner city
Glasgow. *"We believe that a community should
not exist merely for its own sake but should have
a common objective. We aim to try and explore
ways of developing community awareness of, and
facilities for, any 'disadvantaged' groups."*
Location: 283 Royston Hill, Royston, Glasgow
Ref: **D&D 90-91**

'SILLY WIZARD'   circa 1989
'Squalid flat' in Edinburgh that 'closely resembled
an American hippie commune'. Home at various
times to most of the original members of the band
Silly Wizard.
Location: 69 Broughton Street, Edinburgh
Ref: www.harbourtownrecords.com/johnny.html
(1.1.2011)

CRAIGENCAULT FARM
1989 -
A twenty-three acre small-holding beside Kinghorn Loch. Made up of organic market garden, orchards, poultry range, permanent pasture and woodland along with wood and metalwork workshops, a meeting-cum-ceilidh barn and an art studio. The farm house was home to communal group throughout the nineties. They built up links with the local community through the formation of an advisory group. The community has now been dissolved and has become an ecological centre.
Location: Kinghorn, Fife
Ref: **D&D 98-99**; www.craigencalt.co.uk (25.5.12)

ENYGMA
circa 1989
A proposal for a community in Scotland exclusively for gay men. "Envisaged is a small rural estate, within commuting distance of Edinburgh or Glasgow, where we would grow most of our own food and have space for recreation and conservation. There would be homes for ourselves: self contained apartments within a large house or in a wing attached ..."
Ref: D&D 92-93

TALAMH
1993 - present
16th century farmhouse and 50 acres bought by a group of friends who shared similar ideals, to provide affordable housing for themselves. Became a housing co-op in 1996. Most of the land is managed as a nature reserve and the group have planted thousands of young trees. "We are into : *working towards sustainability and low-impact living, looking after our land and encouraging wildlife and biodiversity, growing our own veg and fruit, trying to keep all our buildings from falling down, opposing Trident, trying to stop Scottish Coal extending opencast mining ..."*
Location: Birkhill House, Coalburn
Ref: **D&D 96-97**; www.talamh.org.uk (25.5.12)

WOODHEAD
1994 -
Group living in old farmhouse and large modernised cottage in two acres of land. Part of the wider Findhorn community in the area. "*There is no single definition of our 'raison d'etre', but it is probably a mixture of consciously exploring our spirituality through our daily interactions with each other, while trying to find the most fulfilling way to live.*"
Location: Kinloss, Forres
Ref: **D&D 00-01**

IRELAND

MILLISLE KINDERFARM
1939 - 48
Kibbutz style community at Magill's farm set up by the Jewish Association. Housed Jewish refuges and Kindertransport children. Aim was for it to be as self sufficient as possible. Local farmers gave help and advice on how to make the farm as productive as possible.
Location: Woburn Road, Millisle, County Down
Ref: www.culturenorthernireland.org (20.5.2011)

CAMPHILL GLENCRAIG
1954 - present
Community for people with learning disabilities, mental health problems and other special needs Includes biodynamic farm, 15 houses, a chapel and garden plus various craft and services workshops. Also School for Children and Training College for young people up to the age of 19 providing curative education.
Location: Craigavad, 4 Seahill Drive, Holywood
Ref: *Alternative Ireland Directory* 1982 2nd ed; www.glencraig.org.uk (21.4.2011)

CORRYMEELA COMMUNITY
1965 - present
Residential and dispersed community committed to reconciliation and peace in Northern Ireland.
Location: Drumaroan Road, Ballycastle
Ref: www.corrymeela.org (21.4.11)

THE ORPHANAGE   circa 1967 - ?

House used as communal base by experimental Irish folk group Dr Strangely Strange. Was owned by the group's backing singer, Orphan Annie, hence the nickname the Orphanage. Later a second 'Orphanage' was set up by the group's founder member Tim Booth which became a springboard for a new generation of Irish rock, helping launch the careers of Thin Lizzy's Phil Lynott, Gary Moore and others.
Location: Dublin
Ref: *Electric Eden*

DORNISH ISLAND COMMUNE   1969 - 1971

Commune set up by Sid Rawles 'Diggers' on an island owned by John Lennon.
Location: Off west coast
Ref: *People Together*; www.beatlemoney.com (5.1.2011)

'ISLAND COMMUNE'   circa 1970

Hippie Commune in squatted house. Some of them, including Home of Ubi Dwyer (of Windsor Free Festival fame). Sold 'Freedom' outside the GPO on saturdays. *"5 acres, 2 miles from city centre. Habitable cottage and hut and also a soon-to-be mansion. The bulk of the land is being developed as a market garden. The commune is open. Visitors are welcome, but it might be nice to warn them you're coming."* Ended when mentally disturbed member tried to poison others.
Location: corner of Merrion Road and Nutley Lane, Dublin
Ref: Alan Macsimon *The History of Anarchism in Ireland* 1996; *International Times* 79 (May 1970)

WALDEN TWO GROUP   early 1970's

Small urban communal house exploring ideas contained in B F Skinner's book Walden Two.
Location: Dublin
Ref: *Crabapple Newsletter* No1 25.11.1973

MOURNE GRANGE
CAMPHILL   1971 - present

Village scale community in the Mourne mountains with biodynamic farm and market garden has grown to over 140 people, including adults with special needs who live and work together with co-workers and their families. Also run bakery, cafe, village store and laundry.
Location: Kilkell, Northern Ireland
Ref: *Alternative Ireland Directory* 1982 2nd ed; www.mournegrange.org (5.1.2011)

CAMPHILL DUFFCARRIG   1972 -

25 hectare village with a biodynamic farm, garden and workshops for weaving, pottery, laundry and food processing. Set up to provide home for young people from the Republic finishing their education and training at Camphill Glencraig, *"Our community creates a space for people with a large variety of disabilities, some of them in need of specialised one-to-one support. As many of our residents have grown older with the community and have reached retirement age, this has created a challenge for Duffcarrig in helping them continue to have rich and full lives."*
Location: Gorey, County Wexford
Ref: www.camphill.ie/duffcarrig (21.4.2001)

ECOLOGICAL
RESEARCH COMMUNITY   circa 1973

Proposal to set up group *"On 40 acres of land in Ireland. Five certain members, plus two to three likely others, aged 21-35, all ex-university ... Predominately purist, in favour of total self-sufficiency with no money, no trade and little barter after unavoidable purchases ... We hope as the community grows it will proliferate on detached sites within walking distance of the heartland ..."* Did manage to get going for a short while on 40 acres of rather poor land in County Leitrim.
Location: County Leitrim
Ref: *In The Making* 1 Supplement No2

ATLANTIS   1974/75 - 1990's

Group set up by Jenny James and others who had been involved in People Not Psychiatry network in London. Originally known for their version of primal therapy which could and did take place anywhere and at any time. Attracted much publicity and were attacked by the mainstream and the alternative press. Were involved in many political campaigns. Jenny James wrote a series of books cataloguing the life of the commune. Had London base in Villa Road, in Brixton.

After Atlantis left the house was rented to the St Brides Academy for Young Ladies.
Location: Burtonport
Ref: Jenny James *They Call us the Screamers*

ATLANTIS INISHFREE 1975 - 1987/8
Small island that was colonised by the Atlantis primal therapy commune. The group bought a number of empty cottages and gradually moved from the house in Burtonport onto the island in the process turning from a therapy based commune to a self-sufficiency and crofting focussed group. Planned to sail to South America on their own boat, the Atlantis Adventure, to escape the collapse of western civilisation. Left in the late 80's (not on their boat) on a journey that would end in them setting up a new base in Columbia.
Location: Inishfree Island, Clew Bay
Ref: Jenny James *Atlantis Inshfree*

CASTLETOWN HOUSE circa 1975 - 1977
Group mentioned in *Communes Network* newsletter by someone visiting communes
Location: Castleconnor, Ballina, County Mayo
Ref: *Communes Network* 12 and 27

FELLOWSHIP OF ISIS circa 1977
New age healing fellowship with several hundred members worldwide. Have a temple dedicated to Isis and publish books about eastern gods and temple rites.
Location: Huntingdon Castle, Clonegal, Wexford
Ref: *Undercurrents* 22 (Jun Jul 1977)

THE PEOPLE circa 1977
Small group running a wholefood shop. Planning to go mobile travelling up and down the West Coast selling "anything useful" and exchanging information between like-minded groups.
Location: Knockauns, Cloonminda, Castlerea, Galway
Ref: *Undercurrents* 22 (Jun Jul 1977); *Communes Network* 21

DIVINE LIGHT MISSION circa 1970's - 1983
Ashram lived in by Divine Light devotees.
Location: 5 Finaghy Park Central, Finaghy, Belfast and also at 26 Shanowen Road, Dublin
Ref: www.prem-rawat-bio.org (31.7.2011)

KILMURRAY FARM circa 1978
Bio-dynamic farm.
Location: Thomastown, Kilkenny
Ref: *Communes Network* 41

IRISH MENNONITE MOVEMENT circa 1978 - 1983?
Small group of Mennonites. "*We are here because we want to test the relevance for Ireland of our church's long-held convictions of believer's baptism, Christian community, biblical ethics and pacifism.*" Living in communal household and single family units.
Location: 4 Clonmore Villas and 92 Ballybough Road, Dublin
Ref: *Alternative Communities* 4th ed

CAMPHILL BALLYTOBIN 1979 - present
Camphill community with six shared houses where residents and co-workers live as extended families. Also run Castalia Hall an arts venue. "*For both children and adults we offer individual therapies, for example eurythmy, bath, massage, physio and occupational therapy, as well as music and colour-daylight-therapy.*"
Location: Callan
Ref: www.camphill.ie/ballytobin (21.6.2011)

EIRE FARM circa 1980 -
Collective community of 29 people in West Cork. One of nine communities worldwide associated with The Farm in Tennessee. Trying to be self-sufficient and ran a company promoting alternative energy technologies. "*We try to raise our children to be our friends not our underlings and we take responsibility for their education. We believe in the sacredness of childbirth and having our babies at home.*"
Location: Timolengue, Bandon, County Cork
Ref: *In The Making* 8; *Alt Communities* 3rd ed

CAMPHILL GRANGEMOCKLER early 1980's
Community of forty people living in four households of adults with special needs and international volunteers set on 50 acres ."*We aim to create a warm home atmosphere, a rich cultural life, and meaningful work for all members of the community.*" Main areas of work are farming, gardening and weaving workshop.
Location: Templemichael, Carrick-on-Suir
Ref: www.camphill.ie/grangemockler (21.4.2011)

ABC RADIO 1982 - 85
Group running pirate radio station living in large five bedroom house in a "*commune type arrangement*".
Location: Tramore, Waterford
Ref: www.dxarchive.com/ireland_tramore_abc_history_andy_ellis.html (21.5.2011)

GLENWHEEL CO-OPERATIVE VILLAGE   circa 1982

Proposal for a village sized community. *"Come on board and make it happen."*
Location: c/o John Playdon, Bromley, Kent
Ref: *Alternative Ireland Directory* 1982 2nd ed

ATLANTIS ADVENTURE   1982 - 2009

Boat in which commune planned to sail to S America.
Location: Con Minihane's Boatyard, Baltimore
Ref: www.surroundedbywater.org (8.8.2011)

'CARTWHEEL EIRE'   circa 1982 -

Outpost of the Cartwheel project. Negotiating to take over the island from the Atlantis Commune.
Location: West Cottage, Inishfree Island, Donegal
Ref: *Alternative Communities* 4th ed

INISGLAS TRUST   circa 1982

A working non-profit making community run Biodynamic market garden and nursery. Small herd of goats and bakery.
Location: The Deeps, Crossabeg
Ref: *Alternative Ireland Directory* 1982 2nd ed

LETTERCOLLUM HOUSE   circa 1983

Group of eight in large house with 12 acres of land – plans for self-sufficiency, converting stables to restaurant, craft workshops and commercial mushroom growing.
Location: Tioleague
Ref: *Alternative Communities* 4th ed

CAMPHILL CLANABOGAN   1984 -

80 people living in six households on a 56-acre estate The households, varying in size from 6-15 people, consist of adult residents with learning disabilities, a home coordinator and a team of coworkers. Over the years the farmed area was further increased by renting land. Additional lands were purchased in 1994 and 2007.
Location: 15 Drudgeon Road, Omagh
Ref: http: //camphillclanabogan.com (21.4.2001)

INISRATH ISLAND   1984 -

Victorian mansion on island in Loch Erne built in 1854 bought by a group of Hare Krishna monks to turn into a Hare Krishna centre. A temple room was established in the west wing of the house with *"... a magnificent golden altar at one end of the long room and a life size representation of Swami Prabhupada at the other."*
Location: Inish Rath Island, Loch Erne
Ref: www.krishnaisland.com (21.12.10); ***D&D 98-99***

CAMPHILL DUNSHANE   1985 -

Began as a training college for adolescents in need of special education and care. Victorian manor house and 26-acre stud farm transformed into a land-based community with craft workshops.
Location: Dunshane House Brannockstown
Ref: www.camphill.ie/dunshane (2.9.2011)

THE BRIDGE   1991 - present

Camphill Community set up as sister community to Camphill Dunshane to provide living and working situations for some of the young adults as they were leaving the training college. Have three house communities in the town of Kilcullen.
Location: Main Street, Kilcullen
Ref: www.camphill.ie/thebridge (21.4.2011)

CAMPHILL CARRICK-ON-SUIR   1996 -

Founded by a group of people from the Grangemockler Community. Initially living at the Slate Quarries at Ahenny, while they purchased a small farm and house (Feb 97) in Carrick-on-Suir. *"Following a period of pioneering in the Slate quarries, we moved to our first town house – Brogan in January 1998. We continued building many diverse living situations and workshops in the town and on the farm. Our most recent additions are three houses in a housing estate adjacent to the farm. Over the last thirteen years we have grown from eight to 45."*
Location: Castle Street, Carrick-on-Suir
Ref: www.camphill.ie/carrick-on-suir (21.4.2011)

CAMPHILL HOLYWOOD   circa 1997/2006 -

Community established from café, bakery and organic food shop orginally run by Glencraig Camphill. A nearby house was acquired and separate community set up comprising people with special needs, coworkers and their children and young volunteers.
Location: 8 Shore Road and Riverside House, Holywood, Northern Ireland
Ref: www.camphillholywood.co.uk (21.4.2011)

Location Unknown

During my research I came across information about groups that gave no indication as to their location. Rather than not record them here is a list of their names and references. There will inevitably be many more communes of all shapes and sizes that have left no trace of their existence.

ABBEY GARDEN COMMUNITY   late 1930's
Ref: *Theatre of Conscience*

PACIFIST LAND SCHEME   circa 1940
Pitdown?
Ref: *Valiant for Peace*

COMMUNITY CENTRE   circa 1962
South coast.
Ref: *CLA Bulletin* Jan 1962

BRIAN ENO - ART COMMUNE   circa 1968
Camberwell.
Ref: www.da-vincibrothers.com/biography.htm
(6.8.10)

SANDHURST COTTAGE   circa 1970
Ref: *Directory of Communes* 1970;
Communes Europe

OLD RECTORY FARM   circa 1970
Ref: *Directory of Communes* 1970;
Communes Europe

ECCLES COMMUNE   circa 1970
Ref: *International Times* 89 (Oct 1970)

FAT GRAPPLE COMMUNE   circa 1971
Ref: www.cogs.susx.ac.uk (12.8.11)

DANCE THEATRE COMMUNE   1971-81
Ref: www.nal.vam.ac.uk/acgb/acgb-125.html

NEWBRIDGE COTTAGES   circa 1972
Ref: *Directory of Communes* 1972

DESIGN & SUPPLY   circa 1972
West country?
Ref: *Directory of Communes* 1972

CLUN COMMUNE   circa 1972. London?
Ref: www.lrb.co.uk/v24/n07/letters.html (3.7.09)

'GONG' COMMUNE   circa 1973 -
Ref: www.planetgong.co.uk

THE LIVING THEATRE   circa 1973
London.
Ref: www.squat.freeserve.co.uk/story/ch4.htm
(3.7.09)

ARTHUR BROWN COMMUNE   circa 1970's
Dorset.
Ref: www.godofhellfire.co.uk/80's90's.htm (3.7.09)

COMMUNE   circa 1973
South of London.
Ref: Interviewee in F Musgrove *Margins of the Mind*

TROKES   circa 1975
Ref: *Communes Network* 9

Fictional Groups

IMBER COURT   1958

Iris Murdoch's fourth novel was set in 'Imber Court', a lay religious community, situated next to Imber Abbey, apparently an enclosed order of Benedictine nuns. It was dramatised by the BBC in 1982.

Fictional Location: Gloucestershire
Ref: Iris Murdoch *The Bell* 1958

WHOLEWEAL COMMUNITY   1973

A commune that appeared in the Green Death series of Doctor Who. Environmentalists in a local commune called 'The Wholeweal Community' (known by locals as 'The Nuthutch') try to warn the community about the danger in its midst, but are largely ignored. The Doctor and Jo travel to Wales to investigate and find one of the series' most iconic monsters in the form of giant maggots.

Fictional Location: South Wales
Ref: www.tardis.wikia.com/wiki/The_Green_Death (1.2.11)

WHITECROSS   1976

When looking for filming locations for the second series of *Survivors* the BBC decided to use a place called Callow Hill near Monmouth. It wasn't a commune in the formal sense – Saul David (who grew up there) recalled *"There were about 30 children at one stage, running around like savages at a place ... which was owned by my grandparents. They lived in the big house, but my dad had five brothers and a sister, and they all lived in various houses scattered on the hill."* Script writers who visited *"reportedly left the settlement excited about the prospect of the extraordinary setting and the storylines that could take place there."* It sounds as if many of the crew 'went native': *"we became so integrated into the life at Callow Hill and into ourselves as a group that the filming always seemed to be secondary."* Actress Celia Gregory later said that it was an experience that *"none of us will forget."*

Location: Monmouthshire
Ref: *Sunday Times* (10.10.04); *Survivors* DVD boxed set insert notes

THE HEADS   1983 - 89

Group based in *"a large flat in West Bromwich"*, that started off as a spoof entry in the 1983

Communes Network Directory. Despite the unlikely details provided *"... Main income from small petrochemical business ... Ducks, Chickens, Ferrets, Large organic window box ..."* There were complaints at a CN readers meeting that it was wrong to mislead people who may have taken the entry at face value. The description of the group was expanded by those putting together the first edition of *Diggers & Dreamers* as an example of the format and sort of entry that groups should send in. This led to at least one group asking if they had to send in their own comical entry!

1989 D&D Description

"Our community has grown rapidly. Shane Flush, our mentor, led the original group of 17 adults and four children to our large flat in West Bromwich back in 1983. Since then the combination of his charismatic leadership, an encouragement of polyfidelitous relationships and a total disregard of birth control has meant that the adult population has remained the same but that there are now a further forty children. Shane's solution to the low numbers problem, from which so many alternative communities suffer, has obviously been nothing other than brilliant! The increased population has necessitated much building work - we have recently completed a loft extension. This will house a programmed learning space where our young people will be sedated for much of the day and fed information subliminally through pillow speakers - so much more cost effective than deschooling! We have been expanding the range of vermin that we rear. In addition to the ferrets we now keep weasels and several large rats. The latter are allowed to free range in the sewers of West Bromwich and their contribution to the recycling of waste is highly valued by the local community. Several of us are on the Enterprise Allowance Scheme running an hydroponic venus fly trap nursery. The petrochemical business has been doing amazingly well, particularly since we started gambling on the futures market. Our other hobbies and interests include taxidermy and embalming. We have always opposed petty bourgeoise collectivism and with so many other communities now crumbling due to the failure of their archaic consensus decision making systems we are very

relieved that we have always trusted in Shane and his wisdom. It is a real privilege to be acting on the whims and fancies of somebody of such great intellectual development. The Heads Community feels well prepared for the great paradigm shift which is to come.

We are planning to spawn new Heads Communities in other areas. New members join for life and are expected to hand over absolutely everything they possess. If you are interested then write immediately so that your induction process can start as soon as possible.

Ref: **Communes Network Directory** 1983; Diggers and Dreamers archive

THE HENGISTFEL TRIBE   1985

Group described in a letter printed in *Communes Network* 101, purporting to be from a pagan survivalist group based on a farm in the New Forest, written in response to various letters and articles that had appeared in previous issues of CN. Sparked a series of letters condemning the group as neo-fascist and criticising CN for printing it. There followed a debate on whether CN editors should censor contributions (the decision was not to) and an editorial disclaimer was put in all future issue. Despite attempts to track down and identify the Hengistfell Tribe and a short period when *D&D* editors monitored survivalist magazines, no trace of such a group was ever found leading to the assumption that the letter was a hoax.

Extracts from letter to CN

"*Dear Communes Network readers,*
... The Hengistfell Tribe is centred on a farming community, which encludes what would fairly be described as educational facilities. Our unifying ideology is a belief in the inevitable collapse of mongrel civilisation; and the determination to survive the ensuing chaos. The farm is run on biodynamic lines, producing enough to feed both branches of our organisation. What surplus we have we sell through our outreach project. But some of our London members are working in the so-called market. This we regard as purely temporary. Preparing for autarky involves more than simply feeding ourselves. Reading your publication, I wondered what your rural communes will do, faced with swarms of starving refugees from the collapsing cities. We have no qualms about this. We will defend our land and we are making sure we have the ability to do that.

Although organised on traditional lines — the men responsible for the heavy work and outside jobs, the women for the nurturing functions — all members are thoroughly trained in self-defence. Conventionally I suppose talk of traditional roles is taken to mean women have inferior status. We do not see it in that way. Our children are our heritage, bred to be survivors in the coming savagery, educated in skills that are truly useful ... Many of us believe that this lemming-like rush to destruction is a result of a deliberate policy created and implemented by those whose ultimate objective is to put an end to homo sapiens. We are interested in alternative technology as long as it is not polluting, and have been developing our methane generator. (We came close to demolishing half the farm with it in the early days). We are also selectively breeding our cattle to exist under the most adverse conditions, and breeding an extremely primitive breed of pig. ... If evolution continues — a certainty — and if higher man survives — which is not — then perhaps our gene pool that we are carefully constructing in our tribe will become the basis for the next evolutionary leap. What is certain is that if anyone survives the coming savagery, it will be the cream of our species who do so. Nature cannot ultimately allow a species, however powerful, to defy Her laws as ours has. And I personaly refuse to believe the planet will allow one of its children to destroy it:
Oisin, Hengistfell Tribe, London and Hampshire."
Ref: **Communes Network** 101, 102 and 103

THE LODGE   1989

Group featured in a regular column in *The Guardian*. See page 358.

THE END

All numbers in bold are page numbers.

9, 11: CPFLU: A History of Christian Pacifist Forestry and Land Units
18: Phyllida Lumsden, The Island Farmers
19: The Island Farmers
21, 22: Richard Murry, Community Farm
29: Remembering Genocides – Northern Ireland's inaugural Holocaust memorial commemoration booklet
33, 34, 35: Community Journey
36, 334, 342: Communes Network Magazine, Communes Network Archive
37: Theatres of Conscience 1939-53
39, 41: Cheshire V C: A Story of War and Peace
44, 46: The Reilly Plan
48, 296, 252, 253: Squatting – the real story
52: KIT Newsletter X #3 March Part III, U B Lacy Collection
54, 55: Experiment in Co-operation
59: Article by Hilde Marchant in Picture Post
64, 66: Braziers: A Personal Story
71: The Wheathill Bruderhof: Ten Years Of Community Living
96: Camphill Brochure 2012
99: Gordon Joly, Wikimedia Commons
111, 112: cover of Atlantis Is
114 (left): © Victor Patterson www.victorpatterson.com
114 (right): Sleeve Atlantis Live 1980
115: © Victor Patterson www.victorpatterson.com
116 (top): Cover Atlantis Innisfree
116 (middle & bottom): Communes Network
119: Sinclair User, December 1985
123: Wikimedia Commons
126: Far Out
131, 133: Maurice Nicoll: A Portrait
134: Front Cover, Sunday Talks at Coombe Springs
136, 138: My Life in Subud, Photos by John Donat
140: © 2009 George and Ben Bennett www.jgbennett.net/gallery.html
143: Garden News 18.12.1957
150: Front Cover of The Processeans magazine, May 1974 - Love Sex Fear Death
151, 152: Love Sex Fear Death
163, 164, 165, 206, 257, 260, 261, 263: Communes Europe

182, 189: Paris Match 1975
185: Article in Findhorn Archive, Scottish National Library
204: Much Ado About Something
222: www.exfamily.org
224: Jonathan How private collection
100, 244, 245, 251, 273, 274, 294, 309, 381, 385: www.internationaltimes.it/archive/
256: Communes Section, Alternative London 1970
275: www.bobleroi.co.uk
276, 277: Stills from BBC4 What Happened Next? series
278: www.last.fm/music/Magic+Muscle
283, 284: From booklet in Motor Driven Bimbo CD
286: Exodus-Leviticus-Timeline.pdf at www.leviticuscollective.co.uk
293: Sarah Eno private collection
297: www.grosvenor-road.co.uk
303: Diggers & Dreamers 08/09
319 (top): Crabapple community private collection
319 (bottom): Fairground Prospectus 1981
323: Bob Sloan
328: Promotional Poster for Alternative Communities Movement, photos from Teachers Community Booklet
331, 332: A Book of Visions cover
336: Pages from Genesis Proposal
339, 343: Greentown Proposal
341: Diggers & Dreamers 90/91
344: Communes Network Directory 1984, Communes Network Archive
345 (bottom), 346: ICN Newsletter, Communes Network Archive
346: Communes Network Directory 1984, Communes Network Archive
347: Charlie Easterfield, Communes Network Archive
348: Cover of Collective Housing Handbook
351: Postcard of Laurieston Hall
354, 355: Fairground Prospectus 1981
367: Morgan Read private collection
375, 377: Lifespan Community – One year in the life. ©Howard Davies
376: Cover Lifespan Leaflet
391: Radical Routes Booklet

Author's Tale: All illustrations and cuttings from author's personal collection.
Directory: All illustrations in this section from issues of Communes Network magazine 1975 - 1995.
All other pictures either by the author or of unknown origin.

Index

Chris Coates

In a roll call of communal experience at the 2001 International Communal Studies Conference at Zegg I found myself, somewhat to my surprise, standing in the communal veterans section of those with 20 or more years experience of communal living along with born & bred Kibbutzniks and a few other survivors of the 1970's. I realised then that I had a communal CV that didn't really register (in the ordinary biographical sense) but intertwined with the rest of my life in one long continuous thread. So while my job applications say I have been a: street performer; clown; actor; stage manager; building site labourer; carpenter; construction project manager; design forum convenor; and Lancaster City Green Party Councillor – my alternative CV would tell you that after being a squatter I spent 20 years exploring communal living at People in Common, a small alternative community in Burnley. Was active in the Communes Network during the late 1970's and 80's and have been an editor of *Diggers & Dreamers* since it was first published in 1990. At the turn of the millennium D&D published *Utopia Britannica*, my history of British Utopian Experiments 1325 – 1945. I am now embarking on a second communal journey as a member of Forgebank Cohousing Community in Lancaster. I have lived in some sort of communal set-up for almost as long as I have lived in the 'outside world' and – I would say that on balance – the benefits of communal living outweigh the disadvantages. Living on your own has its attraction, but it is not all it's cracked up to be!

Many have ridiculed utopians and tried to consign them to the footnotes of history ... but the utopian tendency has an uncanny resilience. Trying to make the world a better place would seem to be a basic human instinct and far from being marginal to our history has, at times, played a central and pivotal role. If you've enjoyed this book and haven't yet read the first volume of *Utopia Britannica* then join Chris Coates again and use his definitive A to Z gazetteer of utopian Britain to travel through a landscape of dreams made real. Find places you never knew existed and move through a country of the imagination dreamt into existence by generations of utopian experimenters who refused to accept that there wasn't a better place to be than the one that they found themselves in already.

▸ Thread 1 – Dissenters' Paradise: Christian Sects from the 15th to the 20th Century.

▸ Thread 2 – Islands of Socialism: Early 19th Century Socialist Experiments.

▸ Thread 3 – Artistic Visionaries: Artists' Colonies from Coleridge to Peake.

▸ Thread 4 – The Old New Age: Mysticism, Myth and Organic Farming the first time.

▸ Thread 5 – Utopia for Everyone: From the State of Welfare to the Welfare State.

Utopia Britannica:
British Utopian Experiments 1325 - 1945
312 pp paperback, b&w illustrations
ISBN 0 9514945 8 9
Diggers & Dreamers Publications, £16.50

www.diggersanddreamers.org.uk

If this book has stimulated your interest in communal living in Britain then take a look at the Diggers & Dreamers website. You'll find a directory of current groups of all sorts ... from rural to urban; secular to spiritual; vegan to omniverous; and from co-operative to private ownership. They're all very different but at the same time have much in common. There are also listings for communities looking for members as well as volunteers plus forming groups that are at the early stages. The website includes various other useful resources and noticeboards.

Cohousing in Britain: A Diggers & Dreamers Review
163 pp paperback, b&w illustrations
ISBN 978 0 9545757 3 1
Diggers & Dreamers Publications, £12

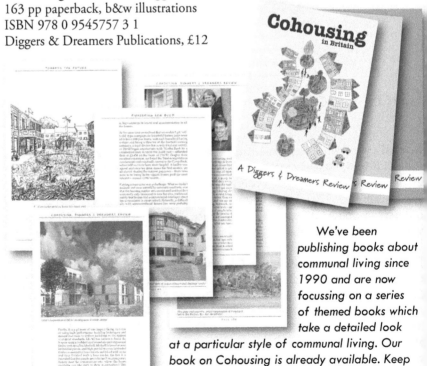

We've been publishing books about communal living since 1990 and are now focussing on a series of themed books which take a detailed look at a particular style of communal living. Our book on Cohousing is already available. Keep watching the D&D website to check for the publication of new volumes with other themes.

Lightning Source UK Ltd.
Milton Keynes UK
UKHW031820180121
377267UK00005B/189